ARCHIVAL QUALITY

AN ONI PRESS PUBLICATION

FROM THE LIBRARY OF:

Written by Ivy Noelle Weir
Illustrated and colored by Steenz

Lettered by Joamette Gil
Flatting assistance by Deb Groves

‡

Designed by Kate Z. Stone
Edited by Robin Herrera

Published by Oni Press, Inc.

Joe Nozemack	founder & chief financial officer
James Lucas Jones	publisher
Charlie Chu	v.p. of creative & business development
Brad Rooks	director of operations
Rachel Reed	marketing manager
Melissa Meszaros	publicity manager
Troy Look	director of design & production
Hilary Thompson	graphic designer
Kate Z. Stone	junior graphic designer
Angie Knowles	digital prepress lead
Ari Yarwood	executive editor
Robin Herrera	senior editor
Desiree Wilson	associate editor
Alissa Salla	administrative assistant
Jung Lee	logistics associate

onipress.com
facebook.com/onipress
twitter.com/onipress
onipress.tumblr.com
instagram.com/onipress

First Edition: March 2018

ISBN 978-1-62010-470-5 ‡ eISBN 978-1-62010-471-2

Archival Quality, March 2018. Published by Oni Press, Inc. 1319 SE Martin Luther King Jr. Blvd., Suite 240, Portland, OR 97214. Archival Quality is ™ & © 2018 Ivy Noelle Weir and Christina Stewart. All rights reserved. Oni Press logo and icon ™ & © 2018 Oni Press, Inc. All rights reserved. Oni Press logo and icon artwork created by Keith A. Wood. The events, institutions, and characters presented in this book are fictional. Any resemblance to actual persons, living or dead, is purely coincidental. No portion of this publication may be reproduced, by any means, without the express written permission of the copyright holders.

Library of Congress Control Number: 2017948855

1 3 5 7 9 10 8 6 4 2

Printed in China

To everyone who believed I could. -INW

To everyone with no drawing skills
who offered to draw the book for me
when I was at my lowest. -S

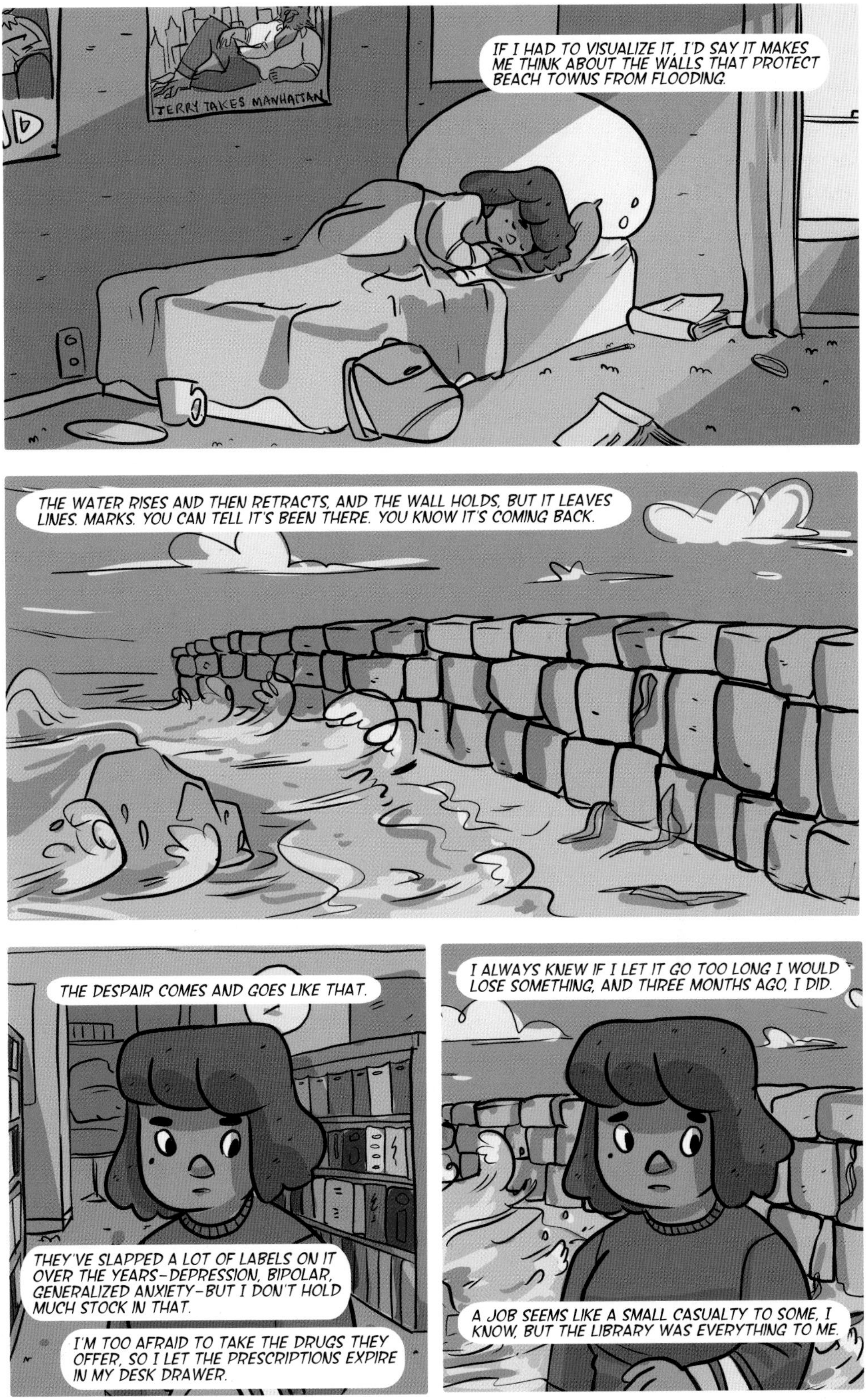
JERRY TAKES MANHATTAN
IF I HAD TO VISUALIZE IT, I'D SAY IT MAKES ME THINK ABOUT THE WALLS THAT PROTECT BEACH TOWNS FROM FLOODING.
THE WATER RISES AND THEN RETRACTS, AND THE WALL HOLDS, BUT IT LEAVES LINES. MARKS. YOU CAN TELL IT'S BEEN THERE. YOU KNOW IT'S COMING BACK.
THE DESPAIR COMES AND GOES LIKE THAT.
THEY'VE SLAPPED A LOT OF LABELS ON IT OVER THE YEARS–DEPRESSION, BIPOLAR, GENERALIZED ANXIETY–BUT I DON'T HOLD MUCH STOCK IN THAT.
I'M TOO AFRAID TO TAKE THE DRUGS THEY OFFER, SO I LET THE PRESCRIPTIONS EXPIRE IN MY DESK DRAWER.
I ALWAYS KNEW IF I LET IT GO TOO LONG I WOULD LOSE SOMETHING, AND THREE MONTHS AGO, I DID.
A JOB SEEMS LIKE A SMALL CASUALTY TO SOME, I KNOW, BUT THE LIBRARY WAS EVERYTHING TO ME.

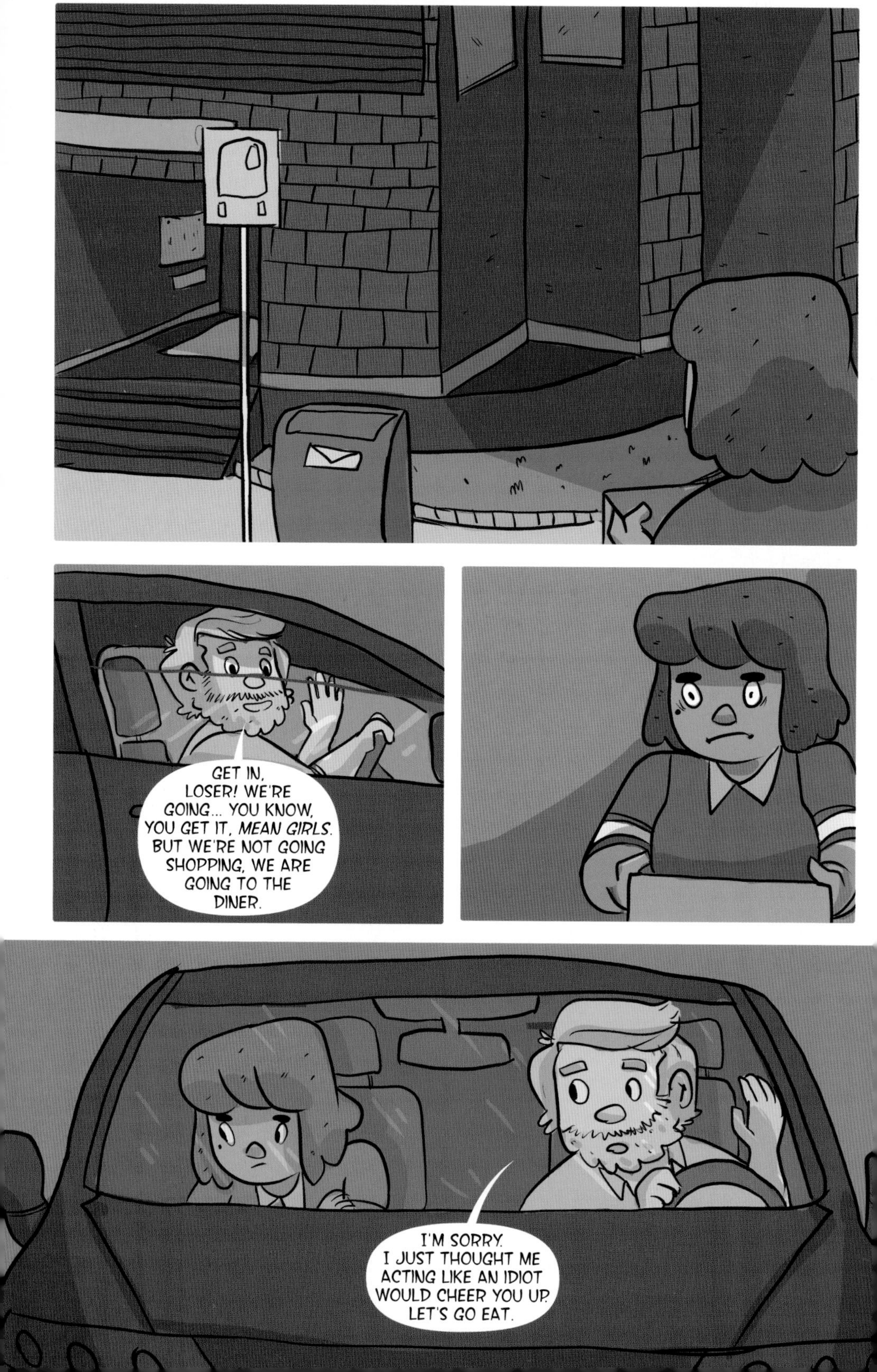

GET IN, LOSER! WE'RE GOING... YOU KNOW, YOU GET IT, *MEAN GIRLS*. BUT WE'RE NOT GOING SHOPPING, WE ARE GOING TO THE DINER.
I'M SORRY. I JUST THOUGHT ME ACTING LIKE AN IDIOT WOULD CHEER YOU UP. LET'S GO EAT.

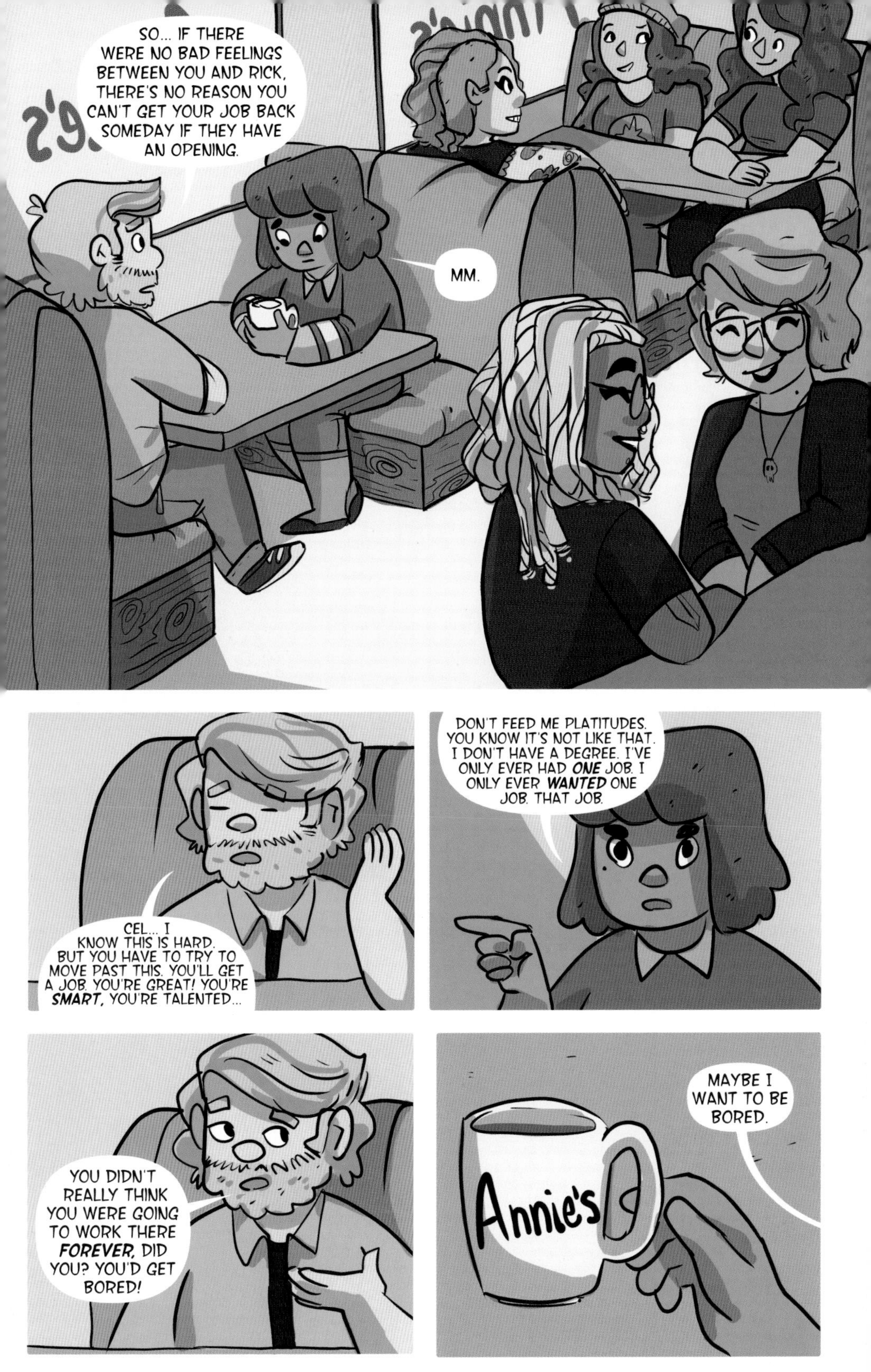
SO... IF THERE WERE NO BAD FEELINGS BETWEEN YOU AND RICK, THERE'S NO REASON YOU CAN'T GET YOUR JOB BACK SOMEDAY IF THEY HAVE AN OPENING.
MM.
CEL... I KNOW THIS IS HARD. BUT YOU HAVE TO TRY TO MOVE PAST THIS. YOU'LL GET A JOB. YOU'RE GREAT! YOU'RE **SMART,** YOU'RE TALENTED...
DON'T FEED ME PLATITUDES. YOU KNOW IT'S NOT LIKE THAT. I DON'T HAVE A DEGREE. I'VE ONLY EVER HAD **ONE** JOB. I ONLY EVER **WANTED** ONE JOB. THAT JOB.
YOU DIDN'T REALLY THINK YOU WERE GOING TO WORK THERE **FOREVER,** DID YOU? YOU'D GET BORED!
Annie's
MAYBE I WANT TO BE BORED.

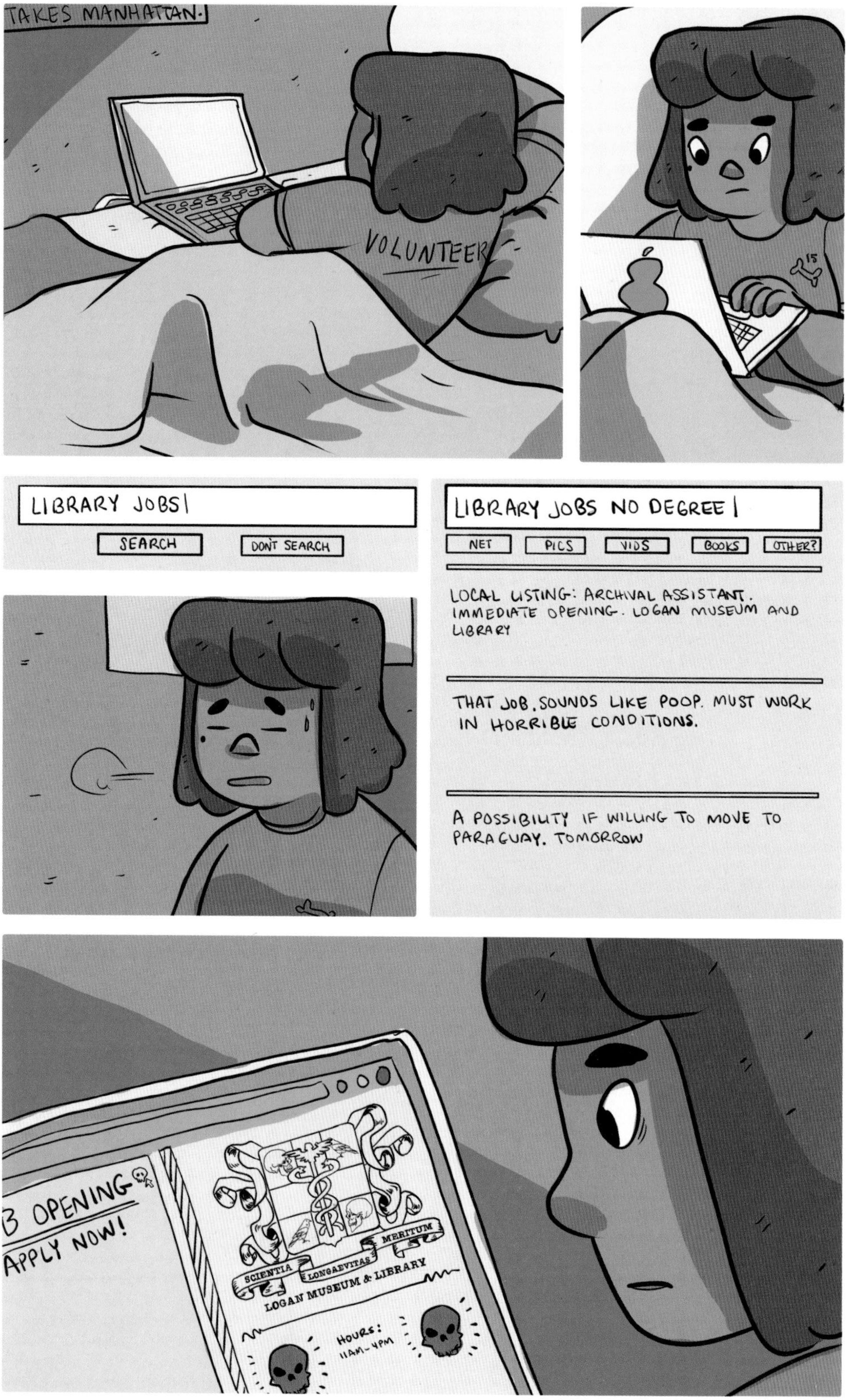
TAKES MANHATTAN.
VOLUNTEER
LIBRARY JOBS|
SEARCH
DON'T SEARCH
LIBRARY JOBS NO DEGREE |
NET
PICS
VIDS
BOOKS
OTHER?
LOCAL LISTING: ARCHIVAL ASSISTANT. IMMEDIATE OPENING. LOGAN MUSEUM AND LIBRARY
THAT JOB, SOUNDS LIKE POOP. MUST WORK IN HORRIBLE CONDITIONS.
A POSSIBILITY IF WILLING TO MOVE TO PARAGUAY. TOMORROW
B OPENING
APPLY NOW!
SCIENTIA
LONGAEVITAS
MERITUM
LOGAN MUSEUM & LIBRARY
HOURS: 11AM-4PM

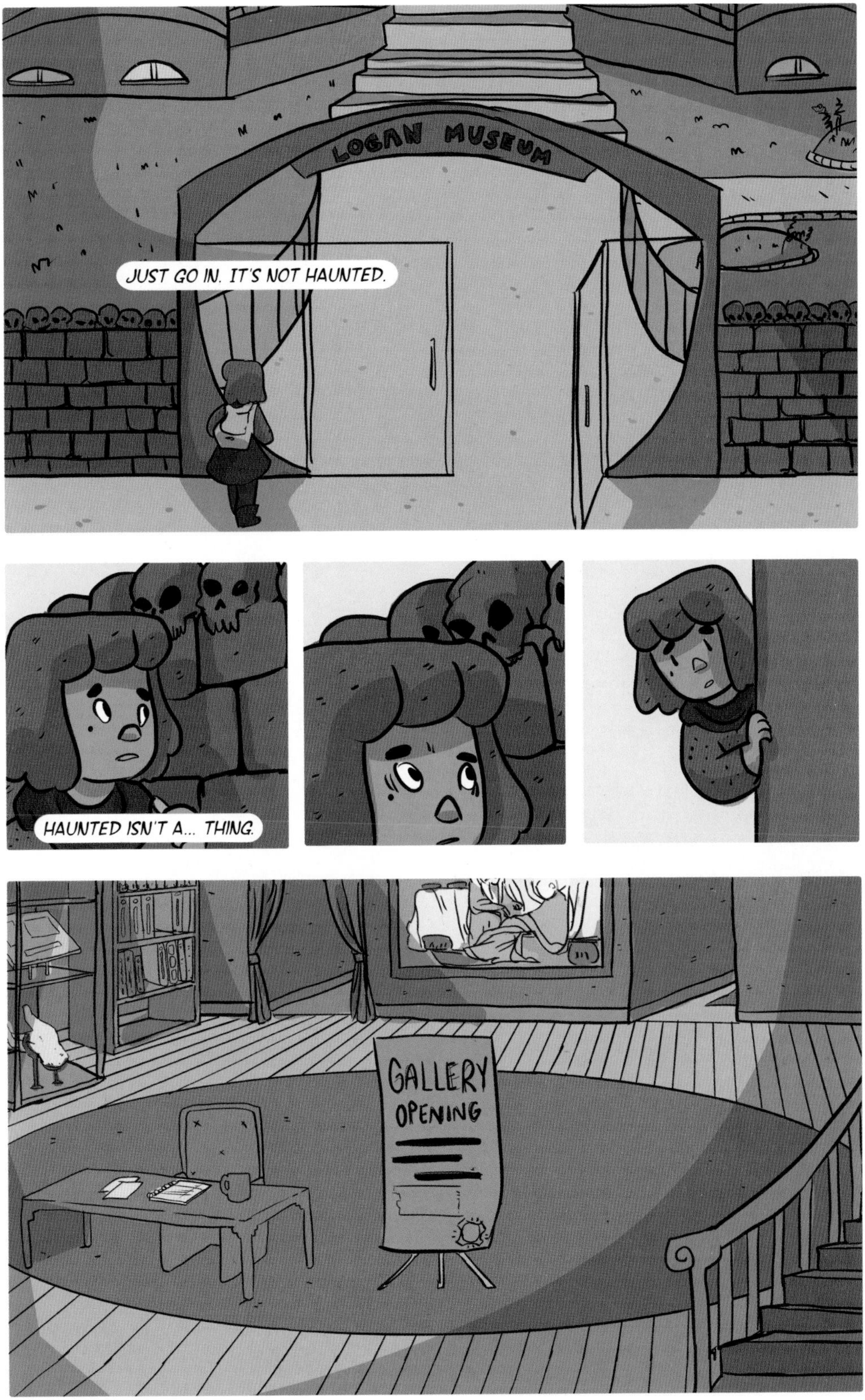
LOGAN MUSEUM
JUST GO IN. IT'S NOT HAUNTED.
HAUNTED ISN'T A... THING.
GALLERY OPENING

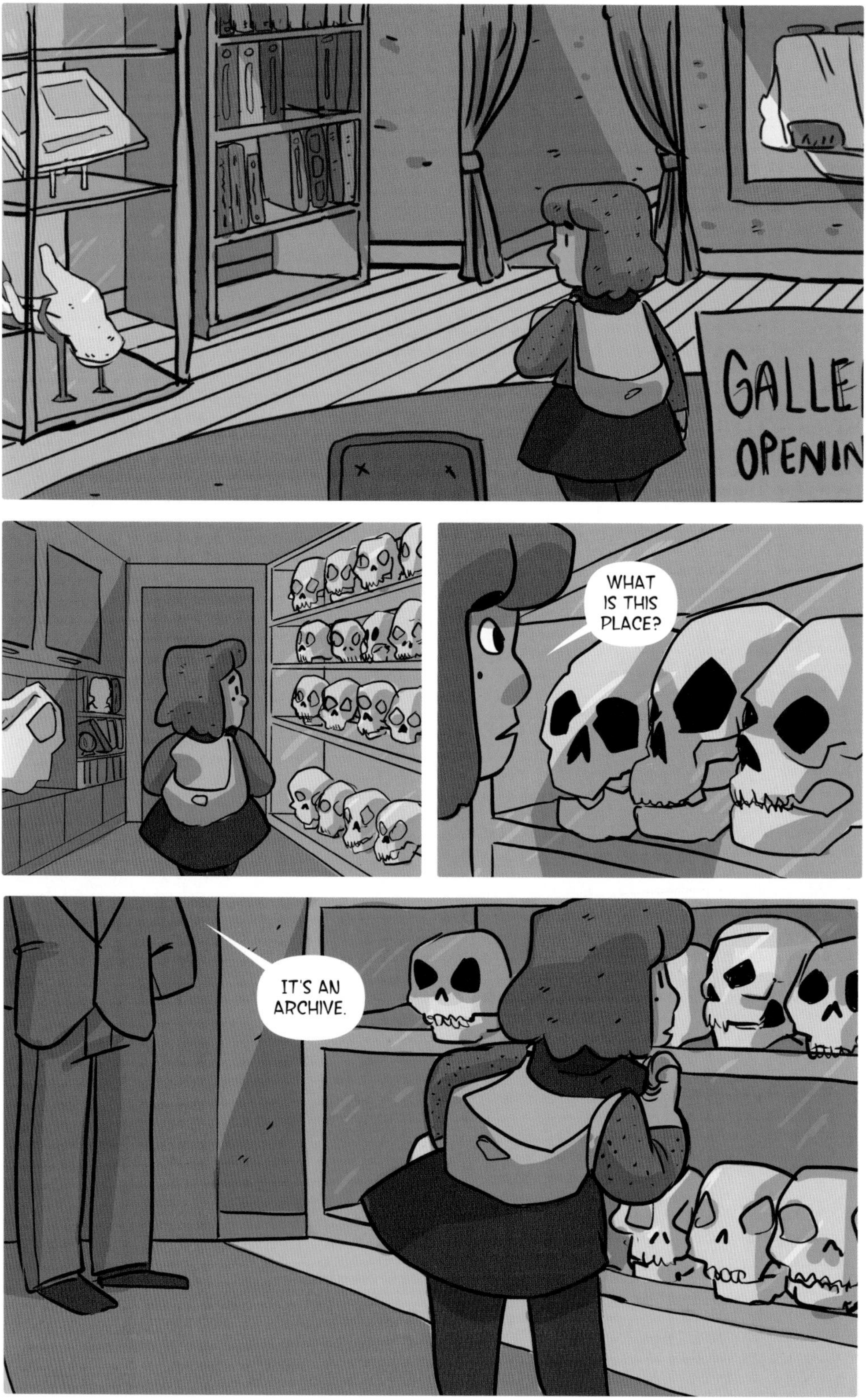
GALLE
OPENIN
WHAT IS THIS PLACE?
IT'S AN ARCHIVE.

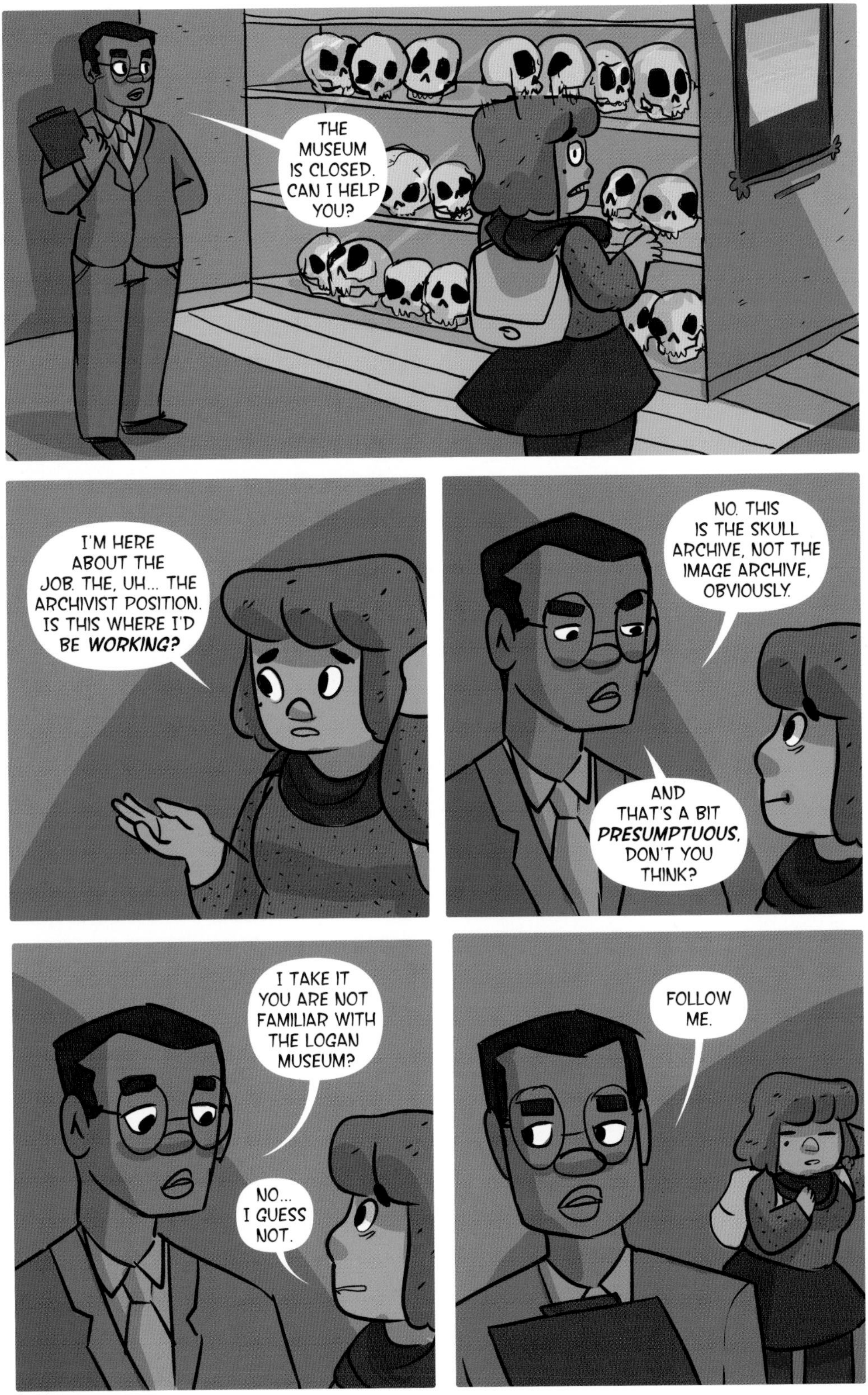
THE MUSEUM IS CLOSED. CAN I HELP YOU?
I'M HERE ABOUT THE JOB. THE, UH... THE ARCHIVIST POSITION. IS THIS WHERE I'D BE *WORKING?*
NO. THIS IS THE SKULL ARCHIVE, NOT THE IMAGE ARCHIVE, OBVIOUSLY.
AND THAT'S A BIT *PRESUMPTUOUS*, DON'T YOU THINK?
I TAKE IT YOU ARE NOT FAMILIAR WITH THE LOGAN MUSEUM?
NO... I GUESS NOT.
FOLLOW ME.

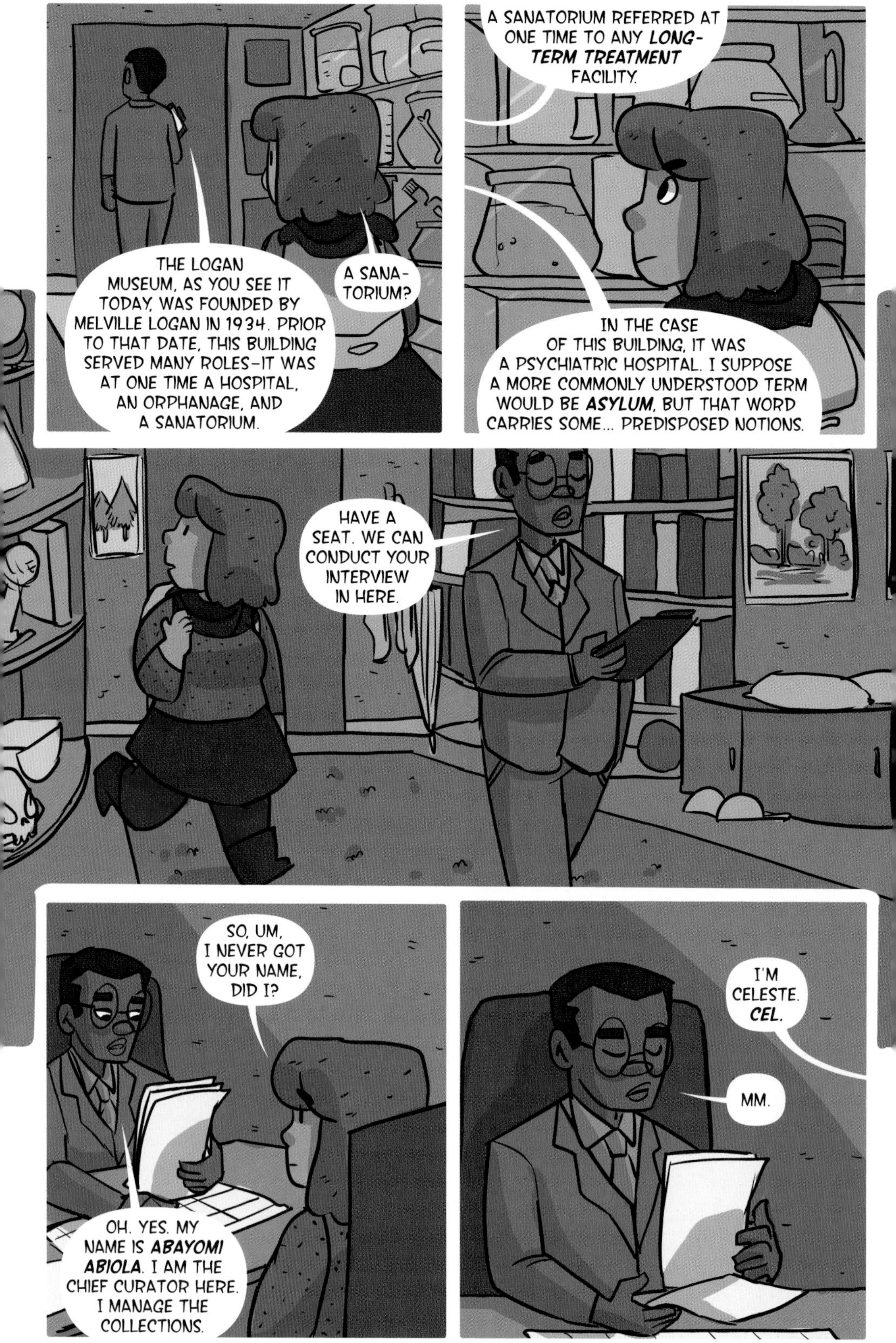
THE LOGAN MUSEUM, AS YOU SEE IT TODAY, WAS FOUNDED BY MELVILLE LOGAN IN 1934. PRIOR TO THAT DATE, THIS BUILDING SERVED MANY ROLES–IT WAS AT ONE TIME A HOSPITAL, AN ORPHANAGE, AND A SANATORIUM.
A SANATORIUM?
A SANATORIUM REFERRED AT ONE TIME TO ANY ***LONG-TERM TREATMENT*** FACILITY.
IN THE CASE OF THIS BUILDING, IT WAS A PSYCHIATRIC HOSPITAL. I SUPPOSE A MORE COMMONLY UNDERSTOOD TERM WOULD BE ***ASYLUM***, BUT THAT WORD CARRIES SOME... PREDISPOSED NOTIONS.
HAVE A SEAT. WE CAN CONDUCT YOUR INTERVIEW IN HERE.
SO, UM, I NEVER GOT YOUR NAME, DID I?
OH. YES. MY NAME IS ***ABAYOMI ABIOLA***. I AM THE CHIEF CURATOR HERE. I MANAGE THE COLLECTIONS.
I'M CELESTE. ***CEL.***
MM.

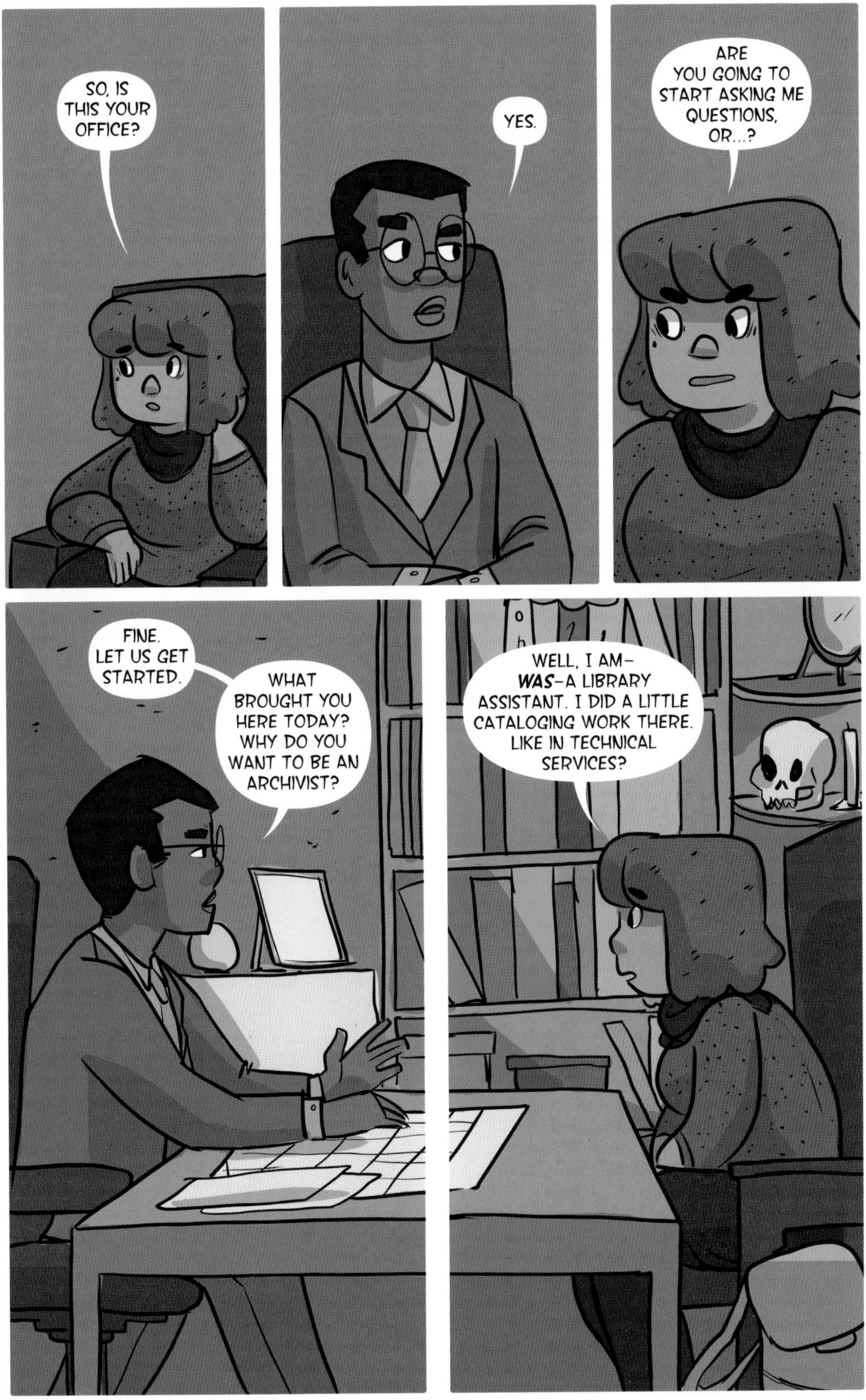
SO, IS THIS YOUR OFFICE?
YES.
ARE YOU GOING TO START ASKING ME QUESTIONS, OR...?
FINE. LET US GET STARTED.
WHAT BROUGHT YOU HERE TODAY? WHY DO YOU WANT TO BE AN ARCHIVIST?
WELL, I AM—*WAS*—A LIBRARY ASSISTANT. I DID A LITTLE CATALOGING WORK THERE. LIKE IN TECHNICAL SERVICES?

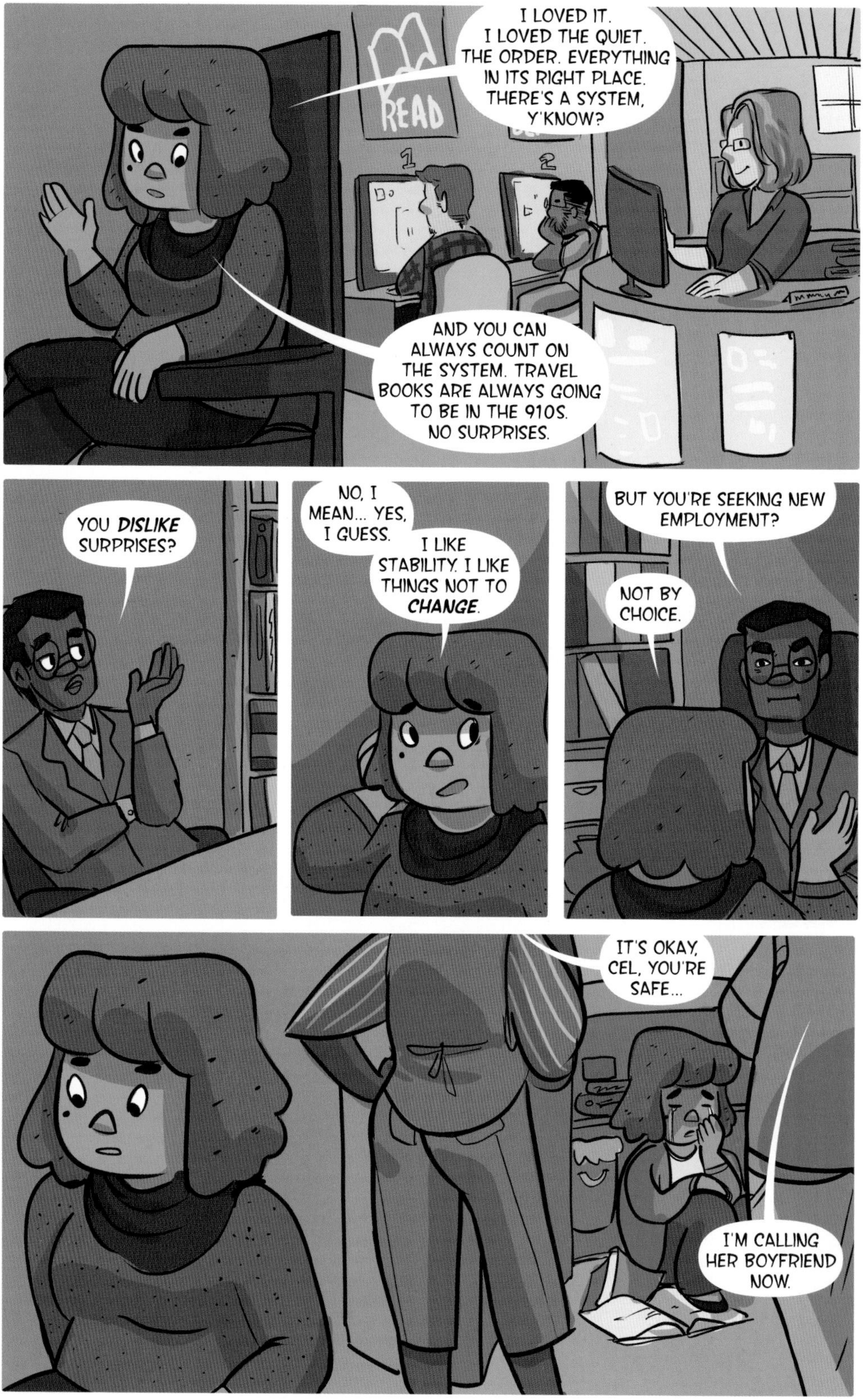
I LOVED IT. I LOVED THE QUIET. THE ORDER. EVERYTHING IN ITS RIGHT PLACE. THERE'S A SYSTEM, Y'KNOW?
READ
AND YOU CAN ALWAYS COUNT ON THE SYSTEM. TRAVEL BOOKS ARE ALWAYS GOING TO BE IN THE 910S. NO SURPRISES.
YOU *DISLIKE* SURPRISES?
NO, I MEAN... YES, I GUESS.
I LIKE STABILITY. I LIKE THINGS NOT TO *CHANGE*.
BUT YOU'RE SEEKING NEW EMPLOYMENT?
NOT BY CHOICE.
IT'S OKAY, CEL, YOU'RE SAFE...
I'M CALLING HER BOYFRIEND NOW.

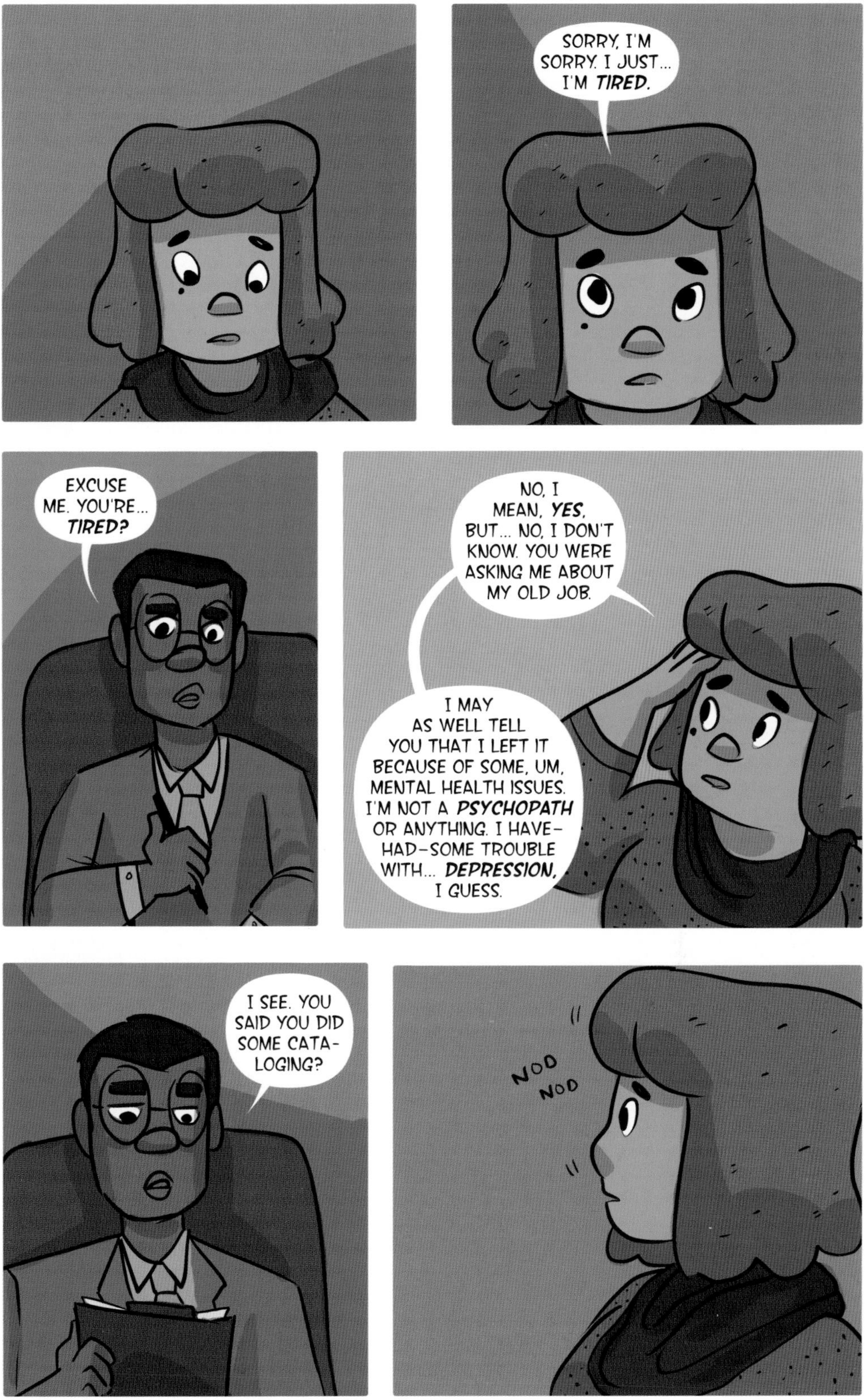
SORRY, I'M SORRY. I JUST... I'M *TIRED.*
EXCUSE ME. YOU'RE... *TIRED?*
NO, I MEAN, *YES,* BUT... NO, I DON'T KNOW. YOU WERE ASKING ME ABOUT MY OLD JOB.
I MAY AS WELL TELL YOU THAT I LEFT IT BECAUSE OF SOME, UM, MENTAL HEALTH ISSUES. I'M NOT A *PSYCHOPATH* OR ANYTHING. I HAVE—HAD—SOME TROUBLE WITH... *DEPRESSION,* I GUESS.
I SEE. YOU SAID YOU DID SOME CATA-LOGING?
NOD NOD

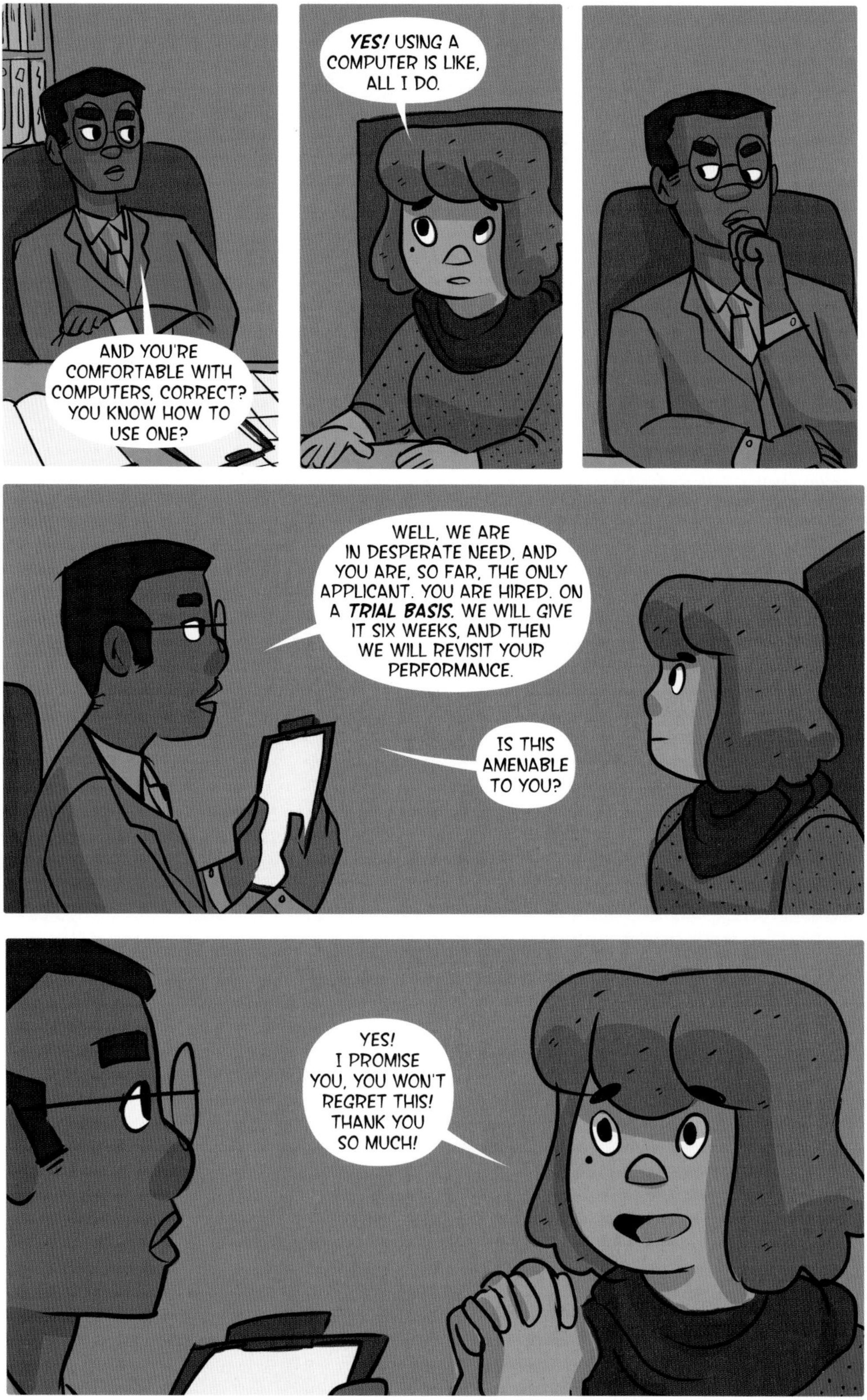
AND YOU'RE COMFORTABLE WITH COMPUTERS, CORRECT? YOU KNOW HOW TO USE ONE?
YES! USING A COMPUTER IS LIKE, ALL I DO.
WELL, WE ARE IN DESPERATE NEED, AND YOU ARE, SO FAR, THE ONLY APPLICANT. YOU ARE HIRED. ON A TRIAL BASIS. WE WILL GIVE IT SIX WEEKS, AND THEN WE WILL REVISIT YOUR PERFORMANCE.
IS THIS AMENABLE TO YOU?
YES! I PROMISE YOU, YOU WON'T REGRET THIS! THANK YOU SO MUCH!

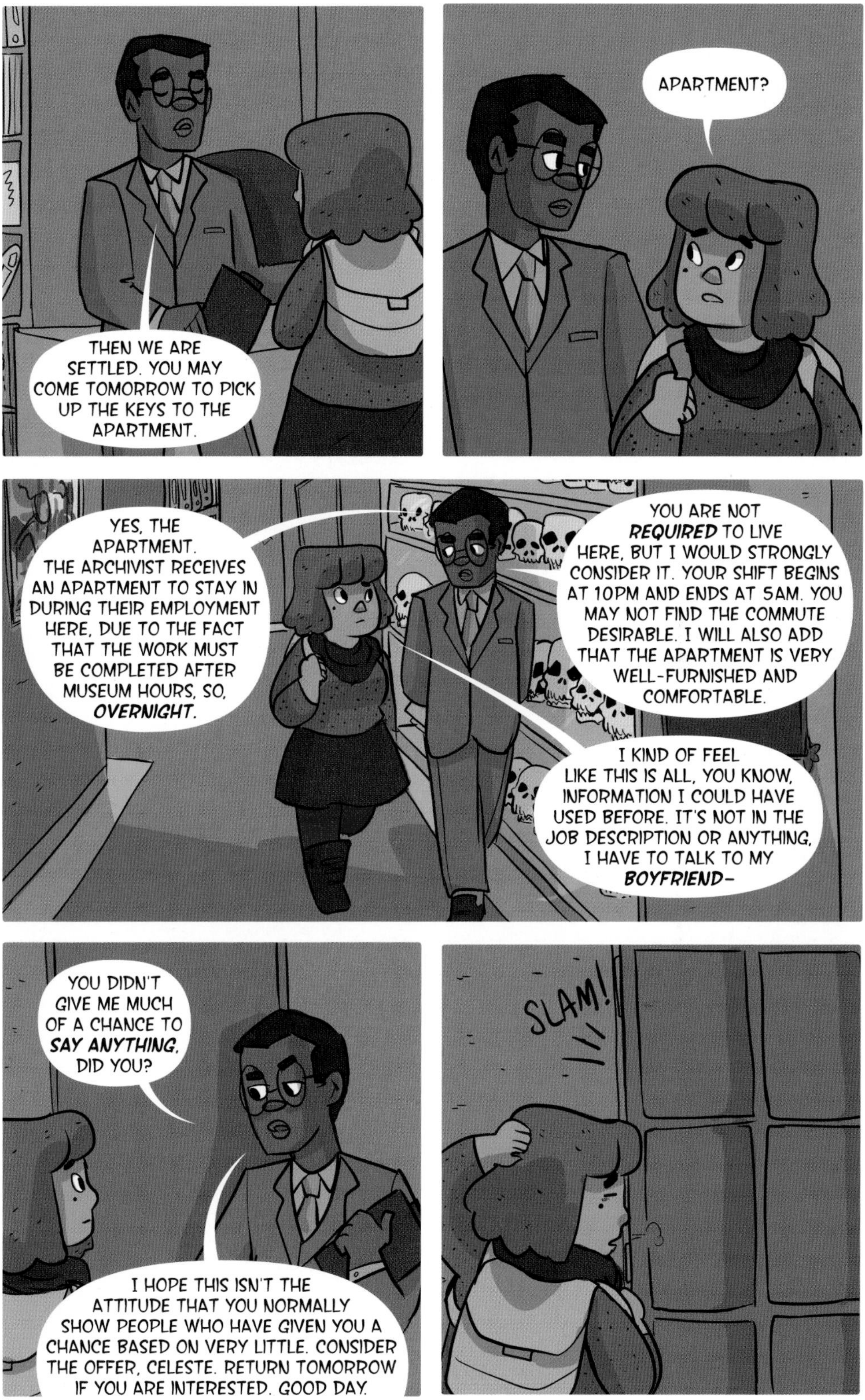
THEN WE ARE SETTLED. YOU MAY COME TOMORROW TO PICK UP THE KEYS TO THE APARTMENT.
APARTMENT?
YES, THE APARTMENT. THE ARCHIVIST RECEIVES AN APARTMENT TO STAY IN DURING THEIR EMPLOYMENT HERE, DUE TO THE FACT THAT THE WORK MUST BE COMPLETED AFTER MUSEUM HOURS, SO, ***OVERNIGHT***.
YOU ARE NOT ***REQUIRED*** TO LIVE HERE, BUT I WOULD STRONGLY CONSIDER IT. YOUR SHIFT BEGINS AT 10PM AND ENDS AT 5AM. YOU MAY NOT FIND THE COMMUTE DESIRABLE. I WILL ALSO ADD THAT THE APARTMENT IS VERY WELL-FURNISHED AND COMFORTABLE.
I KIND OF FEEL LIKE THIS IS ALL, YOU KNOW, INFORMATION I COULD HAVE USED BEFORE. IT'S NOT IN THE JOB DESCRIPTION OR ANYTHING. I HAVE TO TALK TO MY ***BOYFRIEND***-
YOU DIDN'T GIVE ME MUCH OF A CHANCE TO ***SAY ANYTHING***, DID YOU?
I HOPE THIS ISN'T THE ATTITUDE THAT YOU NORMALLY SHOW PEOPLE WHO HAVE GIVEN YOU A CHANCE BASED ON VERY LITTLE. CONSIDER THE OFFER, CELESTE. RETURN TOMORROW IF YOU ARE INTERESTED. GOOD DAY.
SLAM!

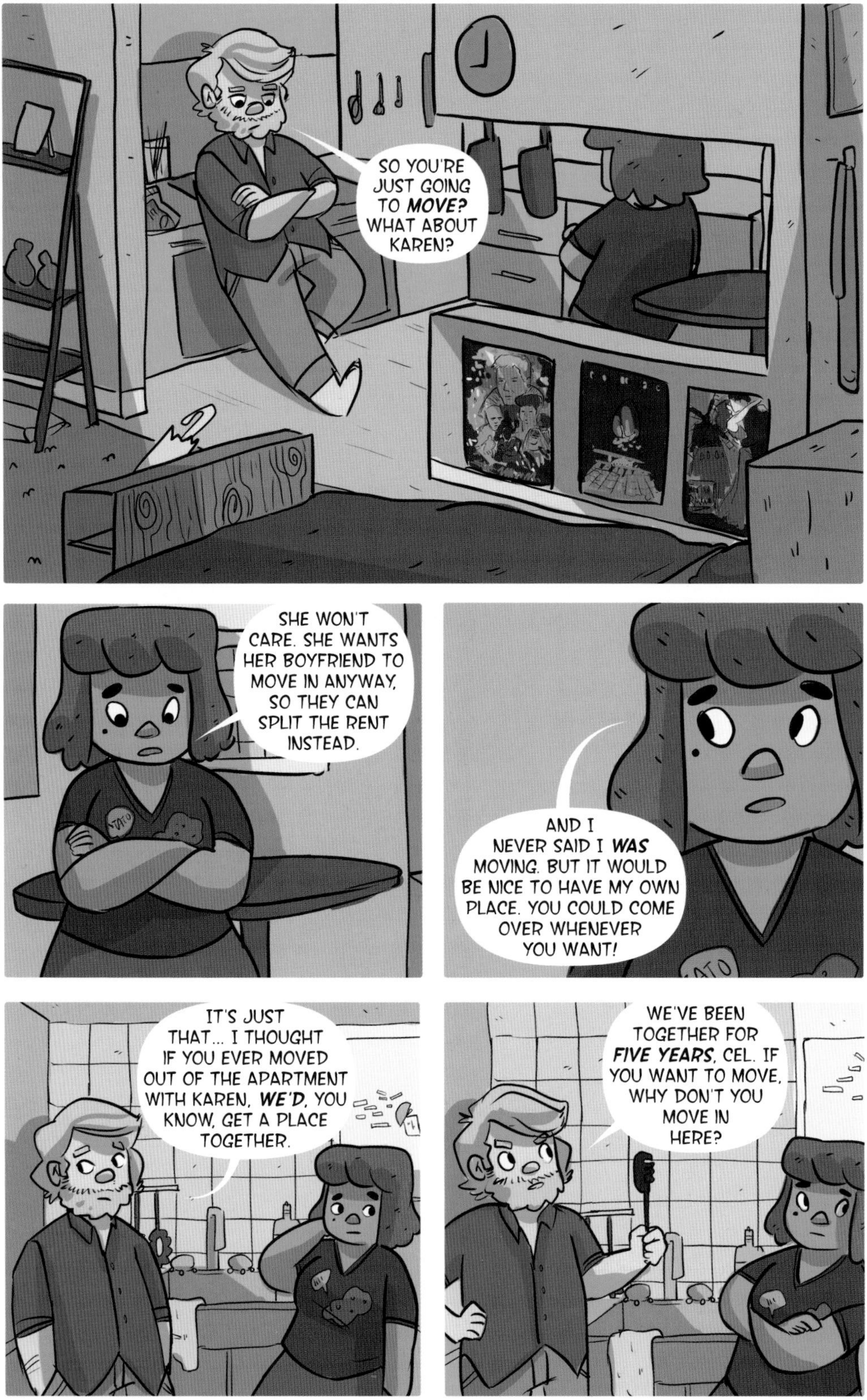
SO YOU'RE JUST GOING TO ***MOVE?*** WHAT ABOUT KAREN?
SHE WON'T CARE. SHE WANTS HER BOYFRIEND TO MOVE IN ANYWAY, SO THEY CAN SPLIT THE RENT INSTEAD.
AND I NEVER SAID I ***WAS*** MOVING. BUT IT WOULD BE NICE TO HAVE MY OWN PLACE. YOU COULD COME OVER WHENEVER YOU WANT!
IT'S JUST THAT... I THOUGHT IF YOU EVER MOVED OUT OF THE APARTMENT WITH KAREN, ***WE'D***, YOU KNOW, GET A PLACE TOGETHER.
WE'VE BEEN TOGETHER FOR ***FIVE YEARS***, CEL. IF YOU WANT TO MOVE, WHY DON'T YOU MOVE IN HERE?

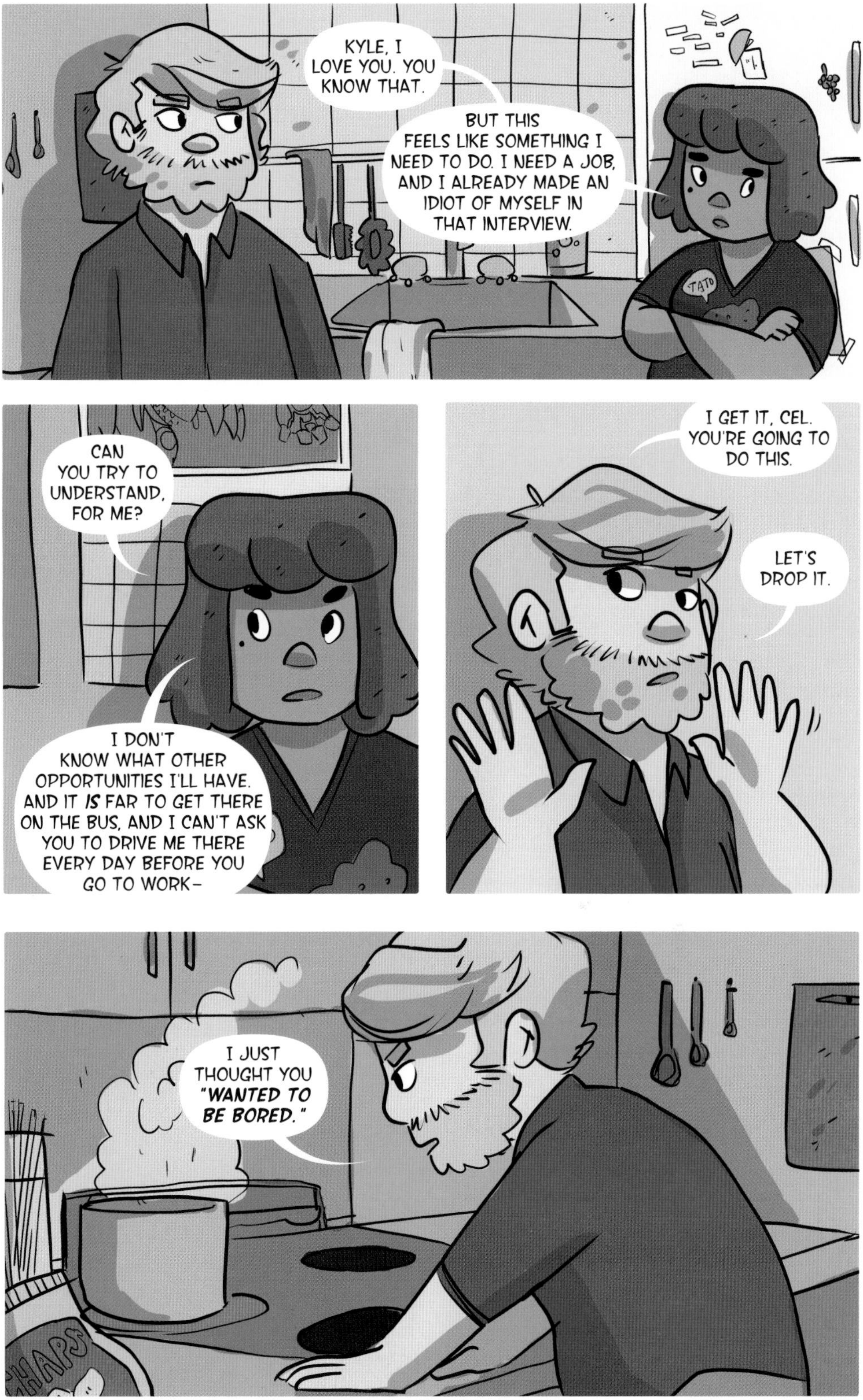
KYLE, I LOVE YOU. YOU KNOW THAT.
BUT THIS FEELS LIKE SOMETHING I NEED TO DO. I NEED A JOB, AND I ALREADY MADE AN IDIOT OF MYSELF IN THAT INTERVIEW.
CAN YOU TRY TO UNDERSTAND, FOR ME?
I DON'T KNOW WHAT OTHER OPPORTUNITIES I'LL HAVE. AND IT *IS* FAR TO GET THERE ON THE BUS, AND I CAN'T ASK YOU TO DRIVE ME THERE EVERY DAY BEFORE YOU GO TO WORK–
I GET IT, CEL. YOU'RE GOING TO DO THIS.
LET'S DROP IT.
I JUST THOUGHT YOU ***"WANTED TO BE BORED."***

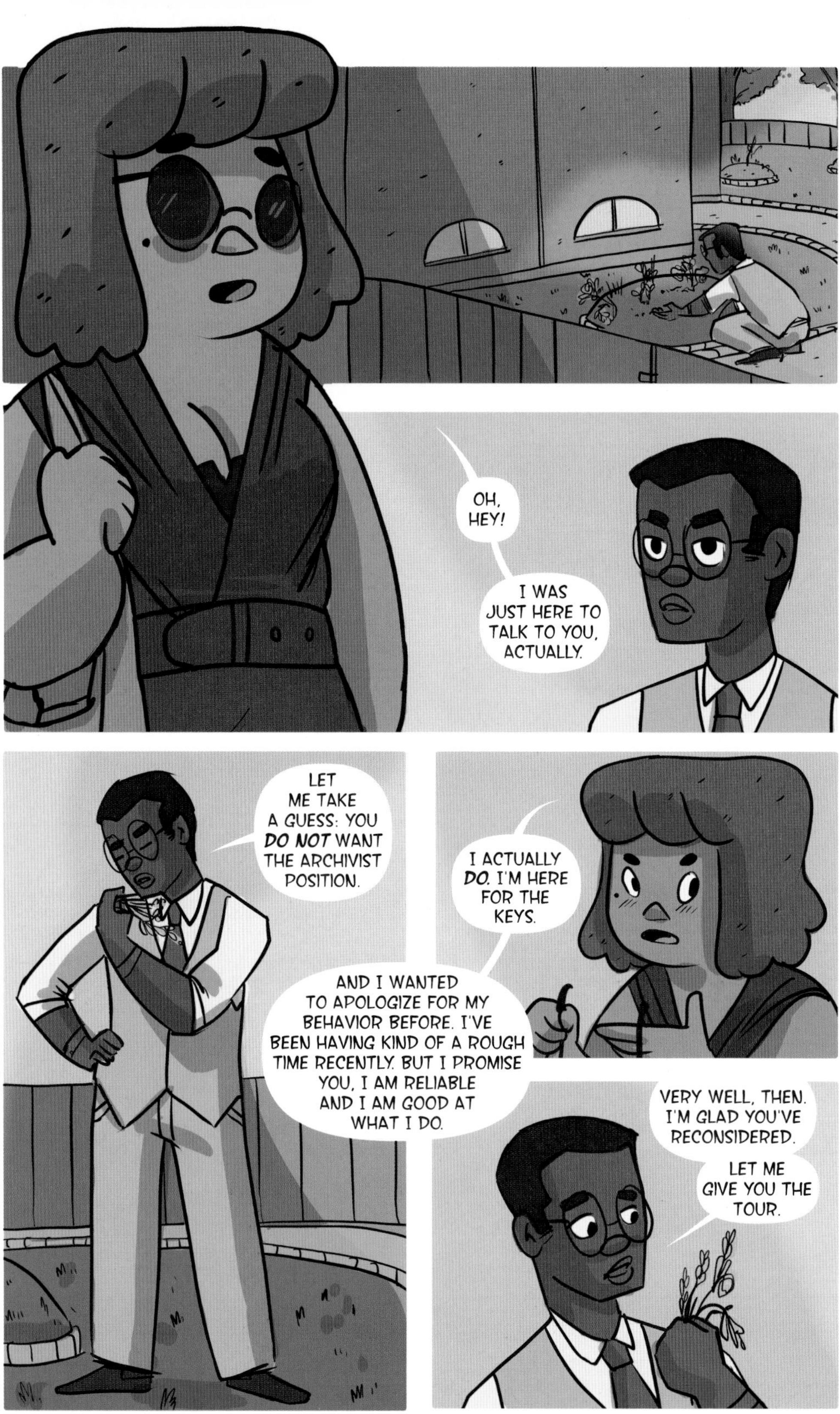
OH, HEY!
I WAS JUST HERE TO TALK TO YOU, ACTUALLY.
LET ME TAKE A GUESS: YOU *DO NOT* WANT THE ARCHIVIST POSITION.
I ACTUALLY *DO.* I'M HERE FOR THE KEYS.
AND I WANTED TO APOLOGIZE FOR MY BEHAVIOR BEFORE. I'VE BEEN HAVING KIND OF A ROUGH TIME RECENTLY. BUT I PROMISE YOU, I AM RELIABLE AND I AM GOOD AT WHAT I DO.
VERY WELL, THEN. I'M GLAD YOU'VE RECONSIDERED.
LET ME GIVE YOU THE TOUR.

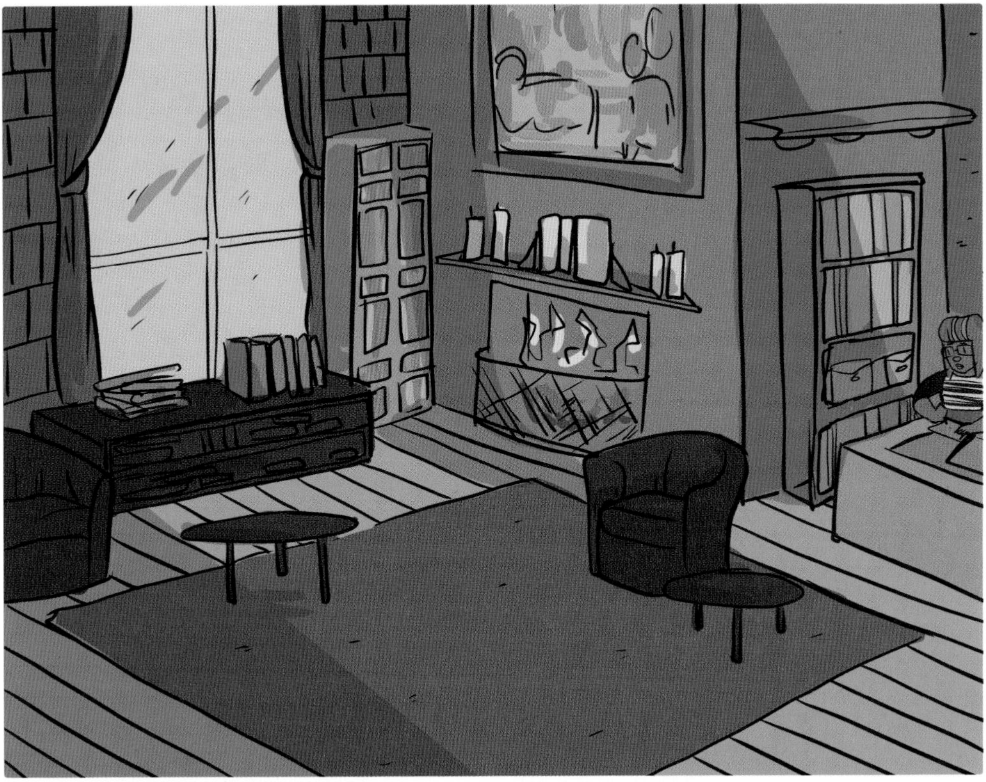

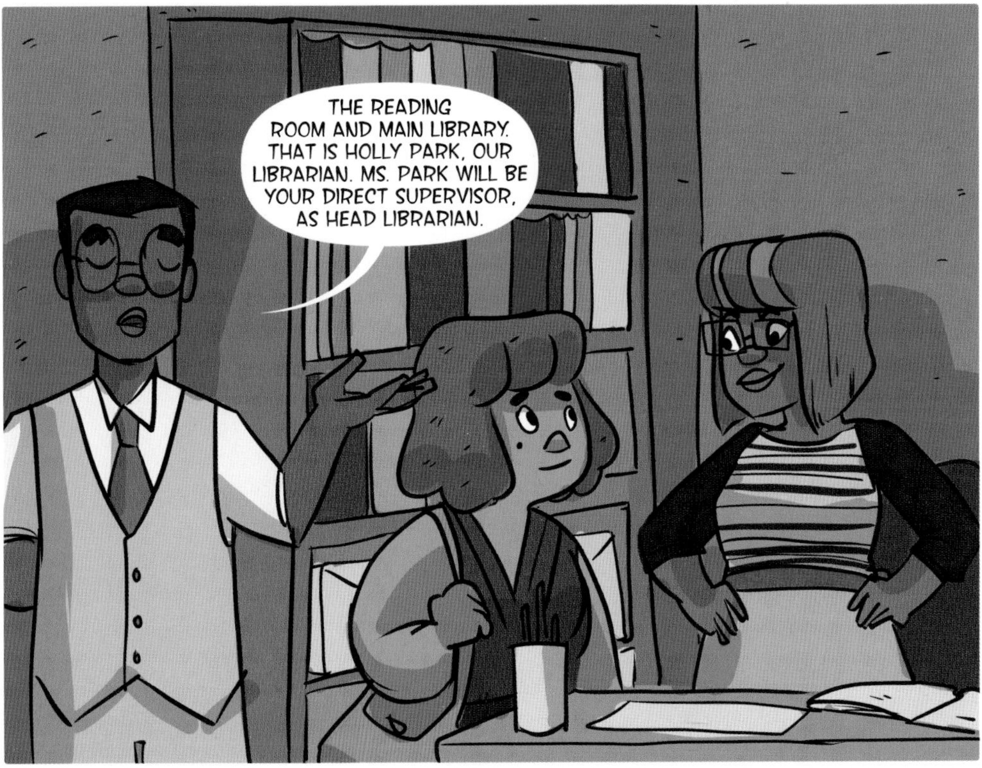

THE READING ROOM AND MAIN LIBRARY. THAT IS HOLLY PARK, OUR LIBRARIAN. MS. PARK WILL BE YOUR DIRECT SUPERVISOR, AS HEAD LIBRARIAN.

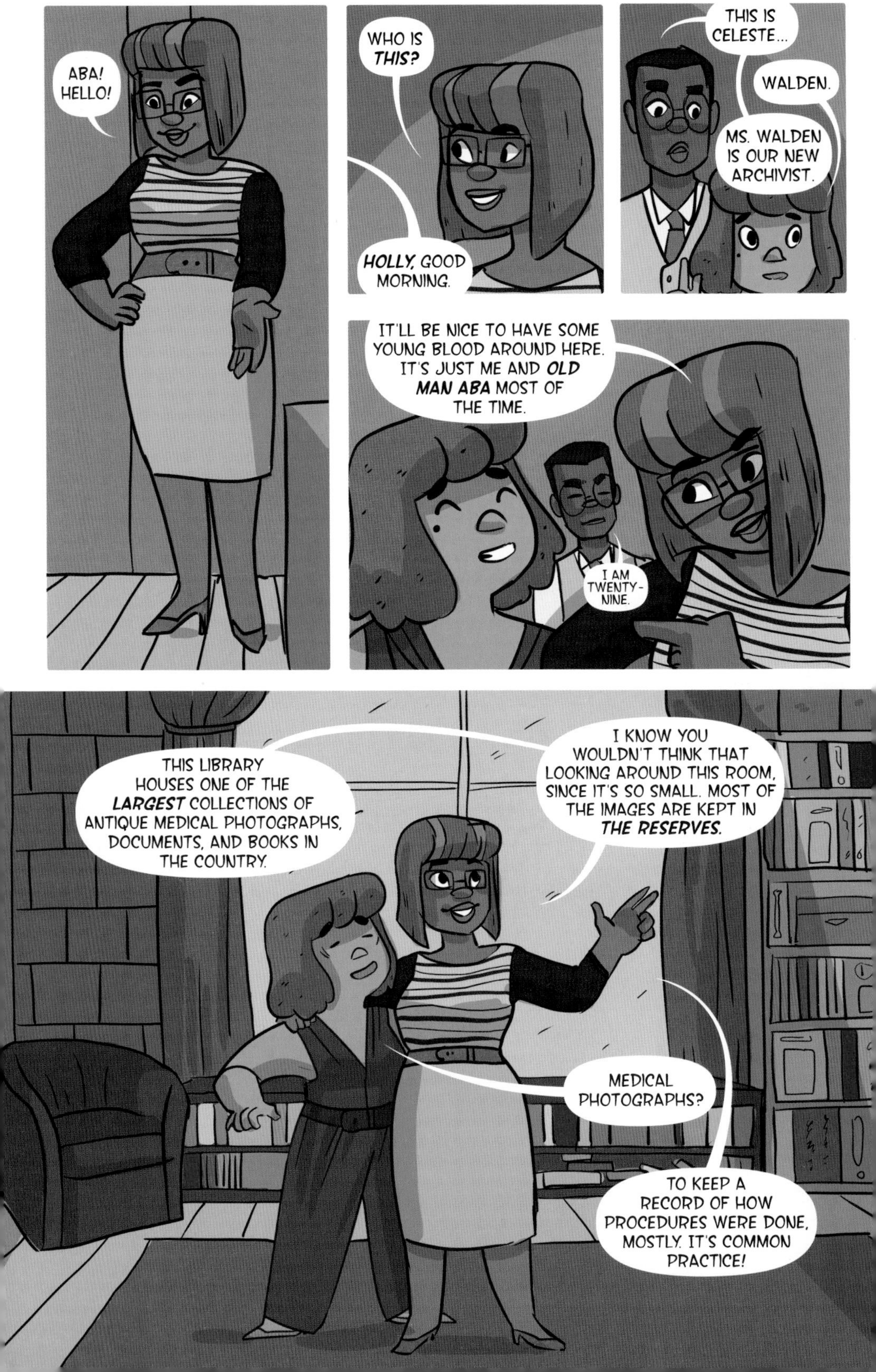
ABA! HELLO!
WHO IS **THIS?**
HOLLY, GOOD MORNING.
THIS IS CELESTE...
WALDEN.
MS. WALDEN IS OUR NEW ARCHIVIST.
IT'LL BE NICE TO HAVE SOME YOUNG BLOOD AROUND HERE. IT'S JUST ME AND ***OLD MAN ABA*** MOST OF THE TIME.
I AM TWENTY-NINE.
THIS LIBRARY HOUSES ONE OF THE ***LARGEST*** COLLECTIONS OF ANTIQUE MEDICAL PHOTOGRAPHS, DOCUMENTS, AND BOOKS IN THE COUNTRY.
I KNOW YOU WOULDN'T THINK THAT LOOKING AROUND THIS ROOM, SINCE IT'S SO SMALL. MOST OF THE IMAGES ARE KEPT IN ***THE RESERVES.***
MEDICAL PHOTOGRAPHS?
TO KEEP A RECORD OF HOW PROCEDURES WERE DONE, MOSTLY. IT'S COMMON PRACTICE!

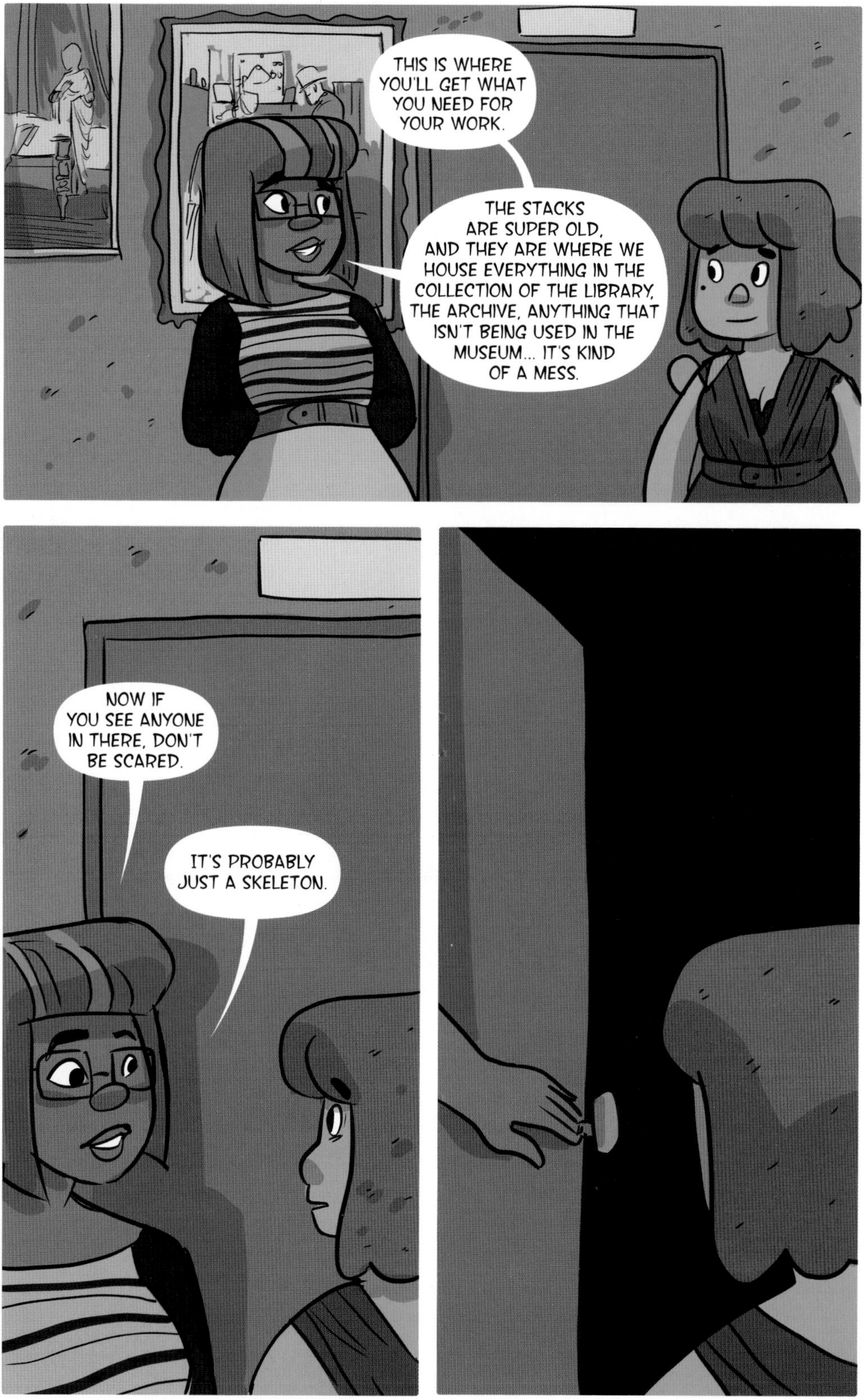
THIS IS WHERE YOU'LL GET WHAT YOU NEED FOR YOUR WORK.
THE STACKS ARE SUPER OLD, AND THEY ARE WHERE WE HOUSE EVERYTHING IN THE COLLECTION OF THE LIBRARY, THE ARCHIVE, ANYTHING THAT ISN'T BEING USED IN THE MUSEUM... IT'S KIND OF A MESS.
NOW IF YOU SEE ANYONE IN THERE, DON'T BE SCARED.
IT'S PROBABLY JUST A SKELETON.

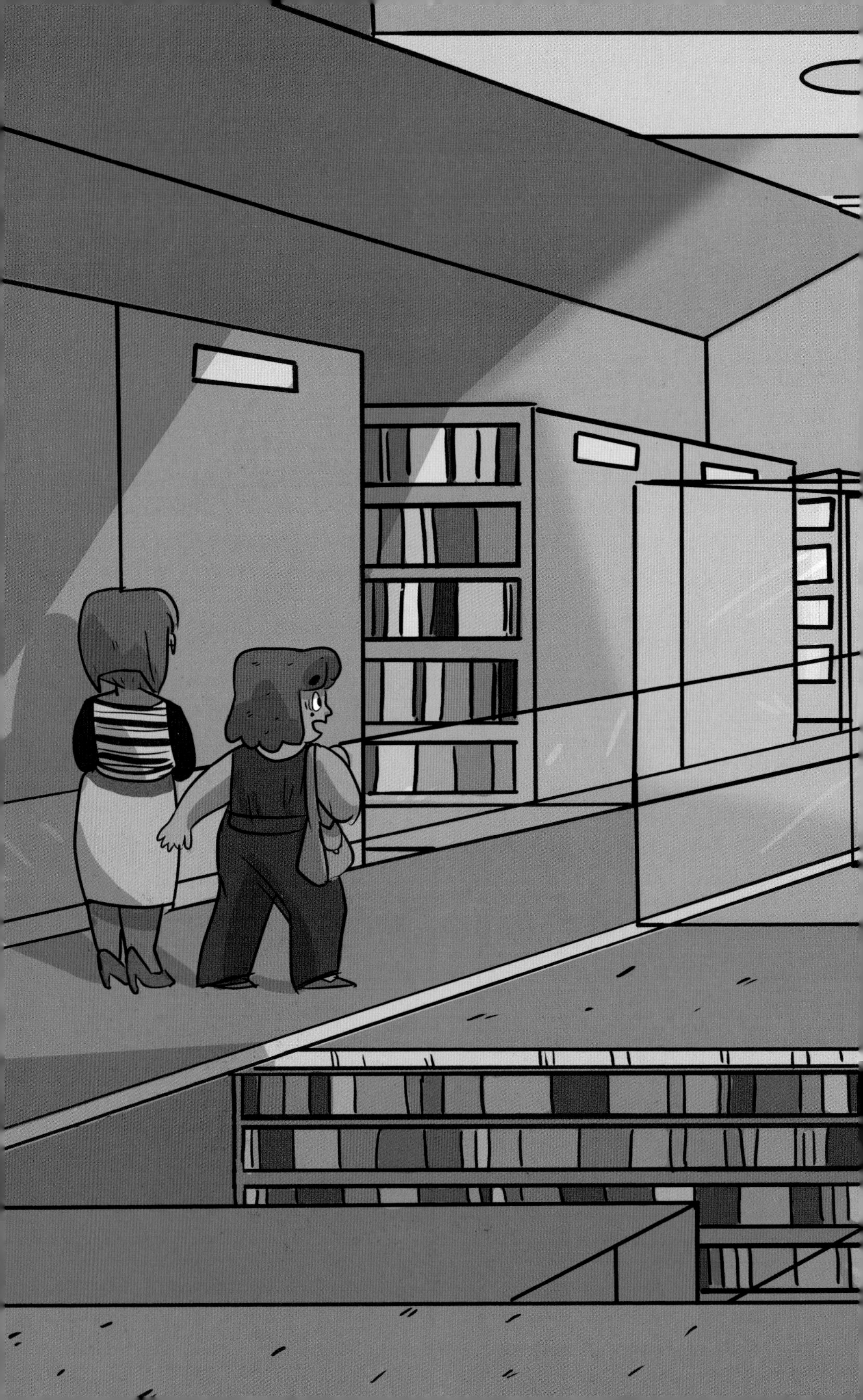

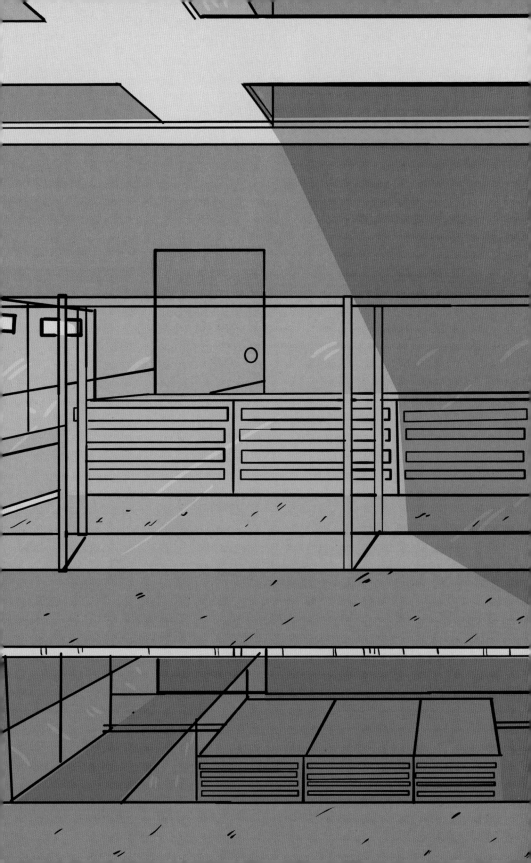

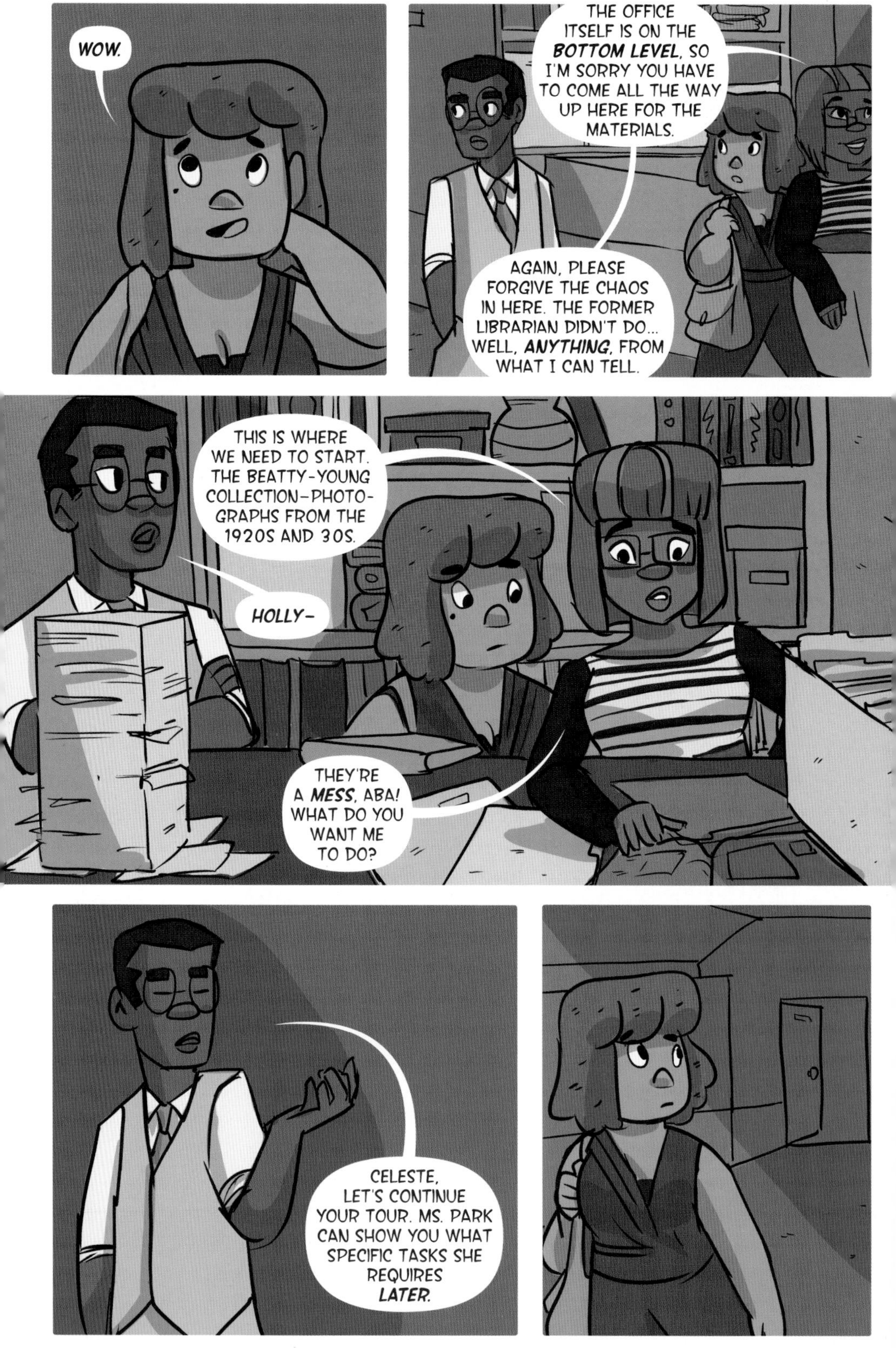
WOW.
THE OFFICE ITSELF IS ON THE BOTTOM LEVEL, SO I'M SORRY YOU HAVE TO COME ALL THE WAY UP HERE FOR THE MATERIALS.
AGAIN, PLEASE FORGIVE THE CHAOS IN HERE. THE FORMER LIBRARIAN DIDN'T DO... WELL, ANYTHING, FROM WHAT I CAN TELL.
THIS IS WHERE WE NEED TO START. THE BEATTY-YOUNG COLLECTION–PHOTOGRAPHS FROM THE 1920S AND 30S.
HOLLY–
THEY'RE A MESS, ABA! WHAT DO YOU WANT ME TO DO?
CELESTE, LET'S CONTINUE YOUR TOUR. MS. PARK CAN SHOW YOU WHAT SPECIFIC TASKS SHE REQUIRES LATER.

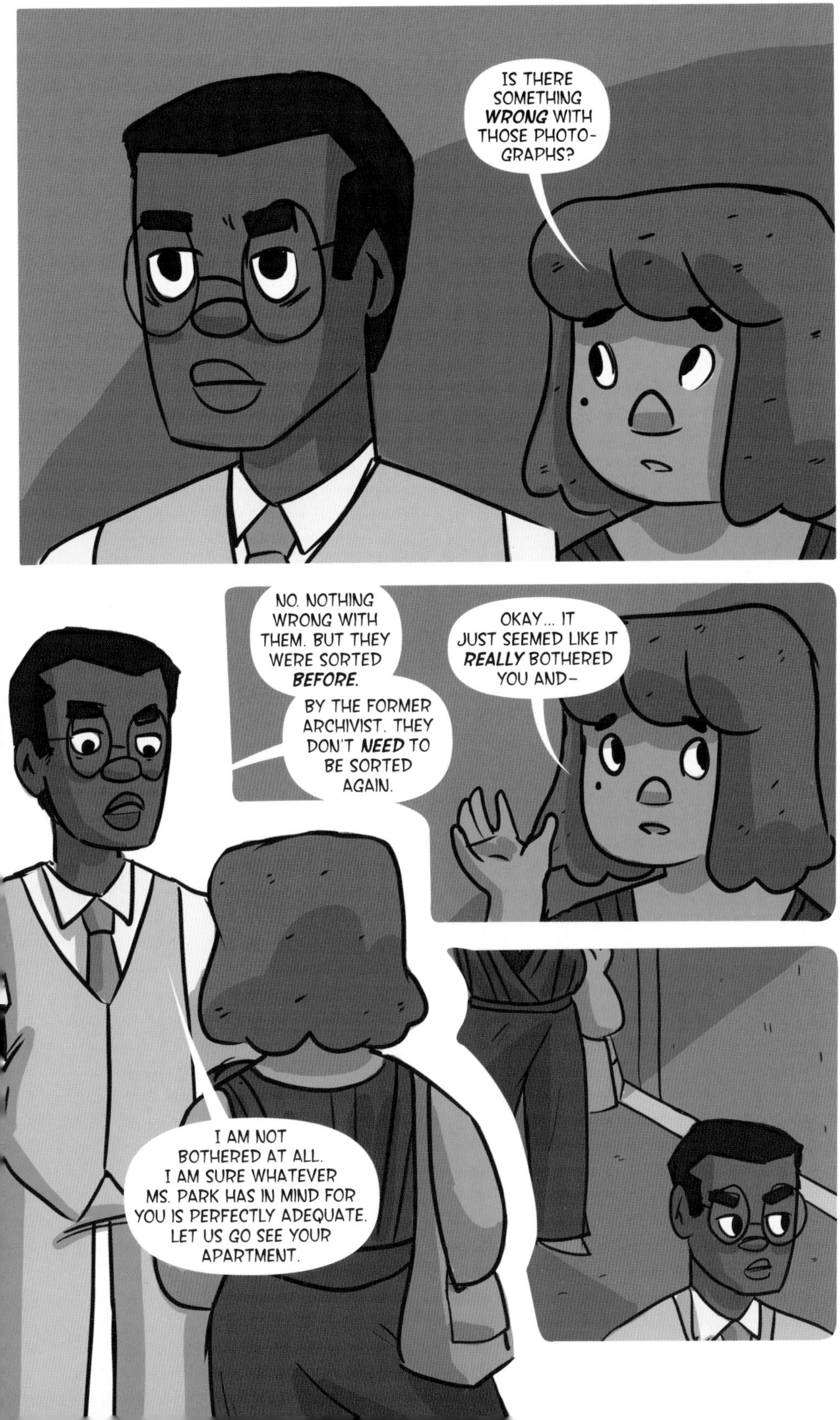
IS THERE SOMETHING WRONG WITH THOSE PHOTO-GRAPHS?
NO. NOTHING WRONG WITH THEM. BUT THEY WERE SORTED BEFORE.
BY THE FORMER ARCHIVIST. THEY DON'T NEED TO BE SORTED AGAIN.
OKAY... IT JUST SEEMED LIKE IT REALLY BOTHERED YOU AND–
I AM NOT BOTHERED AT ALL. I AM SURE WHATEVER MS. PARK HAS IN MIND FOR YOU IS PERFECTLY ADEQUATE. LET US GO SEE YOUR APARTMENT.

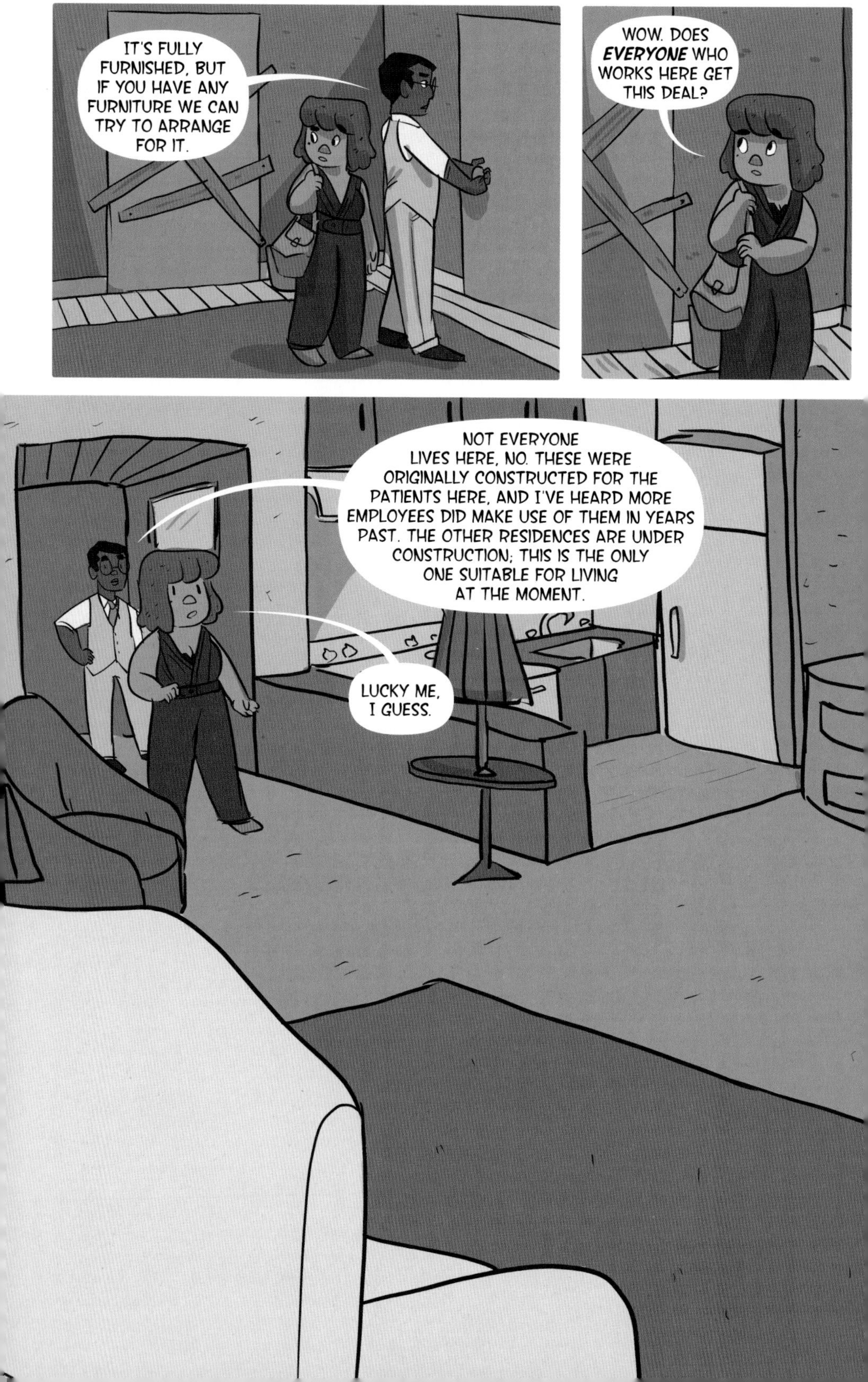
IT'S FULLY FURNISHED, BUT IF YOU HAVE ANY FURNITURE WE CAN TRY TO ARRANGE FOR IT.
WOW. DOES *EVERYONE* WHO WORKS HERE GET THIS DEAL?
NOT EVERYONE LIVES HERE, NO. THESE WERE ORIGINALLY CONSTRUCTED FOR THE PATIENTS HERE, AND I'VE HEARD MORE EMPLOYEES DID MAKE USE OF THEM IN YEARS PAST. THE OTHER RESIDENCES ARE UNDER CONSTRUCTION; THIS IS THE ONLY ONE SUITABLE FOR LIVING AT THE MOMENT.
LUCKY ME, I GUESS.

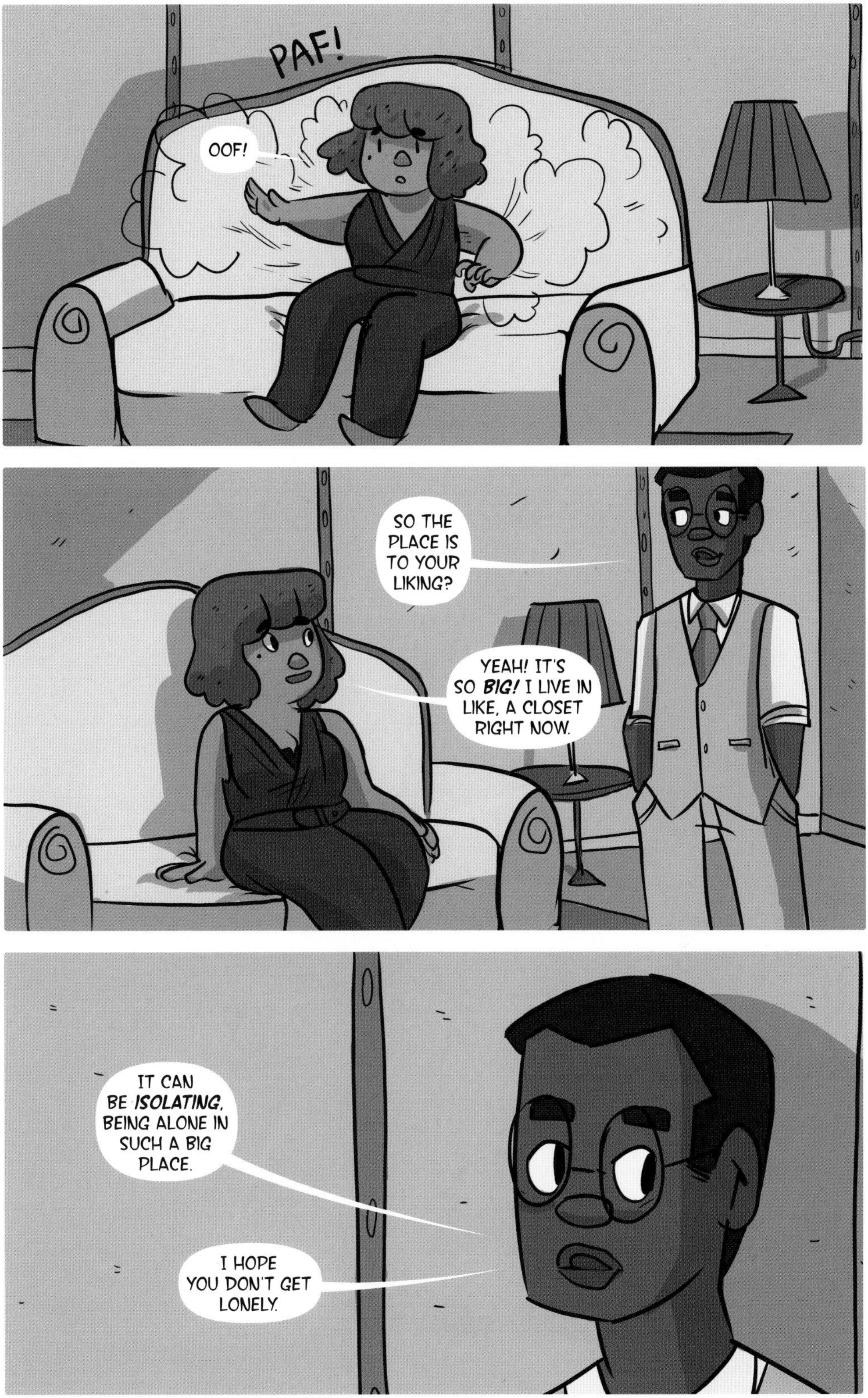
PAF!
OOF!
SO THE PLACE IS TO YOUR LIKING?
YEAH! IT'S SO **BIG!** I LIVE IN LIKE, A CLOSET RIGHT NOW.
IT CAN BE ***ISOLATING***, BEING ALONE IN SUCH A BIG PLACE.
I HOPE YOU DON'T GET LONELY.

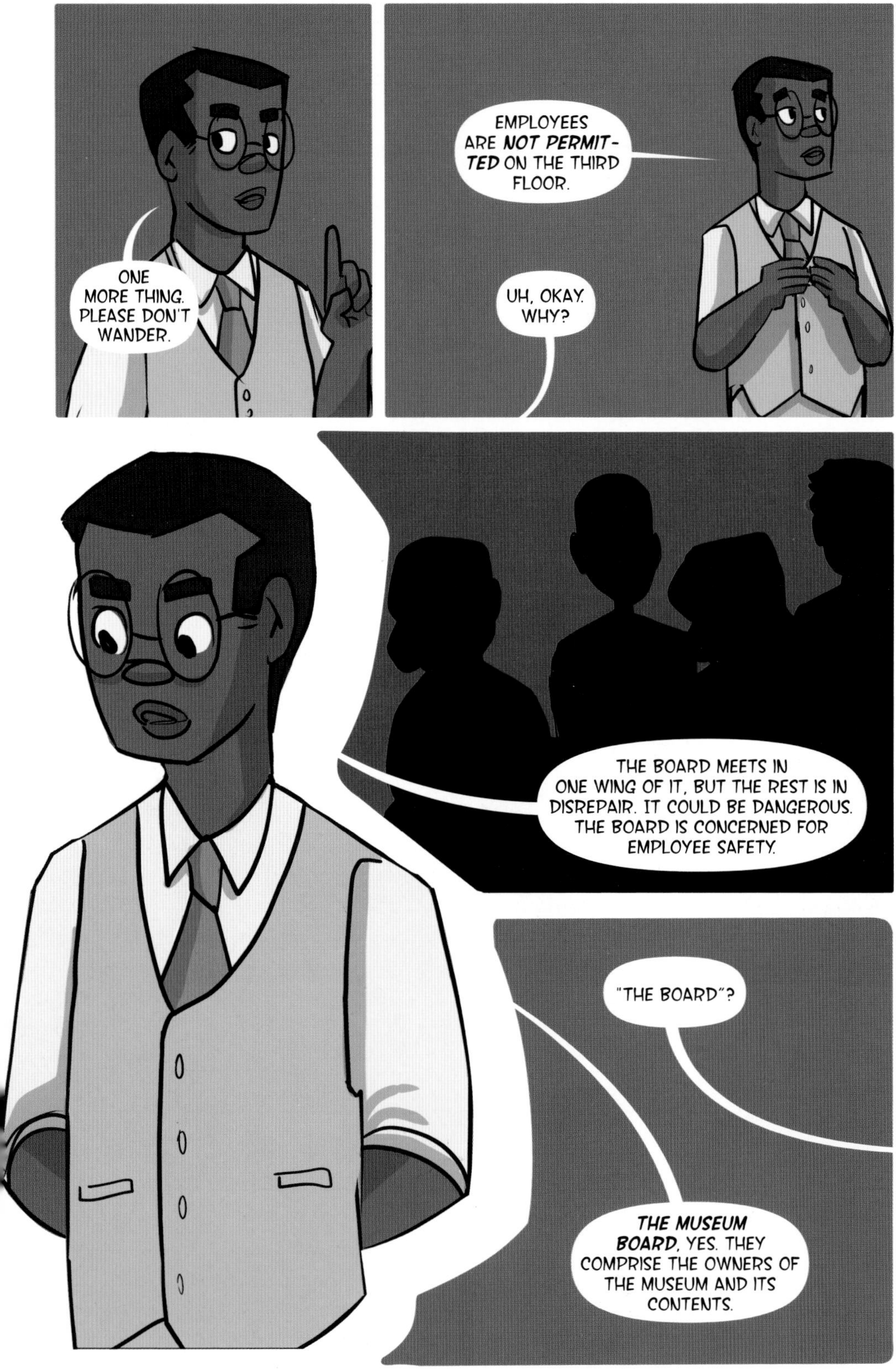
ONE MORE THING. PLEASE DON'T WANDER.
EMPLOYEES ARE **NOT PERMITTED** ON THE THIRD FLOOR.
UH, OKAY. WHY?
THE BOARD MEETS IN ONE WING OF IT, BUT THE REST IS IN DISREPAIR. IT COULD BE DANGEROUS. THE BOARD IS CONCERNED FOR EMPLOYEE SAFETY.
"THE BOARD"?
THE MUSEUM BOARD, YES. THEY COMPRISE THE OWNERS OF THE MUSEUM AND ITS CONTENTS.

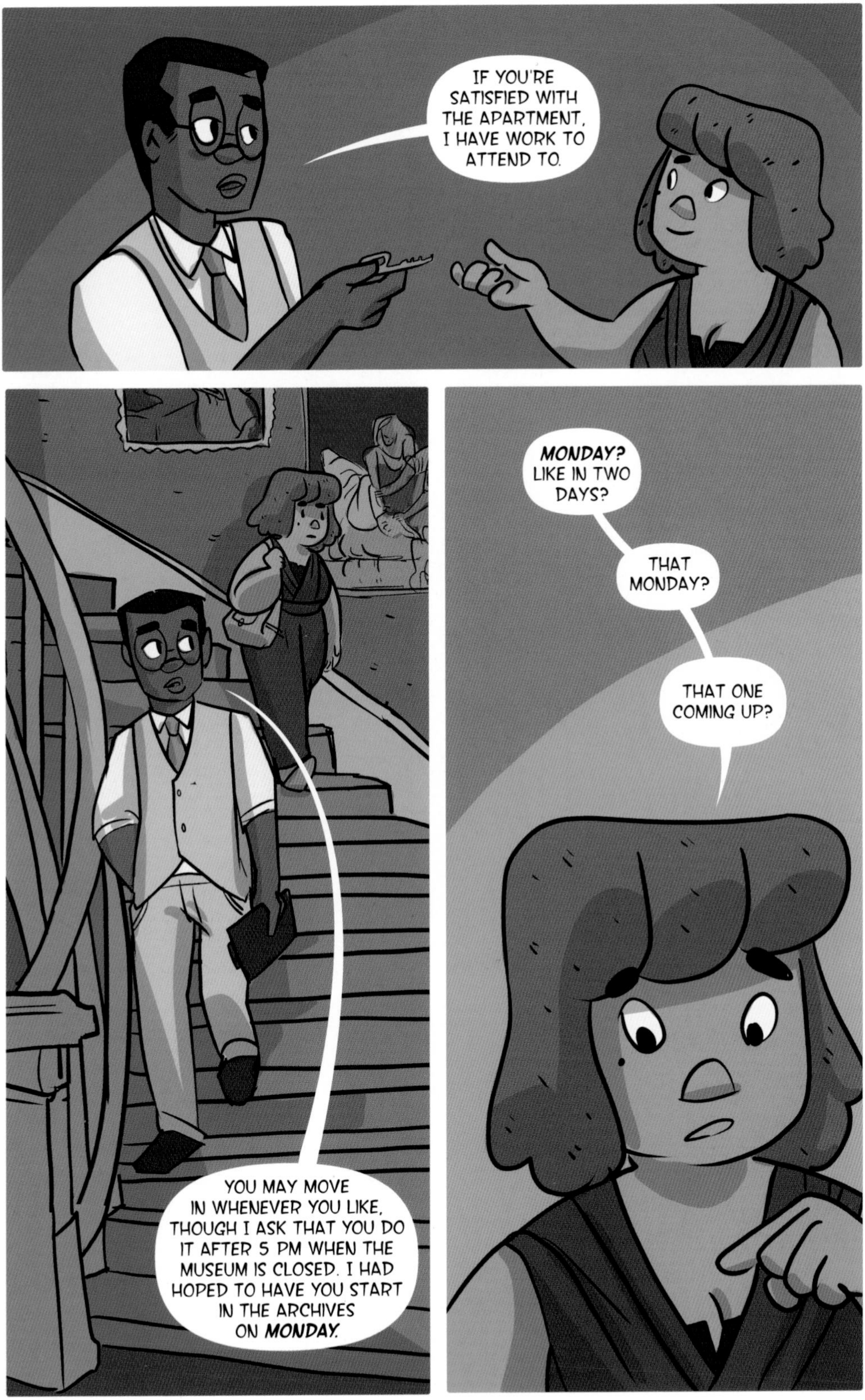
IF YOU'RE SATISFIED WITH THE APARTMENT, I HAVE WORK TO ATTEND TO.
YOU MAY MOVE IN WHENEVER YOU LIKE, THOUGH I ASK THAT YOU DO IT AFTER 5 PM WHEN THE MUSEUM IS CLOSED. I HAD HOPED TO HAVE YOU START IN THE ARCHIVES ON ***MONDAY.***
MONDAY? LIKE IN TWO DAYS?
THAT MONDAY?
THAT ONE COMING UP?

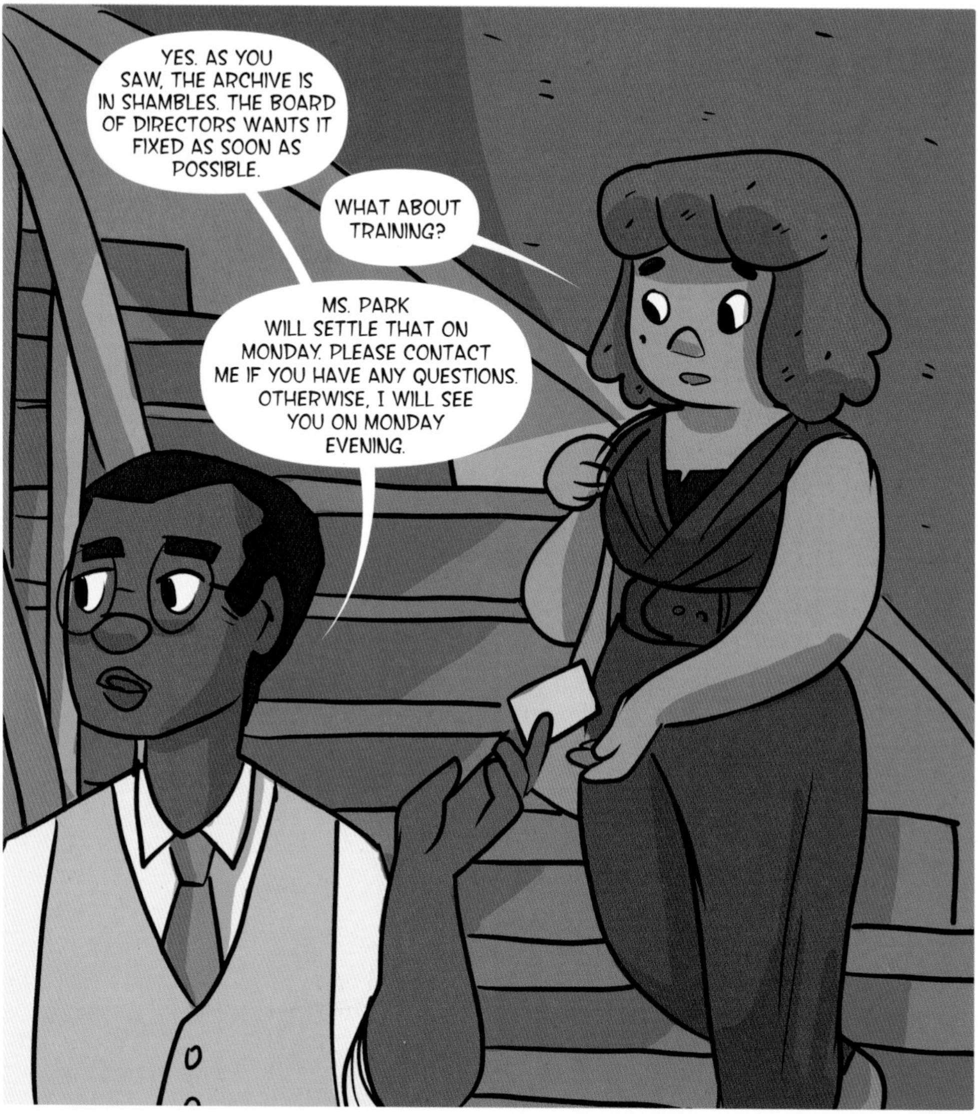
YES. AS YOU SAW, THE ARCHIVE IS IN SHAMBLES. THE BOARD OF DIRECTORS WANTS IT FIXED AS SOON AS POSSIBLE.
WHAT ABOUT TRAINING?
MS. PARK WILL SETTLE THAT ON MONDAY. PLEASE CONTACT ME IF YOU HAVE ANY QUESTIONS. OTHERWISE, I WILL SEE YOU ON MONDAY EVENING.

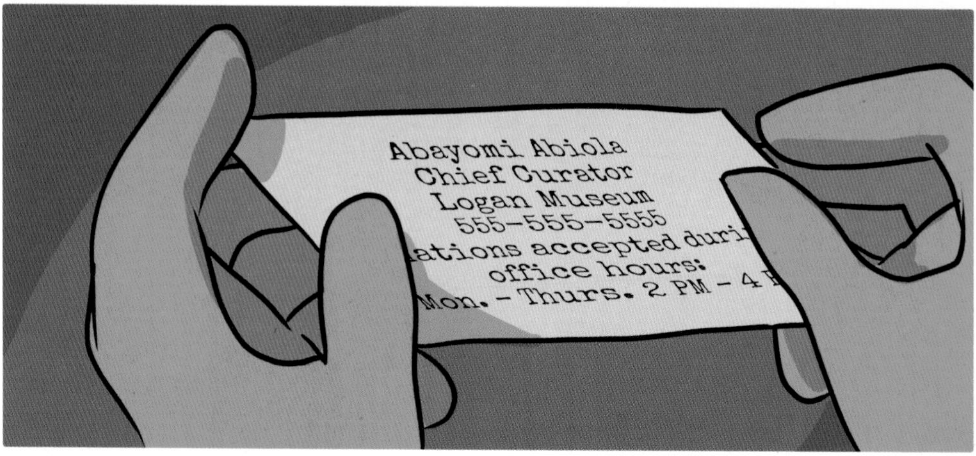
Abayomi Abiola
Chief Curator
Logan Museum
555-555-5555
office hours:

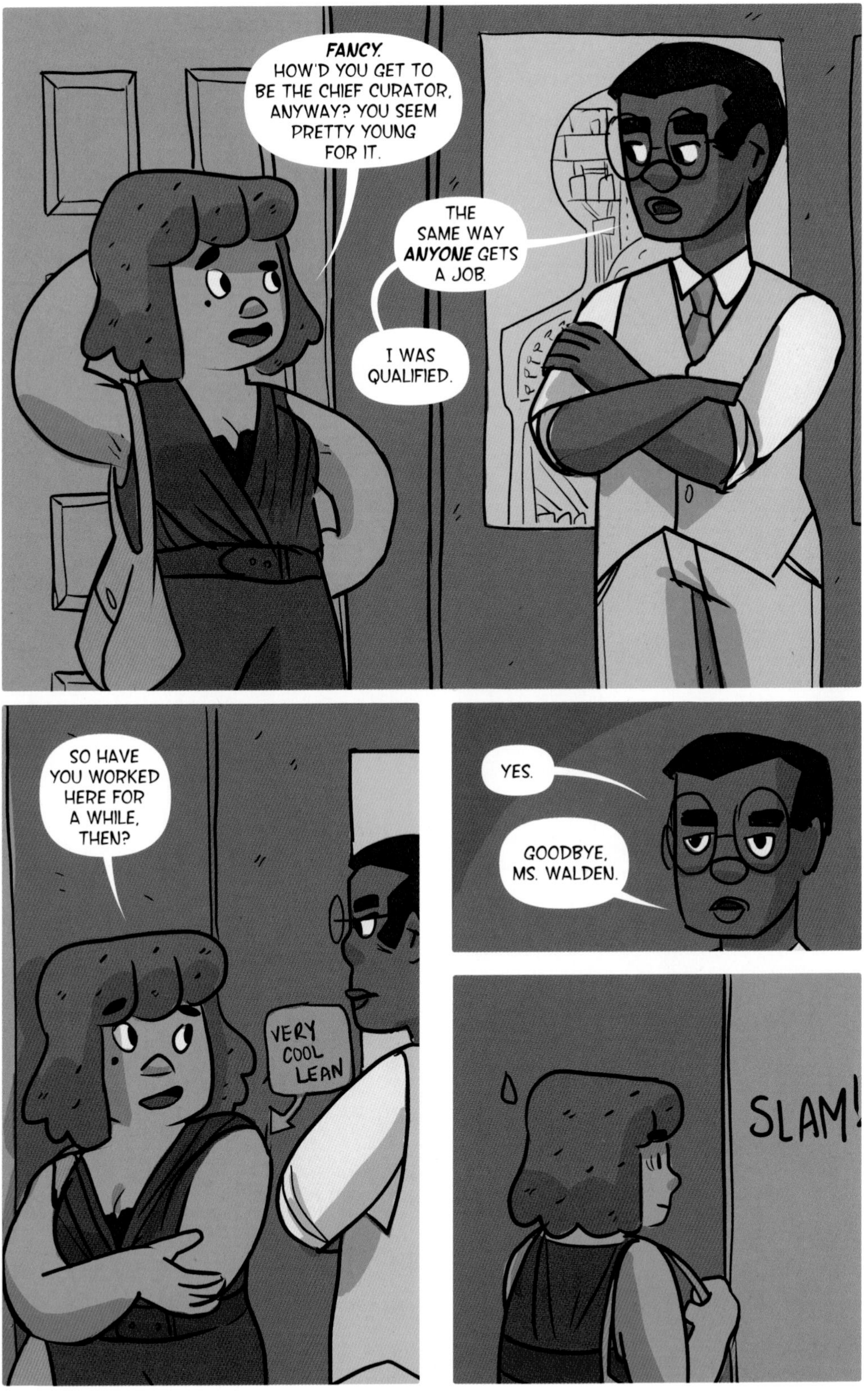
FANCY. HOW'D YOU GET TO BE THE CHIEF CURATOR, ANYWAY? YOU SEEM PRETTY YOUNG FOR IT.
THE SAME WAY ANYONE GETS A JOB.
I WAS QUALIFIED.
SO HAVE YOU WORKED HERE FOR A WHILE, THEN?
VERY COOL LEAN
YES.
GOODBYE, MS. WALDEN.
SLAM!

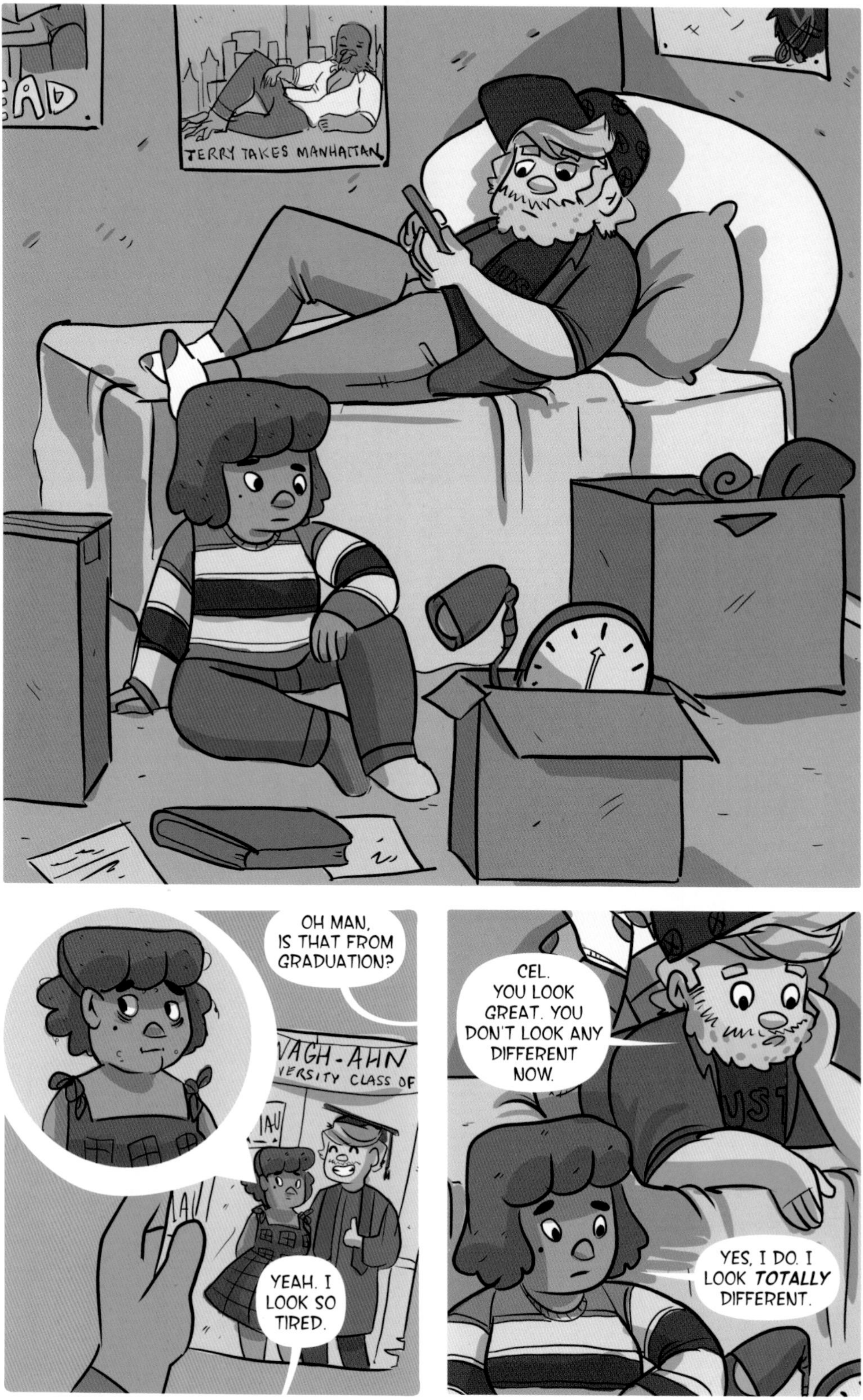

EAD
TERRY TAKES MANHATTAN
OH MAN, IS THAT FROM GRADUATION?
VAGH-AHN
VERSITY CLASS OF
YEAH. I LOOK SO TIRED.
CEL. YOU LOOK GREAT. YOU DON'T LOOK ANY DIFFERENT NOW.
YES, I DO. I LOOK **TOTALLY** DIFFERENT.

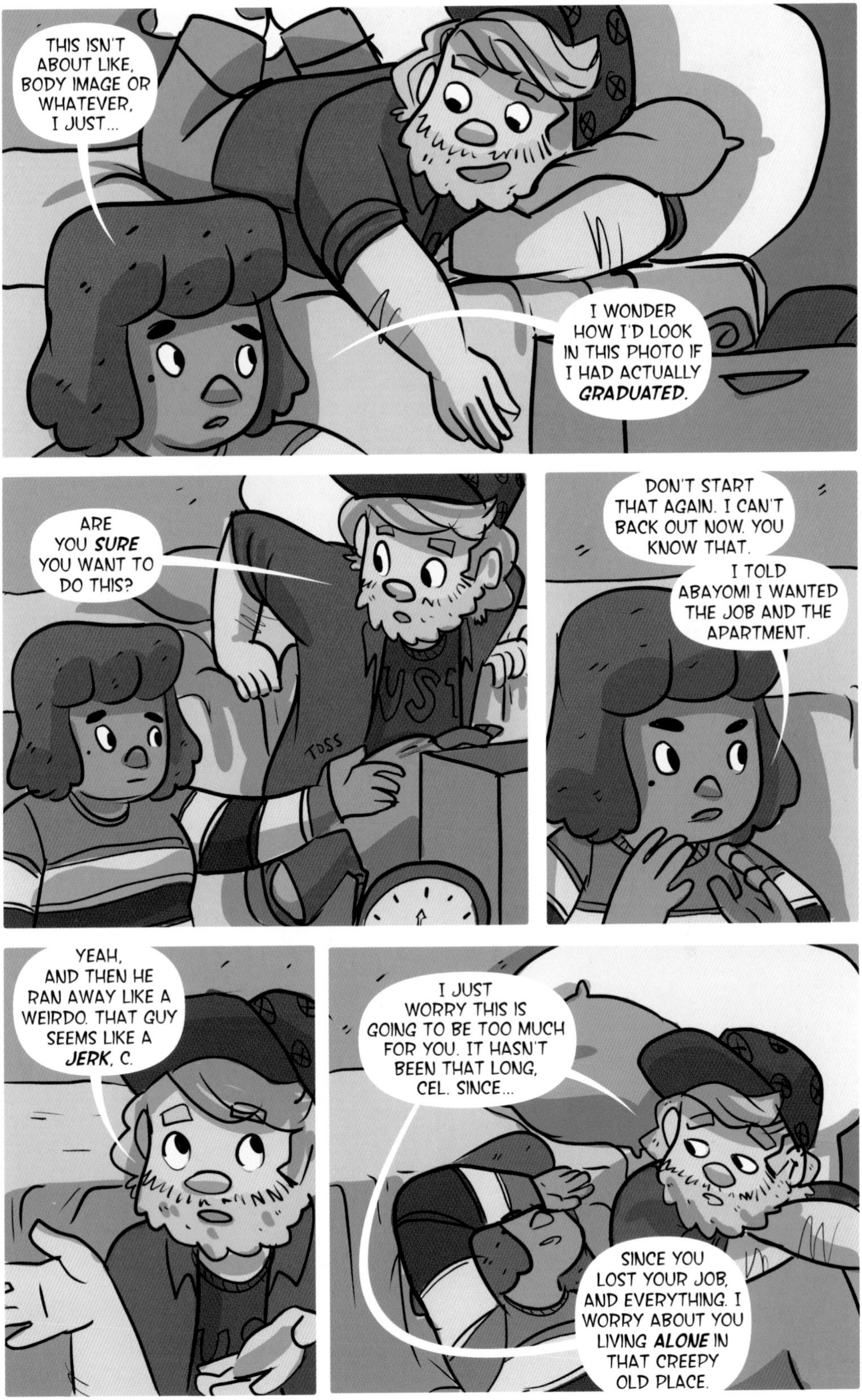
THIS ISN'T ABOUT LIKE, BODY IMAGE OR WHATEVER, I JUST...
I WONDER HOW I'D LOOK IN THIS PHOTO IF I HAD ACTUALLY GRADUATED.
ARE YOU SURE YOU WANT TO DO THIS?
TOSS
DON'T START THAT AGAIN. I CAN'T BACK OUT NOW. YOU KNOW THAT.
I TOLD ABAYOMI I WANTED THE JOB AND THE APARTMENT.
YEAH, AND THEN HE RAN AWAY LIKE A WEIRDO. THAT GUY SEEMS LIKE A JERK, C.
I JUST WORRY THIS IS GOING TO BE TOO MUCH FOR YOU. IT HASN'T BEEN THAT LONG, CEL. SINCE...
SINCE YOU LOST YOUR JOB, AND EVERYTHING. I WORRY ABOUT YOU LIVING ALONE IN THAT CREEPY OLD PLACE.

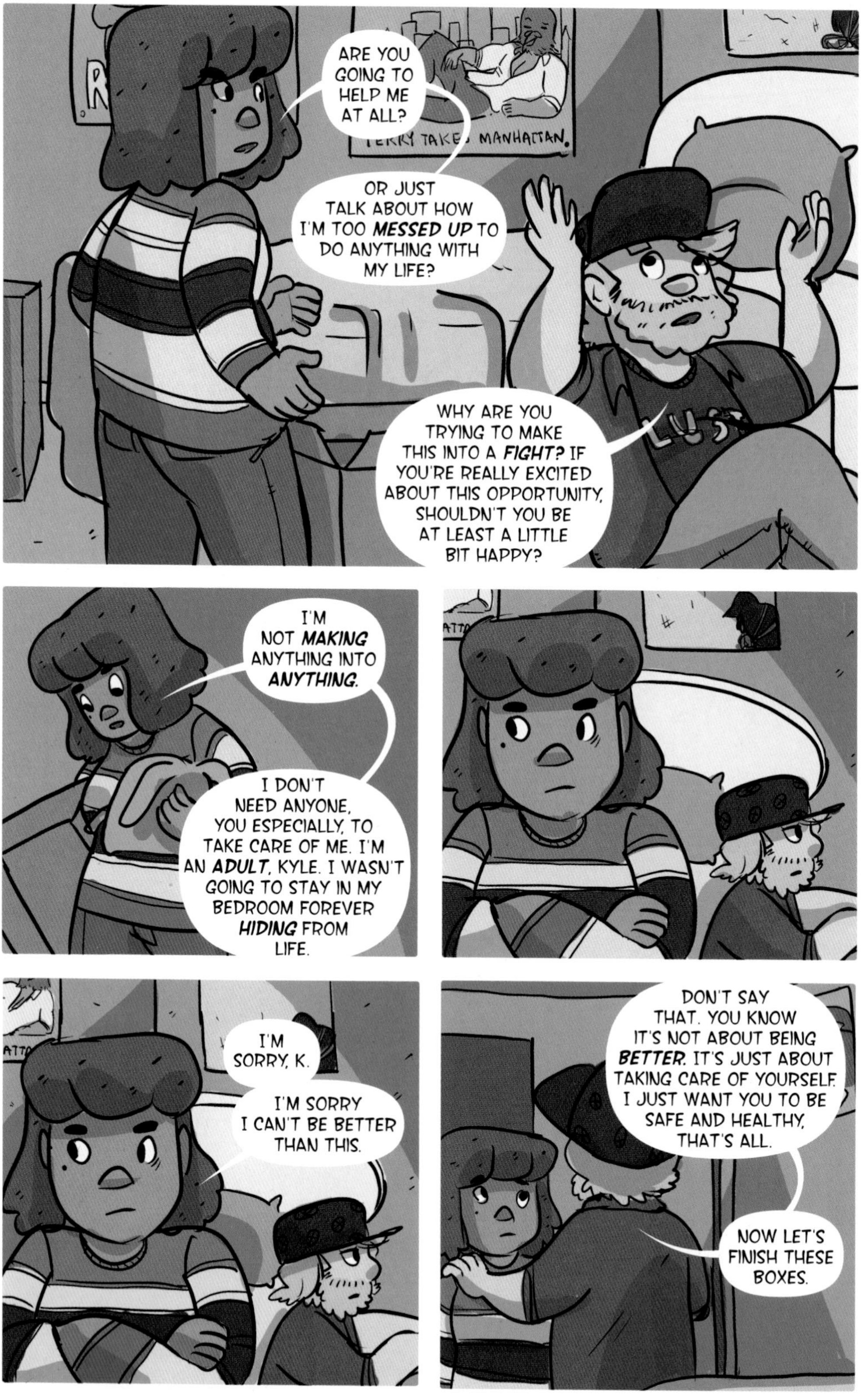
TERRY TAKES MANHATTAN.
ARE YOU GOING TO HELP ME AT ALL?
OR JUST TALK ABOUT HOW I'M TOO MESSED UP TO DO ANYTHING WITH MY LIFE?
WHY ARE YOU TRYING TO MAKE THIS INTO A FIGHT? IF YOU'RE REALLY EXCITED ABOUT THIS OPPORTUNITY, SHOULDN'T YOU BE AT LEAST A LITTLE BIT HAPPY?
I'M NOT MAKING ANYTHING INTO ANYTHING.
I DON'T NEED ANYONE, YOU ESPECIALLY, TO TAKE CARE OF ME. I'M AN ADULT, KYLE. I WASN'T GOING TO STAY IN MY BEDROOM FOREVER HIDING FROM LIFE.
I'M SORRY, K.
I'M SORRY I CAN'T BE BETTER THAN THIS.
DON'T SAY THAT. YOU KNOW IT'S NOT ABOUT BEING BETTER. IT'S JUST ABOUT TAKING CARE OF YOURSELF. I JUST WANT YOU TO BE SAFE AND HEALTHY, THAT'S ALL.
NOW LET'S FINISH THESE BOXES.

TWO DAYS LATER

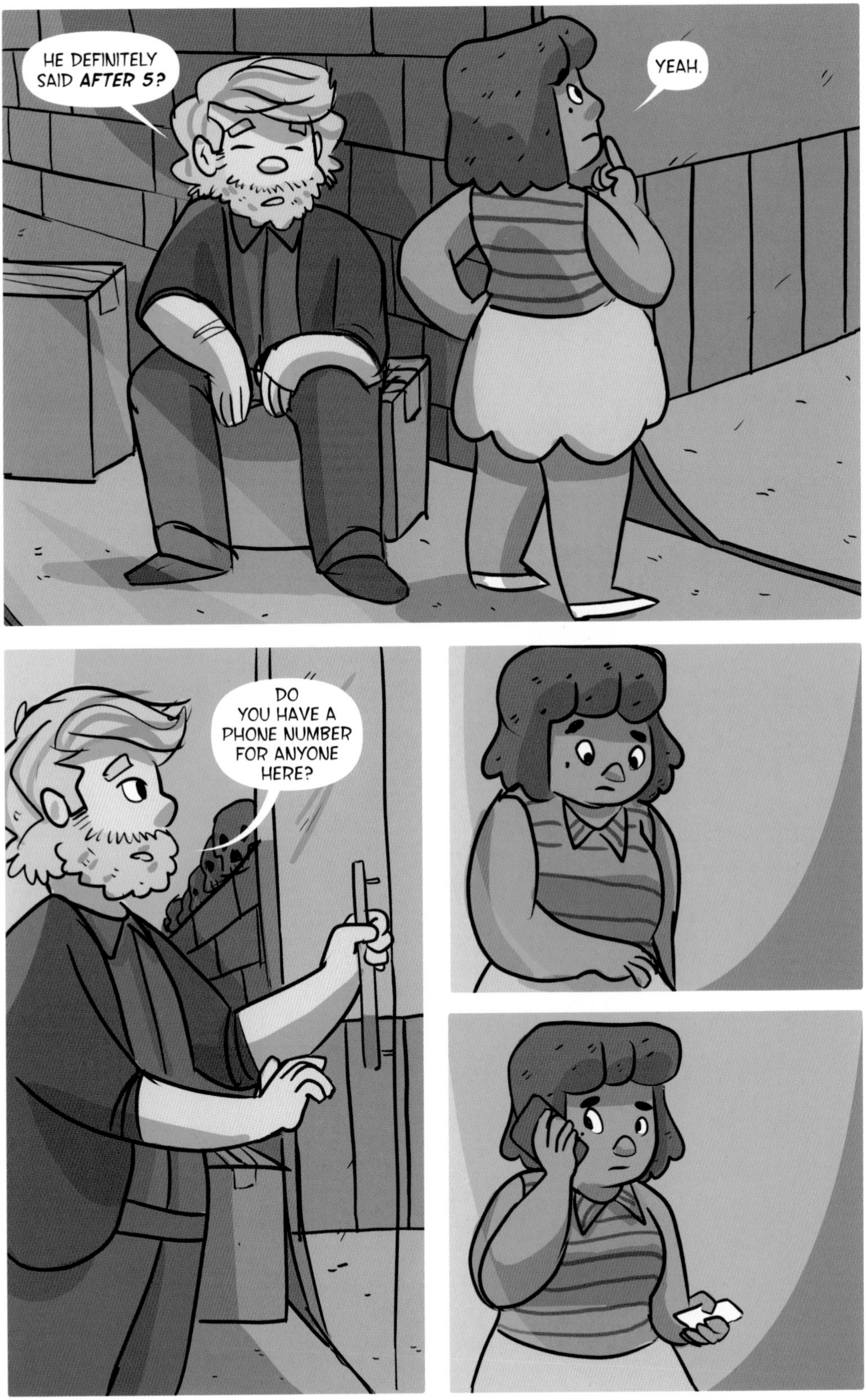
HE DEFINITELY SAID AFTER 5?
YEAH.
DO YOU HAVE A PHONE NUMBER FOR ANYONE HERE?

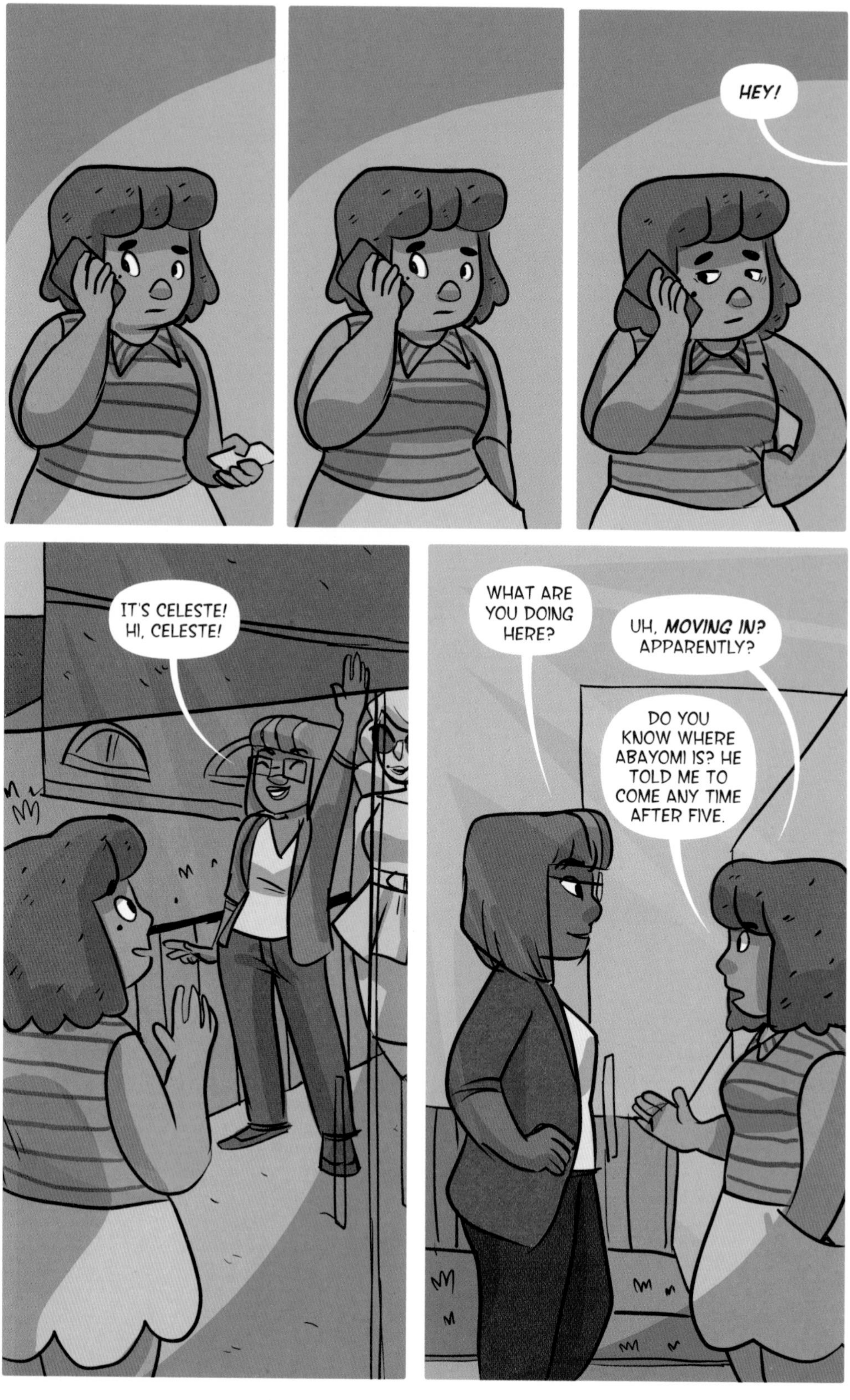
HEY!
IT'S CELESTE! HI, CELESTE!
WHAT ARE YOU DOING HERE?
UH, *MOVING IN?* APPARENTLY?
DO YOU KNOW WHERE ABAYOMI IS? HE TOLD ME TO COME ANY TIME AFTER FIVE.

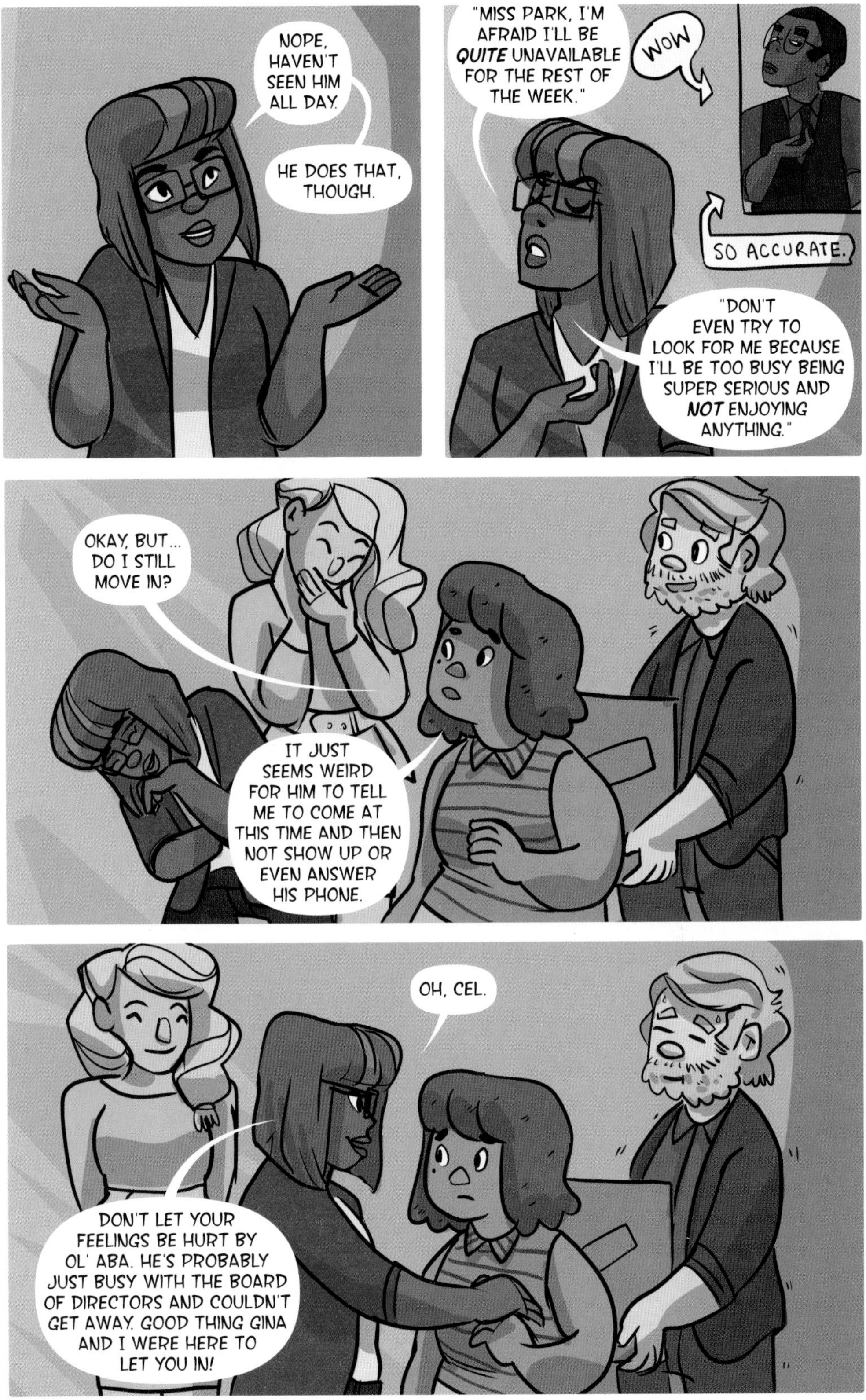
NOPE, HAVEN'T SEEN HIM ALL DAY.
HE DOES THAT, THOUGH.
"MISS PARK, I'M AFRAID I'LL BE QUITE UNAVAILABLE FOR THE REST OF THE WEEK."
WOW
SO ACCURATE.
"DON'T EVEN TRY TO LOOK FOR ME BECAUSE I'LL BE TOO BUSY BEING SUPER SERIOUS AND NOT ENJOYING ANYTHING."
OKAY, BUT... DO I STILL MOVE IN?
IT JUST SEEMS WEIRD FOR HIM TO TELL ME TO COME AT THIS TIME AND THEN NOT SHOW UP OR EVEN ANSWER HIS PHONE.
OH, CEL.
DON'T LET YOUR FEELINGS BE HURT BY OL' ABA. HE'S PROBABLY JUST BUSY WITH THE BOARD OF DIRECTORS AND COULDN'T GET AWAY. GOOD THING GINA AND I WERE HERE TO LET YOU IN!

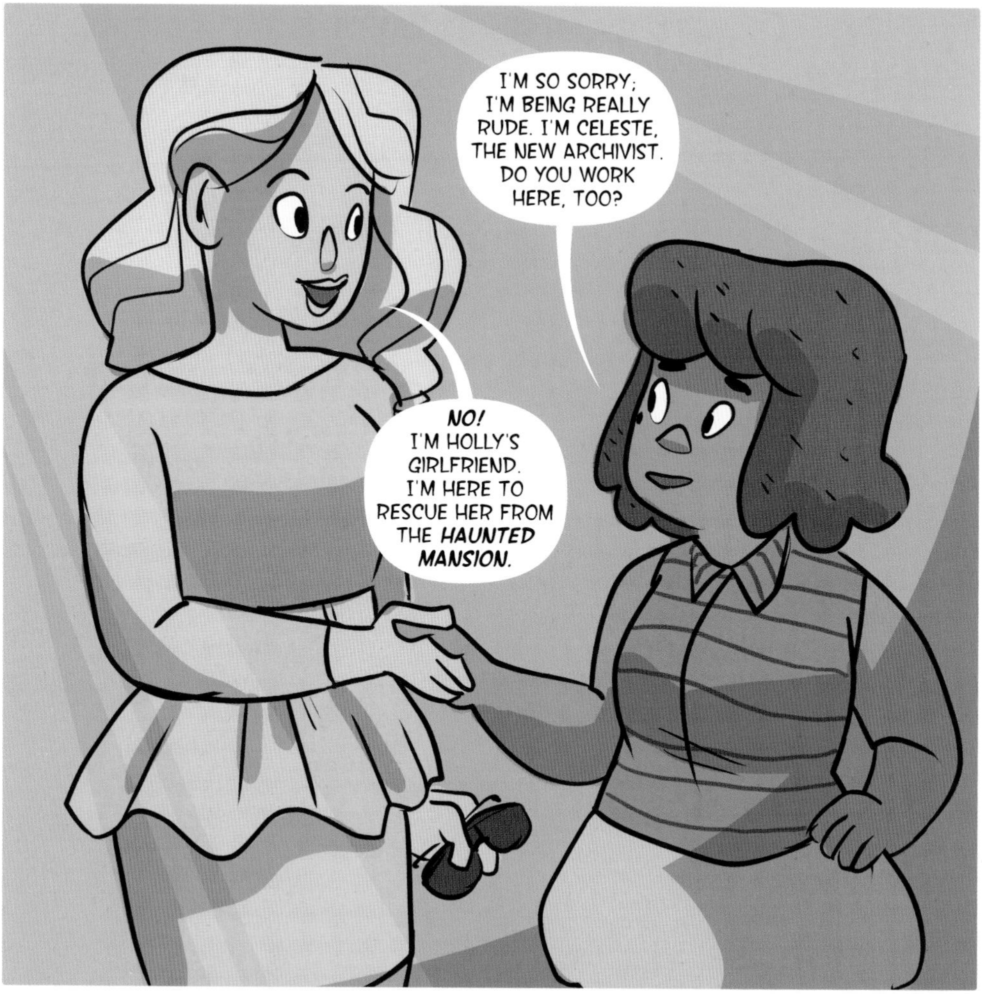
I'M SO SORRY; I'M BEING REALLY RUDE. I'M CELESTE, THE NEW ARCHIVIST. DO YOU WORK HERE, TOO?
NO! I'M HOLLY'S GIRLFRIEND. I'M HERE TO RESCUE HER FROM THE *HAUNTED MANSION.*

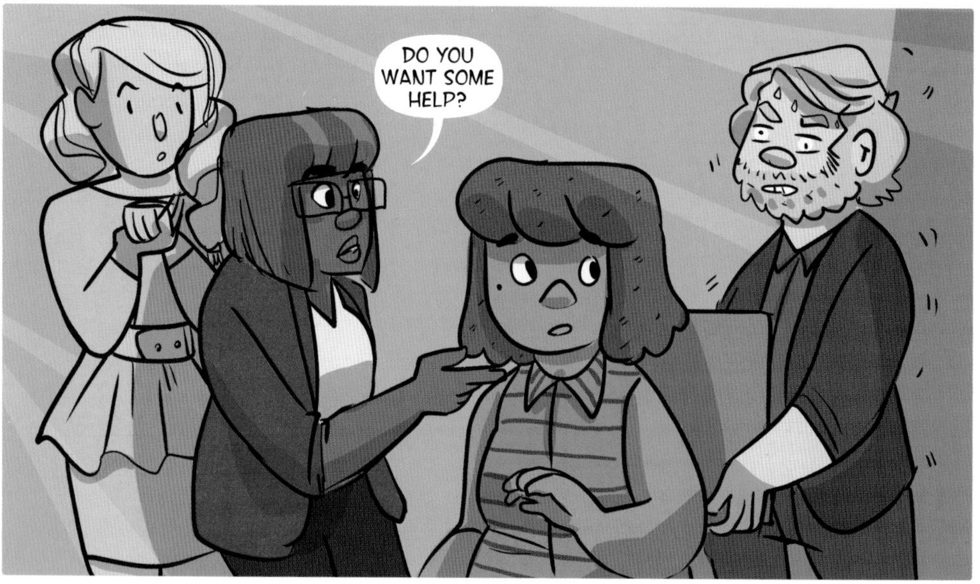
DO YOU WANT SOME HELP?

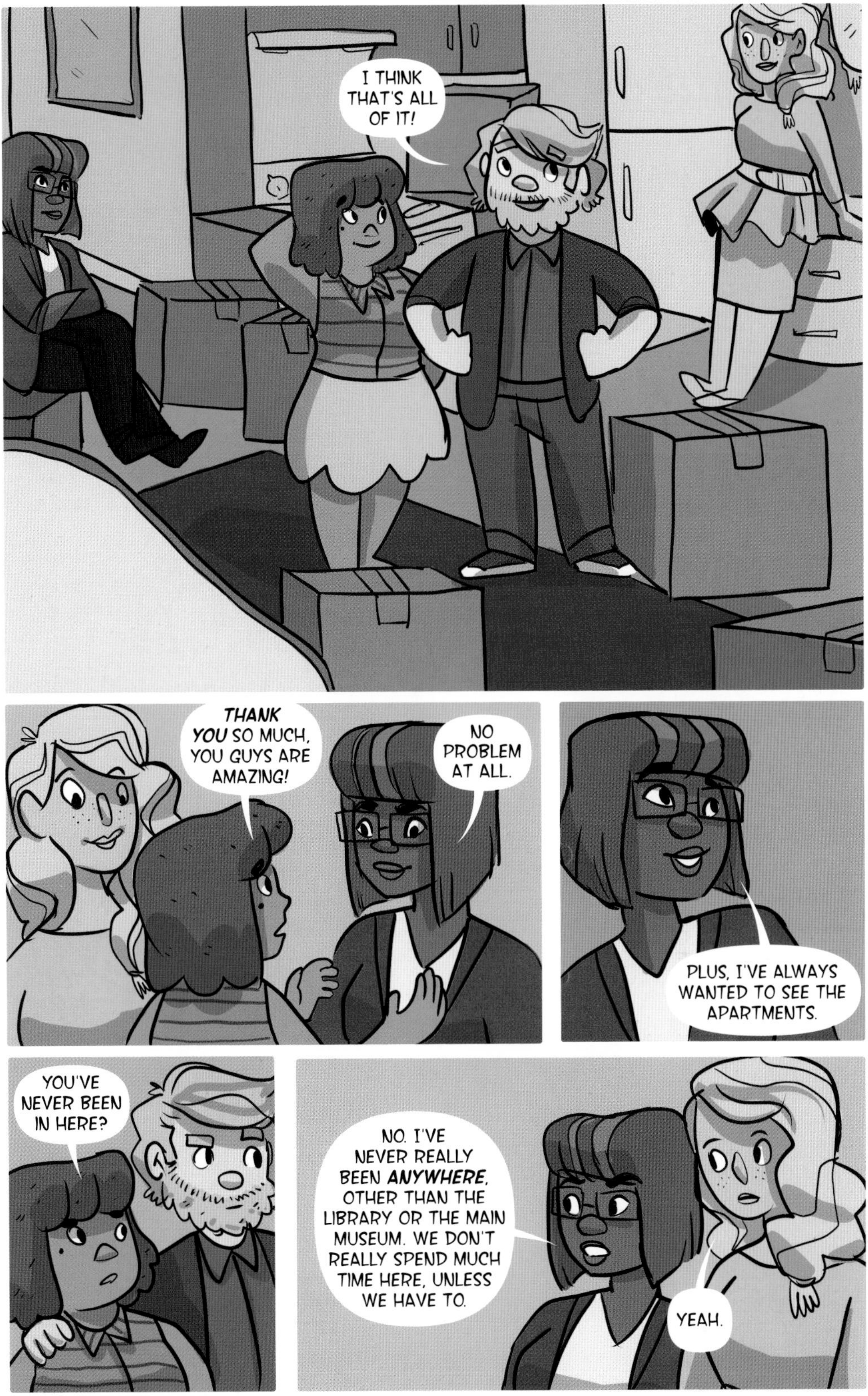

I THINK THAT'S ALL OF IT!
THANK YOU SO MUCH, YOU GUYS ARE AMAZING!
NO PROBLEM AT ALL.
PLUS, I'VE ALWAYS WANTED TO SEE THE APARTMENTS.
YOU'VE NEVER BEEN IN HERE?
NO. I'VE NEVER REALLY BEEN ***ANYWHERE***, OTHER THAN THE LIBRARY OR THE MAIN MUSEUM. WE DON'T REALLY SPEND MUCH TIME HERE, UNLESS WE HAVE TO.
YEAH.

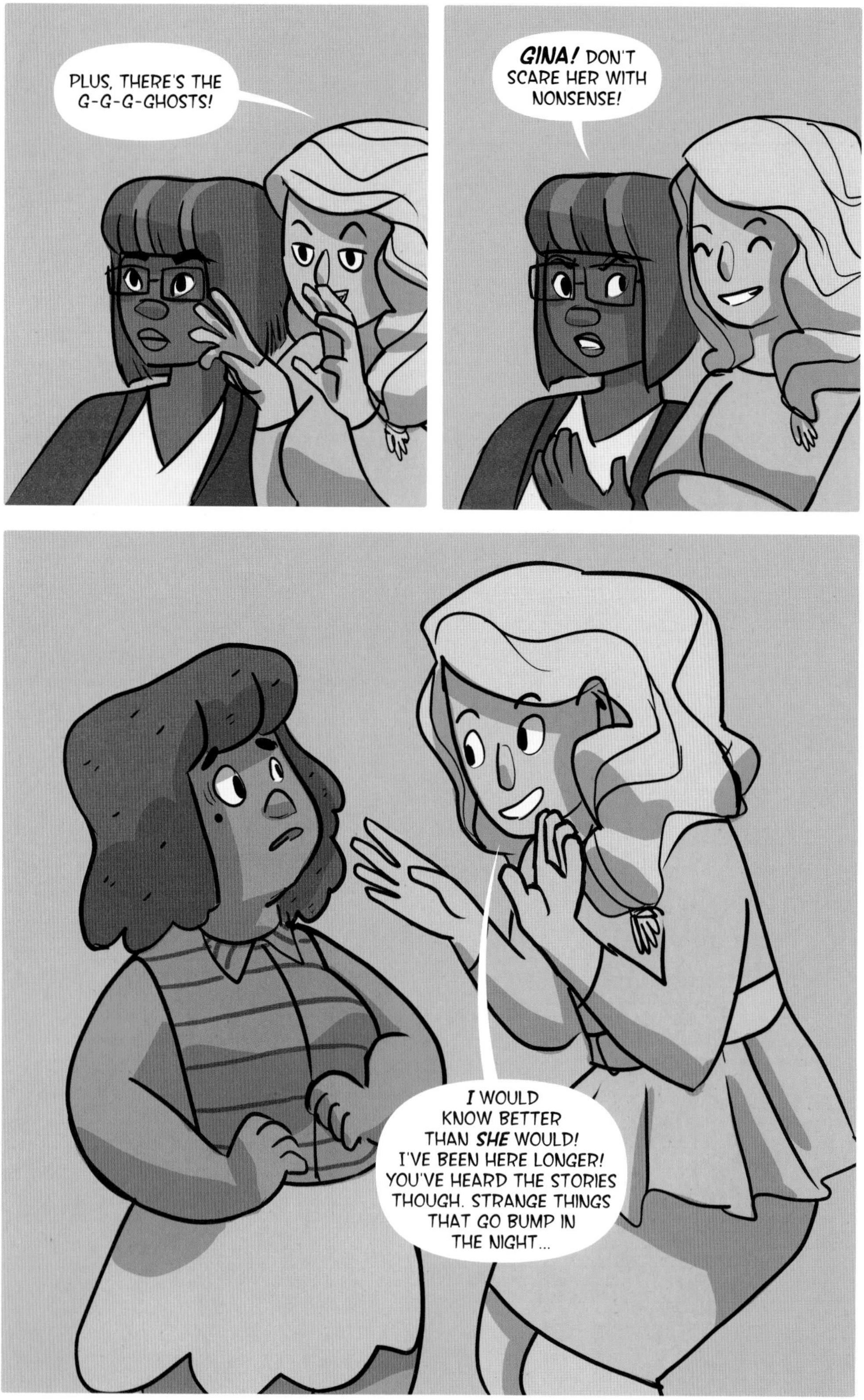
PLUS, THERE'S THE G-G-G-GHOSTS!
GINA! DON'T SCARE HER WITH NONSENSE!
I WOULD KNOW BETTER THAN SHE WOULD! I'VE BEEN HERE LONGER! YOU'VE HEARD THE STORIES THOUGH. STRANGE THINGS THAT GO BUMP IN THE NIGHT...

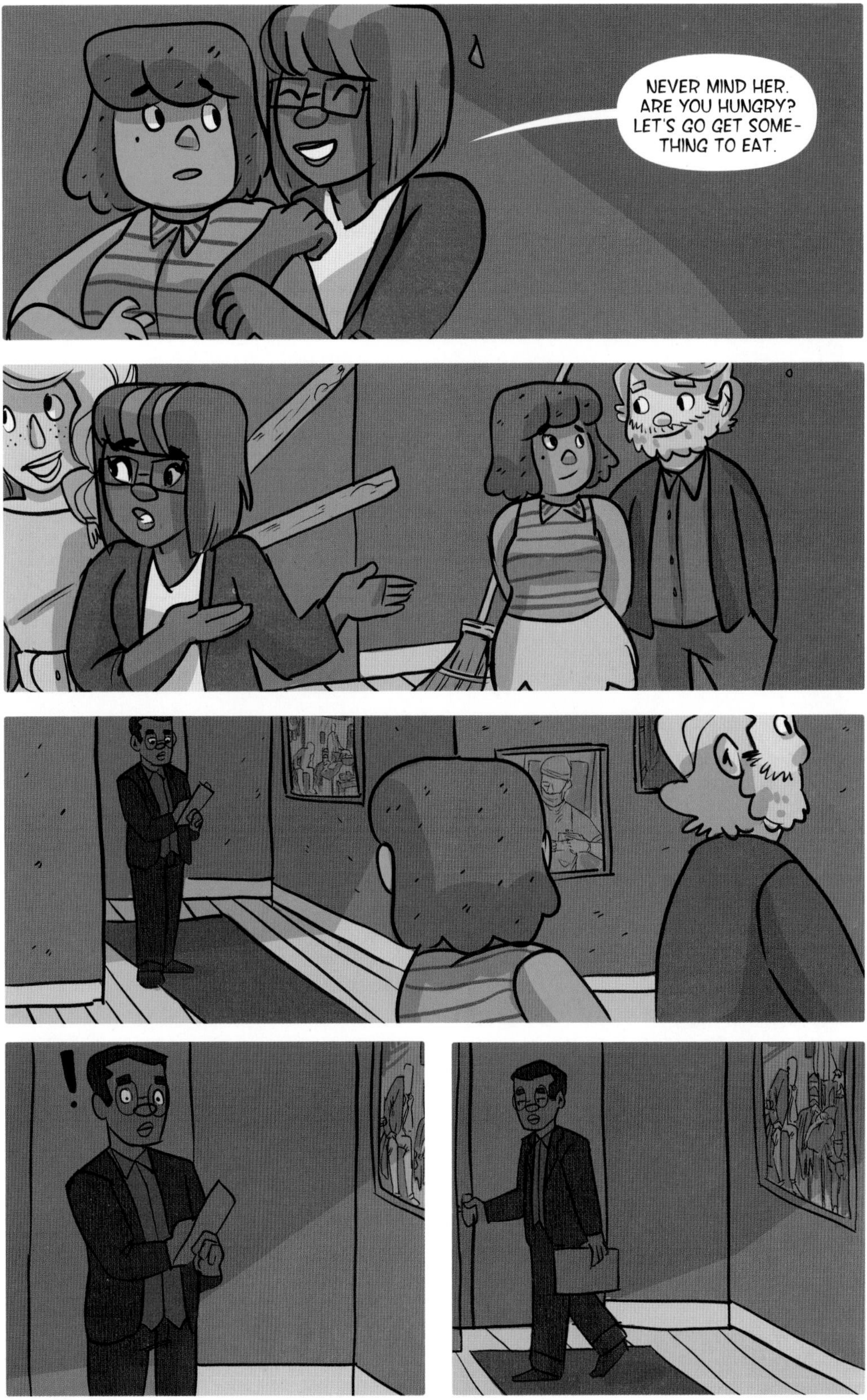
NEVER MIND HER. ARE YOU HUNGRY? LET'S GO GET SOME-THING TO EAT.
!

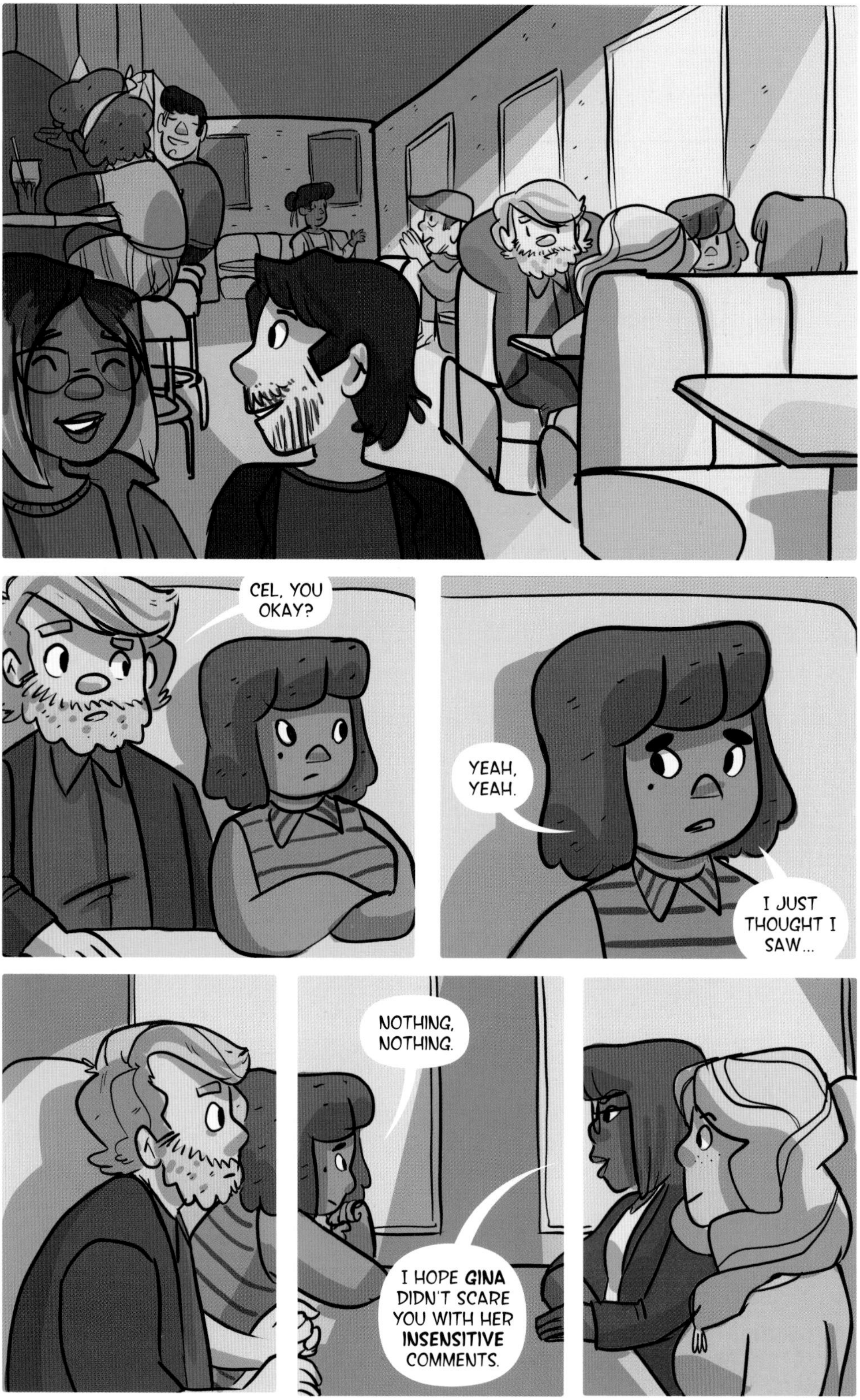
CEL, YOU OKAY?
YEAH, YEAH.
I JUST THOUGHT I SAW...
NOTHING, NOTHING.
I HOPE GINA DIDN'T SCARE YOU WITH HER INSENSITIVE COMMENTS.

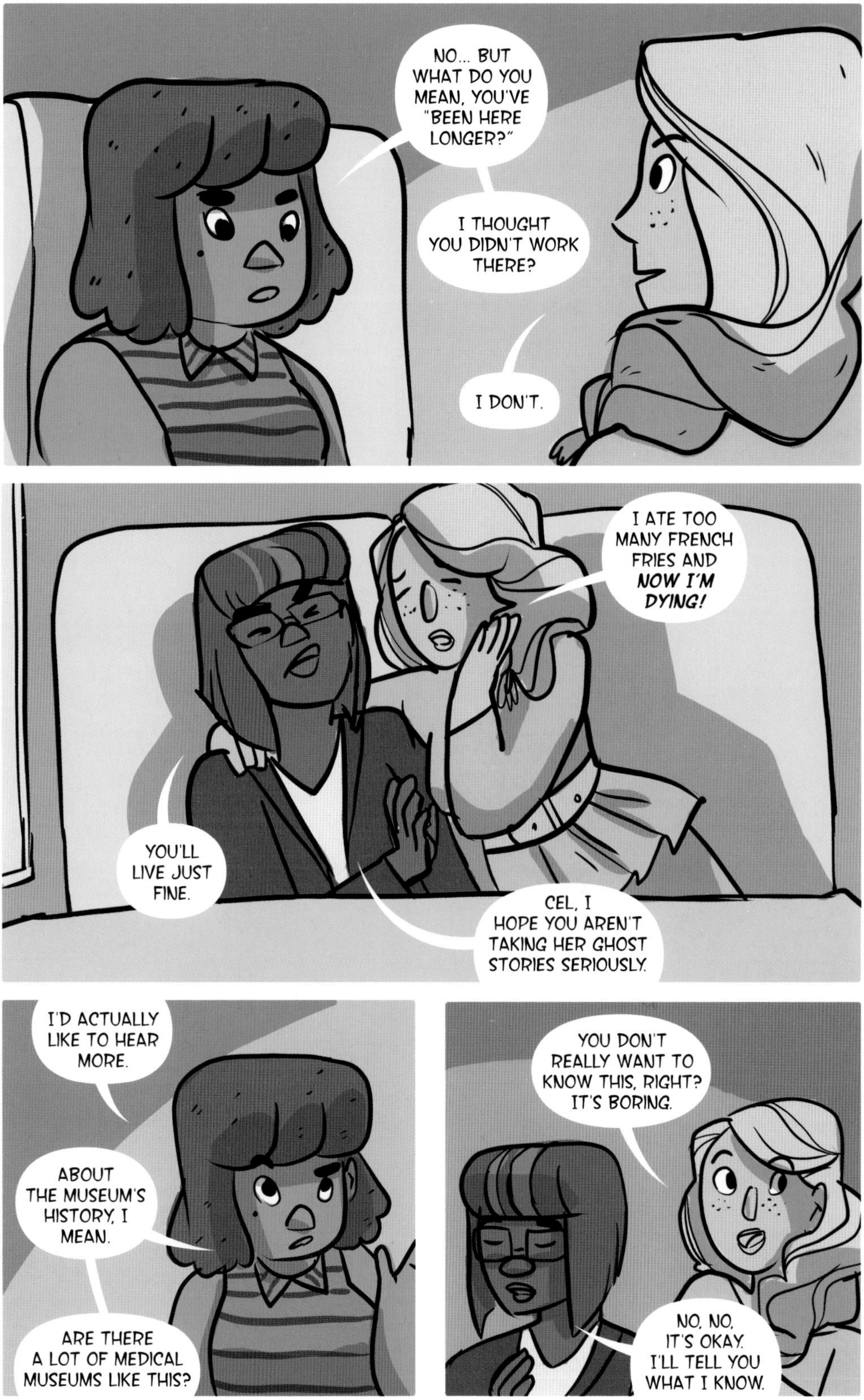
NO... BUT WHAT DO YOU MEAN, YOU'VE "BEEN HERE LONGER?"
I THOUGHT YOU DIDN'T WORK THERE?
I DON'T.
I ATE TOO MANY FRENCH FRIES AND *NOW I'M DYING!*
YOU'LL LIVE JUST FINE.
CEL, I HOPE YOU AREN'T TAKING HER GHOST STORIES SERIOUSLY.
I'D ACTUALLY LIKE TO HEAR MORE.
ABOUT THE MUSEUM'S HISTORY, I MEAN.
ARE THERE A LOT OF MEDICAL MUSEUMS LIKE THIS?
YOU DON'T REALLY WANT TO KNOW THIS, RIGHT? IT'S BORING.
NO, NO, IT'S OKAY. I'LL TELL YOU WHAT I KNOW.

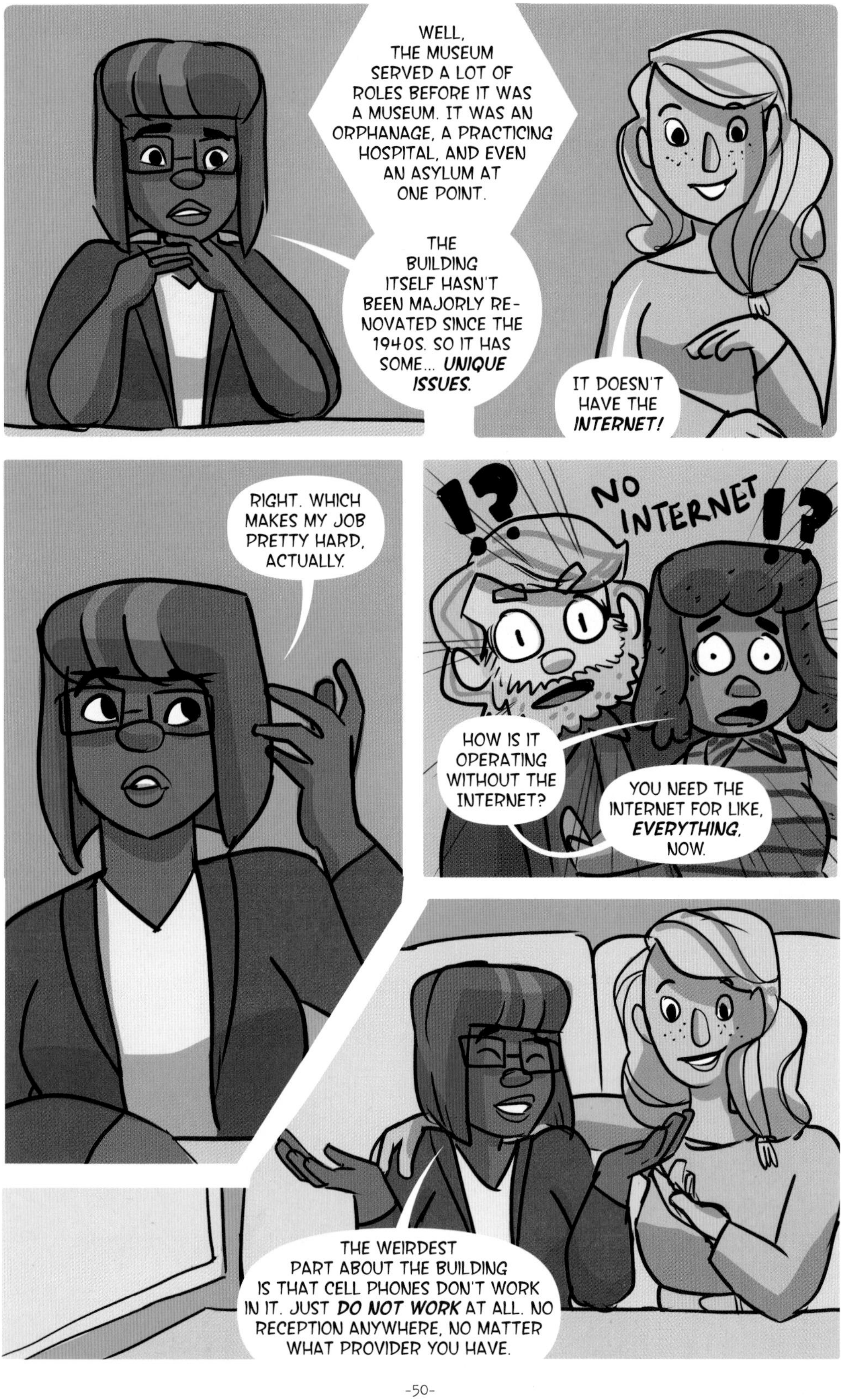
WELL, THE MUSEUM SERVED A LOT OF ROLES BEFORE IT WAS A MUSEUM. IT WAS AN ORPHANAGE, A PRACTICING HOSPITAL, AND EVEN AN ASYLUM AT ONE POINT.
THE BUILDING ITSELF HASN'T BEEN MAJORLY RE-NOVATED SINCE THE 1940S. SO IT HAS SOME... ***UNIQUE ISSUES.***
IT DOESN'T HAVE THE ***INTERNET!***
RIGHT. WHICH MAKES MY JOB PRETTY HARD, ACTUALLY.
!?
NO INTERNET
!?
HOW IS IT OPERATING WITHOUT THE INTERNET?
YOU NEED THE INTERNET FOR LIKE, ***EVERYTHING,*** NOW.
THE WEIRDEST PART ABOUT THE BUILDING IS THAT CELL PHONES DON'T WORK IN IT. JUST ***DO NOT WORK*** AT ALL. NO RECEPTION ANYWHERE, NO MATTER WHAT PROVIDER YOU HAVE.

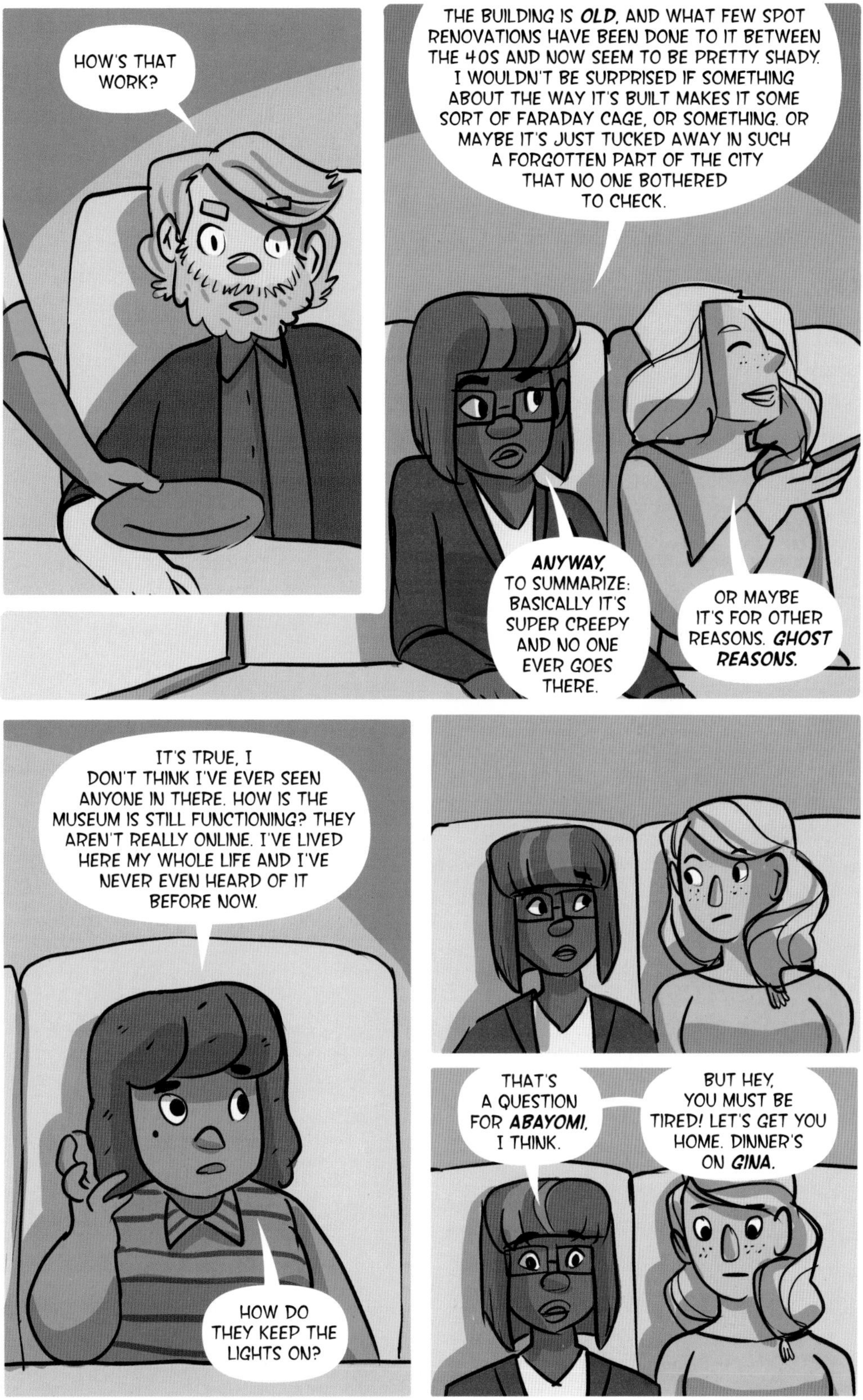
HOW'S THAT WORK?
THE BUILDING IS OLD, AND WHAT FEW SPOT RENOVATIONS HAVE BEEN DONE TO IT BETWEEN THE 40S AND NOW SEEM TO BE PRETTY SHADY. I WOULDN'T BE SURPRISED IF SOMETHING ABOUT THE WAY IT'S BUILT MAKES IT SOME SORT OF FARADAY CAGE, OR SOMETHING. OR MAYBE IT'S JUST TUCKED AWAY IN SUCH A FORGOTTEN PART OF THE CITY THAT NO ONE BOTHERED TO CHECK.
ANYWAY, TO SUMMARIZE: BASICALLY IT'S SUPER CREEPY AND NO ONE EVER GOES THERE.
OR MAYBE IT'S FOR OTHER REASONS. GHOST REASONS.
IT'S TRUE, I DON'T THINK I'VE EVER SEEN ANYONE IN THERE. HOW IS THE MUSEUM IS STILL FUNCTIONING? THEY AREN'T REALLY ONLINE. I'VE LIVED HERE MY WHOLE LIFE AND I'VE NEVER EVEN HEARD OF IT BEFORE NOW.
HOW DO THEY KEEP THE LIGHTS ON?
THAT'S A QUESTION FOR ABAYOMI, I THINK.
BUT HEY, YOU MUST BE TIRED! LET'S GET YOU HOME. DINNER'S ON GINA.

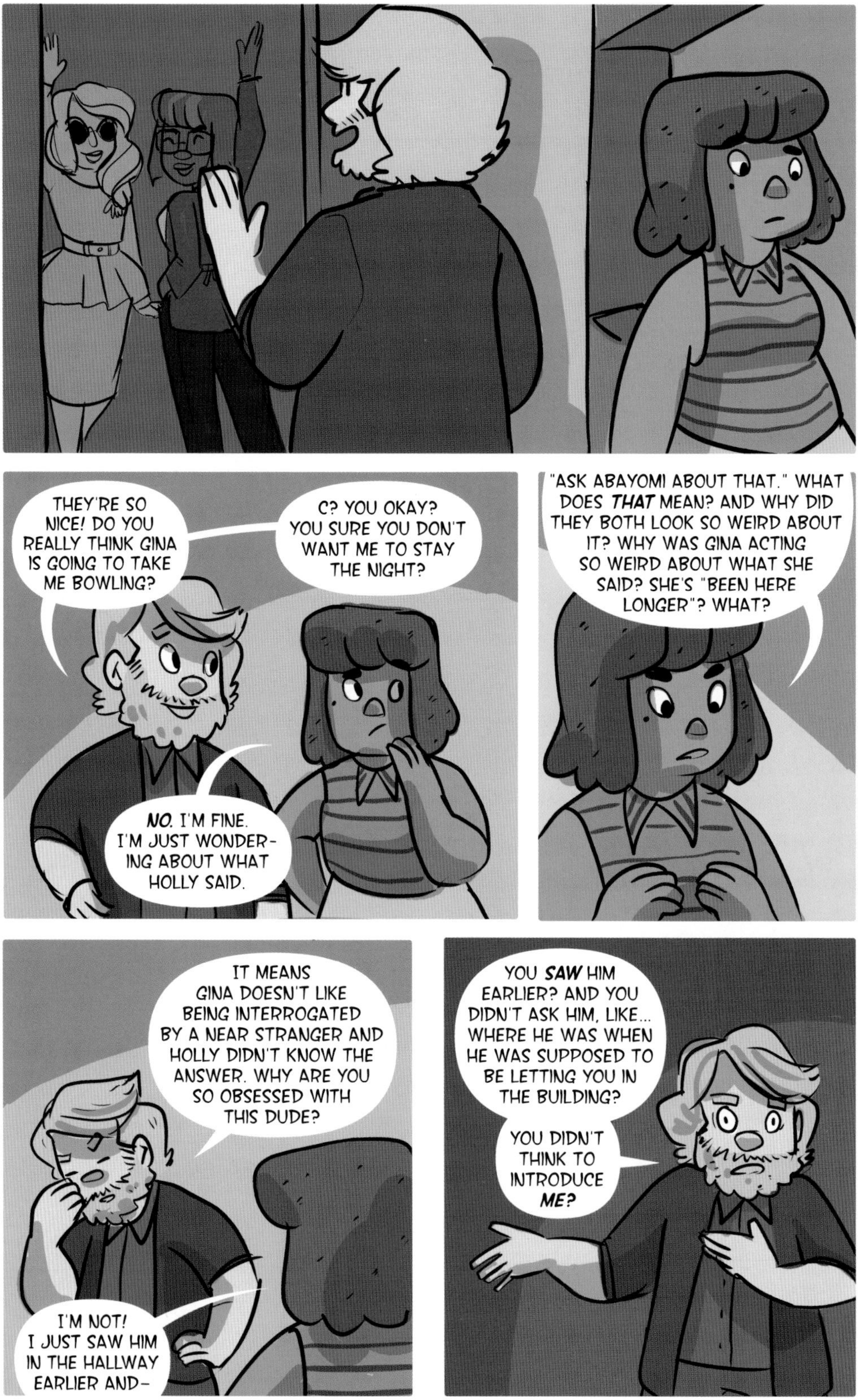
THEY'RE SO NICE! DO YOU REALLY THINK GINA IS GOING TO TAKE ME BOWLING?
C? YOU OKAY? YOU SURE YOU DON'T WANT ME TO STAY THE NIGHT?
NO. I'M FINE. I'M JUST WONDERING ABOUT WHAT HOLLY SAID.
"ASK ABAYOMI ABOUT THAT." WHAT DOES THAT MEAN? AND WHY DID THEY BOTH LOOK SO WEIRD ABOUT IT? WHY WAS GINA ACTING SO WEIRD ABOUT WHAT SHE SAID? SHE'S "BEEN HERE LONGER"? WHAT?
IT MEANS GINA DOESN'T LIKE BEING INTERROGATED BY A NEAR STRANGER AND HOLLY DIDN'T KNOW THE ANSWER. WHY ARE YOU SO OBSESSED WITH THIS DUDE?
I'M NOT! I JUST SAW HIM IN THE HALLWAY EARLIER AND–
YOU SAW HIM EARLIER? AND YOU DIDN'T ASK HIM, LIKE... WHERE HE WAS WHEN HE WAS SUPPOSED TO BE LETTING YOU IN THE BUILDING?
YOU DIDN'T THINK TO INTRODUCE ME?

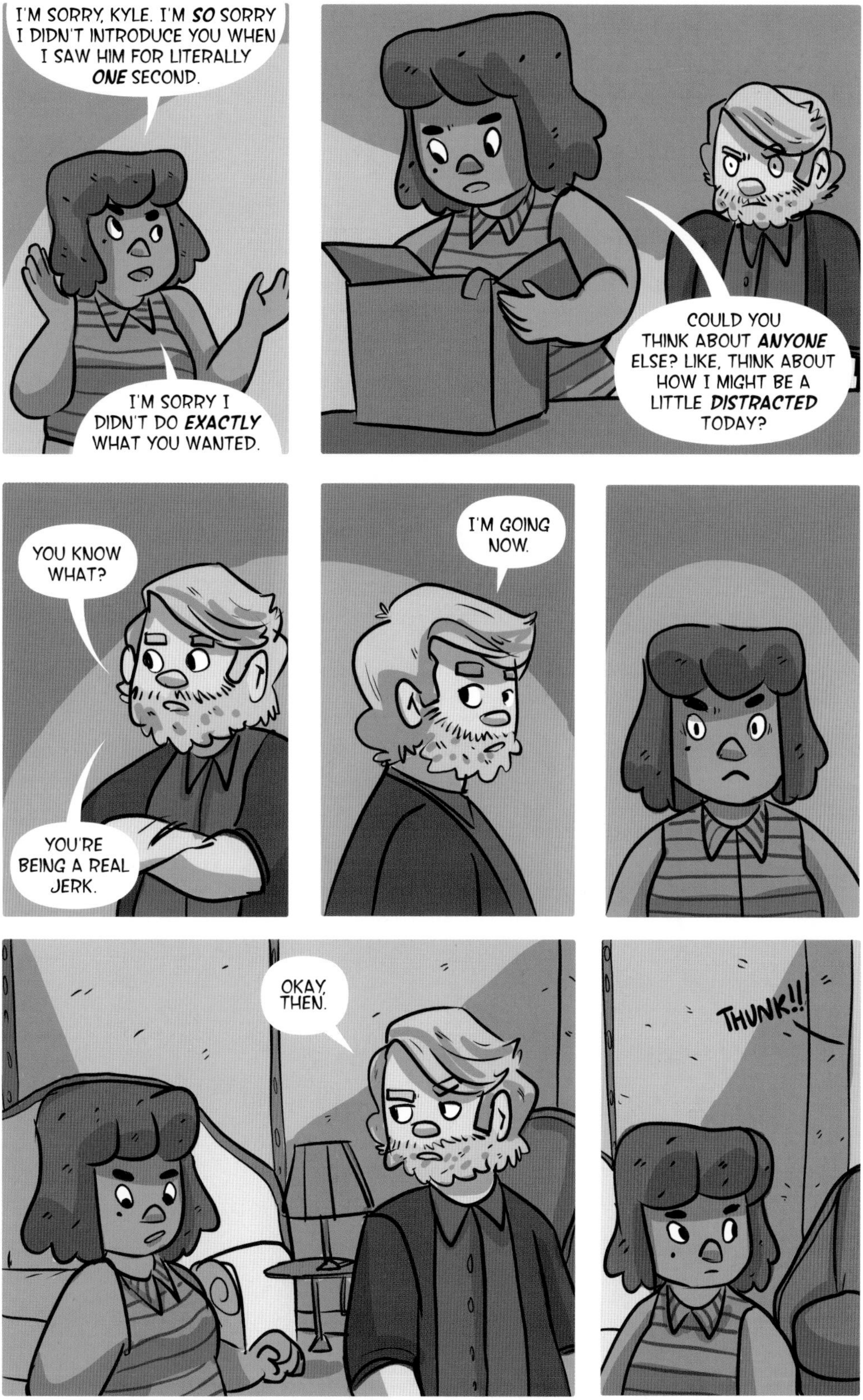
I'M SORRY, KYLE. I'M SO SORRY I DIDN'T INTRODUCE YOU WHEN I SAW HIM FOR LITERALLY ONE SECOND.
I'M SORRY I DIDN'T DO EXACTLY WHAT YOU WANTED.
COULD YOU THINK ABOUT ANYONE ELSE? LIKE, THINK ABOUT HOW I MIGHT BE A LITTLE DISTRACTED TODAY?
YOU KNOW WHAT?
YOU'RE BEING A REAL JERK.
I'M GOING NOW.
OKAY, THEN.
THUNK!!

CLICK!

CLICK!

CLICK!

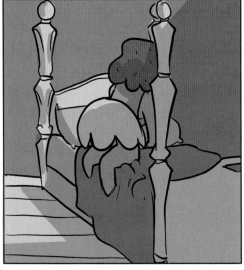

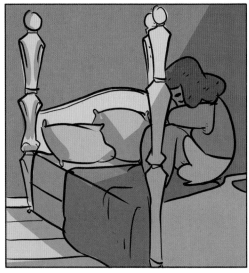

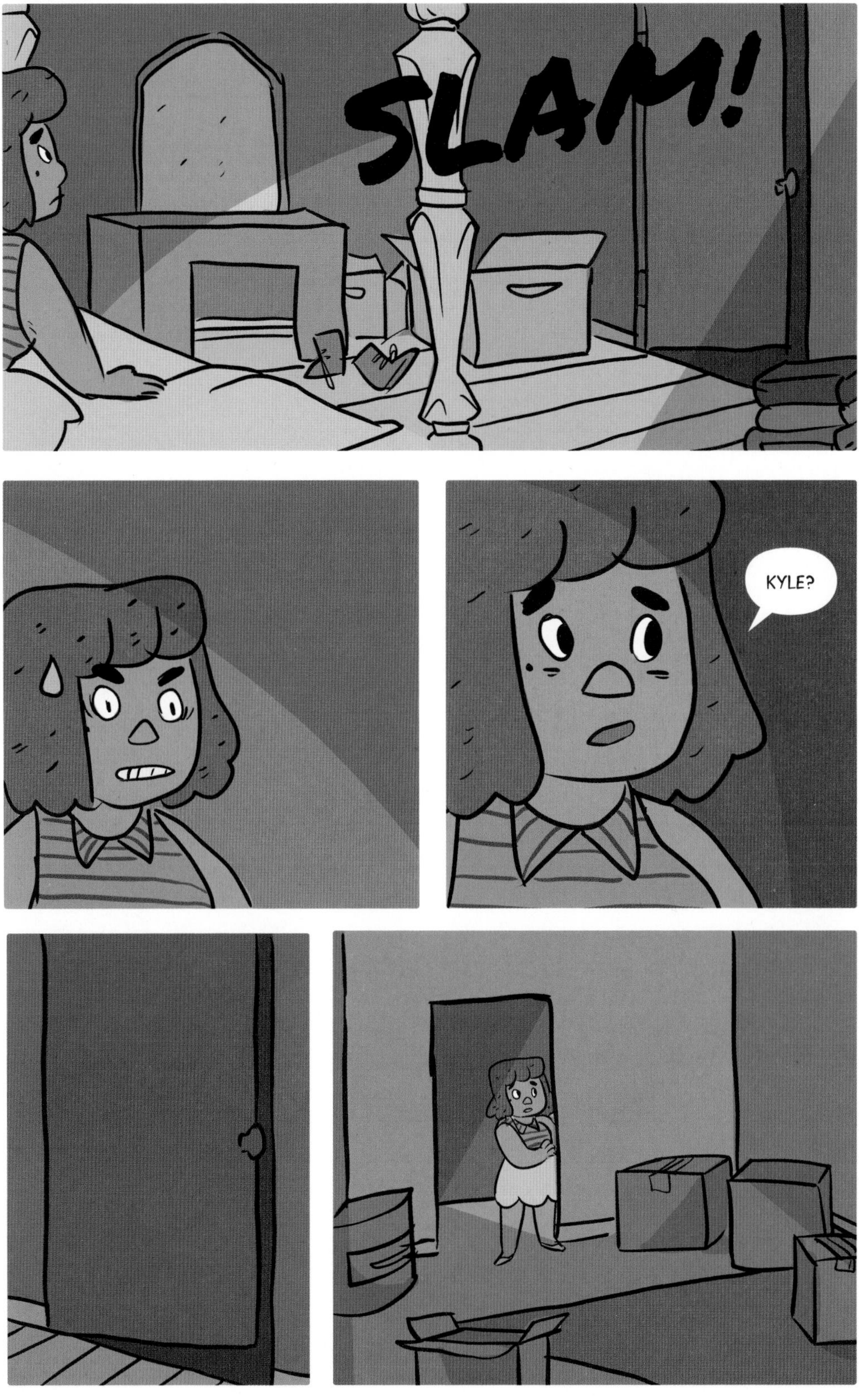
SLAM!
KYLE?

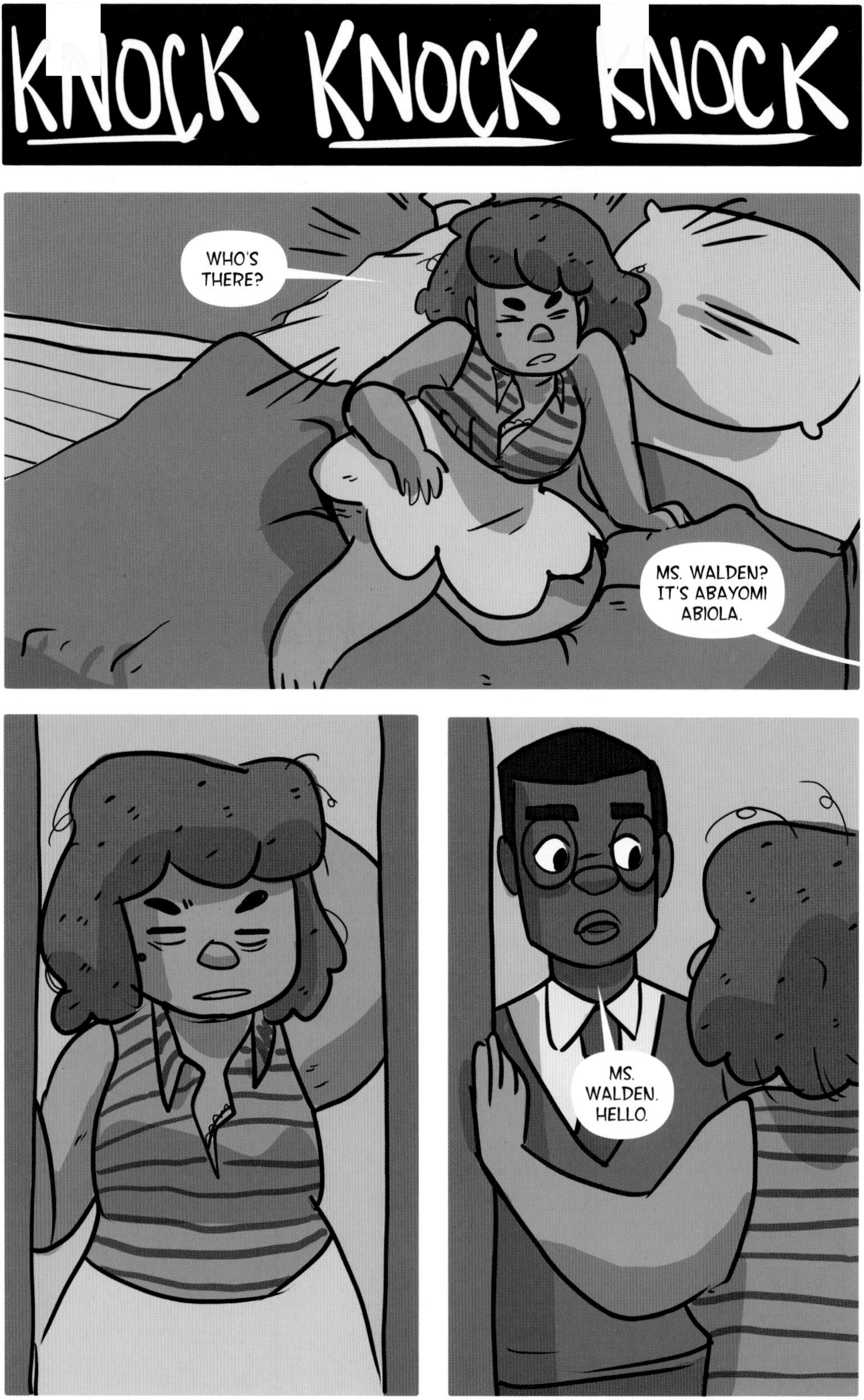
KNOCK KNOCK KNOCK
WHO'S THERE?
MS. WALDEN? IT'S ABAYOMI ABIOLA.
MS. WALDEN. HELLO.

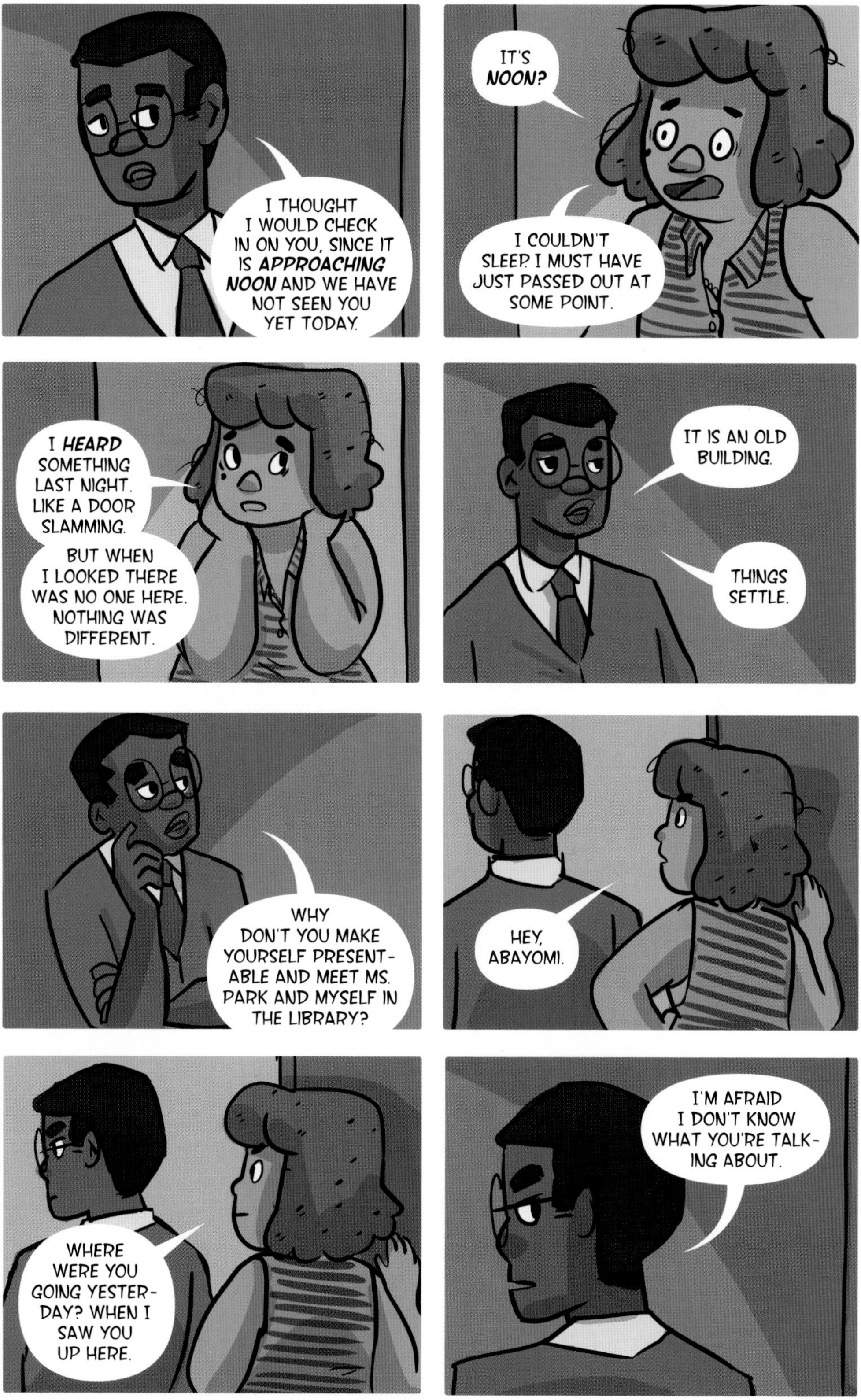
I THOUGHT I WOULD CHECK IN ON YOU, SINCE IT IS **APPROACHING NOON** AND WE HAVE NOT SEEN YOU YET TODAY.
IT'S **NOON?**
I COULDN'T SLEEP. I MUST HAVE JUST PASSED OUT AT SOME POINT.
I **HEARD** SOMETHING LAST NIGHT. LIKE A DOOR SLAMMING.
BUT WHEN I LOOKED THERE WAS NO ONE HERE. NOTHING WAS DIFFERENT.
IT IS AN OLD BUILDING.
THINGS SETTLE.
WHY DON'T YOU MAKE YOURSELF PRESENT-ABLE AND MEET MS. PARK AND MYSELF IN THE LIBRARY?
HEY, ABAYOMI.
WHERE WERE YOU GOING YESTER-DAY? WHEN I SAW YOU UP HERE.
I'M AFRAID I DON'T KNOW WHAT YOU'RE TALK-ING ABOUT.

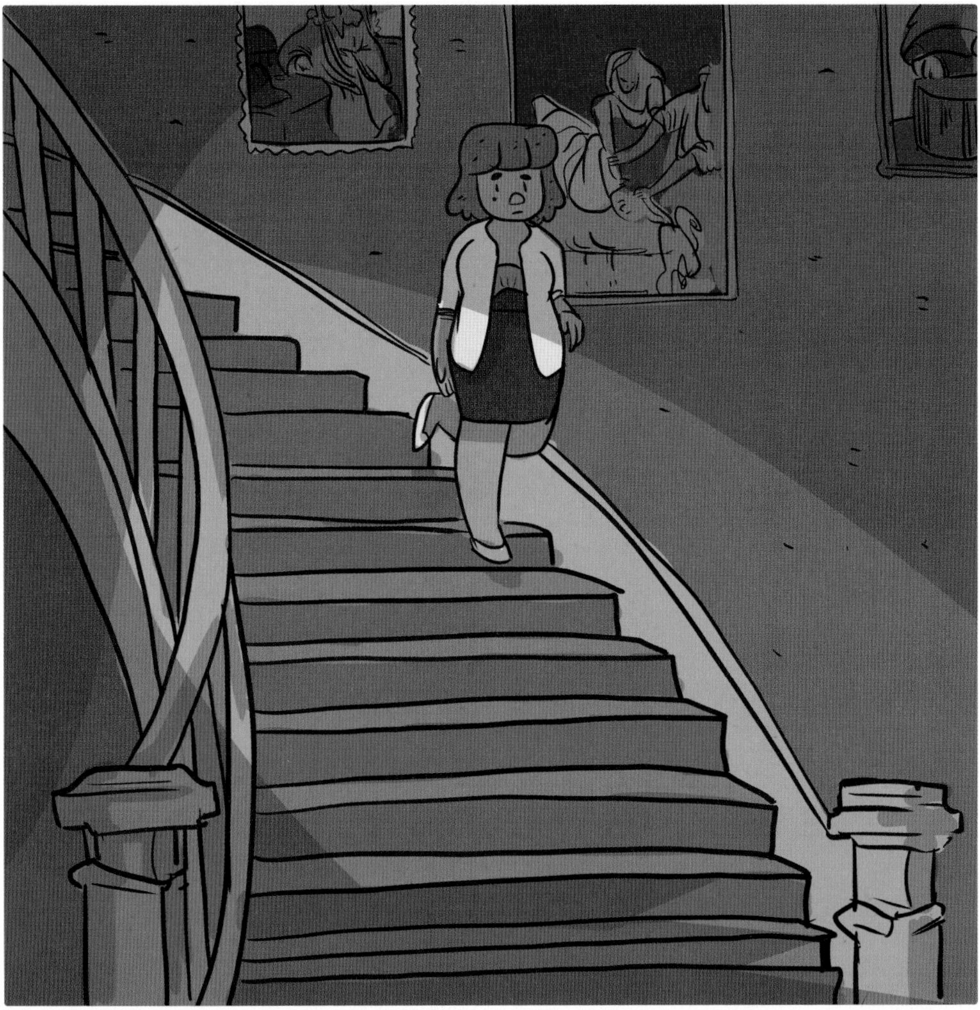

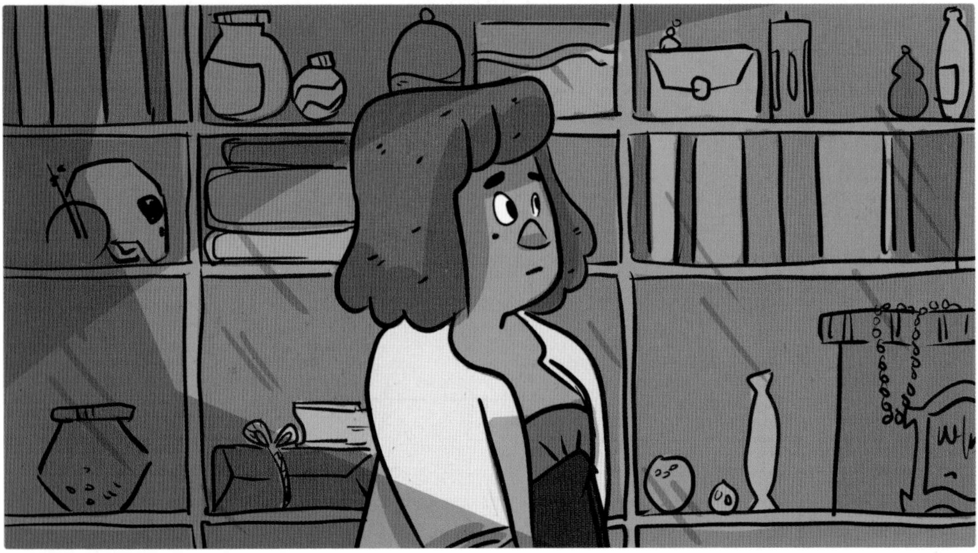

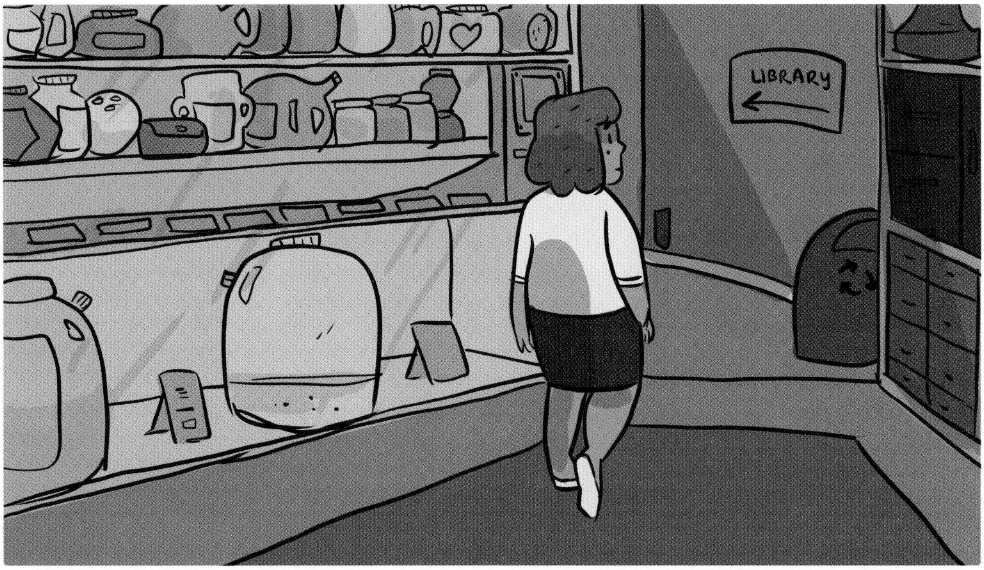
LIBRARY

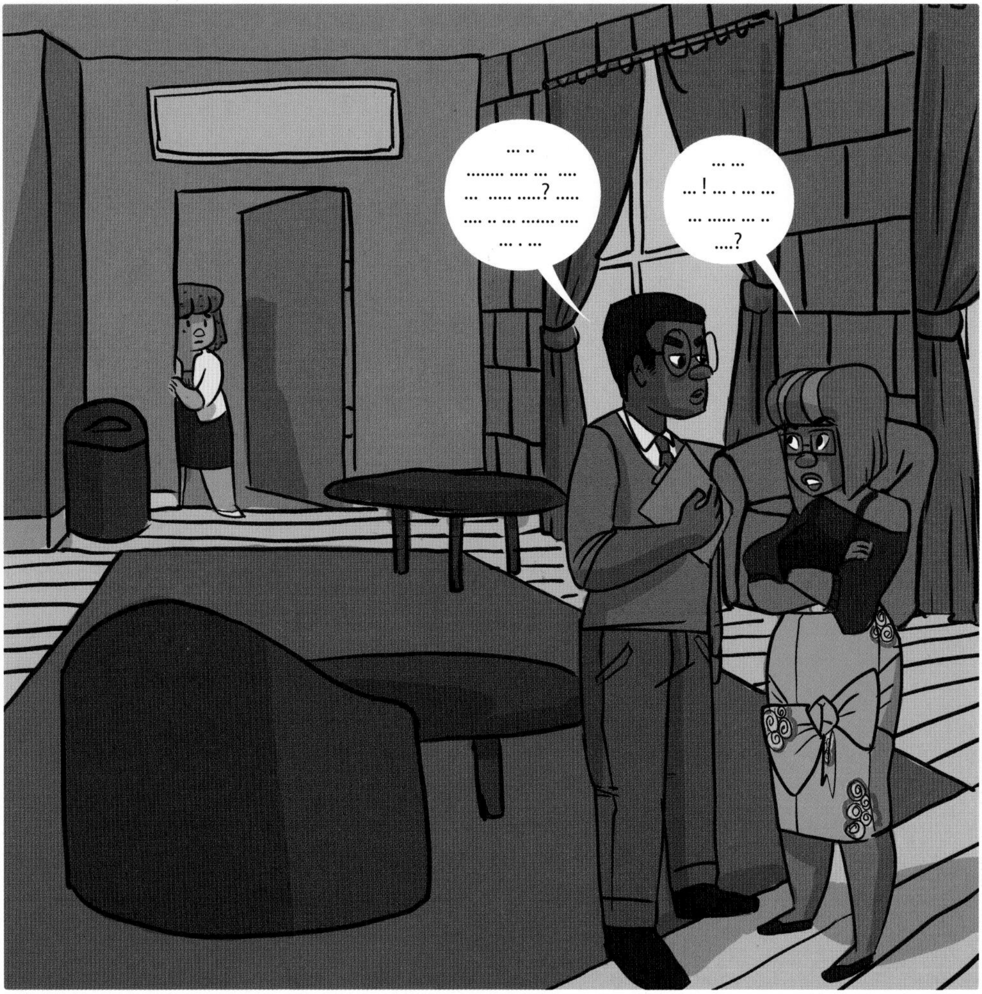

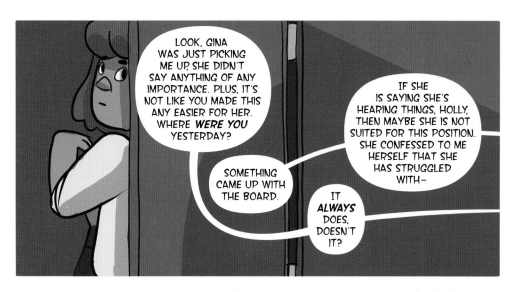

LOOK, GINA WAS JUST PICKING ME UP. SHE DIDN'T SAY ANYTHING OF ANY IMPORTANCE. PLUS, IT'S NOT LIKE YOU MADE THIS ANY EASIER FOR HER. WHERE *WERE YOU* YESTERDAY?

IF SHE IS SAYING SHE'S HEARING THINGS, HOLLY, THEN MAYBE SHE IS NOT SUITED FOR THIS POSITION. SHE CONFESSED TO ME HERSELF THAT SHE HAS STRUGGLED WITH—

SOMETHING CAME UP WITH THE BOARD.

IT *ALWAYS* DOES, DOESN'T IT?

HEY.

CEL! OH MY GOD! YOU SCARED ME!

DID YOU GET LOST? HOW'D YOU END UP OVER THERE?

YEAH. I GOT A LITTLE TURNED AROUND.

NO WORRIES! IT'S LIKE A MAZE IN HERE.

ARE YOU EXCITED TO START YOUR TRAINING? I'M *SO* EXCITED!

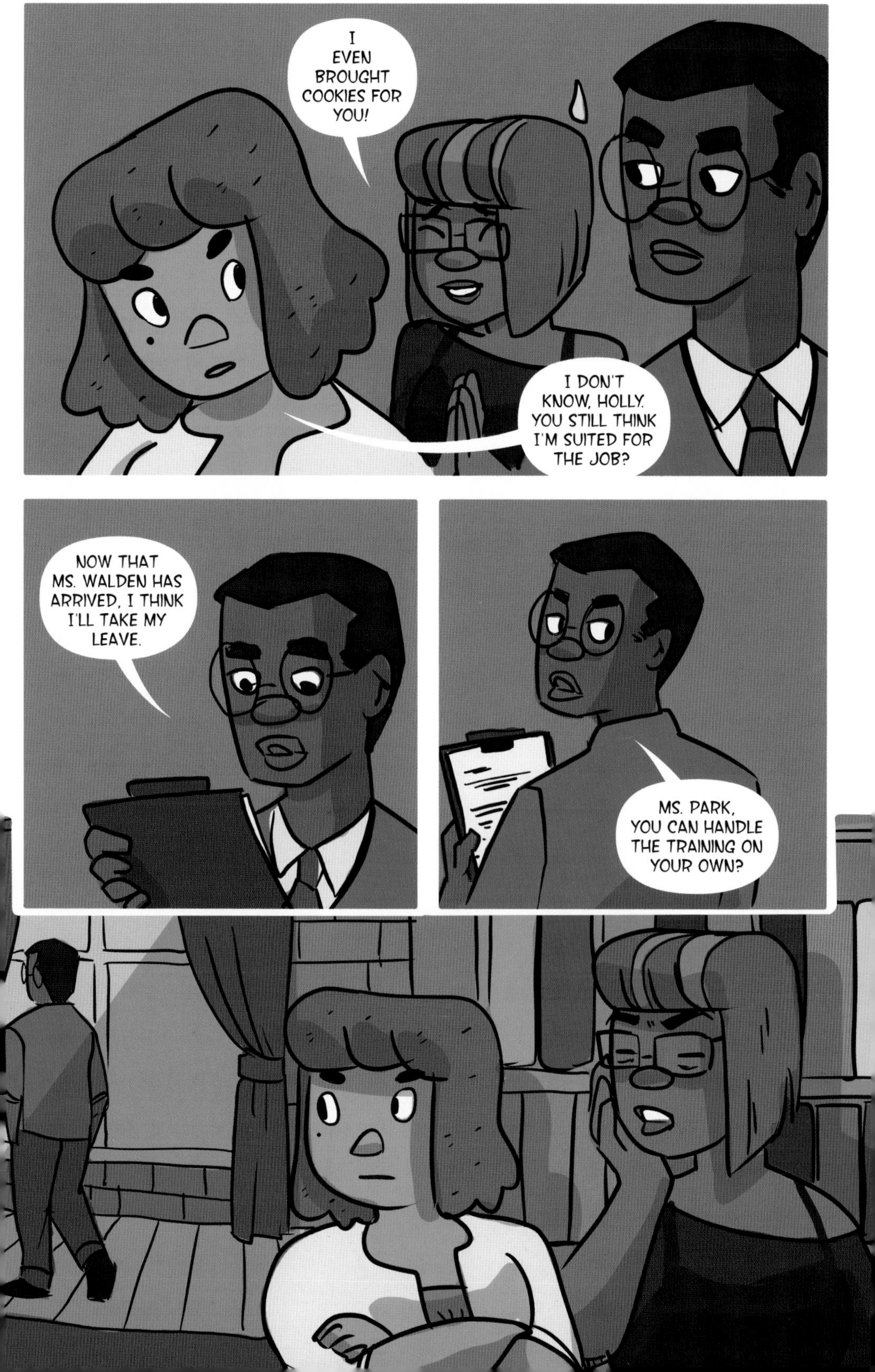
I EVEN BROUGHT COOKIES FOR YOU!
I DON'T KNOW, HOLLY. YOU STILL THINK I'M SUITED FOR THE JOB?
NOW THAT MS. WALDEN HAS ARRIVED, I THINK I'LL TAKE MY LEAVE.
MS. PARK, YOU CAN HANDLE THE TRAINING ON YOUR OWN?

WELCOME TO YOUR NEW JOB!

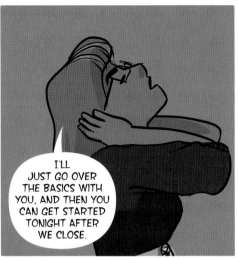

I'LL JUST GO OVER THE BASICS WITH YOU, AND THEN YOU CAN GET STARTED TONIGHT AFTER WE CLOSE.

I'LL GIVE YOU ONE BOX TO START. HERE WE GO! THE BEATTY-YOUNG COLLECTION.

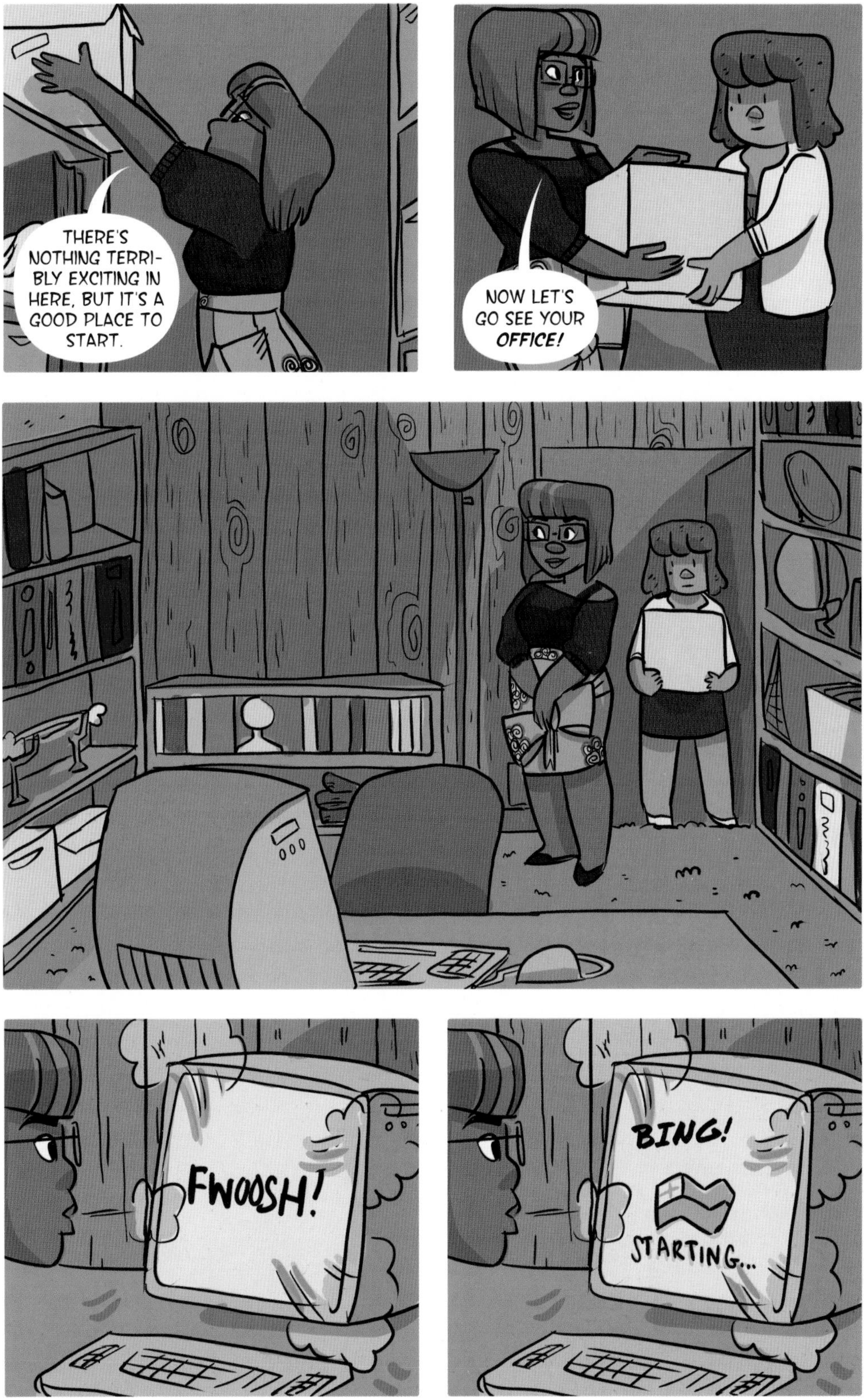
THERE'S NOTHING TERRI-BLY EXCITING IN HERE, BUT IT'S A GOOD PLACE TO START.
NOW LET'S GO SEE YOUR *OFFICE!*
FWOOSH!
BING!
STARTING...

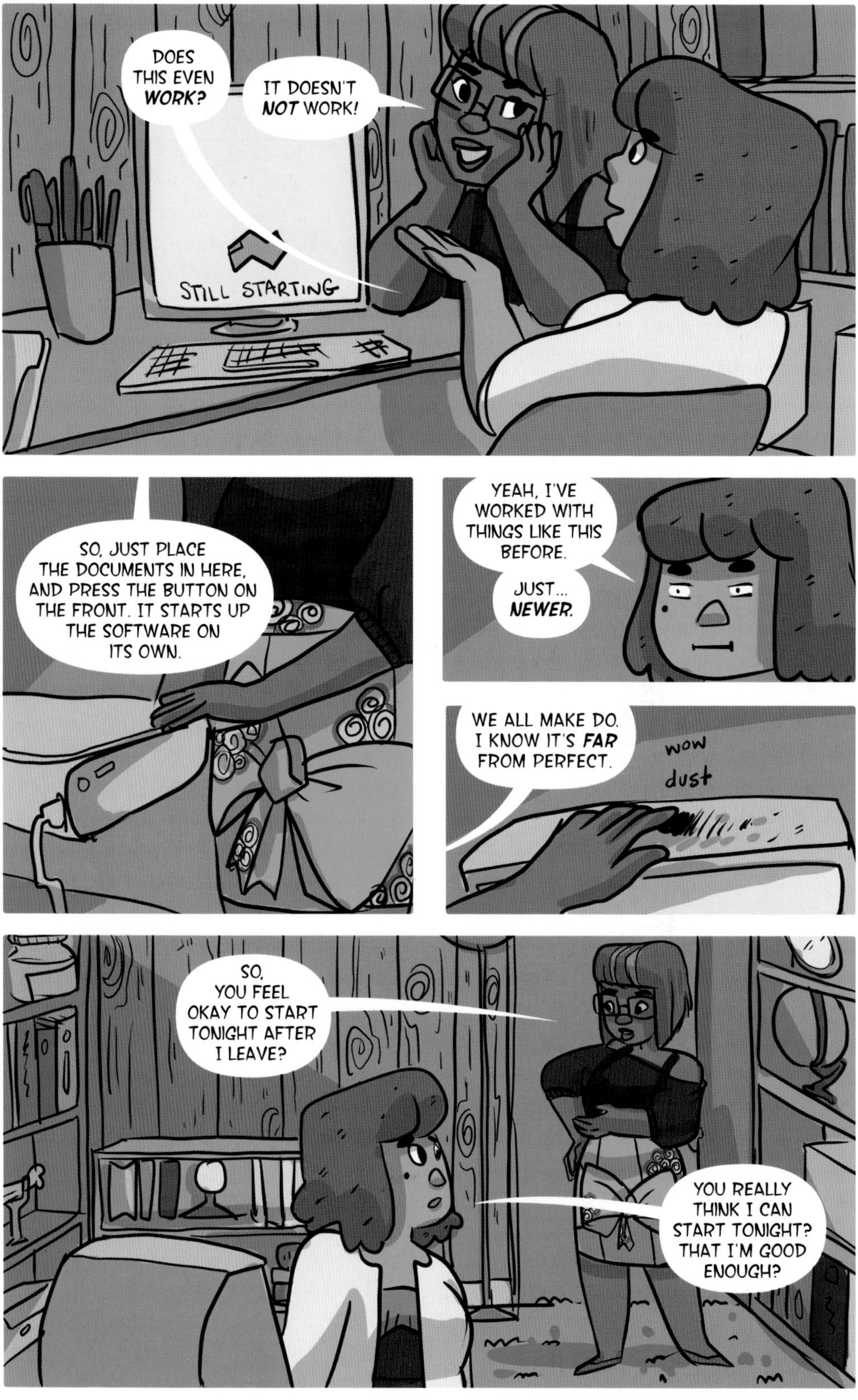
DOES THIS EVEN WORK?
IT DOESN'T NOT WORK!
STILL STARTING
SO, JUST PLACE THE DOCUMENTS IN HERE, AND PRESS THE BUTTON ON THE FRONT. IT STARTS UP THE SOFTWARE ON ITS OWN.
YEAH, I'VE WORKED WITH THINGS LIKE THIS BEFORE.
JUST... NEWER.
WE ALL MAKE DO. I KNOW IT'S FAR FROM PERFECT.
wow
dust
SO, YOU FEEL OKAY TO START TONIGHT AFTER I LEAVE?
YOU REALLY THINK I CAN START TONIGHT? THAT I'M GOOD ENOUGH?

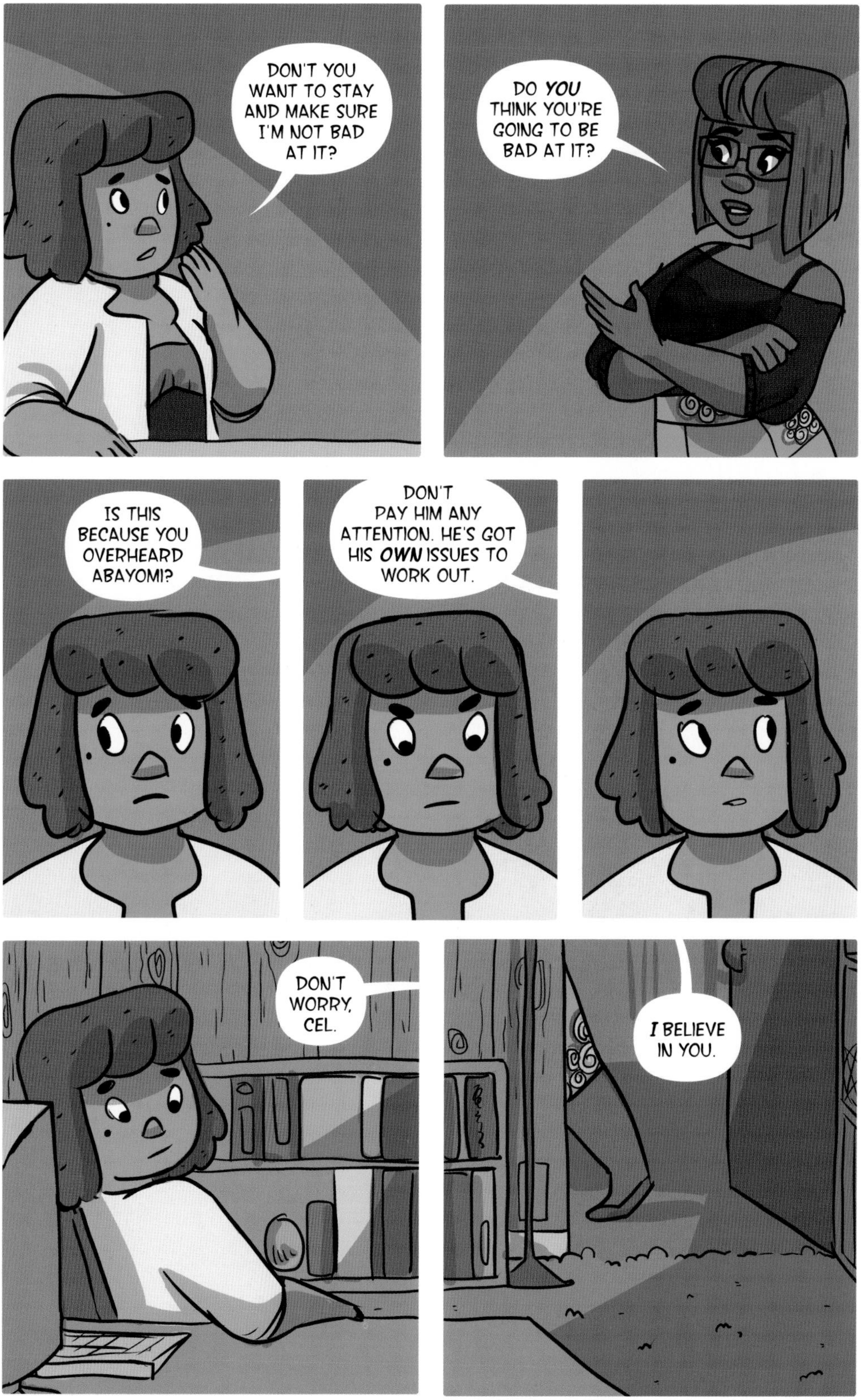
DON'T YOU WANT TO STAY AND MAKE SURE I'M NOT BAD AT IT?
DO *YOU* THINK YOU'RE GOING TO BE BAD AT IT?
IS THIS BECAUSE YOU OVERHEARD ABAYOMI?
DON'T PAY HIM ANY ATTENTION. HE'S GOT HIS *OWN* ISSUES TO WORK OUT.
DON'T WORRY, CEL.
I BELIEVE IN YOU.

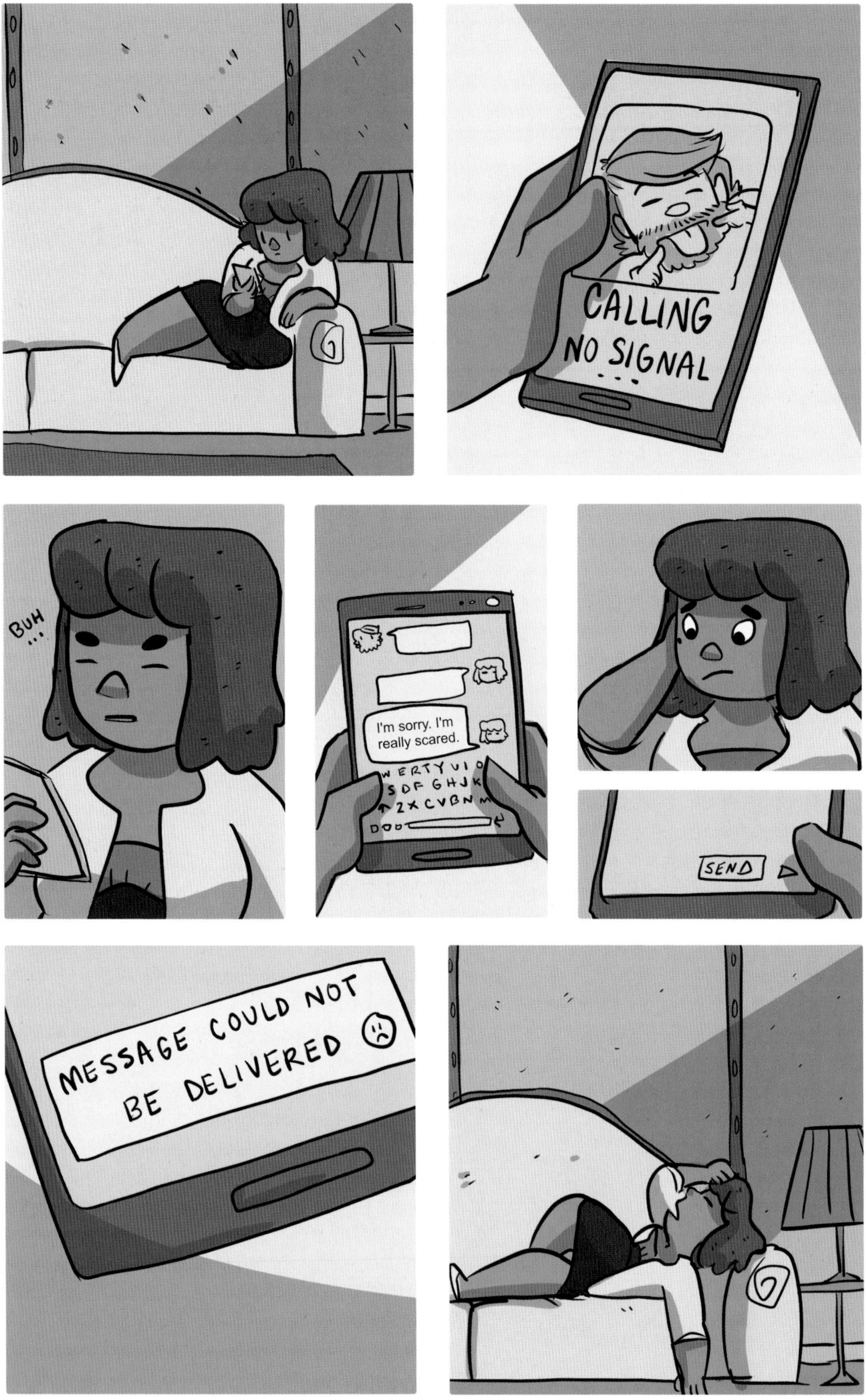
CALLING
NO SIGNAL
...
BUH
...
I'm sorry. I'm really scared.
SEND
MESSAGE COULD NOT BE DELIVERED

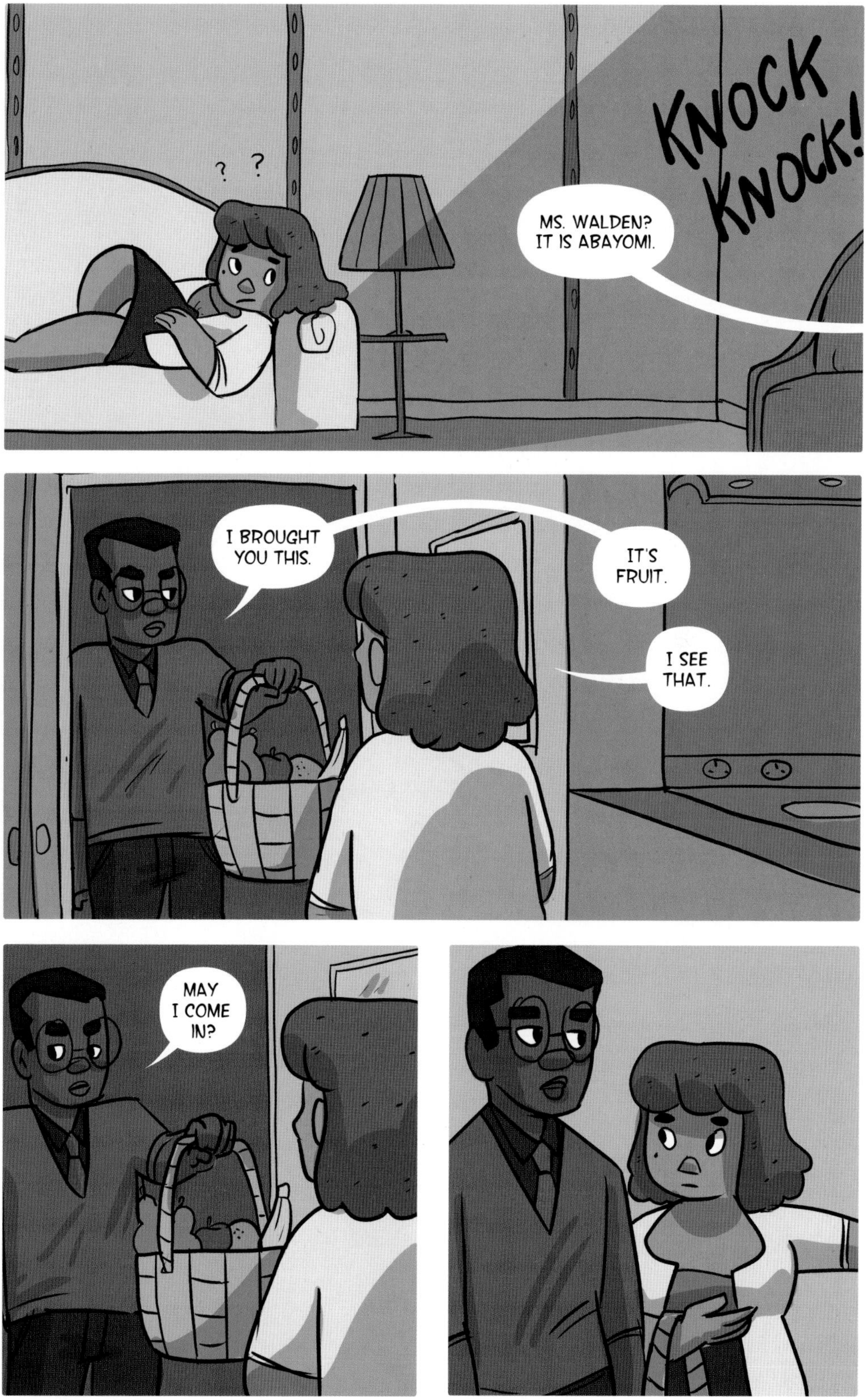
? ?
KNOCK KNOCK!
MS. WALDEN? IT IS ABAYOMI.
I BROUGHT YOU THIS.
IT'S FRUIT.
I SEE THAT.
MAY I COME IN?

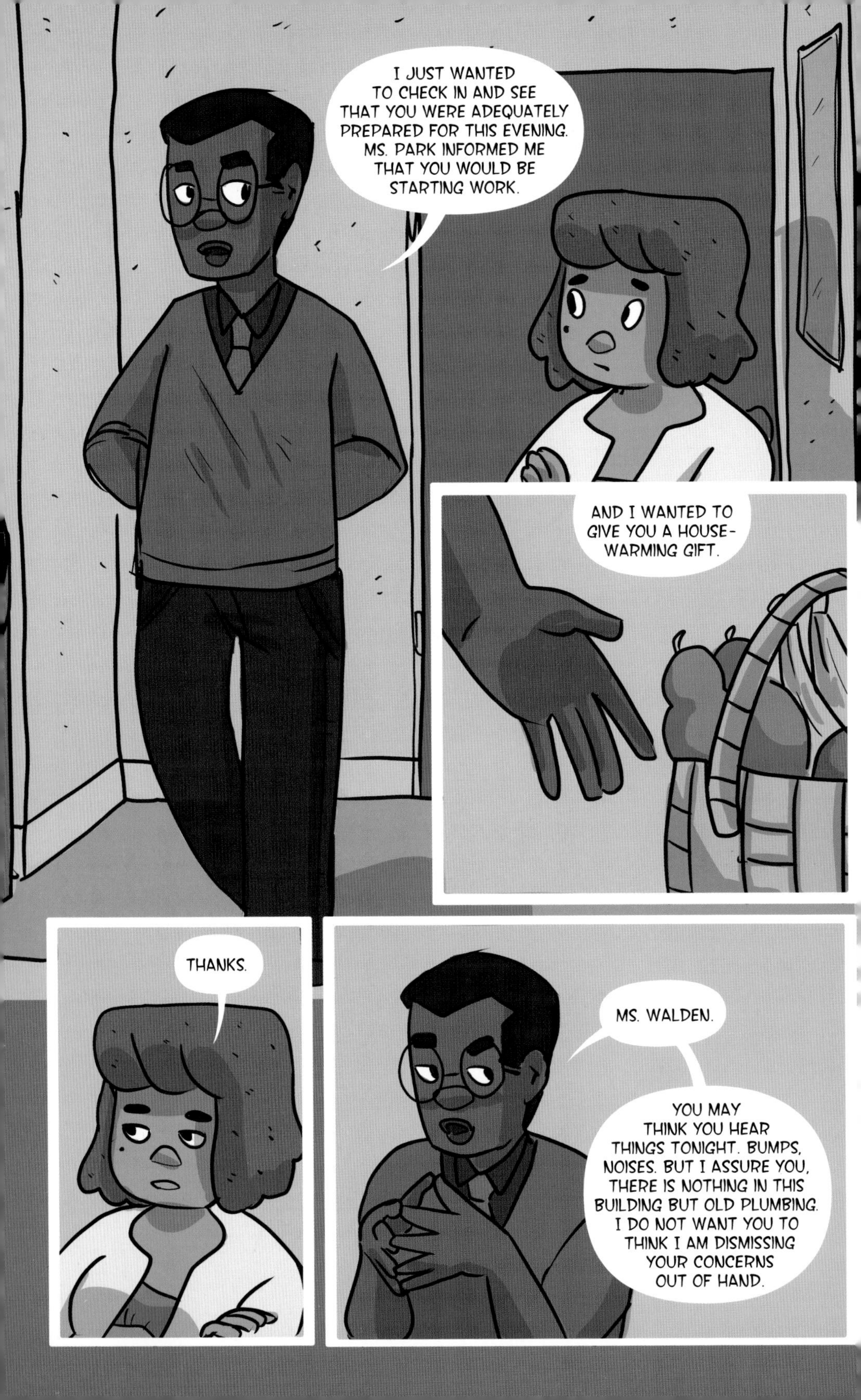
I JUST WANTED TO CHECK IN AND SEE THAT YOU WERE ADEQUATELY PREPARED FOR THIS EVENING. MS. PARK INFORMED ME THAT YOU WOULD BE STARTING WORK.
AND I WANTED TO GIVE YOU A HOUSE-WARMING GIFT.
THANKS.
MS. WALDEN.
YOU MAY THINK YOU HEAR THINGS TONIGHT. BUMPS, NOISES. BUT I ASSURE YOU, THERE IS NOTHING IN THIS BUILDING BUT OLD PLUMBING. I DO NOT WANT YOU TO THINK I AM DISMISSING YOUR CONCERNS OUT OF HAND.

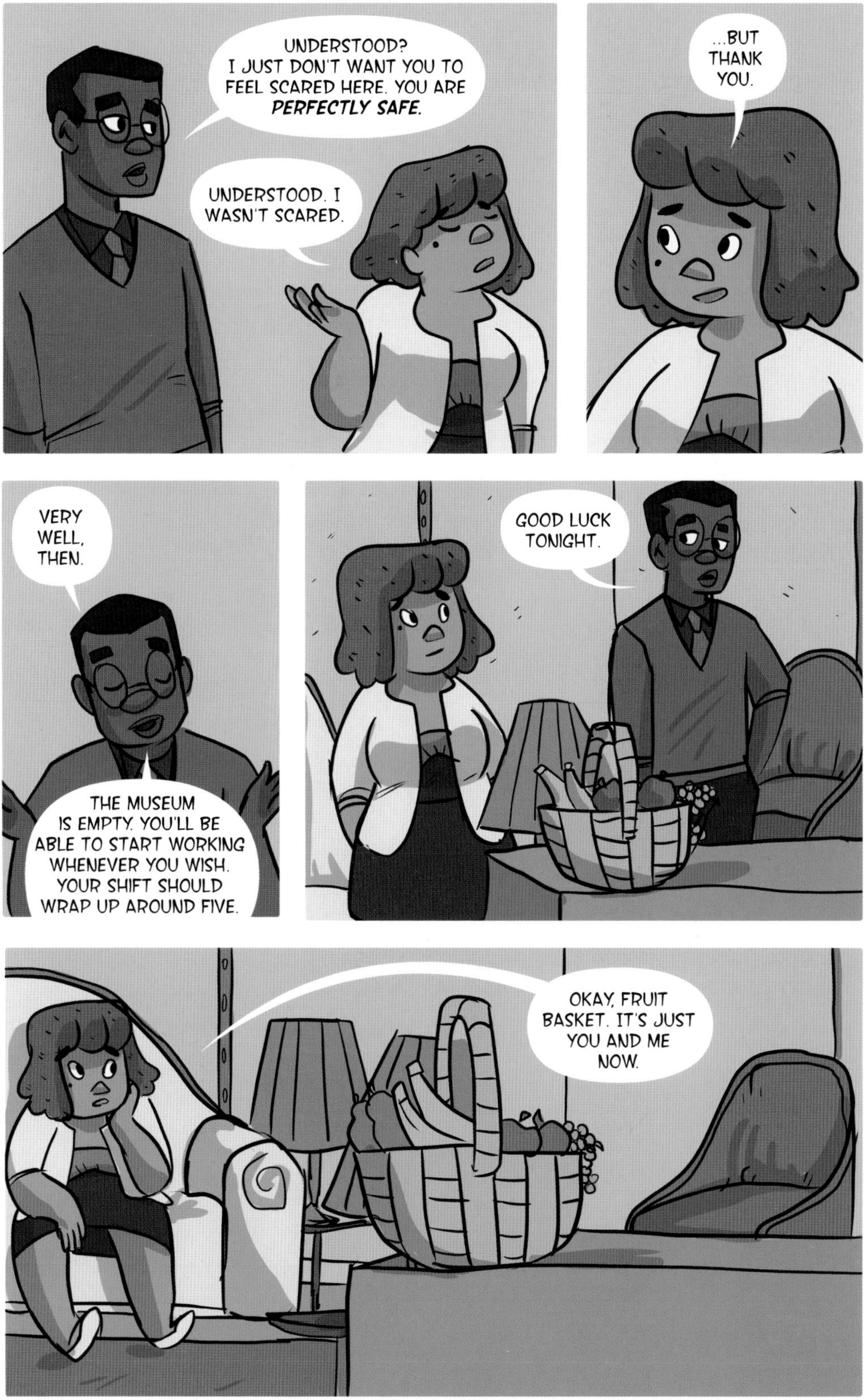
UNDERSTOOD? I JUST DON'T WANT YOU TO FEEL SCARED HERE. YOU ARE *PERFECTLY SAFE.*
UNDERSTOOD. I WASN'T SCARED.
...BUT THANK YOU.
VERY WELL, THEN.
THE MUSEUM IS EMPTY. YOU'LL BE ABLE TO START WORKING WHENEVER YOU WISH. YOUR SHIFT SHOULD WRAP UP AROUND FIVE.
GOOD LUCK TONIGHT.
OKAY, FRUIT BASKET. IT'S JUST YOU AND ME NOW.

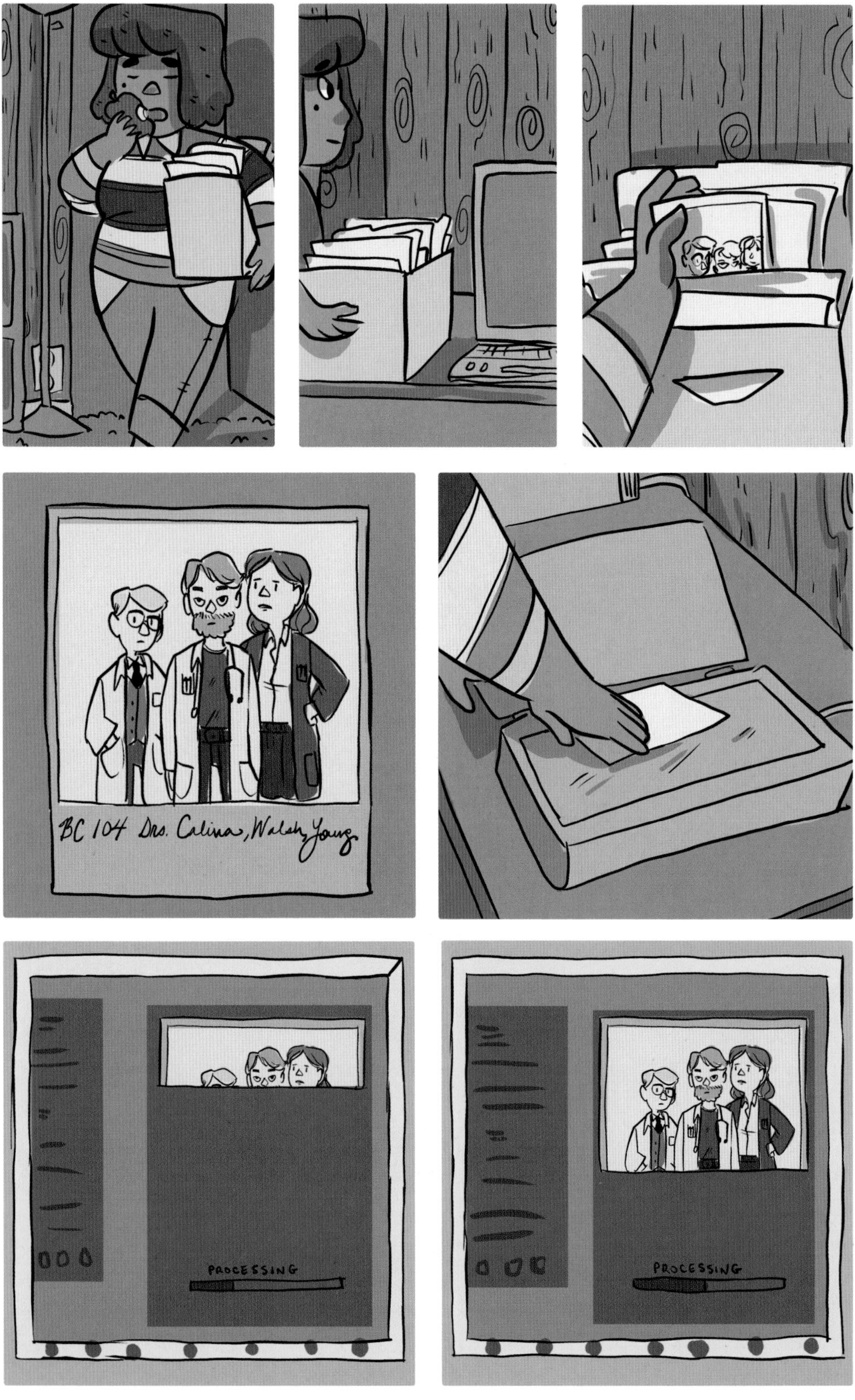
BC 104 Drs. Calina, Walsh, Young
PROCESSING
PROCESSING

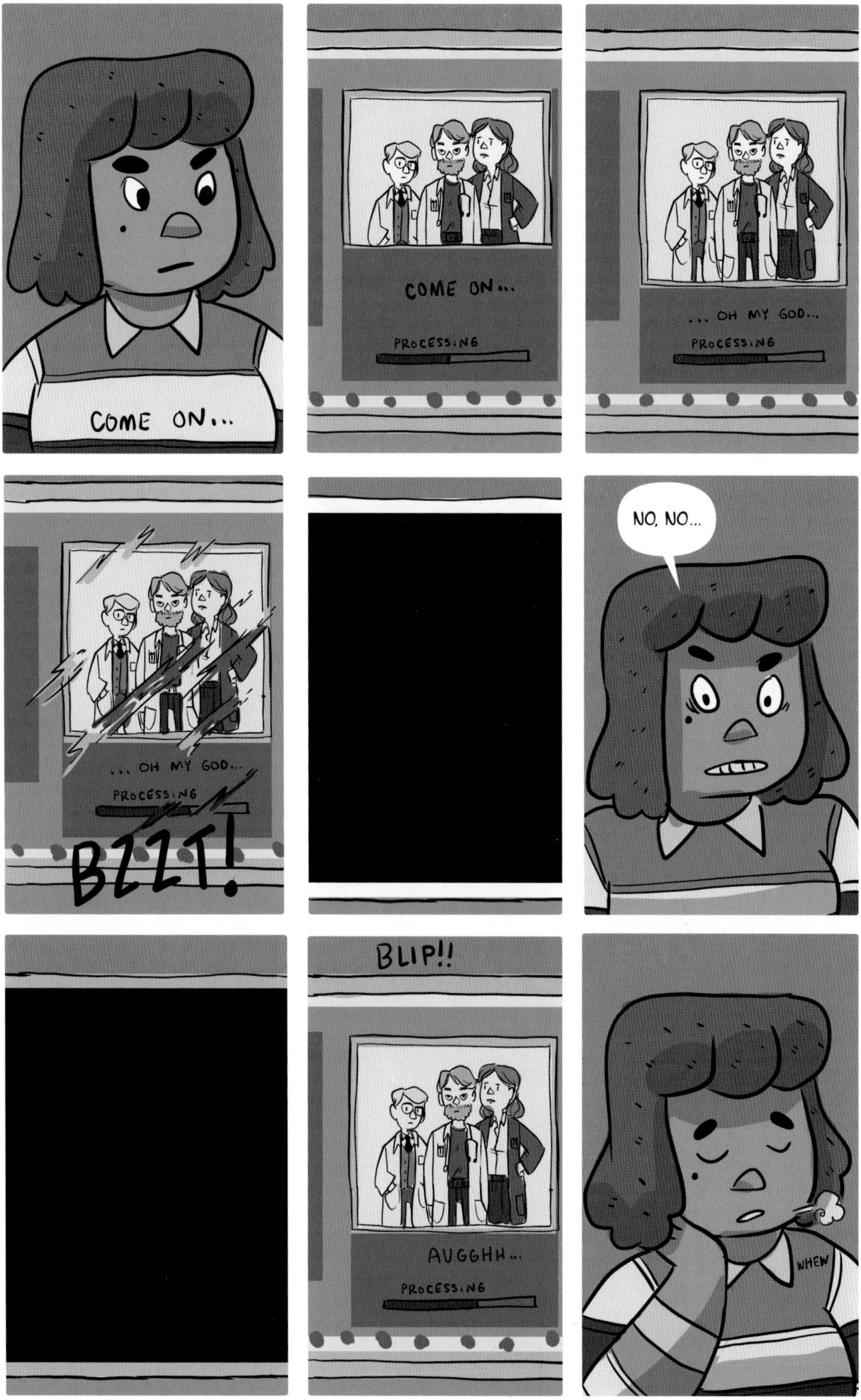

COME ON...
COME ON...
PROCESSING
... OH MY GOD...
PROCESSING
... OH MY GOD...
PROCESSING
BZZT!
NO, NO...
BLIP!!
AUGGHH...
PROCESSING
WHEW

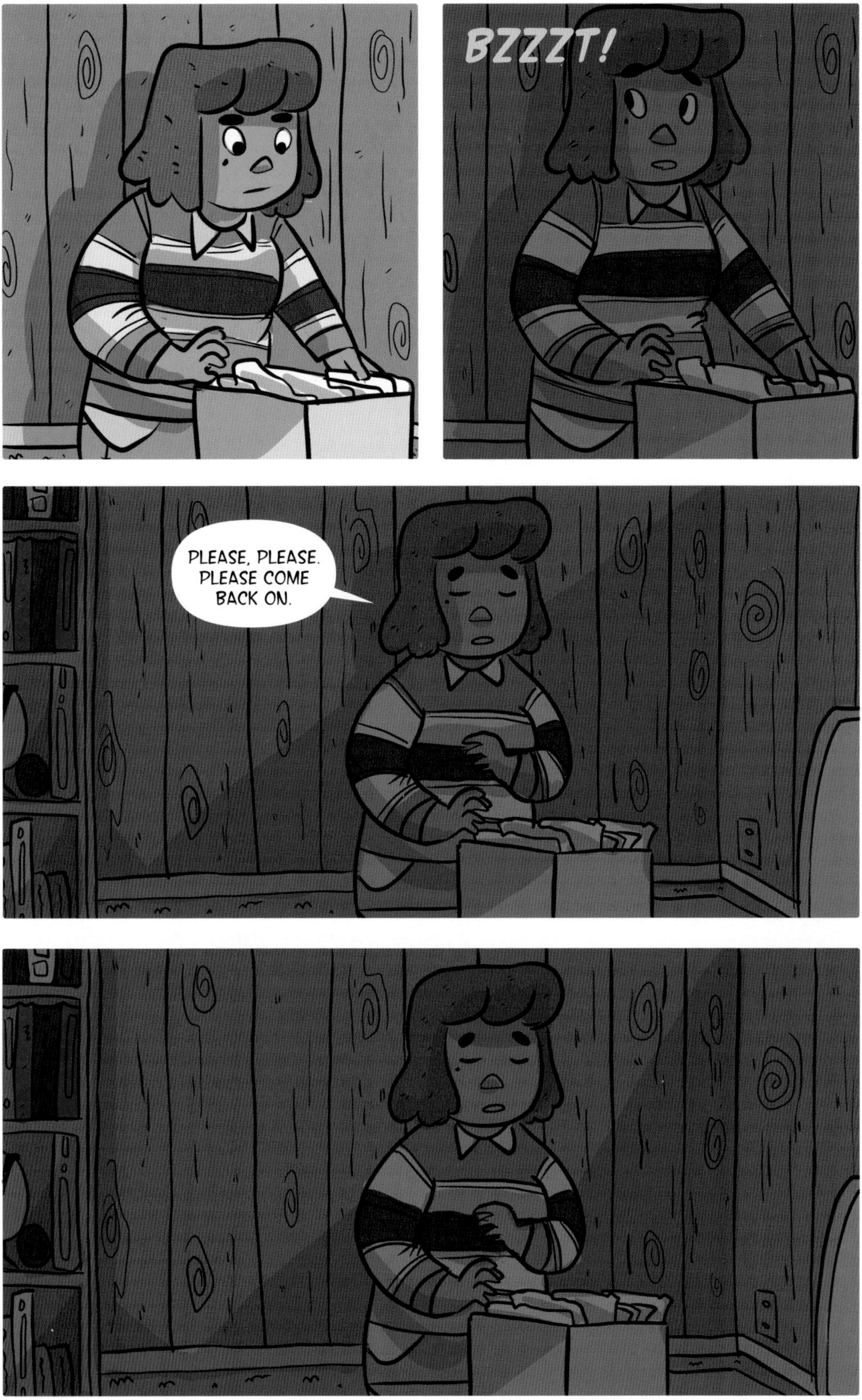
BZZZT!
PLEASE, PLEASE. PLEASE COME BACK ON.

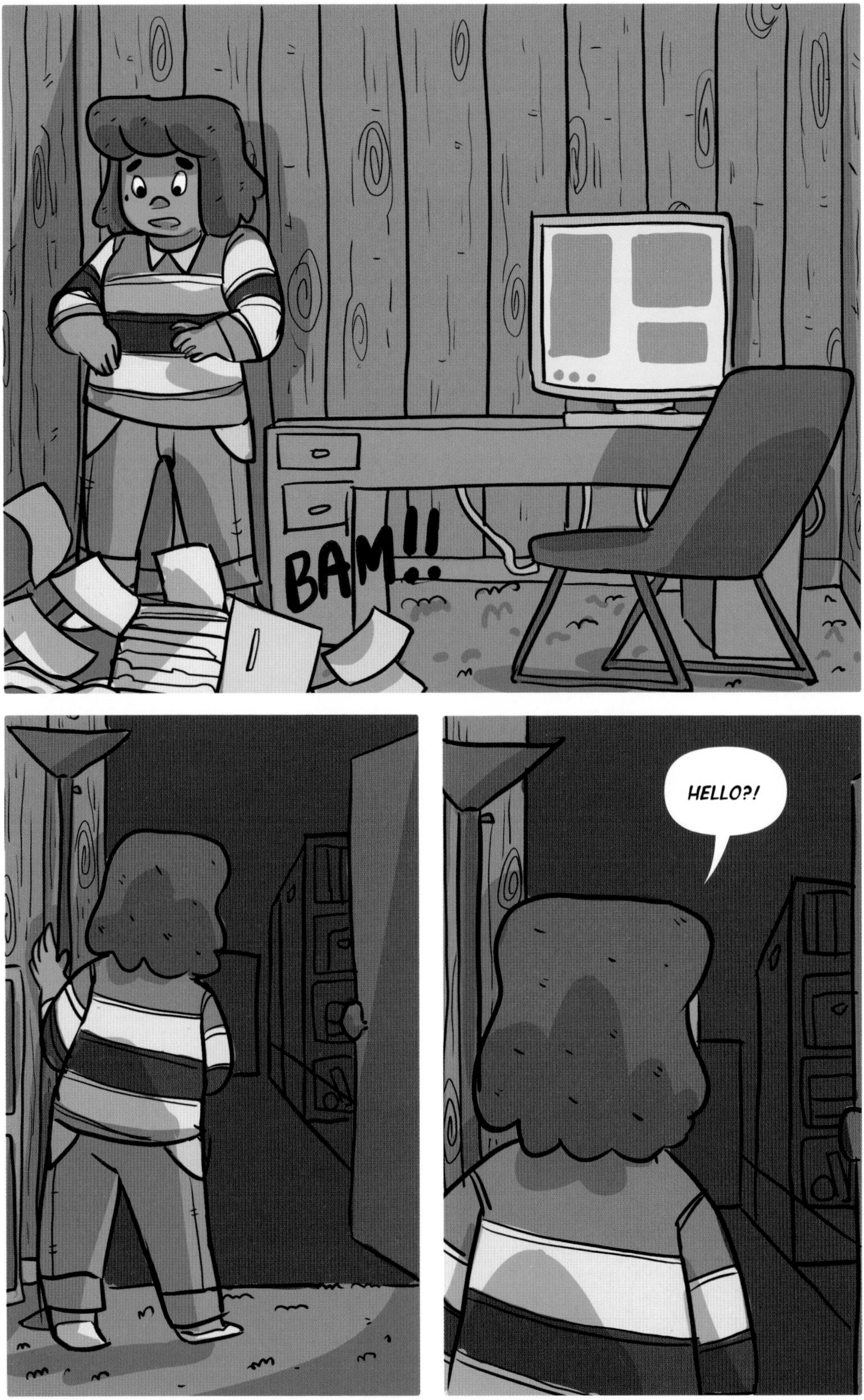
BAM!!
HELLO?!

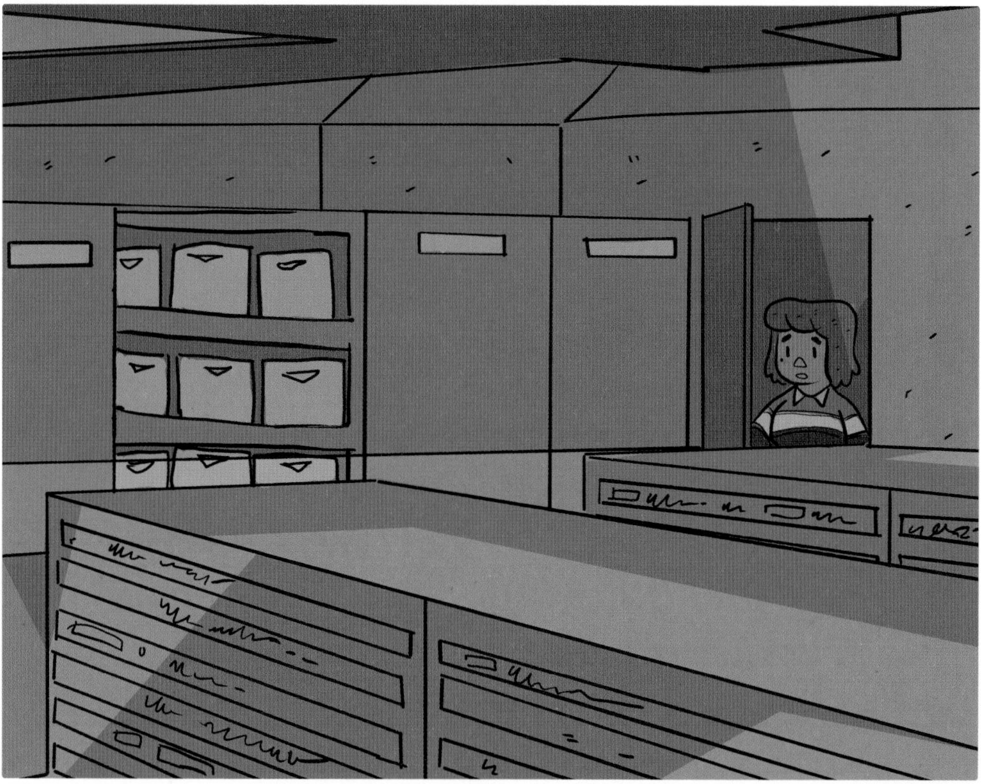

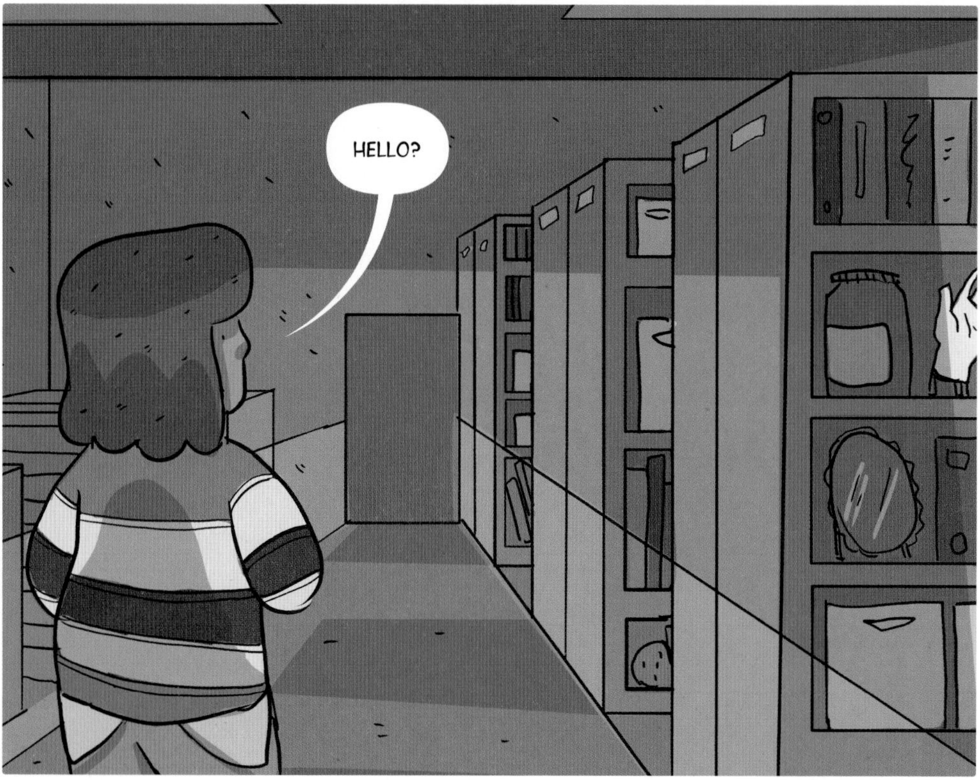
HELLO?

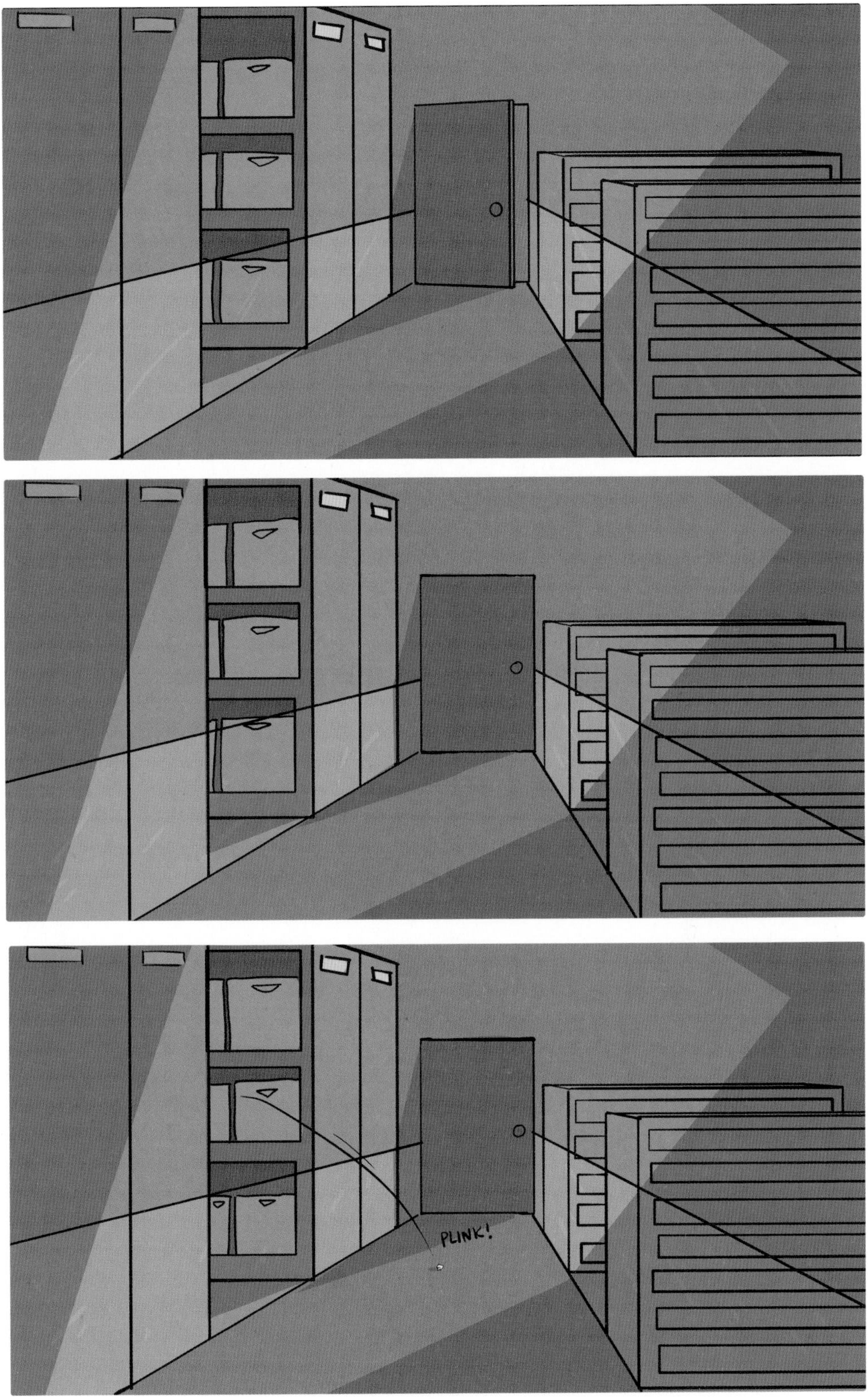
PLINK!

THE NEXT MORNING

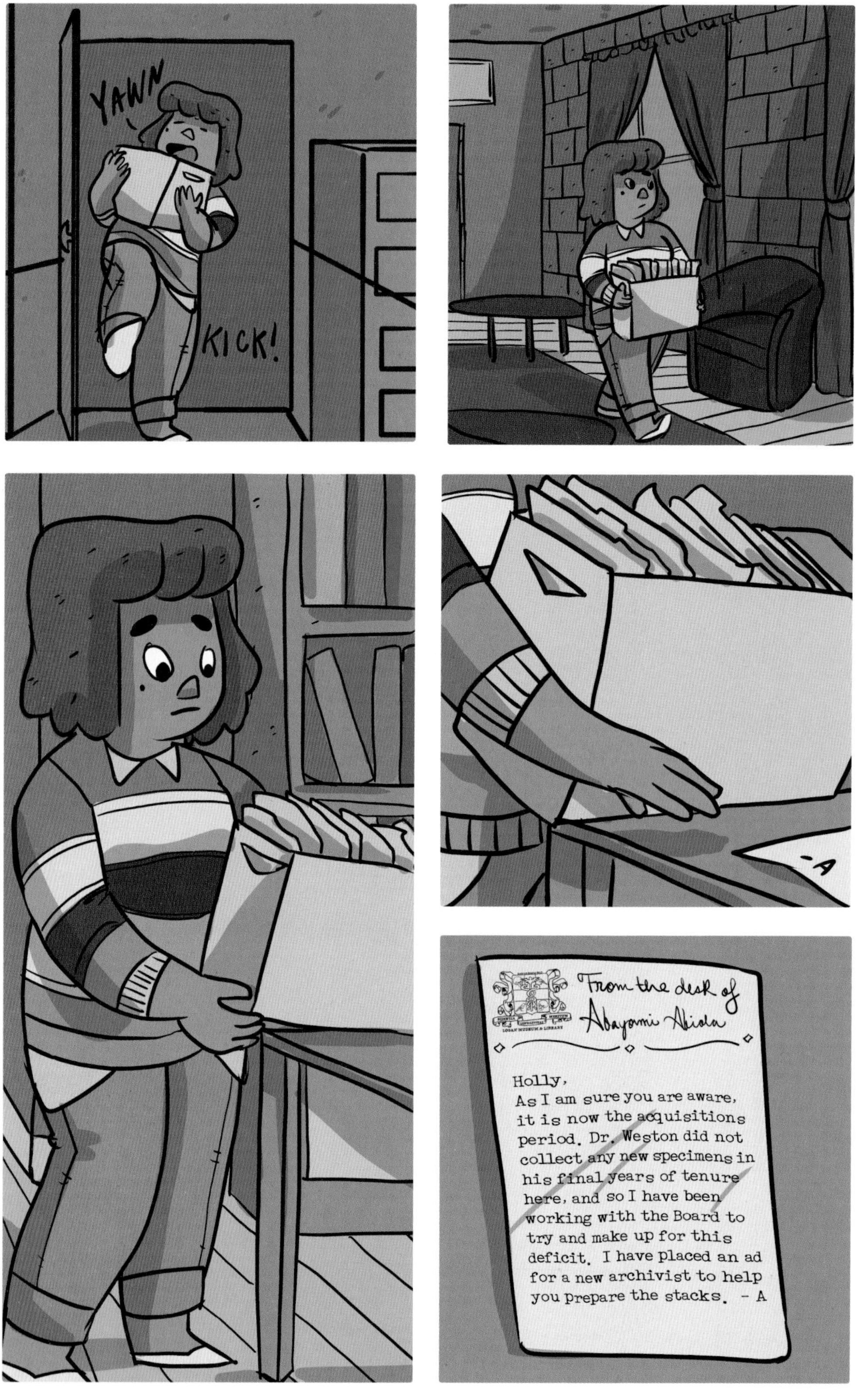
YAWN
KICK!
-A
From the desk of
Abayomi Abiola
LOGAN MUSEUM & LIBRARY
Holly,
As I am sure you are aware,
it is now the acquisitions
period. Dr. Weston did not
collect any new specimens in
his final years of tenure
here, and so I have been
working with the Board to
try and make up for this
deficit. I have placed an ad
for a new archivist to help
you prepare the stacks. - A

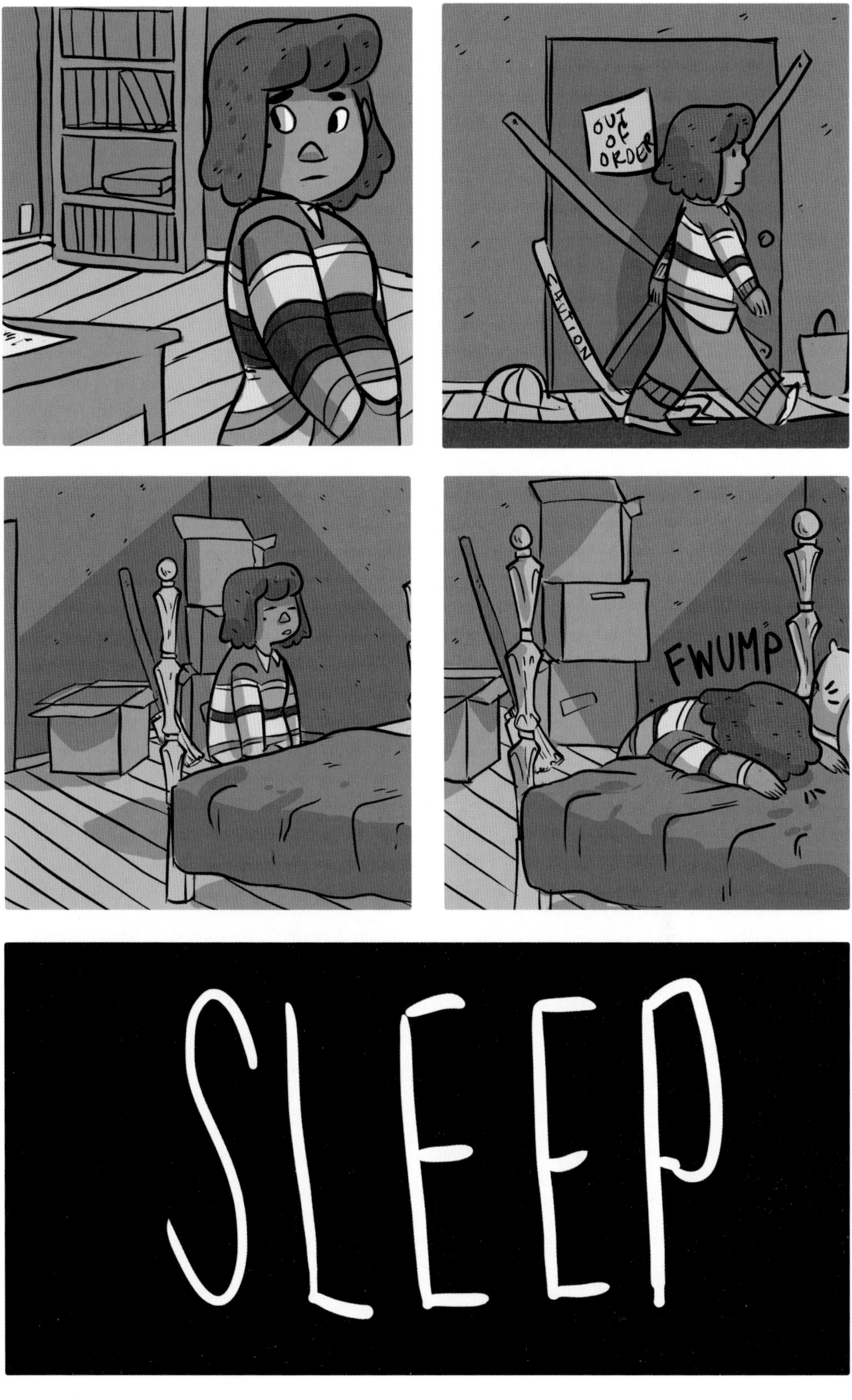
OUT OF ORDER
CAUTION
FWUMP
SLEEP

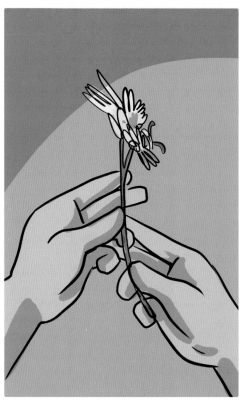

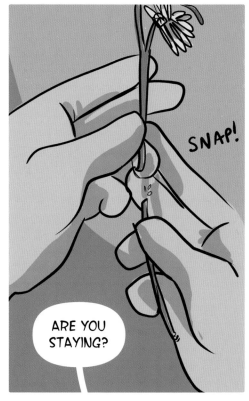

SNAP!

ARE YOU STAYING?

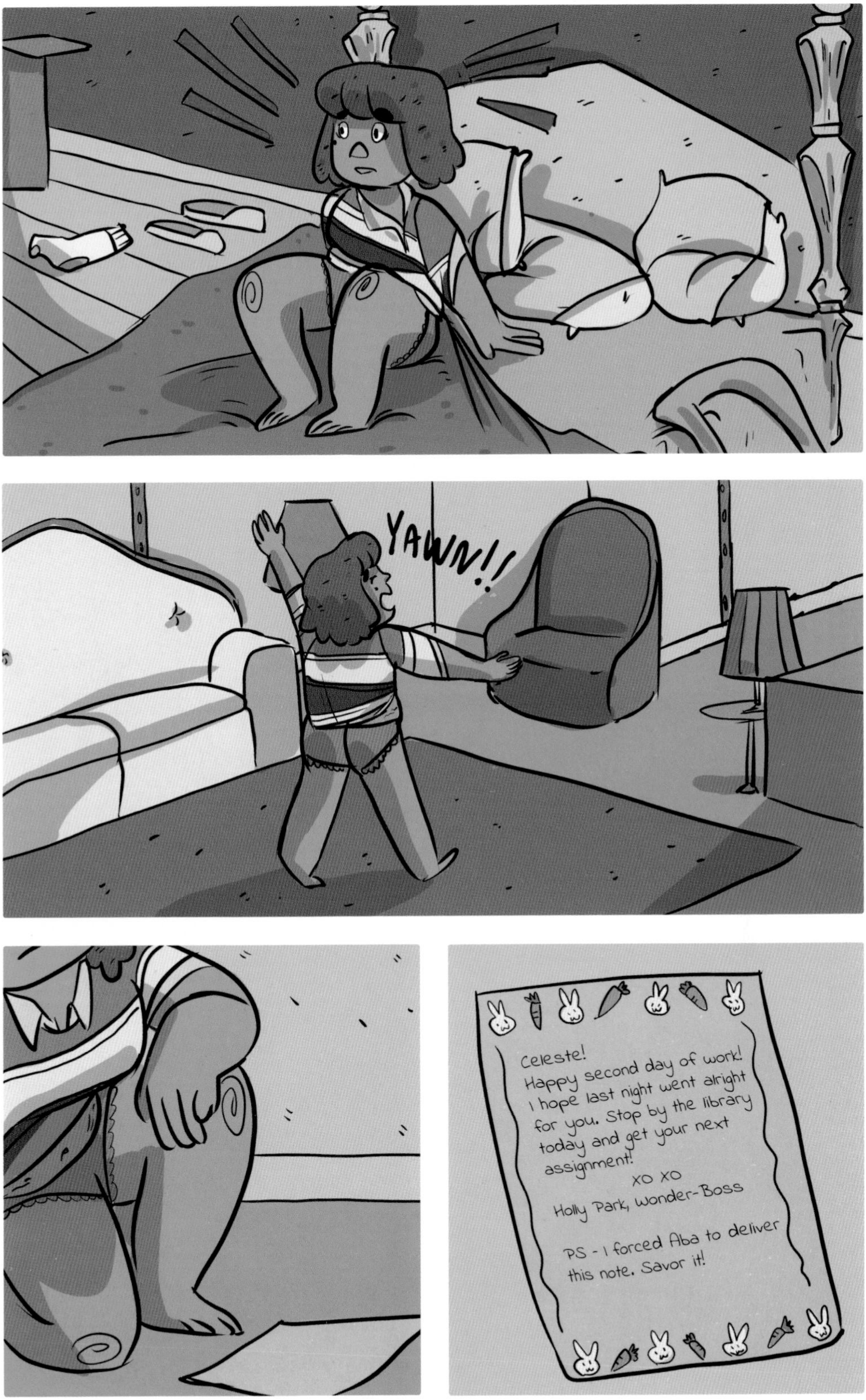
YAWN!!
Celeste!
Happy second day of work!
I hope last night went alright
for you. Stop by the library
today and get your next
assignment!
XO XO
Holly Park, Wonder-Boss
PS - I forced Aba to deliver
this note. Savor it!

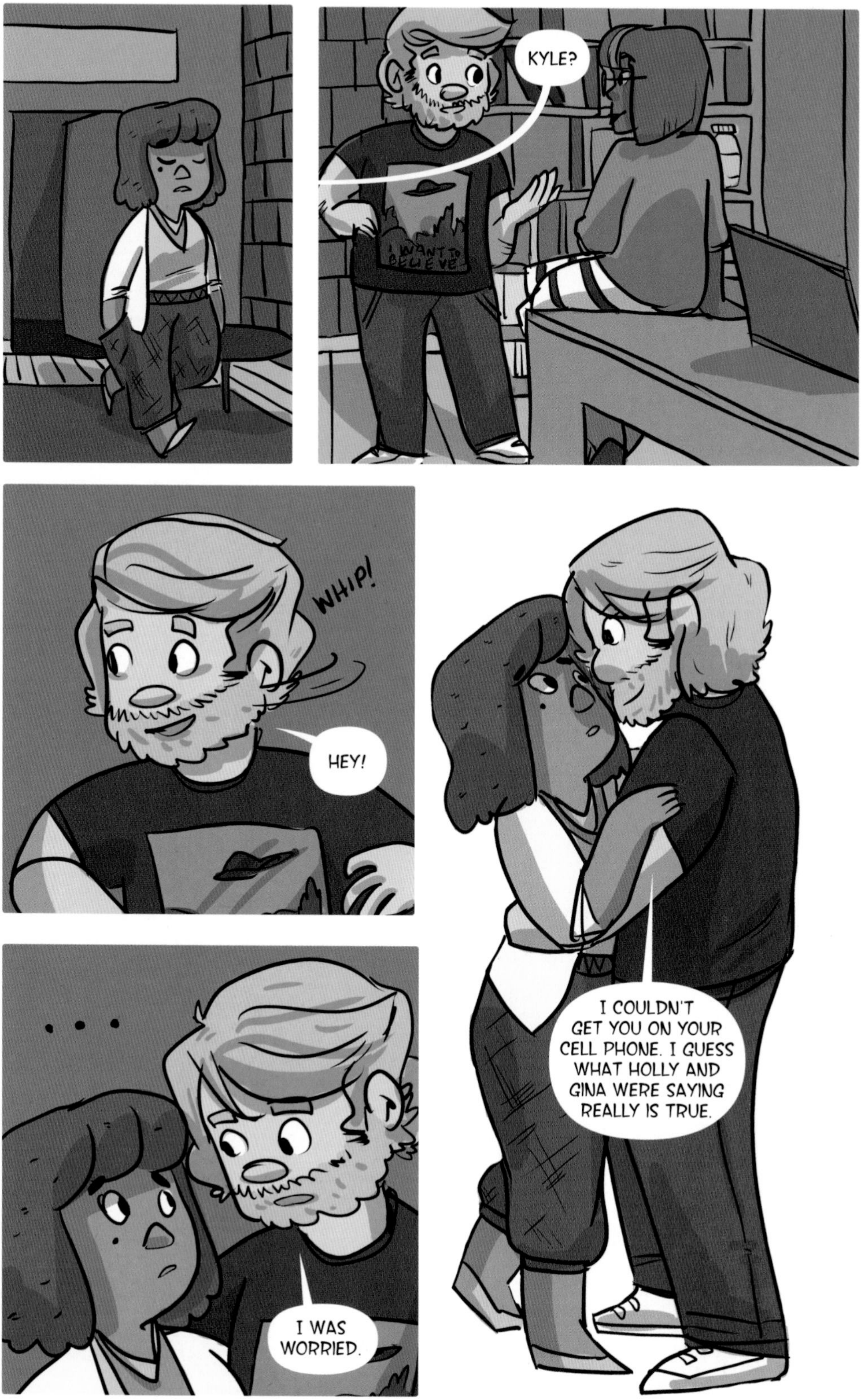
KYLE?
I WANT TO BELIEVE
WHIP!
HEY!
...
I WAS WORRIED.
I COULDN'T GET YOU ON YOUR CELL PHONE. I GUESS WHAT HOLLY AND GINA WERE SAYING REALLY IS TRUE.

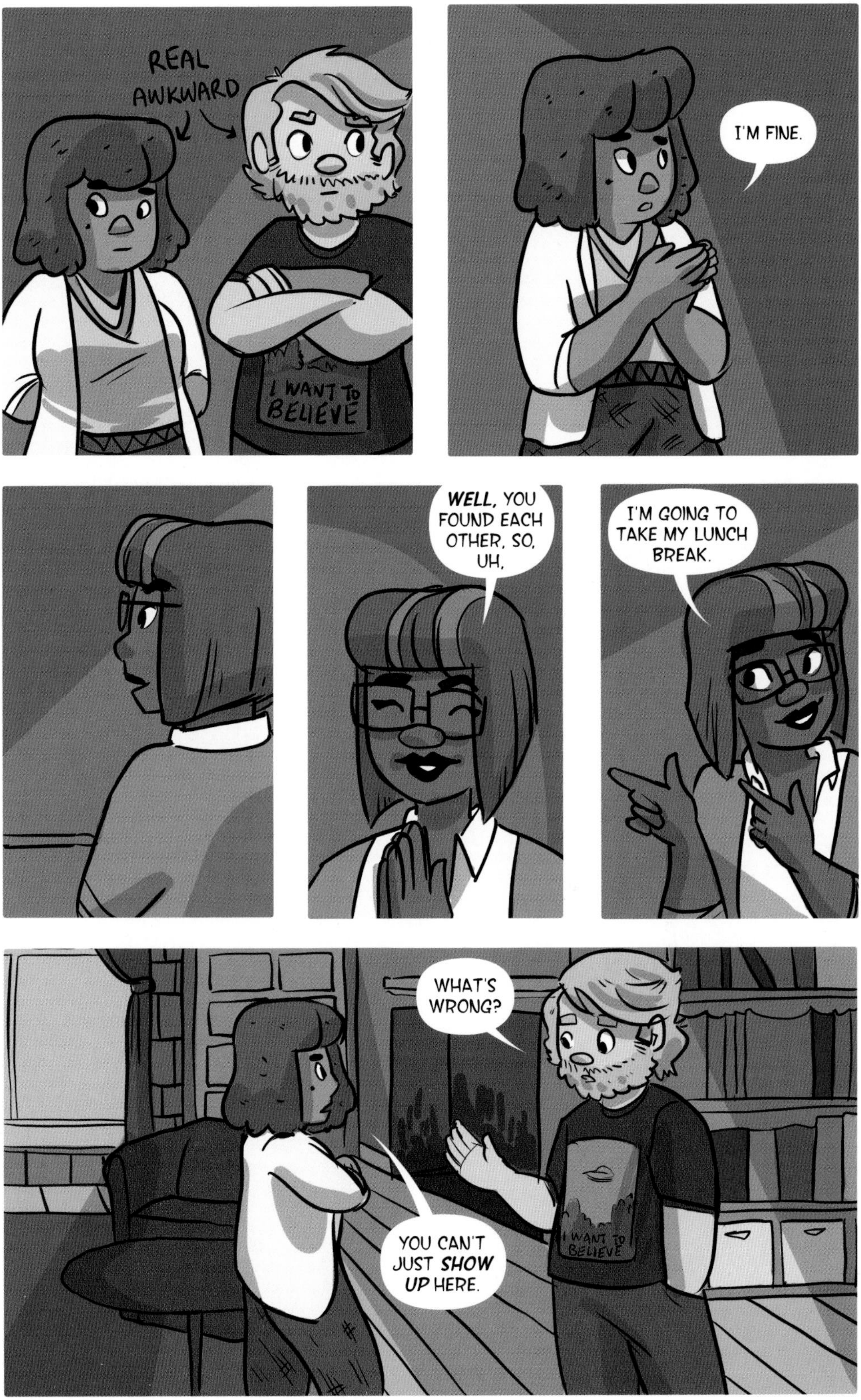
REAL AWKWARD
I WANT TO BELIEVE
I'M FINE.
WELL, YOU FOUND EACH OTHER, SO, UH,
I'M GOING TO TAKE MY LUNCH BREAK.
WHAT'S WRONG?
YOU CAN'T JUST SHOW UP HERE.
I WANT TO BELIEVE

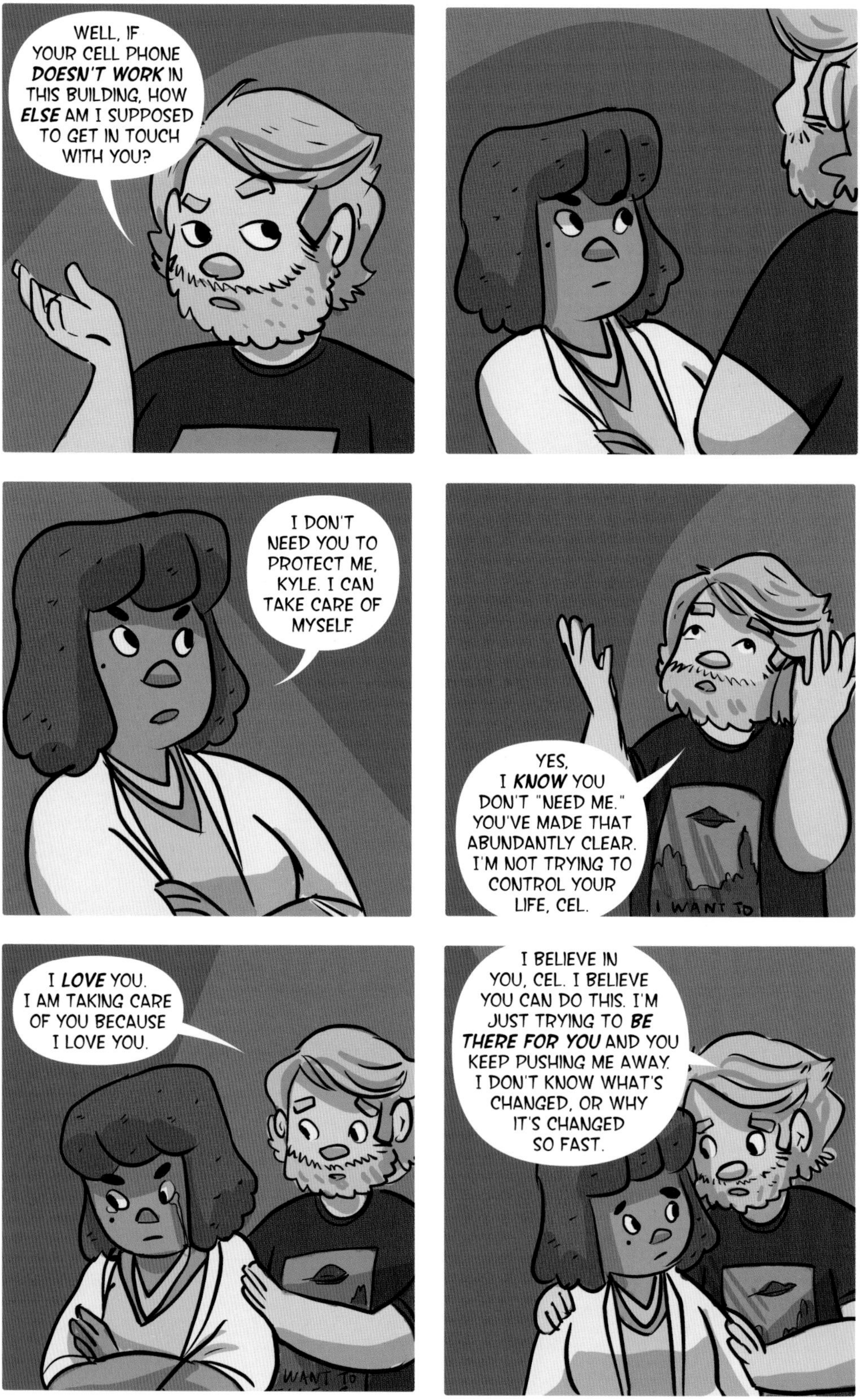
WELL, IF YOUR CELL PHONE **DOESN'T WORK** IN THIS BUILDING, HOW **ELSE** AM I SUPPOSED TO GET IN TOUCH WITH YOU?
I DON'T NEED YOU TO PROTECT ME, KYLE. I CAN TAKE CARE OF MYSELF.
YES, I **KNOW** YOU DON'T "NEED ME." YOU'VE MADE THAT ABUNDANTLY CLEAR. I'M NOT TRYING TO CONTROL YOUR LIFE, CEL.
I WANT TO
I **LOVE** YOU. I AM TAKING CARE OF YOU BECAUSE I LOVE YOU.
WANT TO
I BELIEVE IN YOU, CEL. I BELIEVE YOU CAN DO THIS. I'M JUST TRYING TO **BE THERE FOR YOU** AND YOU KEEP PUSHING ME AWAY. I DON'T KNOW WHAT'S CHANGED, OR WHY IT'S CHANGED SO FAST.

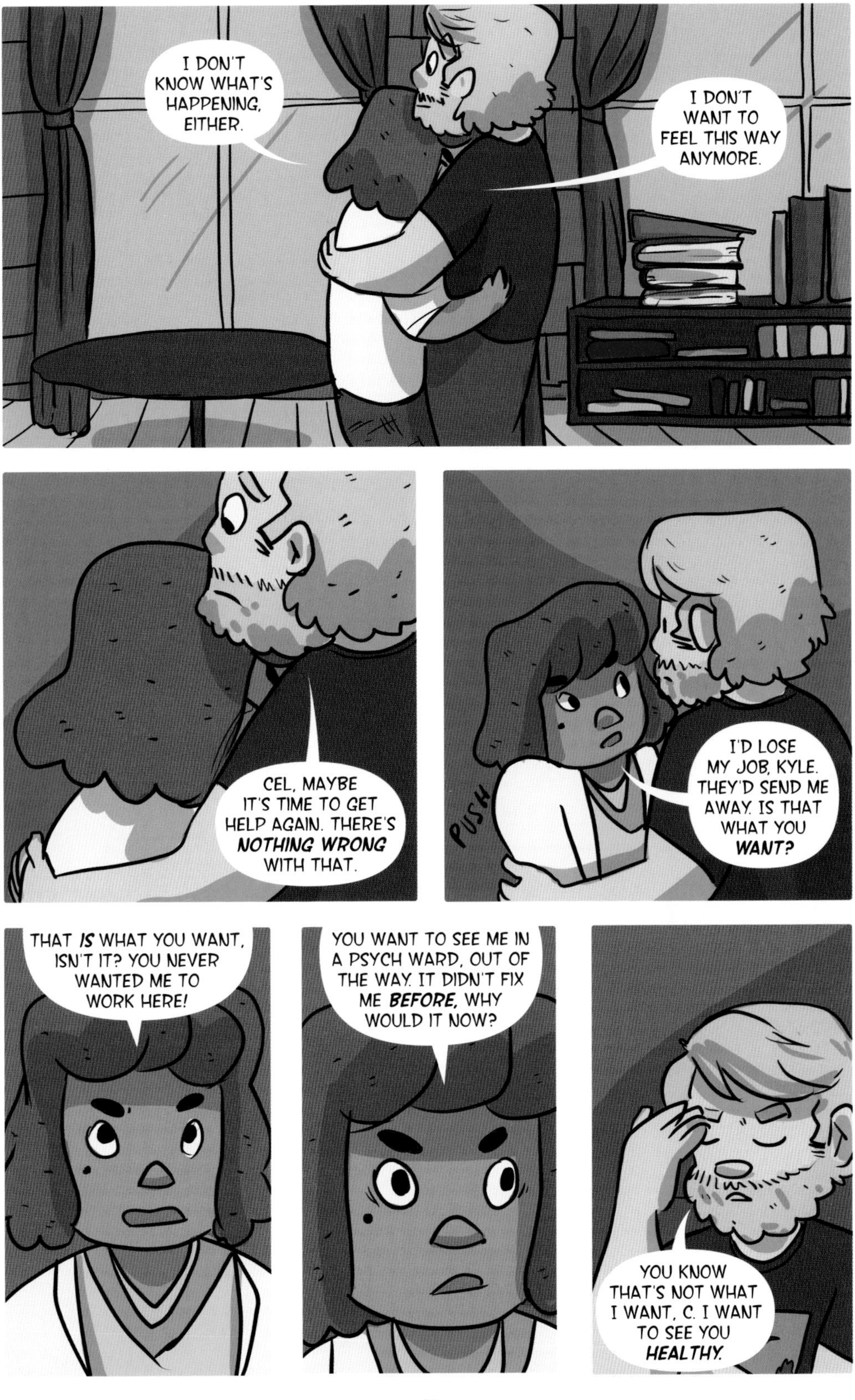
I DON'T KNOW WHAT'S HAPPENING, EITHER.
I DON'T WANT TO FEEL THIS WAY ANYMORE.
CEL, MAYBE IT'S TIME TO GET HELP AGAIN. THERE'S ***NOTHING WRONG*** WITH THAT.
PUSH
I'D LOSE MY JOB, KYLE. THEY'D SEND ME AWAY. IS THAT WHAT YOU ***WANT?***
THAT ***IS*** WHAT YOU WANT, ISN'T IT? YOU NEVER WANTED ME TO WORK HERE!
YOU WANT TO SEE ME IN A PSYCH WARD, OUT OF THE WAY. IT DIDN'T FIX ME ***BEFORE,*** WHY WOULD IT NOW?
YOU KNOW THAT'S NOT WHAT I WANT, C. I WANT TO SEE YOU ***HEALTHY.***

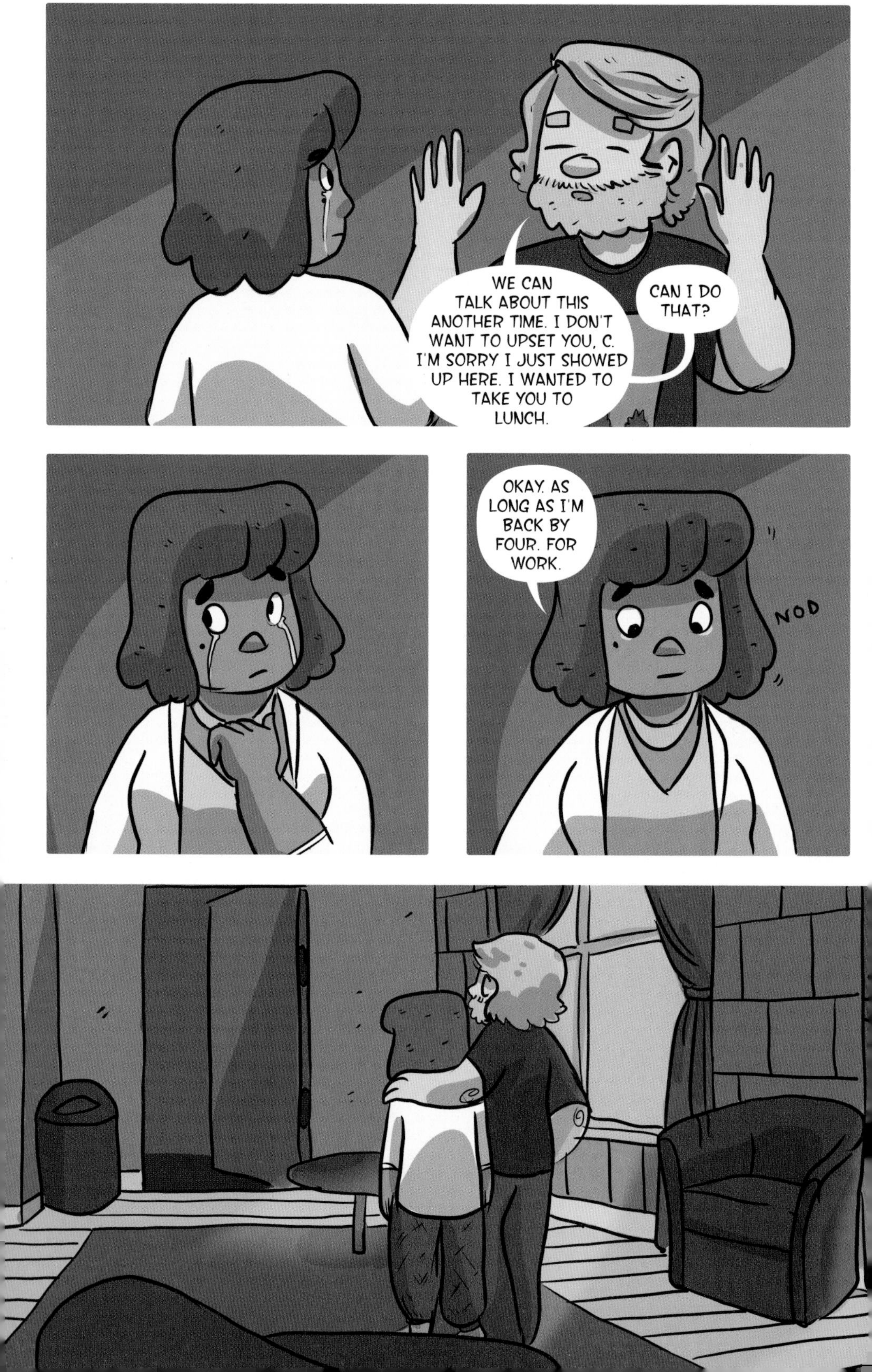
WE CAN TALK ABOUT THIS ANOTHER TIME. I DON'T WANT TO UPSET YOU, C. I'M SORRY I JUST SHOWED UP HERE. I WANTED TO TAKE YOU TO LUNCH.
CAN I DO THAT?
OKAY. AS LONG AS I'M BACK BY FOUR. FOR WORK.
NOD

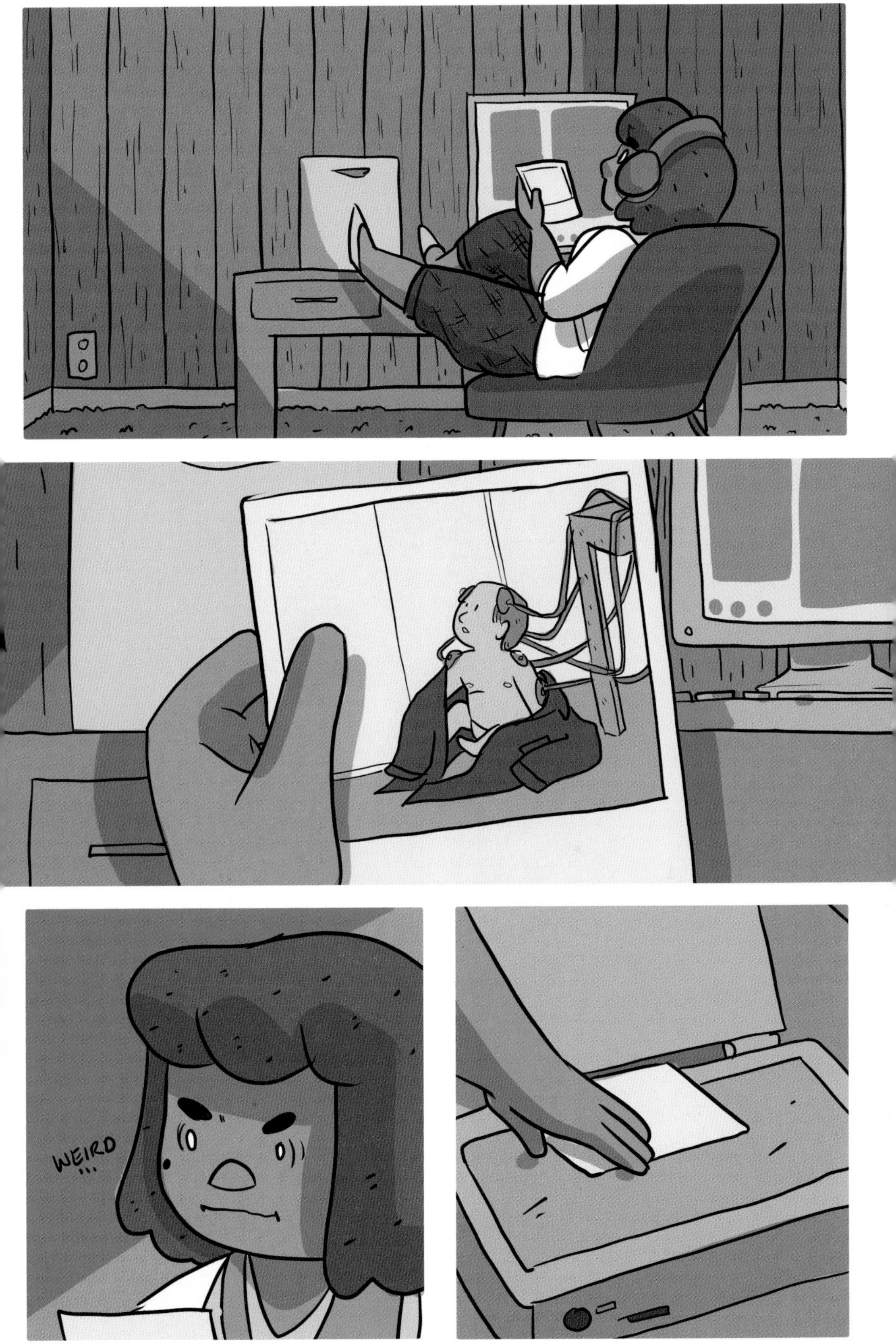
WEIRD...

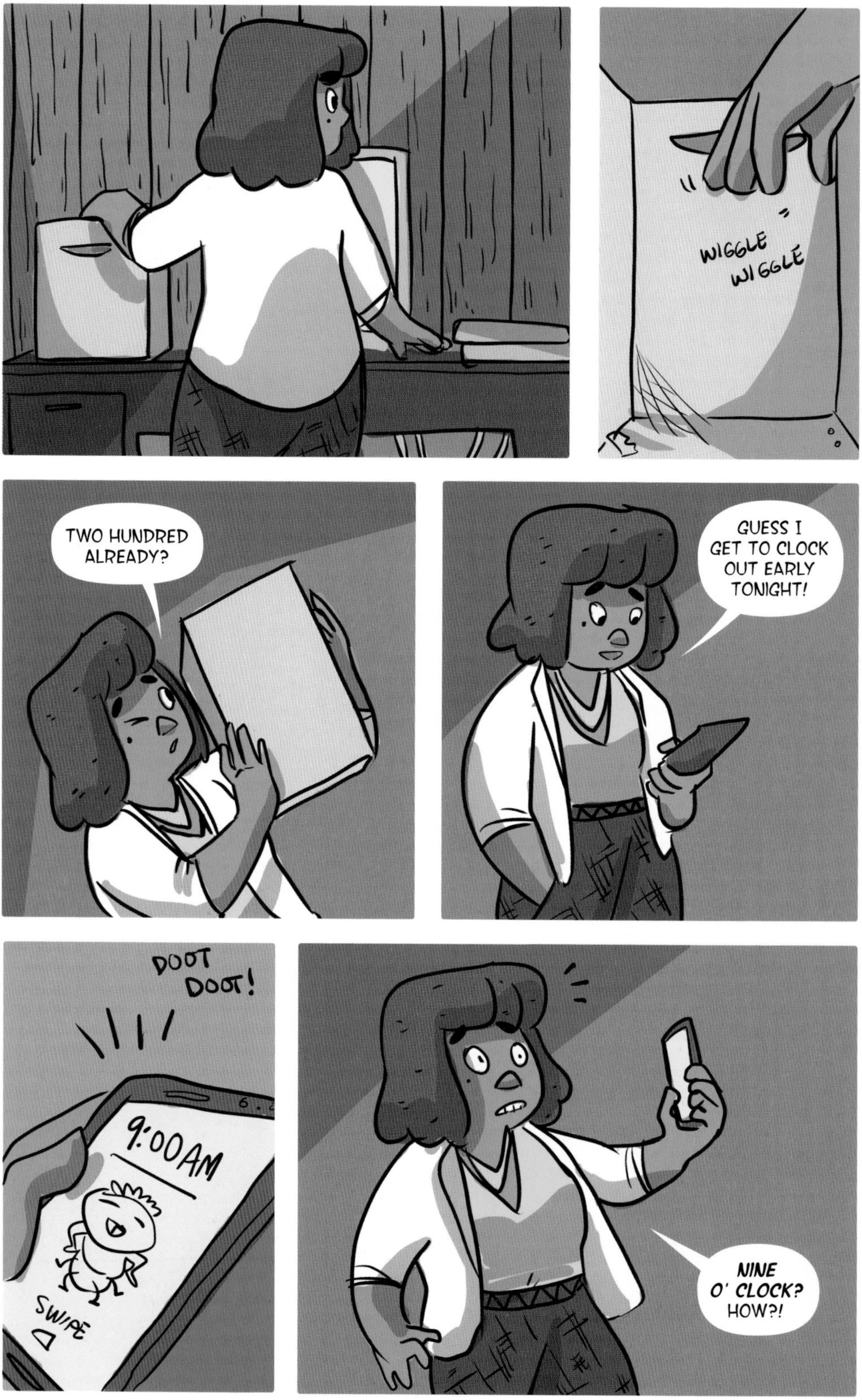
WIGGLE
WIGGLE
TWO HUNDRED ALREADY?
GUESS I GET TO CLOCK OUT EARLY TONIGHT!
DOOT DOOT!
9:00AM
SWIPE
NINE O' CLOCK? HOW?!

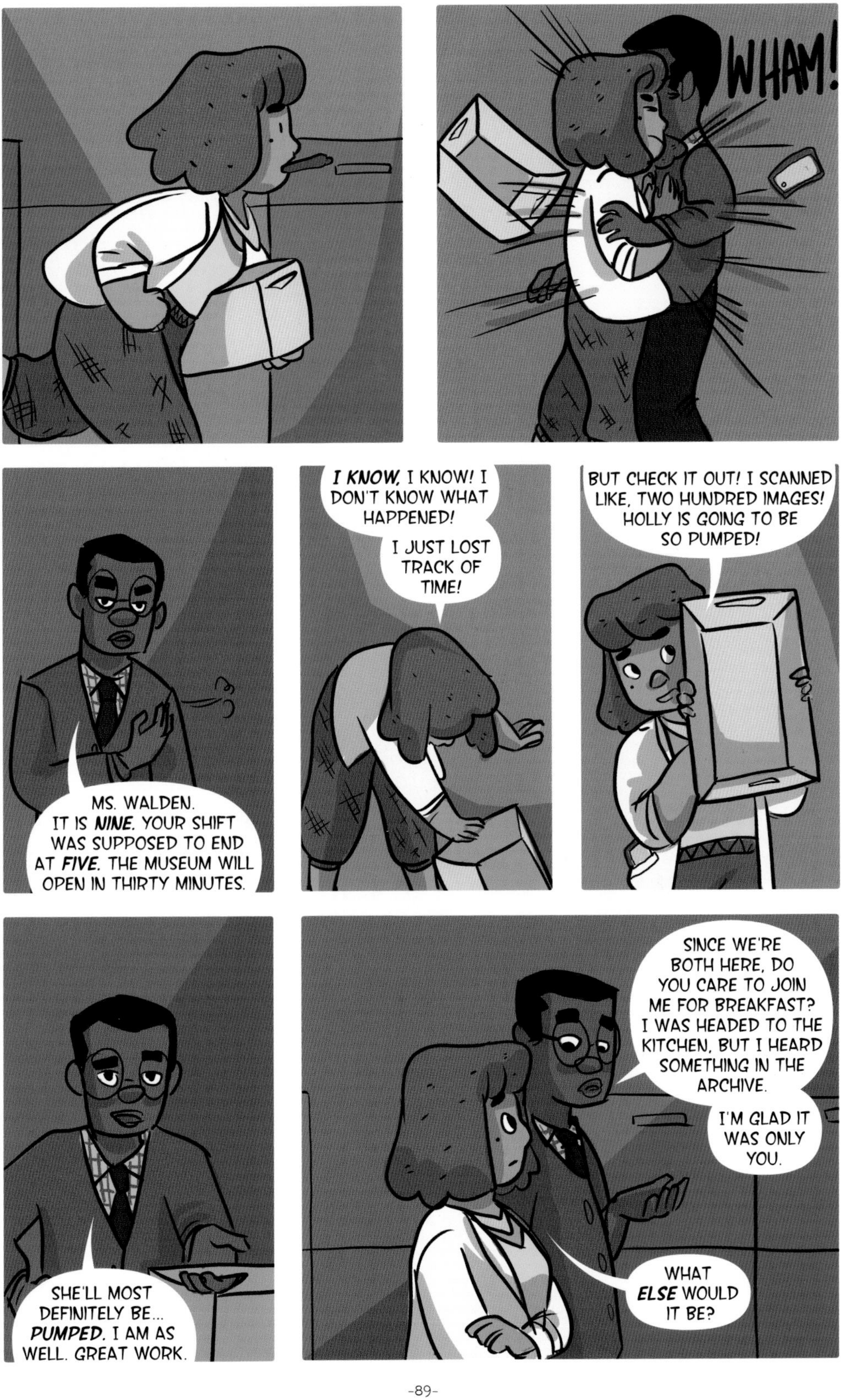
WHAM!
MS. WALDEN. IT IS NINE. YOUR SHIFT WAS SUPPOSED TO END AT FIVE. THE MUSEUM WILL OPEN IN THIRTY MINUTES.
I KNOW, I KNOW! I DON'T KNOW WHAT HAPPENED!
I JUST LOST TRACK OF TIME!
BUT CHECK IT OUT! I SCANNED LIKE, TWO HUNDRED IMAGES! HOLLY IS GOING TO BE SO PUMPED!
SHE'LL MOST DEFINITELY BE... PUMPED. I AM AS WELL. GREAT WORK.
SINCE WE'RE BOTH HERE, DO YOU CARE TO JOIN ME FOR BREAKFAST? I WAS HEADED TO THE KITCHEN, BUT I HEARD SOMETHING IN THE ARCHIVE.
I'M GLAD IT WAS ONLY YOU.
WHAT ELSE WOULD IT BE?

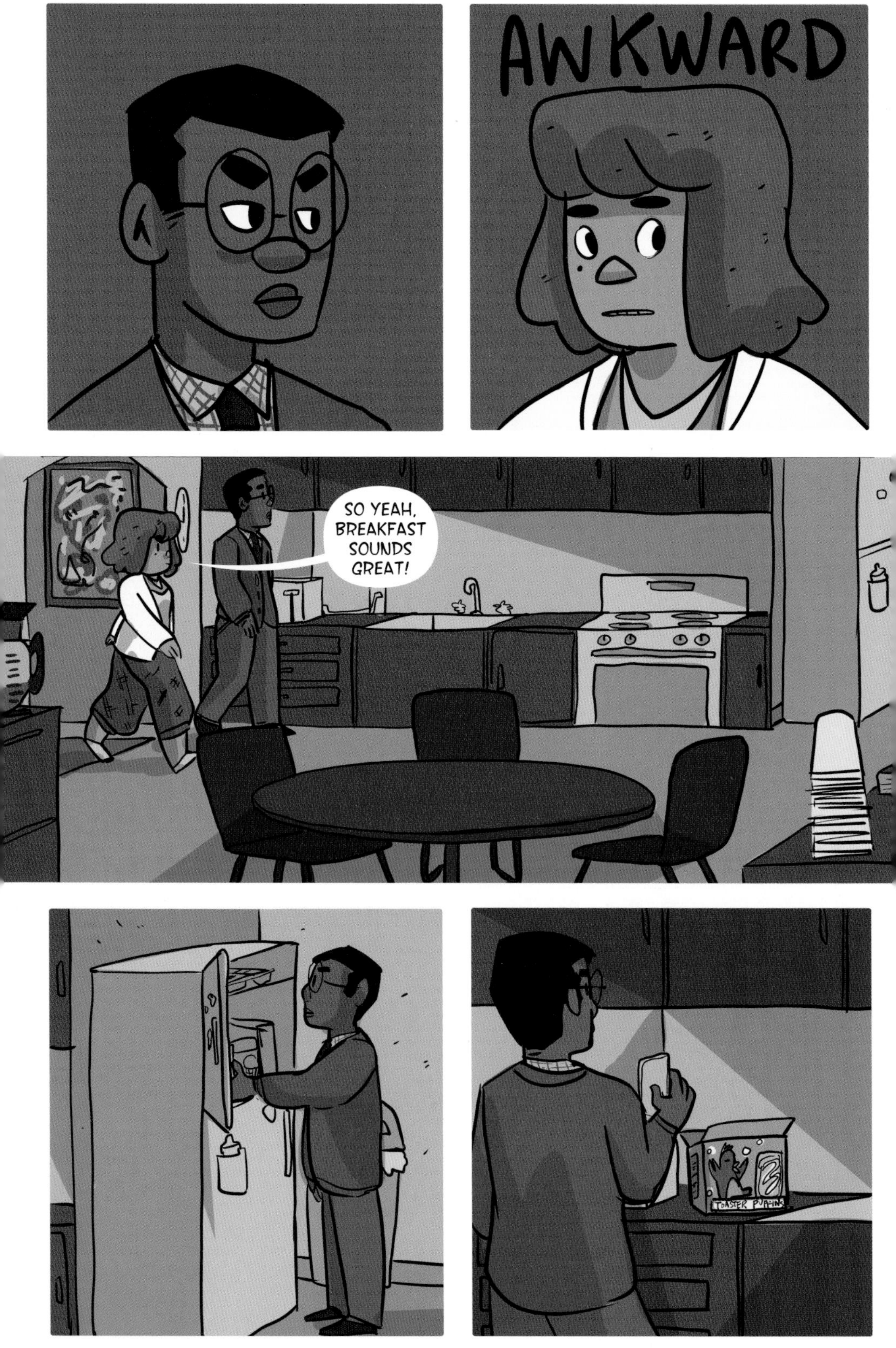
AWKWARD
SO YEAH, BREAKFAST SOUNDS GREAT!
TOASTER PUFFINS

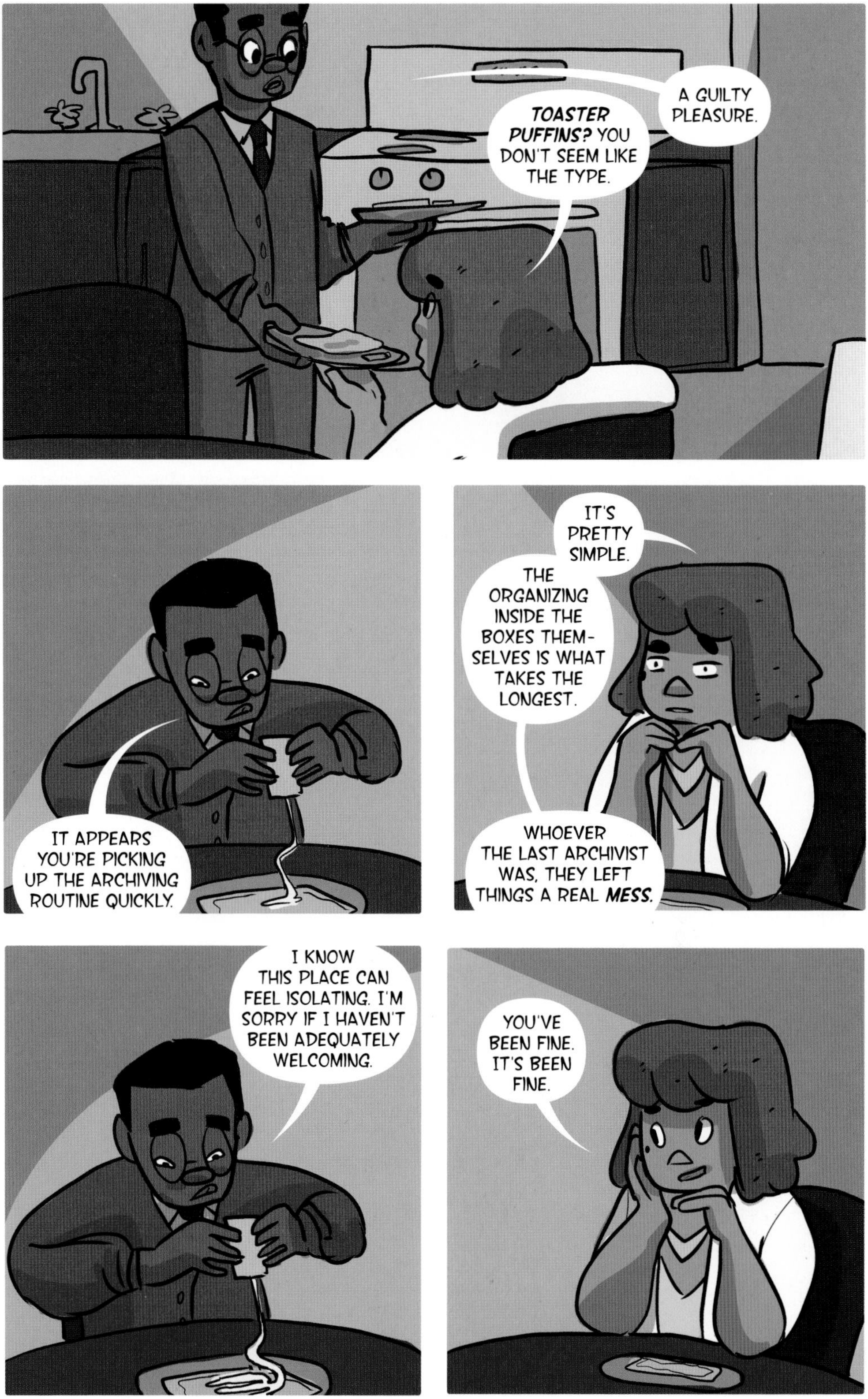
TOASTER PUFFINS? YOU DON'T SEEM LIKE THE TYPE.
A GUILTY PLEASURE.
IT APPEARS YOU'RE PICKING UP THE ARCHIVING ROUTINE QUICKLY.
IT'S PRETTY SIMPLE.
THE ORGANIZING INSIDE THE BOXES THEM-SELVES IS WHAT TAKES THE LONGEST.
WHOEVER THE LAST ARCHIVIST WAS, THEY LEFT THINGS A REAL MESS.
I KNOW THIS PLACE CAN FEEL ISOLATING. I'M SORRY IF I HAVEN'T BEEN ADEQUATELY WELCOMING.
YOU'VE BEEN FINE. IT'S BEEN FINE.

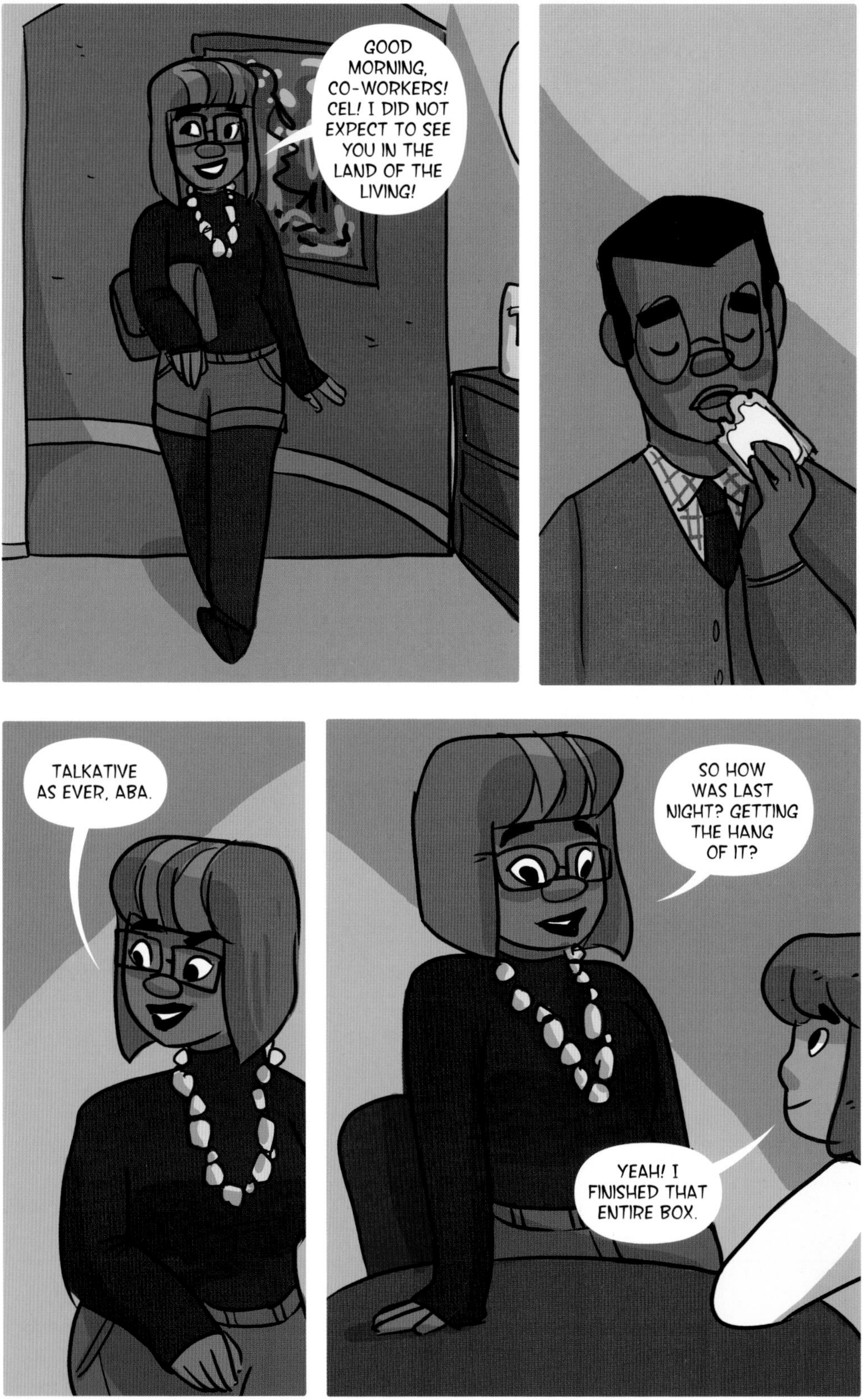
GOOD MORNING, CO-WORKERS! CEL! I DID NOT EXPECT TO SEE YOU IN THE LAND OF THE LIVING!
TALKATIVE AS EVER, ABA.
SO HOW WAS LAST NIGHT? GETTING THE HANG OF IT?
YEAH! I FINISHED THAT ENTIRE BOX.

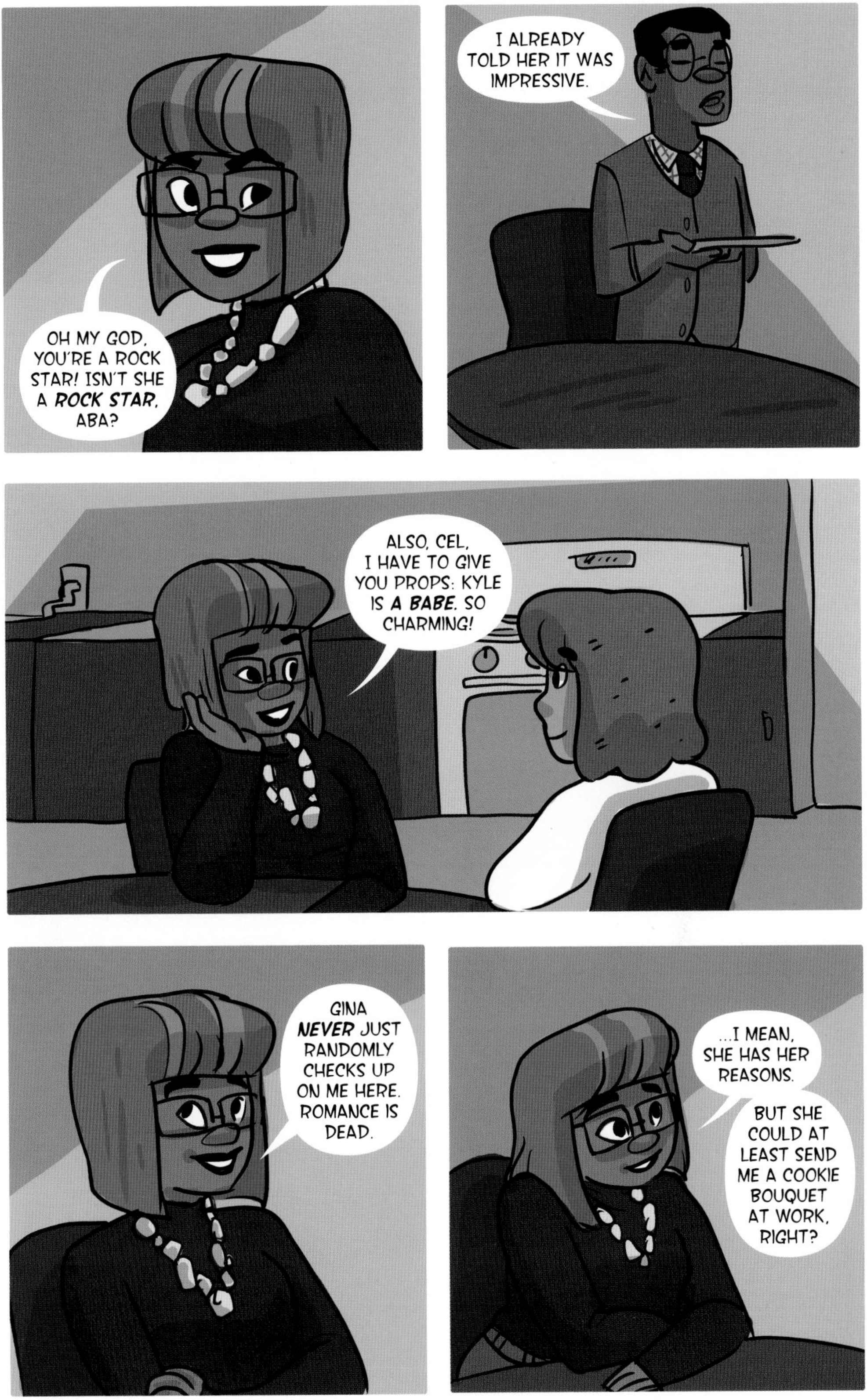
OH MY GOD, YOU'RE A ROCK STAR! ISN'T SHE A ROCK STAR, ABA?
I ALREADY TOLD HER IT WAS IMPRESSIVE.
ALSO, CEL, I HAVE TO GIVE YOU PROPS: KYLE IS A BABE. SO CHARMING!
GINA NEVER JUST RANDOMLY CHECKS UP ON ME HERE. ROMANCE IS DEAD.
...I MEAN, SHE HAS HER REASONS.
BUT SHE COULD AT LEAST SEND ME A COOKIE BOUQUET AT WORK, RIGHT?

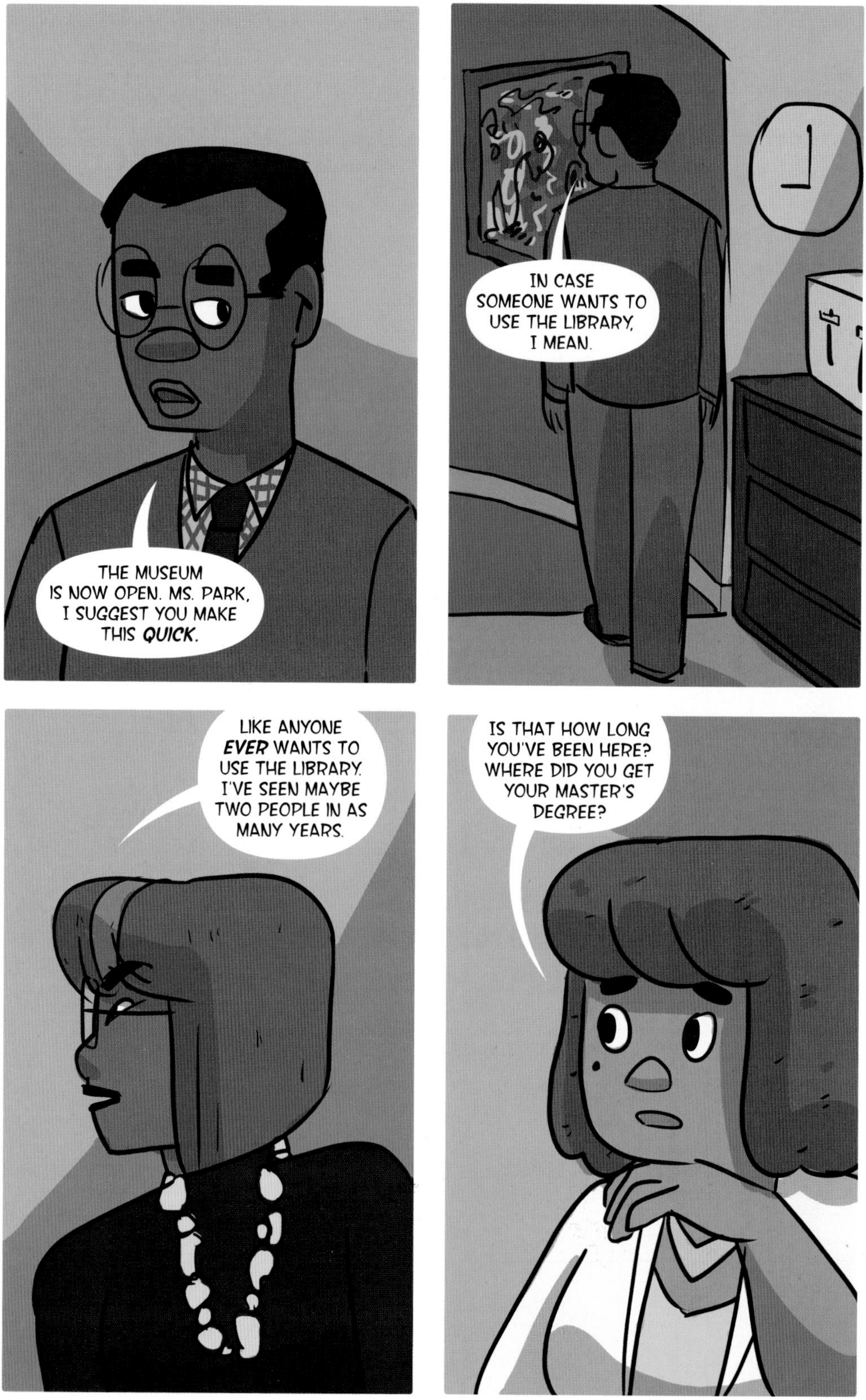
THE MUSEUM IS NOW OPEN. MS. PARK, I SUGGEST YOU MAKE THIS **QUICK**.
IN CASE SOMEONE WANTS TO USE THE LIBRARY, I MEAN.
LIKE ANYONE **EVER** WANTS TO USE THE LIBRARY. I'VE SEEN MAYBE TWO PEOPLE IN AS MANY YEARS.
IS THAT HOW LONG YOU'VE BEEN HERE? WHERE DID YOU GET YOUR MASTER'S DEGREE?

DON'T HAVE ONE! THIS IS MY FIRST LIBRARY. I WAS A MEDICAL STUDENT BEFORE.

OH. *I* WAS A LIBRARIAN BEFORE.

AND YOU'RE A LIBRARIAN NOW! WHAT DO *YOU* CALL WHAT YOU DO?

I GUESS YOU'RE RIGHT. I LIKE THE JOB, SO FAR. IT'S SO MEDITATIVE. I MEAN, WHEN THE POWER ISN'T GOING OUT.

WHAT MADE YOU LEAVE MEDICAL SCHOOL?

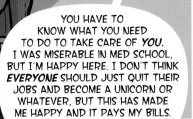

IT WAS WHAT MY *PARENTS* WANTED ME TO DO. MY DAD IS STILL MAD ABOUT IT, HONESTLY. BUT I LIKE WHAT I DO NOW. I'VE BEEN HERE THREE YEARS AND I DON'T SEE MYSELF LEAVING.

YOU HAVE TO KNOW WHAT YOU NEED TO DO TO TAKE CARE OF *YOU.* I WAS MISERABLE IN MED SCHOOL, BUT I'M HAPPY HERE. I DON'T THINK *EVERYONE* SHOULD JUST QUIT THEIR JOBS AND BECOME A UNICORN OR WHATEVER, BUT THIS HAS MADE ME HAPPY AND IT PAYS MY BILLS.

I WISH I KNEW HOW TO DO THAT. BE HAPPY, I MEAN.

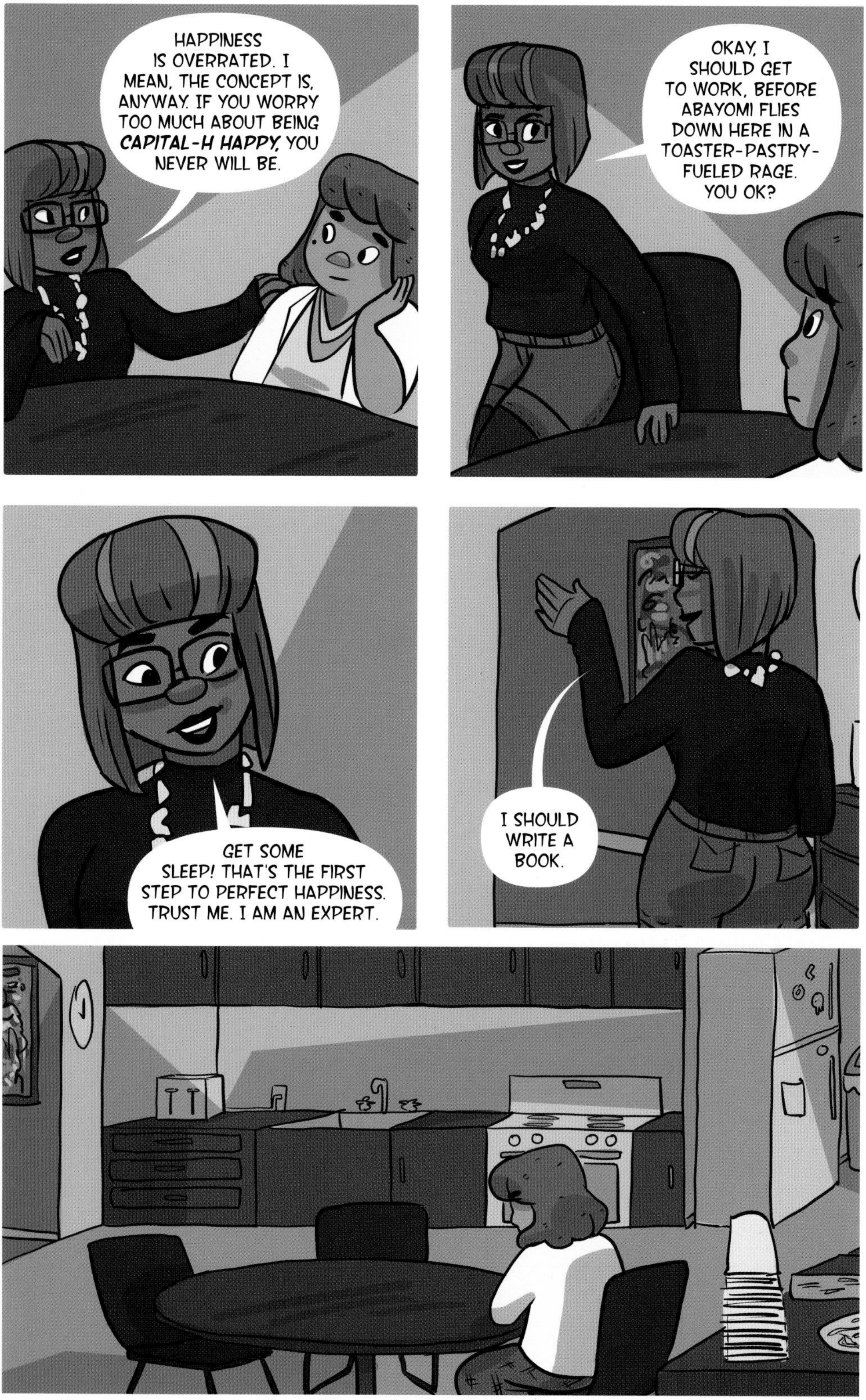
HAPPINESS IS OVERRATED. I MEAN, THE CONCEPT IS, ANYWAY. IF YOU WORRY TOO MUCH ABOUT BEING *CAPITAL-H HAPPY,* YOU NEVER WILL BE.
OKAY, I SHOULD GET TO WORK, BEFORE ABAYOMI FLIES DOWN HERE IN A TOASTER-PASTRY-FUELED RAGE. YOU OK?
GET SOME SLEEP! THAT'S THE FIRST STEP TO PERFECT HAPPINESS. TRUST ME. I AM AN EXPERT.
I SHOULD WRITE A BOOK.

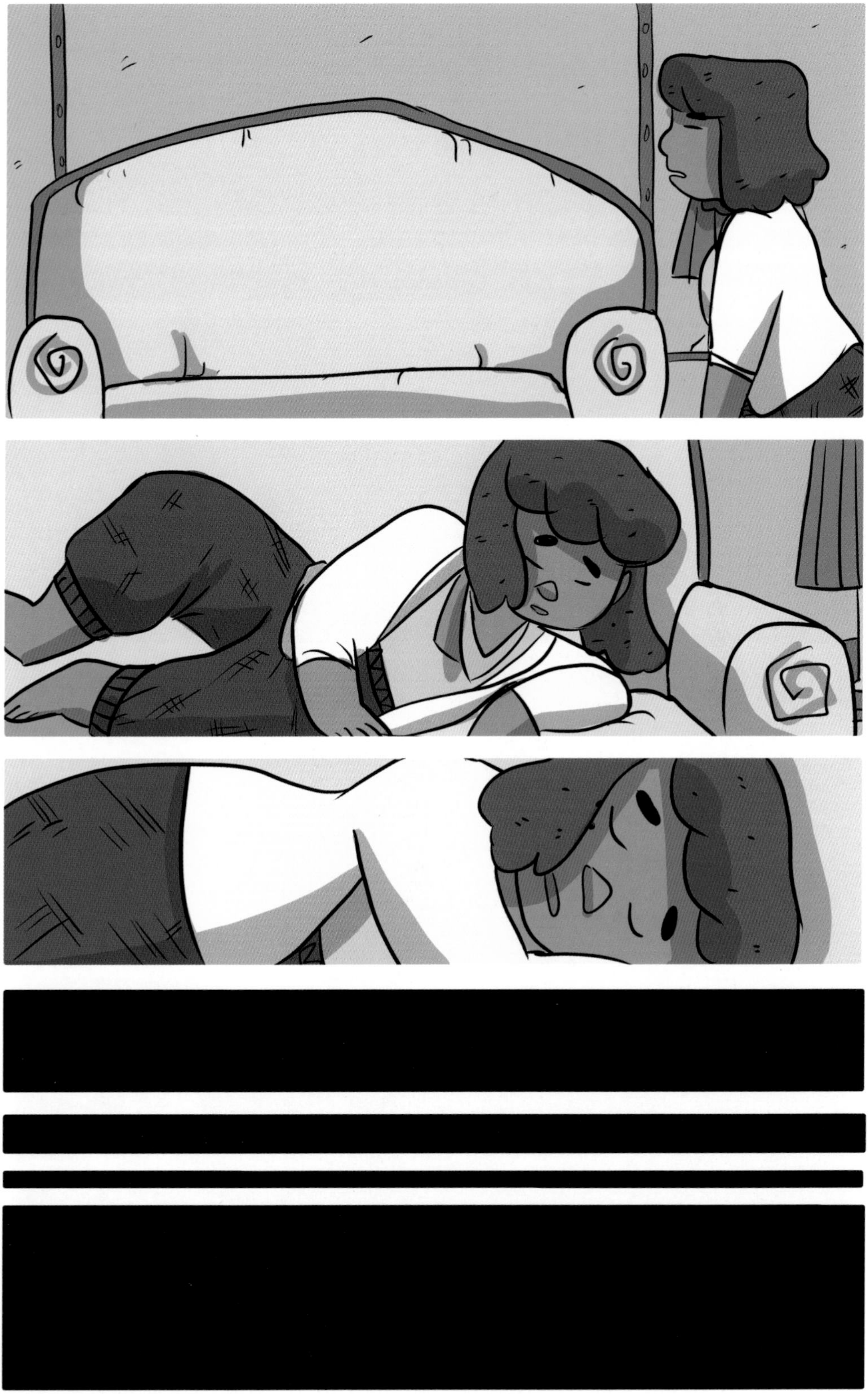

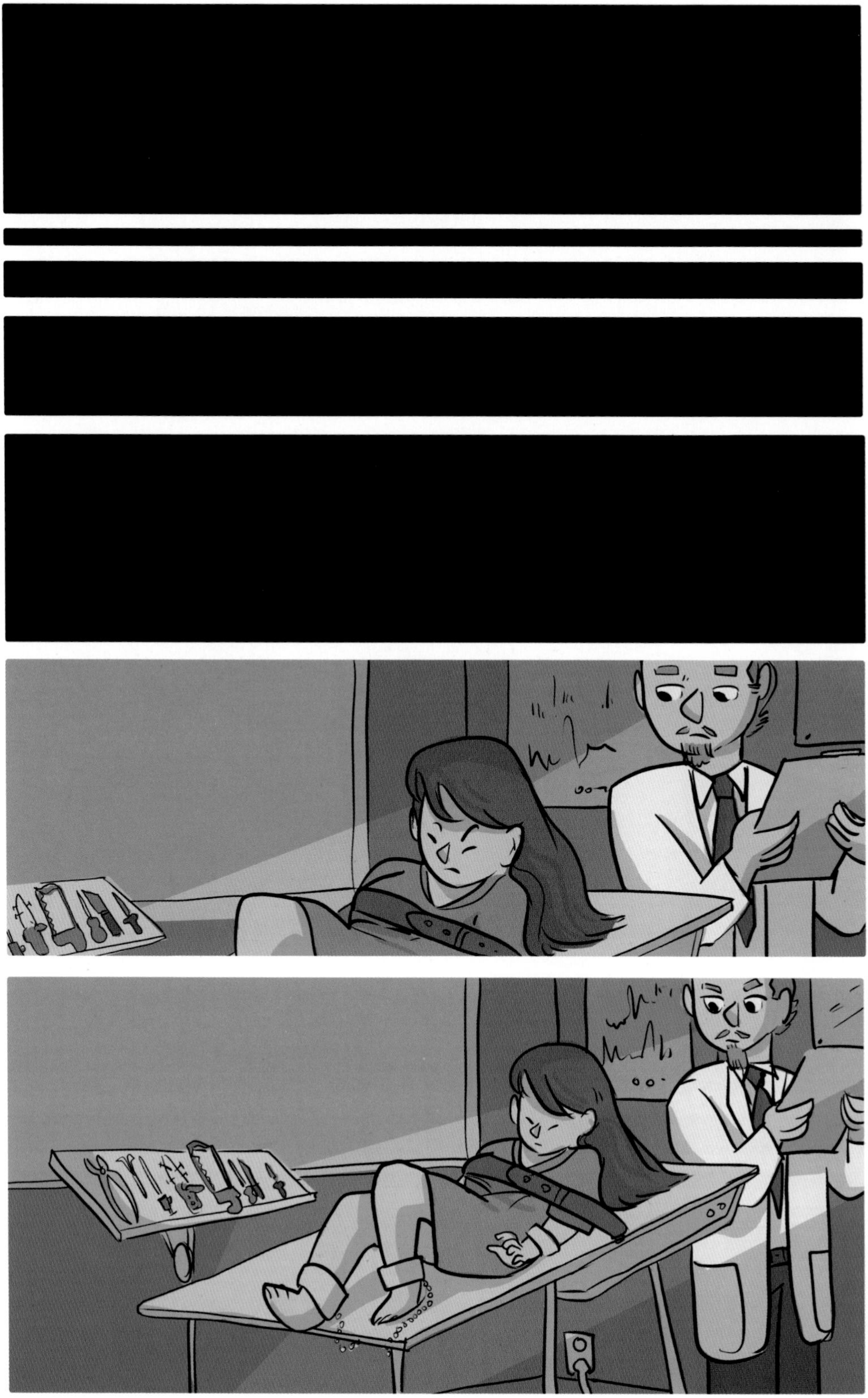

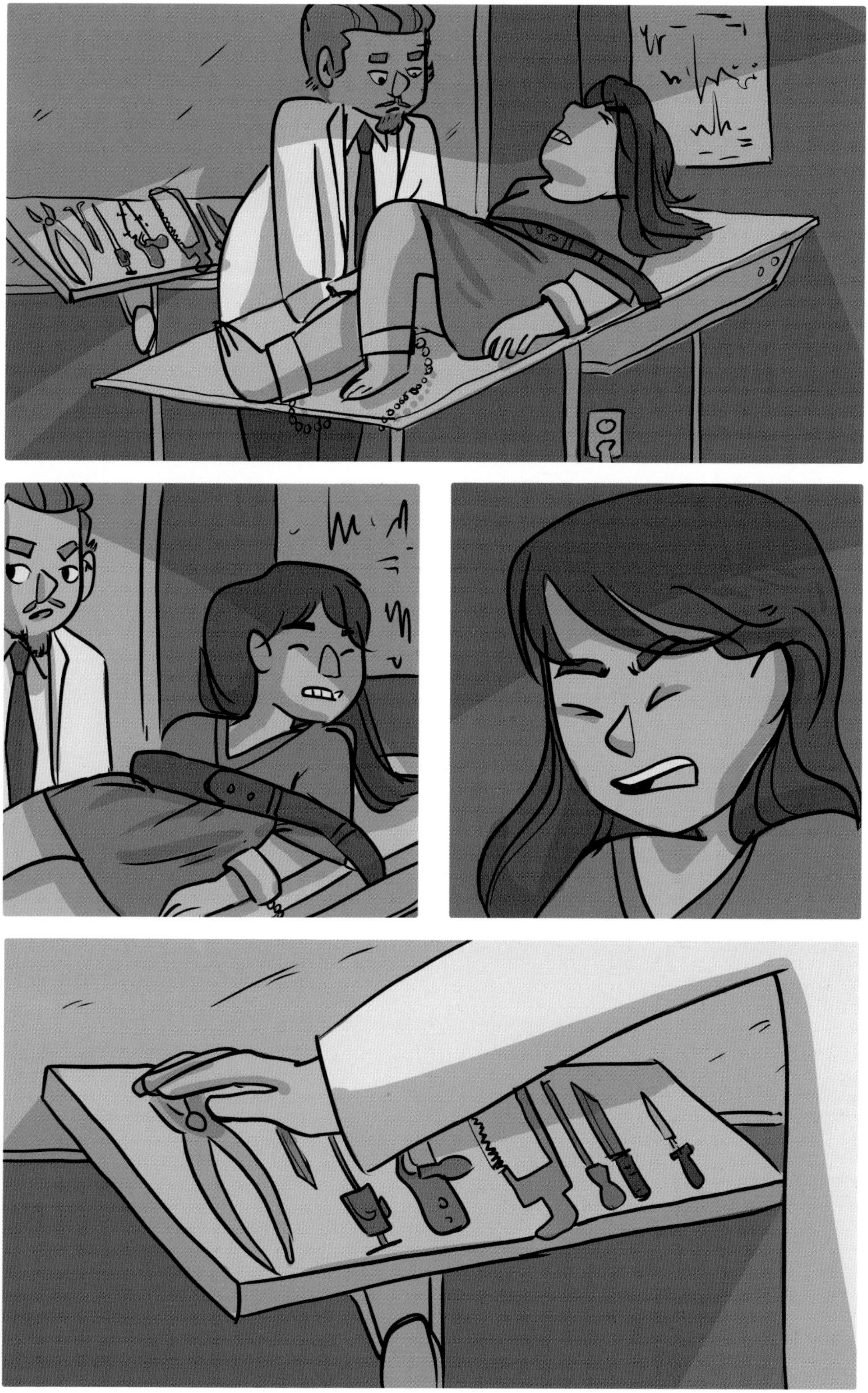

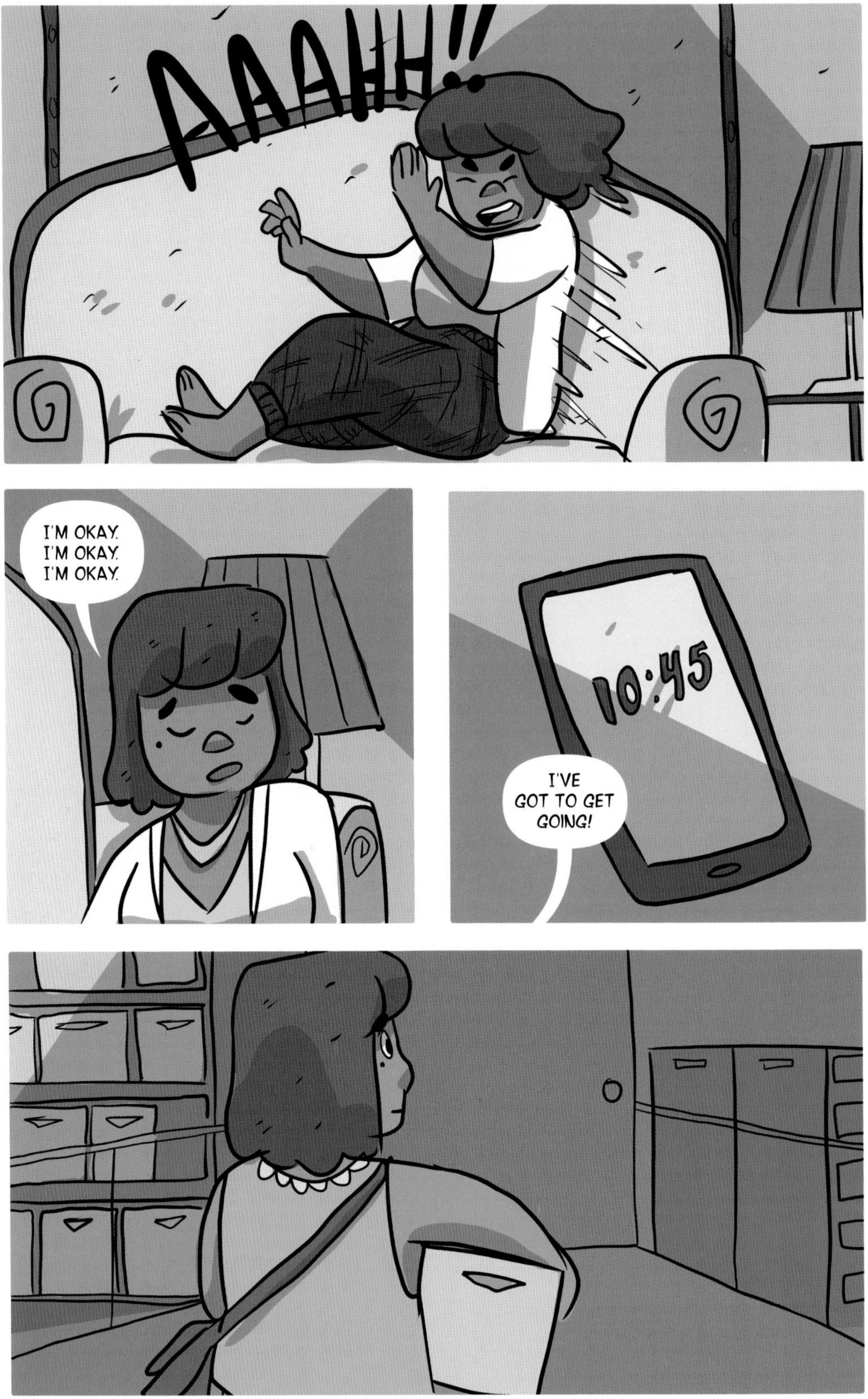
AAAHH!!
I'M OKAY.
I'M OKAY.
I'M OKAY.
10:45
I'VE GOT TO GET GOING!

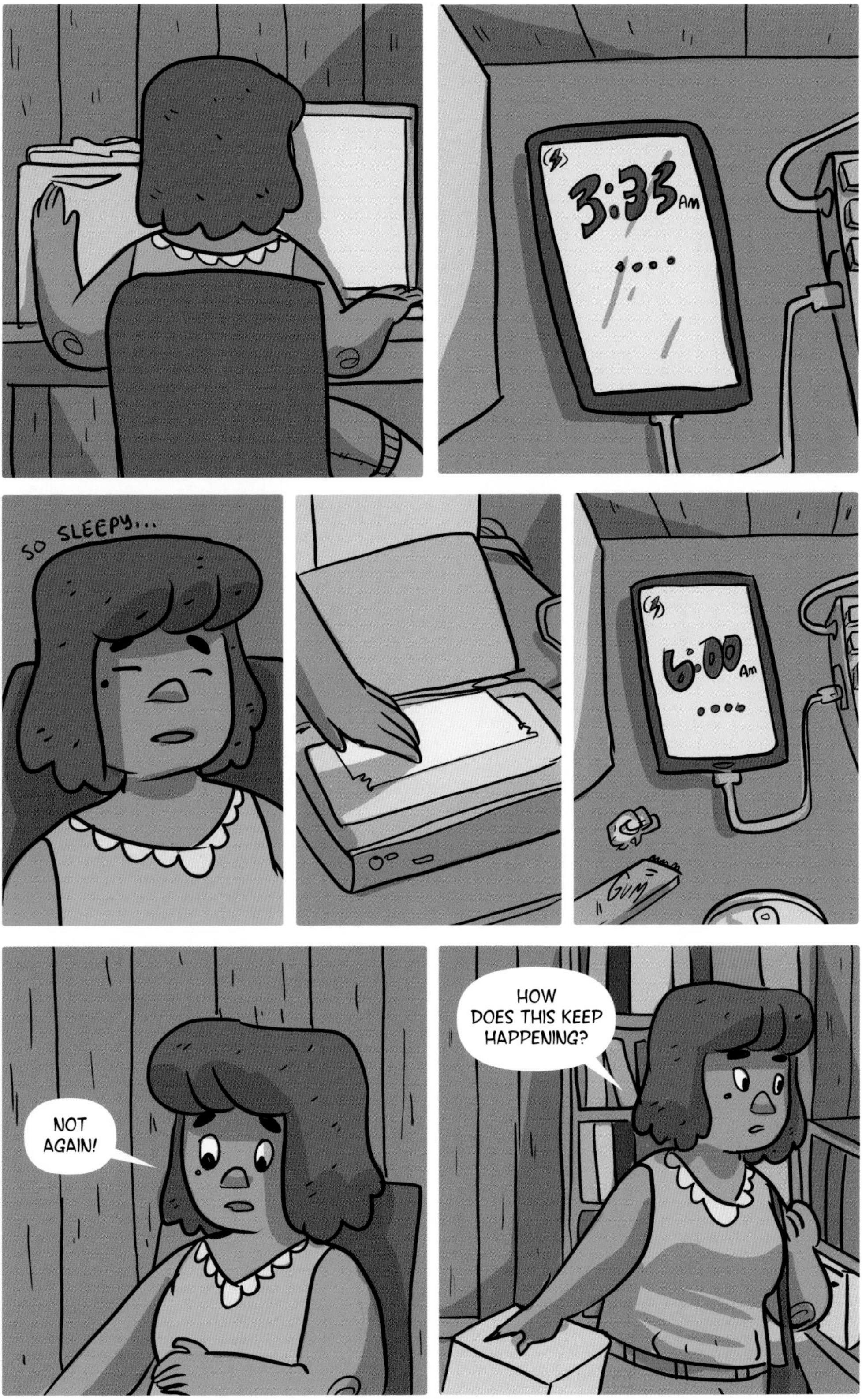
3:33 AM
SO SLEEPY...
6:00 AM
GUM
NOT AGAIN!
HOW DOES THIS KEEP HAPPENING?

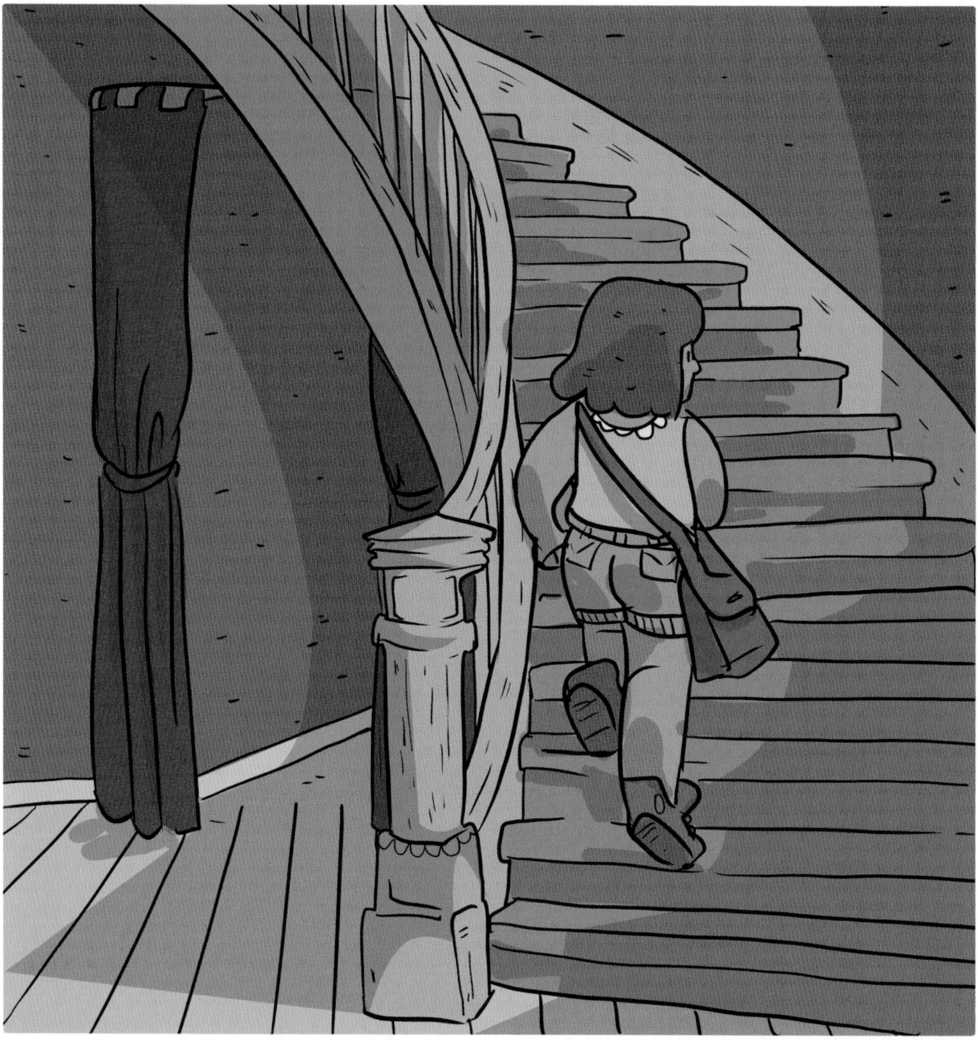

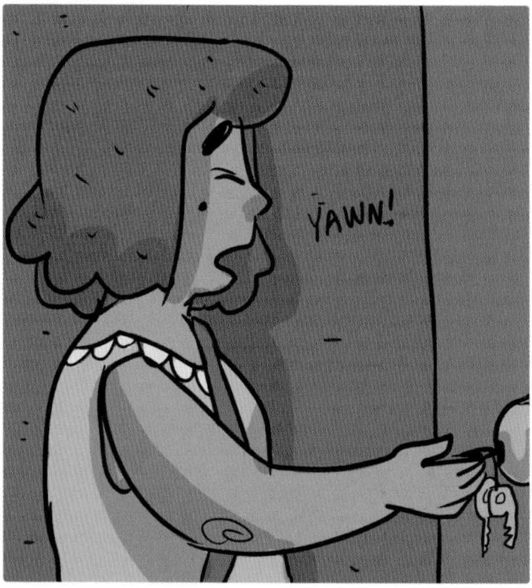
YAWN!

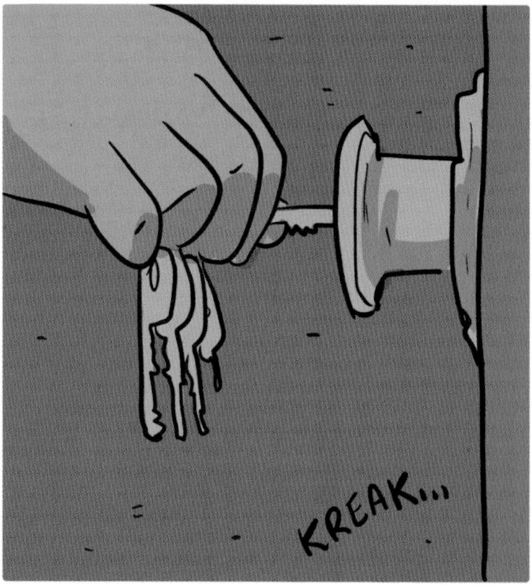
KREAK...

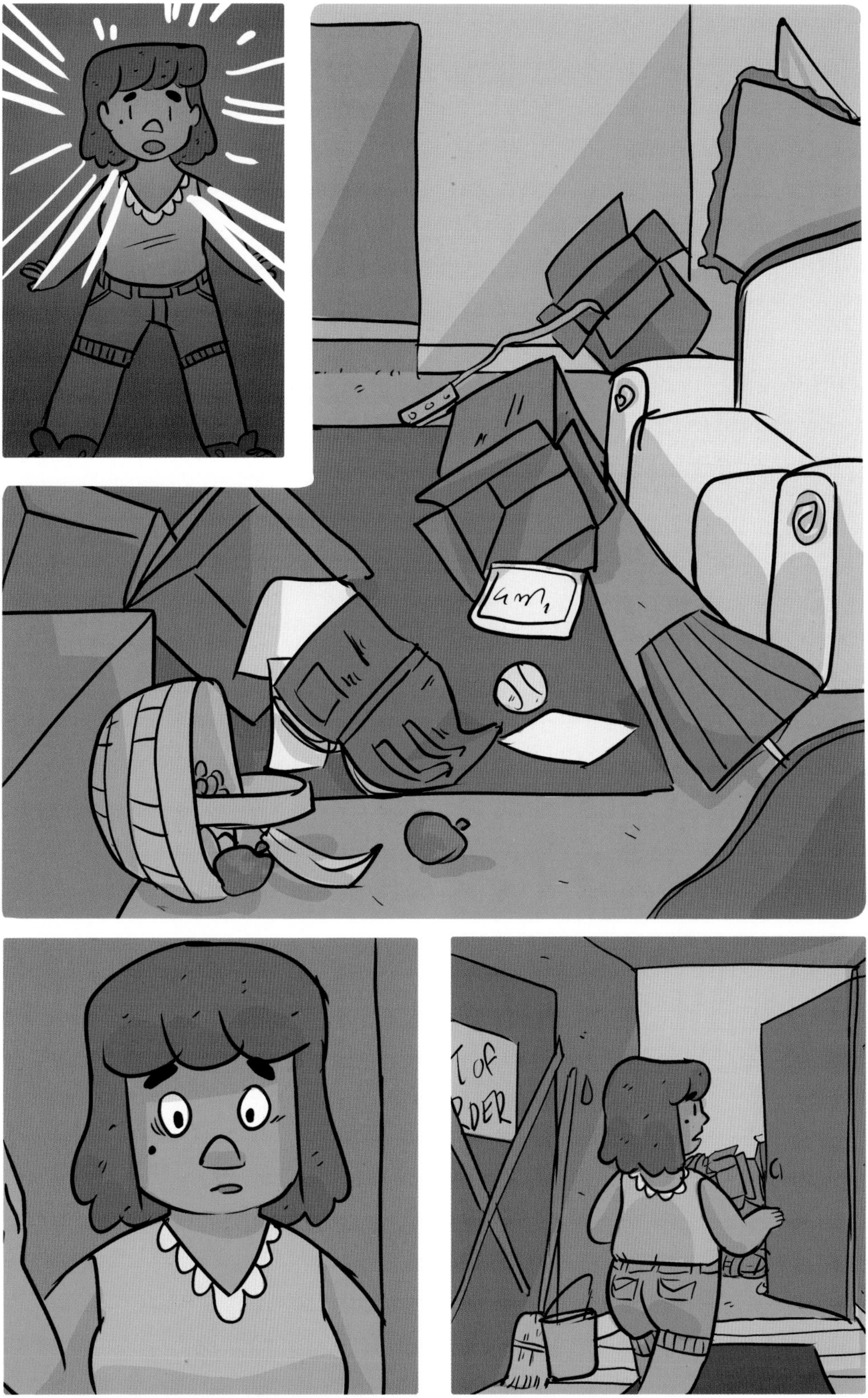

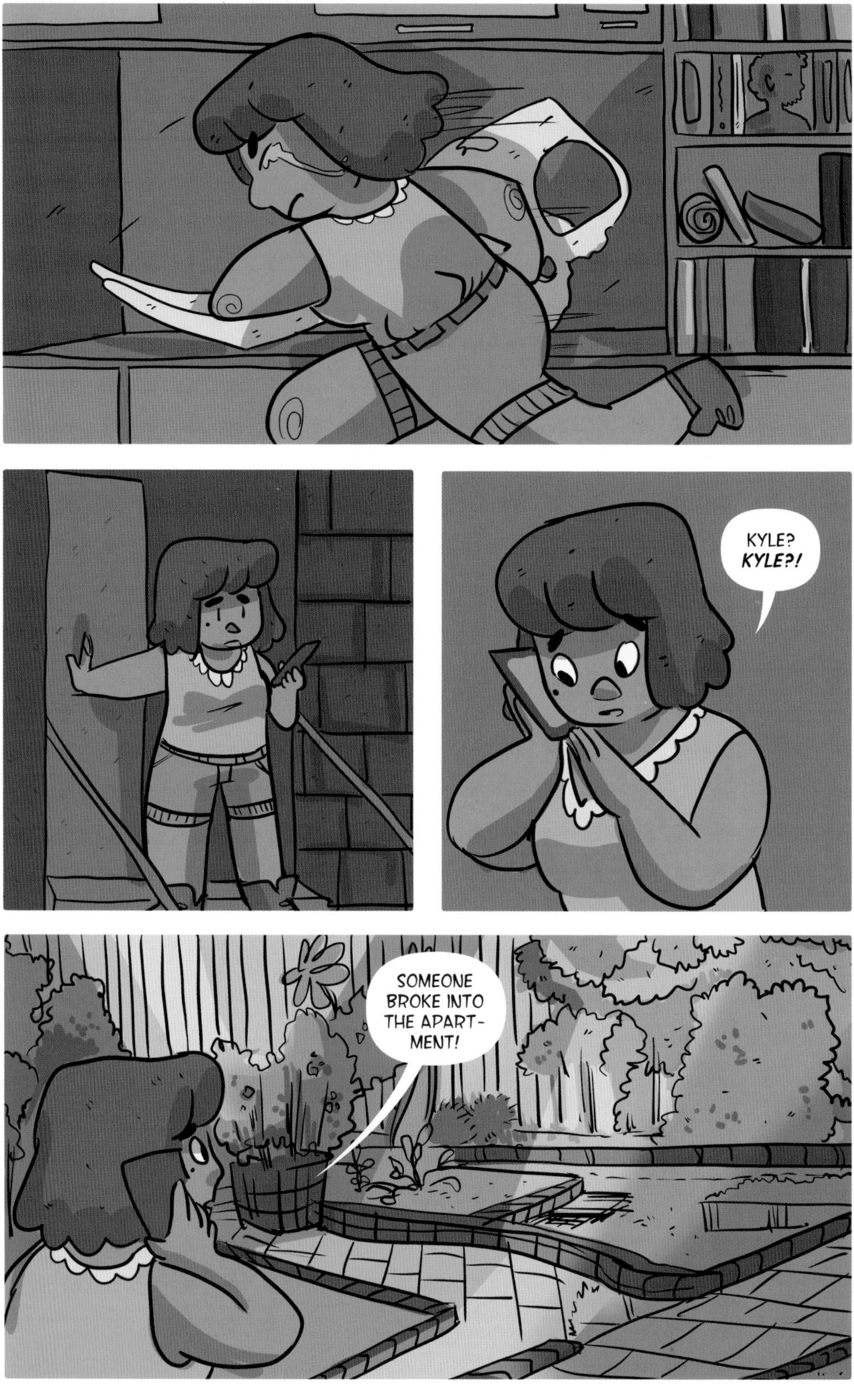
KYLE?
KYLE?!
SOMEONE BROKE INTO THE APART-MENT!

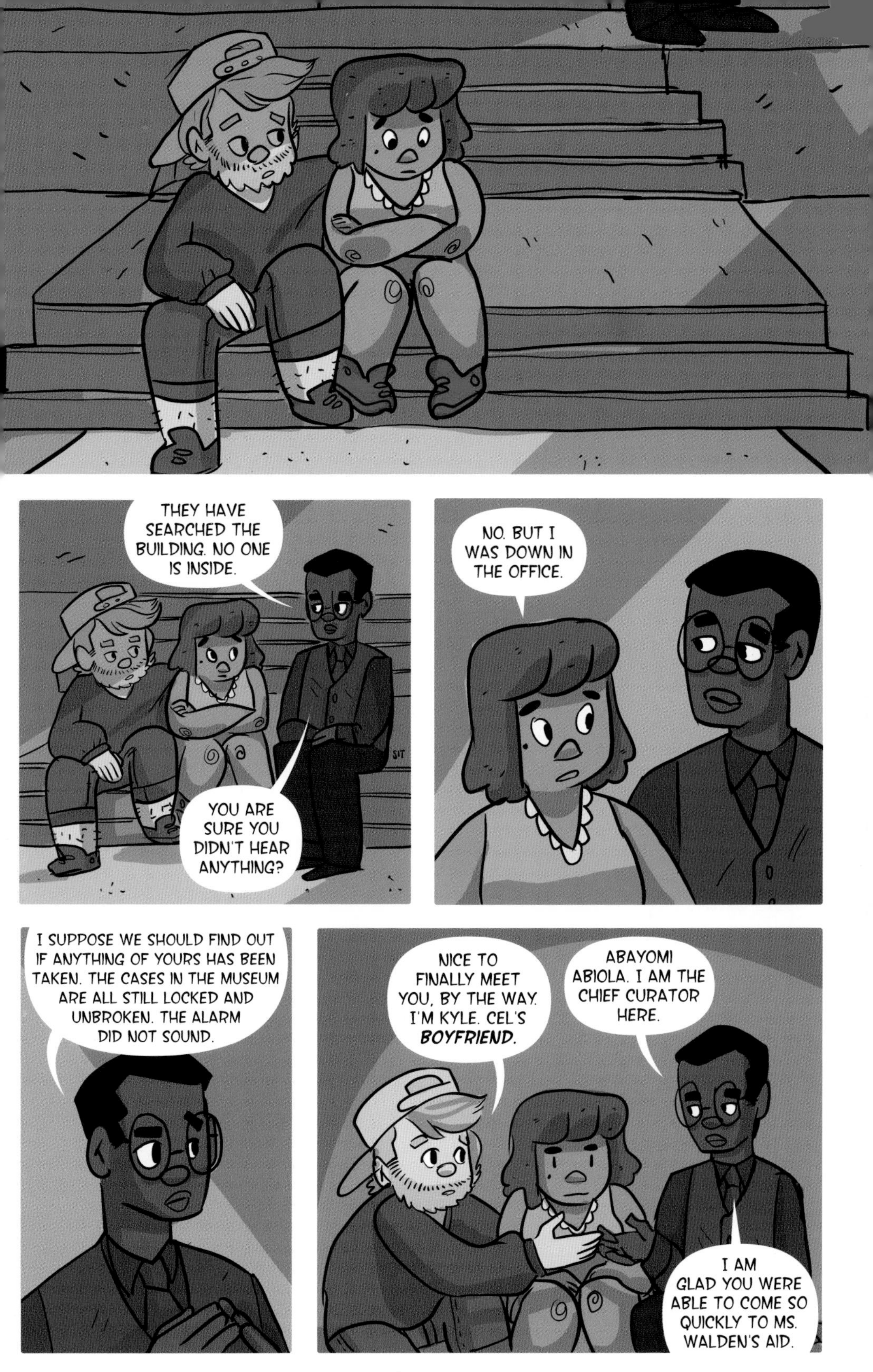
THEY HAVE SEARCHED THE BUILDING. NO ONE IS INSIDE.
SIT
YOU ARE SURE YOU DIDN'T HEAR ANYTHING?
NO. BUT I WAS DOWN IN THE OFFICE.
I SUPPOSE WE SHOULD FIND OUT IF ANYTHING OF YOURS HAS BEEN TAKEN. THE CASES IN THE MUSEUM ARE ALL STILL LOCKED AND UNBROKEN. THE ALARM DID NOT SOUND.
NICE TO FINALLY MEET YOU, BY THE WAY. I'M KYLE. CEL'S ***BOYFRIEND.***
ABAYOMI ABIOLA. I AM THE CHIEF CURATOR HERE.
I AM GLAD YOU WERE ABLE TO COME SO QUICKLY TO MS. WALDEN'S AID.

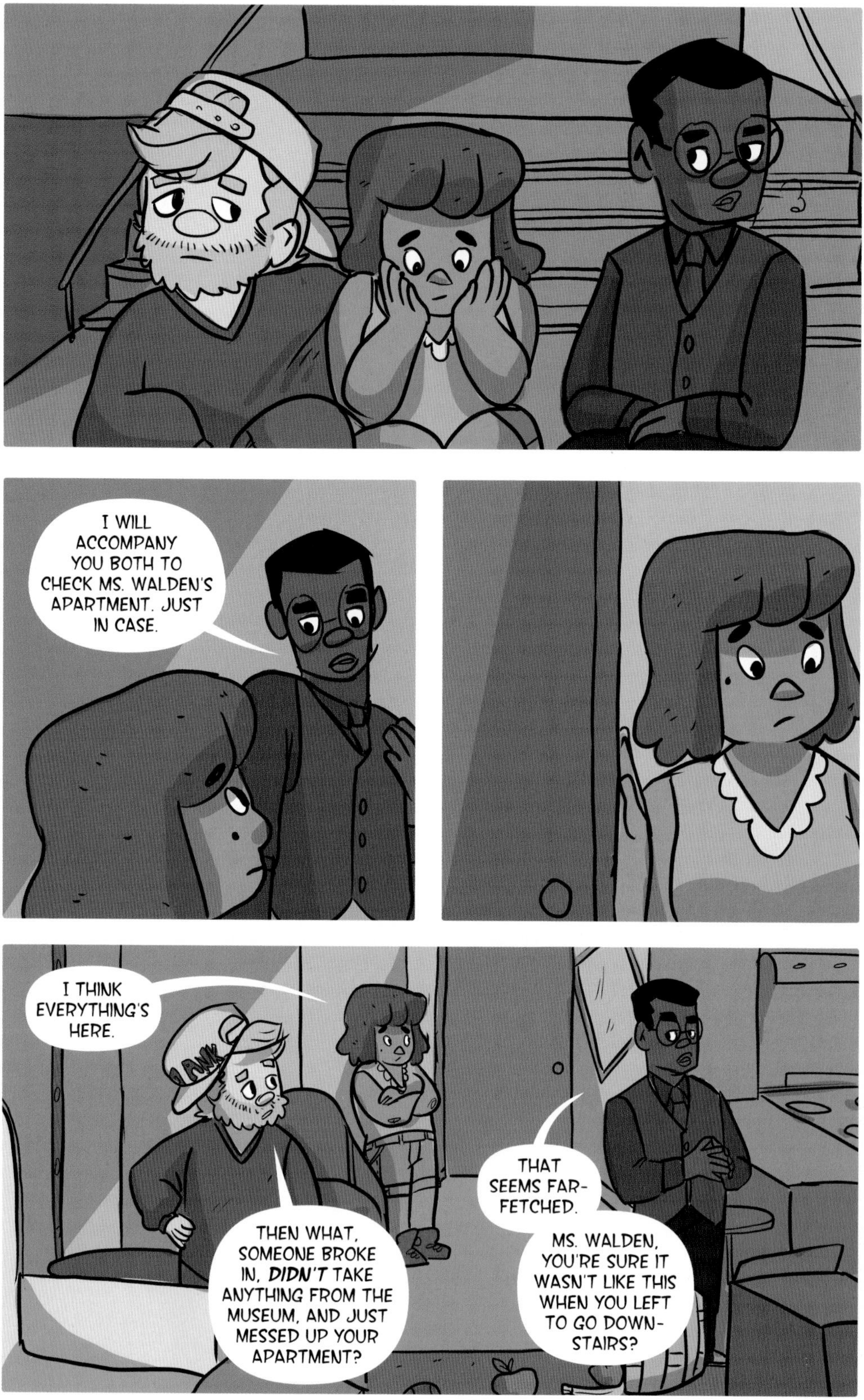
I WILL ACCOMPANY YOU BOTH TO CHECK MS. WALDEN'S APARTMENT. JUST IN CASE.
I THINK EVERYTHING'S HERE.
THEN WHAT, SOMEONE BROKE IN, *DIDN'T* TAKE ANYTHING FROM THE MUSEUM, AND JUST MESSED UP YOUR APARTMENT?
THAT SEEMS FAR-FETCHED.
MS. WALDEN, YOU'RE SURE IT WASN'T LIKE THIS WHEN YOU LEFT TO GO DOWN-STAIRS?

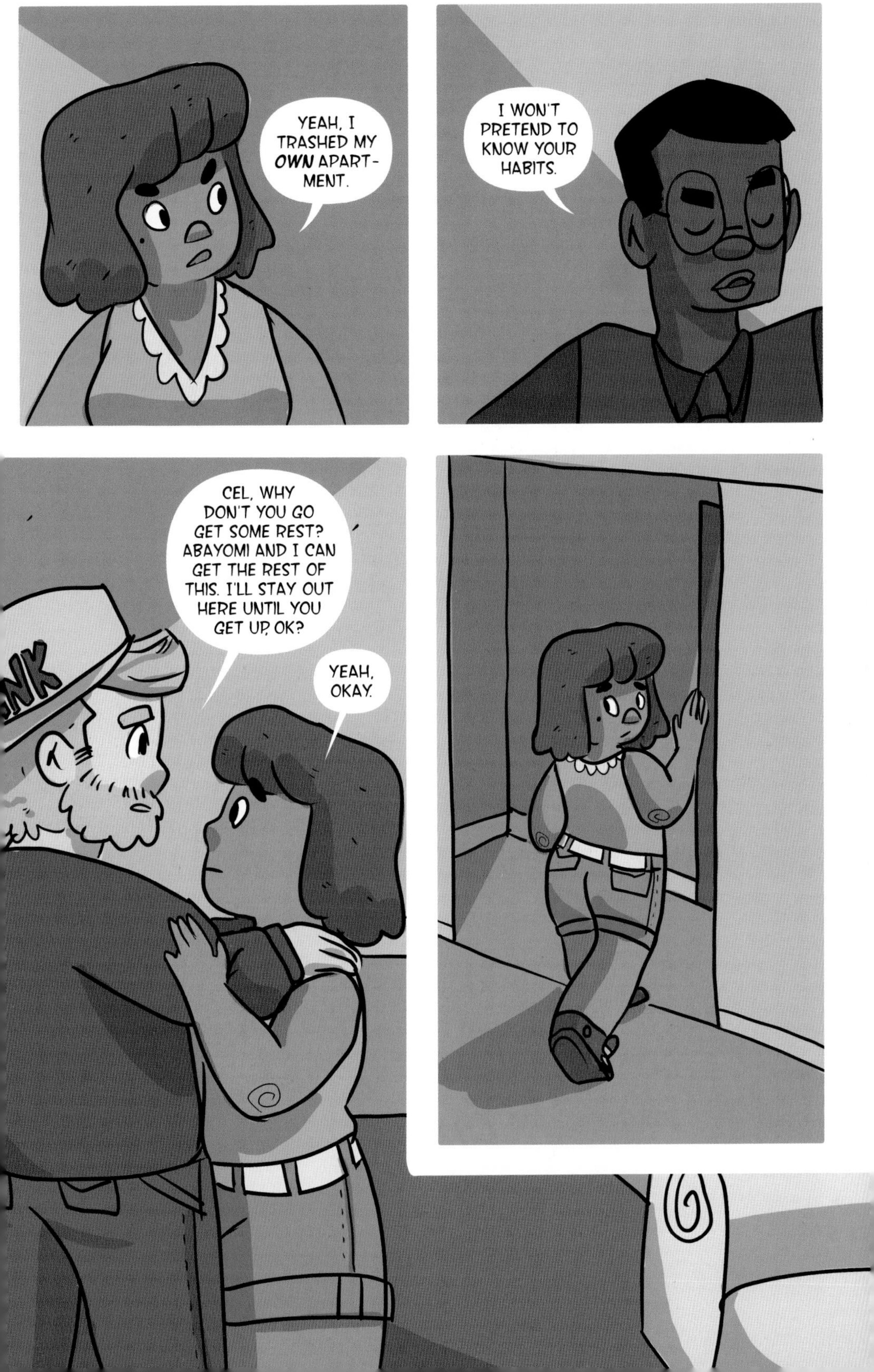
YEAH, I TRASHED MY OWN APARTMENT.
I WON'T PRETEND TO KNOW YOUR HABITS.
CEL, WHY DON'T YOU GO GET SOME REST? ABAYOMI AND I CAN GET THE REST OF THIS. I'LL STAY OUT HERE UNTIL YOU GET UP, OK?
YEAH, OKAY.

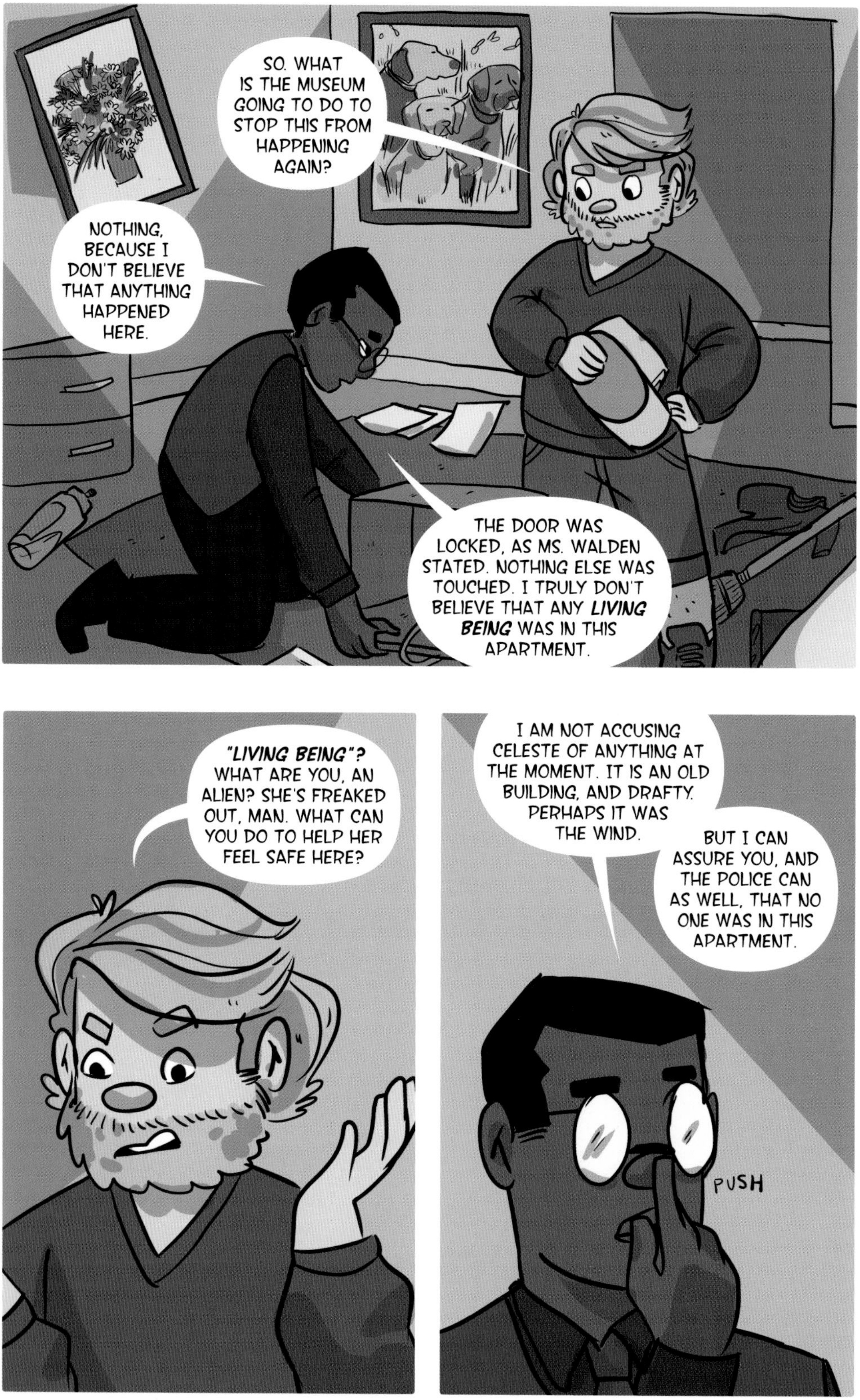
SO. WHAT IS THE MUSEUM GOING TO DO TO STOP THIS FROM HAPPENING AGAIN?
NOTHING, BECAUSE I DON'T BELIEVE THAT ANYTHING HAPPENED HERE.
THE DOOR WAS LOCKED, AS MS. WALDEN STATED. NOTHING ELSE WAS TOUCHED. I TRULY DON'T BELIEVE THAT ANY *LIVING BEING* WAS IN THIS APARTMENT.
"LIVING BEING"? WHAT ARE YOU, AN ALIEN? SHE'S FREAKED OUT, MAN. WHAT CAN YOU DO TO HELP HER FEEL SAFE HERE?
I AM NOT ACCUSING CELESTE OF ANYTHING AT THE MOMENT. IT IS AN OLD BUILDING, AND DRAFTY. PERHAPS IT WAS THE WIND.
BUT I CAN ASSURE YOU, AND THE POLICE CAN AS WELL, THAT NO ONE WAS IN THIS APARTMENT.
PUSH

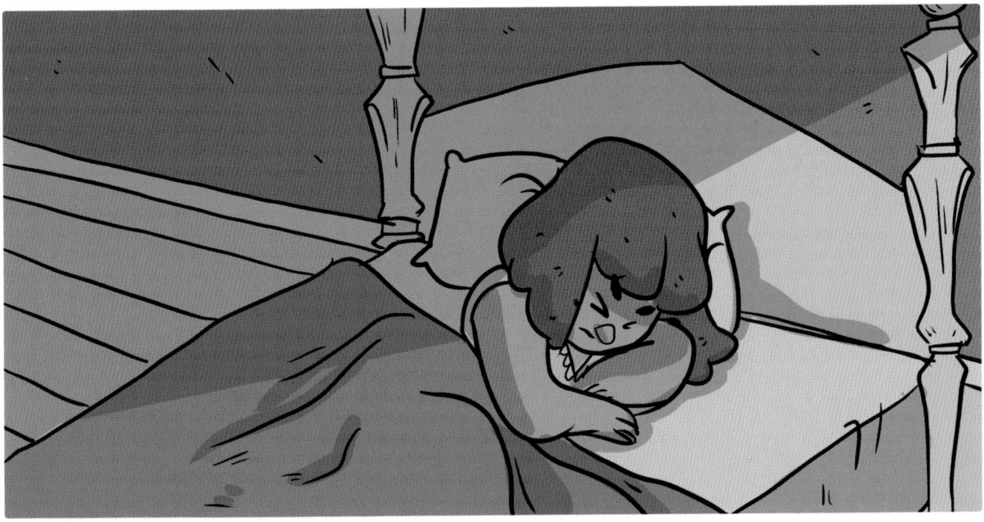

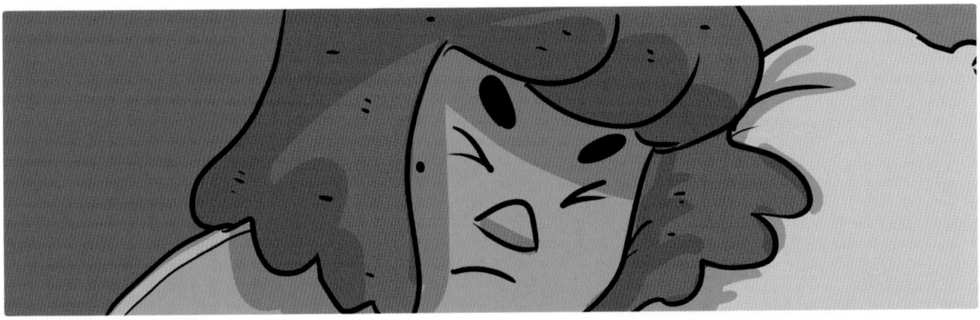

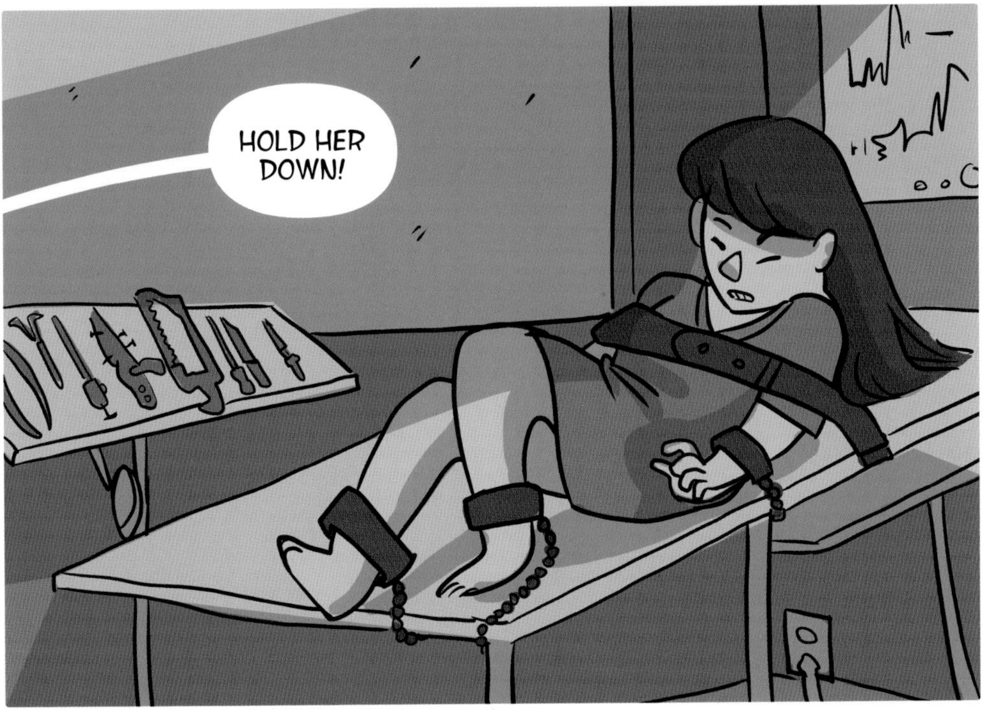
HOLD HER DOWN!

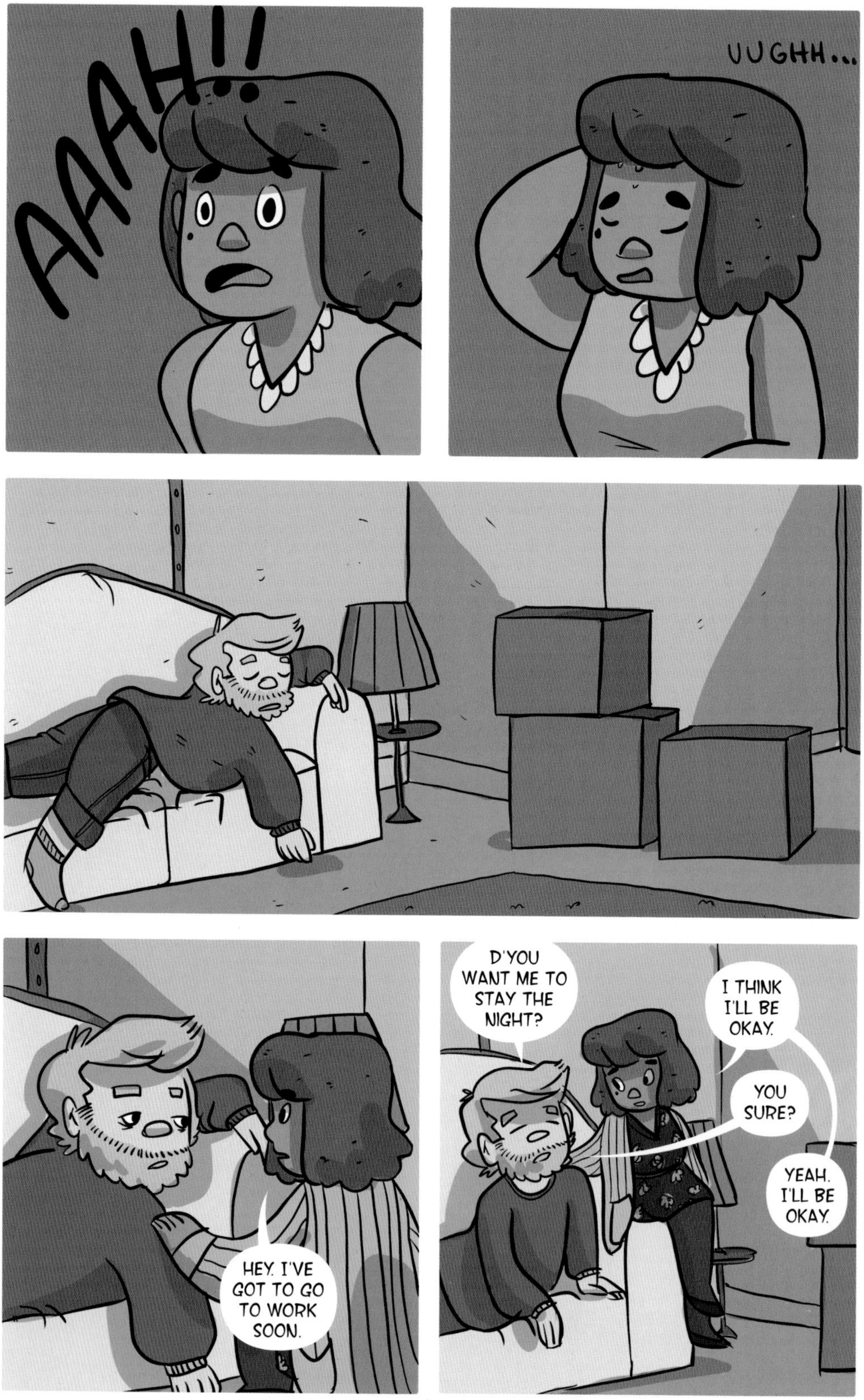
AAAH!!!
UUGHH...
HEY. I'VE GOT TO GO TO WORK SOON.
D'YOU WANT ME TO STAY THE NIGHT?
I THINK I'LL BE OKAY.
YOU SURE?
YEAH. I'LL BE OKAY.

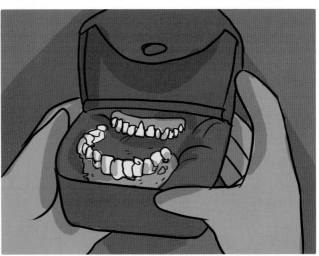

BLEH

SNAP! ///

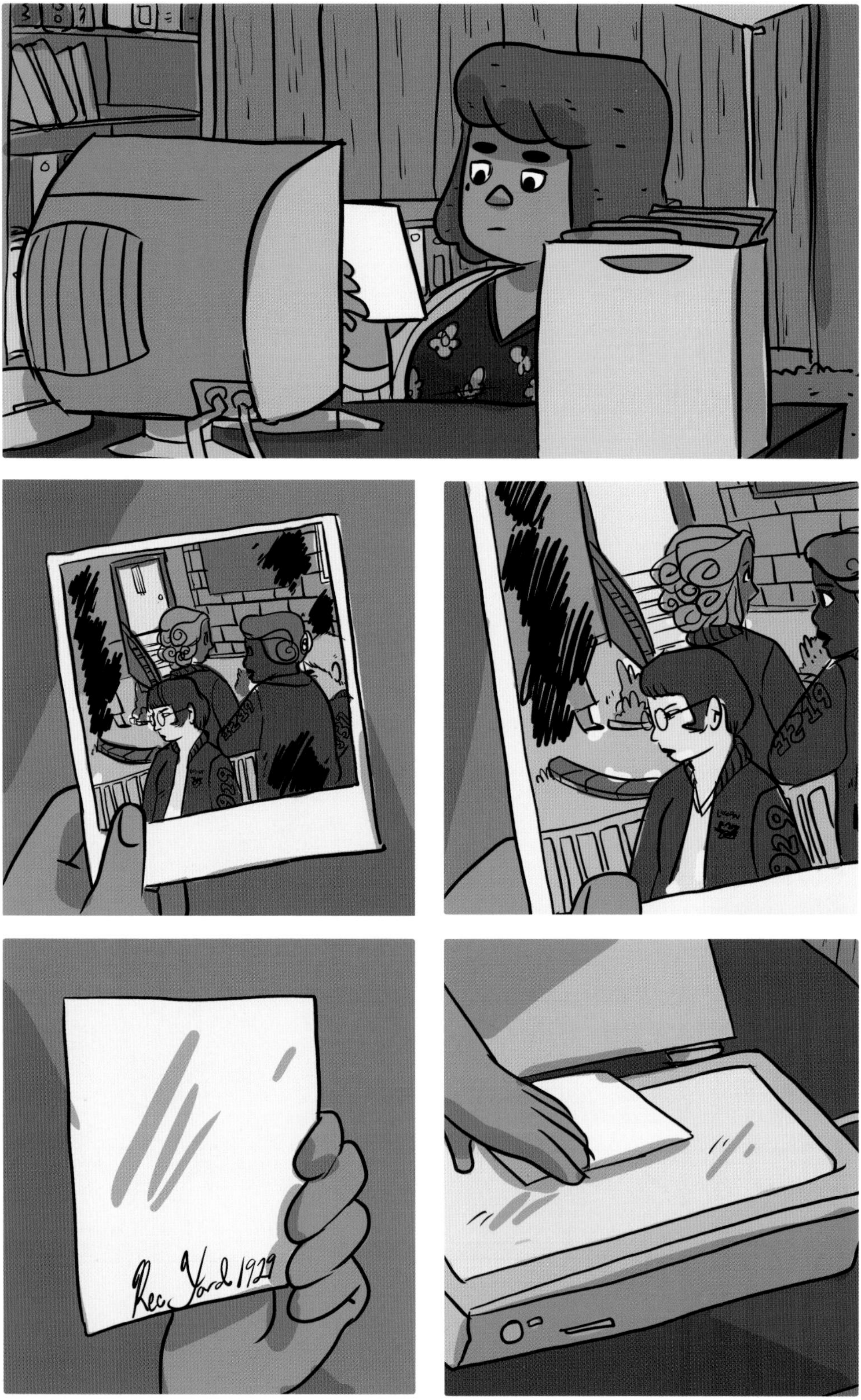
Rec Yard 1929

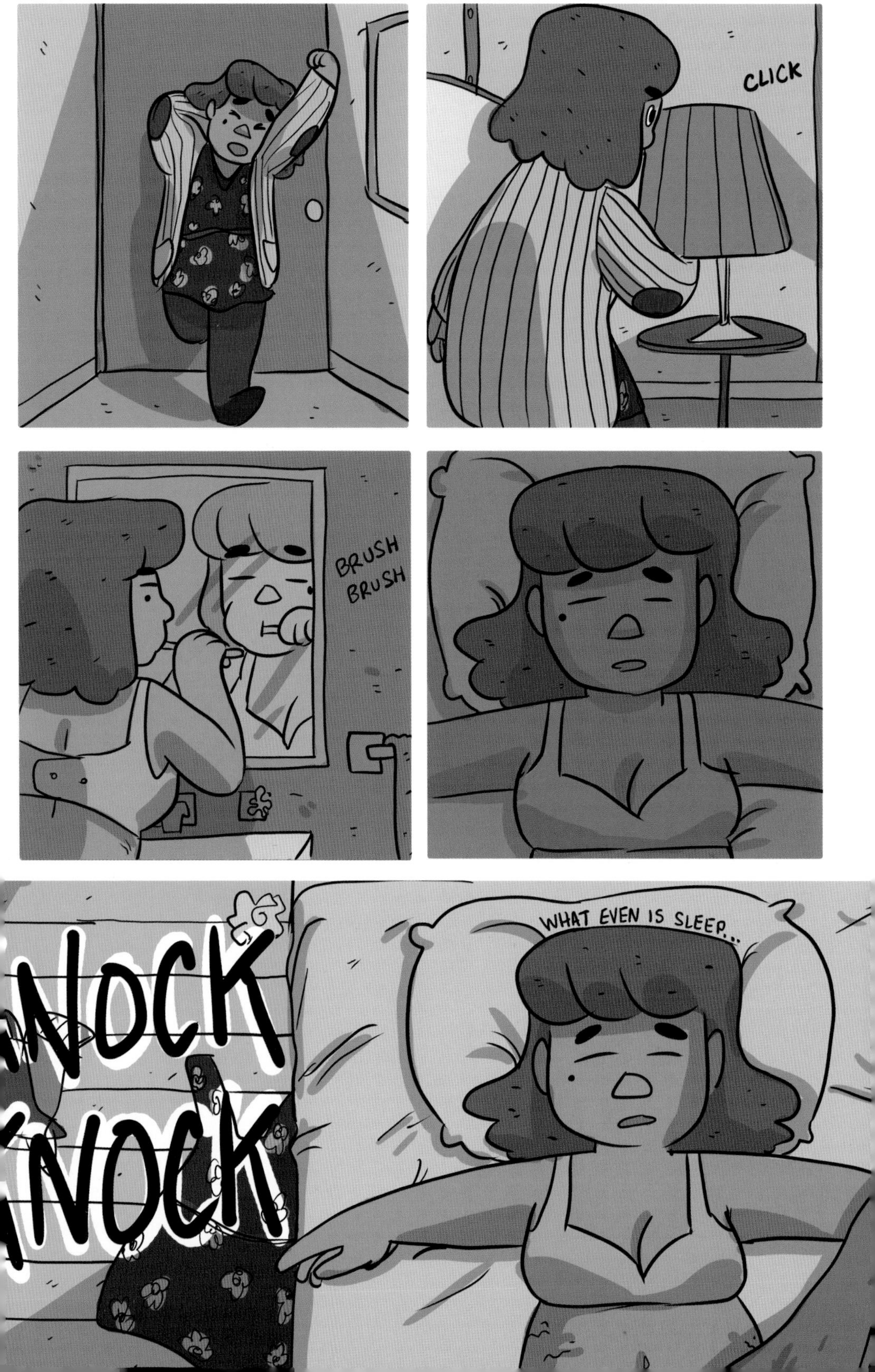
CLICK
BRUSH
BRUSH
WHAT EVEN IS SLEEP...
NOCK
NOCK

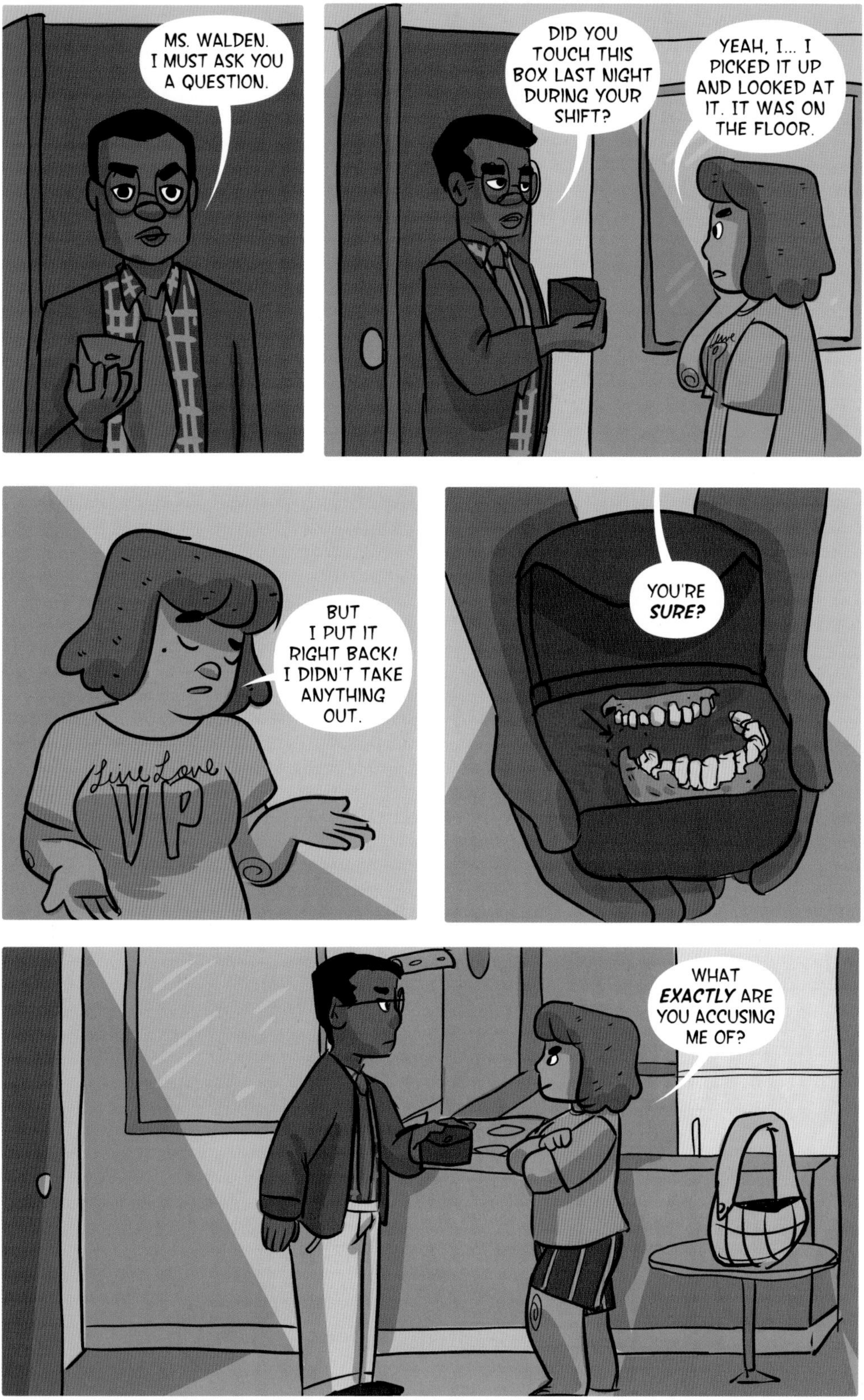
MS. WALDEN. I MUST ASK YOU A QUESTION.
DID YOU TOUCH THIS BOX LAST NIGHT DURING YOUR SHIFT?
YEAH, I... I PICKED IT UP AND LOOKED AT IT. IT WAS ON THE FLOOR.
BUT I PUT IT RIGHT BACK! I DIDN'T TAKE ANYTHING OUT.
Live Love VP
YOU'RE *SURE?*
WHAT *EXACTLY* ARE YOU ACCUSING ME OF?

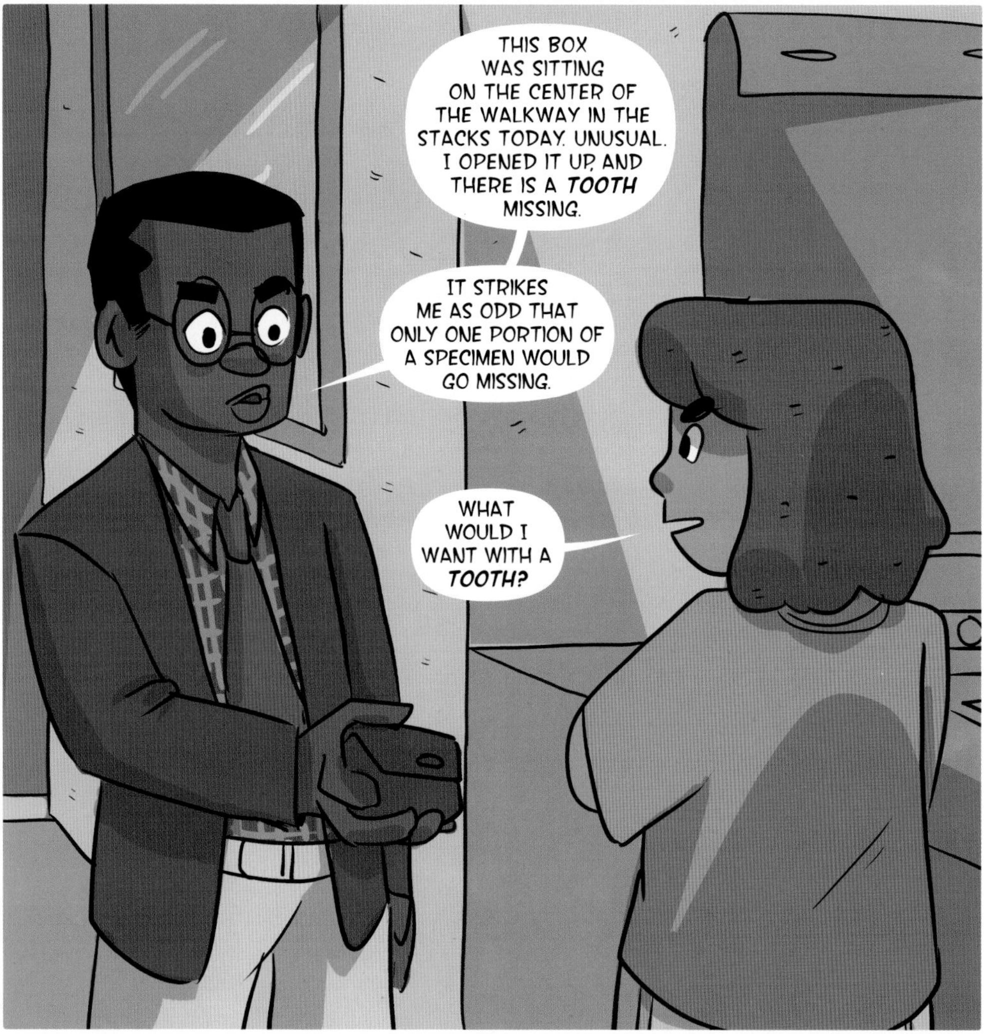
THIS BOX WAS SITTING ON THE CENTER OF THE WALKWAY IN THE STACKS TODAY. UNUSUAL. I OPENED IT UP, AND THERE IS A *TOOTH* MISSING.
IT STRIKES ME AS ODD THAT ONLY ONE PORTION OF A SPECIMEN WOULD GO MISSING.
WHAT WOULD I WANT WITH A *TOOTH?*

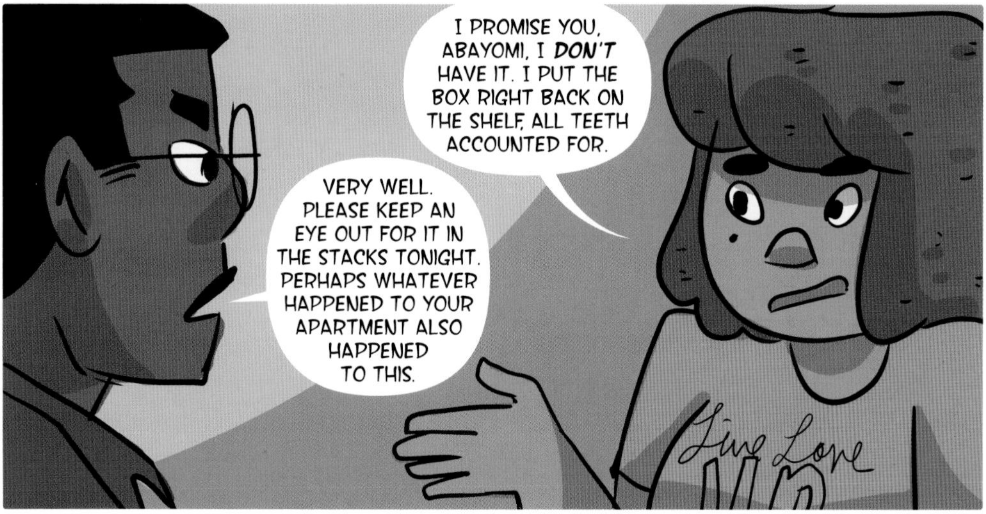
I PROMISE YOU, ABAYOMI, I *DON'T* HAVE IT. I PUT THE BOX RIGHT BACK ON THE SHELF, ALL TEETH ACCOUNTED FOR.
VERY WELL. PLEASE KEEP AN EYE OUT FOR IT IN THE STACKS TONIGHT. PERHAPS WHATEVER HAPPENED TO YOUR APARTMENT ALSO HAPPENED TO THIS.

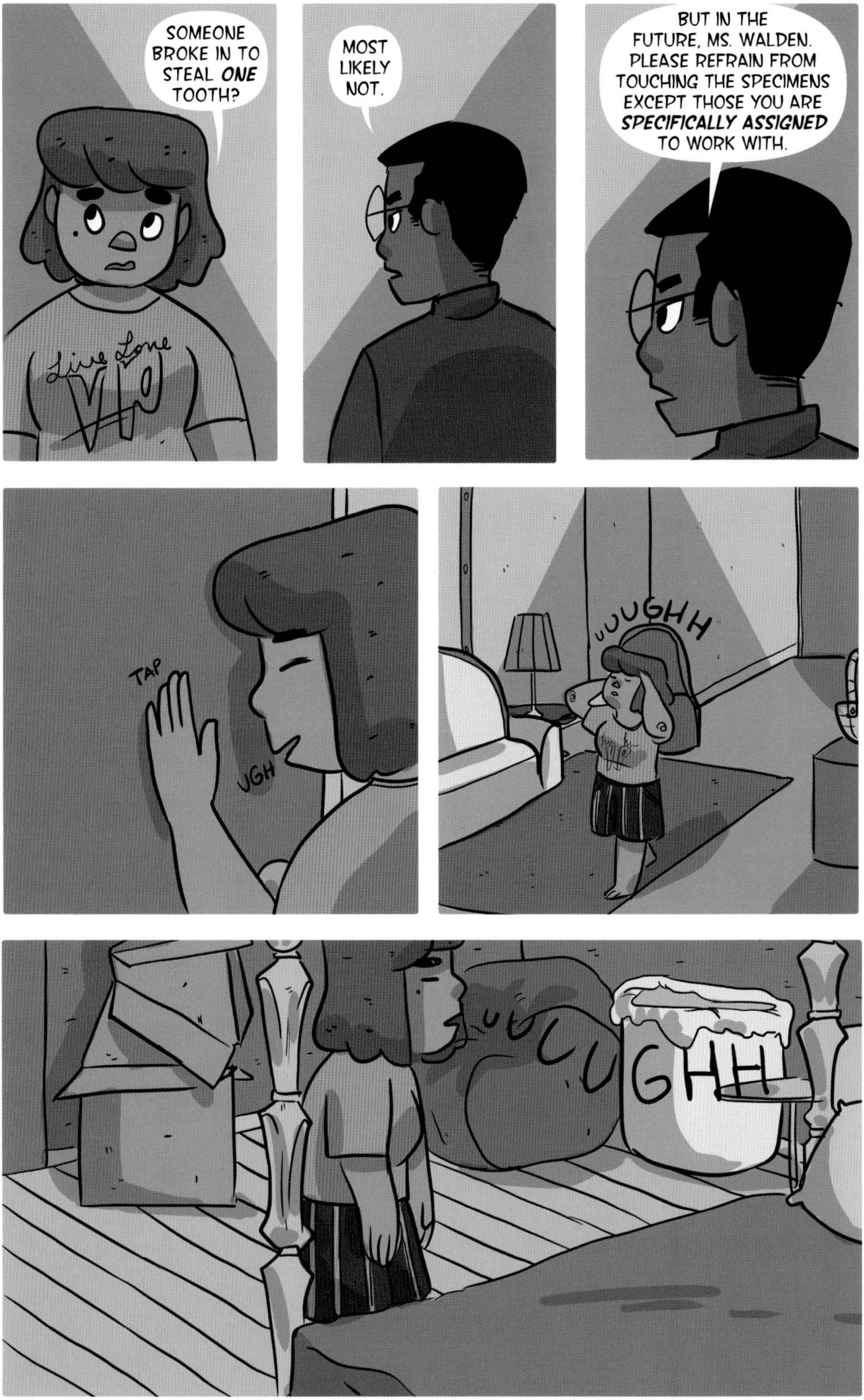
SOMEONE BROKE IN TO STEAL *ONE* TOOTH?
MOST LIKELY NOT.
BUT IN THE FUTURE, MS. WALDEN. PLEASE REFRAIN FROM TOUCHING THE SPECIMENS EXCEPT THOSE YOU ARE ***SPECIFICALLY ASSIGNED*** TO WORK WITH.
TAP
UGH
uUUGHH
UUUUGHH

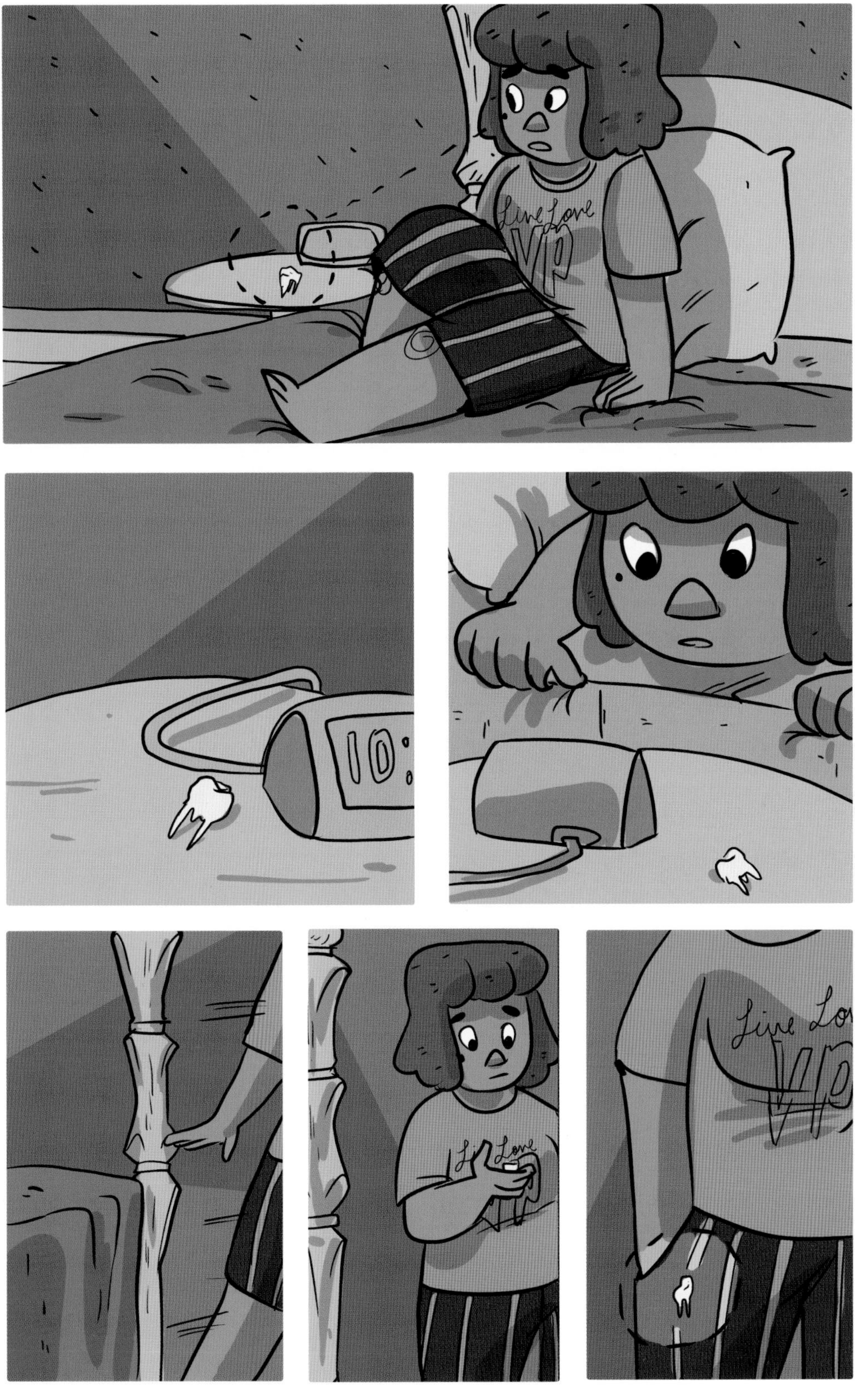
Live Love
VP
10:

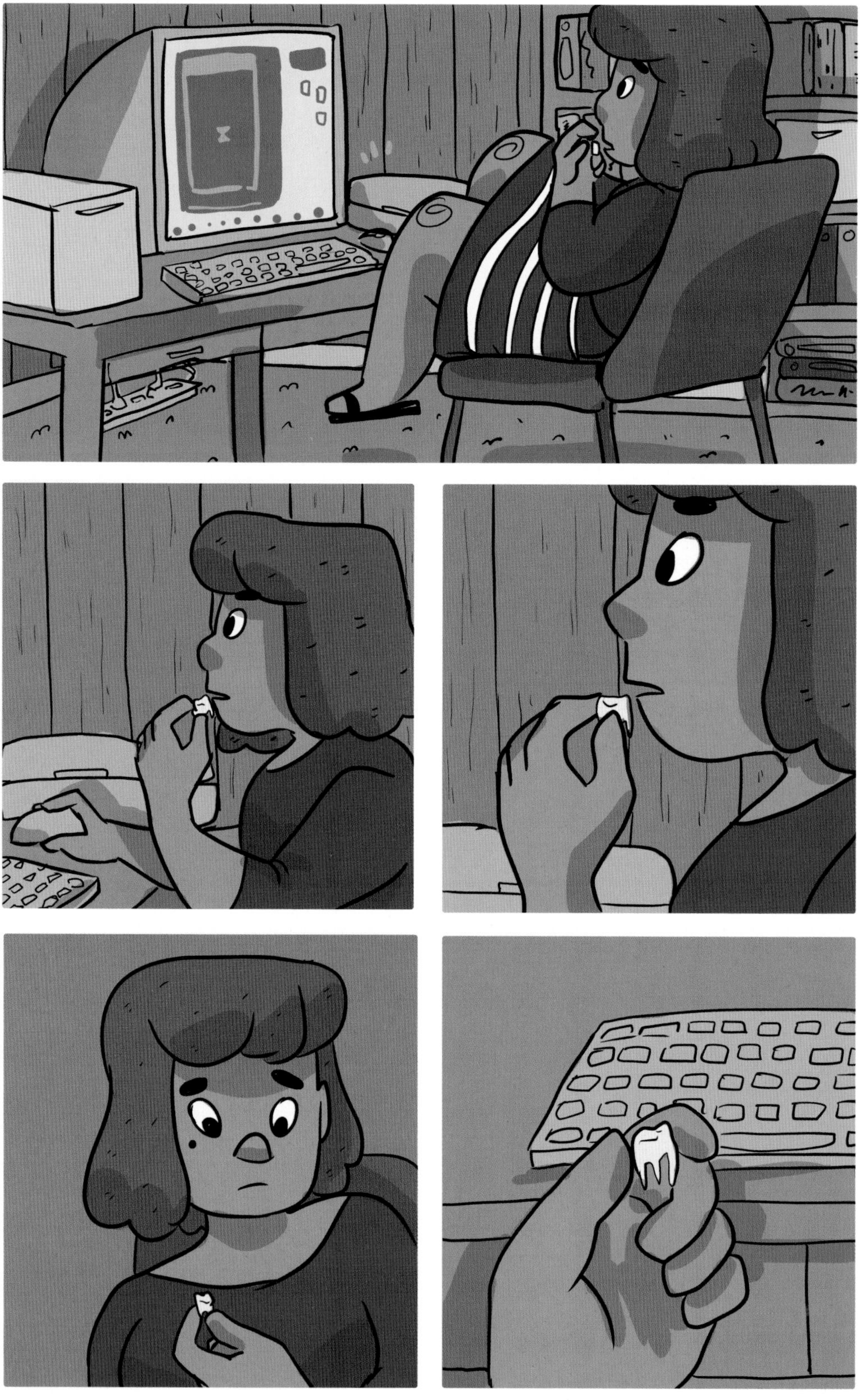

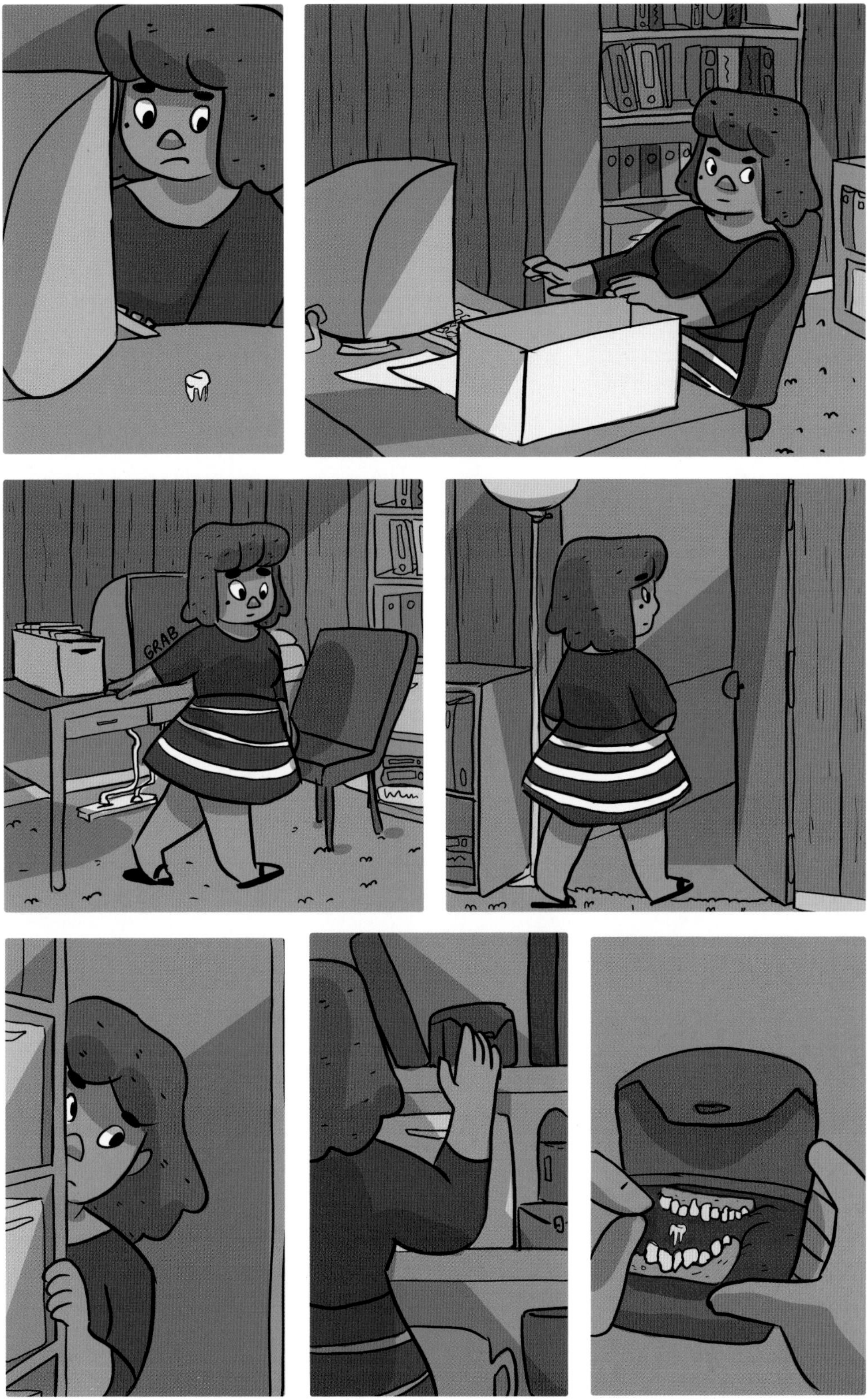
GRAB

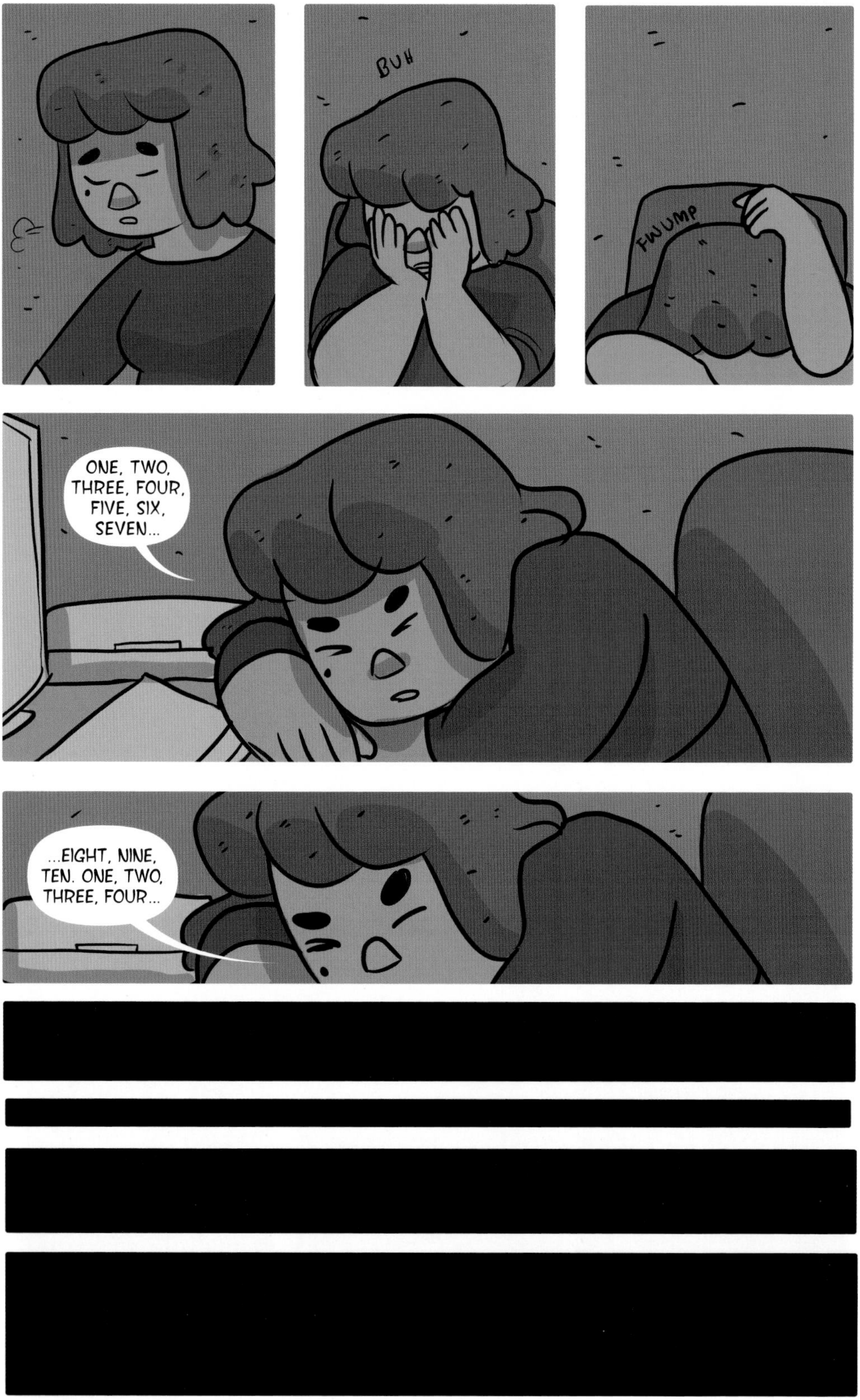
BUH
FWUMP
ONE, TWO, THREE, FOUR, FIVE, SIX, SEVEN...
...EIGHT, NINE, TEN. ONE, TWO, THREE, FOUR...

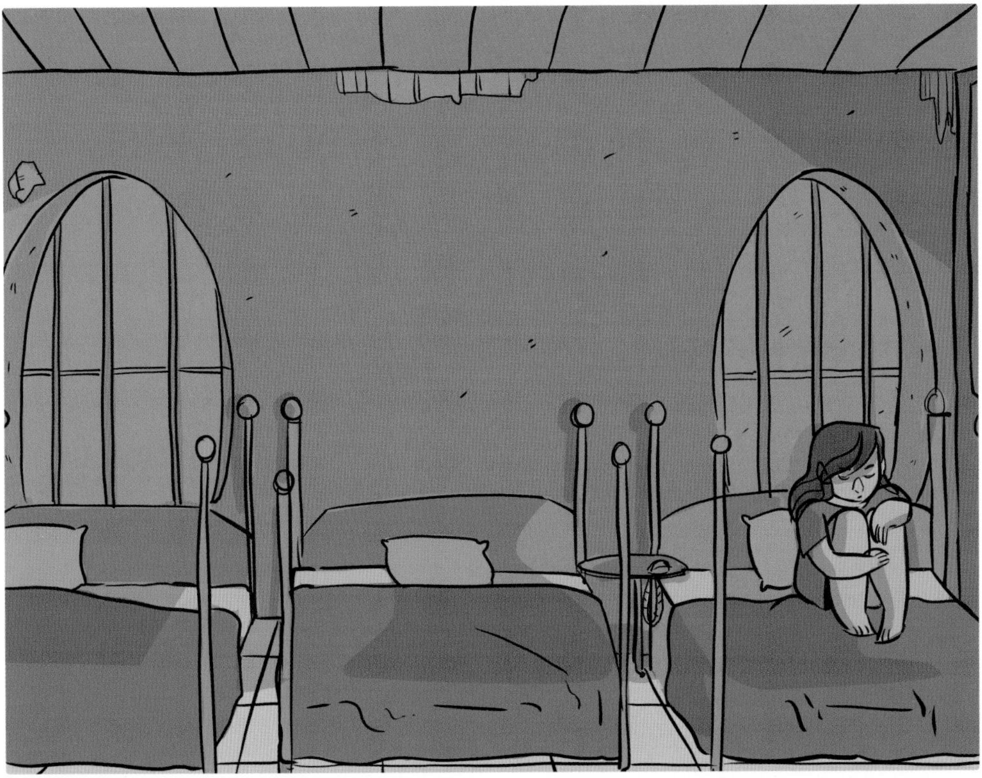

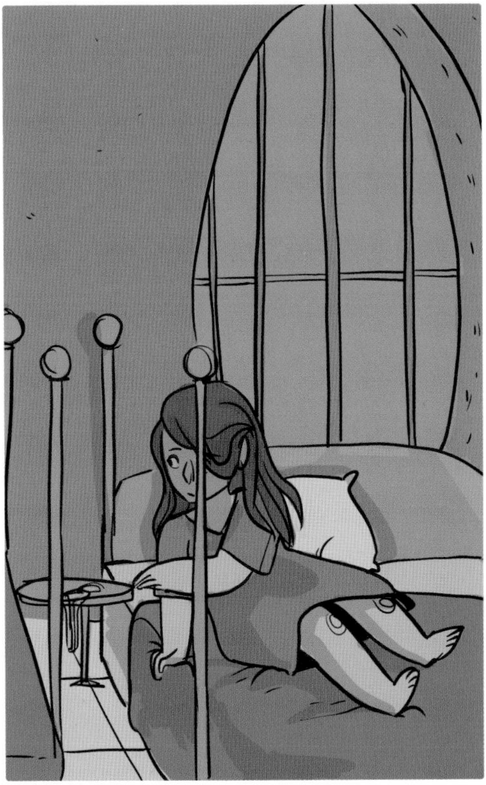

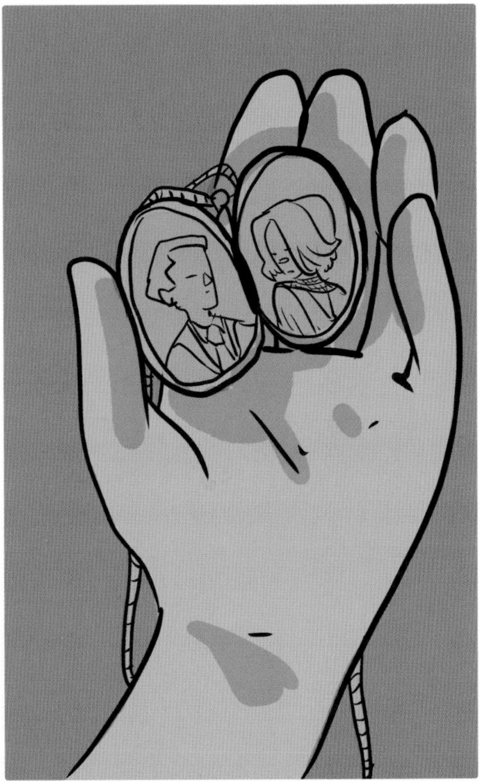

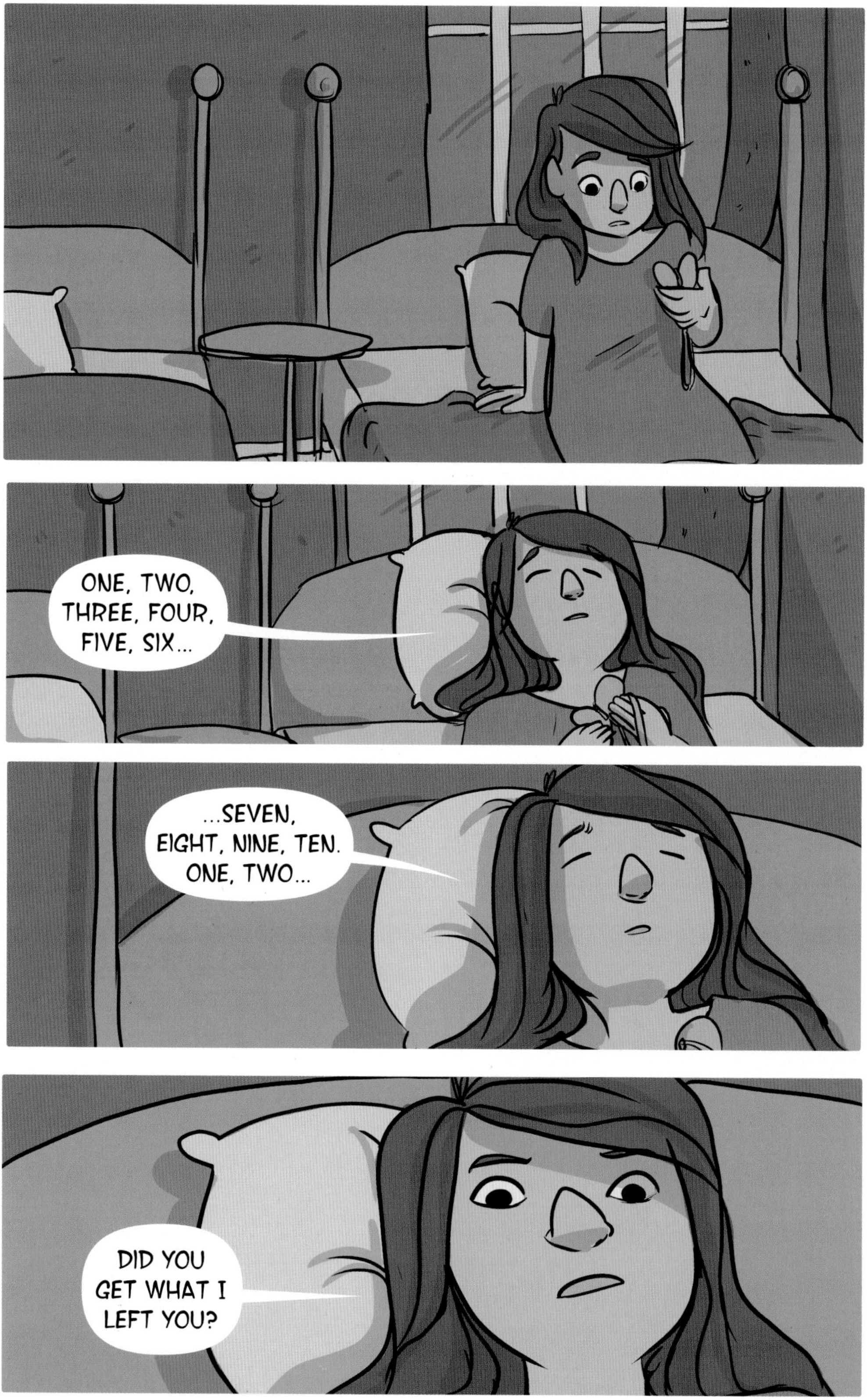
ONE, TWO, THREE, FOUR, FIVE, SIX...
...SEVEN, EIGHT, NINE, TEN. ONE, TWO...
DID YOU GET WHAT I LEFT YOU?

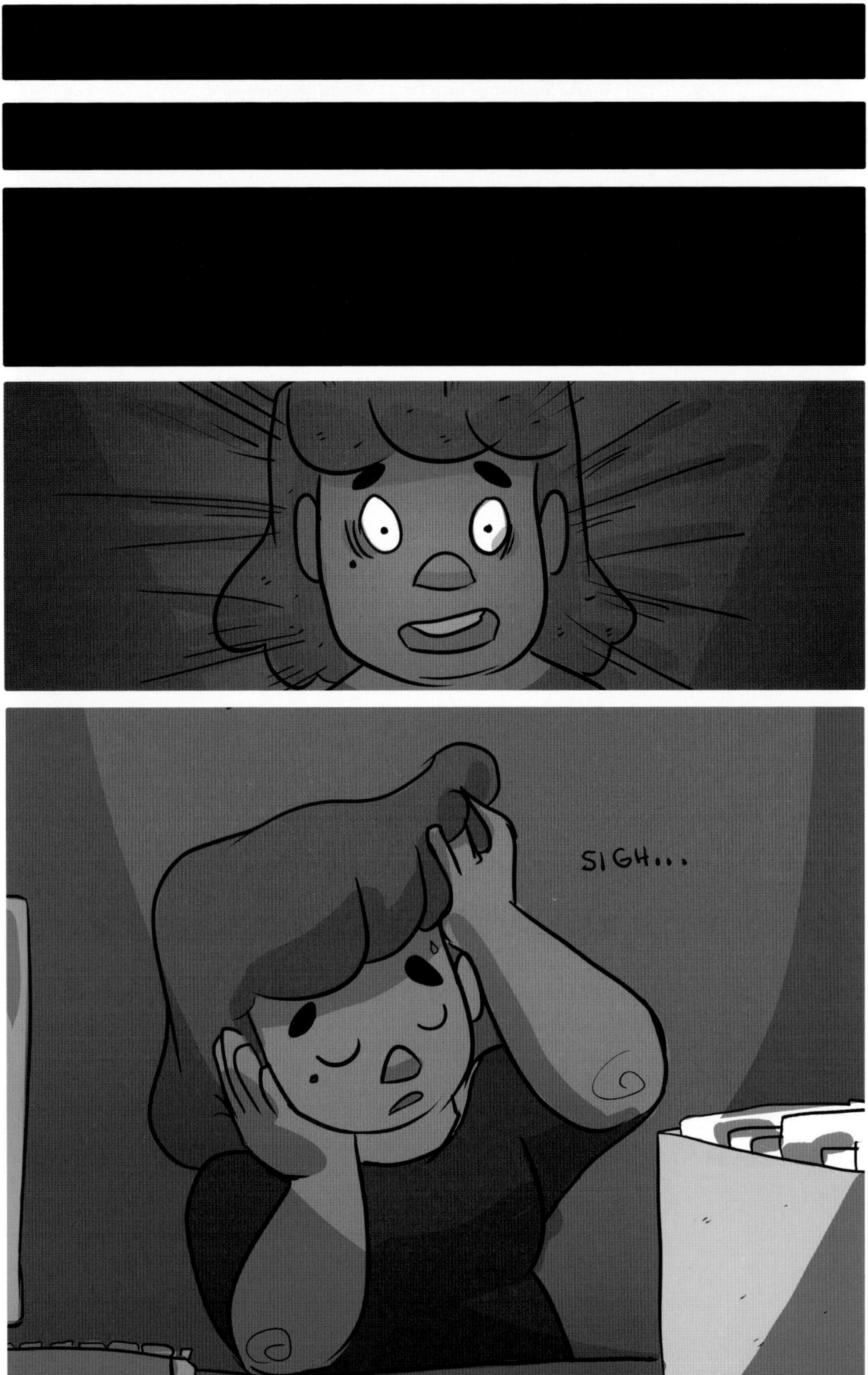
SIGH...

TWO WEEKS LATER

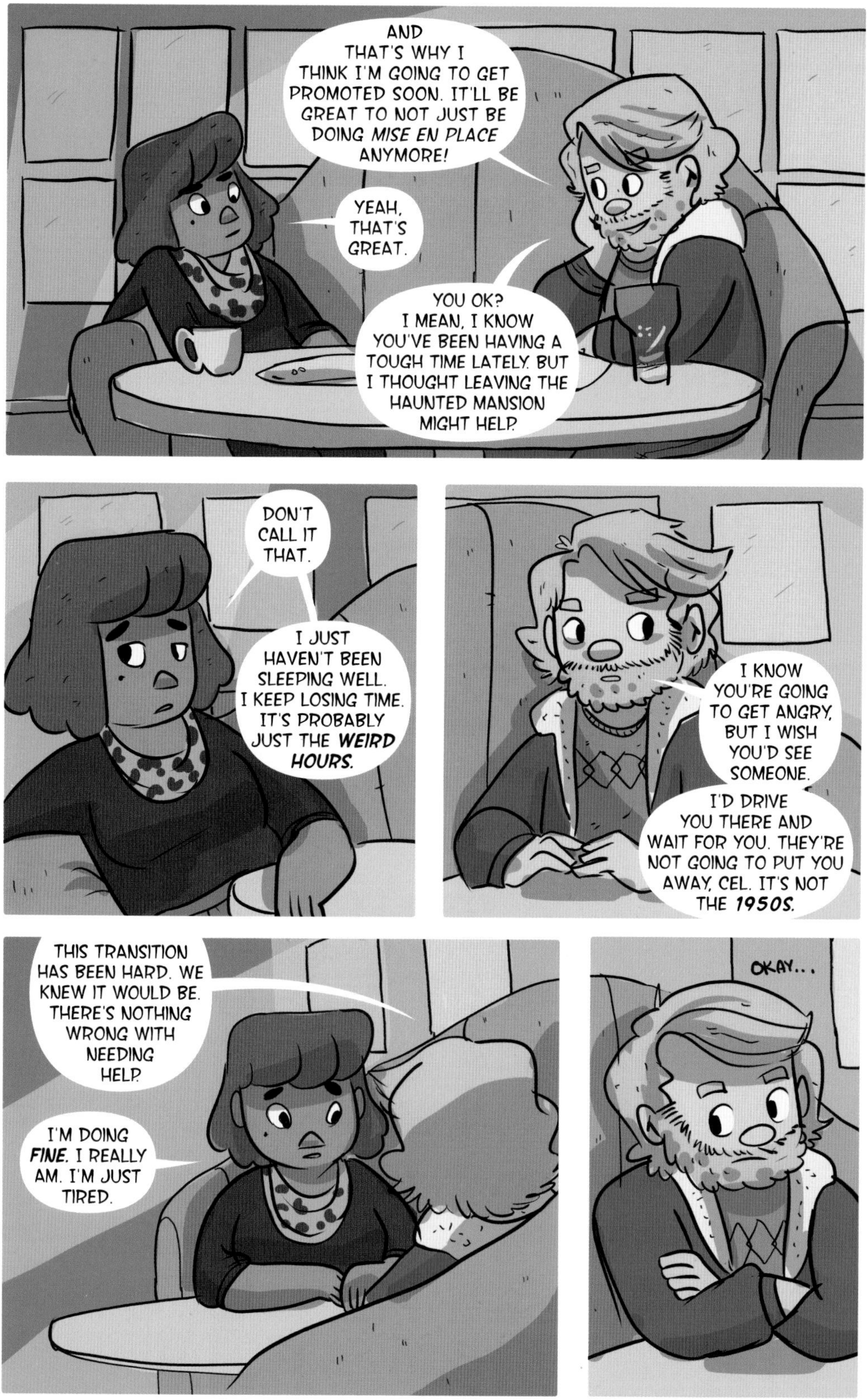
AND THAT'S WHY I THINK I'M GOING TO GET PROMOTED SOON. IT'LL BE GREAT TO NOT JUST BE DOING *MISE EN PLACE* ANYMORE!
YEAH, THAT'S GREAT.
YOU OK? I MEAN, I KNOW YOU'VE BEEN HAVING A TOUGH TIME LATELY. BUT I THOUGHT LEAVING THE HAUNTED MANSION MIGHT HELP.
DON'T CALL IT THAT.
I JUST HAVEN'T BEEN SLEEPING WELL. I KEEP LOSING TIME. IT'S PROBABLY JUST THE **WEIRD HOURS.**
I KNOW YOU'RE GOING TO GET ANGRY, BUT I WISH YOU'D SEE SOMEONE.
I'D DRIVE YOU THERE AND WAIT FOR YOU. THEY'RE NOT GOING TO PUT YOU AWAY, CEL. IT'S NOT THE **1950S.**
THIS TRANSITION HAS BEEN HARD. WE KNEW IT WOULD BE. THERE'S NOTHING WRONG WITH NEEDING HELP.
I'M DOING **FINE.** I REALLY AM. I'M JUST TIRED.
OKAY...

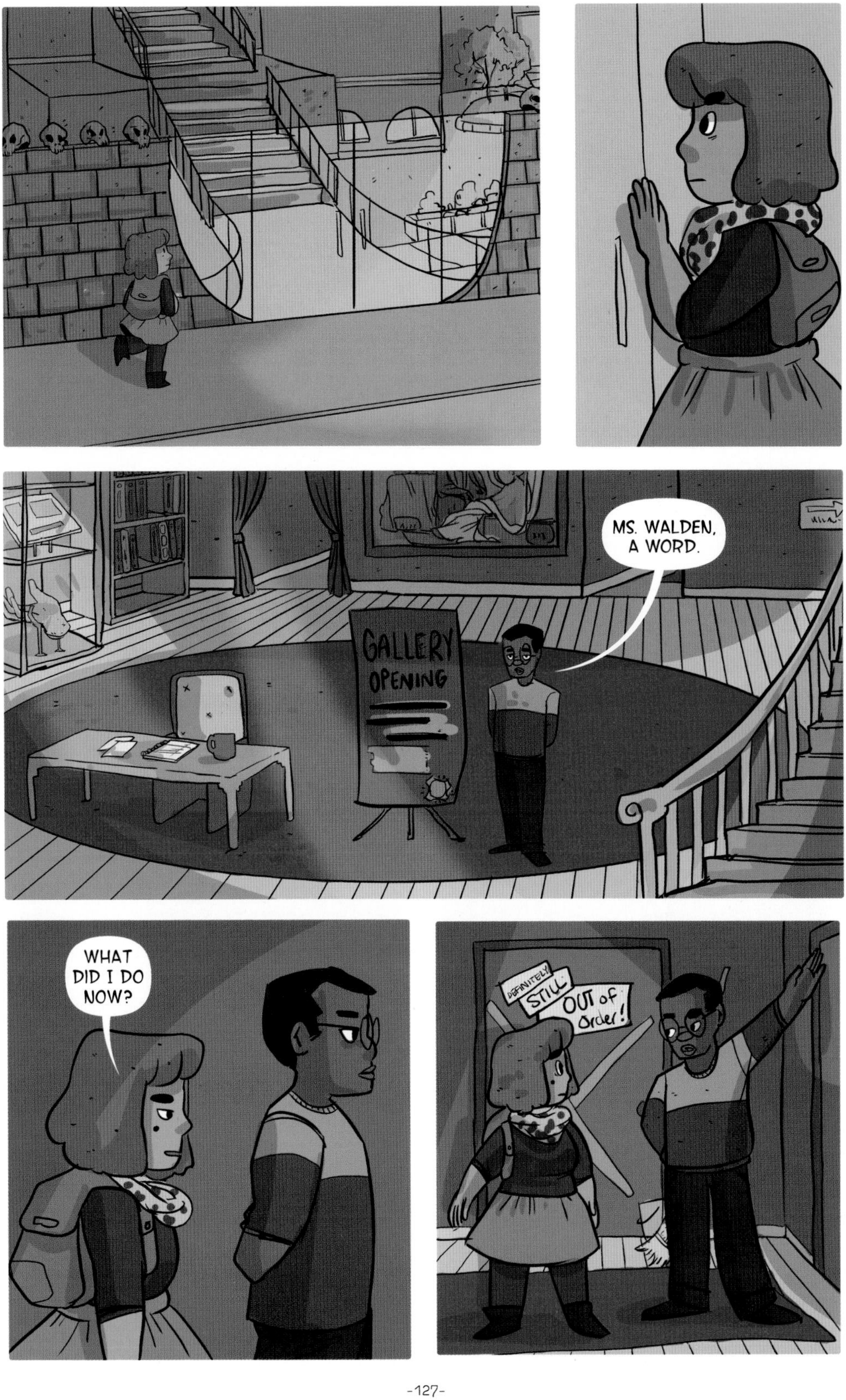
MS. WALDEN, A WORD.
GALLERY OPENING
WHAT DID I DO NOW?
DEFINITELY STILL OUT of Order!

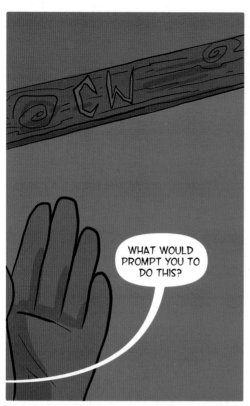

WHAT WOULD PROMPT YOU TO DO THIS?

WHOA—I DID *NOT* DO THAT!

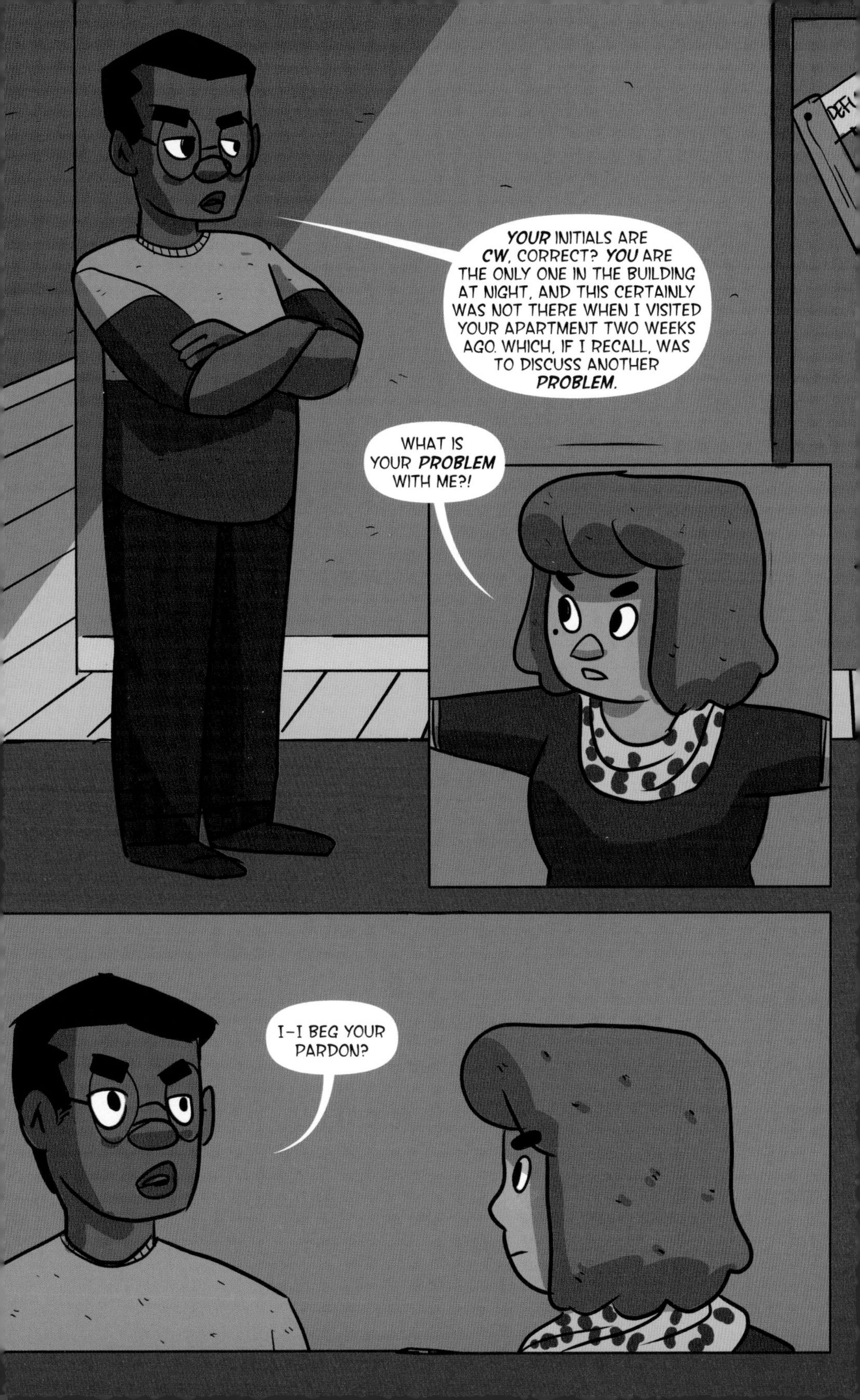
YOUR INITIALS ARE CW, CORRECT? YOU ARE THE ONLY ONE IN THE BUILDING AT NIGHT, AND THIS CERTAINLY WAS NOT THERE WHEN I VISITED YOUR APARTMENT TWO WEEKS AGO. WHICH, IF I RECALL, WAS TO DISCUSS ANOTHER PROBLEM.
WHAT IS YOUR PROBLEM WITH ME?!
I-I BEG YOUR PARDON?

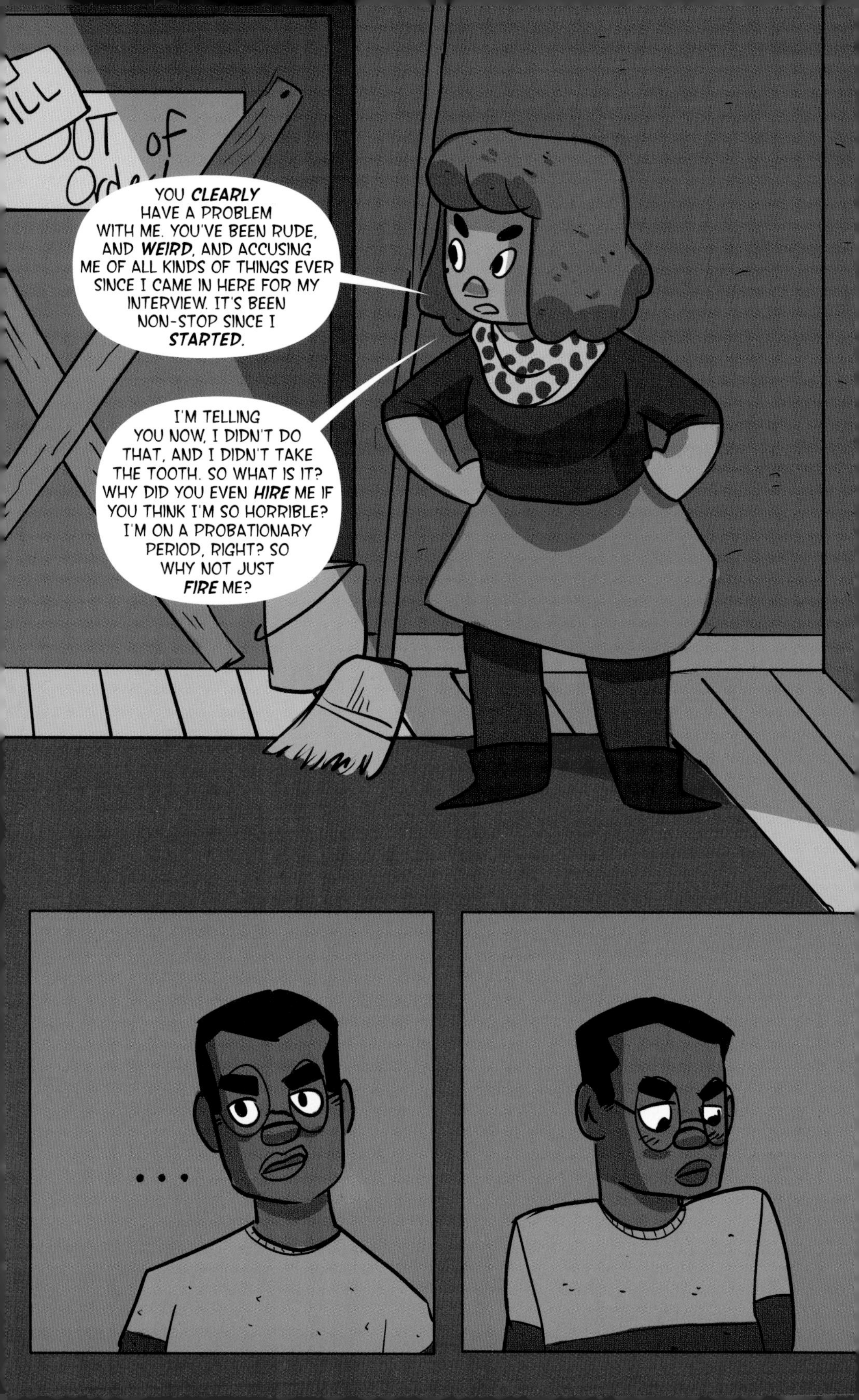

OUT of Order
YOU CLEARLY HAVE A PROBLEM WITH ME. YOU'VE BEEN RUDE, AND WEIRD, AND ACCUSING ME OF ALL KINDS OF THINGS EVER SINCE I CAME IN HERE FOR MY INTERVIEW. IT'S BEEN NON-STOP SINCE I STARTED.
I'M TELLING YOU NOW, I DIDN'T DO THAT, AND I DIDN'T TAKE THE TOOTH. SO WHAT IS IT? WHY DID YOU EVEN HIRE ME IF YOU THINK I'M SO HORRIBLE? I'M ON A PROBATIONARY PERIOD, RIGHT? SO WHY NOT JUST FIRE ME?
...

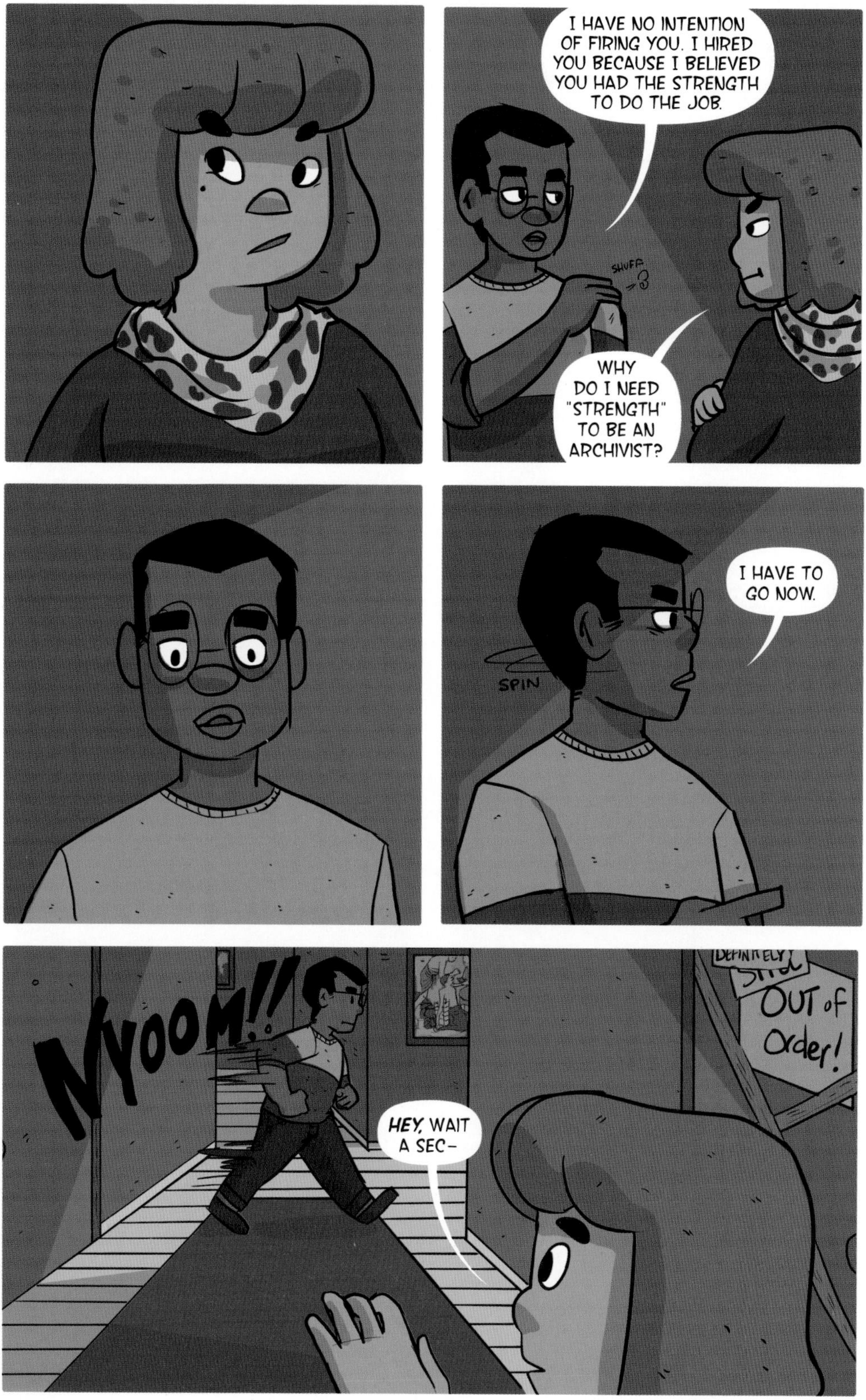
I HAVE NO INTENTION OF FIRING YOU. I HIRED YOU BECAUSE I BELIEVED YOU HAD THE STRENGTH TO DO THE JOB.
SHUFF
WHY DO I NEED "STRENGTH" TO BE AN ARCHIVIST?
SPIN
I HAVE TO GO NOW.
NYOOM!!
OUT of Order!
HEY, WAIT A SEC–

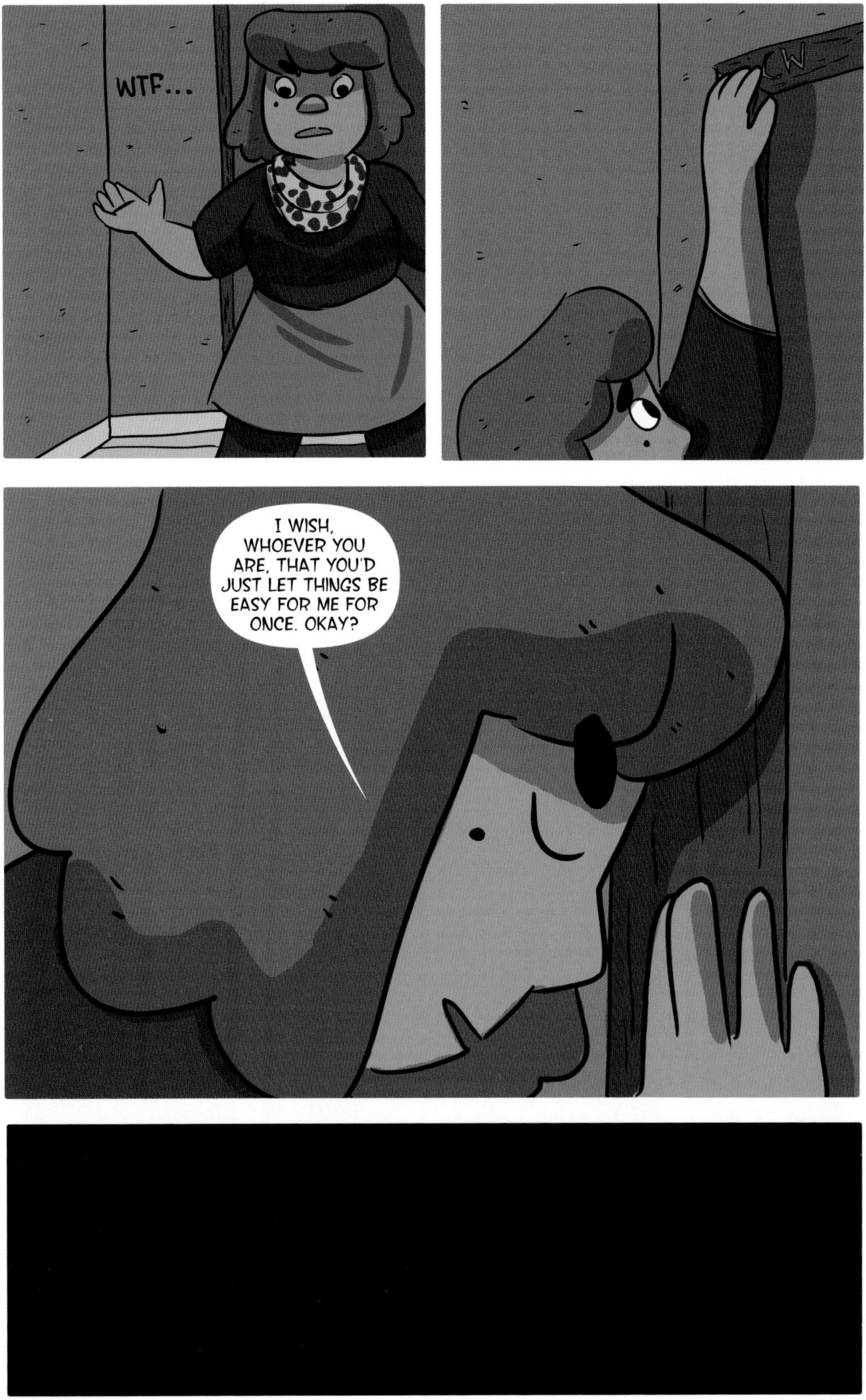
WTF...
CW
I WISH, WHOEVER YOU ARE, THAT YOU'D JUST LET THINGS BE EASY FOR ME FOR ONCE. OKAY?

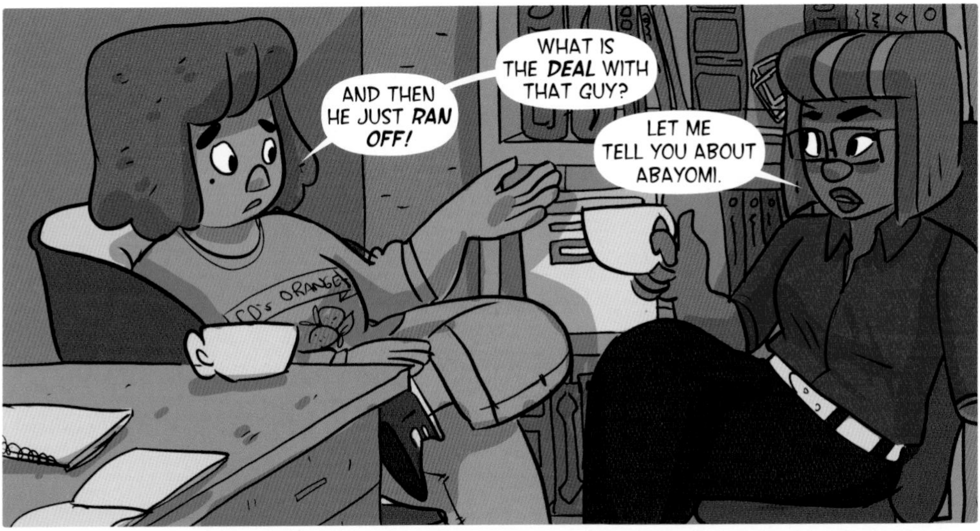
AND THEN HE JUST RAN OFF!
WHAT IS THE DEAL WITH THAT GUY?
LET ME TELL YOU ABOUT ABAYOMI.
CJ's ORANGE

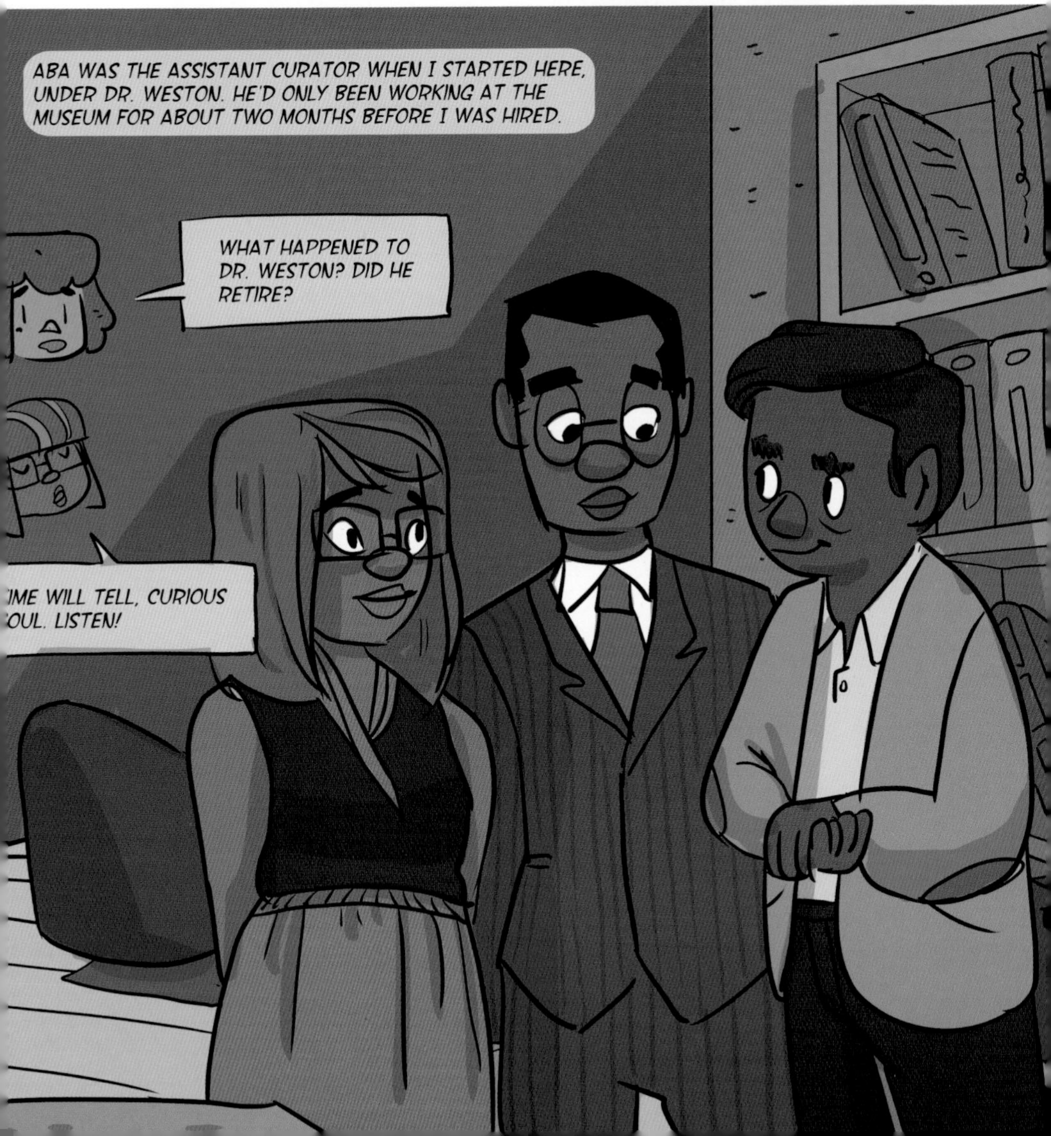
ABA WAS THE ASSISTANT CURATOR WHEN I STARTED HERE, UNDER DR. WESTON. HE'D ONLY BEEN WORKING AT THE MUSEUM FOR ABOUT TWO MONTHS BEFORE I WAS HIRED.
WHAT HAPPENED TO DR. WESTON? DID HE RETIRE?
IME WILL TELL, CURIOUS OUL. LISTEN!

DR. WESTON WAS SO KIND, AND SO WELCOMING. HE HIRED ME IN SPITE OF MY LACK OF EXPERIENCE, AND TRAINED ME *HIMSELF.*

AND ABA, HE WAS A TEACHER'S PET. HE LOVED DR. WESTON LIKE A FATHER, BUT I DON'T THINK IT WAS NECESSARILY *RECIPROCATED.*

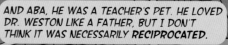

ABA WAS OBSESSED WITH GETTING THE DOCTOR'S APPROVAL, AND STUDIED THE COLLECTION AND HISTORY OF THE MUSEUM LIKE IT WAS HIS JOB.

WELL... WASN'T IT?

WHY DO YOU HATE GOOD STORYTELLING, CELESTE?

WHEN DR. WESTON VANISHED, ABAYOMI TOOK IT *REALLY* HARD. WE *BOTH* DID.

WAIT, *"VANISHED"?* HE DIDN'T JUST LIKE... *RETIRE,* OR SOMETHING?

HE JUST *DISAPPEARED.*

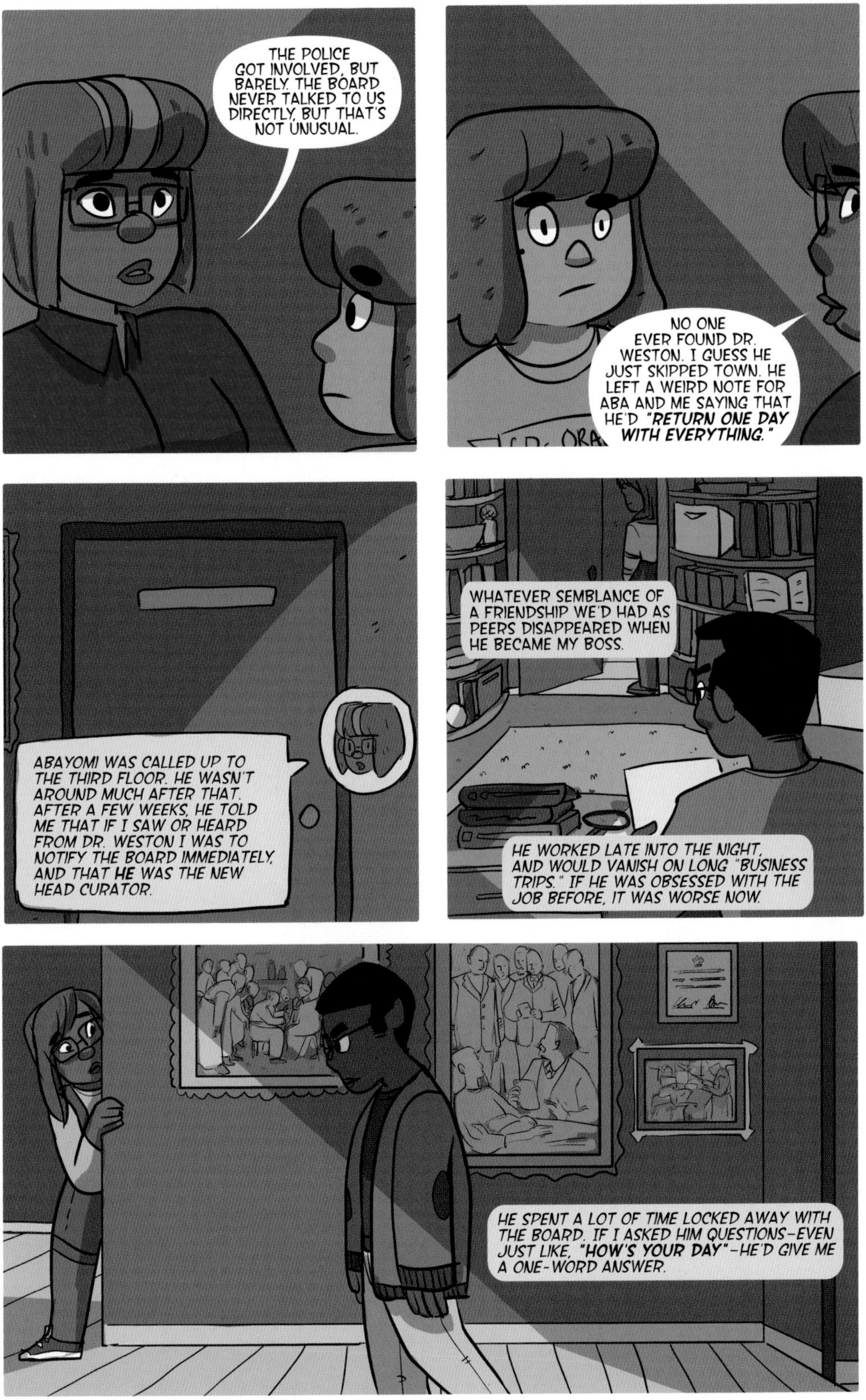
THE POLICE GOT INVOLVED, BUT BARELY. THE BOARD NEVER TALKED TO US DIRECTLY, BUT THAT'S NOT UNUSUAL.
NO ONE EVER FOUND DR. WESTON. I GUESS HE JUST SKIPPED TOWN. HE LEFT A WEIRD NOTE FOR ABA AND ME SAYING THAT HE'D "RETURN ONE DAY WITH EVERYTHING."
ABAYOMI WAS CALLED UP TO THE THIRD FLOOR. HE WASN'T AROUND MUCH AFTER THAT. AFTER A FEW WEEKS, HE TOLD ME THAT IF I SAW OR HEARD FROM DR. WESTON I WAS TO NOTIFY THE BOARD IMMEDIATELY, AND THAT HE WAS THE NEW HEAD CURATOR.
WHATEVER SEMBLANCE OF A FRIENDSHIP WE'D HAD AS PEERS DISAPPEARED WHEN HE BECAME MY BOSS.
HE WORKED LATE INTO THE NIGHT, AND WOULD VANISH ON LONG "BUSINESS TRIPS." IF HE WAS OBSESSED WITH THE JOB BEFORE, IT WAS WORSE NOW.
HE SPENT A LOT OF TIME LOCKED AWAY WITH THE BOARD. IF I ASKED HIM QUESTIONS—EVEN JUST LIKE, "HOW'S YOUR DAY"—HE'D GIVE ME A ONE-WORD ANSWER.

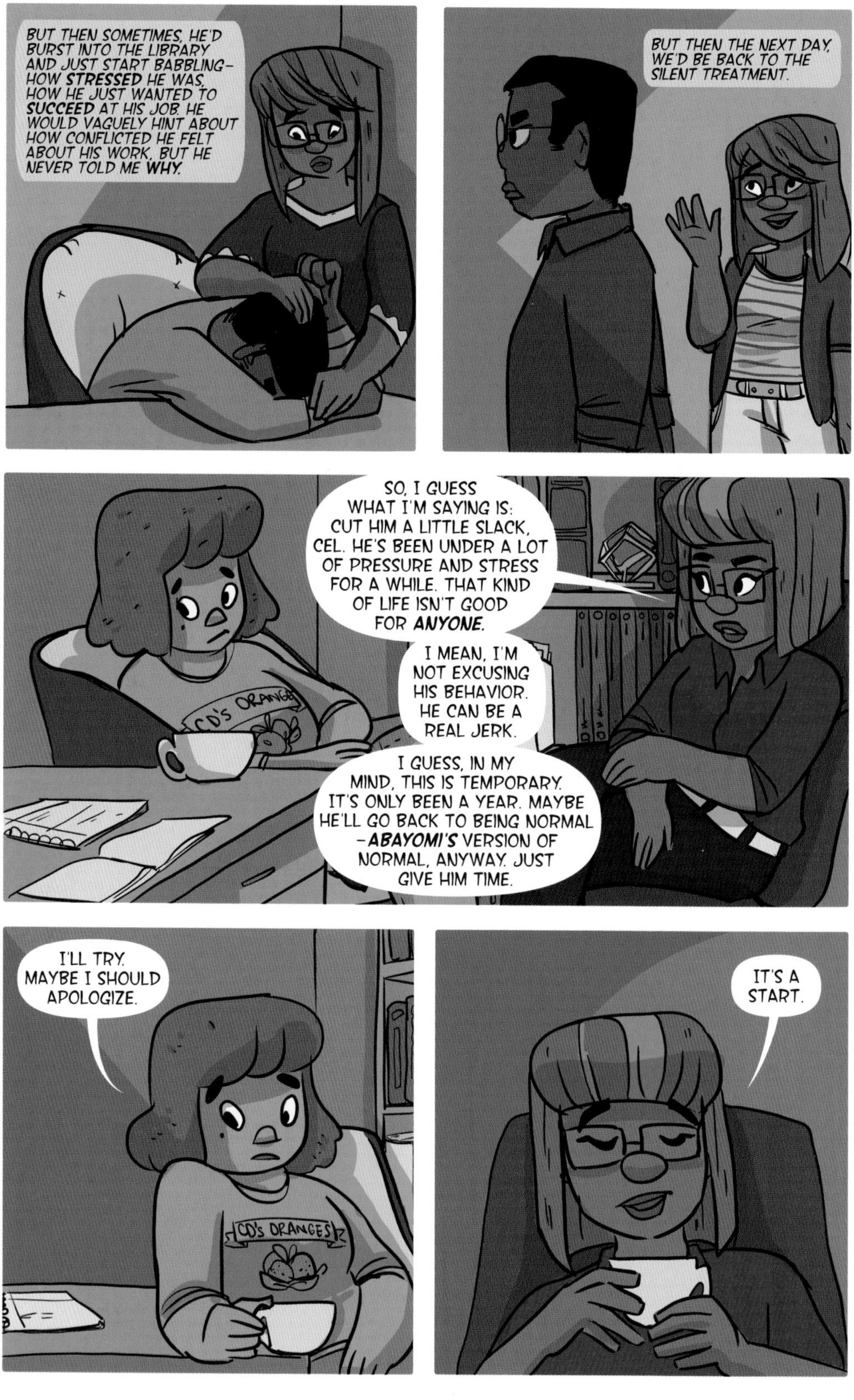
BUT THEN SOMETIMES, HE'D BURST INTO THE LIBRARY AND JUST START BABBLING– HOW **STRESSED** HE WAS, HOW HE JUST WANTED TO **SUCCEED** AT HIS JOB. HE WOULD VAGUELY HINT ABOUT HOW CONFLICTED HE FELT ABOUT HIS WORK, BUT HE NEVER TOLD ME **WHY**.
BUT THEN THE NEXT DAY, WE'D BE BACK TO THE SILENT TREATMENT.
SO, I GUESS WHAT I'M SAYING IS: CUT HIM A LITTLE SLACK, CEL. HE'S BEEN UNDER A LOT OF PRESSURE AND STRESS FOR A WHILE. THAT KIND OF LIFE ISN'T GOOD FOR **ANYONE.**
I MEAN, I'M NOT EXCUSING HIS BEHAVIOR. HE CAN BE A REAL JERK.
I GUESS, IN MY MIND, THIS IS TEMPORARY. IT'S ONLY BEEN A YEAR. MAYBE HE'LL GO BACK TO BEING NORMAL –**ABAYOMI'S** VERSION OF NORMAL, ANYWAY. JUST GIVE HIM TIME.
CD's ORANGES
I'LL TRY. MAYBE I SHOULD APOLOGIZE.
IT'S A START.

THREE DAYS LATER

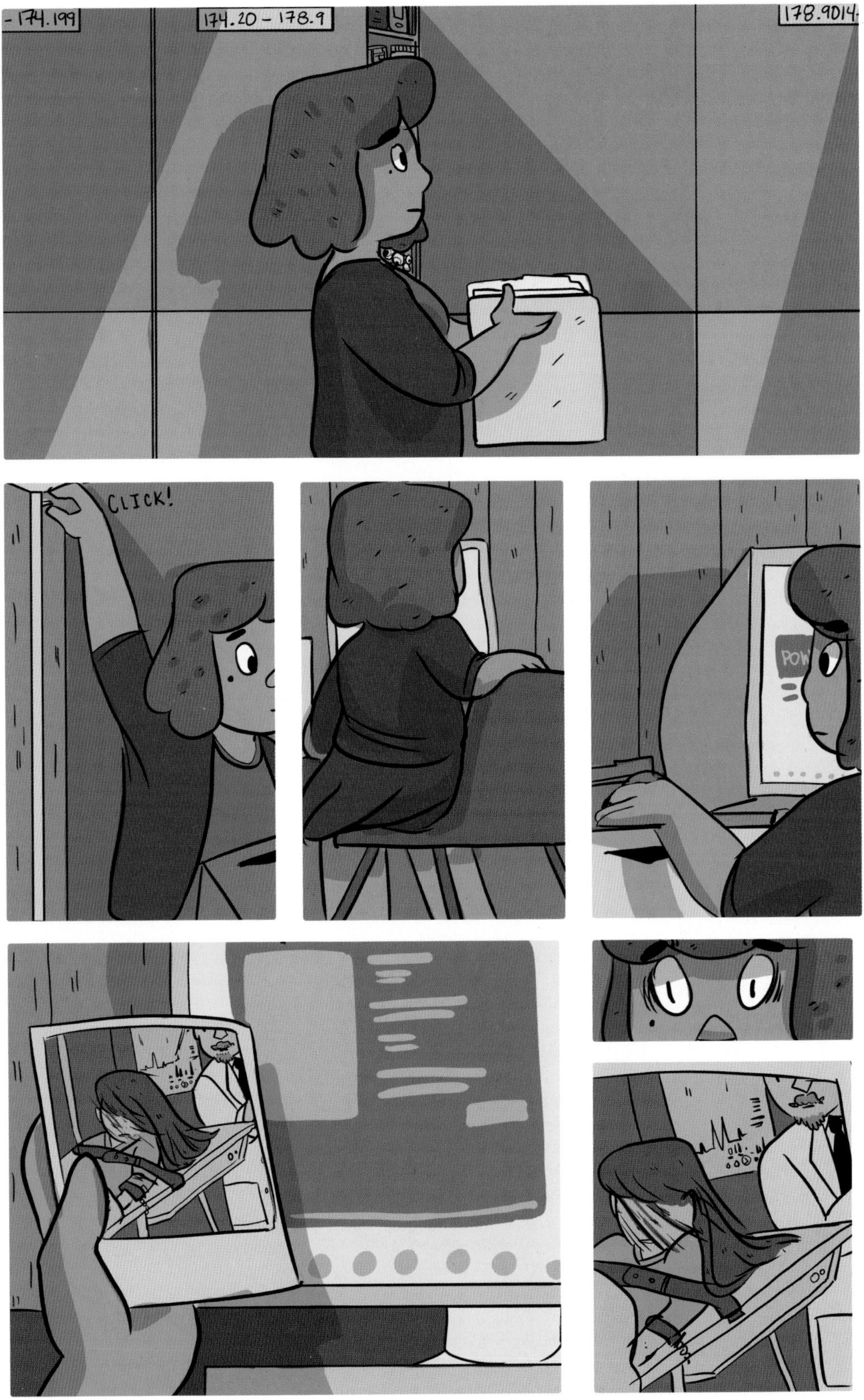

-174.199
174.20 - 178.9
178.9014-
CLICK!
POW

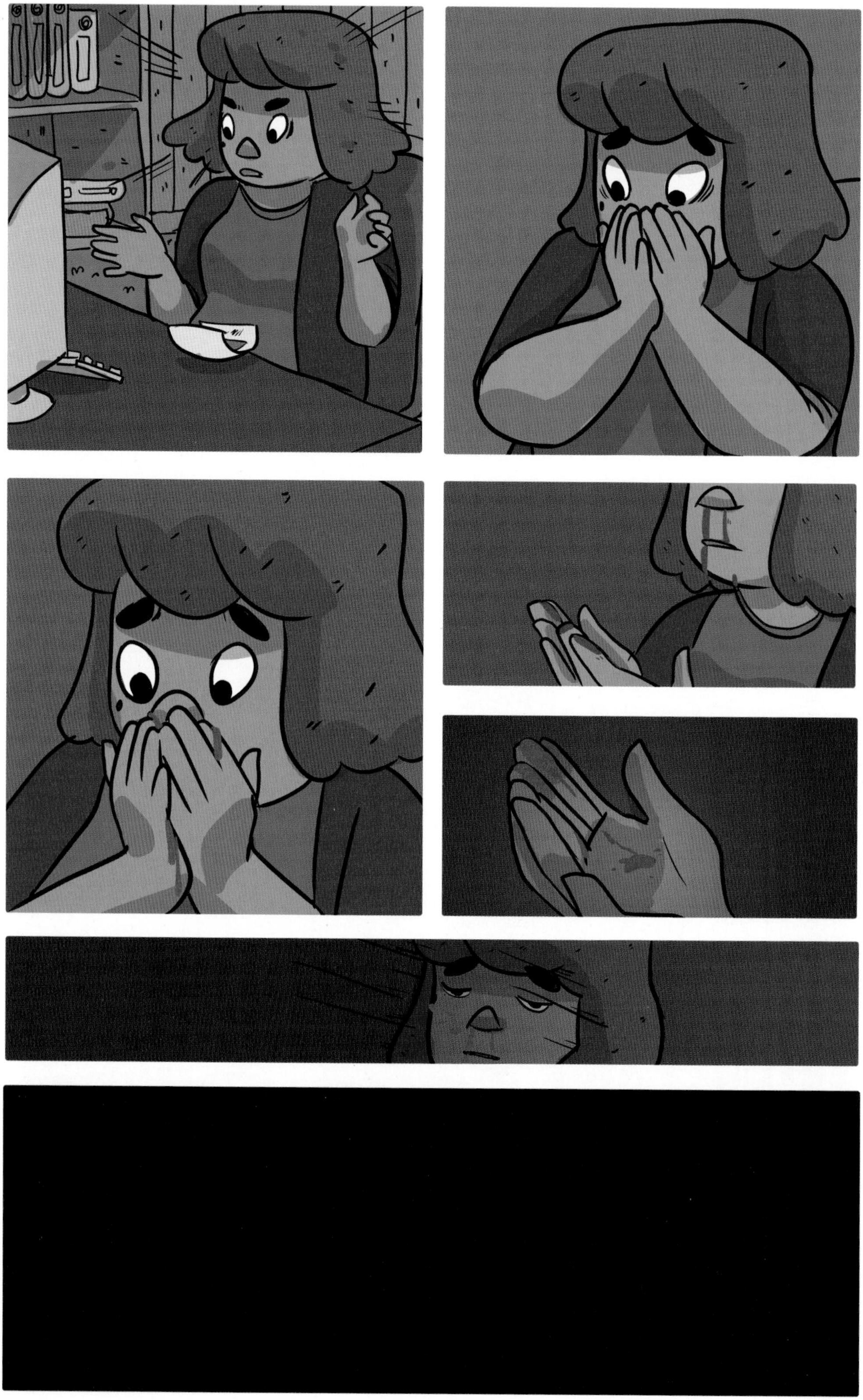

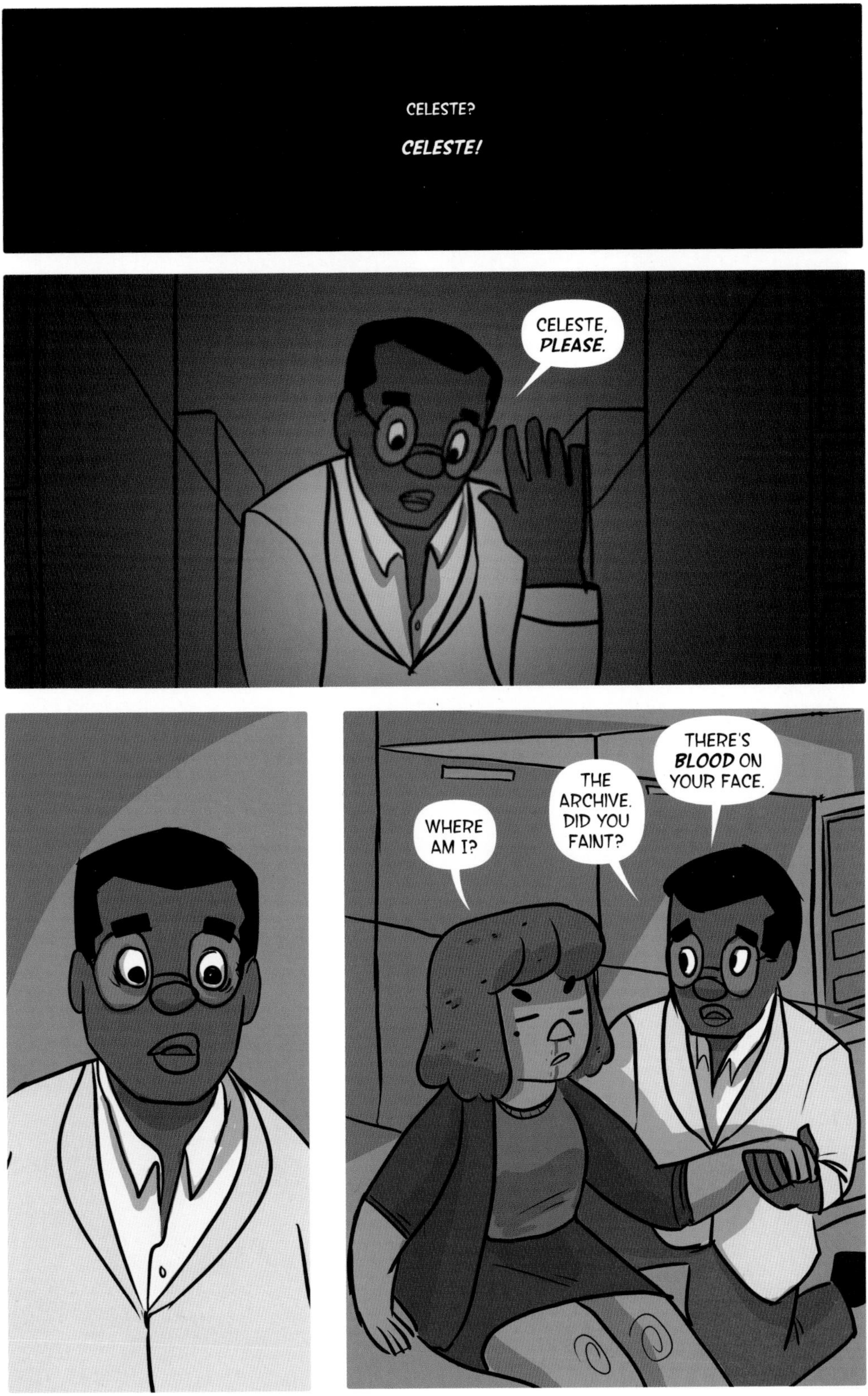
CELESTE?
CELESTE!
CELESTE, *PLEASE.*
WHERE AM I?
THE ARCHIVE. DID YOU FAINT?
THERE'S *BLOOD* ON YOUR FACE.

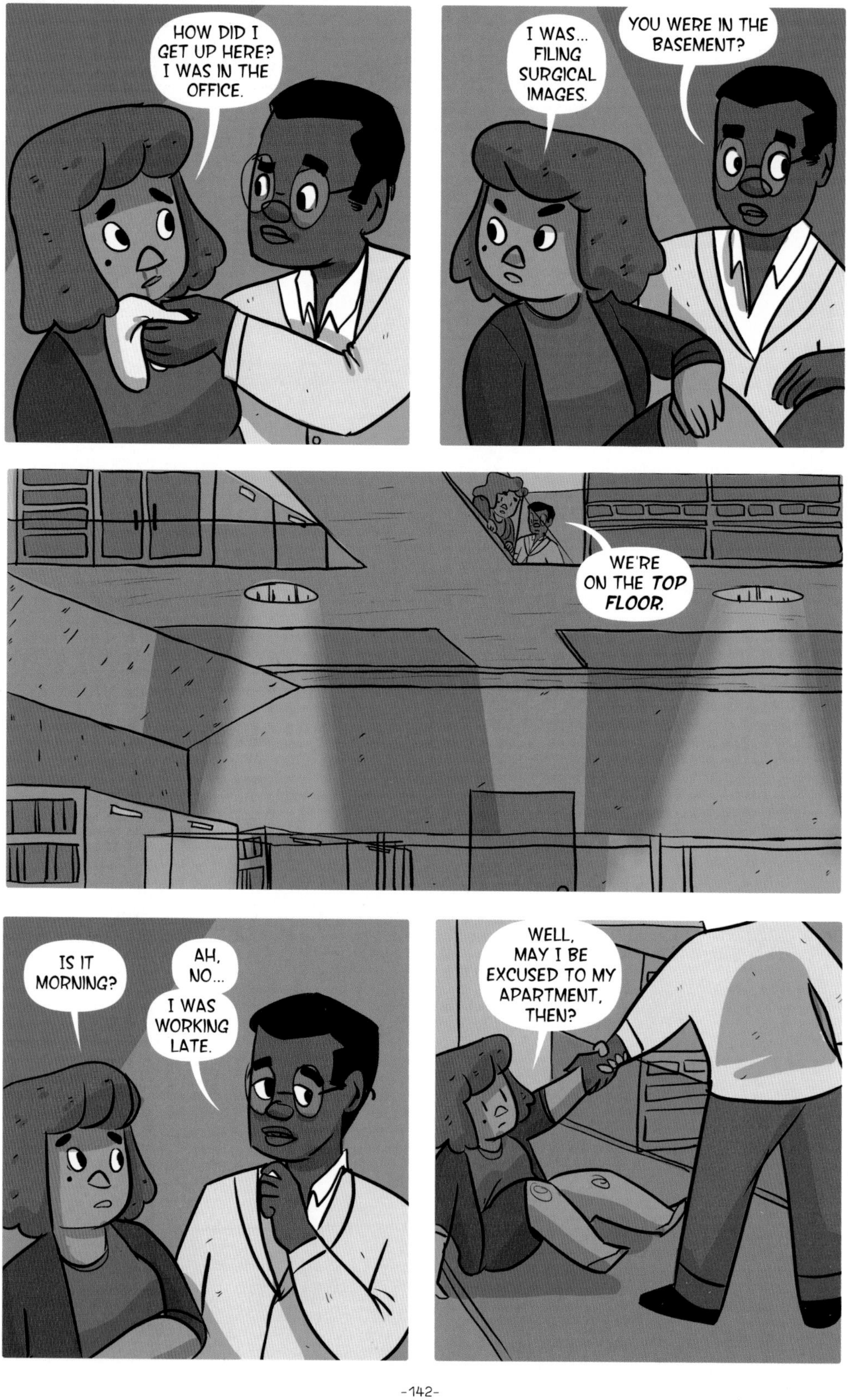
HOW DID I GET UP HERE? I WAS IN THE OFFICE.
I WAS... FILING SURGICAL IMAGES.
YOU WERE IN THE BASEMENT?
WE'RE ON THE *TOP FLOOR.*
IS IT MORNING?
AH, NO...
I WAS WORKING LATE.
WELL, MAY I BE EXCUSED TO MY APARTMENT, THEN?

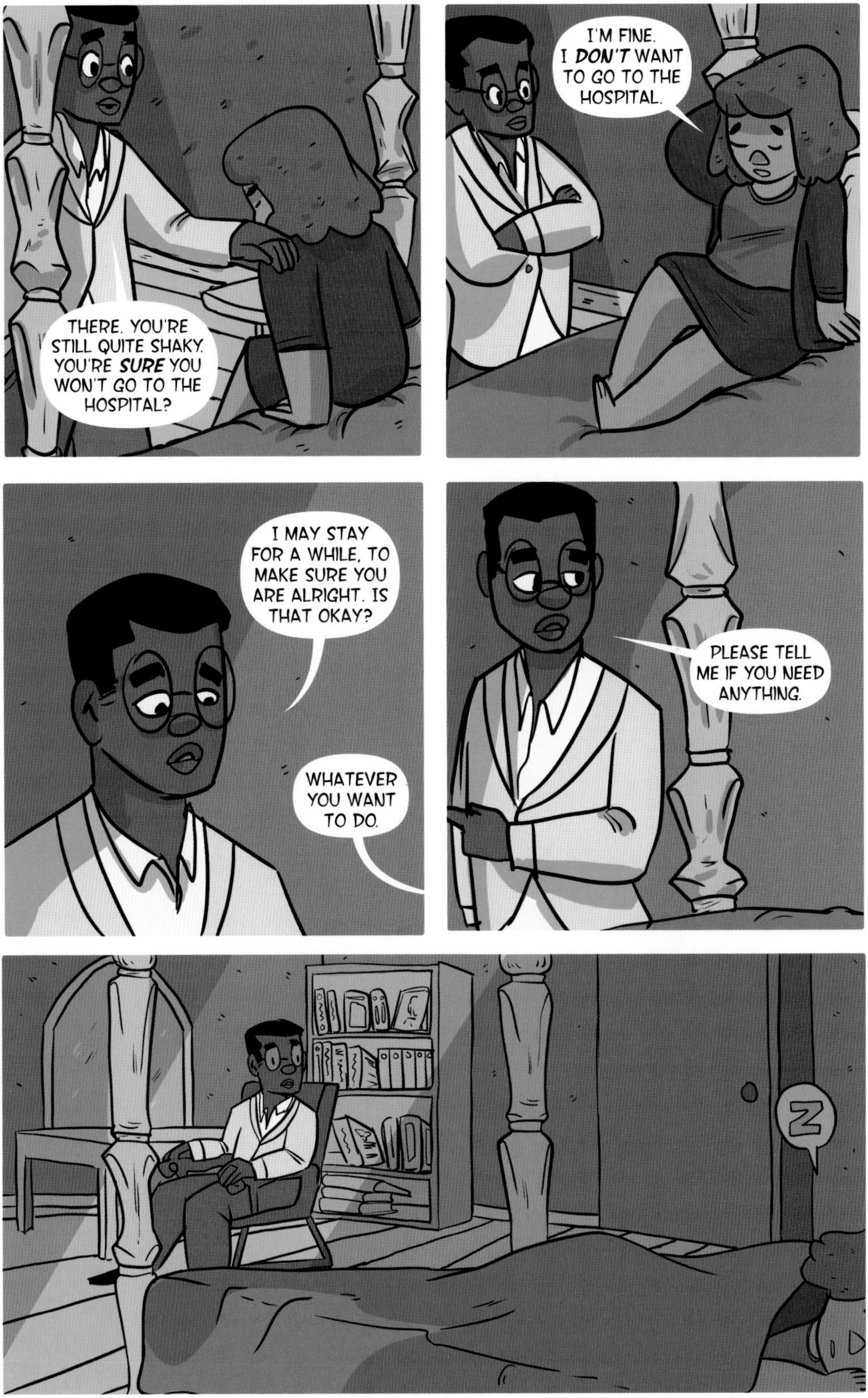
THERE. YOU'RE STILL QUITE SHAKY. YOU'RE **SURE** YOU WON'T GO TO THE HOSPITAL?
I'M FINE. I **DON'T** WANT TO GO TO THE HOSPITAL.
I MAY STAY FOR A WHILE, TO MAKE SURE YOU ARE ALRIGHT. IS THAT OKAY?
WHATEVER YOU WANT TO DO.
PLEASE TELL ME IF YOU NEED ANYTHING.
Z

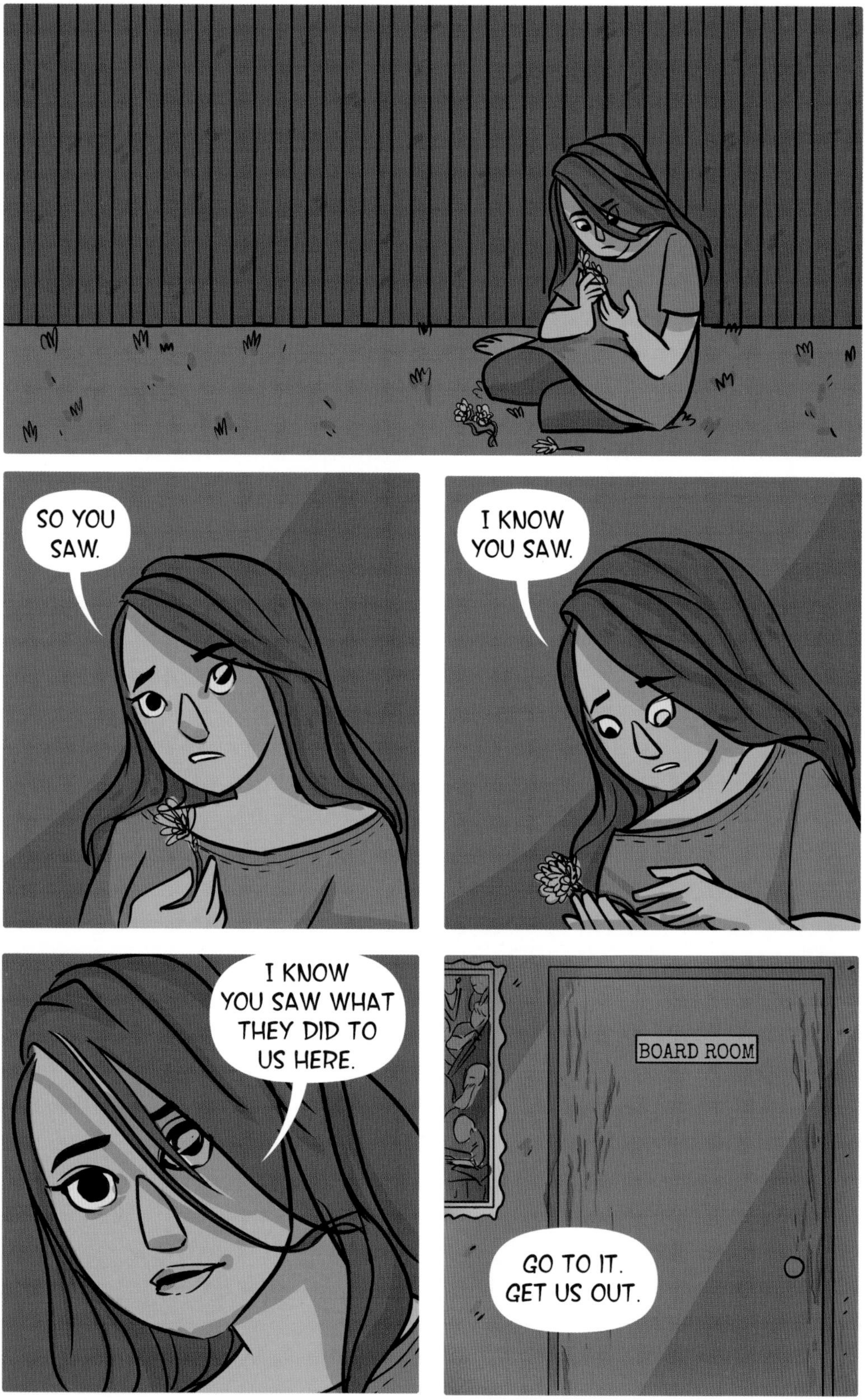
SO YOU SAW.
I KNOW YOU SAW.
I KNOW YOU SAW WHAT THEY DID TO US HERE.
BOARD ROOM
GO TO IT. GET US OUT.

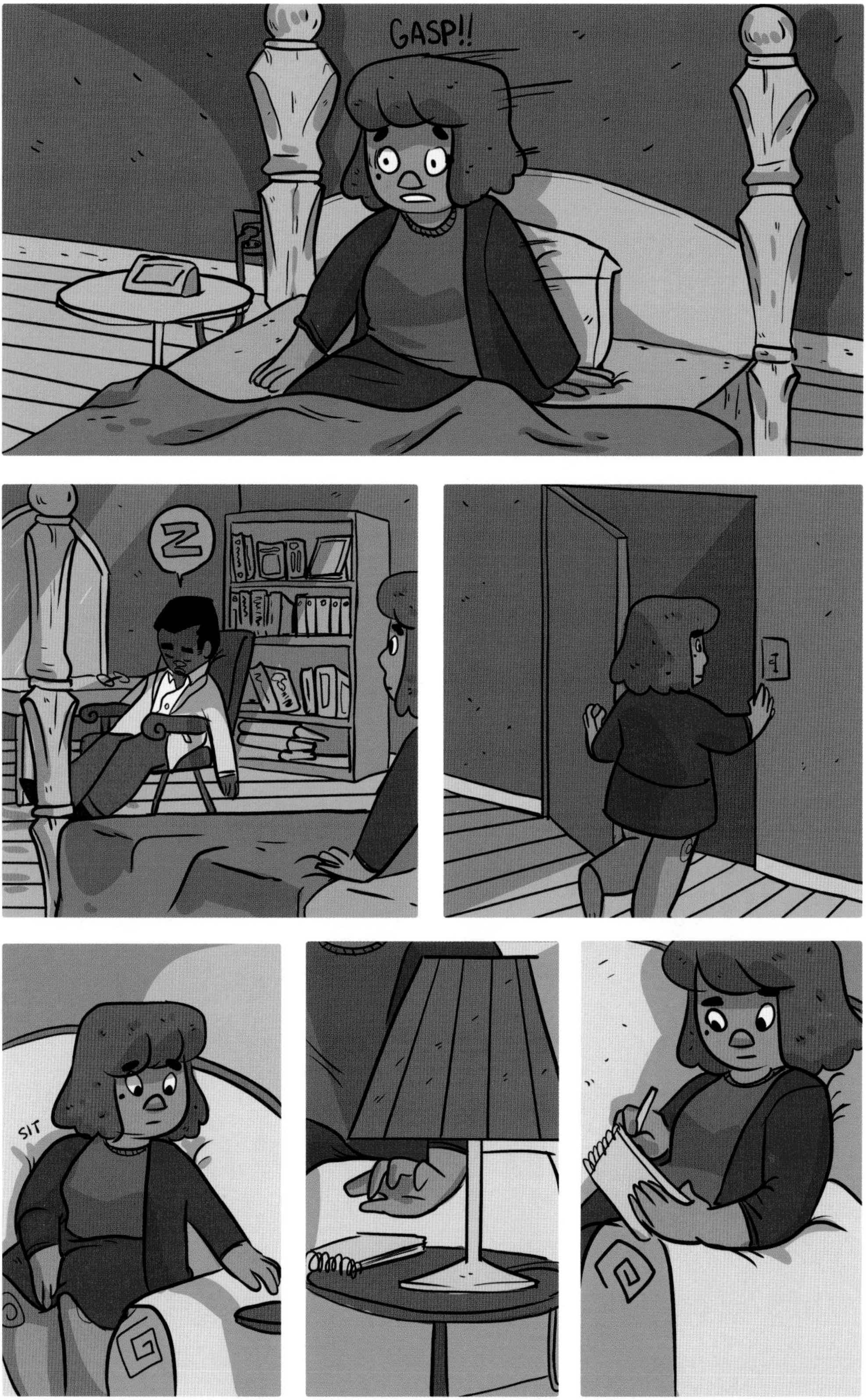
GASP!!
Z
SIT

HEY.

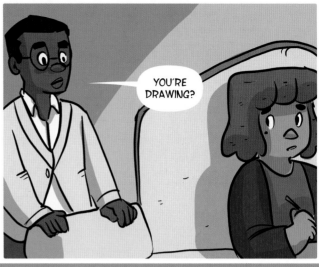

YOU'RE DRAWING?

CALL MOM 11/27

WELL, YOU SEEM BETTER. I'LL BE GOING NOW.

OKAY?

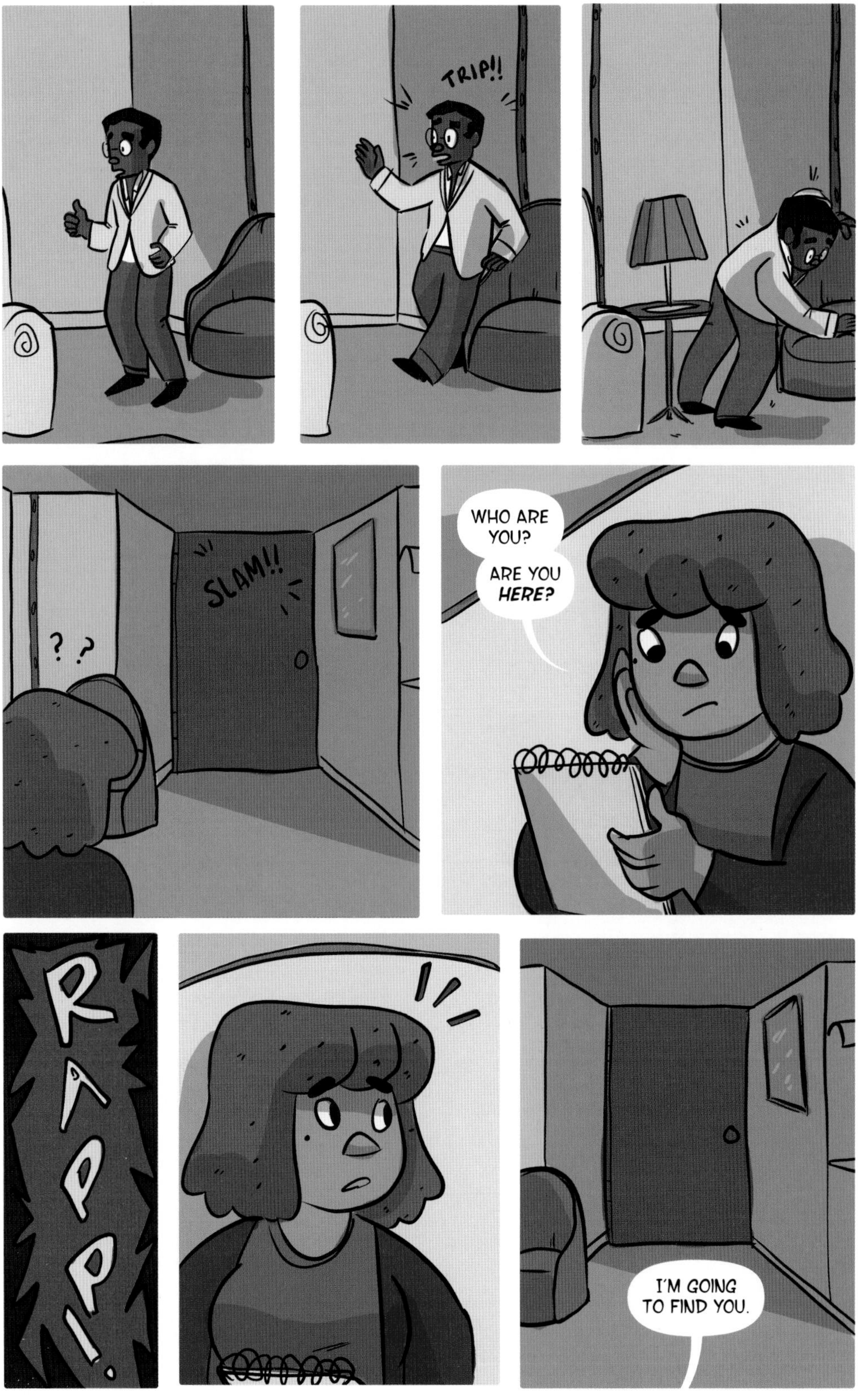
TRIP!!
SLAM!!
? ?
WHO ARE YOU?
ARE YOU *HERE?*
RAPP!
I'M GOING TO FIND YOU.

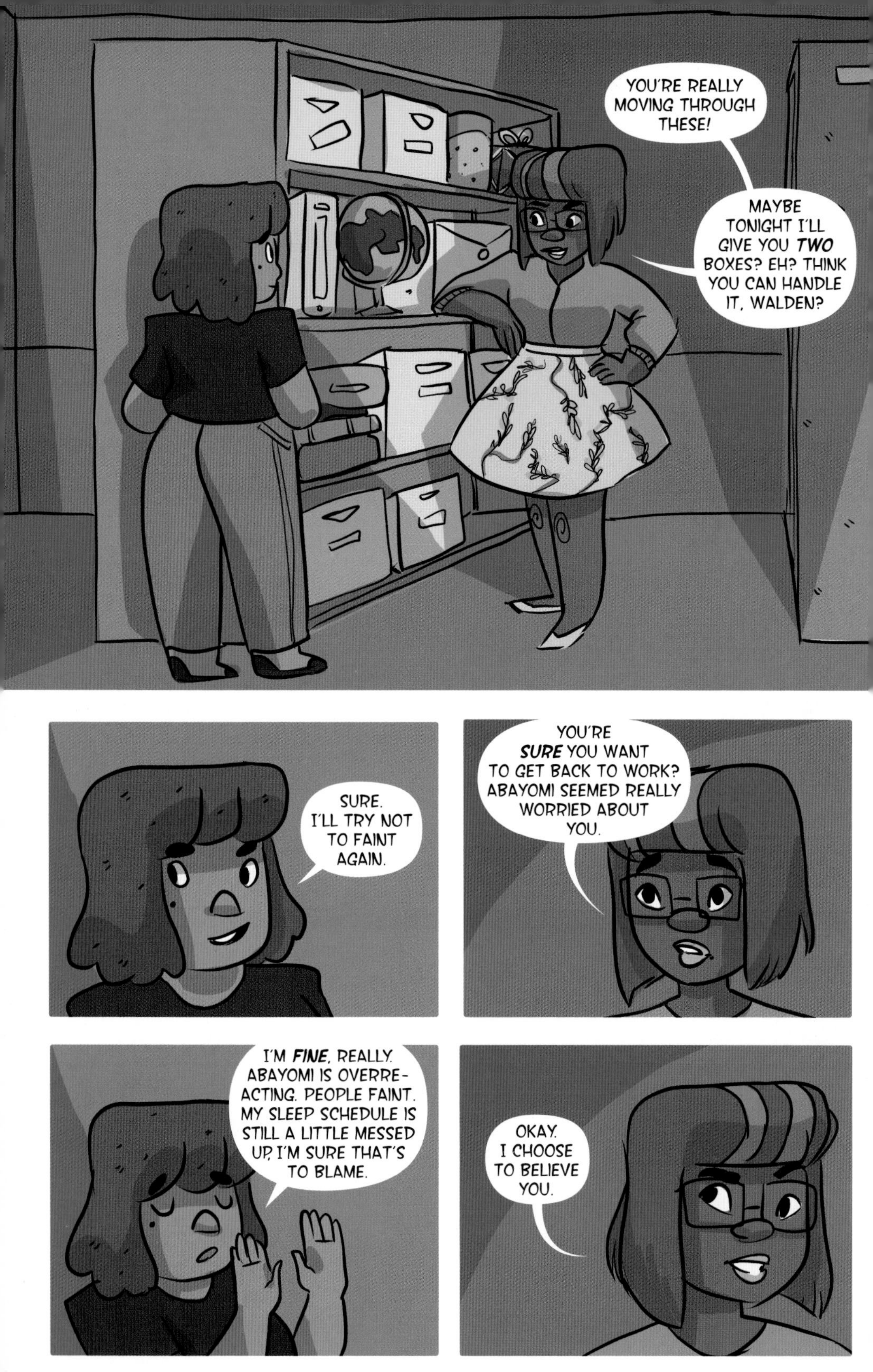
YOU'RE REALLY MOVING THROUGH THESE!
MAYBE TONIGHT I'LL GIVE YOU ***TWO*** BOXES? EH? THINK YOU CAN HANDLE IT, WALDEN?
SURE. I'LL TRY NOT TO FAINT AGAIN.
YOU'RE ***SURE*** YOU WANT TO GET BACK TO WORK? ABAYOMI SEEMED REALLY WORRIED ABOUT YOU.
I'M ***FINE***, REALLY. ABAYOMI IS OVERRE-ACTING. PEOPLE FAINT. MY SLEEP SCHEDULE IS STILL A LITTLE MESSED UP, I'M SURE THAT'S TO BLAME.
OKAY. I CHOOSE TO BELIEVE YOU.

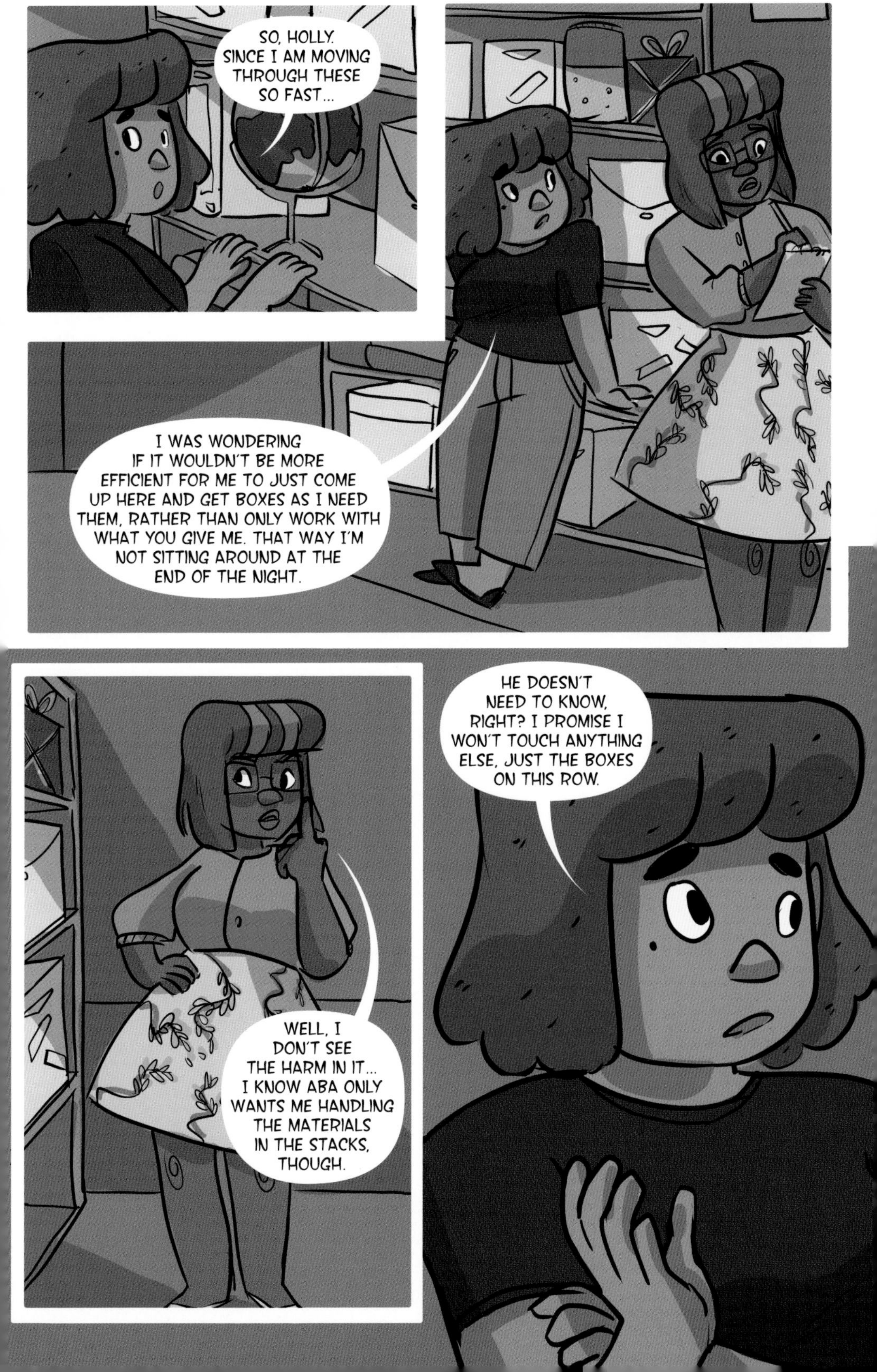
SO, HOLLY. SINCE I AM MOVING THROUGH THESE SO FAST...
I WAS WONDERING IF IT WOULDN'T BE MORE EFFICIENT FOR ME TO JUST COME UP HERE AND GET BOXES AS I NEED THEM, RATHER THAN ONLY WORK WITH WHAT YOU GIVE ME. THAT WAY I'M NOT SITTING AROUND AT THE END OF THE NIGHT.
WELL, I DON'T SEE THE HARM IN IT... I KNOW ABA ONLY WANTS ME HANDLING THE MATERIALS IN THE STACKS, THOUGH.
HE DOESN'T NEED TO KNOW, RIGHT? I PROMISE I WON'T TOUCH ANYTHING ELSE, JUST THE BOXES ON THIS ROW.

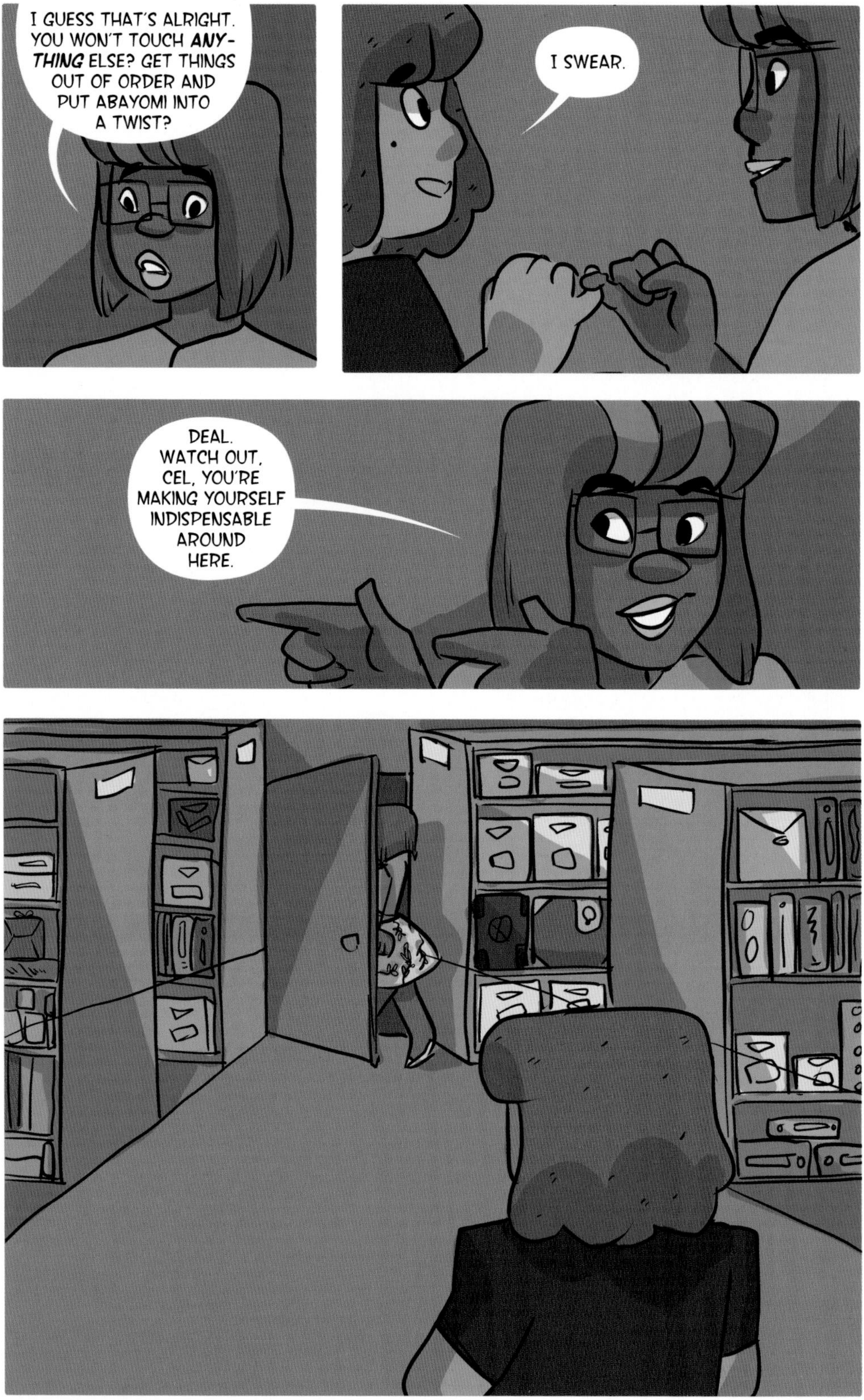
I GUESS THAT'S ALRIGHT. YOU WON'T TOUCH **ANYTHING** ELSE? GET THINGS OUT OF ORDER AND PUT ABAYOMI INTO A TWIST?
I SWEAR.
DEAL. WATCH OUT, CEL, YOU'RE MAKING YOURSELF INDISPENSABLE AROUND HERE.

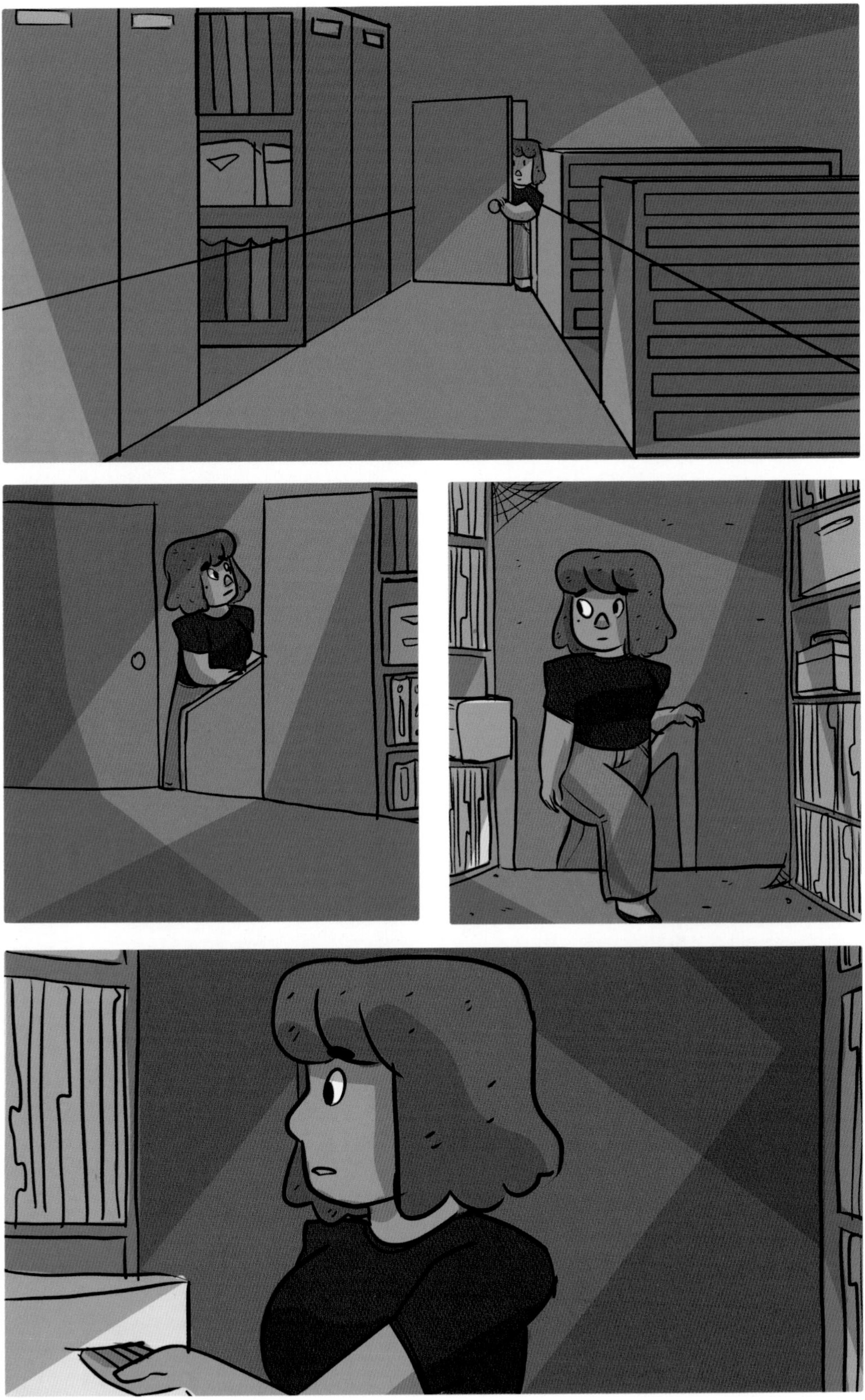

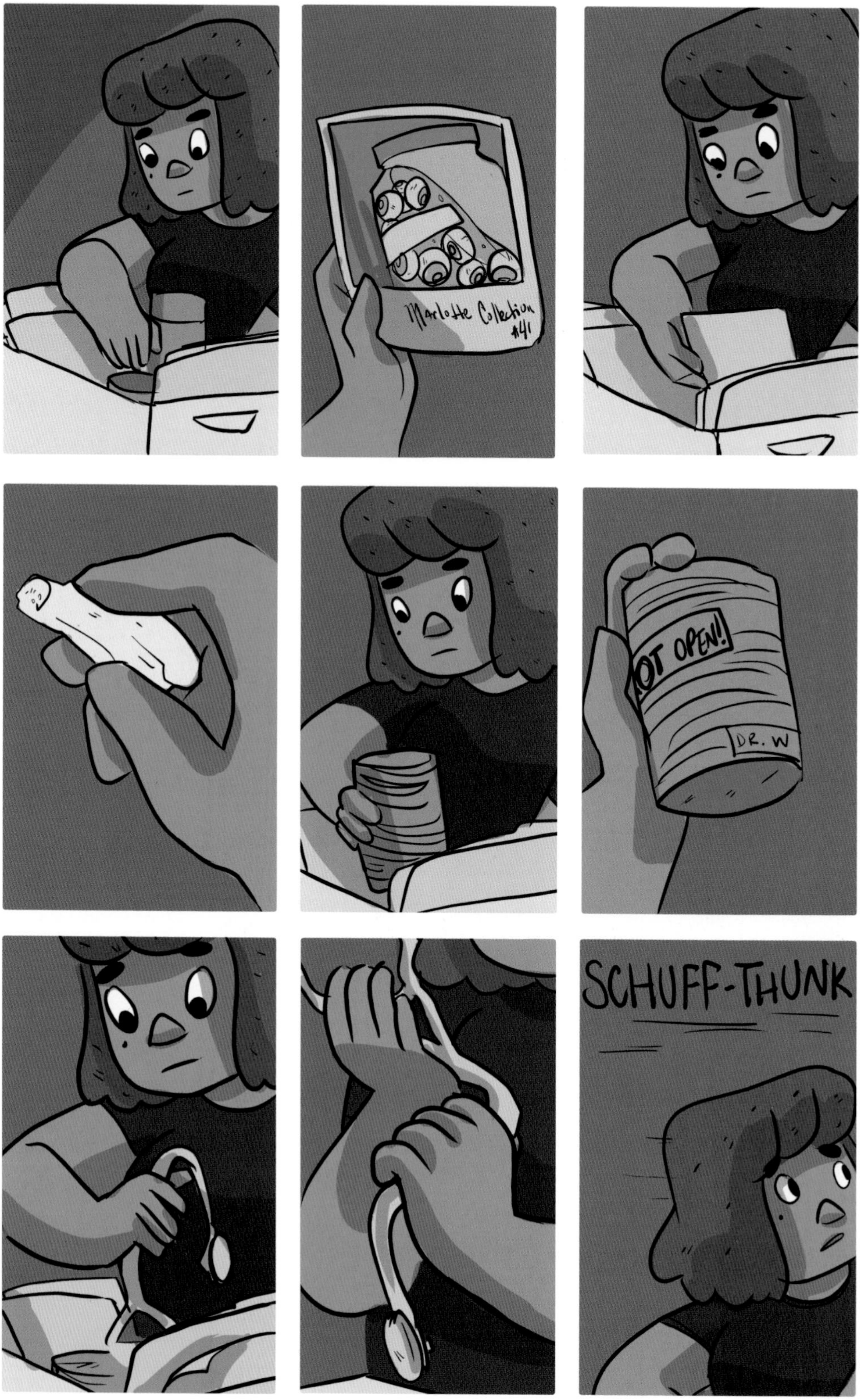
Marlotte Collection #41
OT OPEN!
DR. W
SCHUFF-THUNK

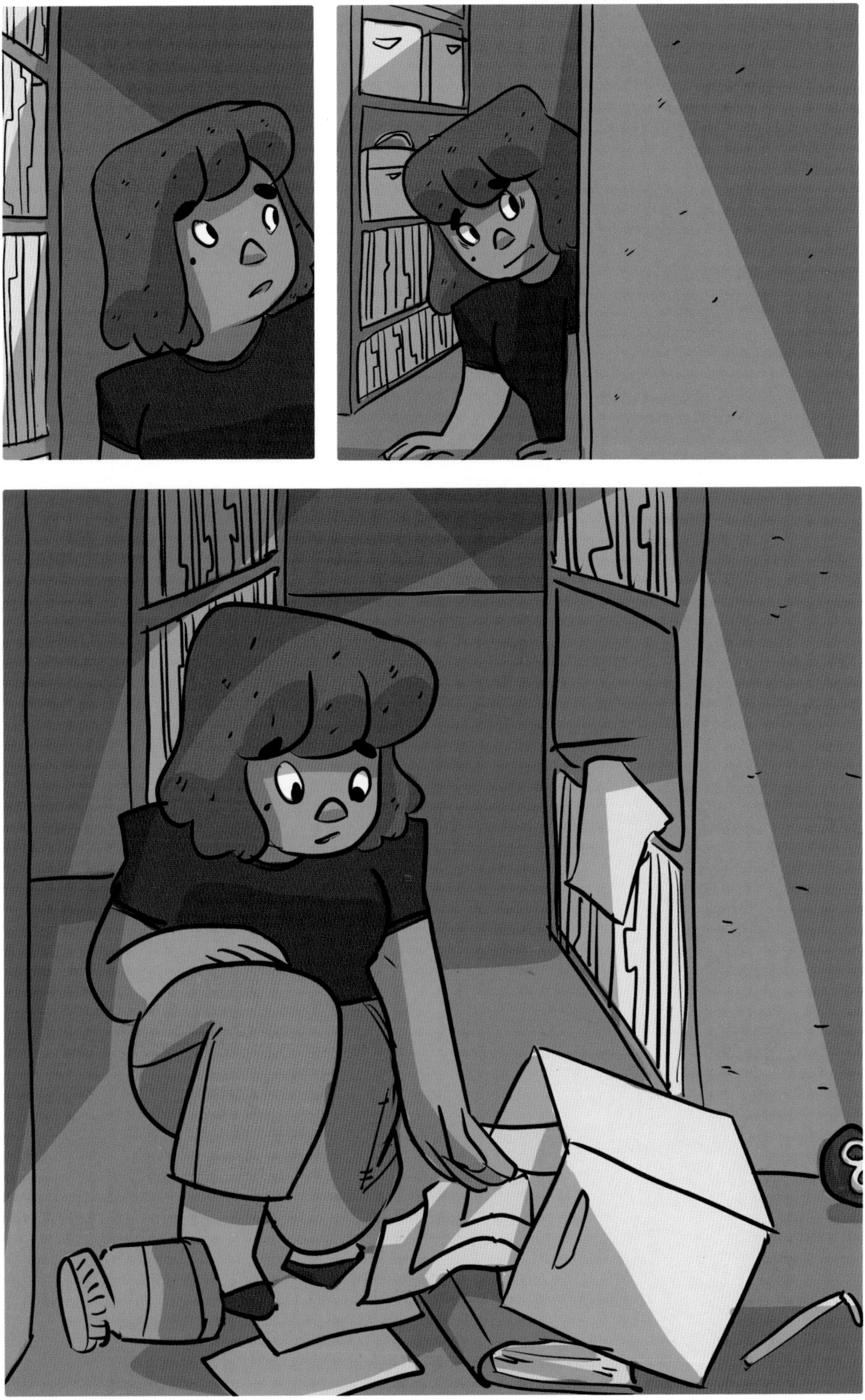

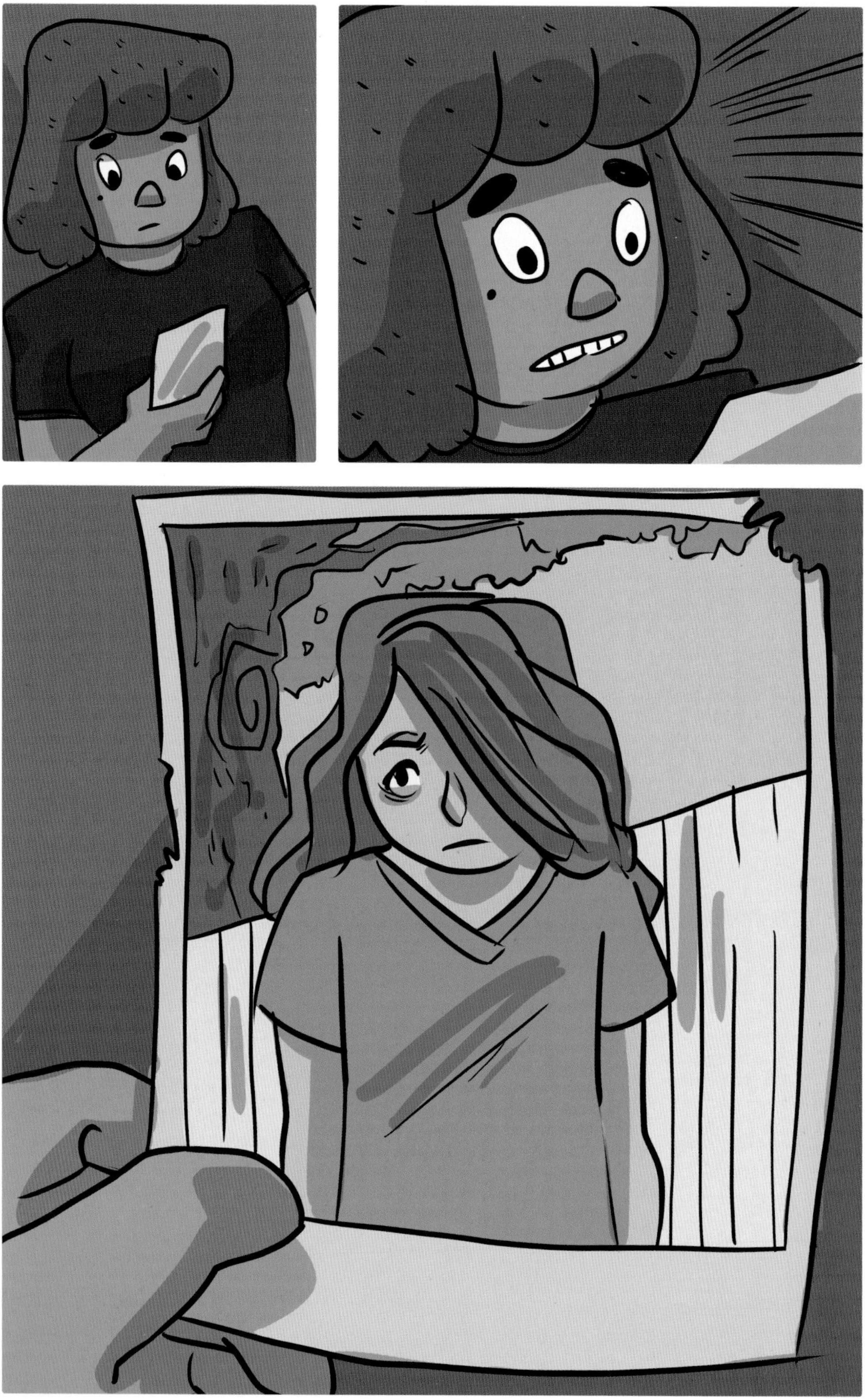

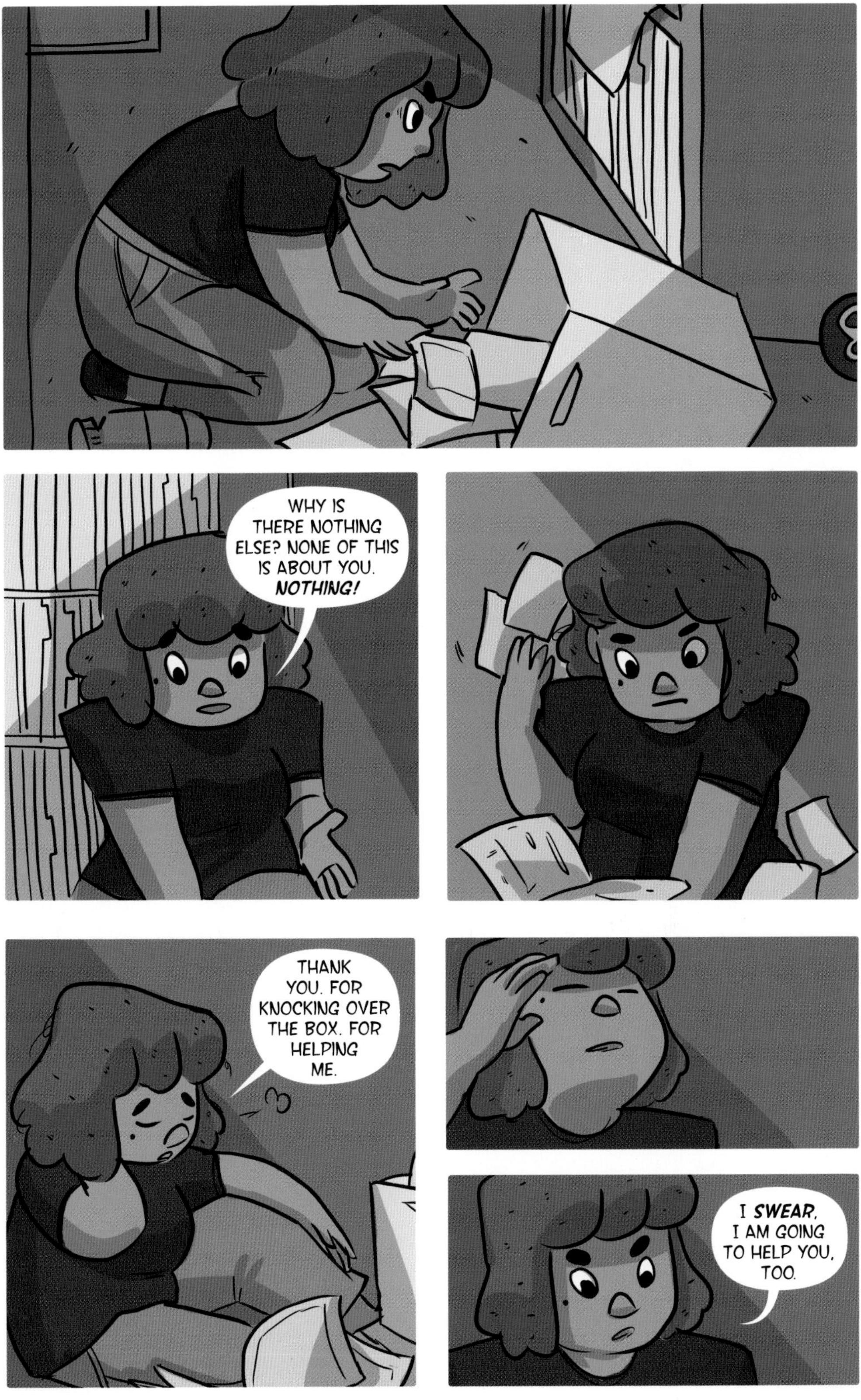
WHY IS THERE NOTHING ELSE? NONE OF THIS IS ABOUT YOU. *NOTHING!*
THANK YOU. FOR KNOCKING OVER THE BOX. FOR HELPING ME.
I *SWEAR*, I AM GOING TO HELP YOU, TOO.

ONE WEEK LATER

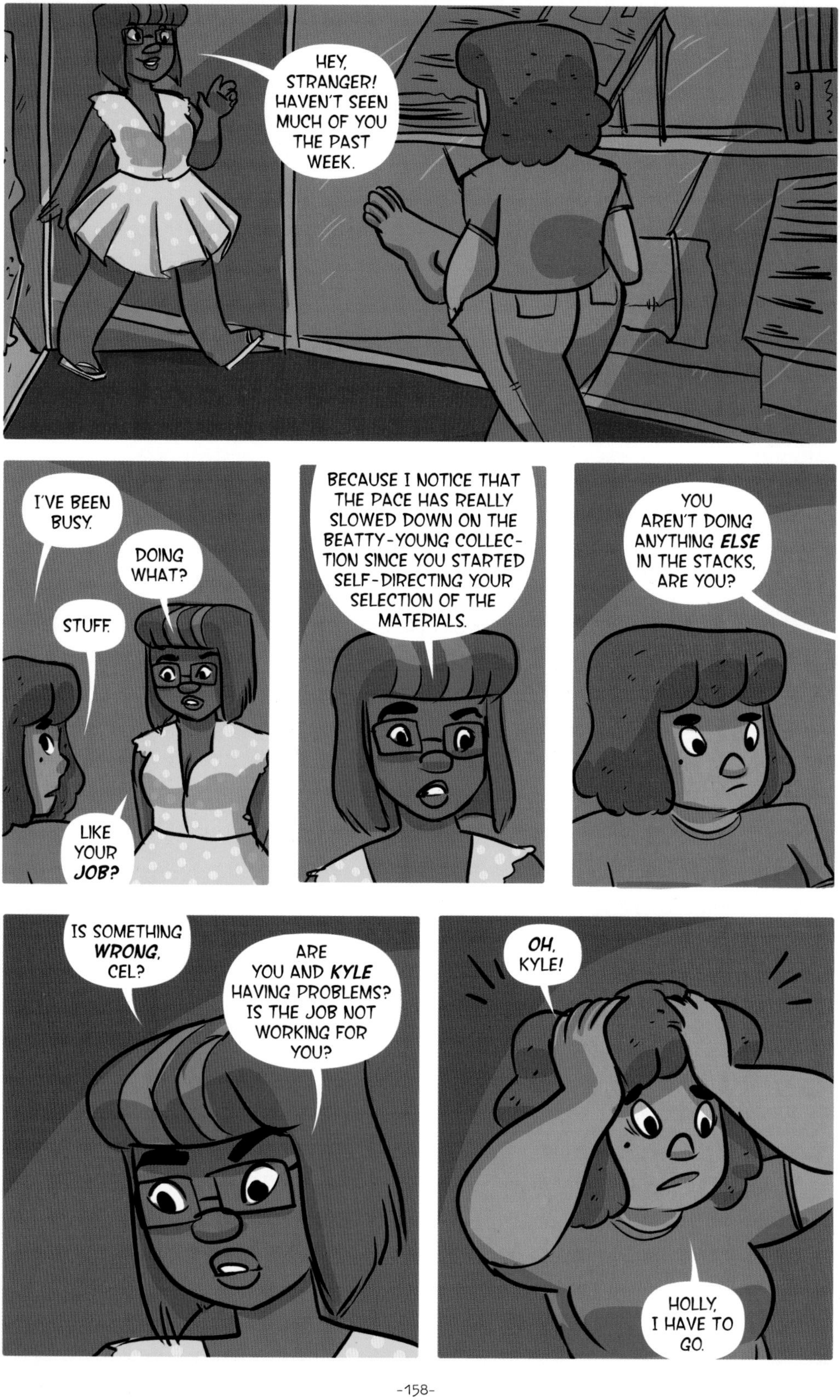
HEY, STRANGER! HAVEN'T SEEN MUCH OF YOU THE PAST WEEK.
I'VE BEEN BUSY.
DOING WHAT?
STUFF.
LIKE YOUR JOB?
BECAUSE I NOTICE THAT THE PACE HAS REALLY SLOWED DOWN ON THE BEATTY-YOUNG COLLECTION SINCE YOU STARTED SELF-DIRECTING YOUR SELECTION OF THE MATERIALS.
YOU AREN'T DOING ANYTHING ELSE IN THE STACKS, ARE YOU?
IS SOMETHING WRONG, CEL?
ARE YOU AND KYLE HAVING PROBLEMS? IS THE JOB NOT WORKING FOR YOU?
OH, KYLE!
HOLLY, I HAVE TO GO.

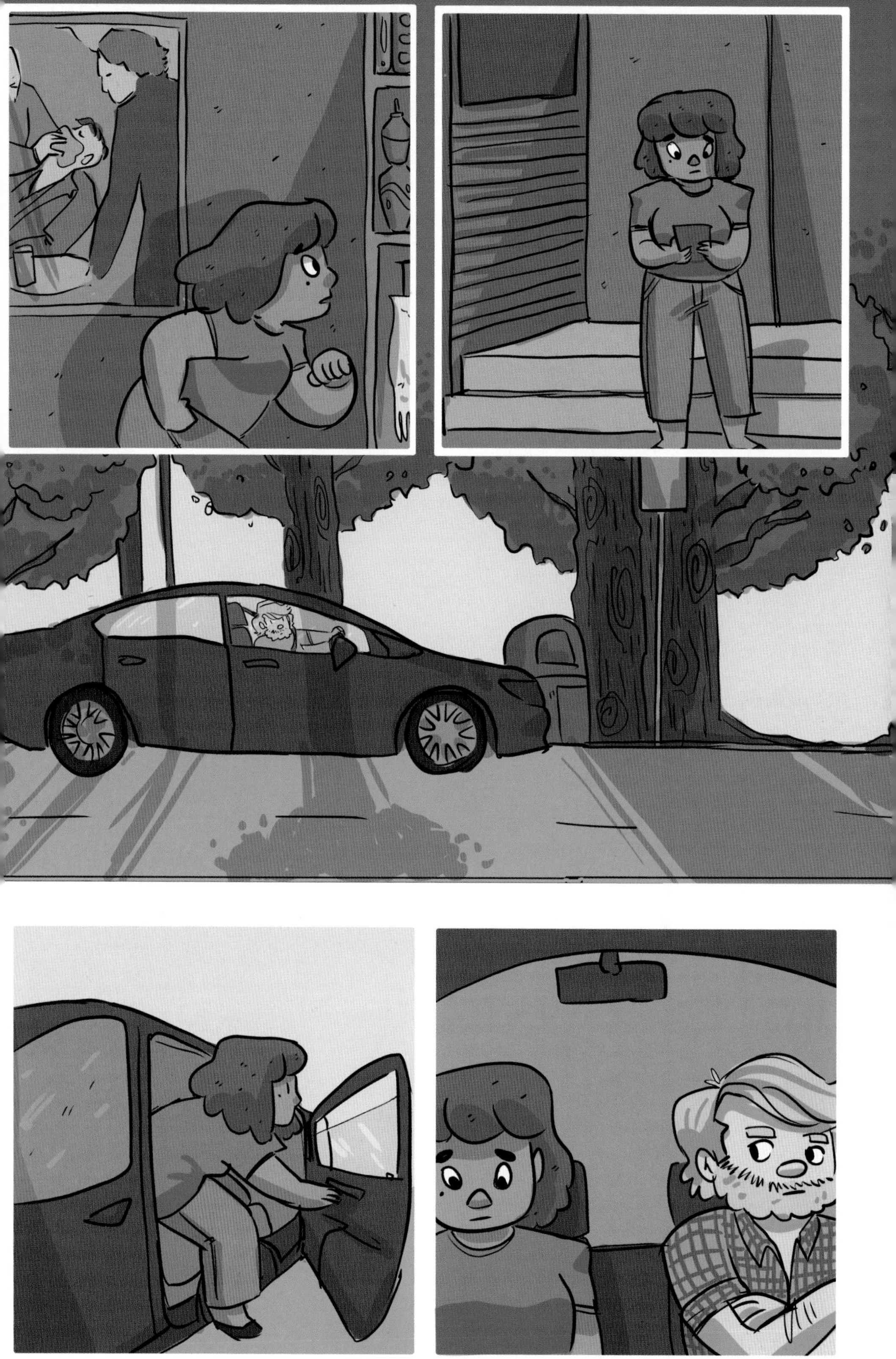

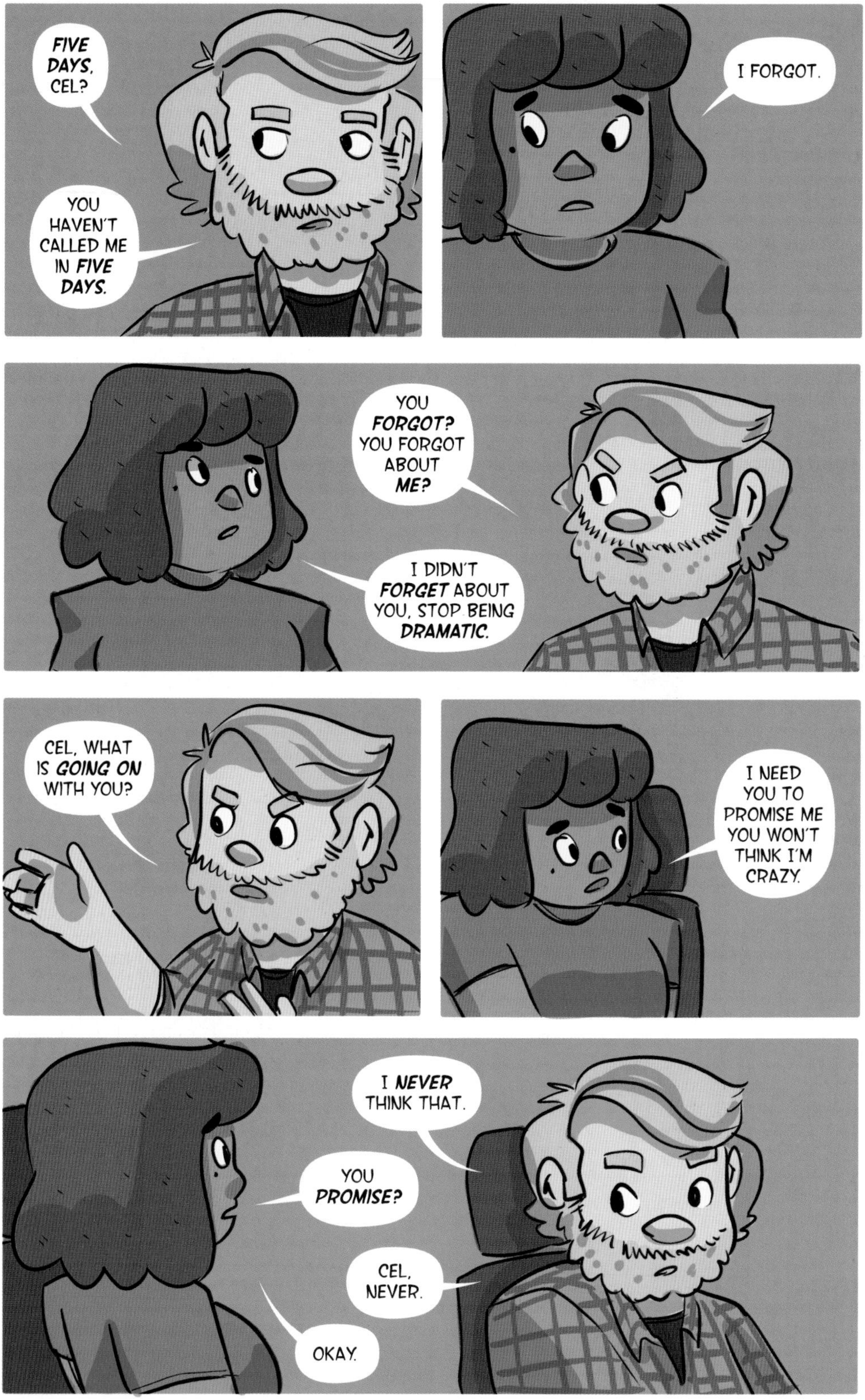
FIVE DAYS, CEL?
YOU HAVEN'T CALLED ME IN FIVE DAYS.
I FORGOT.
YOU FORGOT? YOU FORGOT ABOUT ME?
I DIDN'T FORGET ABOUT YOU, STOP BEING DRAMATIC.
CEL, WHAT IS GOING ON WITH YOU?
I NEED YOU TO PROMISE ME YOU WON'T THINK I'M CRAZY.
I NEVER THINK THAT.
YOU PROMISE?
CEL, NEVER.
OKAY.

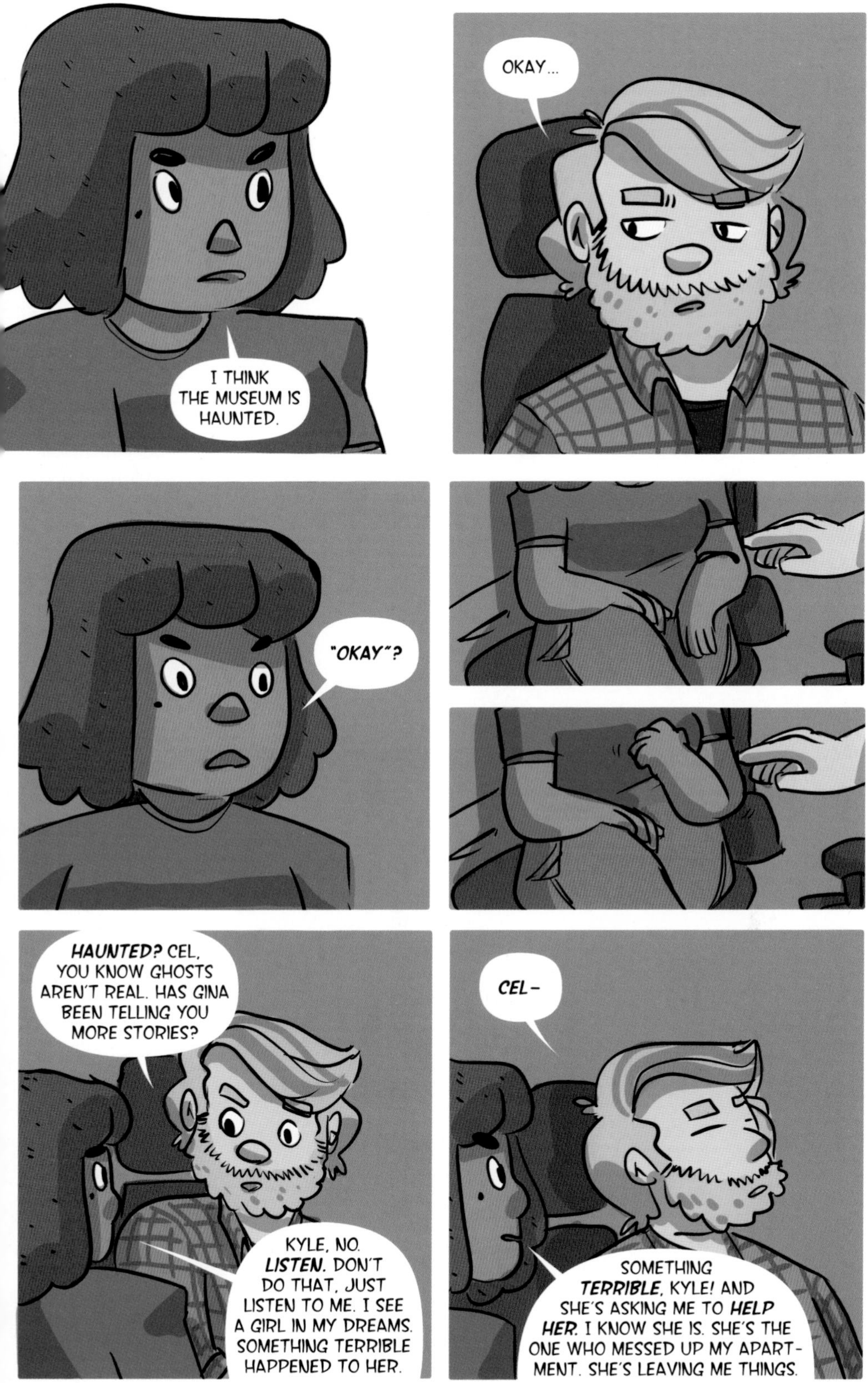
I THINK THE MUSEUM IS HAUNTED.
OKAY...
"OKAY"?
HAUNTED? CEL, YOU KNOW GHOSTS AREN'T REAL. HAS GINA BEEN TELLING YOU MORE STORIES?
KYLE, NO. LISTEN. DON'T DO THAT, JUST LISTEN TO ME. I SEE A GIRL IN MY DREAMS. SOMETHING TERRIBLE HAPPENED TO HER.
CEL-
SOMETHING TERRIBLE, KYLE! AND SHE'S ASKING ME TO HELP HER. I KNOW SHE IS. SHE'S THE ONE WHO MESSED UP MY APARTMENT. SHE'S LEAVING ME THINGS.

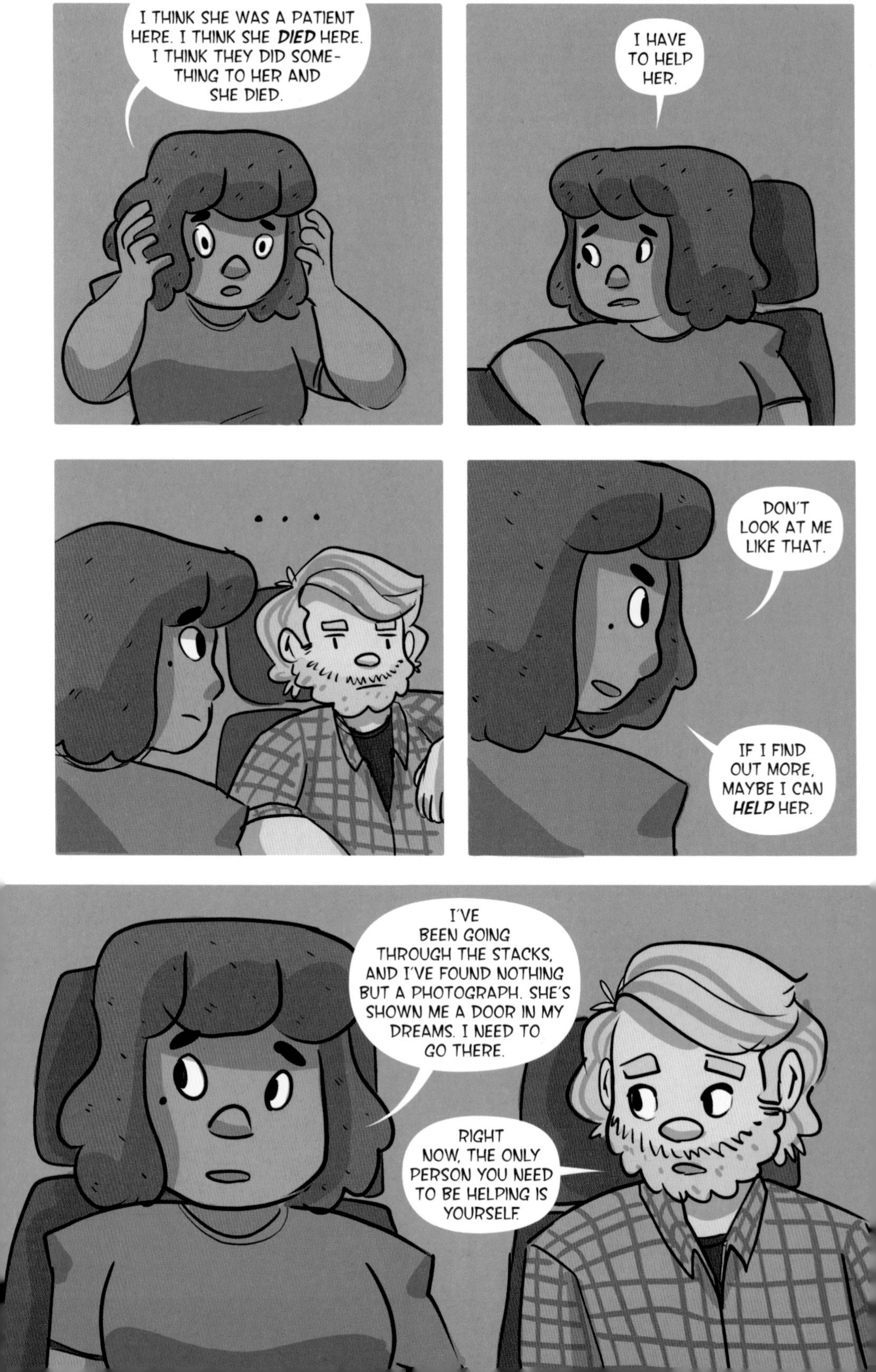
I THINK SHE WAS A PATIENT HERE. I THINK SHE *DIED* HERE. I THINK THEY DID SOME-THING TO HER AND SHE DIED.
I HAVE TO HELP HER.
. . .
DON'T LOOK AT ME LIKE THAT.
IF I FIND OUT MORE, MAYBE I CAN *HELP* HER.
I'VE BEEN GOING THROUGH THE STACKS, AND I'VE FOUND NOTHING BUT A PHOTOGRAPH. SHE'S SHOWN ME A DOOR IN MY DREAMS. I NEED TO GO THERE.
RIGHT NOW, THE ONLY PERSON YOU NEED TO BE HELPING IS YOURSELF.

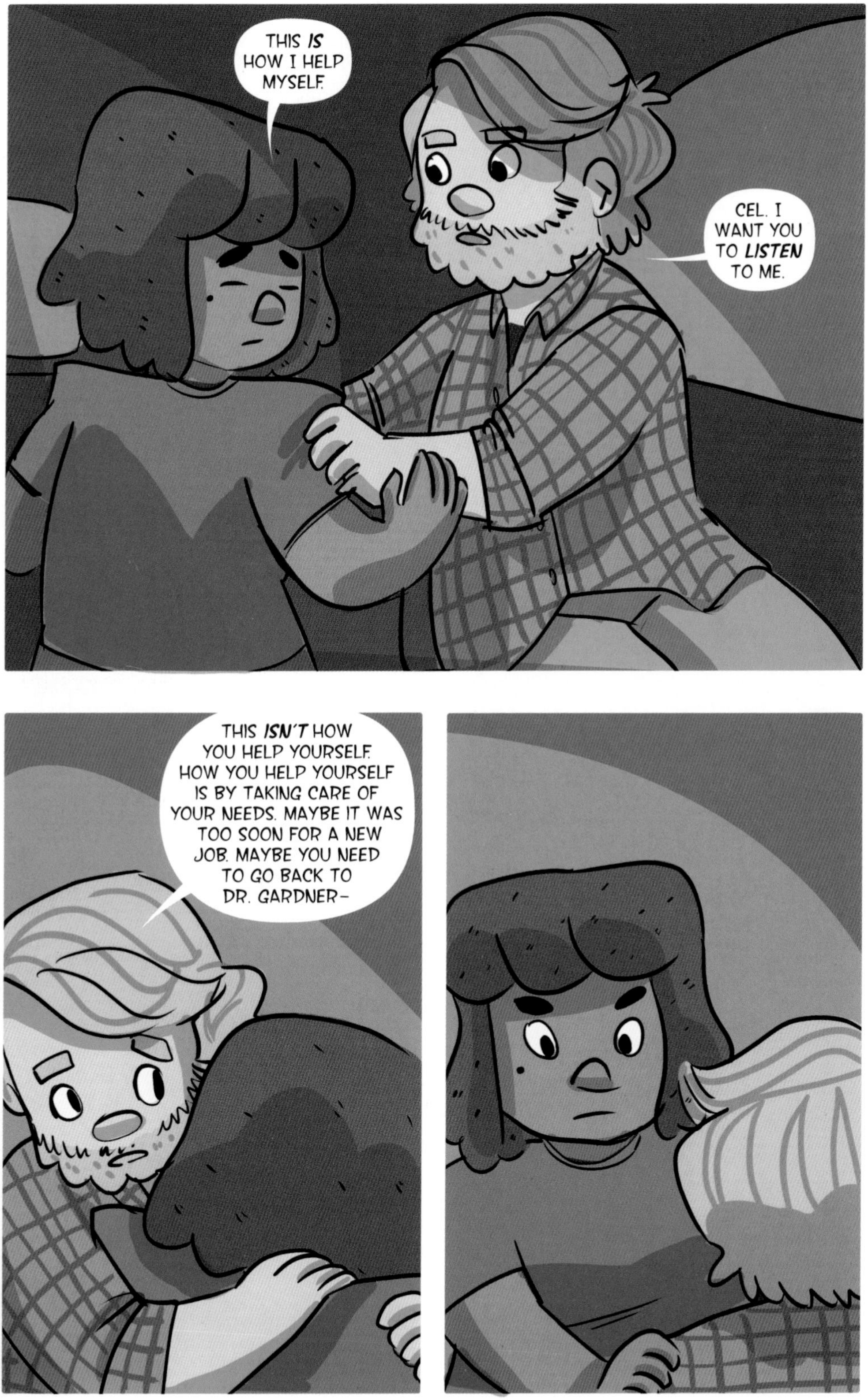
THIS IS HOW I HELP MYSELF.
CEL. I WANT YOU TO LISTEN TO ME.
THIS ISN'T HOW YOU HELP YOURSELF. HOW YOU HELP YOURSELF IS BY TAKING CARE OF YOUR NEEDS. MAYBE IT WAS TOO SOON FOR A NEW JOB. MAYBE YOU NEED TO GO BACK TO DR. GARDNER-

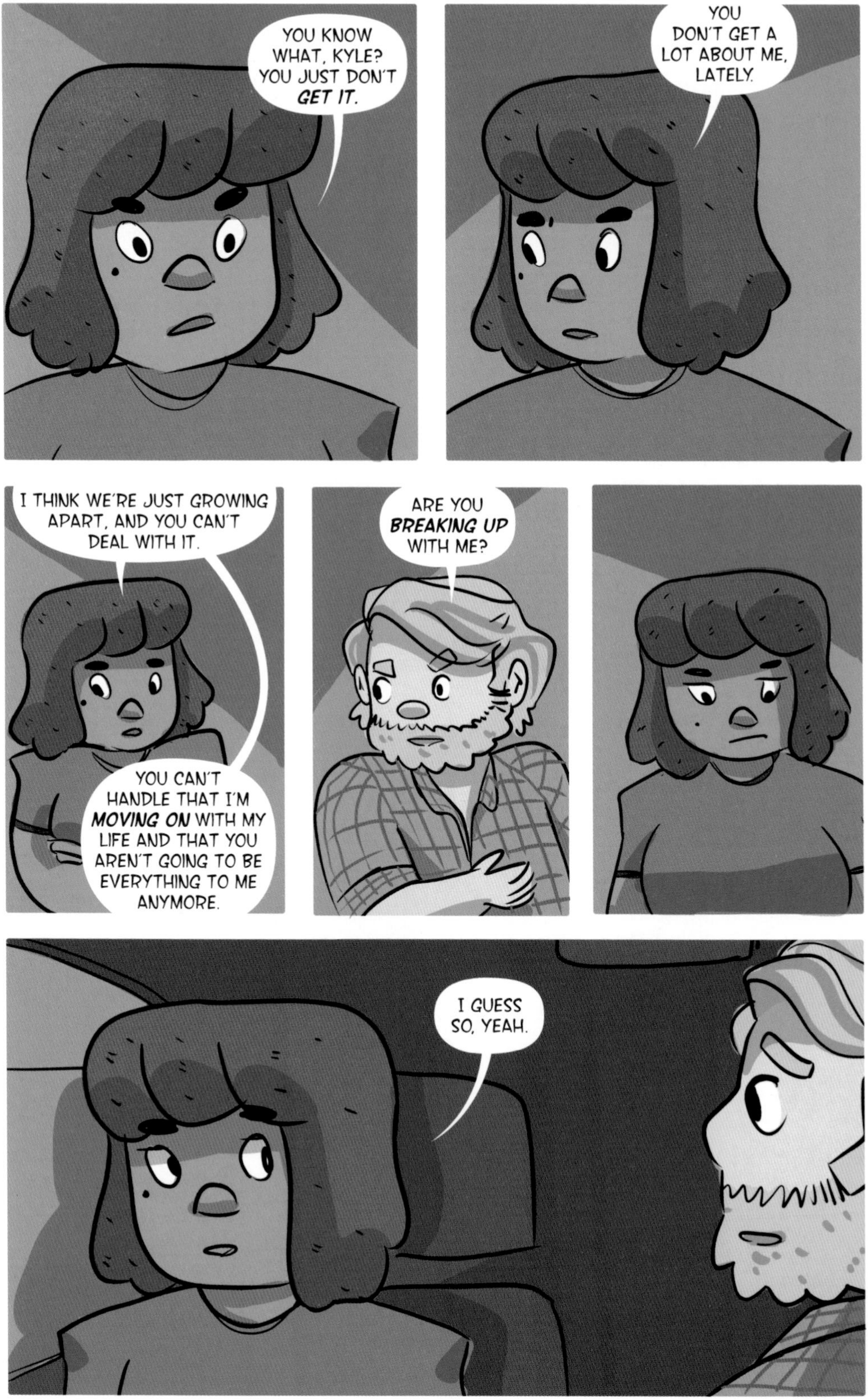
YOU KNOW WHAT, KYLE? YOU JUST DON'T **GET IT**.
YOU DON'T GET A LOT ABOUT ME, LATELY.
I THINK WE'RE JUST GROWING APART, AND YOU CAN'T DEAL WITH IT.
YOU CAN'T HANDLE THAT I'M **MOVING ON** WITH MY LIFE AND THAT YOU AREN'T GOING TO BE EVERYTHING TO ME ANYMORE.
ARE YOU **BREAKING UP** WITH ME?
I GUESS SO, YEAH.

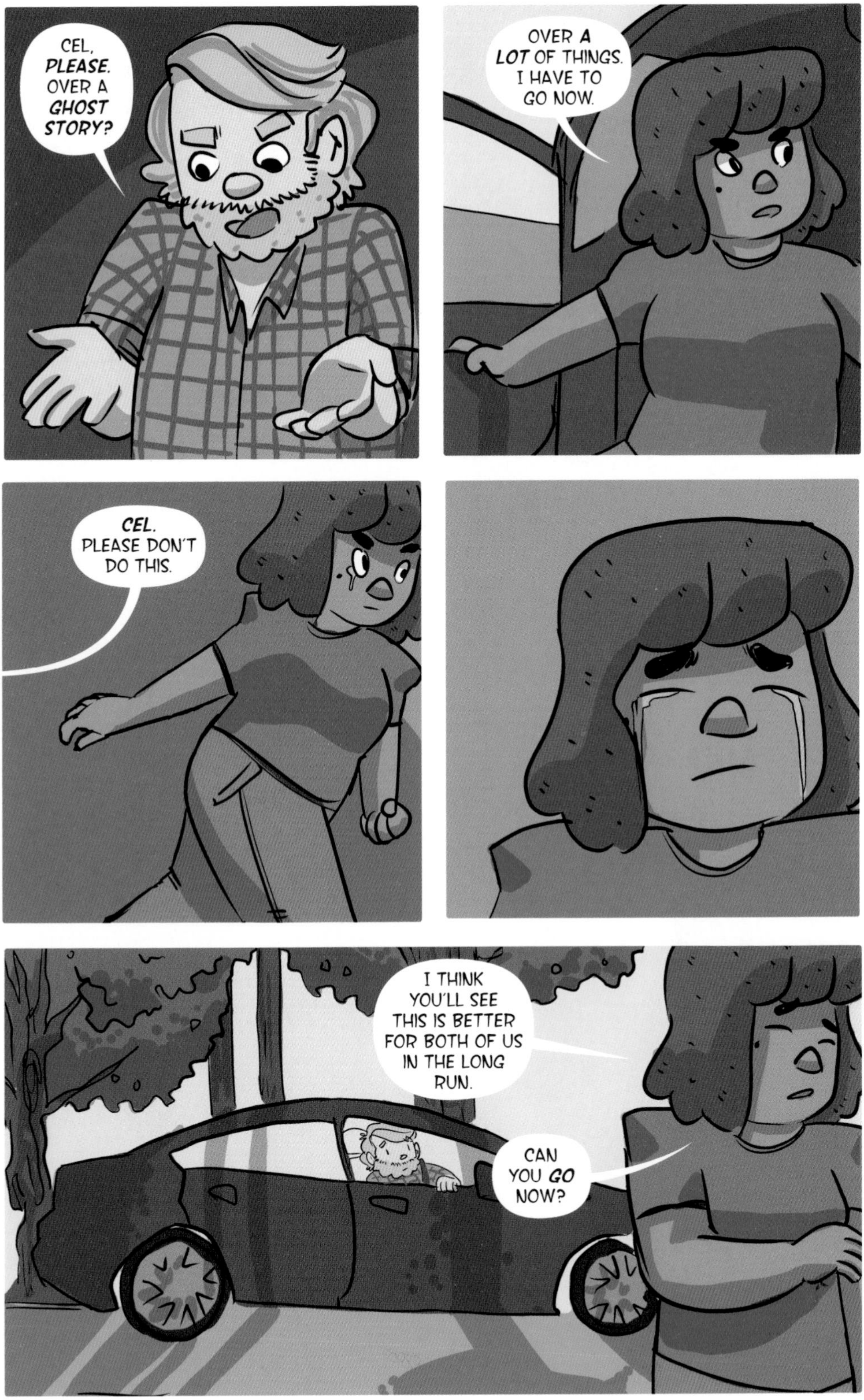
CEL, PLEASE. OVER A GHOST STORY?
OVER A LOT OF THINGS. I HAVE TO GO NOW.
CEL. PLEASE DON'T DO THIS.
I THINK YOU'LL SEE THIS IS BETTER FOR BOTH OF US IN THE LONG RUN.
CAN YOU GO NOW?

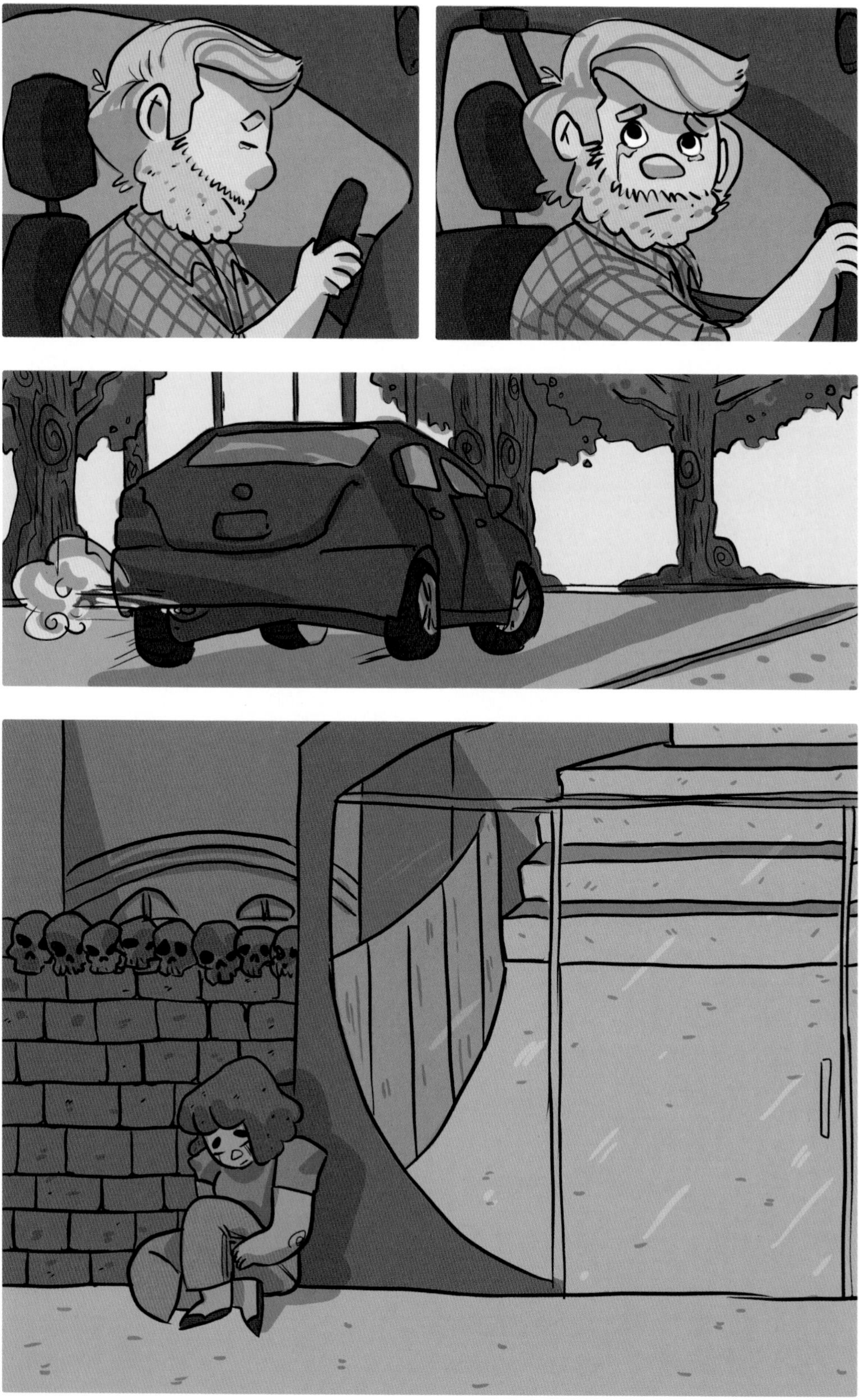

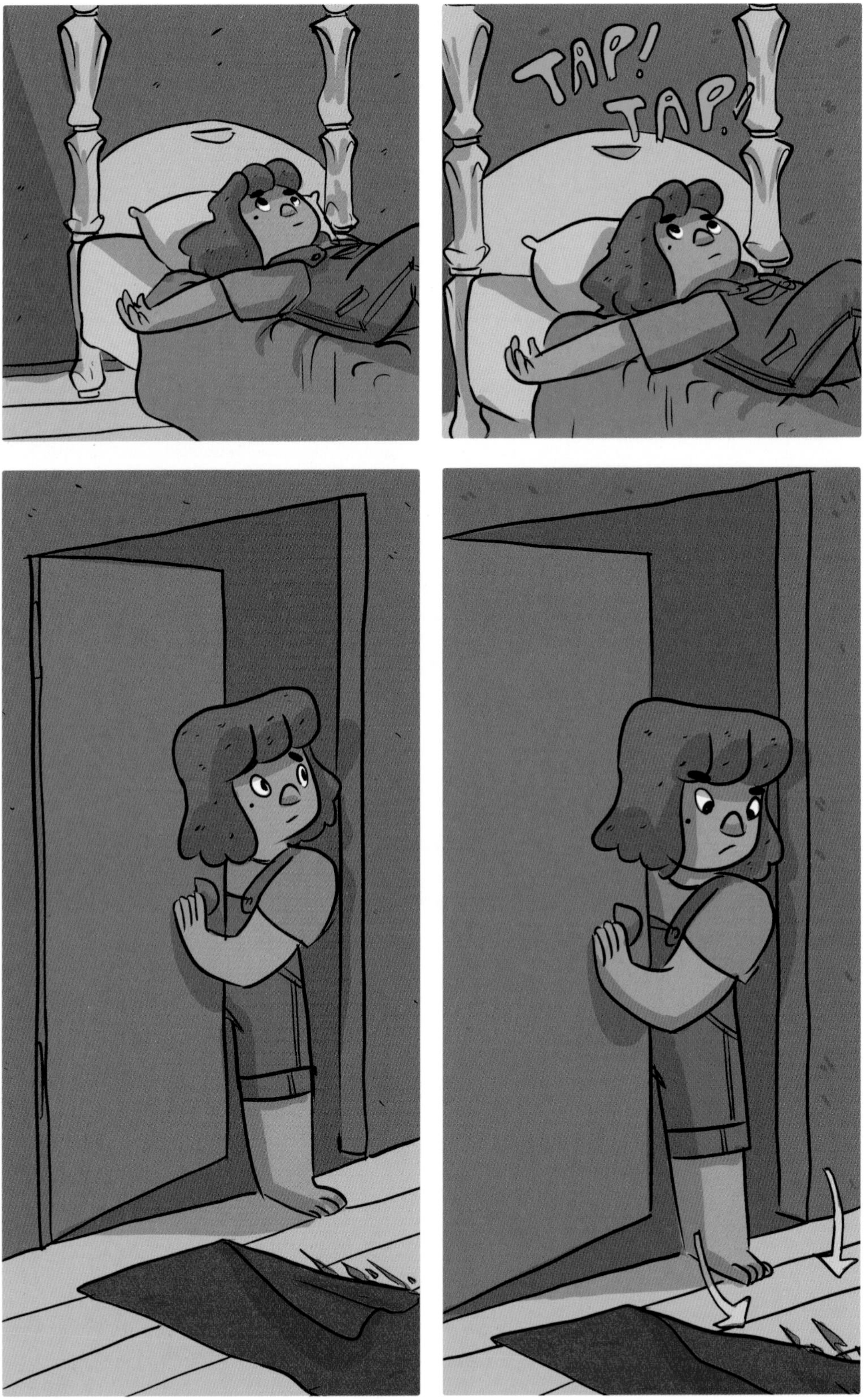
TAP!
TAP!

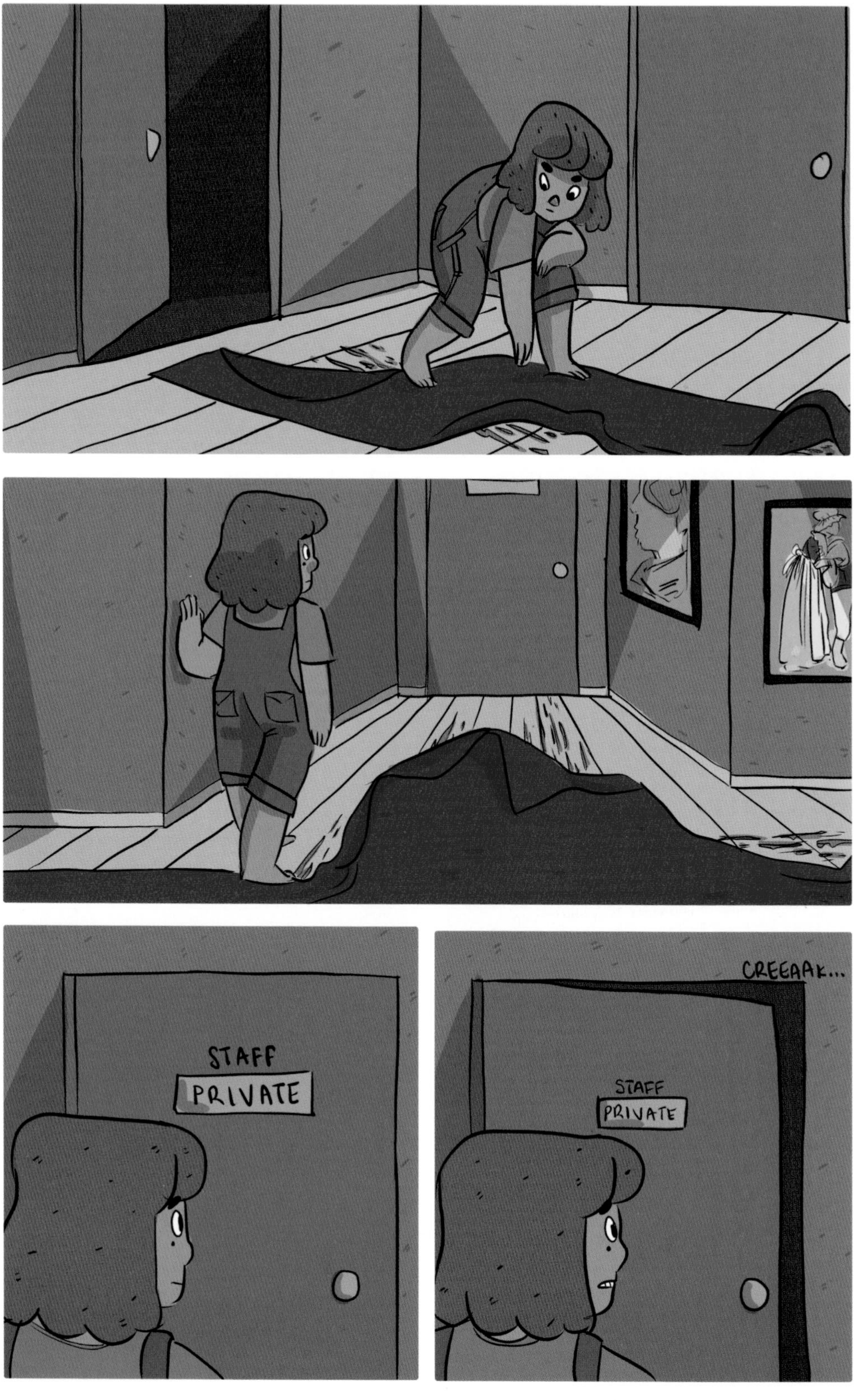
STAFF
PRIVATE
CREEAAK...
STAFF
PRIVATE

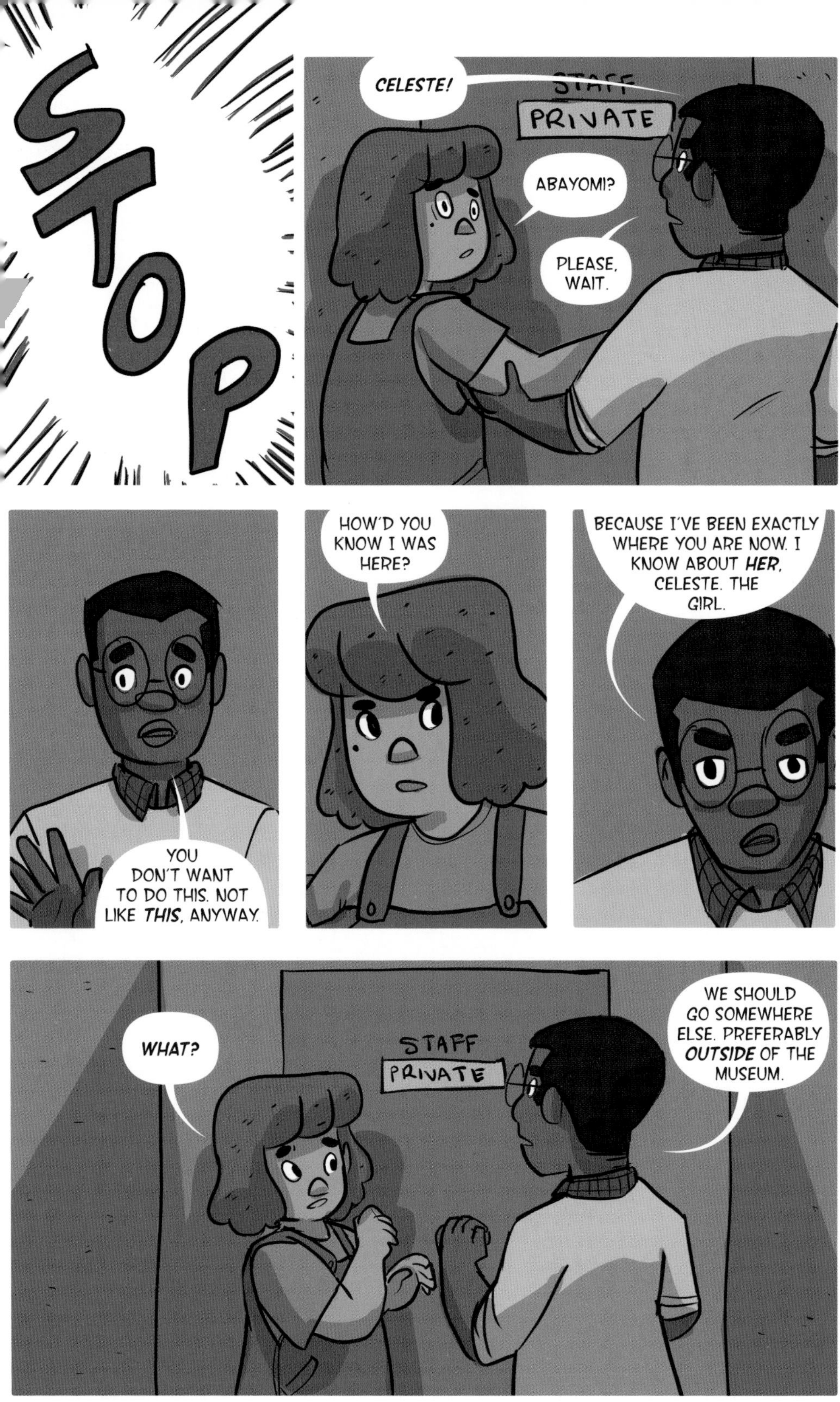
STOP
CELESTE!
STAFF
PRIVATE
ABAYOMI?
PLEASE, WAIT.
YOU DON'T WANT TO DO THIS. NOT LIKE THIS, ANYWAY.
HOW'D YOU KNOW I WAS HERE?
BECAUSE I'VE BEEN EXACTLY WHERE YOU ARE NOW. I KNOW ABOUT HER, CELESTE. THE GIRL.
WHAT?
STAFF
PRIVATE
WE SHOULD GO SOMEWHERE ELSE. PREFERABLY OUTSIDE OF THE MUSEUM.

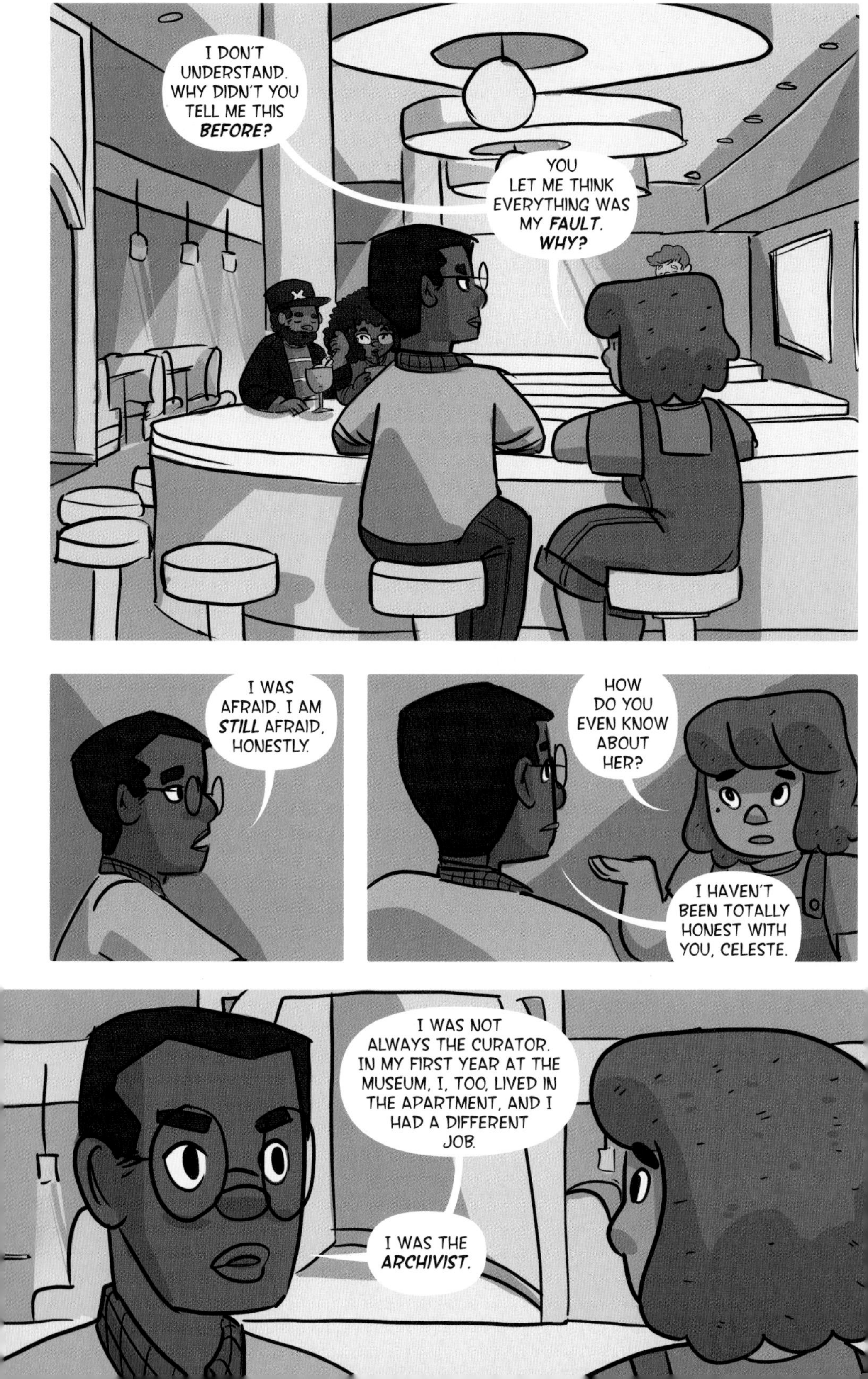
I DON'T UNDERSTAND. WHY DIDN'T YOU TELL ME THIS BEFORE?
YOU LET ME THINK EVERYTHING WAS MY FAULT. WHY?
I WAS AFRAID. I AM STILL AFRAID, HONESTLY.
HOW DO YOU EVEN KNOW ABOUT HER?
I HAVEN'T BEEN TOTALLY HONEST WITH YOU, CELESTE.
I WAS NOT ALWAYS THE CURATOR. IN MY FIRST YEAR AT THE MUSEUM, I, TOO, LIVED IN THE APARTMENT, AND I HAD A DIFFERENT JOB.
I WAS THE ARCHIVIST.

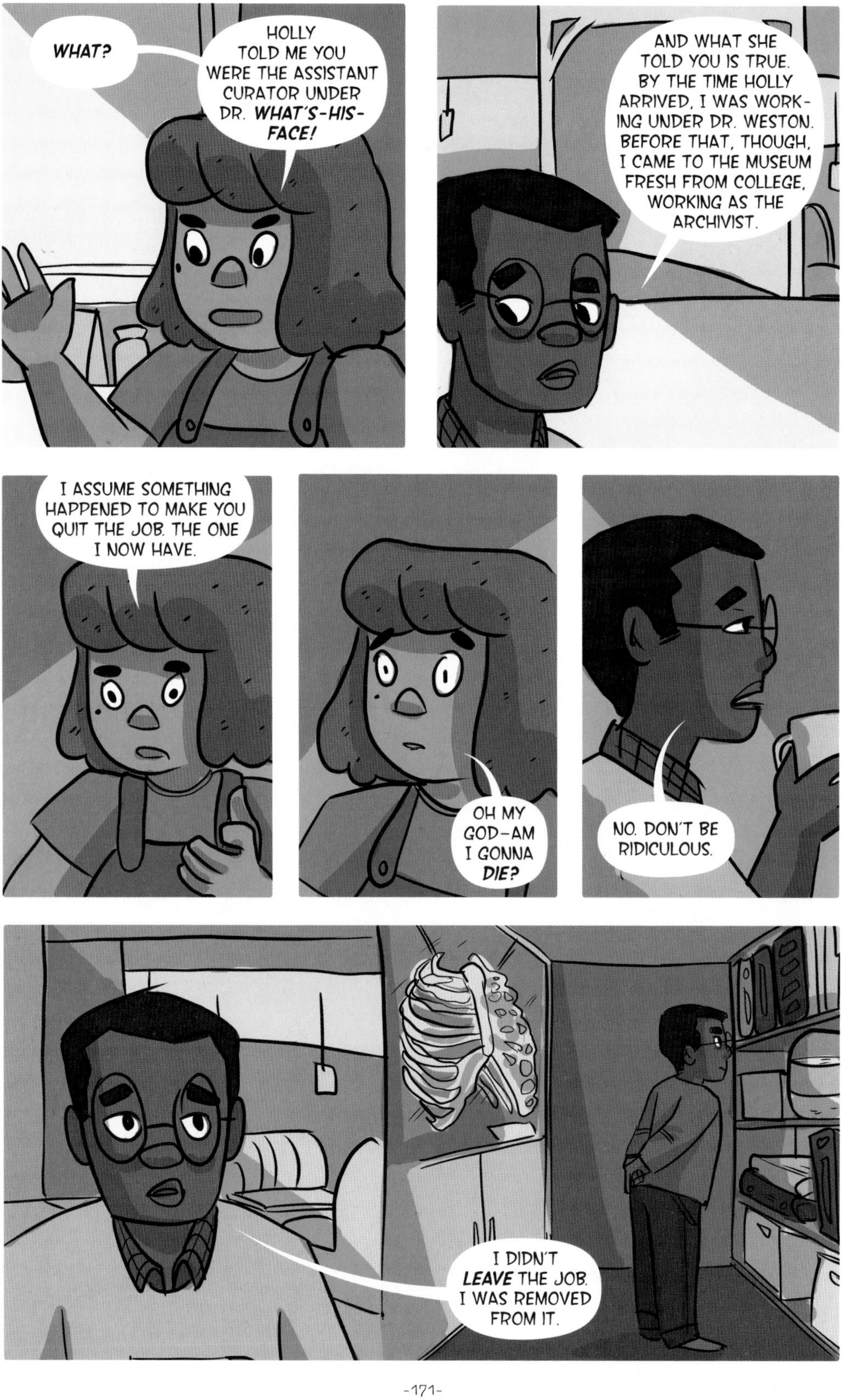
WHAT?
HOLLY TOLD ME YOU WERE THE ASSISTANT CURATOR UNDER DR. WHAT'S-HIS-FACE!
AND WHAT SHE TOLD YOU IS TRUE. BY THE TIME HOLLY ARRIVED, I WAS WORKING UNDER DR. WESTON. BEFORE THAT, THOUGH, I CAME TO THE MUSEUM FRESH FROM COLLEGE, WORKING AS THE ARCHIVIST.
I ASSUME SOMETHING HAPPENED TO MAKE YOU QUIT THE JOB. THE ONE I NOW HAVE.
OH MY GOD—AM I GONNA DIE?
NO. DON'T BE RIDICULOUS.
I DIDN'T LEAVE THE JOB. I WAS REMOVED FROM IT.

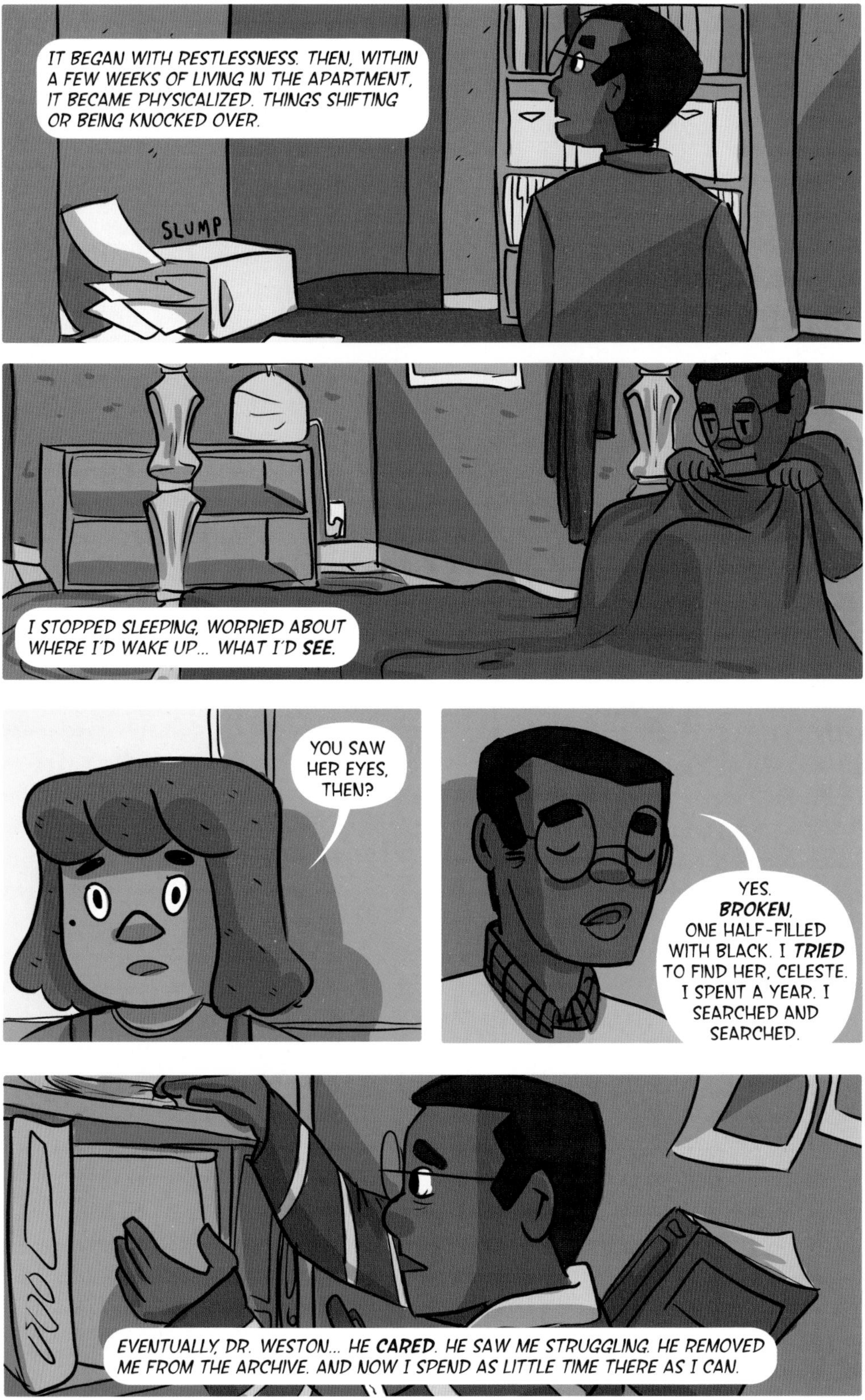
IT BEGAN WITH RESTLESSNESS. THEN, WITHIN A FEW WEEKS OF LIVING IN THE APARTMENT, IT BECAME PHYSICALIZED. THINGS SHIFTING OR BEING KNOCKED OVER.
SLUMP
I STOPPED SLEEPING, WORRIED ABOUT WHERE I'D WAKE UP... WHAT I'D **SEE.**
YOU SAW HER EYES, THEN?
YES. **BROKEN**, ONE HALF-FILLED WITH BLACK. I **TRIED** TO FIND HER, CELESTE. I SPENT A YEAR. I SEARCHED AND SEARCHED.
EVENTUALLY, DR. WESTON... HE **CARED**. HE SAW ME STRUGGLING. HE REMOVED ME FROM THE ARCHIVE. AND NOW I SPEND AS LITTLE TIME THERE AS I CAN.

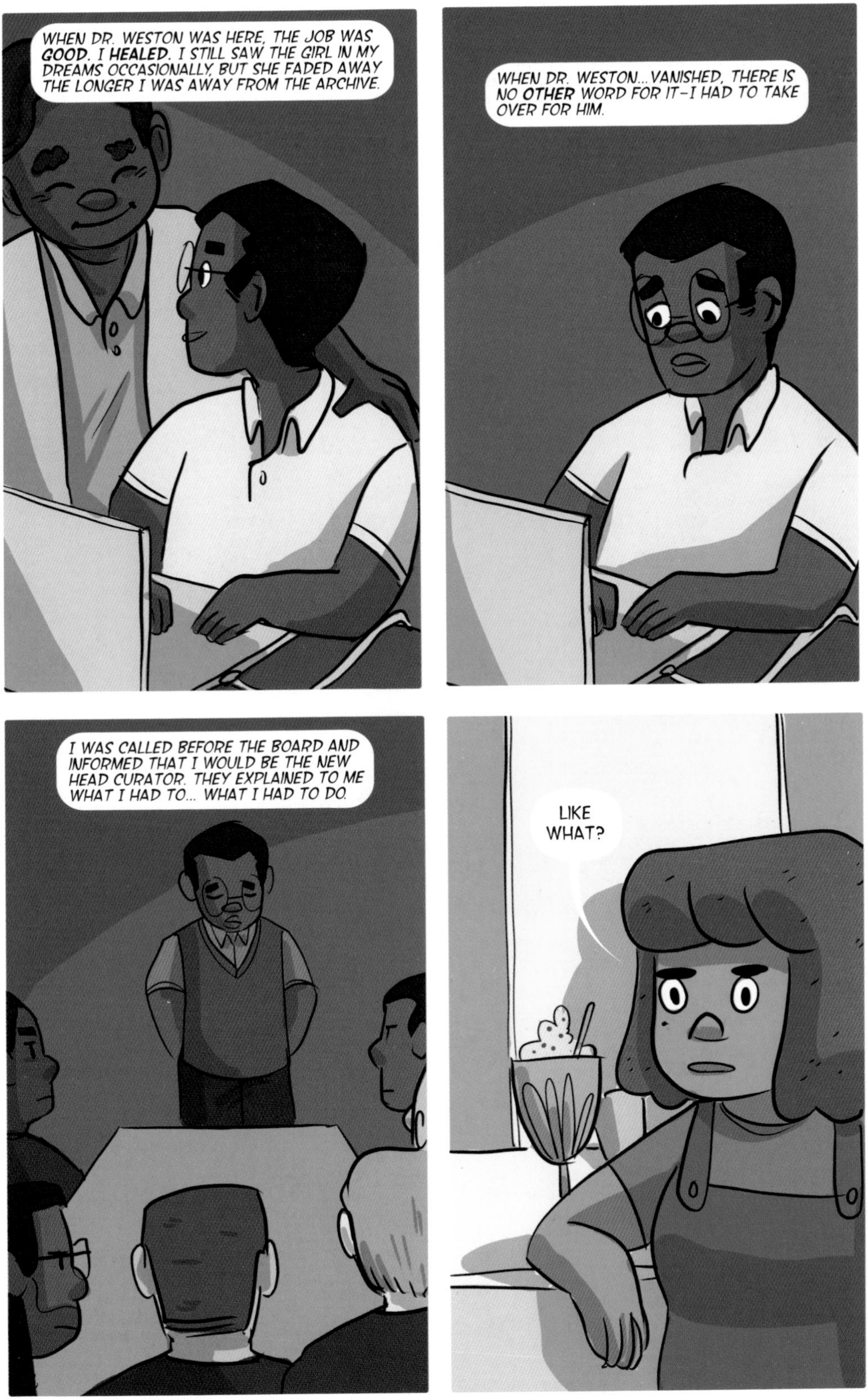
WHEN DR. WESTON WAS HERE, THE JOB WAS **GOOD**. I **HEALED**. I STILL SAW THE GIRL IN MY DREAMS OCCASIONALLY, BUT SHE FADED AWAY THE LONGER I WAS AWAY FROM THE ARCHIVE.
WHEN DR. WESTON... VANISHED, THERE IS NO **OTHER** WORD FOR IT—I HAD TO TAKE OVER FOR HIM.
I WAS CALLED BEFORE THE BOARD AND INFORMED THAT I WOULD BE THE NEW HEAD CURATOR. THEY EXPLAINED TO ME WHAT I HAD TO... WHAT I HAD TO DO.
LIKE WHAT?

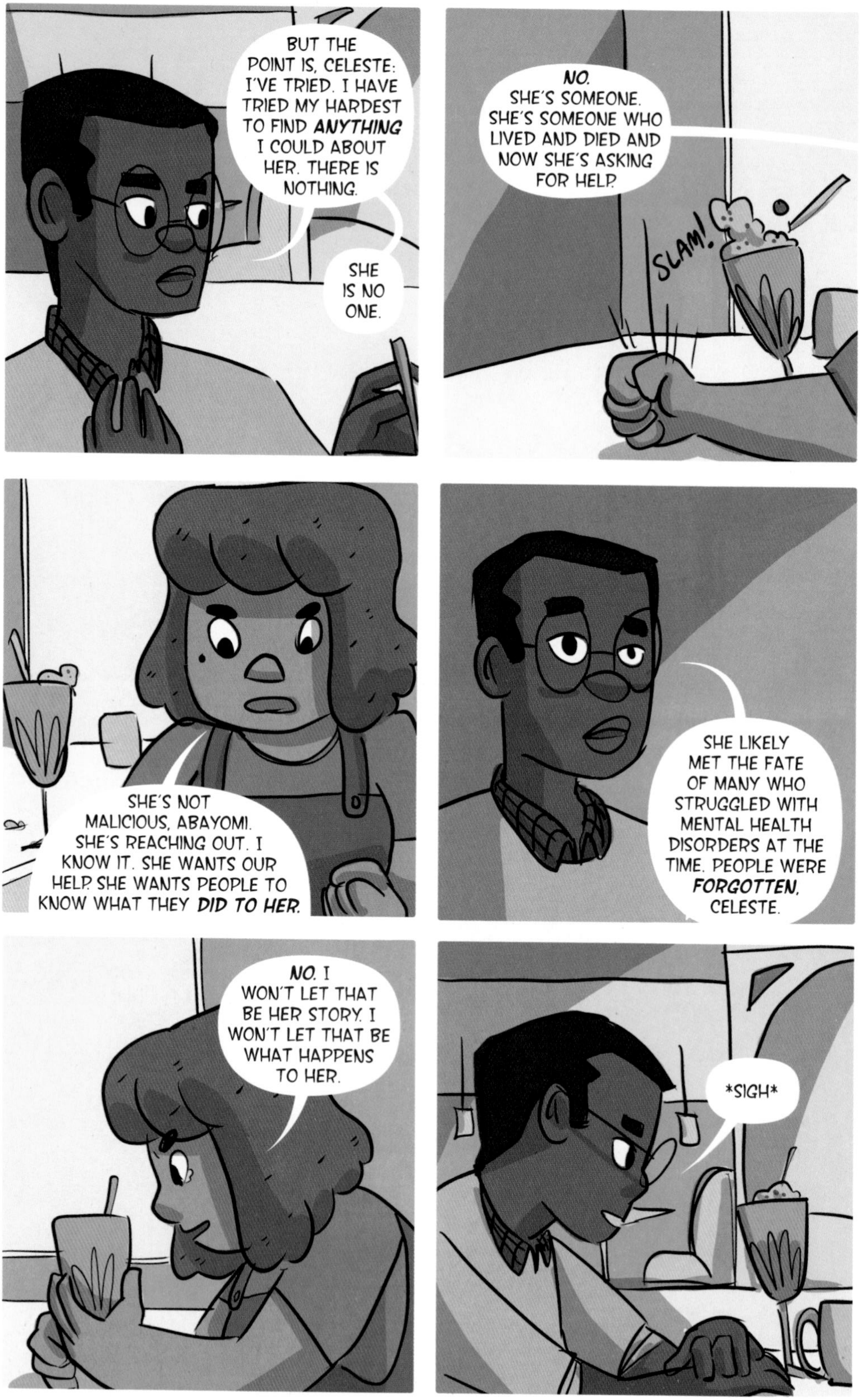
BUT THE POINT IS, CELESTE: I'VE TRIED. I HAVE TRIED MY HARDEST TO FIND **ANYTHING** I COULD ABOUT HER. THERE IS NOTHING.
SHE IS NO ONE.
NO. SHE'S SOMEONE. SHE'S SOMEONE WHO LIVED AND DIED AND NOW SHE'S ASKING FOR HELP.
SLAM!
SHE'S NOT MALICIOUS, ABAYOMI. SHE'S REACHING OUT. I KNOW IT. SHE WANTS OUR HELP. SHE WANTS PEOPLE TO KNOW WHAT THEY **DID TO HER.**
SHE LIKELY MET THE FATE OF MANY WHO STRUGGLED WITH MENTAL HEALTH DISORDERS AT THE TIME. PEOPLE WERE **FORGOTTEN,** CELESTE.
NO. I WON'T LET THAT BE HER STORY. I WON'T LET THAT BE WHAT HAPPENS TO HER.
SIGH

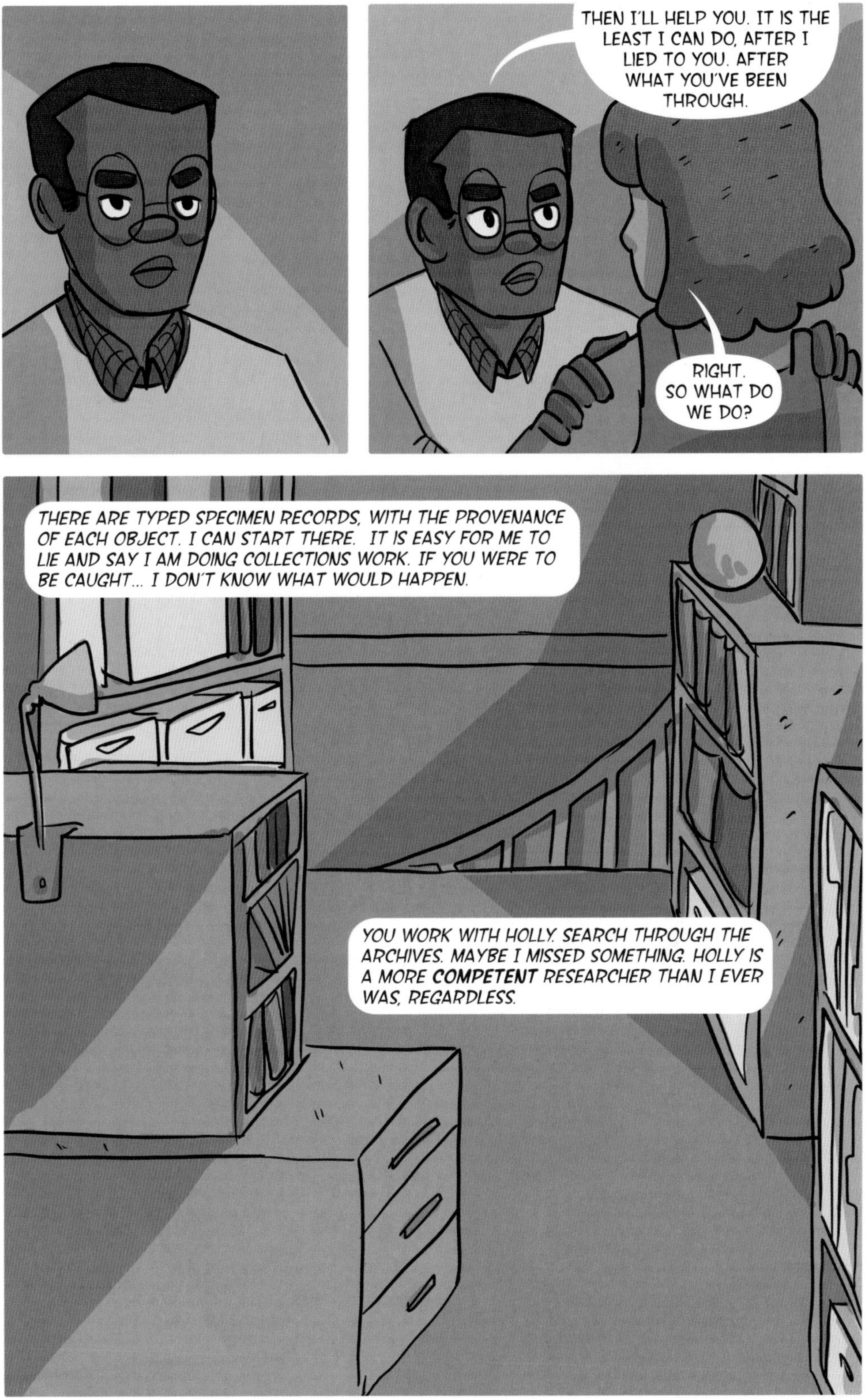
THEN I'LL HELP YOU. IT IS THE LEAST I CAN DO, AFTER I LIED TO YOU. AFTER WHAT YOU'VE BEEN THROUGH.
RIGHT. SO WHAT DO WE DO?
THERE ARE TYPED SPECIMEN RECORDS, WITH THE PROVENANCE OF EACH OBJECT. I CAN START THERE. IT IS EASY FOR ME TO LIE AND SAY I AM DOING COLLECTIONS WORK. IF YOU WERE TO BE CAUGHT... I DON'T KNOW WHAT WOULD HAPPEN.
YOU WORK WITH HOLLY. SEARCH THROUGH THE ARCHIVES. MAYBE I MISSED SOMETHING. HOLLY IS A MORE **COMPETENT** RESEARCHER THAN I EVER WAS, REGARDLESS.

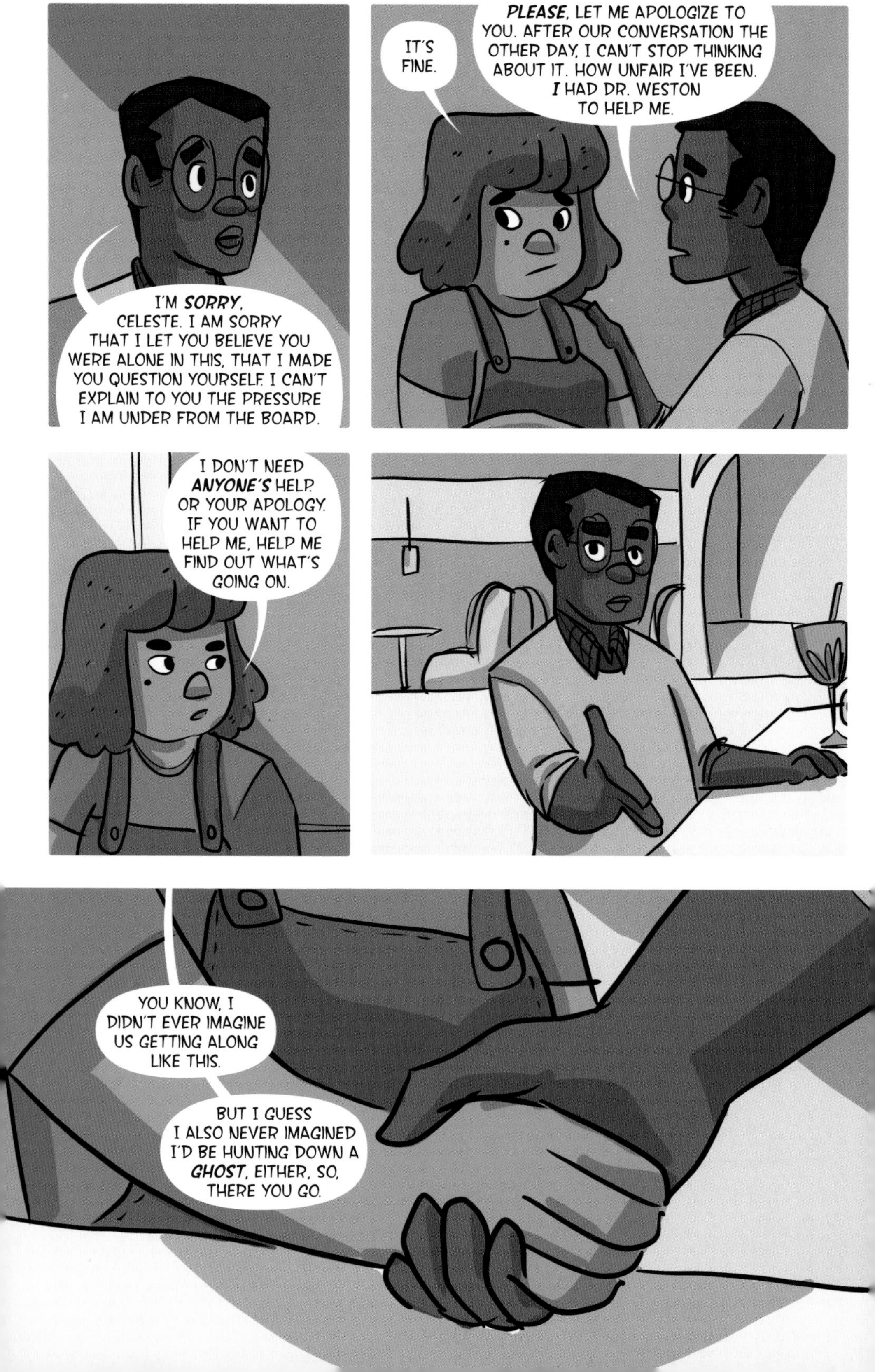
I'M **SORRY**, CELESTE. I AM SORRY THAT I LET YOU BELIEVE YOU WERE ALONE IN THIS, THAT I MADE YOU QUESTION YOURSELF. I CAN'T EXPLAIN TO YOU THE PRESSURE I AM UNDER FROM THE BOARD.
IT'S FINE.
PLEASE, LET ME APOLOGIZE TO YOU. AFTER OUR CONVERSATION THE OTHER DAY, I CAN'T STOP THINKING ABOUT IT. HOW UNFAIR I'VE BEEN. ***I*** HAD DR. WESTON TO HELP ME.
I DON'T NEED **ANYONE'S** HELP. OR YOUR APOLOGY. IF YOU WANT TO HELP ME, HELP ME FIND OUT WHAT'S GOING ON.
YOU KNOW, I DIDN'T EVER IMAGINE US GETTING ALONG LIKE THIS.
BUT I GUESS I ALSO NEVER IMAGINED I'D BE HUNTING DOWN A **GHOST**, EITHER, SO, THERE YOU GO.

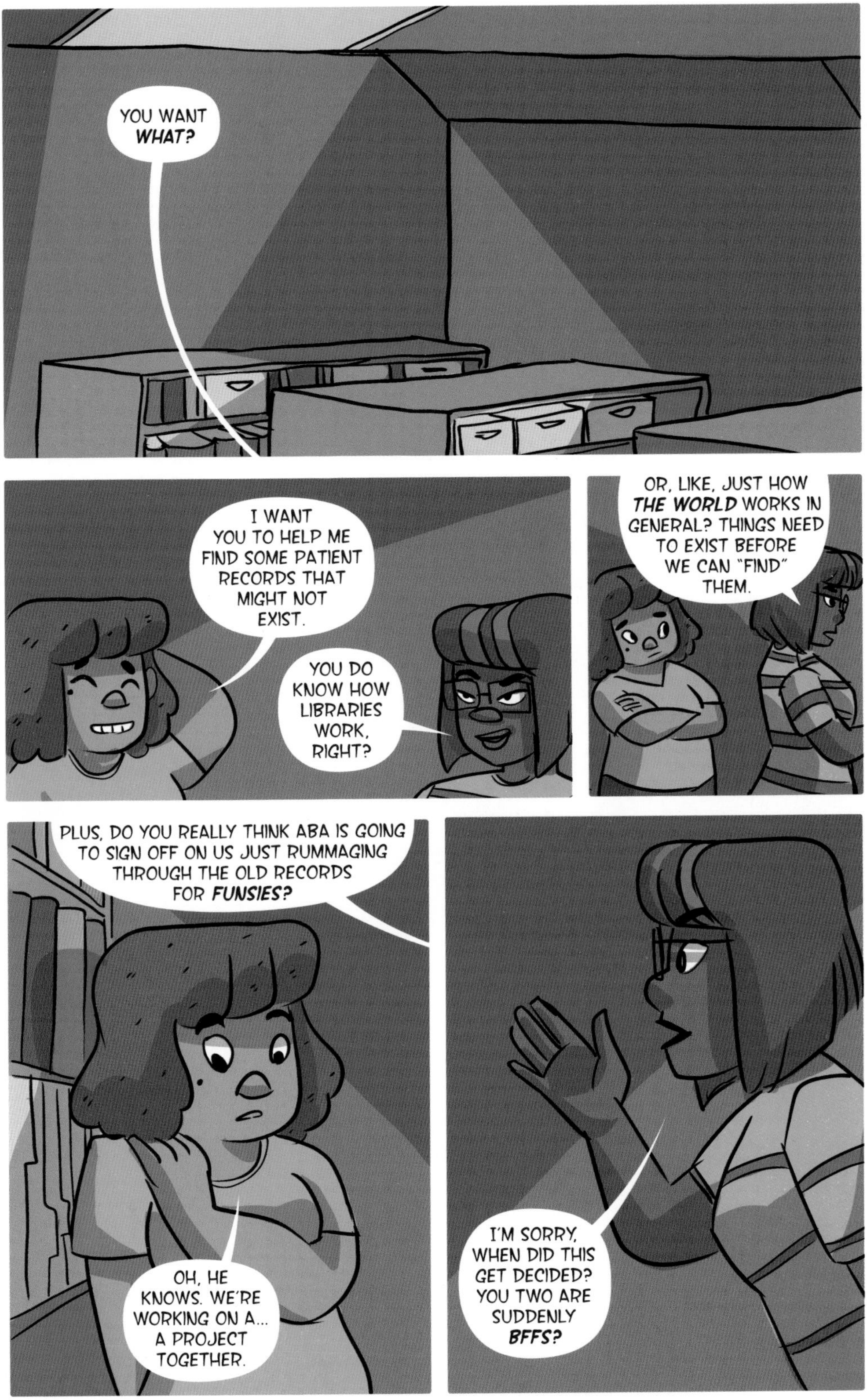
YOU WANT **WHAT?**
I WANT YOU TO HELP ME FIND SOME PATIENT RECORDS THAT MIGHT NOT EXIST.
YOU DO KNOW HOW LIBRARIES WORK, RIGHT?
OR, LIKE, JUST HOW **THE WORLD** WORKS IN GENERAL? THINGS NEED TO EXIST BEFORE WE CAN "FIND" THEM.
PLUS, DO YOU REALLY THINK ABA IS GOING TO SIGN OFF ON US JUST RUMMAGING THROUGH THE OLD RECORDS FOR **FUNSIES?**
OH, HE KNOWS. WE'RE WORKING ON A... A PROJECT TOGETHER.
I'M SORRY, WHEN DID THIS GET DECIDED? YOU TWO ARE SUDDENLY **BFFS?**

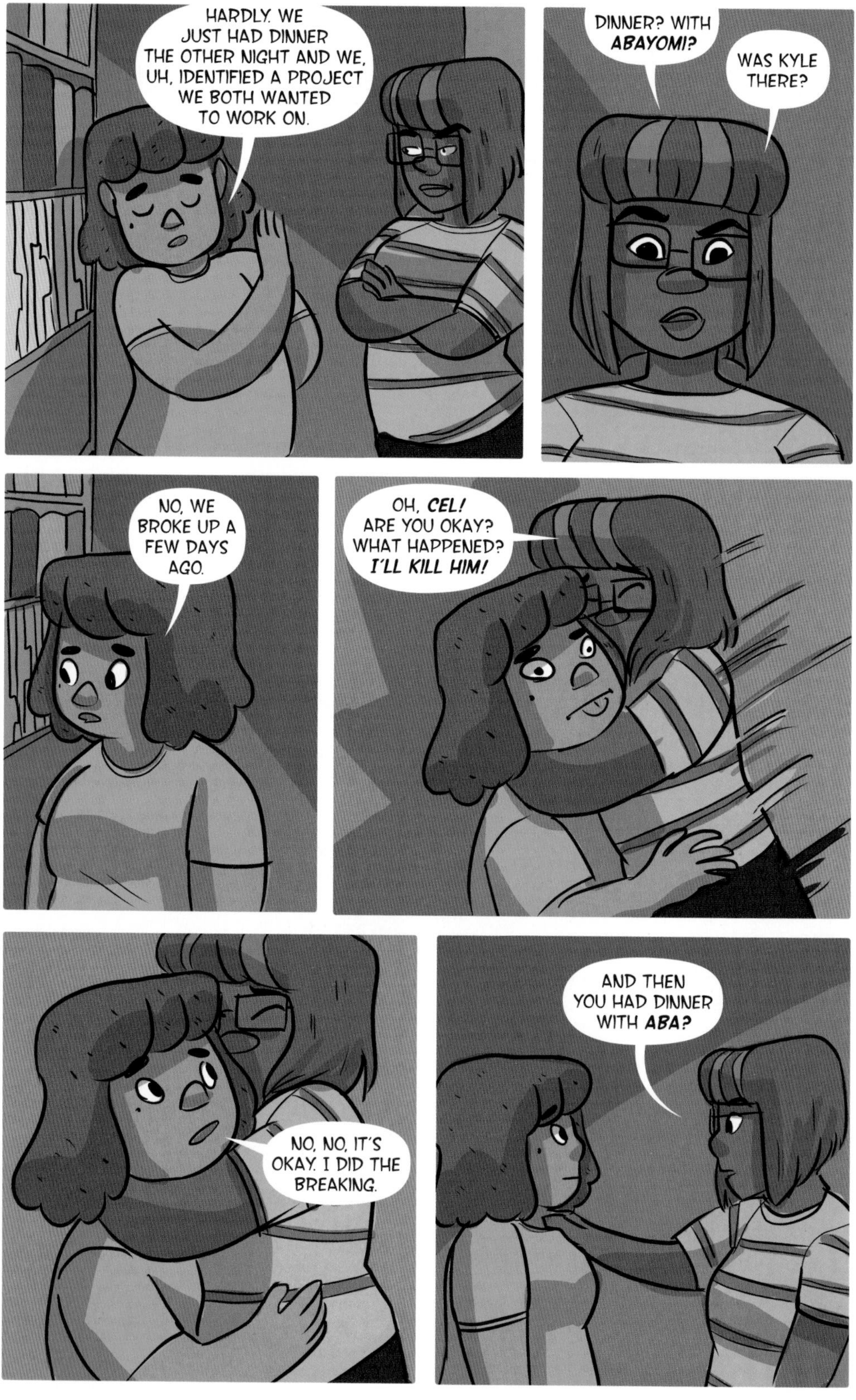
HARDLY. WE JUST HAD DINNER THE OTHER NIGHT AND WE, UH, IDENTIFIED A PROJECT WE BOTH WANTED TO WORK ON.
DINNER? WITH ABAYOMI?
WAS KYLE THERE?
NO, WE BROKE UP A FEW DAYS AGO.
OH, CEL! ARE YOU OKAY? WHAT HAPPENED? I'LL KILL HIM!
NO, NO, IT'S OKAY. I DID THE BREAKING.
AND THEN YOU HAD DINNER WITH ABA?

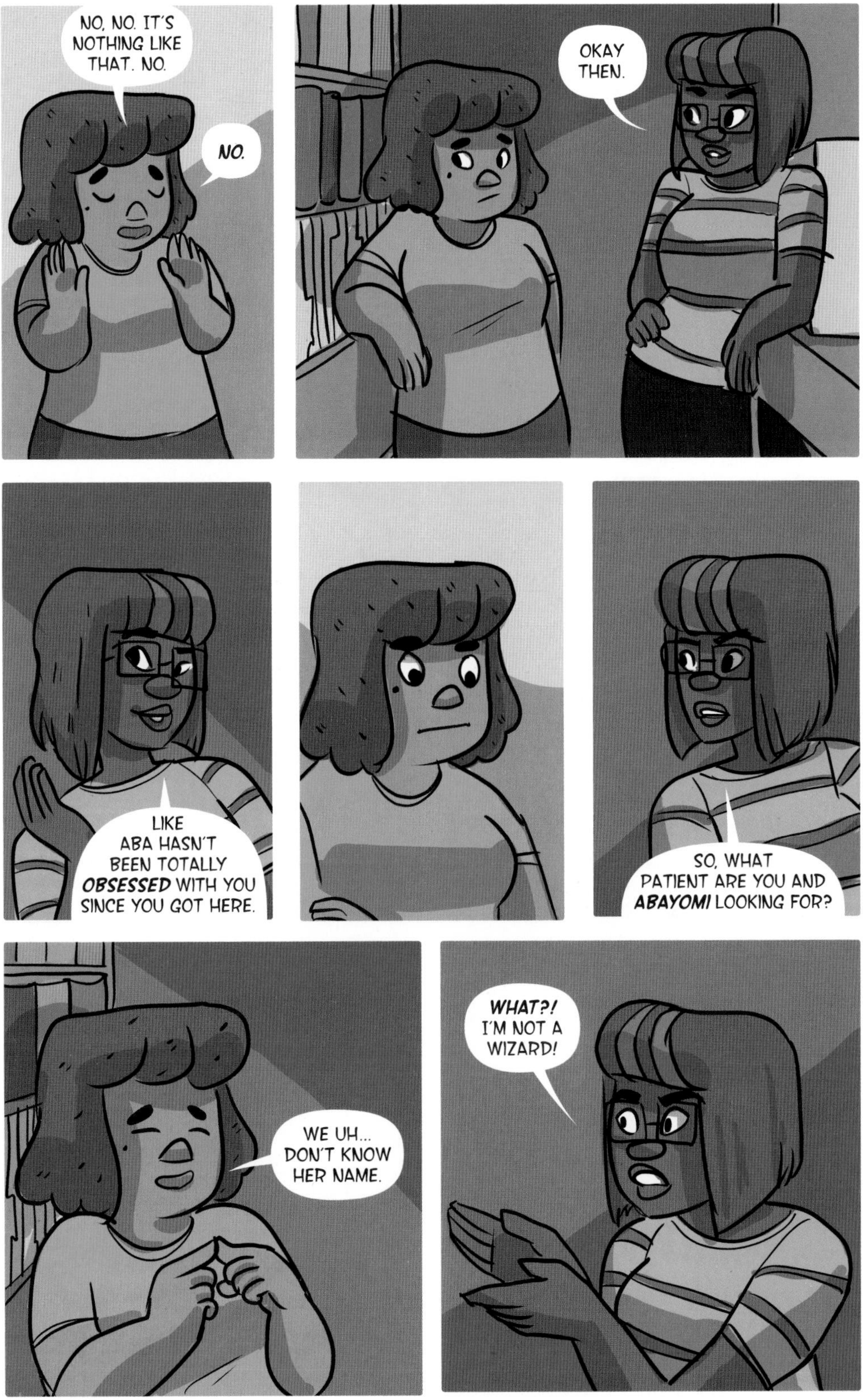
NO, NO. IT'S NOTHING LIKE THAT. NO.
NO.
OKAY THEN.
LIKE ABA HASN'T BEEN TOTALLY OBSESSED WITH YOU SINCE YOU GOT HERE.
SO, WHAT PATIENT ARE YOU AND ABAYOMI LOOKING FOR?
WE UH... DON'T KNOW HER NAME.
WHAT?! I'M NOT A WIZARD!

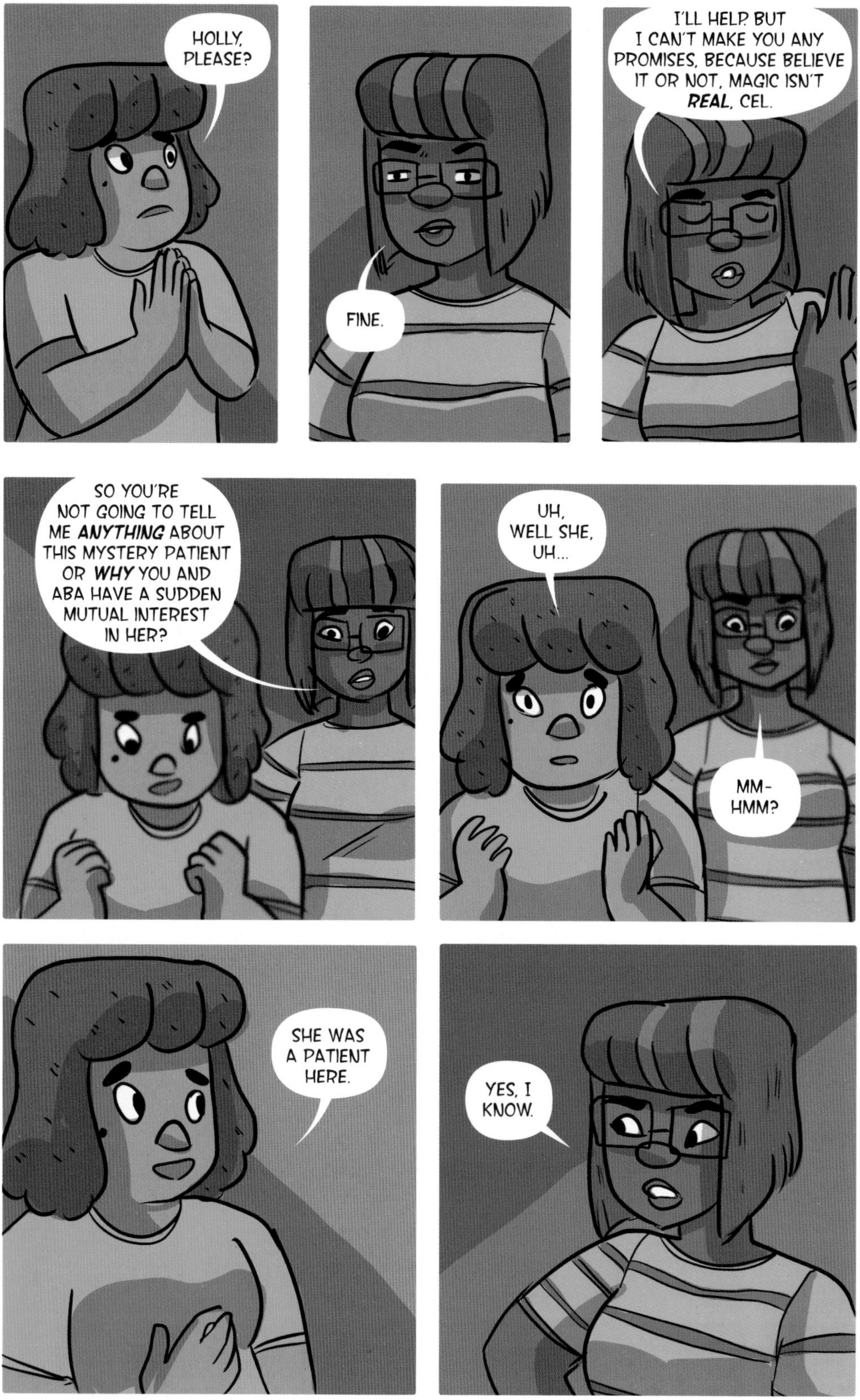
HOLLY, PLEASE?
FINE.
I'LL HELP. BUT I CAN'T MAKE YOU ANY PROMISES, BECAUSE BELIEVE IT OR NOT, MAGIC ISN'T REAL, CEL.
SO YOU'RE NOT GOING TO TELL ME ANYTHING ABOUT THIS MYSTERY PATIENT OR WHY YOU AND ABA HAVE A SUDDEN MUTUAL INTEREST IN HER?
UH, WELL SHE, UH...
MM-HMM?
SHE WAS A PATIENT HERE.
YES, I KNOW.

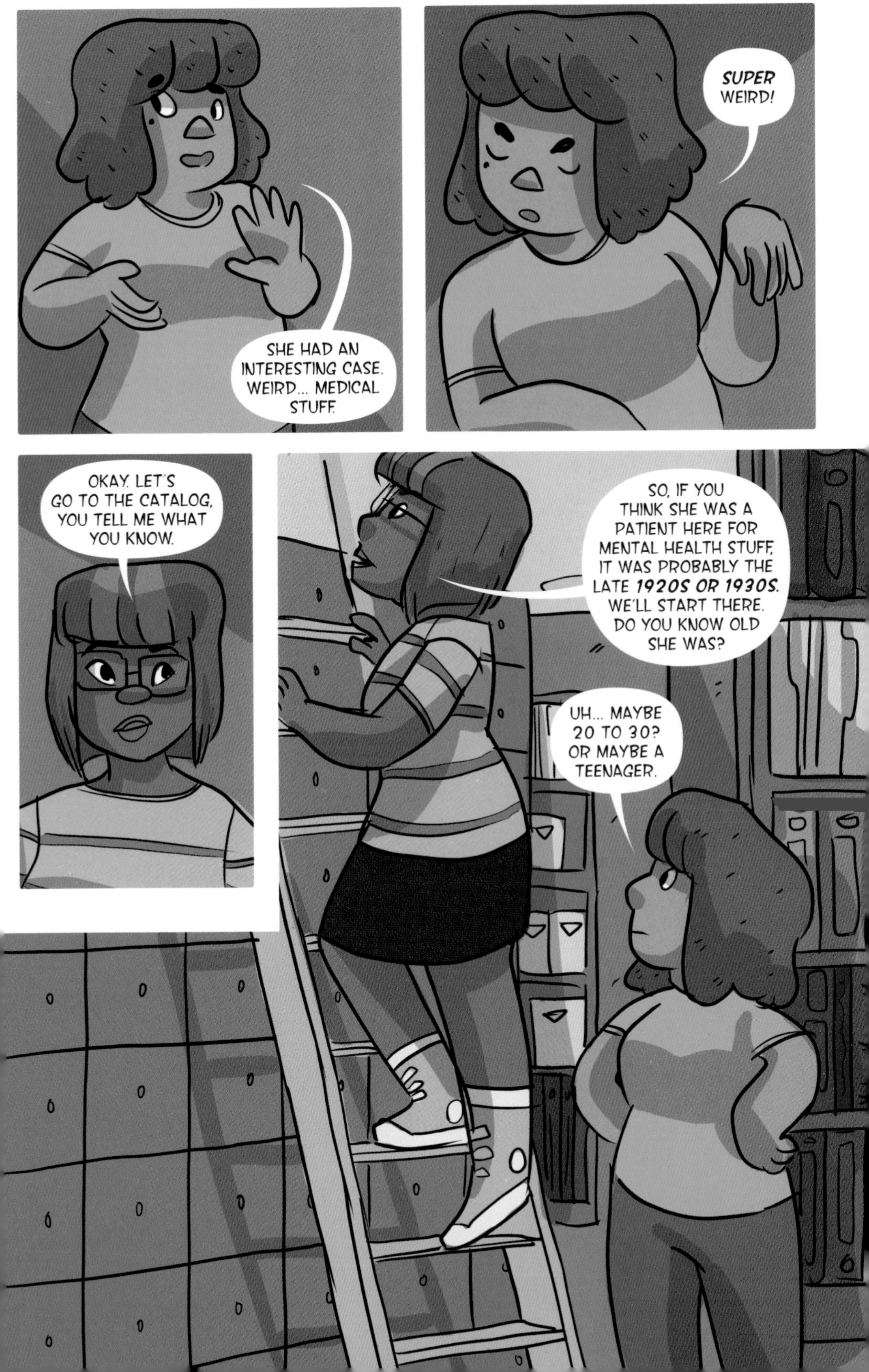
SHE HAD AN INTERESTING CASE. WEIRD... MEDICAL STUFF.
SUPER WEIRD!
OKAY. LET'S GO TO THE CATALOG, YOU TELL ME WHAT YOU KNOW.
SO, IF YOU THINK SHE WAS A PATIENT HERE FOR MENTAL HEALTH STUFF, IT WAS PROBABLY THE LATE 1920S OR 1930S. WE'LL START THERE. DO YOU KNOW OLD SHE WAS?
UH... MAYBE 20 TO 30? OR MAYBE A TEENAGER.

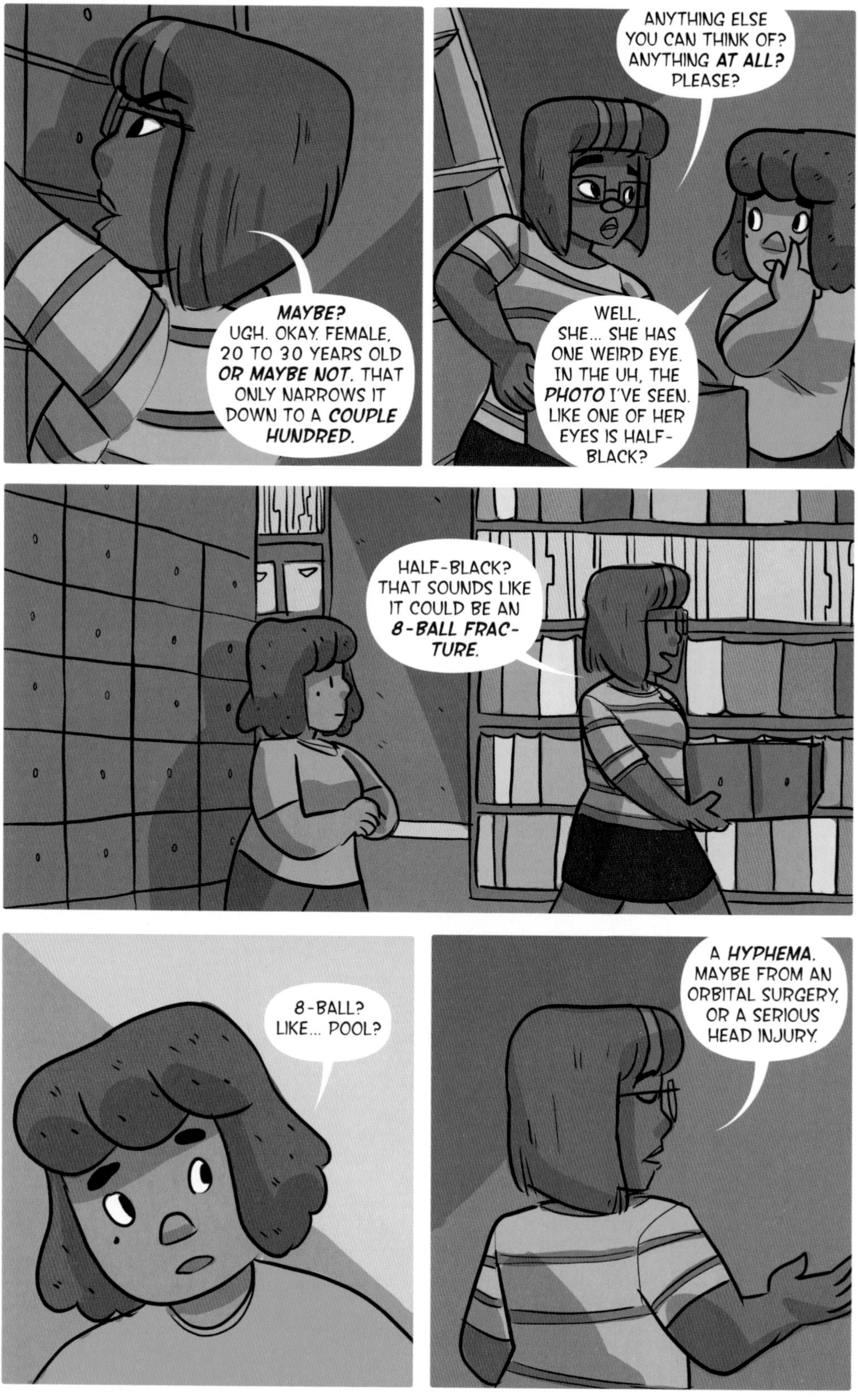
MAYBE? UGH. OKAY. FEMALE, 20 TO 30 YEARS OLD OR MAYBE NOT. THAT ONLY NARROWS IT DOWN TO A COUPLE HUNDRED.
ANYTHING ELSE YOU CAN THINK OF? ANYTHING AT ALL? PLEASE?
WELL, SHE... SHE HAS ONE WEIRD EYE. IN THE UH, THE PHOTO I'VE SEEN. LIKE ONE OF HER EYES IS HALF-BLACK?
HALF-BLACK? THAT SOUNDS LIKE IT COULD BE AN 8-BALL FRACTURE.
8-BALL? LIKE... POOL?
A HYPHEMA. MAYBE FROM AN ORBITAL SURGERY, OR A SERIOUS HEAD INJURY.

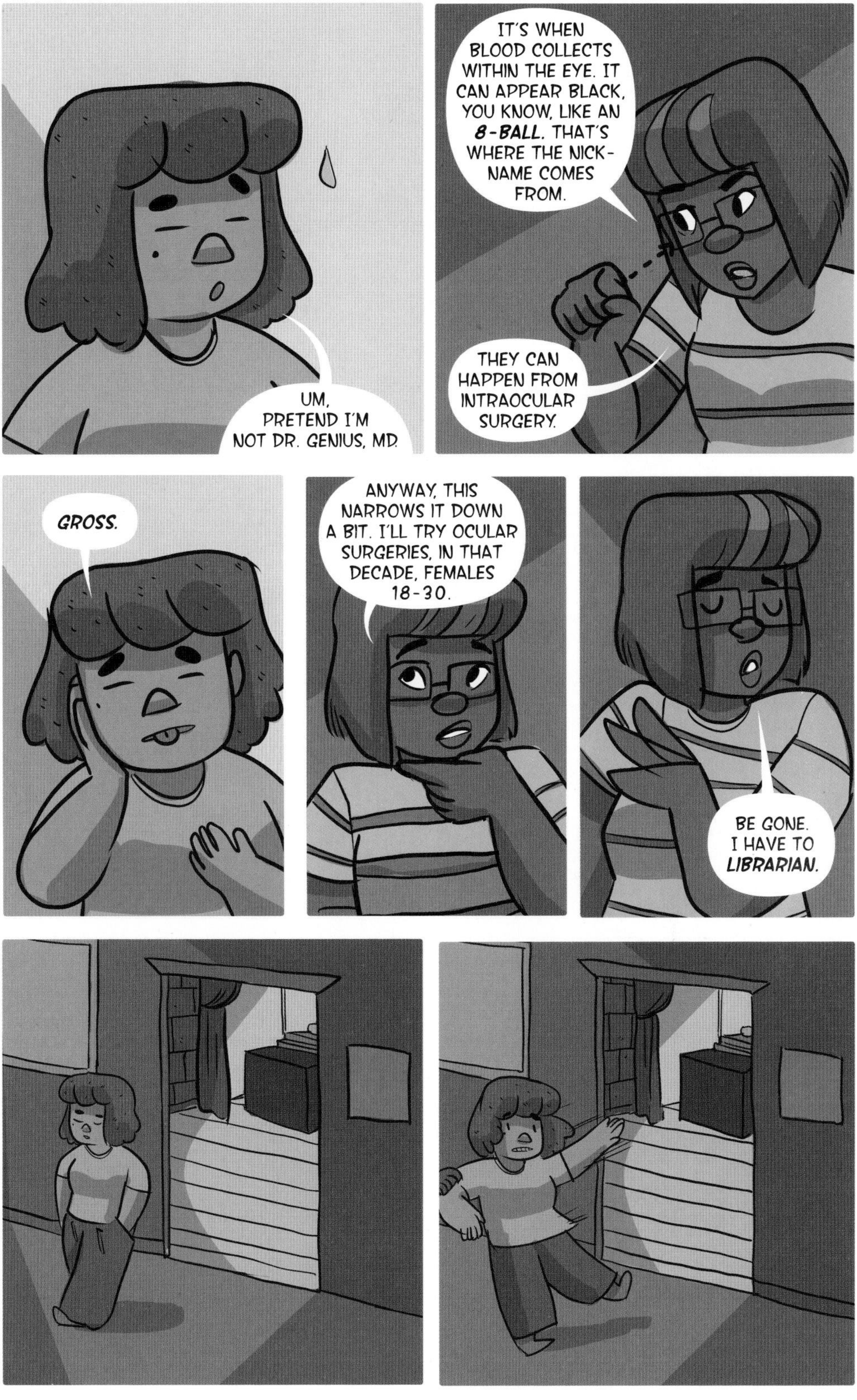
UM, PRETEND I'M NOT DR. GENIUS, MD.
IT'S WHEN BLOOD COLLECTS WITHIN THE EYE. IT CAN APPEAR BLACK, YOU KNOW, LIKE AN **8-BALL**. THAT'S WHERE THE NICK-NAME COMES FROM.
THEY CAN HAPPEN FROM INTRAOCULAR SURGERY.
GROSS.
ANYWAY, THIS NARROWS IT DOWN A BIT. I'LL TRY OCULAR SURGERIES, IN THAT DECADE, FEMALES 18-30.
BE GONE. I HAVE TO ***LIBRARIAN.***

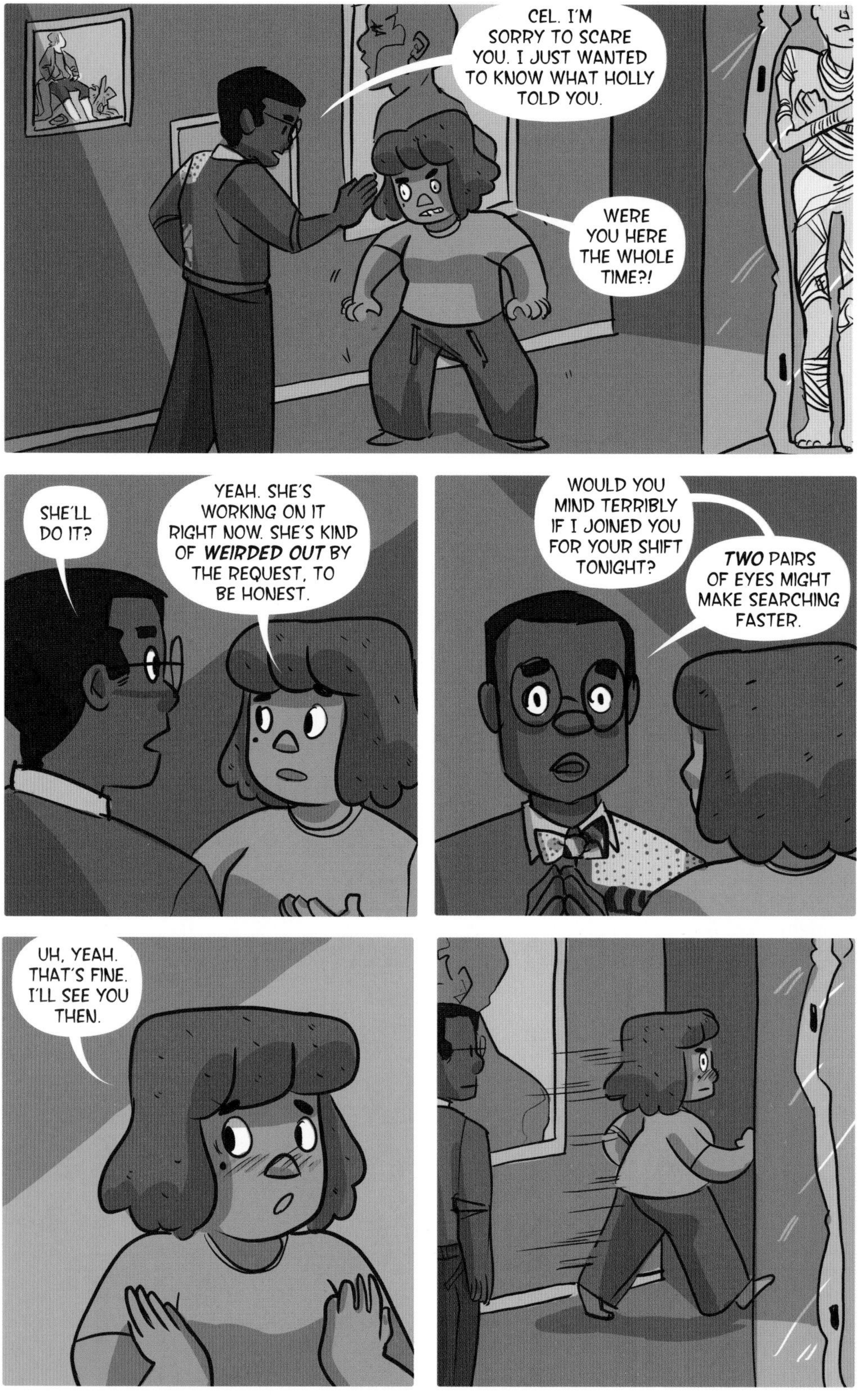
CEL. I'M SORRY TO SCARE YOU. I JUST WANTED TO KNOW WHAT HOLLY TOLD YOU.
WERE YOU HERE THE WHOLE TIME?!
SHE'LL DO IT?
YEAH. SHE'S WORKING ON IT RIGHT NOW. SHE'S KIND OF **WEIRDED OUT** BY THE REQUEST, TO BE HONEST.
WOULD YOU MIND TERRIBLY IF I JOINED YOU FOR YOUR SHIFT TONIGHT?
TWO PAIRS OF EYES MIGHT MAKE SEARCHING FASTER.
UH, YEAH. THAT'S FINE. I'LL SEE YOU THEN.

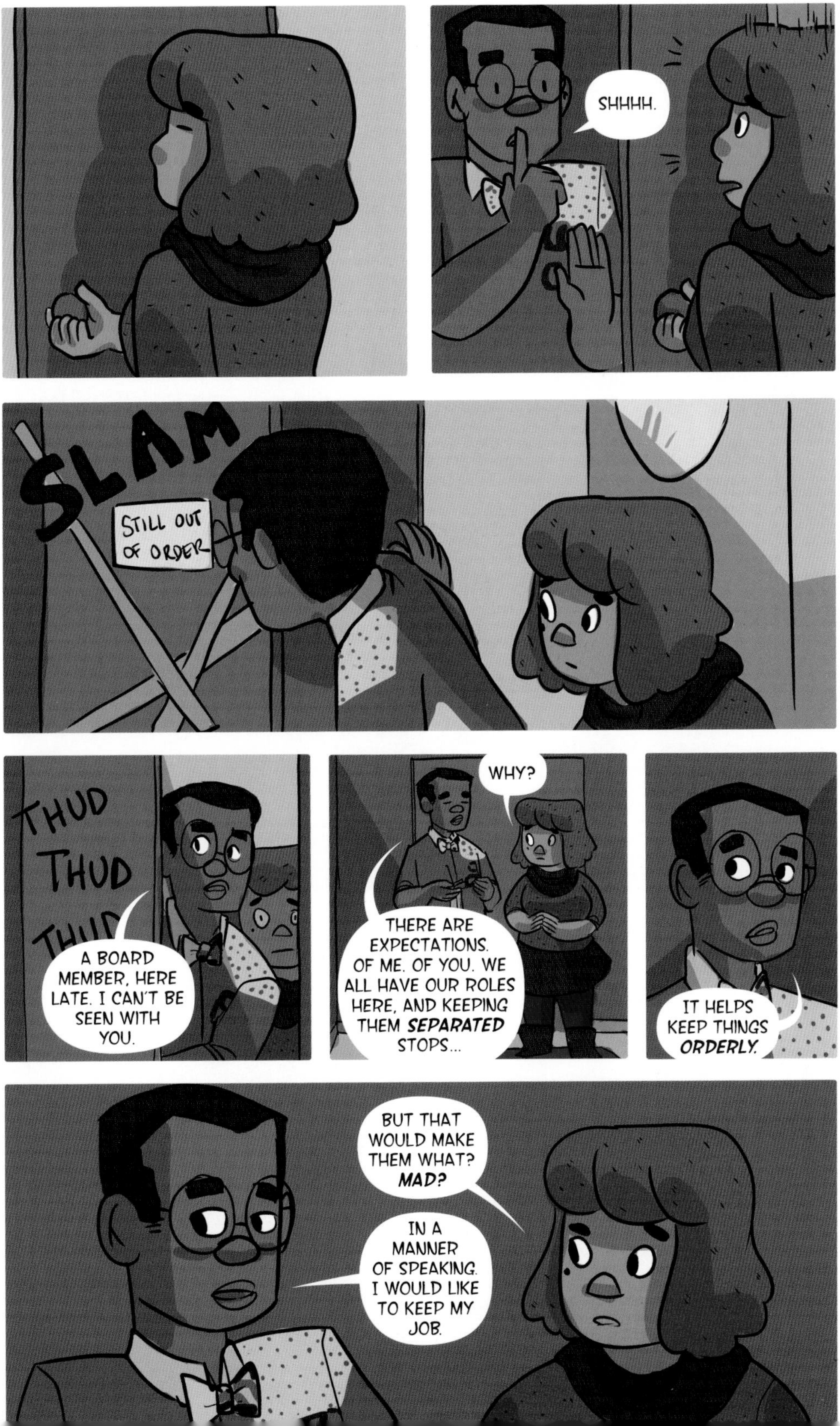
SHHHH.
SLAM
STILL OUT OF ORDER
THUD
THUD
A BOARD MEMBER, HERE LATE. I CAN'T BE SEEN WITH YOU.
WHY?
THERE ARE EXPECTATIONS. OF ME. OF YOU. WE ALL HAVE OUR ROLES HERE, AND KEEPING THEM SEPARATED STOPS...
IT HELPS KEEP THINGS ORDERLY.
BUT THAT WOULD MAKE THEM WHAT? MAD?
IN A MANNER OF SPEAKING. I WOULD LIKE TO KEEP MY JOB.

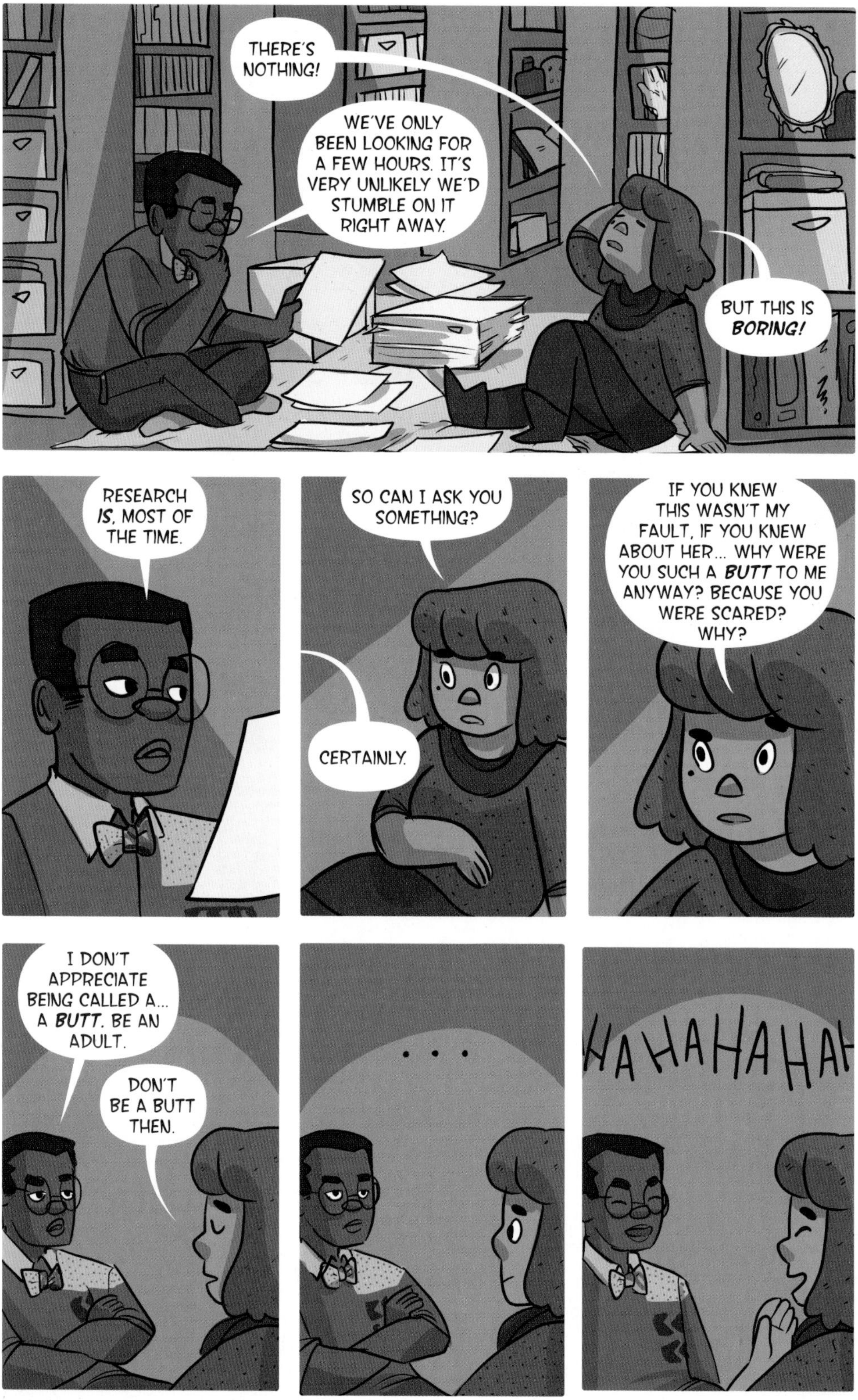
THERE'S NOTHING!
WE'VE ONLY BEEN LOOKING FOR A FEW HOURS. IT'S VERY UNLIKELY WE'D STUMBLE ON IT RIGHT AWAY.
BUT THIS IS *BORING!*
RESEARCH *IS*, MOST OF THE TIME.
SO CAN I ASK YOU SOMETHING?
CERTAINLY.
IF YOU KNEW THIS WASN'T MY FAULT, IF YOU KNEW ABOUT HER... WHY WERE YOU SUCH A *BUTT* TO ME ANYWAY? BECAUSE YOU WERE SCARED? WHY?
I DON'T APPRECIATE BEING CALLED A... A *BUTT*. BE AN ADULT.
DON'T BE A BUTT THEN.
. . .
HAHAHAHAH

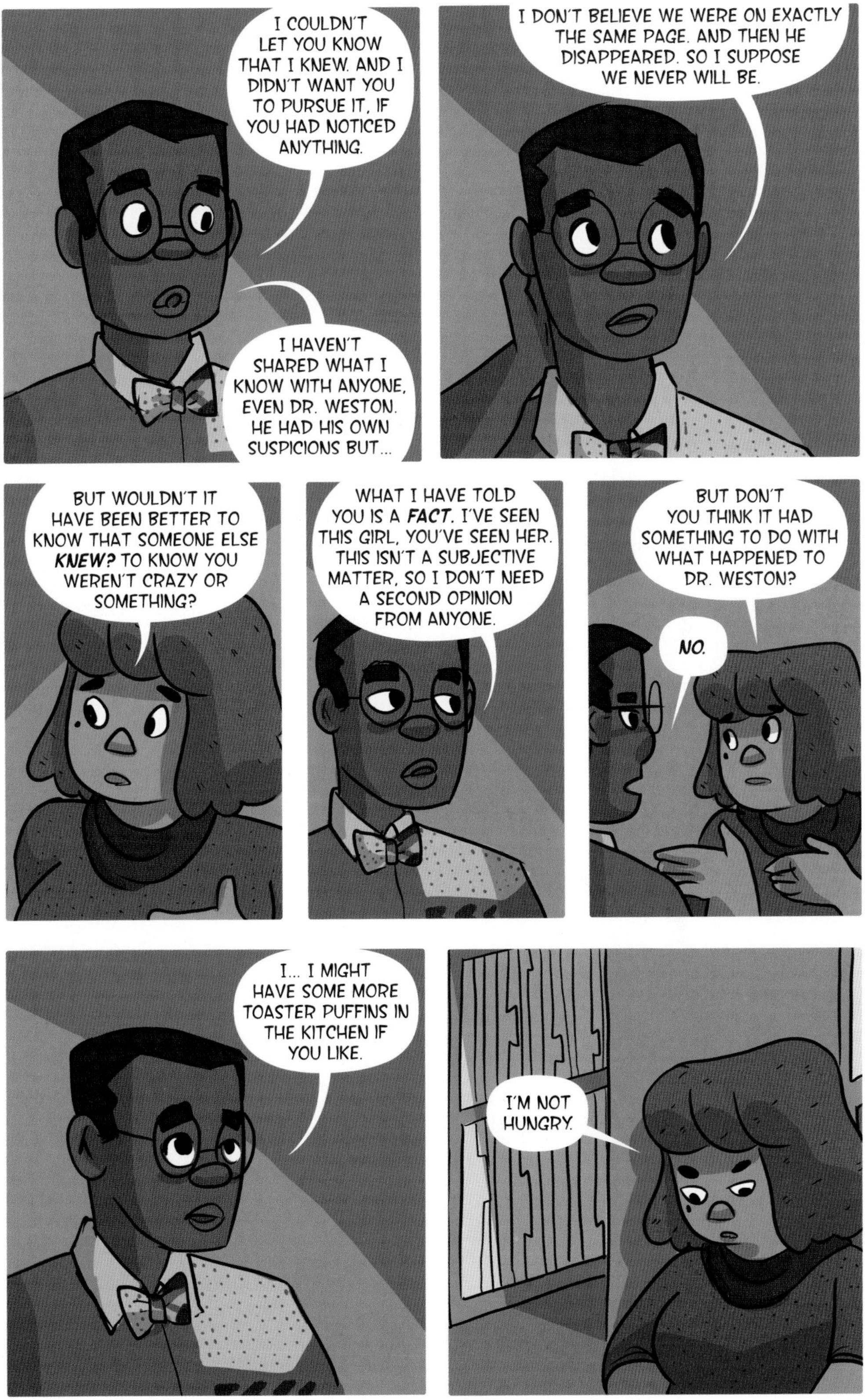
I COULDN'T LET YOU KNOW THAT I KNEW. AND I DIDN'T WANT YOU TO PURSUE IT, IF YOU HAD NOTICED ANYTHING.
I HAVEN'T SHARED WHAT I KNOW WITH ANYONE, EVEN DR. WESTON. HE HAD HIS OWN SUSPICIONS BUT...
I DON'T BELIEVE WE WERE ON EXACTLY THE SAME PAGE. AND THEN HE DISAPPEARED. SO I SUPPOSE WE NEVER WILL BE.
BUT WOULDN'T IT HAVE BEEN BETTER TO KNOW THAT SOMEONE ELSE ***KNEW?*** TO KNOW YOU WEREN'T CRAZY OR SOMETHING?
WHAT I HAVE TOLD YOU IS A ***FACT.*** I'VE SEEN THIS GIRL, YOU'VE SEEN HER. THIS ISN'T A SUBJECTIVE MATTER, SO I DON'T NEED A SECOND OPINION FROM ANYONE.
BUT DON'T YOU THINK IT HAD SOMETHING TO DO WITH WHAT HAPPENED TO DR. WESTON?
NO.
I... I MIGHT HAVE SOME MORE TOASTER PUFFINS IN THE KITCHEN IF YOU LIKE.
I'M NOT HUNGRY.

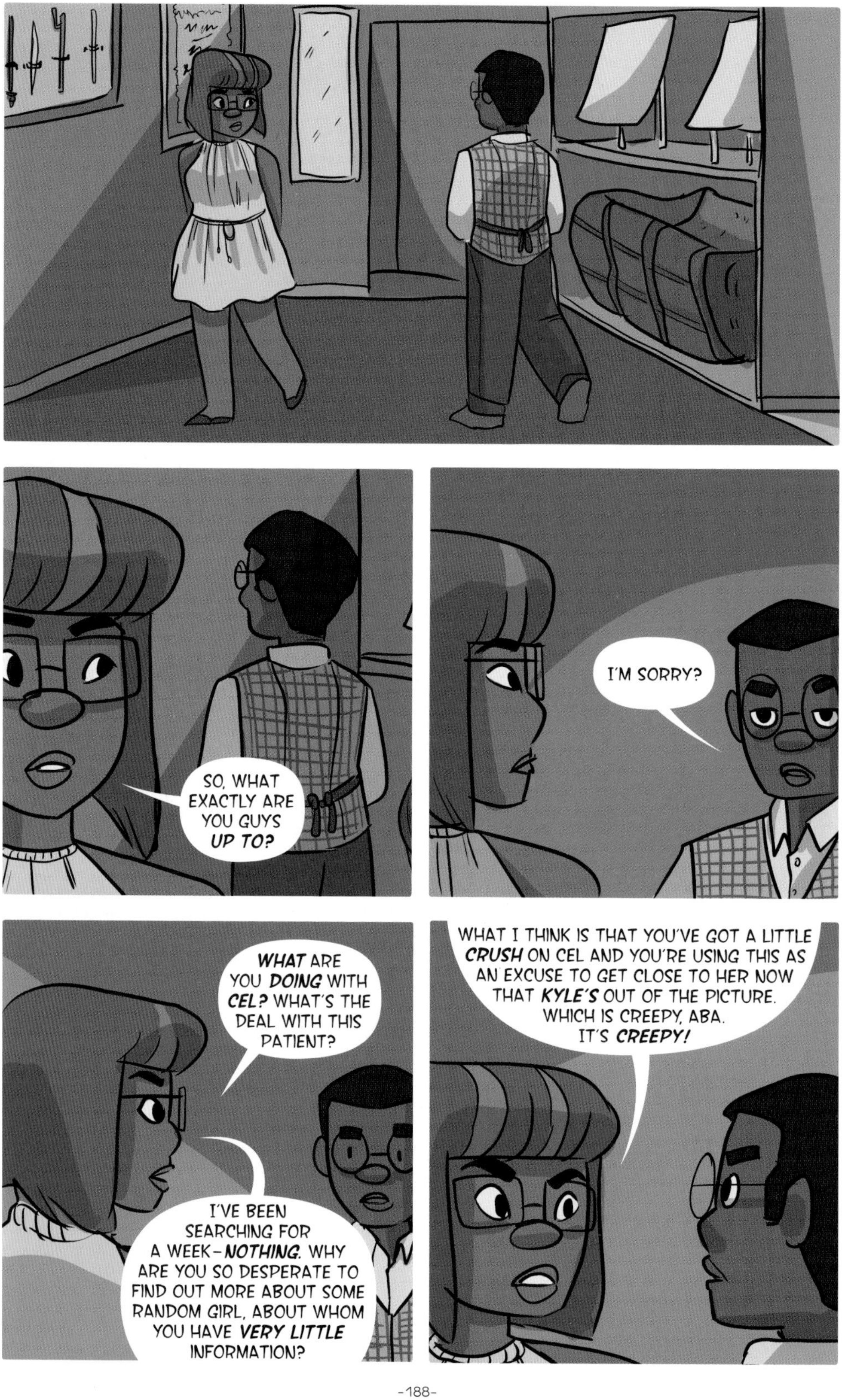
SO, WHAT EXACTLY ARE YOU GUYS UP TO?
I'M SORRY?
WHAT ARE YOU DOING WITH CEL? WHAT'S THE DEAL WITH THIS PATIENT?
I'VE BEEN SEARCHING FOR A WEEK–NOTHING. WHY ARE YOU SO DESPERATE TO FIND OUT MORE ABOUT SOME RANDOM GIRL, ABOUT WHOM YOU HAVE VERY LITTLE INFORMATION?
WHAT I THINK IS THAT YOU'VE GOT A LITTLE CRUSH ON CEL AND YOU'RE USING THIS AS AN EXCUSE TO GET CLOSE TO HER NOW THAT KYLE'S OUT OF THE PICTURE. WHICH IS CREEPY, ABA. IT'S CREEPY!

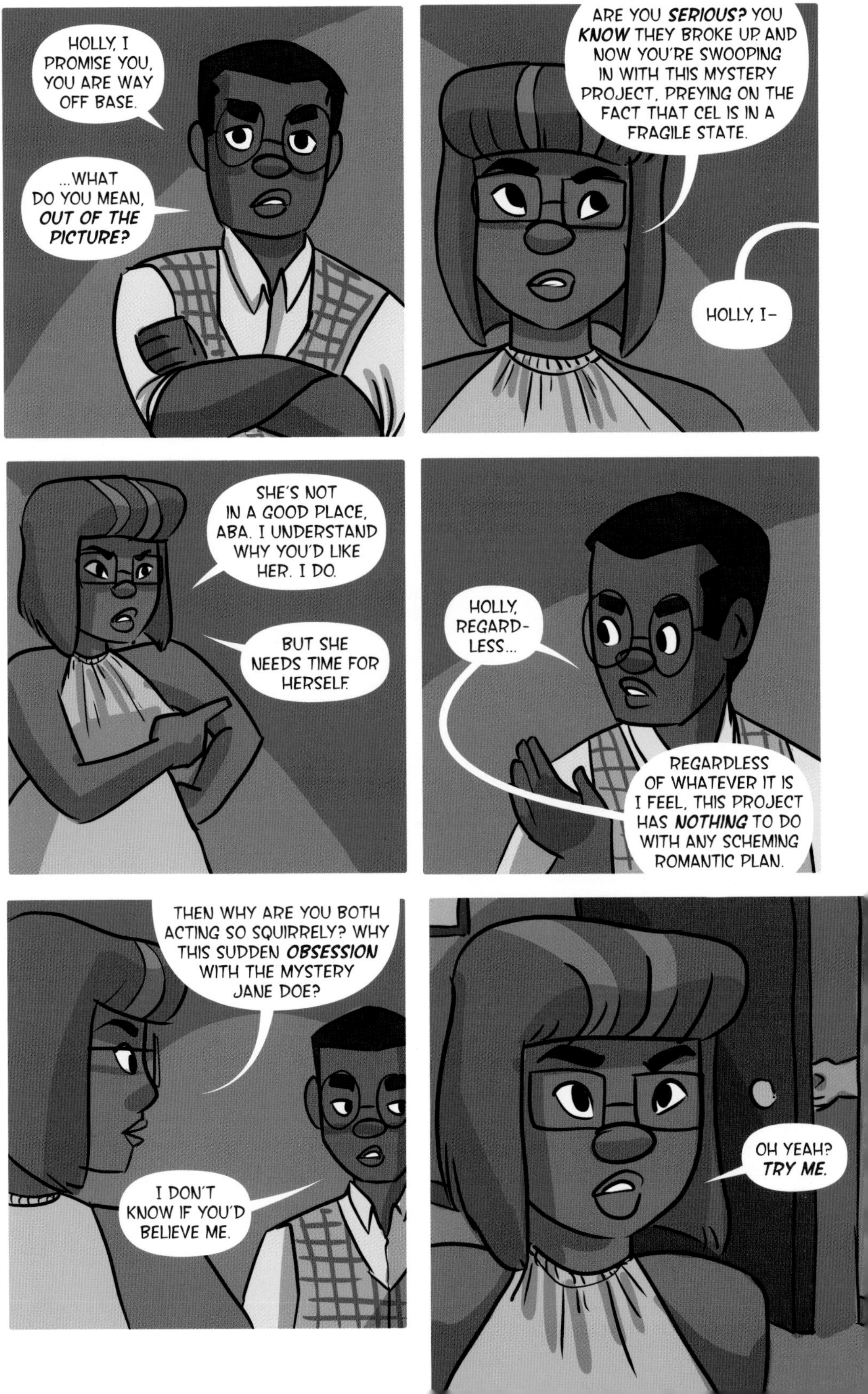
HOLLY, I PROMISE YOU, YOU ARE WAY OFF BASE.
...WHAT DO YOU MEAN, *OUT OF THE PICTURE?*
ARE YOU ***SERIOUS?*** YOU ***KNOW*** THEY BROKE UP. AND NOW YOU'RE SWOOPING IN WITH THIS MYSTERY PROJECT, PREYING ON THE FACT THAT CEL IS IN A FRAGILE STATE.
HOLLY, I–
SHE'S NOT IN A GOOD PLACE, ABA. I UNDERSTAND WHY YOU'D LIKE HER. I DO.
BUT SHE NEEDS TIME FOR HERSELF.
HOLLY, REGARDLESS...
REGARDLESS OF WHATEVER IT IS I FEEL, THIS PROJECT HAS ***NOTHING*** TO DO WITH ANY SCHEMING ROMANTIC PLAN.
THEN WHY ARE YOU BOTH ACTING SO SQUIRRELY? WHY THIS SUDDEN ***OBSESSION*** WITH THE MYSTERY JANE DOE?
I DON'T KNOW IF YOU'D BELIEVE ME.
OH YEAH? ***TRY ME.***

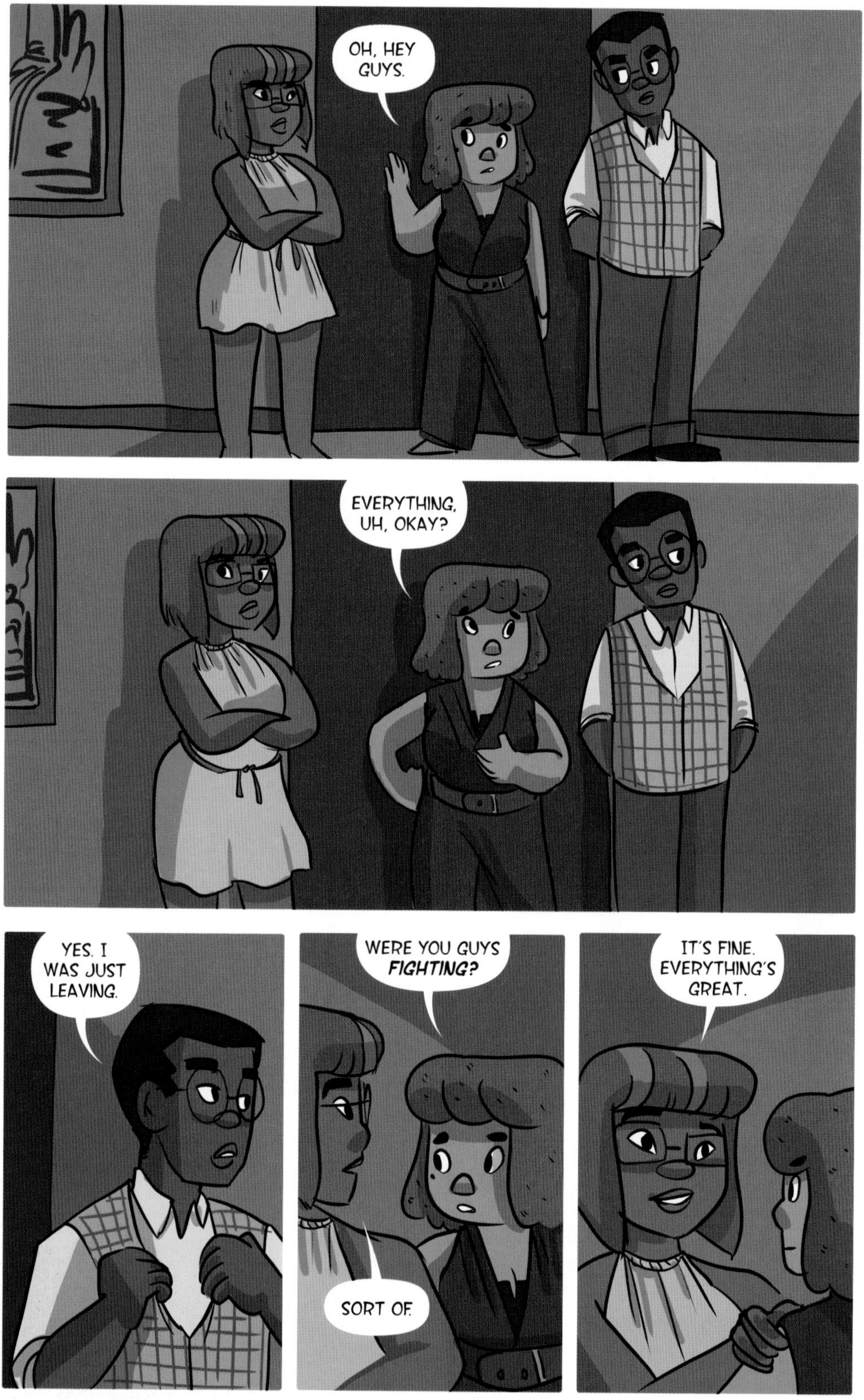
OH, HEY GUYS.
EVERYTHING, UH, OKAY?
YES. I WAS JUST LEAVING.
WERE YOU GUYS *FIGHTING?*
SORT OF.
IT'S FINE. EVERYTHING'S GREAT.

TWO WEEKS LATER

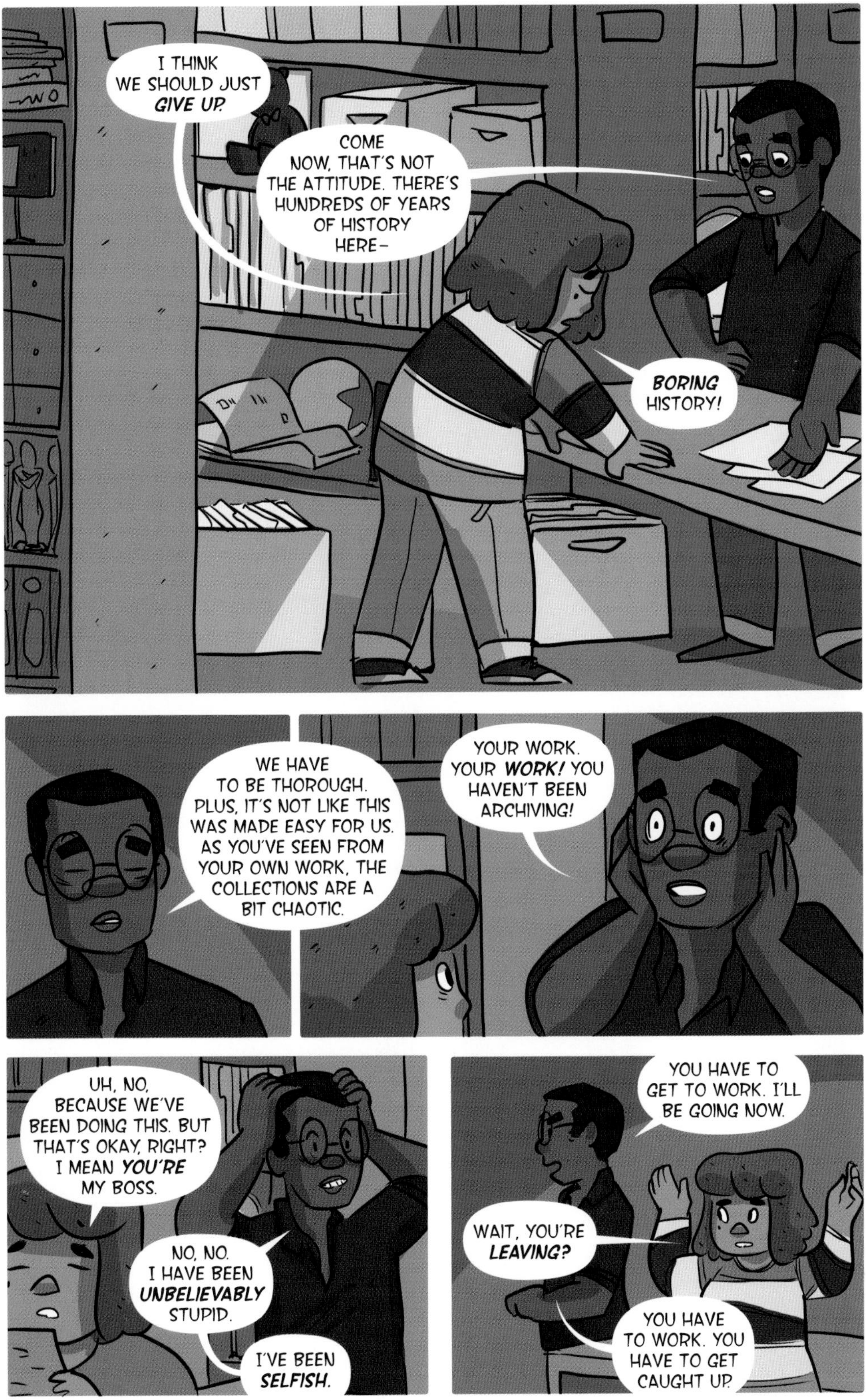
I THINK WE SHOULD JUST GIVE UP.
COME NOW, THAT'S NOT THE ATTITUDE. THERE'S HUNDREDS OF YEARS OF HISTORY HERE-
BORING HISTORY!
WE HAVE TO BE THOROUGH. PLUS, IT'S NOT LIKE THIS WAS MADE EASY FOR US. AS YOU'VE SEEN FROM YOUR OWN WORK, THE COLLECTIONS ARE A BIT CHAOTIC.
YOUR WORK. YOUR WORK! YOU HAVEN'T BEEN ARCHIVING!
UH, NO, BECAUSE WE'VE BEEN DOING THIS. BUT THAT'S OKAY, RIGHT? I MEAN YOU'RE MY BOSS.
NO, NO. I HAVE BEEN UNBELIEVABLY STUPID.
I'VE BEEN SELFISH.
YOU HAVE TO GET TO WORK. I'LL BE GOING NOW.
WAIT, YOU'RE LEAVING?
YOU HAVE TO WORK. YOU HAVE TO GET CAUGHT UP.

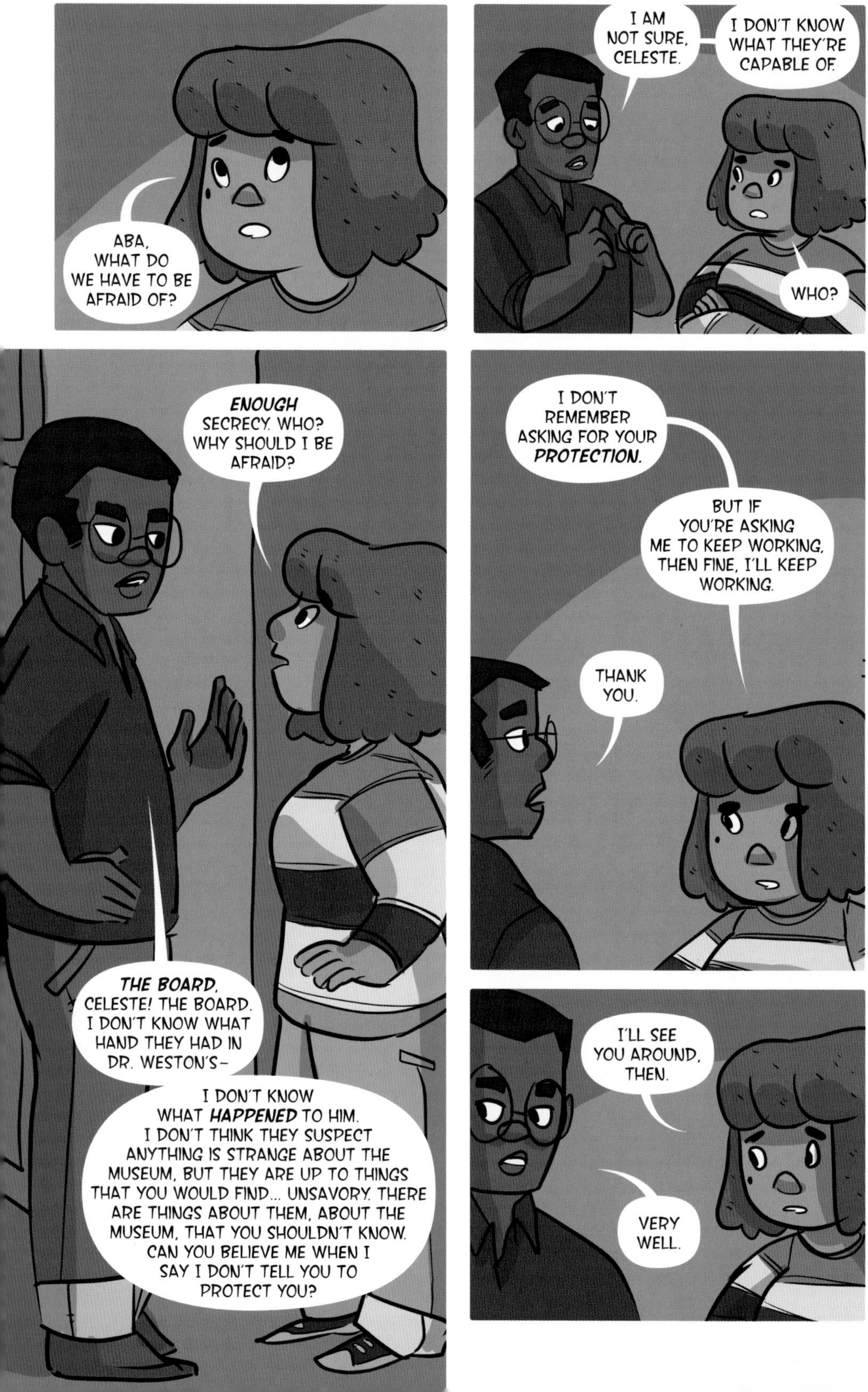
ABA, WHAT DO WE HAVE TO BE AFRAID OF?
I AM NOT SURE, CELESTE.
I DON'T KNOW WHAT THEY'RE CAPABLE OF.
WHO?
ENOUGH SECRECY. WHO? WHY SHOULD I BE AFRAID?
THE BOARD, CELESTE! THE BOARD. I DON'T KNOW WHAT HAND THEY HAD IN DR. WESTON'S–
I DON'T KNOW WHAT HAPPENED TO HIM. I DON'T THINK THEY SUSPECT ANYTHING IS STRANGE ABOUT THE MUSEUM, BUT THEY ARE UP TO THINGS THAT YOU WOULD FIND... UNSAVORY. THERE ARE THINGS ABOUT THEM, ABOUT THE MUSEUM, THAT YOU SHOULDN'T KNOW. CAN YOU BELIEVE ME WHEN I SAY I DON'T TELL YOU TO PROTECT YOU?
I DON'T REMEMBER ASKING FOR YOUR PROTECTION.
BUT IF YOU'RE ASKING ME TO KEEP WORKING, THEN FINE, I'LL KEEP WORKING.
THANK YOU.
I'LL SEE YOU AROUND, THEN.
VERY WELL.

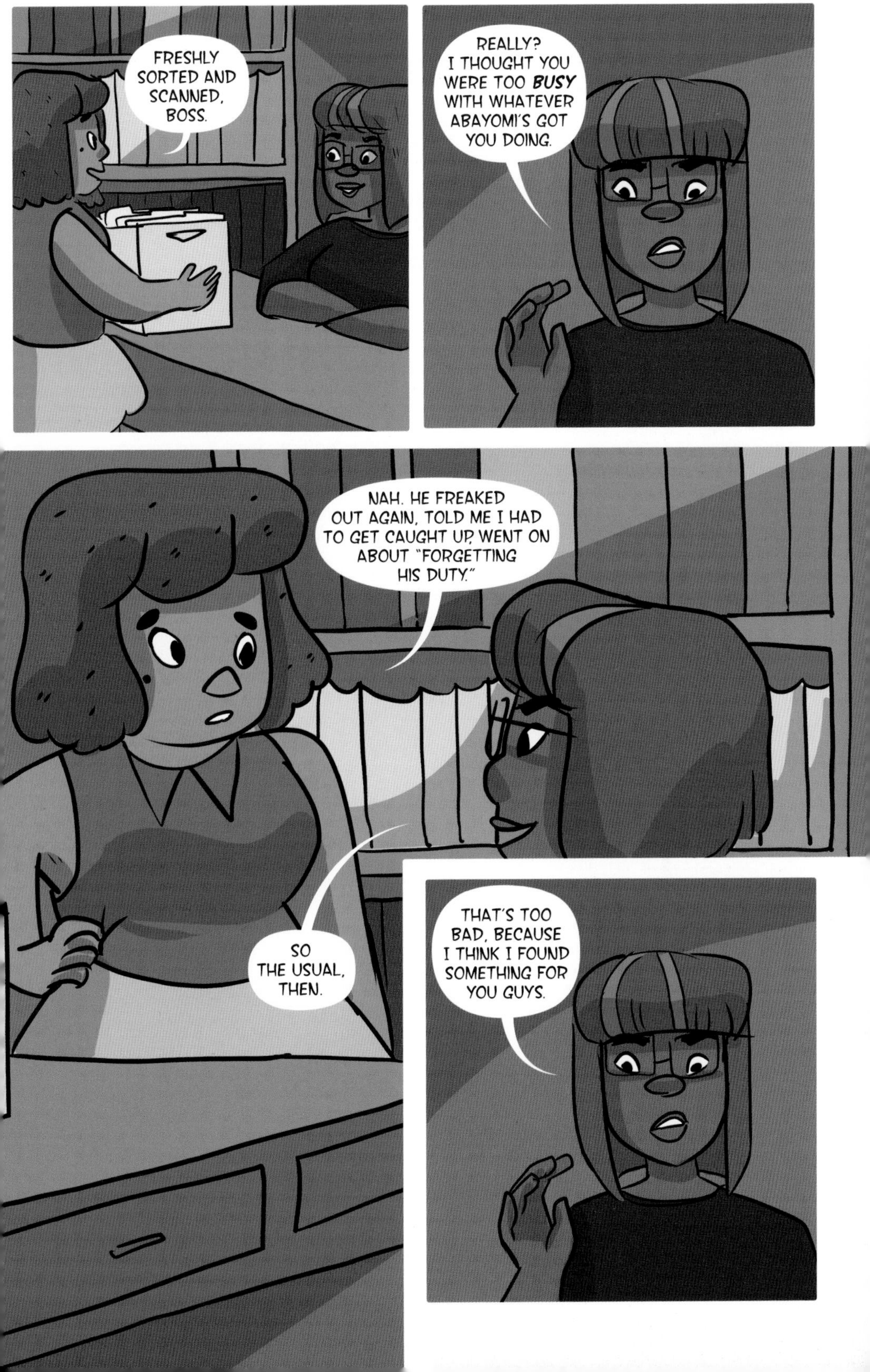
FRESHLY SORTED AND SCANNED, BOSS.
REALLY? I THOUGHT YOU WERE TOO **BUSY** WITH WHATEVER ABAYOMI'S GOT YOU DOING.
NAH. HE FREAKED OUT AGAIN, TOLD ME I HAD TO GET CAUGHT UP, WENT ON ABOUT "FORGETTING HIS DUTY."
SO THE USUAL, THEN.
THAT'S TOO BAD, BECAUSE I THINK I FOUND SOMETHING FOR YOU GUYS.

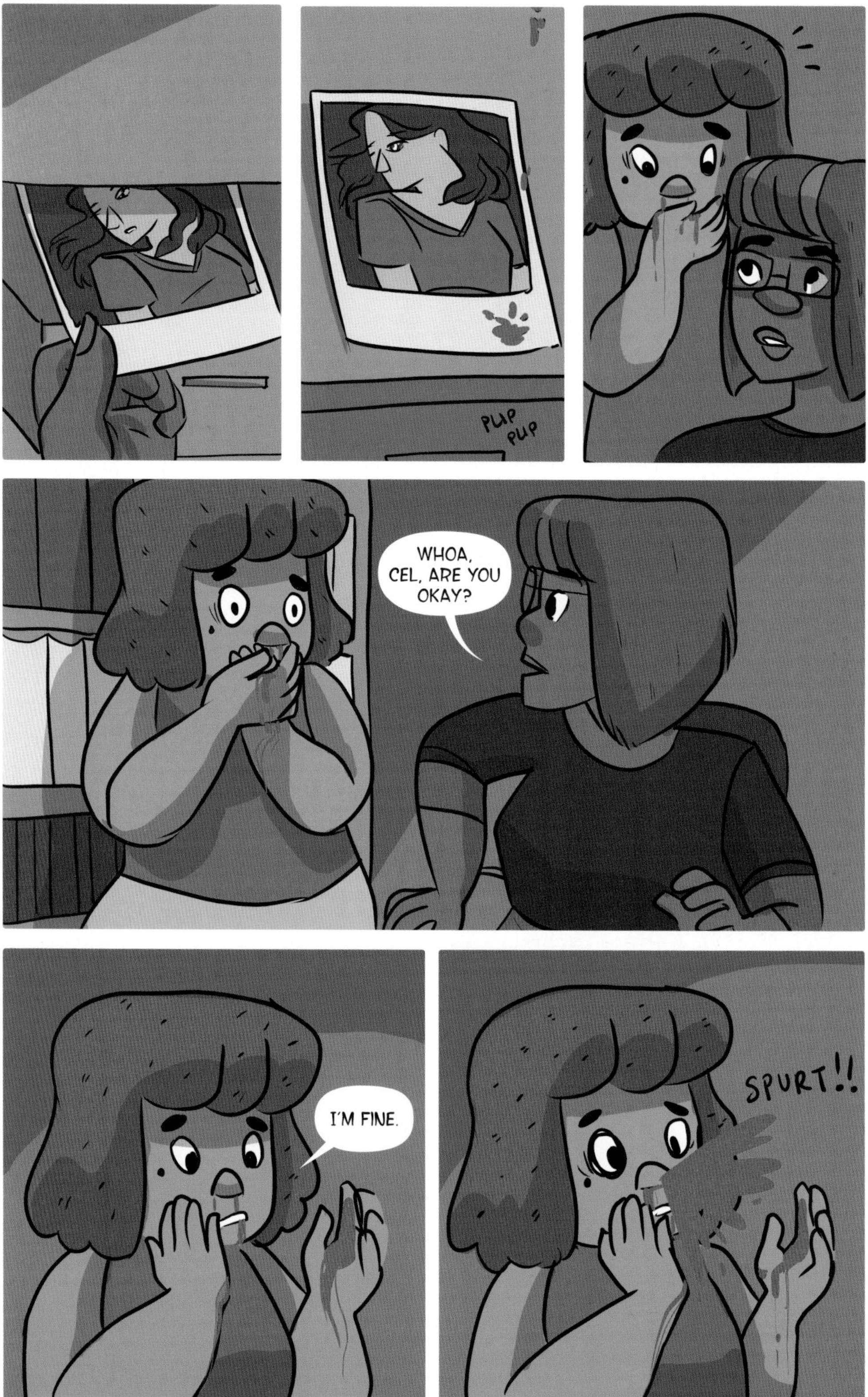
PLIP PLIP
WHOA, CEL, ARE YOU OKAY?
I'M FINE.
SPURT!!

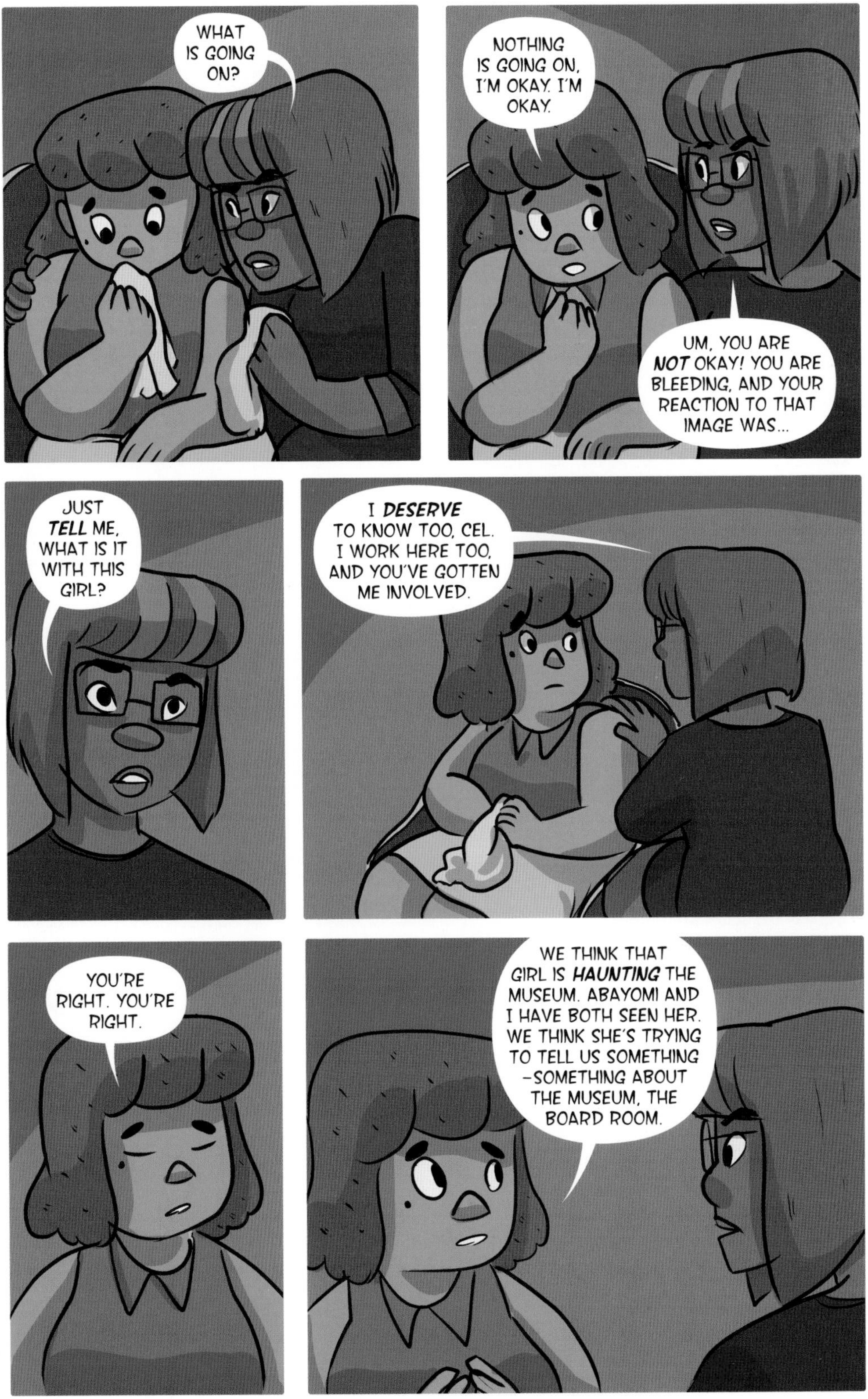
WHAT IS GOING ON?
NOTHING IS GOING ON, I'M OKAY. I'M OKAY.
UM, YOU ARE NOT OKAY! YOU ARE BLEEDING, AND YOUR REACTION TO THAT IMAGE WAS...
JUST TELL ME, WHAT IS IT WITH THIS GIRL?
I DESERVE TO KNOW TOO, CEL. I WORK HERE TOO, AND YOU'VE GOTTEN ME INVOLVED.
YOU'RE RIGHT. YOU'RE RIGHT.
WE THINK THAT GIRL IS HAUNTING THE MUSEUM. ABAYOMI AND I HAVE BOTH SEEN HER. WE THINK SHE'S TRYING TO TELL US SOMETHING -SOMETHING ABOUT THE MUSEUM, THE BOARD ROOM.

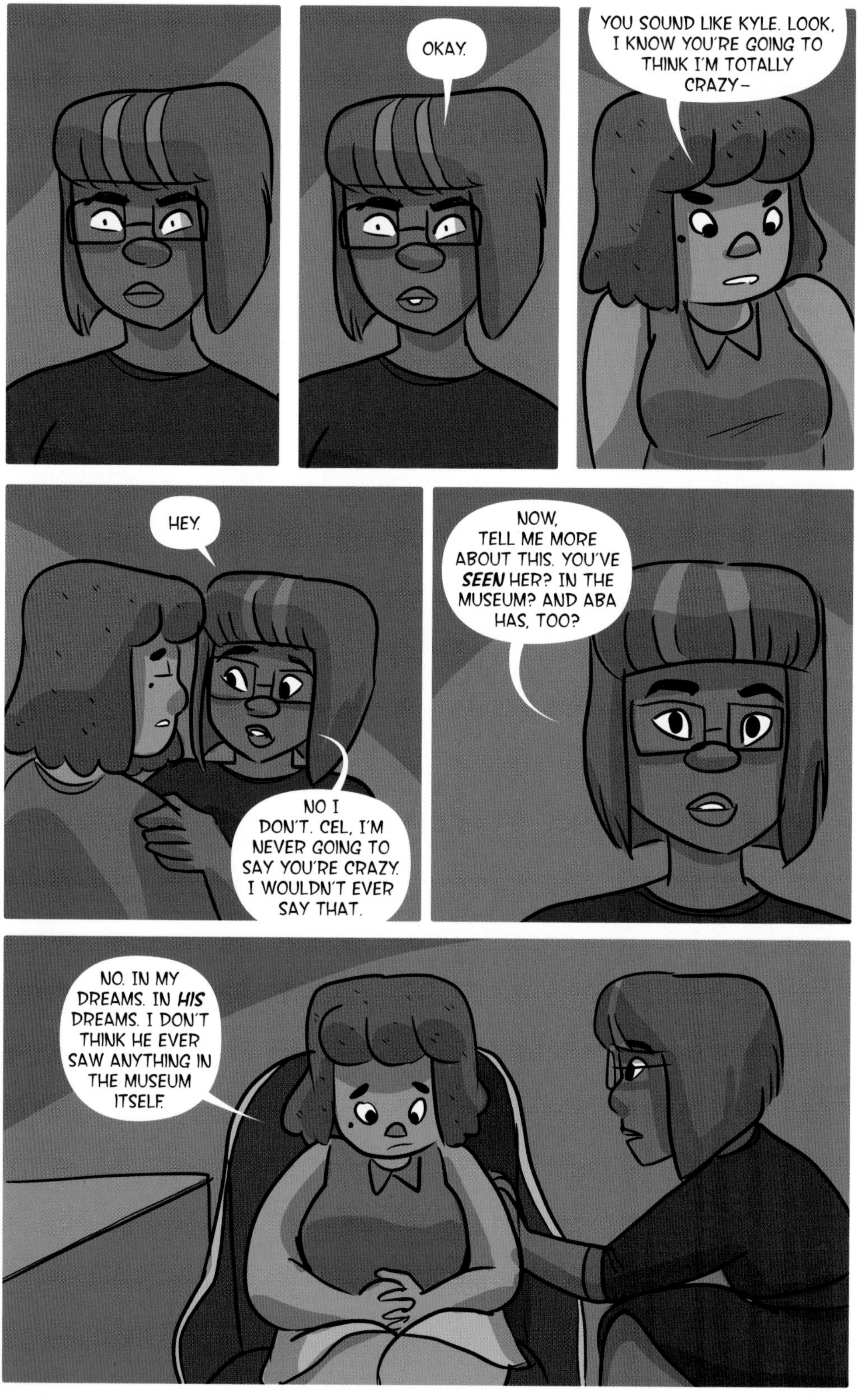
OKAY.
YOU SOUND LIKE KYLE. LOOK, I KNOW YOU'RE GOING TO THINK I'M TOTALLY CRAZY–
HEY.
NO I DON'T. CEL, I'M NEVER GOING TO SAY YOU'RE CRAZY. I WOULDN'T EVER SAY THAT.
NOW, TELL ME MORE ABOUT THIS. YOU'VE ***SEEN*** HER? IN THE MUSEUM? AND ABA HAS, TOO?
NO. IN MY DREAMS. IN ***HIS*** DREAMS. I DON'T THINK HE EVER SAW ANYTHING IN THE MUSEUM ITSELF.

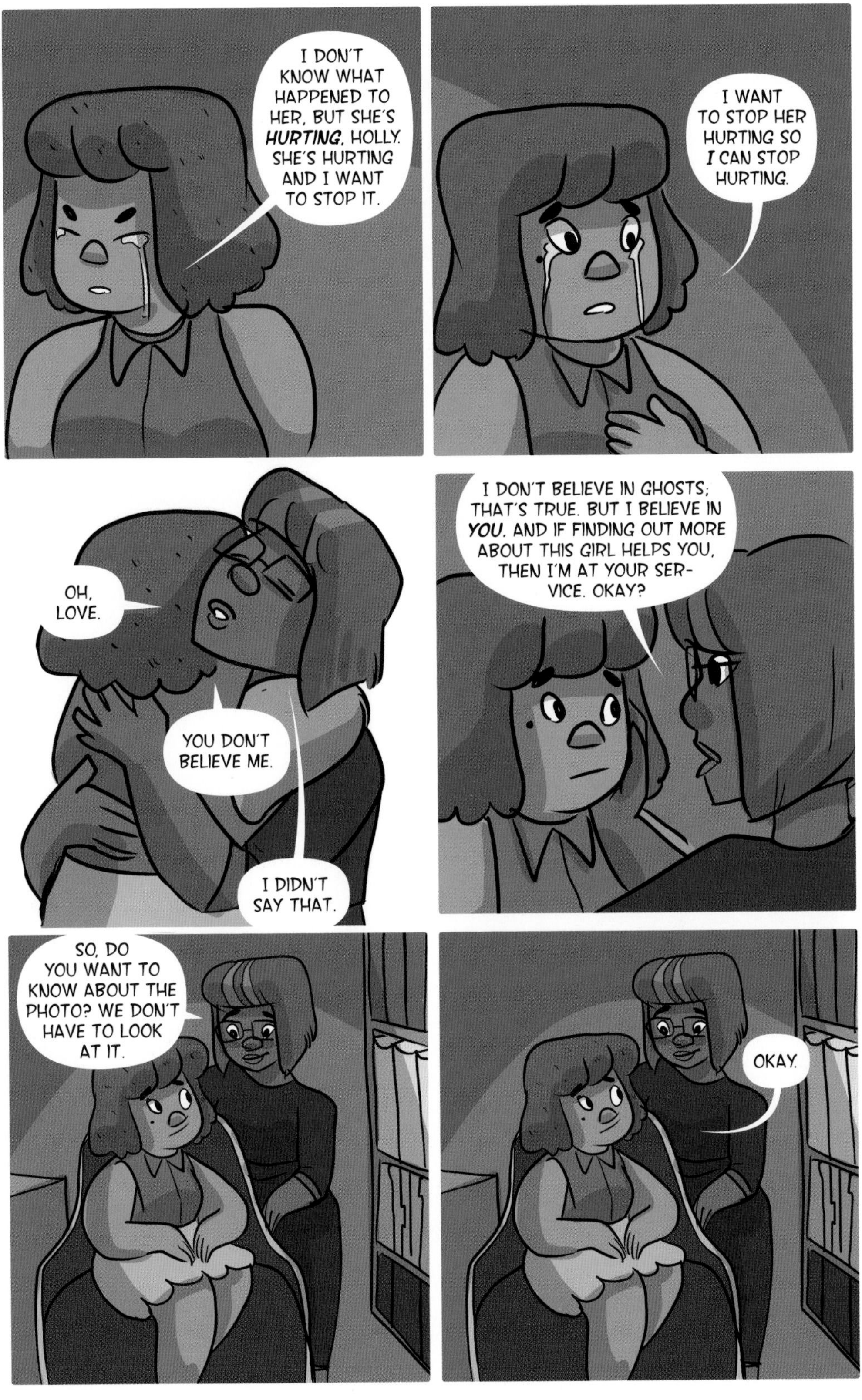
I DON'T KNOW WHAT HAPPENED TO HER, BUT SHE'S HURTING, HOLLY. SHE'S HURTING AND I WANT TO STOP IT.
I WANT TO STOP HER HURTING SO I CAN STOP HURTING.
OH, LOVE.
YOU DON'T BELIEVE ME.
I DIDN'T SAY THAT.
I DON'T BELIEVE IN GHOSTS; THAT'S TRUE. BUT I BELIEVE IN YOU. AND IF FINDING OUT MORE ABOUT THIS GIRL HELPS YOU, THEN I'M AT YOUR SER-VICE. OKAY?
SO, DO YOU WANT TO KNOW ABOUT THE PHOTO? WE DON'T HAVE TO LOOK AT IT.
OKAY.

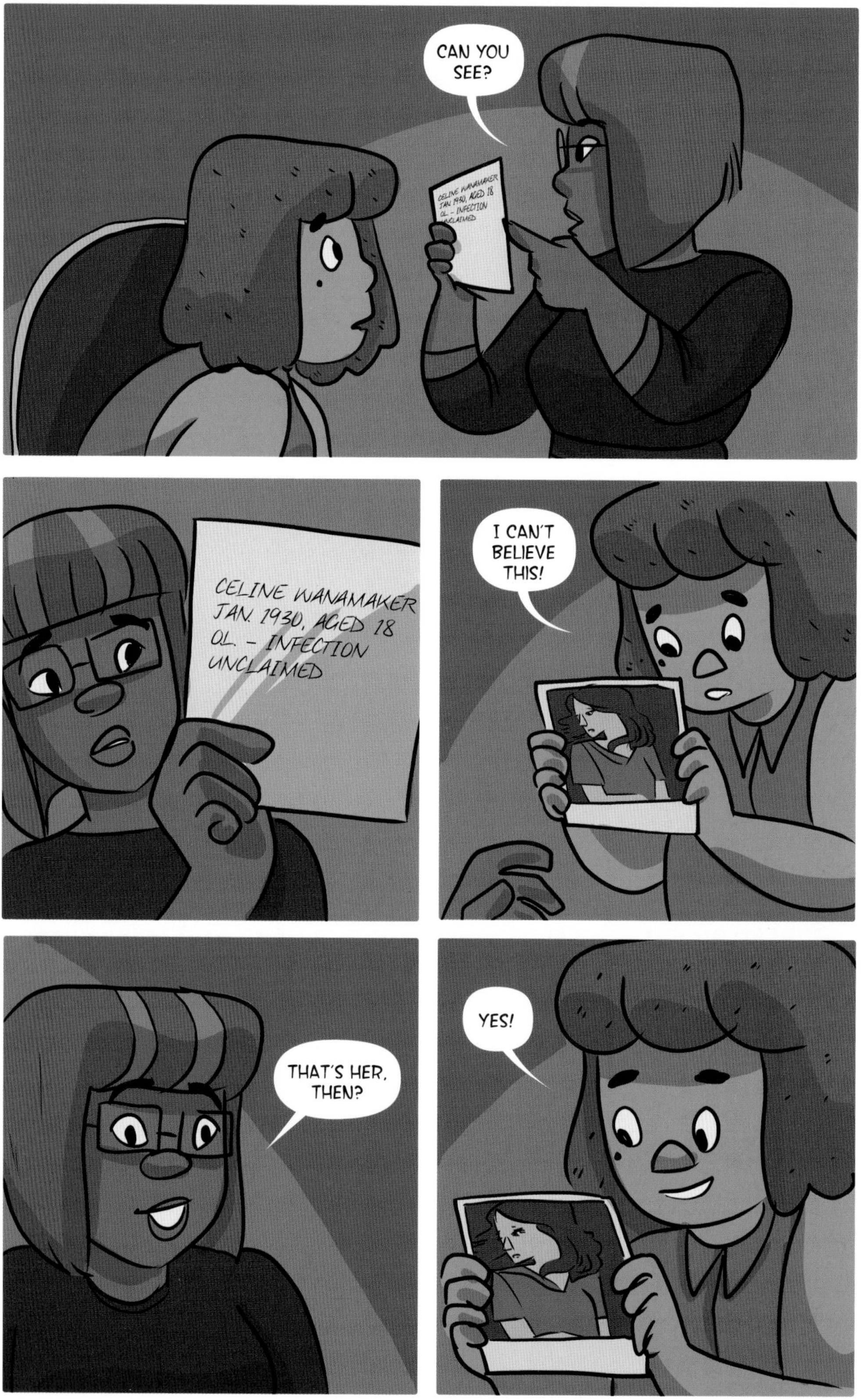
CAN YOU SEE?
CELINE WANAMAKER
JAN. 1930, AGED 18
OL. - INFECTION
UNCLAIMED
I CAN'T BELIEVE THIS!
THAT'S HER, THEN?
YES!

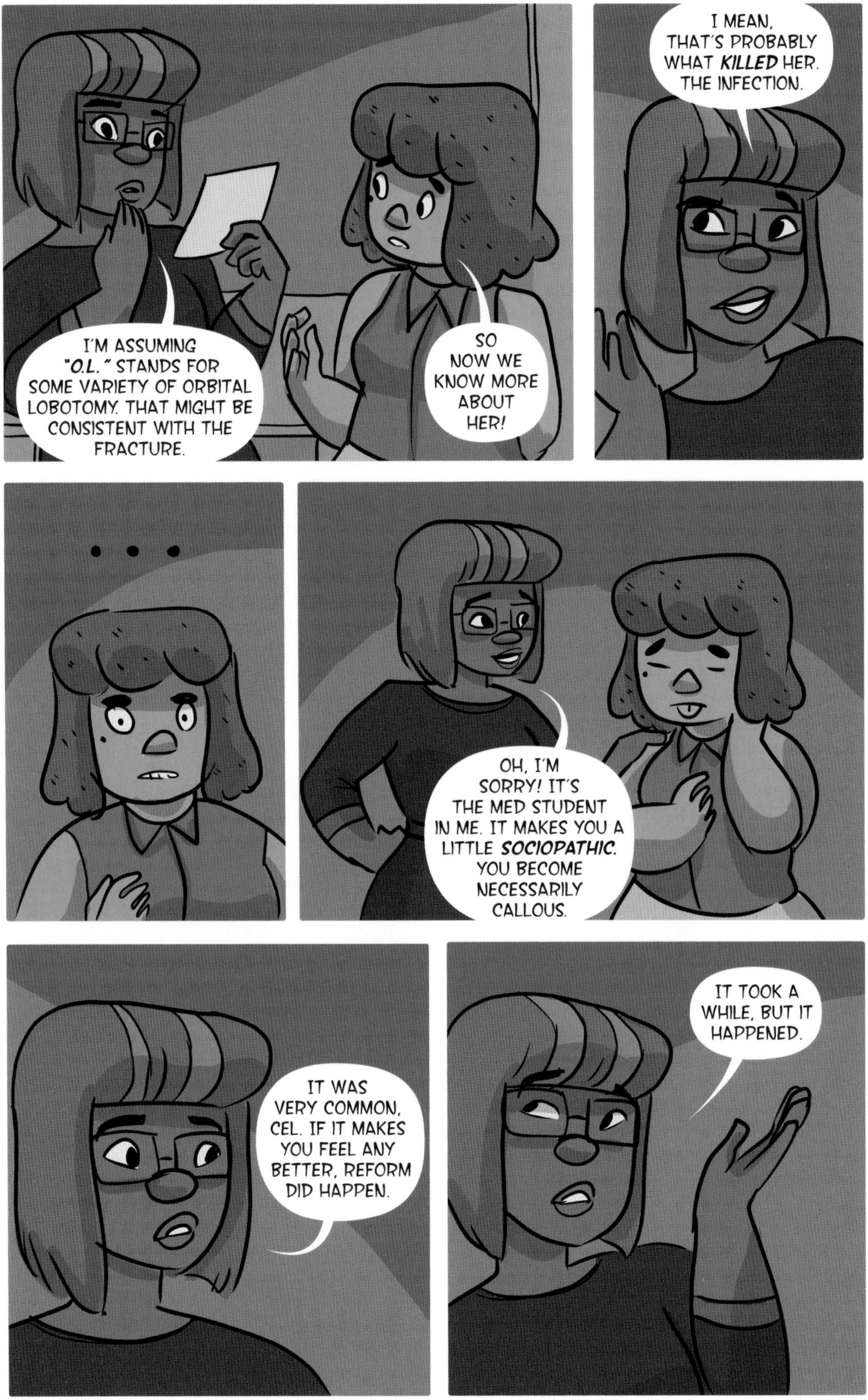
I'M ASSUMING "O.L." STANDS FOR SOME VARIETY OF ORBITAL LOBOTOMY. THAT MIGHT BE CONSISTENT WITH THE FRACTURE.
SO NOW WE KNOW MORE ABOUT HER!
I MEAN, THAT'S PROBABLY WHAT KILLED HER. THE INFECTION.
...
OH, I'M SORRY! IT'S THE MED STUDENT IN ME. IT MAKES YOU A LITTLE SOCIOPATHIC. YOU BECOME NECESSARILY CALLOUS.
IT WAS VERY COMMON, CEL. IF IT MAKES YOU FEEL ANY BETTER, REFORM DID HAPPEN.
IT TOOK A WHILE, BUT IT HAPPENED.

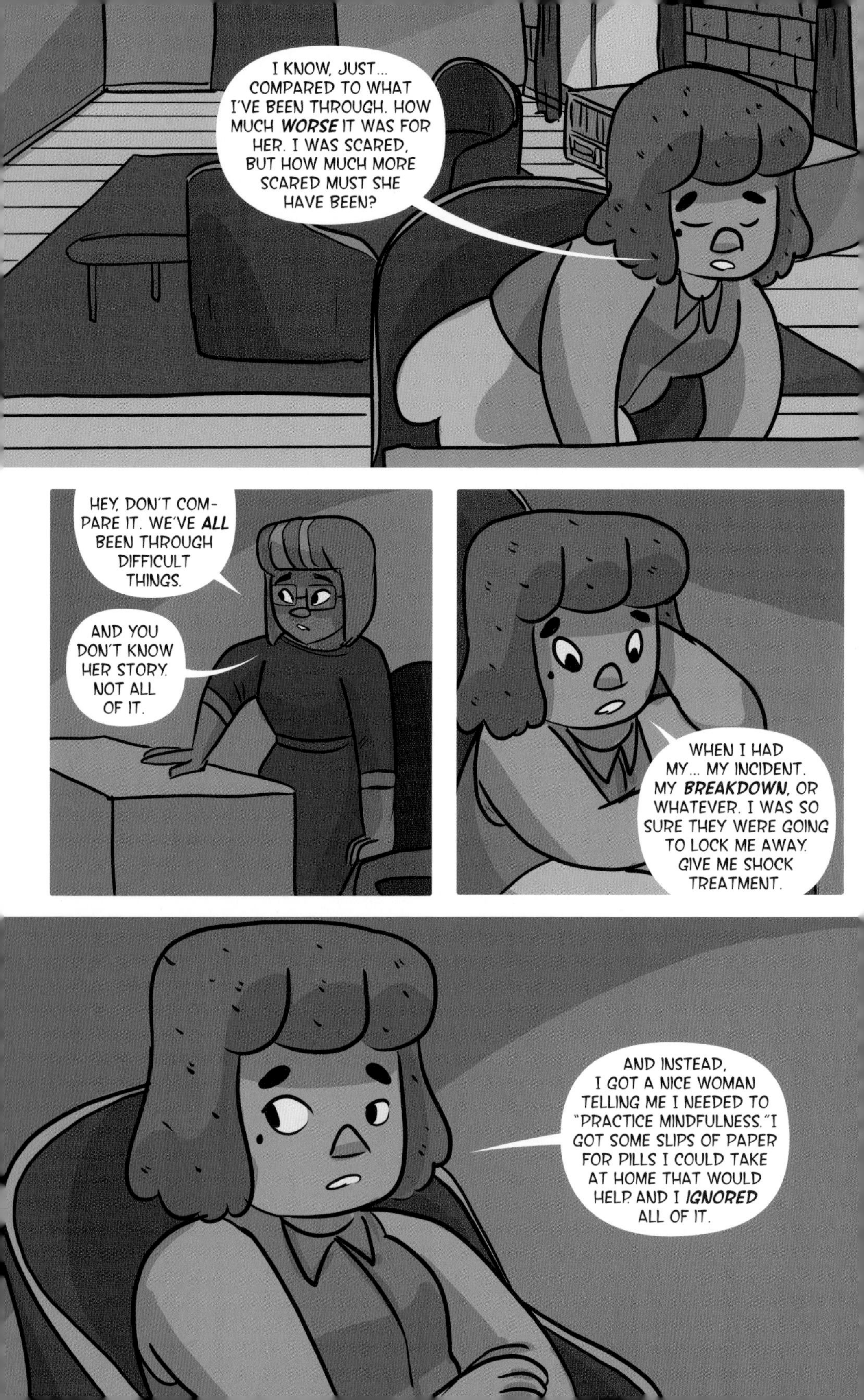
I KNOW, JUST... COMPARED TO WHAT I'VE BEEN THROUGH. HOW MUCH WORSE IT WAS FOR HER. I WAS SCARED, BUT HOW MUCH MORE SCARED MUST SHE HAVE BEEN?
HEY, DON'T COM-PARE IT. WE'VE ALL BEEN THROUGH DIFFICULT THINGS.
AND YOU DON'T KNOW HER STORY. NOT ALL OF IT.
WHEN I HAD MY... MY INCIDENT. MY BREAKDOWN, OR WHATEVER. I WAS SO SURE THEY WERE GOING TO LOCK ME AWAY. GIVE ME SHOCK TREATMENT.
AND INSTEAD, I GOT A NICE WOMAN TELLING ME I NEEDED TO "PRACTICE MINDFULNESS." I GOT SOME SLIPS OF PAPER FOR PILLS I COULD TAKE AT HOME THAT WOULD HELP. AND I IGNORED ALL OF IT.

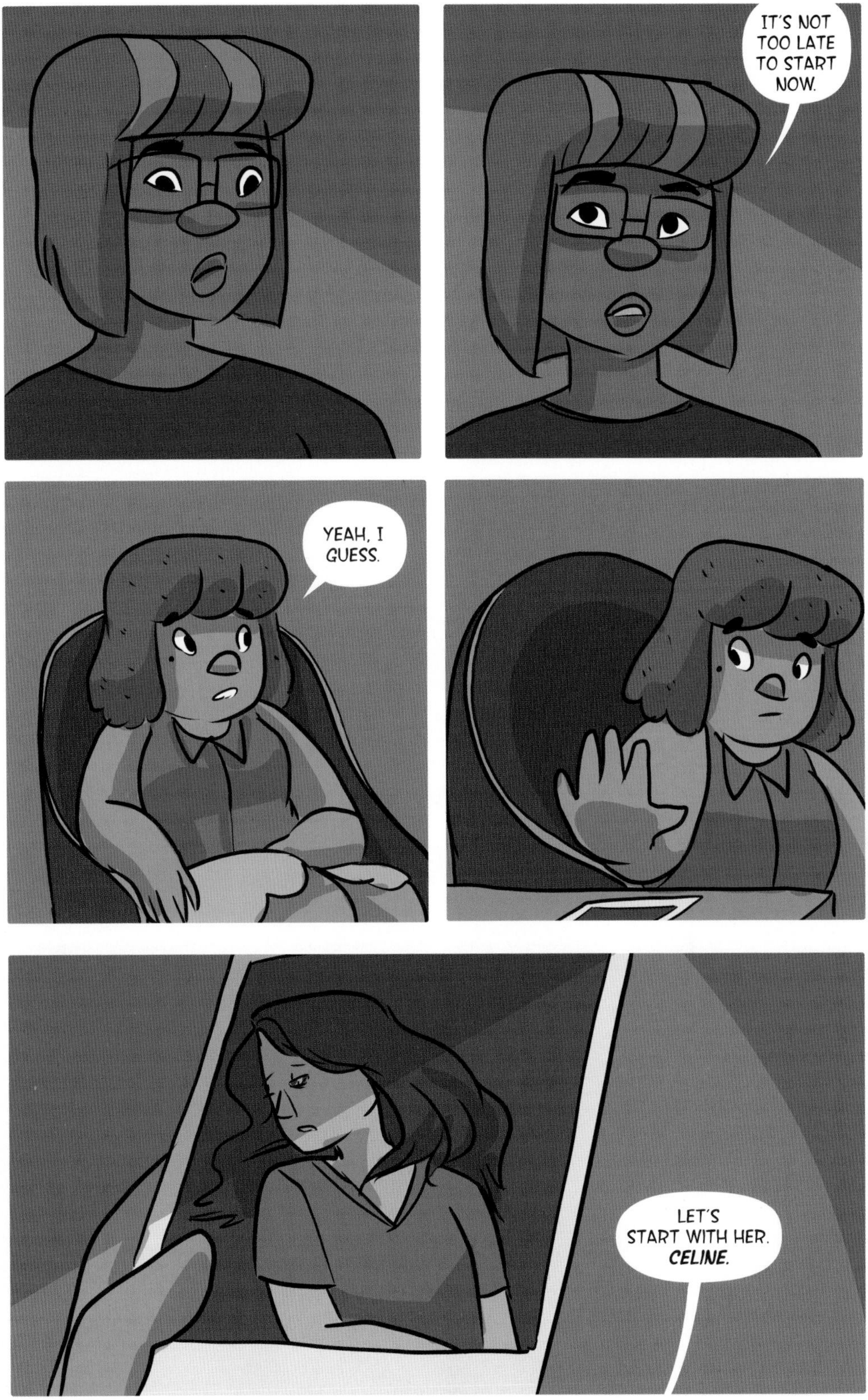
IT'S NOT TOO LATE TO START NOW.
YEAH, I GUESS.
LET'S START WITH HER. CELINE.

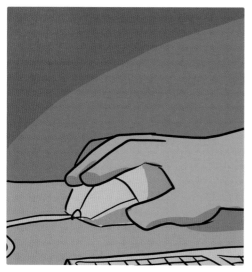

CEL.

JEEZ! YOU SCARED ME TO DEATH!

WHERE HAVE YOU *BEEN?* I HAVEN'T SEEN YOU IN DAYS!

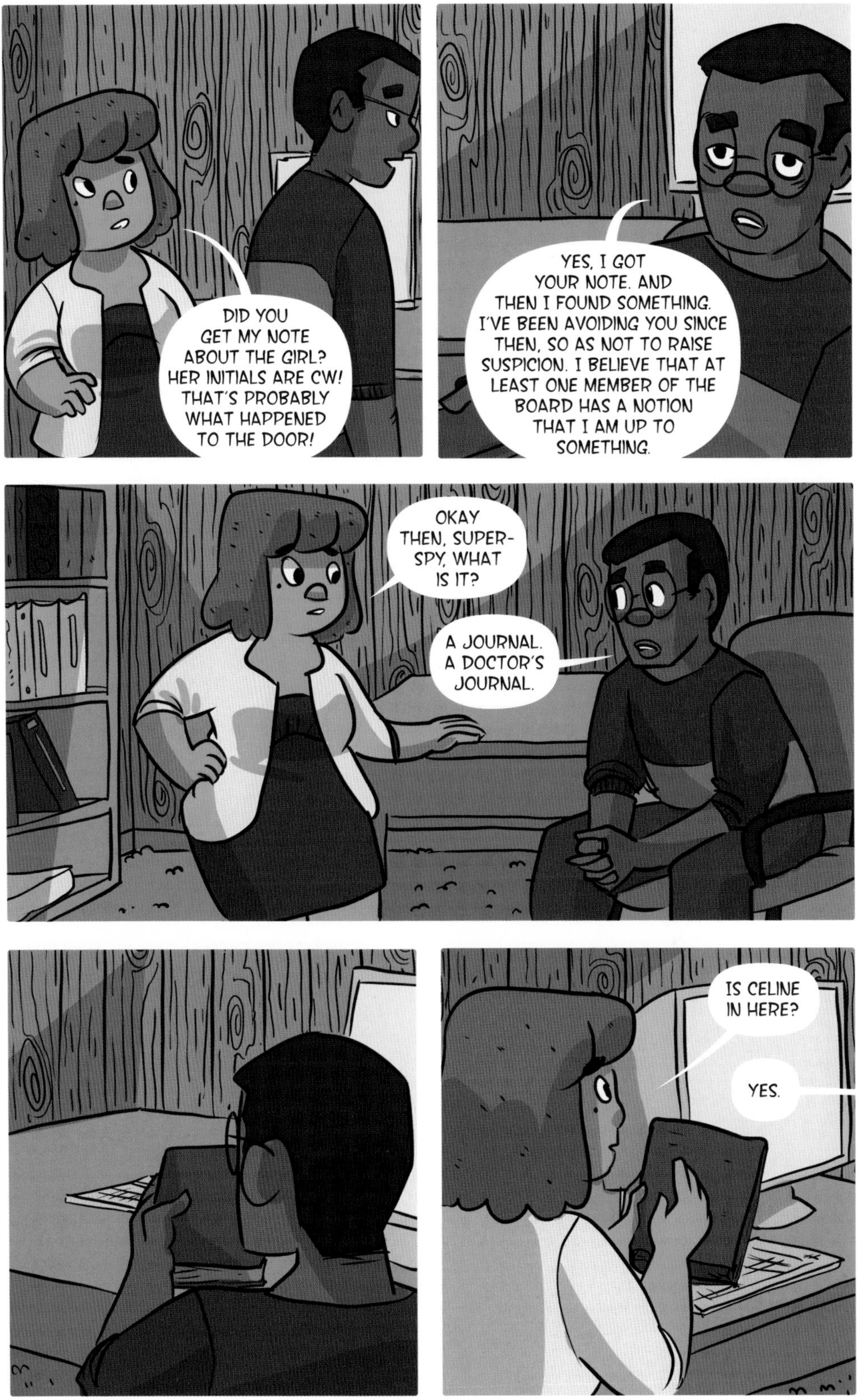
DID YOU GET MY NOTE ABOUT THE GIRL? HER INITIALS ARE CW! THAT'S PROBABLY WHAT HAPPENED TO THE DOOR!
YES, I GOT YOUR NOTE. AND THEN I FOUND SOMETHING. I'VE BEEN AVOIDING YOU SINCE THEN, SO AS NOT TO RAISE SUSPICION. I BELIEVE THAT AT LEAST ONE MEMBER OF THE BOARD HAS A NOTION THAT I AM UP TO SOMETHING.
OKAY THEN, SUPER-SPY, WHAT IS IT?
A JOURNAL. A DOCTOR'S JOURNAL.
IS CELINE IN HERE?
YES.

IT APPEARS HOLLY WAS RIGHT.

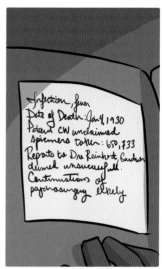

Infection, fever
Date of Death: Jan 4, 1930
Patient CW unclaimed
Specimens taken: 650,733
Reports to Drs. Reinhardt Gardner
deemed unsuccessful.
Continuations of
papinosurgery likely.

IF THEY STILL REMAIN ON THE PROPERTY, IT IS VERY LIKELY THOSE SPECIMENS ARE SOMEWHERE IN THE MUSEUM.

IF THEY WERE FRAGMENTS OF SKULL OR BRAIN TISSUE, I THINK I CAN LOCATE THEM SOMEWHAT EASILY. UNLESS THEY'VE ALREADY BEEN...

UNLESS I CAN'T *FIND* THEM.

SO THERE'S... *PIECES* OF HER? IN THE MUSEUM?

THERE WERE PIECES OF *A LOT* OF PEOPLE IN THE MUSEUM.

ARE. THERE *ARE* PIECES OF A LOT OF PEOPLE.

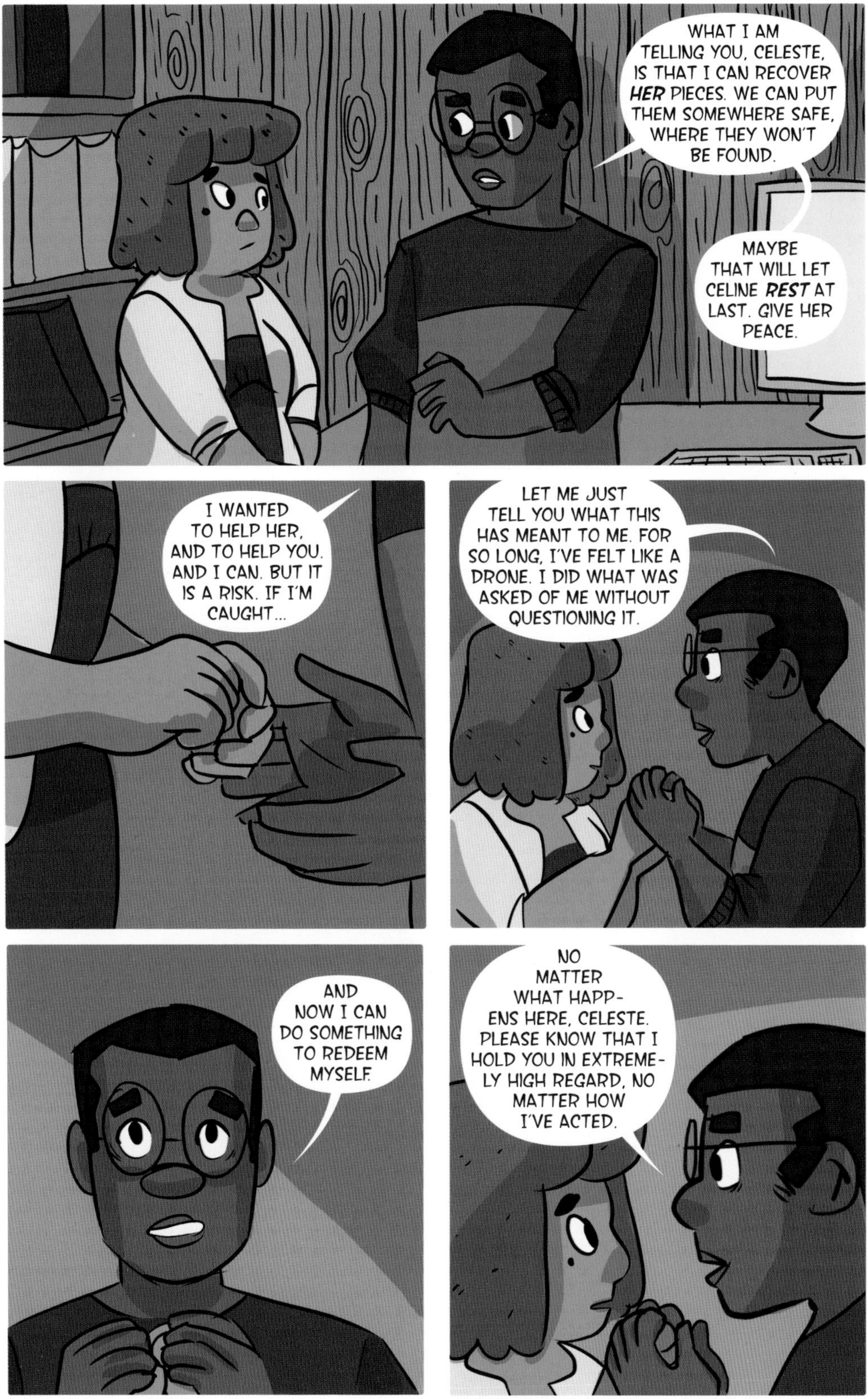
WHAT I AM TELLING YOU, CELESTE, IS THAT I CAN RECOVER HER PIECES. WE CAN PUT THEM SOMEWHERE SAFE, WHERE THEY WON'T BE FOUND.
MAYBE THAT WILL LET CELINE REST AT LAST. GIVE HER PEACE.
I WANTED TO HELP HER, AND TO HELP YOU. AND I CAN. BUT IT IS A RISK. IF I'M CAUGHT...
LET ME JUST TELL YOU WHAT THIS HAS MEANT TO ME. FOR SO LONG, I'VE FELT LIKE A DRONE. I DID WHAT WAS ASKED OF ME WITHOUT QUESTIONING IT.
AND NOW I CAN DO SOMETHING TO REDEEM MYSELF.
NO MATTER WHAT HAPP-ENS HERE, CELESTE. PLEASE KNOW THAT I HOLD YOU IN EXTREME-LY HIGH REGARD, NO MATTER HOW I'VE ACTED.

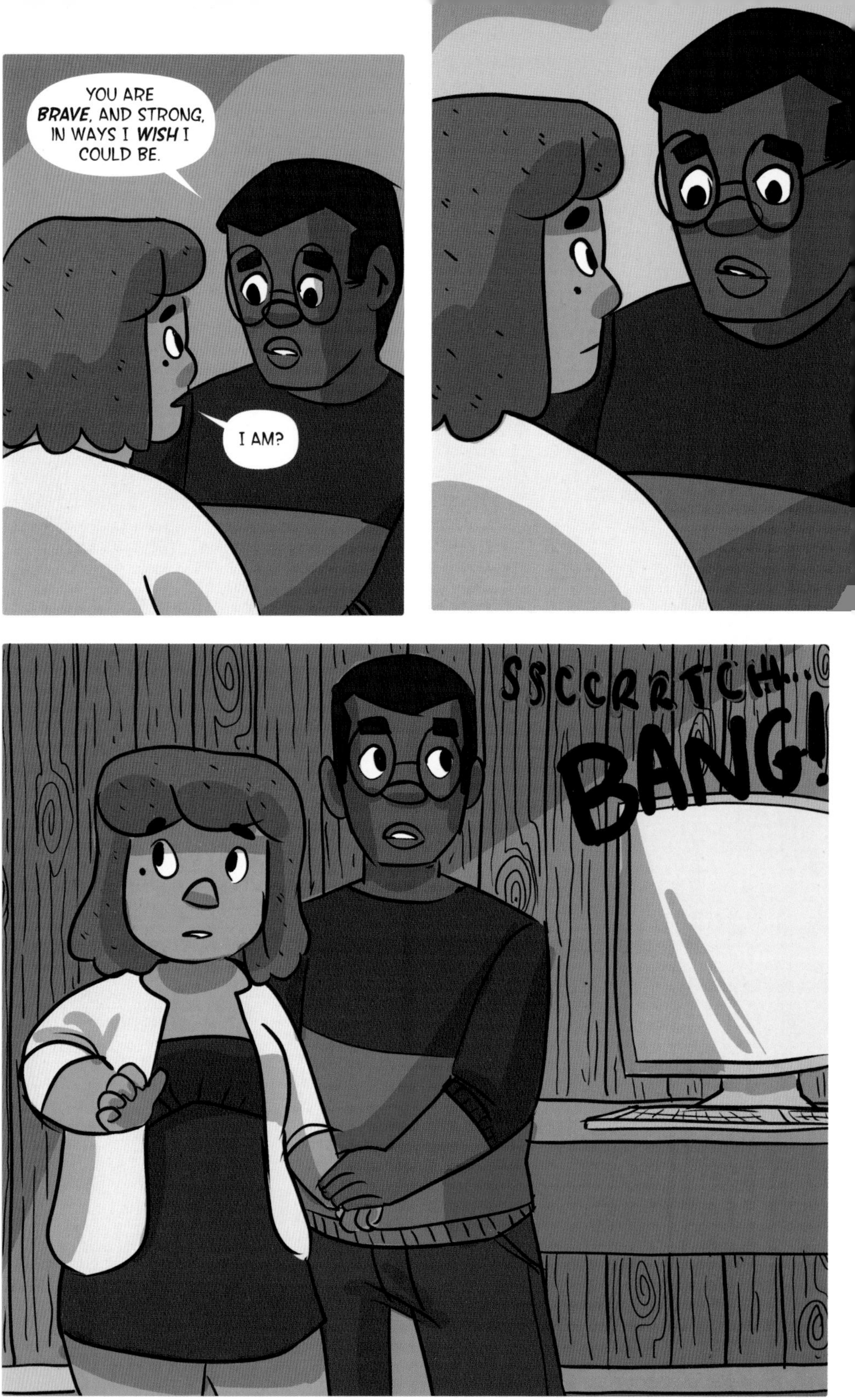
YOU ARE BRAVE, AND STRONG, IN WAYS I WISH I COULD BE.
I AM?
SSCCRRRTCH...
BANG!!

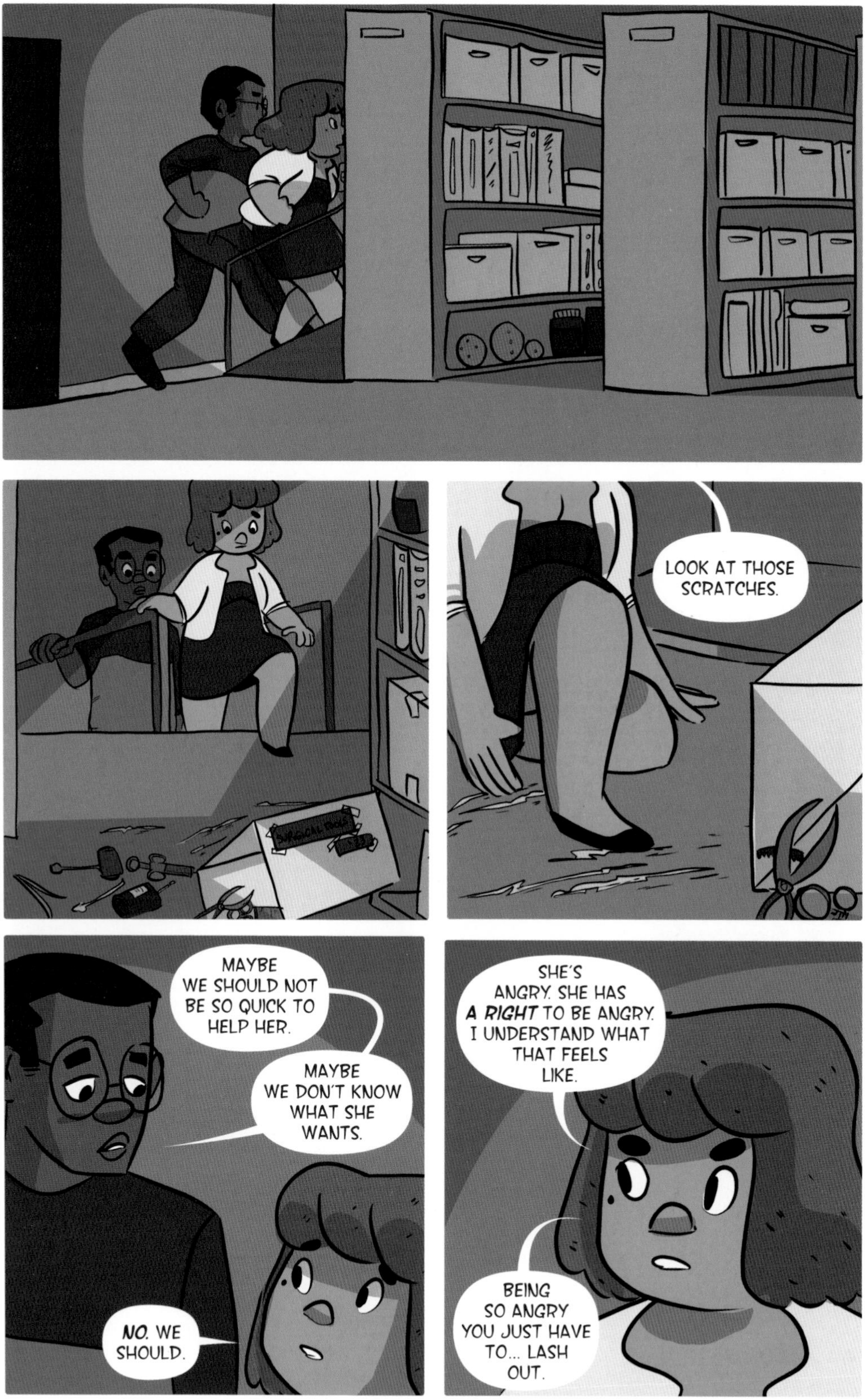
LOOK AT THOSE SCRATCHES.
MAYBE WE SHOULD NOT BE SO QUICK TO HELP HER.
MAYBE WE DON'T KNOW WHAT SHE WANTS.
NO. WE SHOULD.
SHE'S ANGRY. SHE HAS A RIGHT TO BE ANGRY. I UNDERSTAND WHAT THAT FEELS LIKE.
BEING SO ANGRY YOU JUST HAVE TO... LASH OUT.

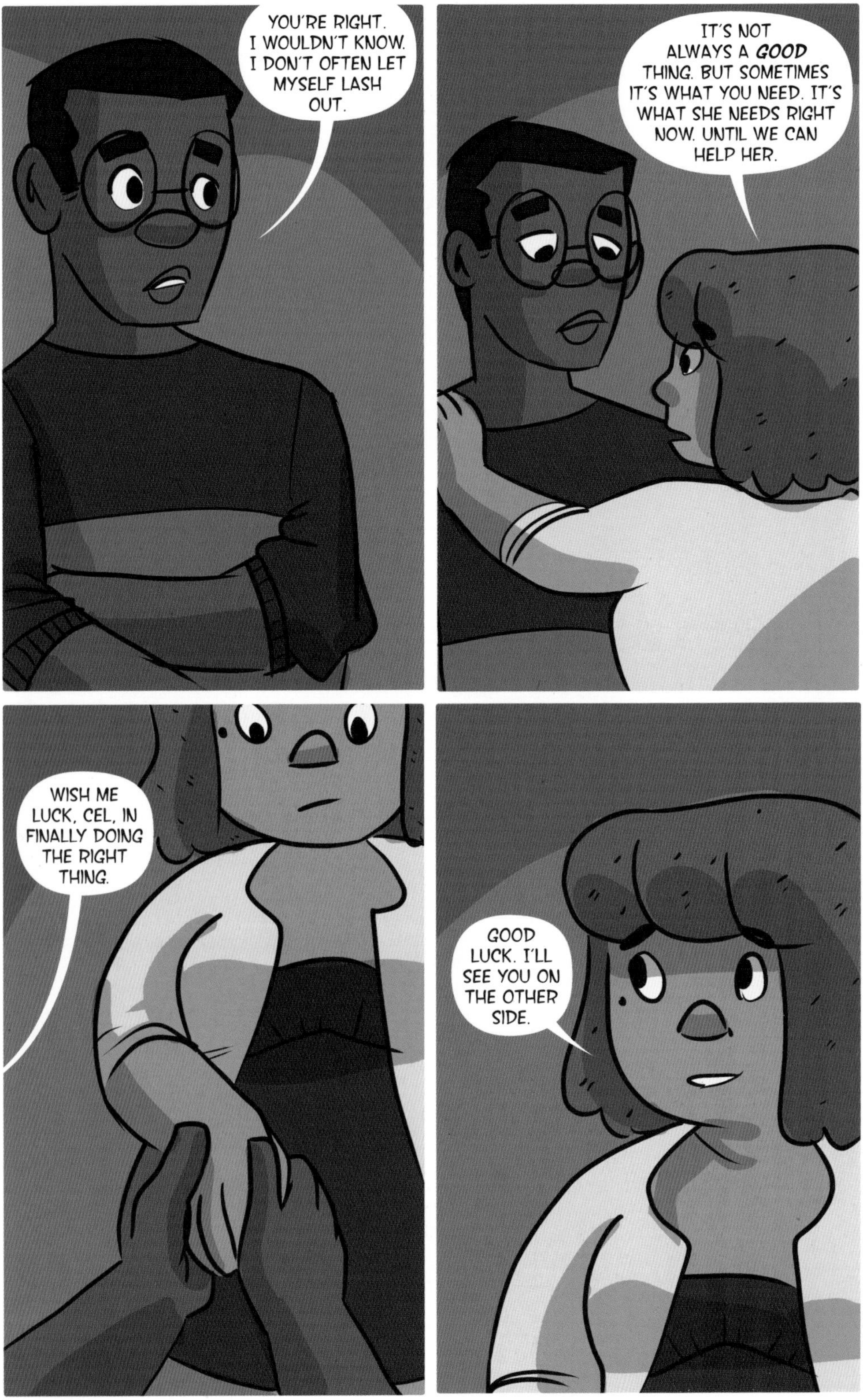
YOU'RE RIGHT. I WOULDN'T KNOW. I DON'T OFTEN LET MYSELF LASH OUT.
IT'S NOT ALWAYS A **GOOD** THING. BUT SOMETIMES IT'S WHAT YOU NEED. IT'S WHAT SHE NEEDS RIGHT NOW. UNTIL WE CAN HELP HER.
WISH ME LUCK, CEL, IN FINALLY DOING THE RIGHT THING.
GOOD LUCK. I'LL SEE YOU ON THE OTHER SIDE.

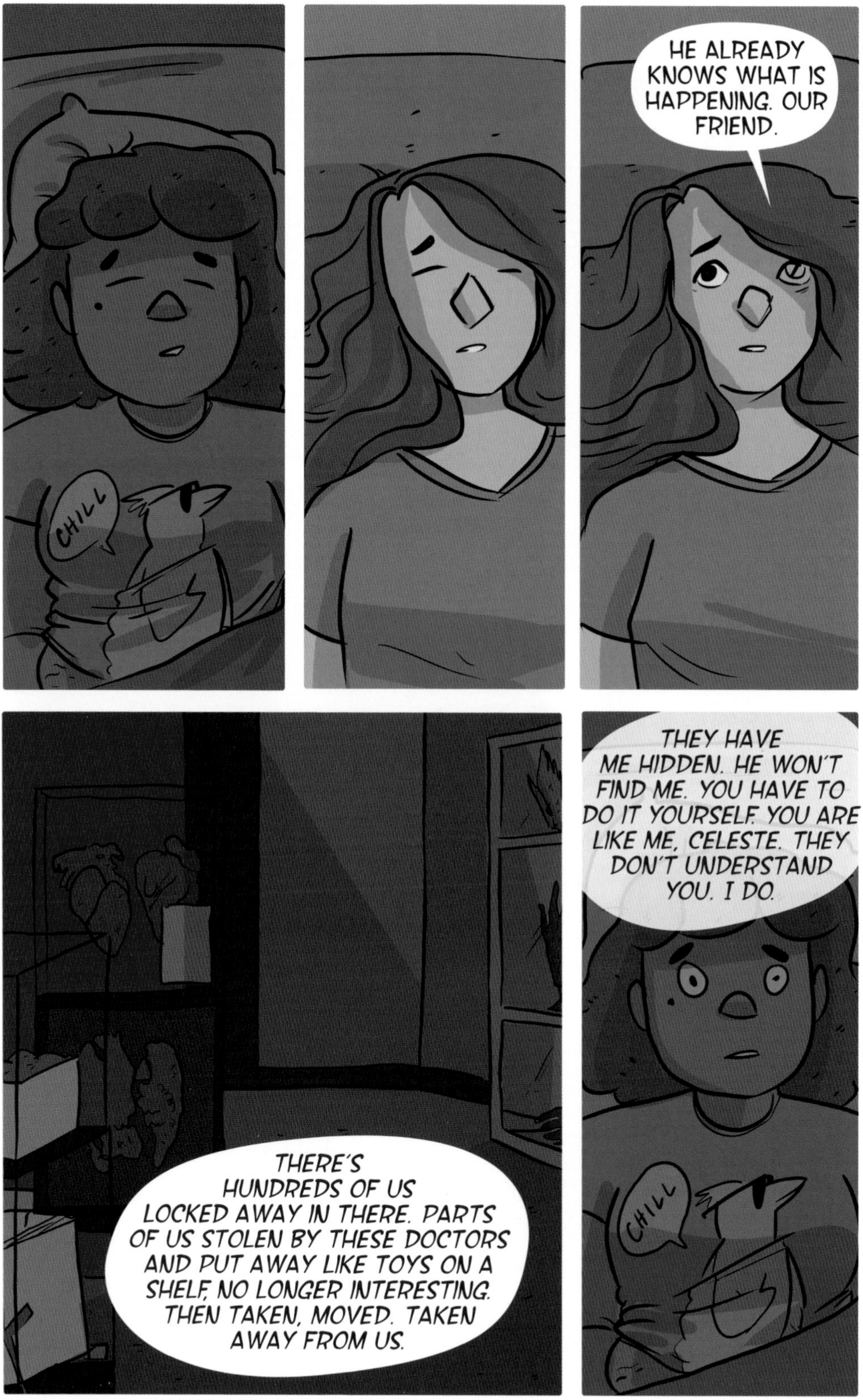
CHILL
HE ALREADY KNOWS WHAT IS HAPPENING. OUR FRIEND.
THERE'S HUNDREDS OF US LOCKED AWAY IN THERE. PARTS OF US STOLEN BY THESE DOCTORS AND PUT AWAY LIKE TOYS ON A SHELF, NO LONGER INTERESTING. THEN TAKEN, MOVED. TAKEN AWAY FROM US.
THEY HAVE ME HIDDEN. HE WON'T FIND ME. YOU HAVE TO DO IT YOURSELF. YOU ARE LIKE ME, CELESTE. THEY DON'T UNDERSTAND YOU. I DO.
CHILL

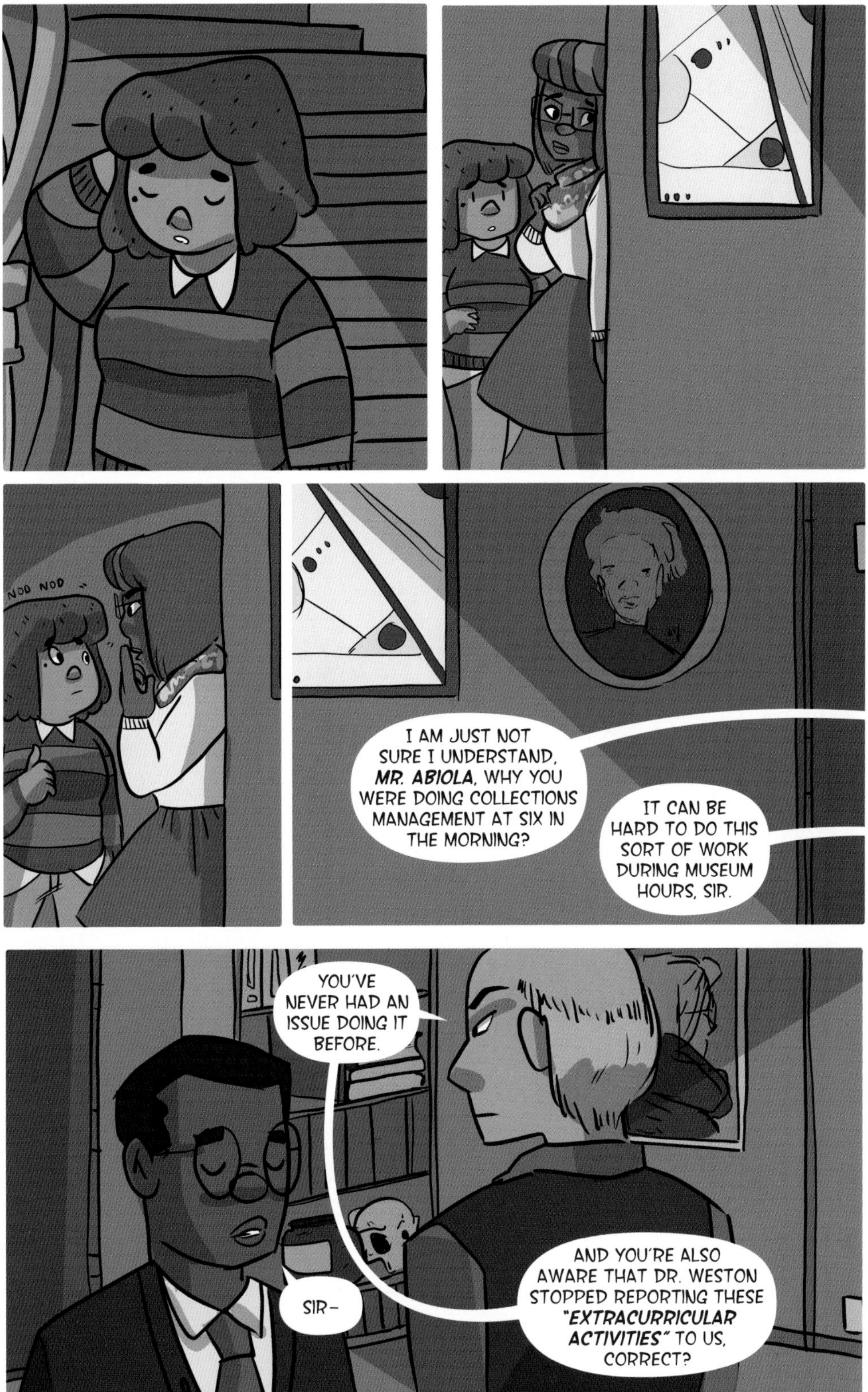
NOD NOD
I AM JUST NOT SURE I UNDERSTAND, ***MR. ABIOLA,*** WHY YOU WERE DOING COLLECTIONS MANAGEMENT AT SIX IN THE MORNING?
IT CAN BE HARD TO DO THIS SORT OF WORK DURING MUSEUM HOURS, SIR.
YOU'VE NEVER HAD AN ISSUE DOING IT BEFORE.
SIR–
AND YOU'RE ALSO AWARE THAT DR. WESTON STOPPED REPORTING THESE ***"EXTRACURRICULAR ACTIVITIES"*** TO US, CORRECT?

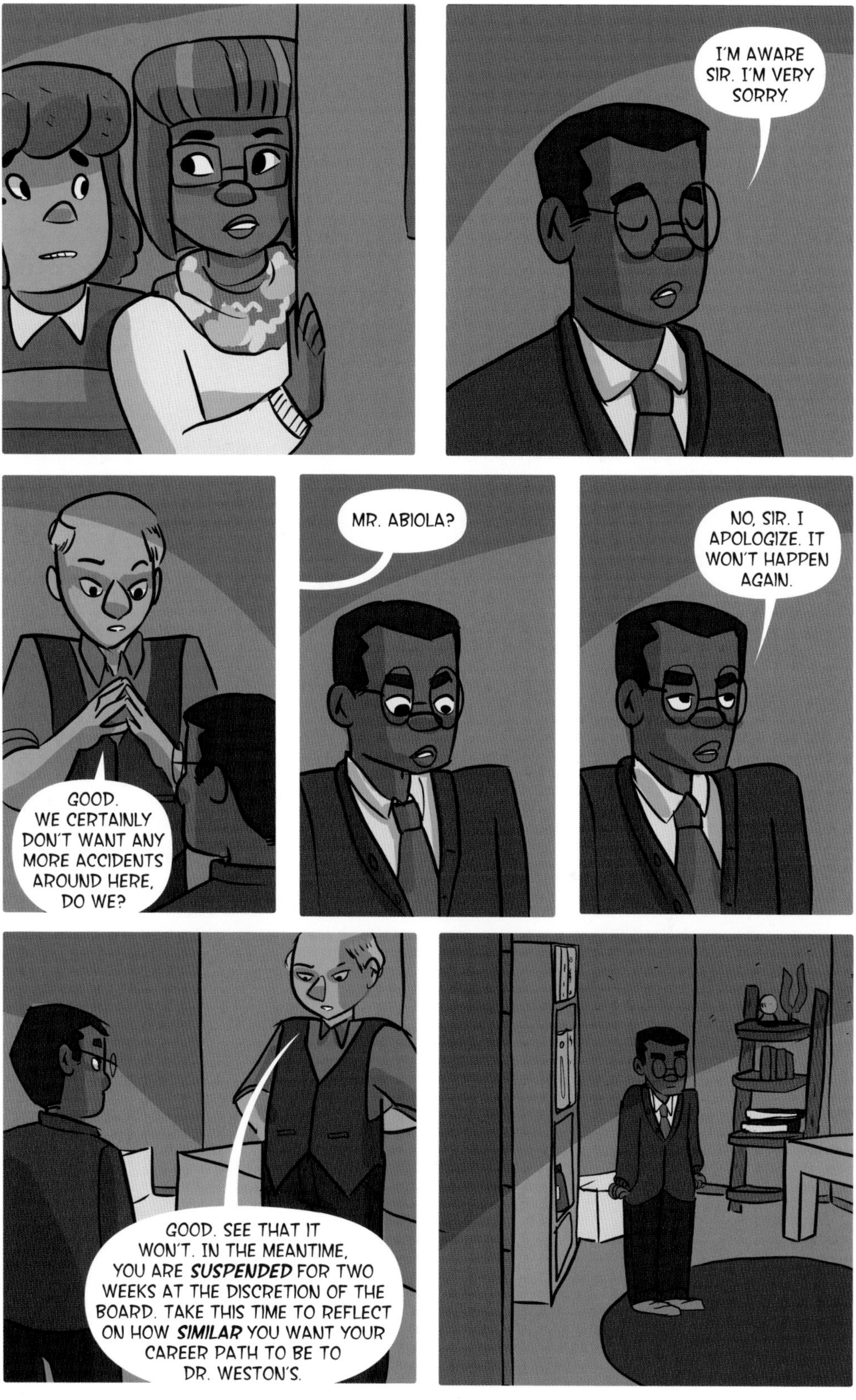
I'M AWARE SIR. I'M VERY SORRY.
GOOD. WE CERTAINLY DON'T WANT ANY MORE ACCIDENTS AROUND HERE, DO WE?
MR. ABIOLA?
NO, SIR. I APOLOGIZE. IT WON'T HAPPEN AGAIN.
GOOD. SEE THAT IT WON'T. IN THE MEANTIME, YOU ARE ***SUSPENDED*** FOR TWO WEEKS AT THE DISCRETION OF THE BOARD. TAKE THIS TIME TO REFLECT ON HOW ***SIMILAR*** YOU WANT YOUR CAREER PATH TO BE TO DR. WESTON'S.

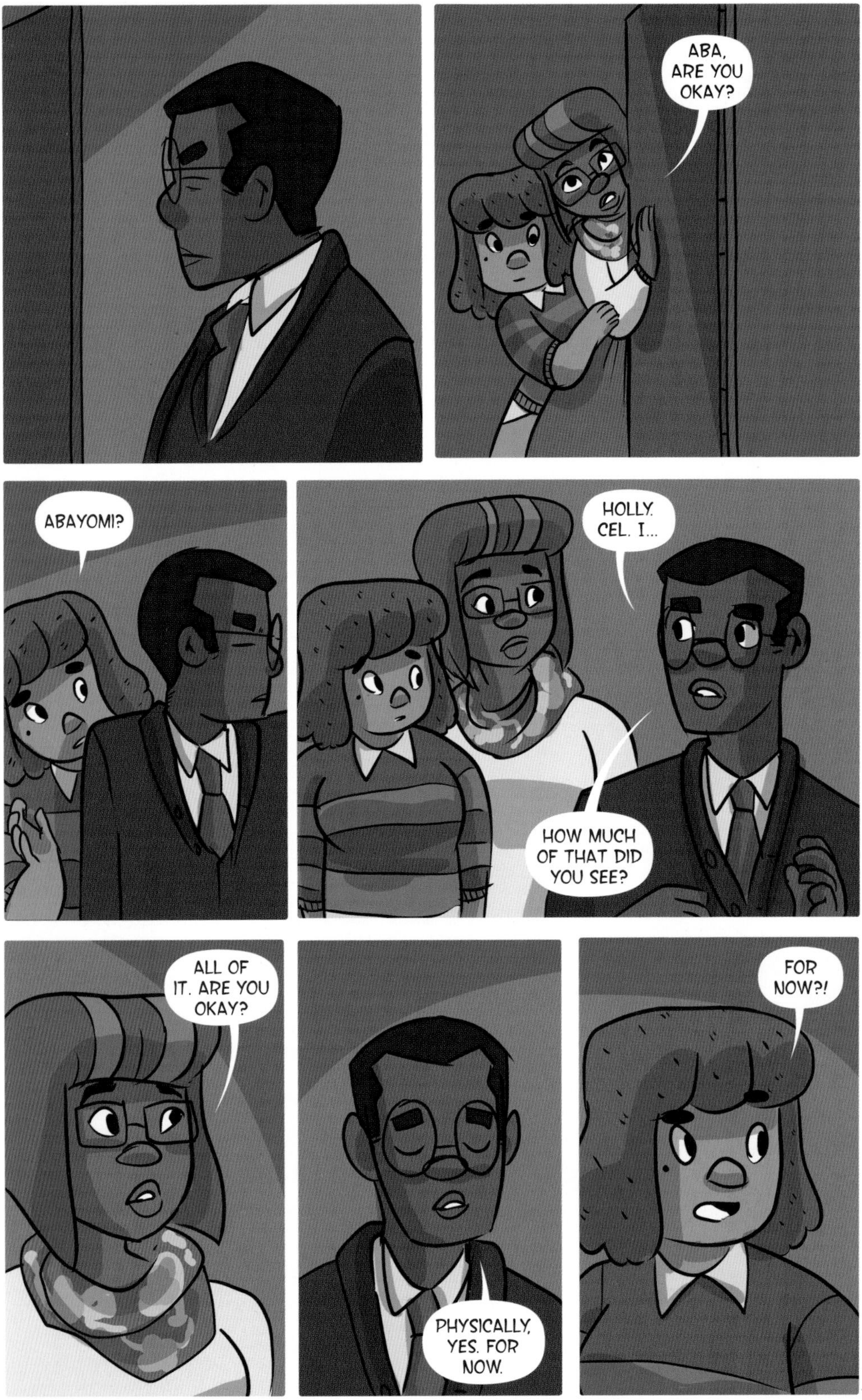
ABA, ARE YOU OKAY?
ABAYOMI?
HOLLY. CEL. I...
HOW MUCH OF THAT DID YOU SEE?
ALL OF IT. ARE YOU OKAY?
PHYSICALLY, YES. FOR NOW.
FOR NOW?!

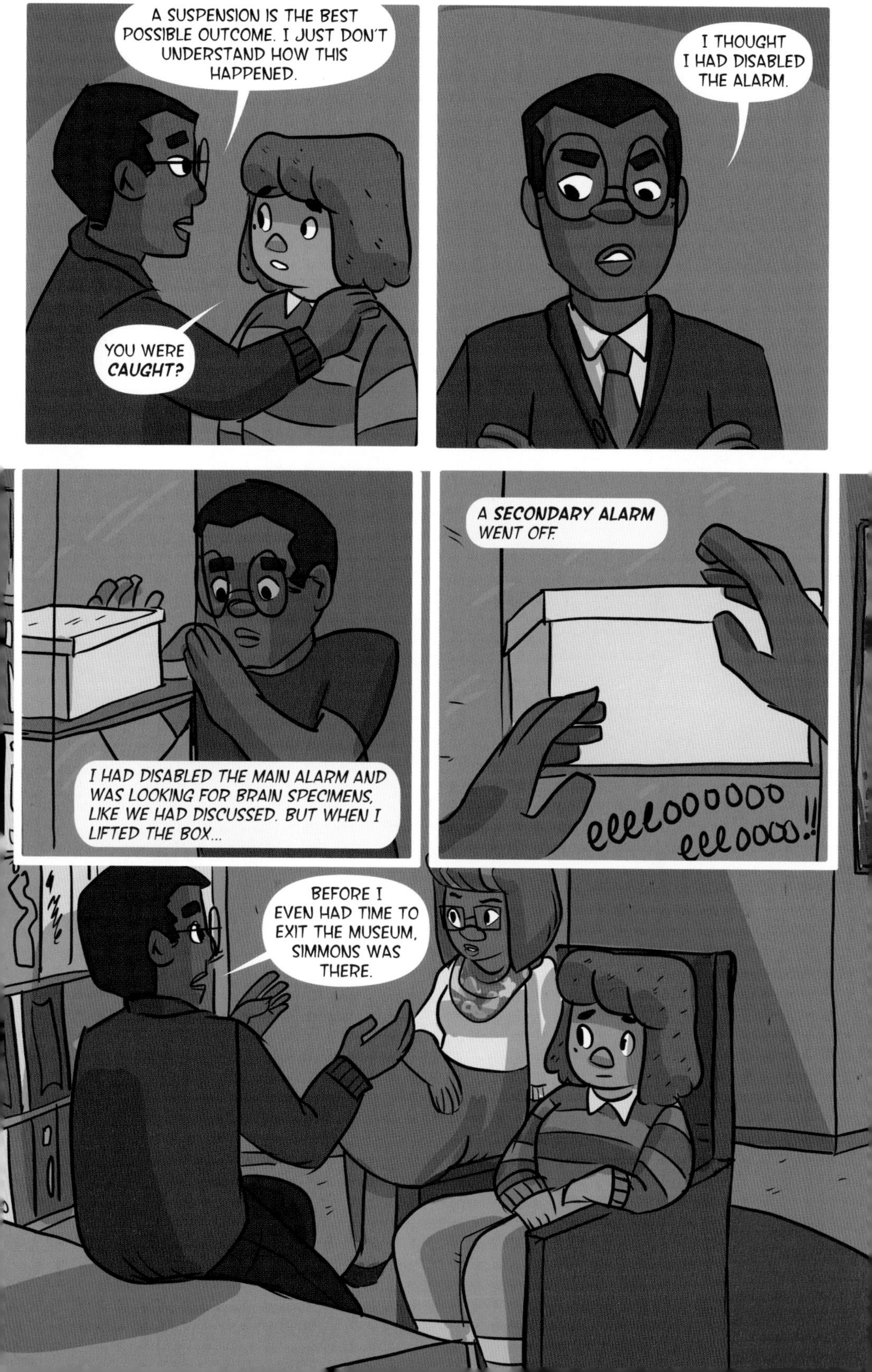
A SUSPENSION IS THE BEST POSSIBLE OUTCOME. I JUST DON'T UNDERSTAND HOW THIS HAPPENED.
YOU WERE *CAUGHT?*
I THOUGHT I HAD DISABLED THE ALARM.
I HAD DISABLED THE MAIN ALARM AND WAS LOOKING FOR BRAIN SPECIMENS, LIKE WE HAD DISCUSSED. BUT WHEN I LIFTED THE BOX...
A **SECONDARY ALARM** WENT OFF.
eeeeooooooo eeeoooo!!
BEFORE I EVEN HAD TIME TO EXIT THE MUSEUM, SIMMONS WAS THERE.

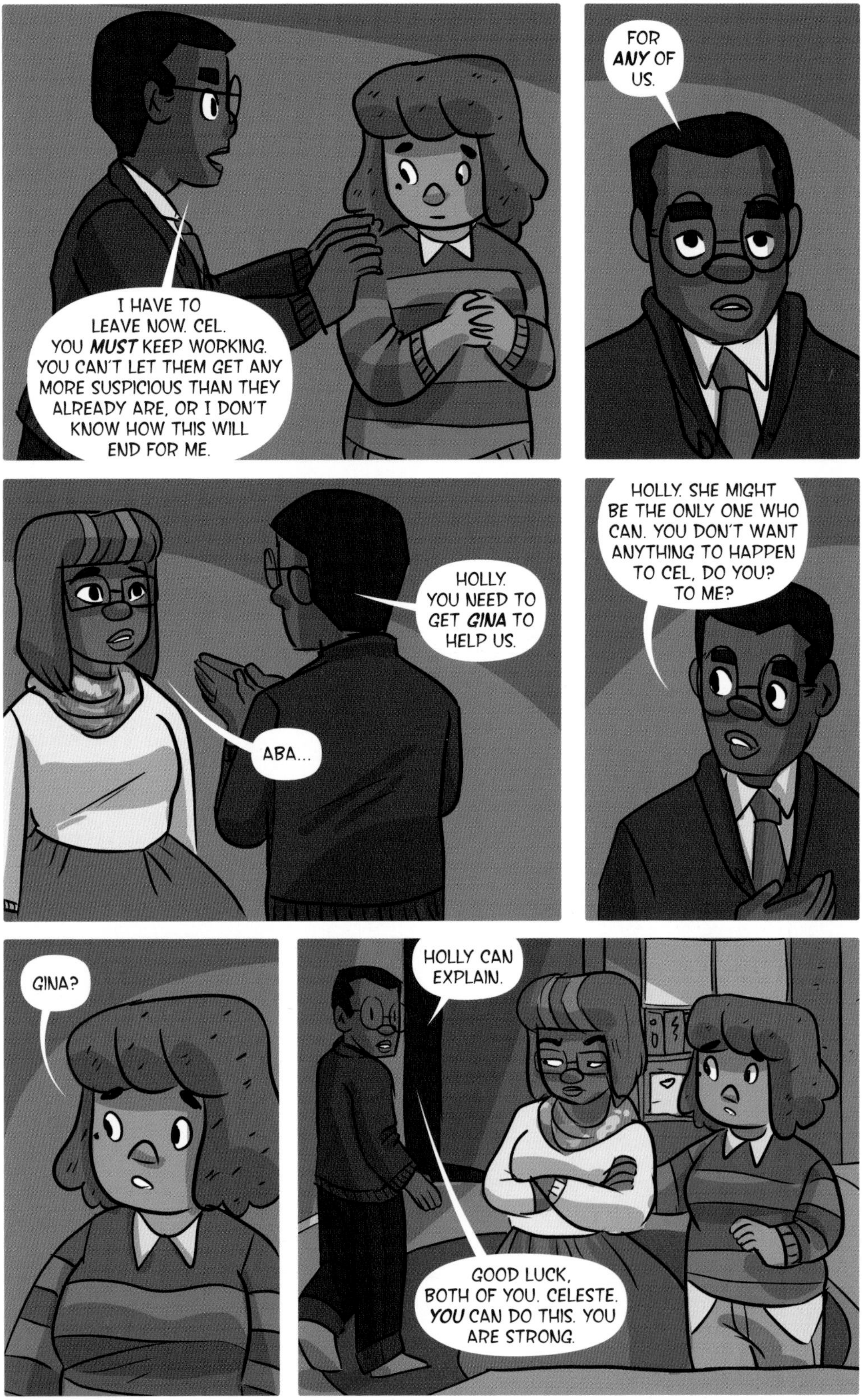
I HAVE TO LEAVE NOW. CEL. YOU MUST KEEP WORKING. YOU CAN'T LET THEM GET ANY MORE SUSPICIOUS THAN THEY ALREADY ARE, OR I DON'T KNOW HOW THIS WILL END FOR ME.
FOR ANY OF US.
HOLLY. YOU NEED TO GET GINA TO HELP US.
ABA...
HOLLY. SHE MIGHT BE THE ONLY ONE WHO CAN. YOU DON'T WANT ANYTHING TO HAPPEN TO CEL, DO YOU? TO ME?
GINA?
HOLLY CAN EXPLAIN.
GOOD LUCK, BOTH OF YOU. CELESTE. YOU CAN DO THIS. YOU ARE STRONG.

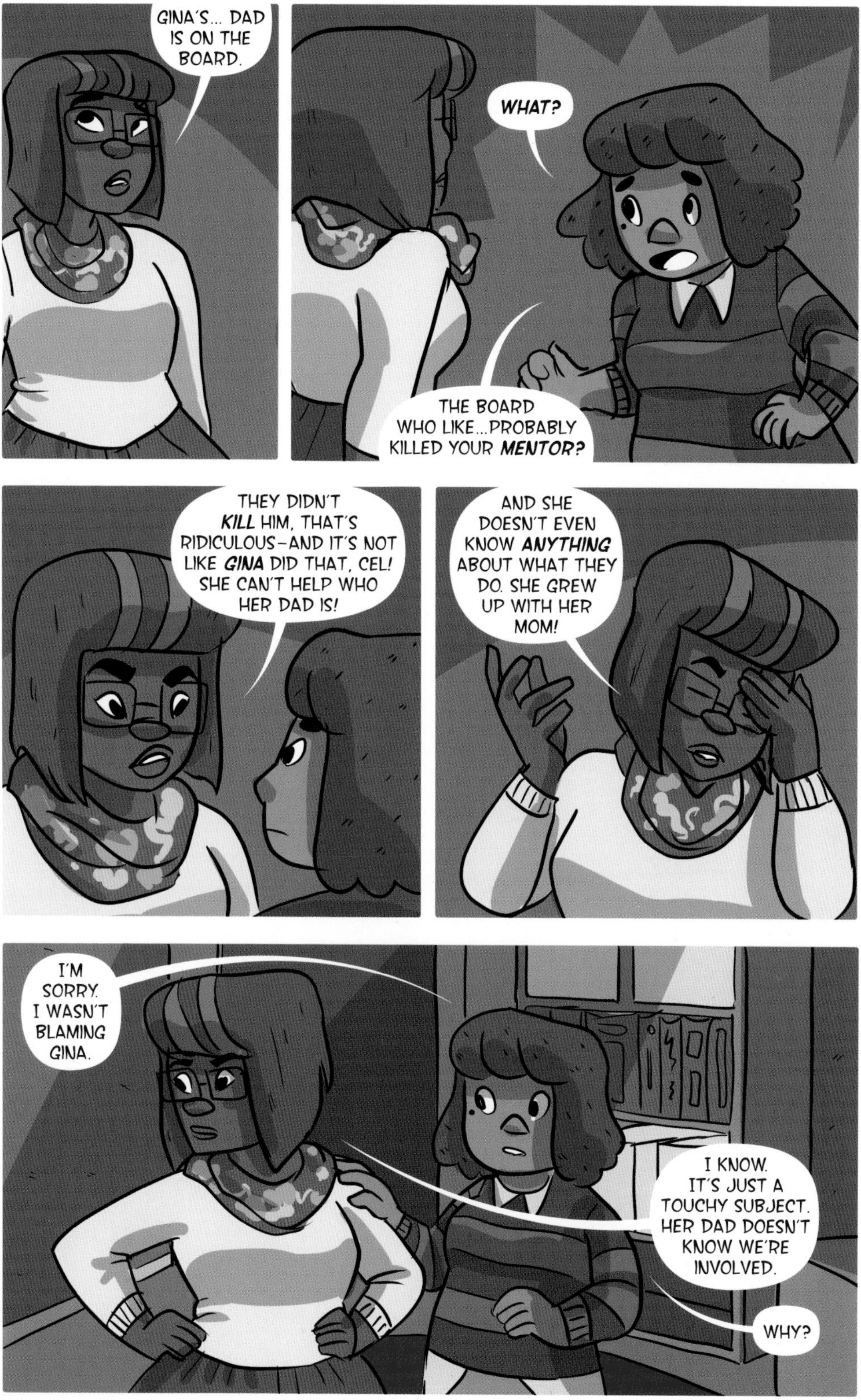
GINA'S... DAD IS ON THE BOARD.
WHAT?
THE BOARD WHO LIKE...PROBABLY KILLED YOUR MENTOR?
THEY DIDN'T KILL HIM, THAT'S RIDICULOUS–AND IT'S NOT LIKE GINA DID THAT, CEL! SHE CAN'T HELP WHO HER DAD IS!
AND SHE DOESN'T EVEN KNOW ANYTHING ABOUT WHAT THEY DO. SHE GREW UP WITH HER MOM!
I'M SORRY. I WASN'T BLAMING GINA.
I KNOW. IT'S JUST A TOUCHY SUBJECT. HER DAD DOESN'T KNOW WE'RE INVOLVED.
WHY?

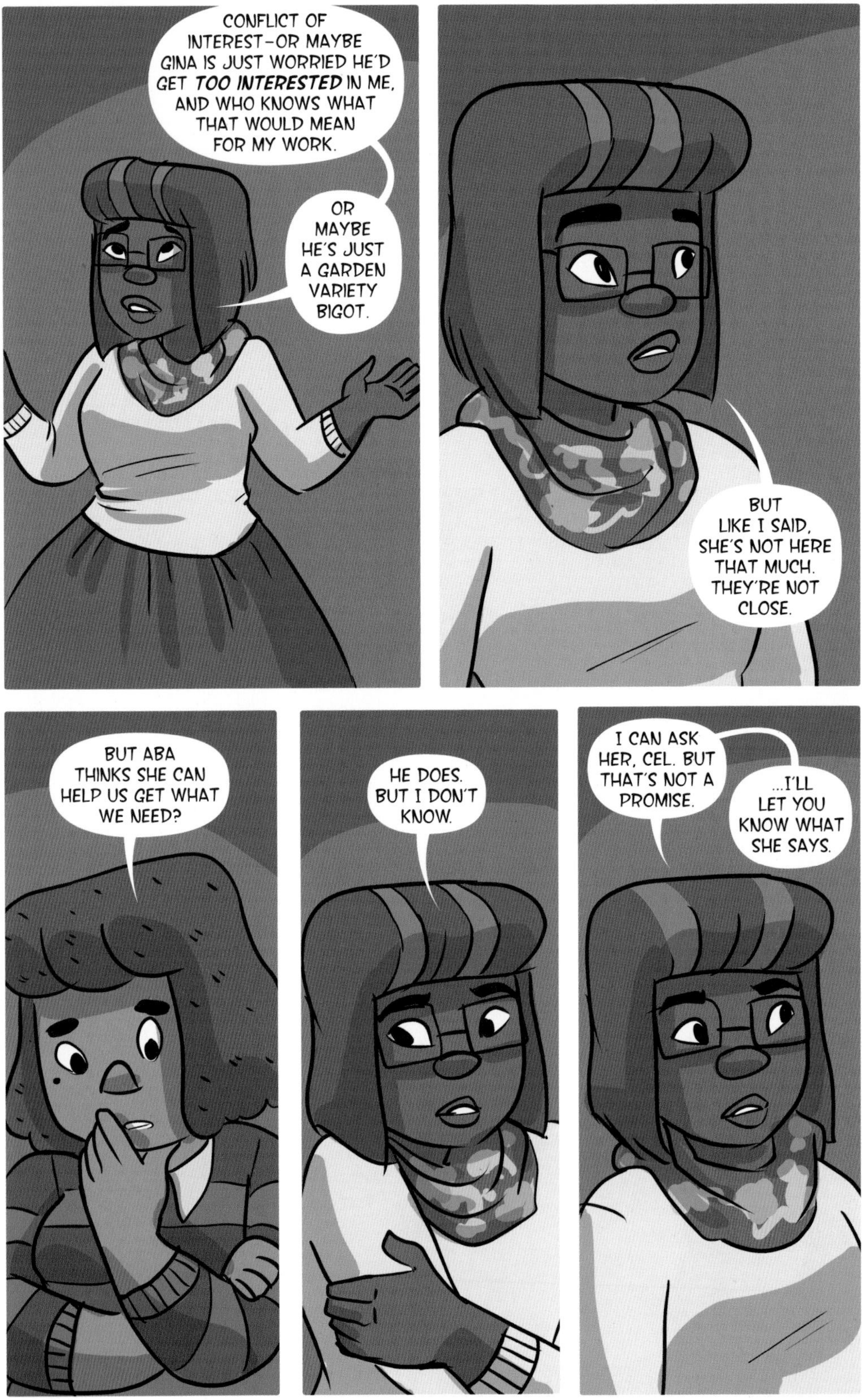
CONFLICT OF INTEREST–OR MAYBE GINA IS JUST WORRIED HE'D GET *TOO INTERESTED* IN ME, AND WHO KNOWS WHAT THAT WOULD MEAN FOR MY WORK.
OR MAYBE HE'S JUST A GARDEN VARIETY BIGOT.
BUT LIKE I SAID, SHE'S NOT HERE THAT MUCH. THEY'RE NOT CLOSE.
BUT ABA THINKS SHE CAN HELP US GET WHAT WE NEED?
HE DOES. BUT I DON'T KNOW.
I CAN ASK HER, CEL. BUT THAT'S NOT A PROMISE.
...I'LL LET YOU KNOW WHAT SHE SAYS.

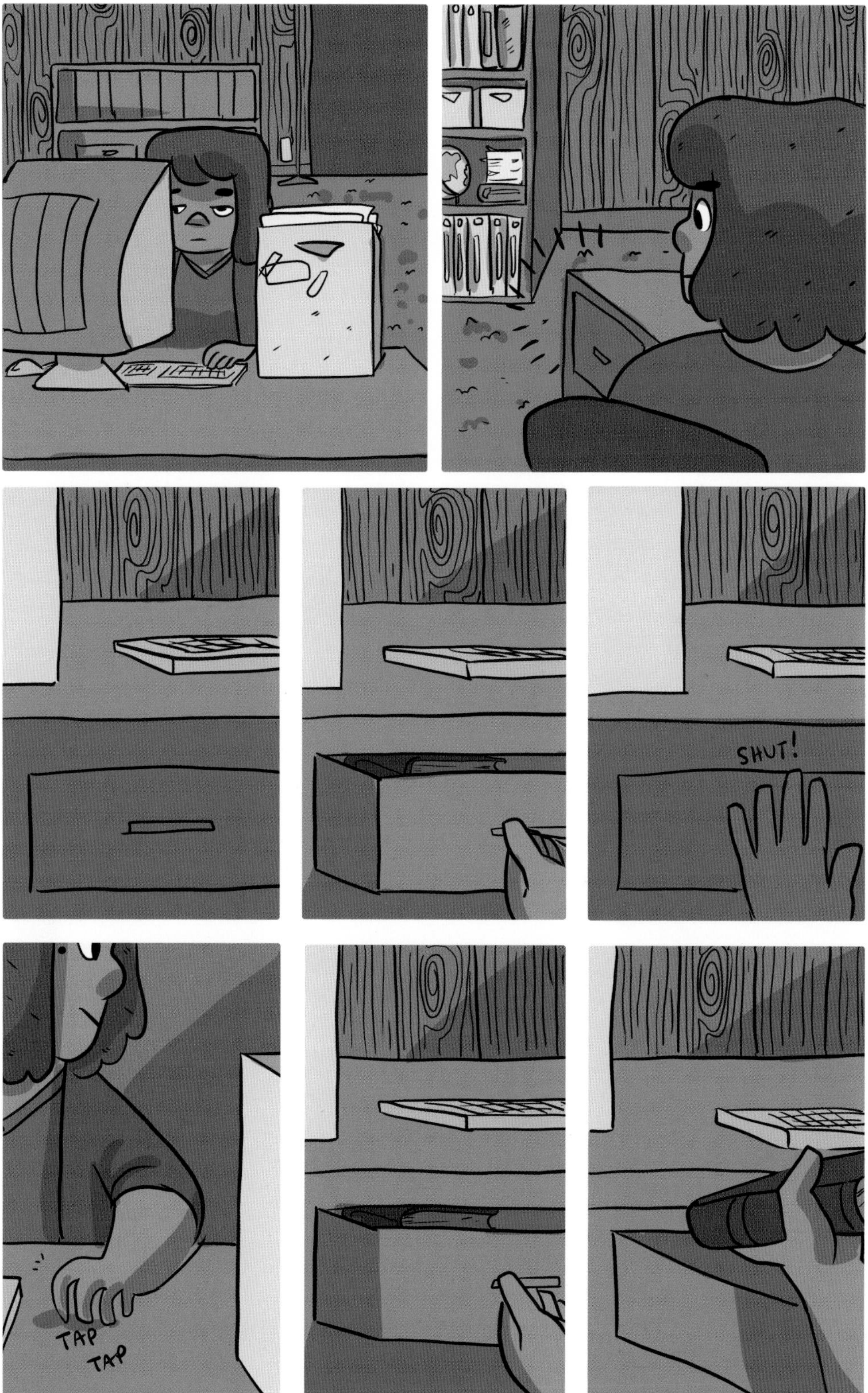
SHUT!
TAP
TAP

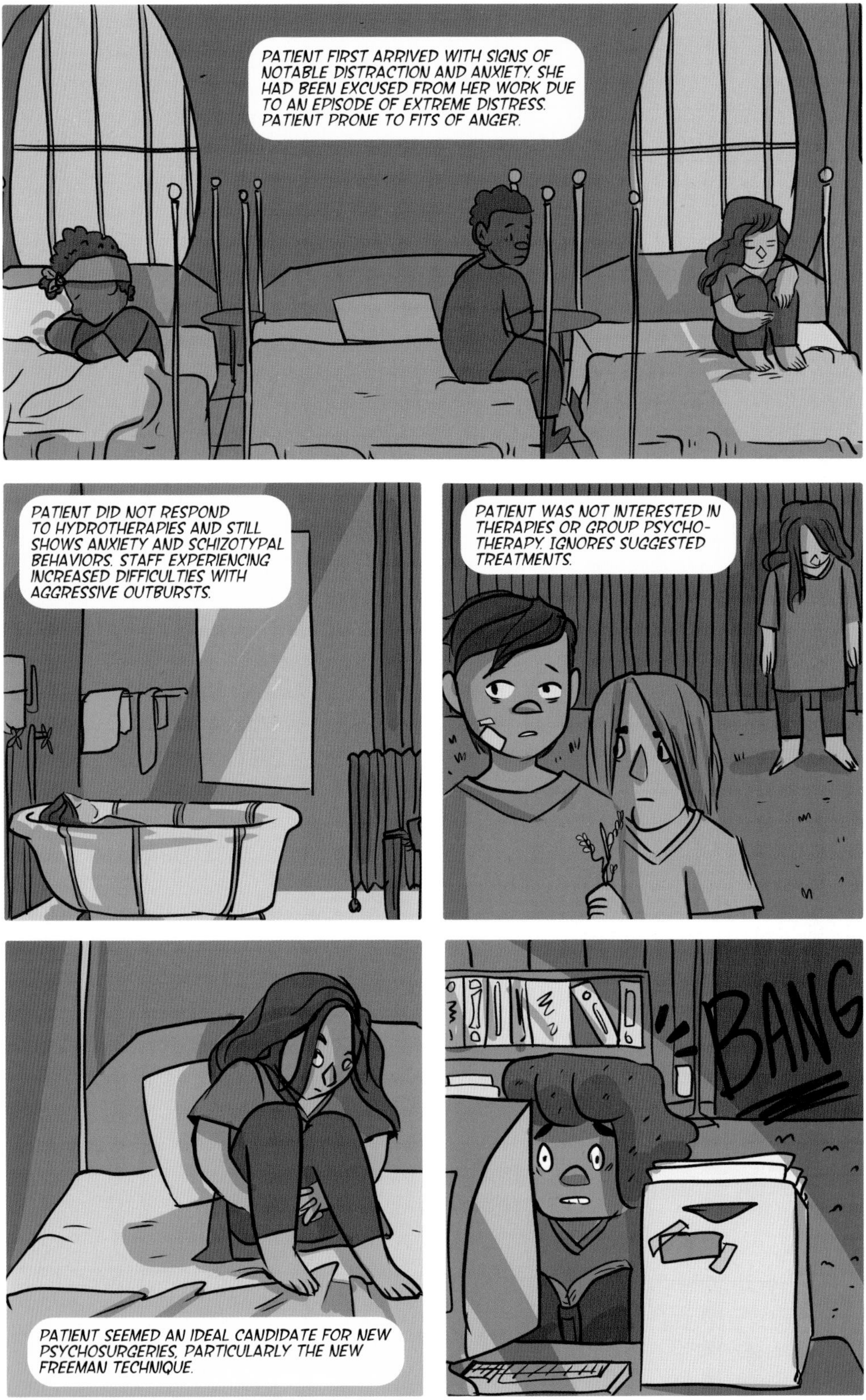
PATIENT FIRST ARRIVED WITH SIGNS OF NOTABLE DISTRACTION AND ANXIETY. SHE HAD BEEN EXCUSED FROM HER WORK DUE TO AN EPISODE OF EXTREME DISTRESS. PATIENT PRONE TO FITS OF ANGER.
PATIENT DID NOT RESPOND TO HYDROTHERAPIES AND STILL SHOWS ANXIETY AND SCHIZOTYPAL BEHAVIORS. STAFF EXPERIENCING INCREASED DIFFICULTIES WITH AGGRESSIVE OUTBURSTS.
PATIENT WAS NOT INTERESTED IN THERAPIES OR GROUP PSYCHOTHERAPY. IGNORES SUGGESTED TREATMENTS.
PATIENT SEEMED AN IDEAL CANDIDATE FOR NEW PSYCHOSURGERIES, PARTICULARLY THE NEW FREEMAN TECHNIQUE.
BANG

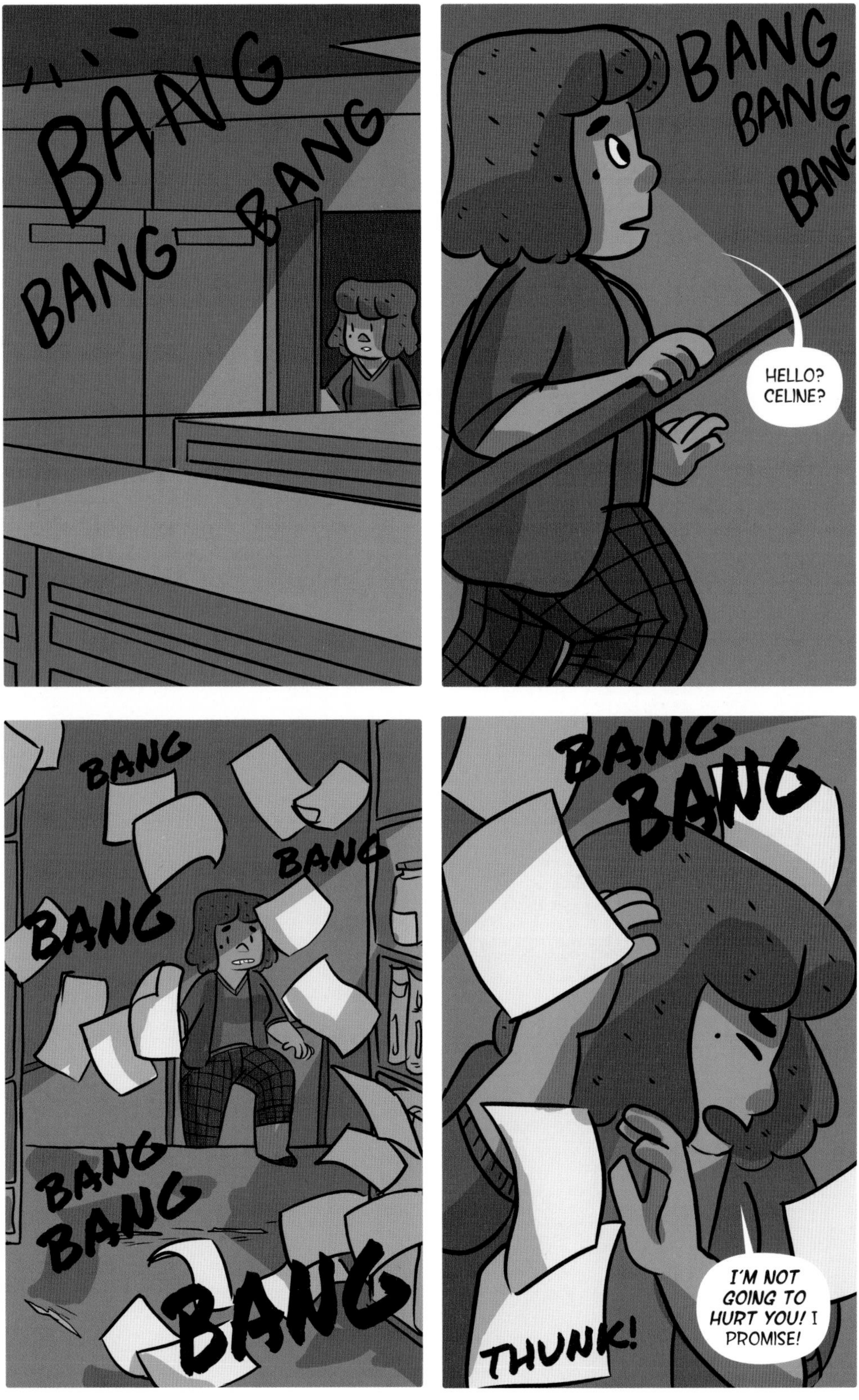
BANG
BANG
BANG
BANG
BANG
BANG
HELLO? CELINE?
BANG
BANG
BANG
BANG
BANG
BANG
BANG
BANG
I'M NOT GOING TO HURT YOU! I PROMISE!
THUNK!

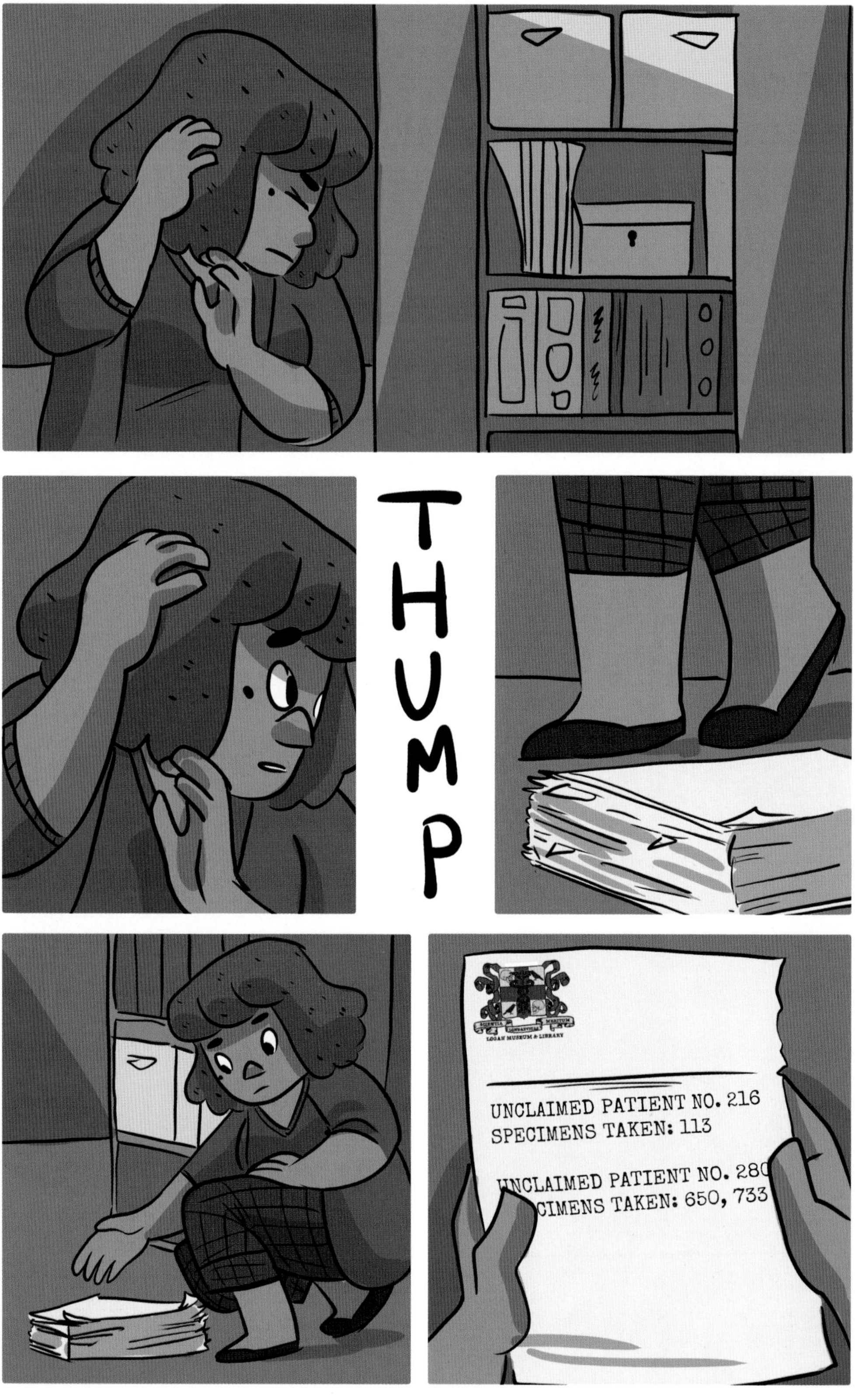
THUMP
SCIENTIA
MERITUM
LOGAN MUSEUM & LIBRARY
UNCLAIMED PATIENT NO. 216
SPECIMENS TAKEN: 113
UNCLAIMED PATIENT NO. 28
CIMENS TAKEN: 650, 733

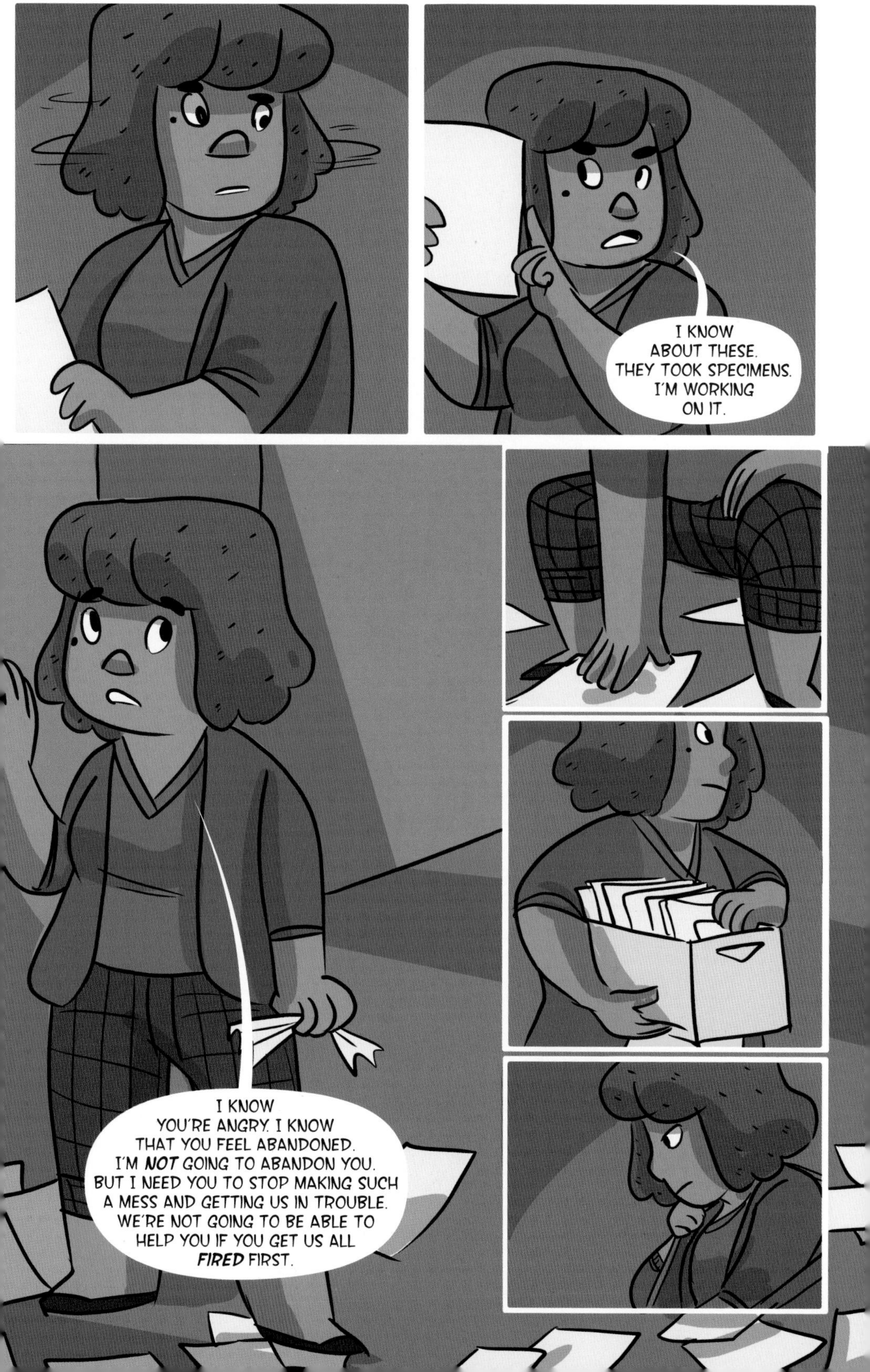
I KNOW ABOUT THESE. THEY TOOK SPECIMENS. I'M WORKING ON IT.
I KNOW YOU'RE ANGRY. I KNOW THAT YOU FEEL ABANDONED. I'M ***NOT*** GOING TO ABANDON YOU. BUT I NEED YOU TO STOP MAKING SUCH A MESS AND GETTING US IN TROUBLE. WE'RE NOT GOING TO BE ABLE TO HELP YOU IF YOU GET US ALL ***FIRED*** FIRST.

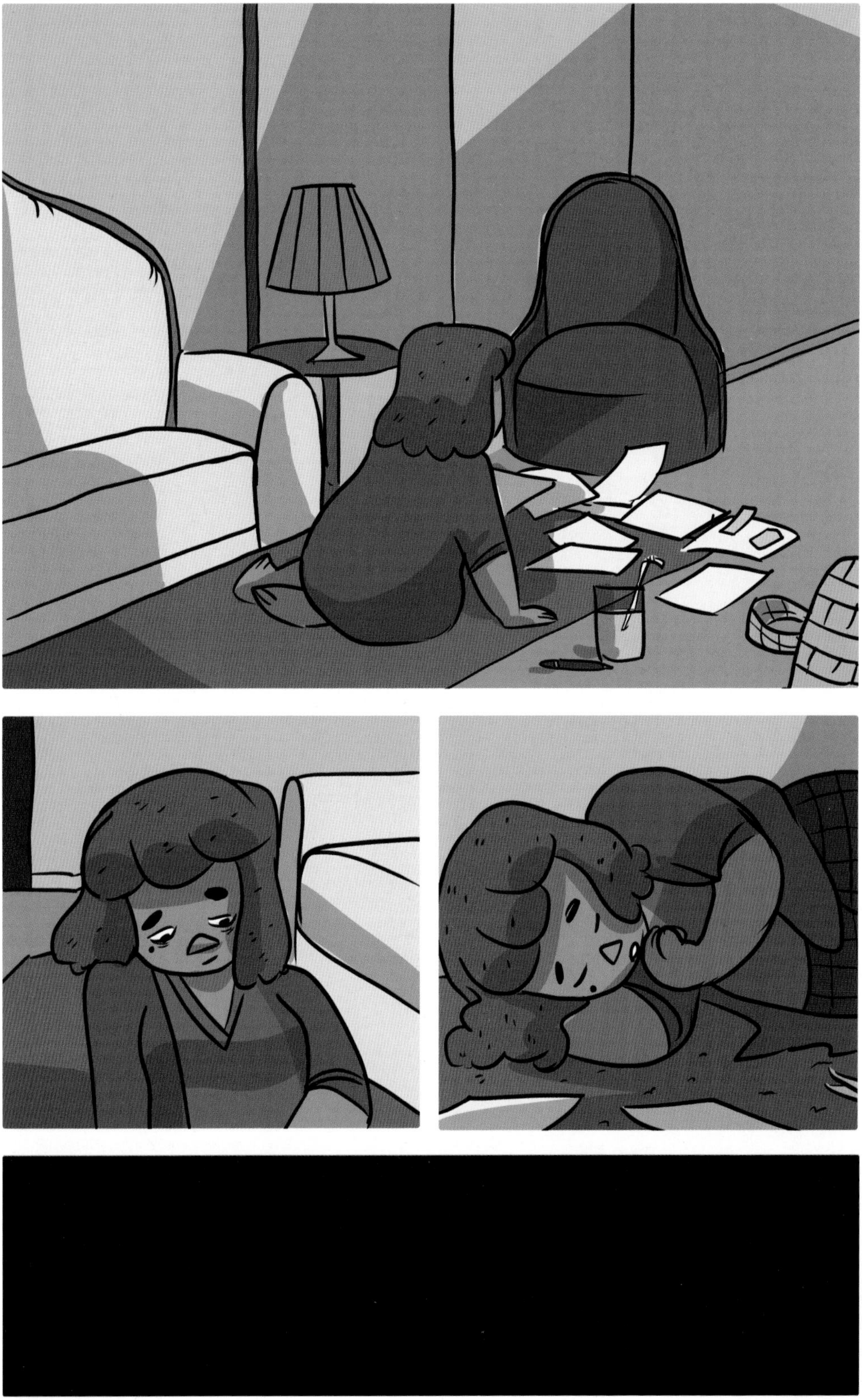

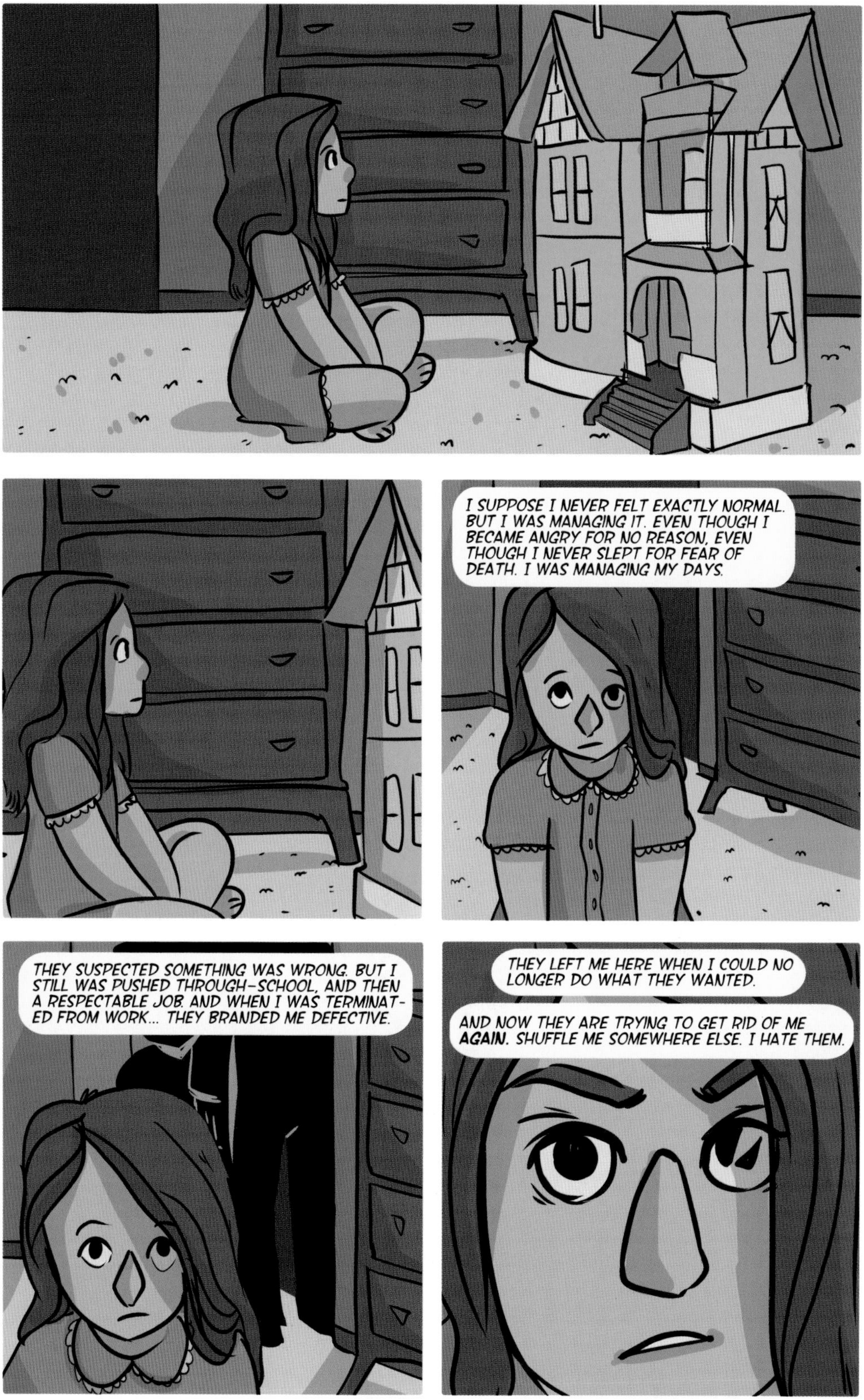
I SUPPOSE I NEVER FELT EXACTLY NORMAL. BUT I WAS MANAGING IT. EVEN THOUGH I BECAME ANGRY FOR NO REASON, EVEN THOUGH I NEVER SLEPT FOR FEAR OF DEATH. I WAS MANAGING MY DAYS.
THEY SUSPECTED SOMETHING WAS WRONG. BUT I STILL WAS PUSHED THROUGH–SCHOOL, AND THEN A RESPECTABLE JOB. AND WHEN I WAS TERMINATED FROM WORK... THEY BRANDED ME DEFECTIVE.
THEY LEFT ME HERE WHEN I COULD NO LONGER DO WHAT THEY WANTED.
AND NOW THEY ARE TRYING TO GET RID OF ME **AGAIN.** SHUFFLE ME SOMEWHERE ELSE. I HATE THEM.

CRAACK!!

STAF
PRIVAT

STAFF
PRIVATE

STAF
PRIVATE

ONE WEEK LATER

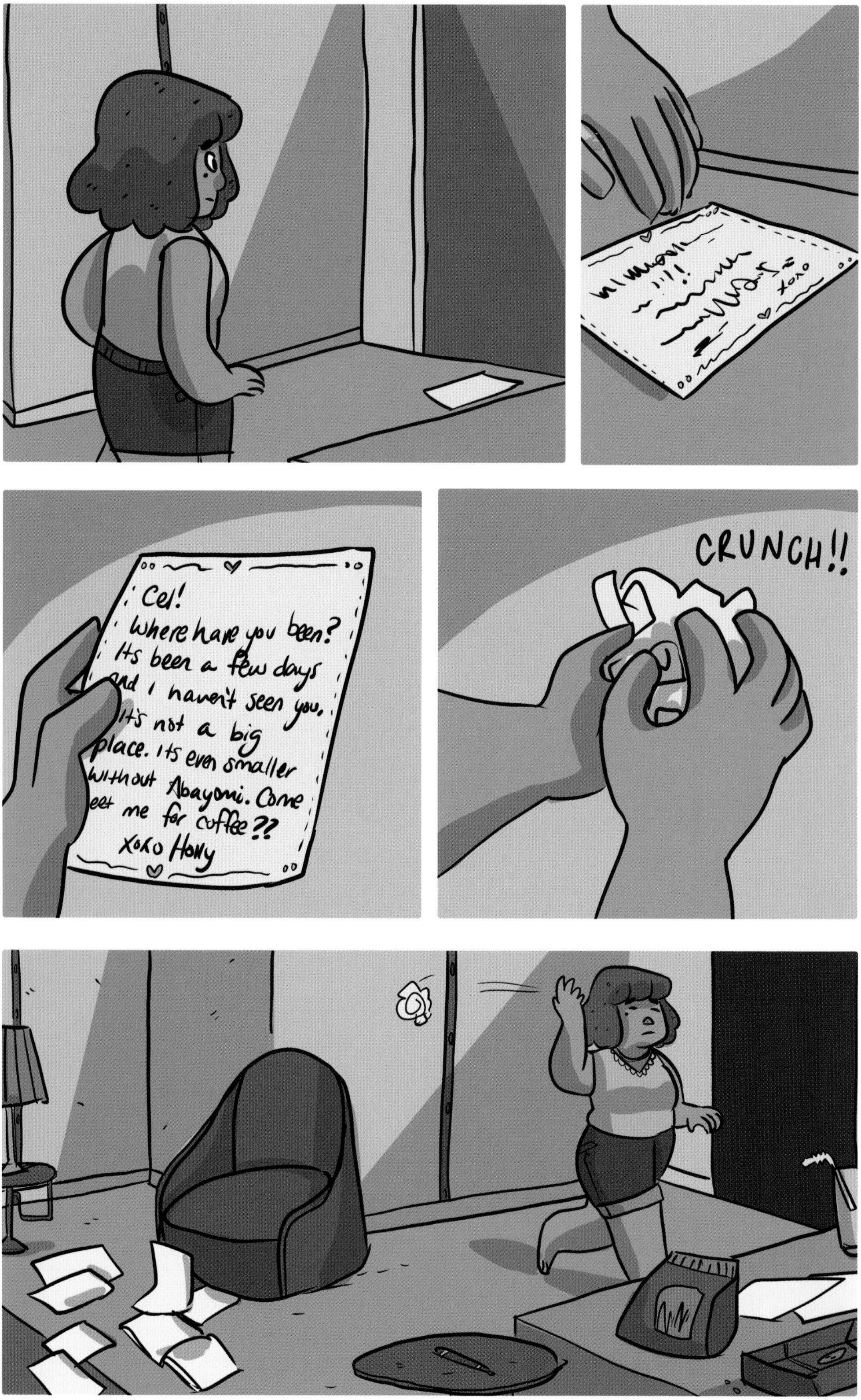
Cel!
Where have you been? It's been a few days and I haven't seen you. It's not a big place. It's even smaller without Abayomi. Come meet me for coffee??
XOXO Holly
CRUNCH!!

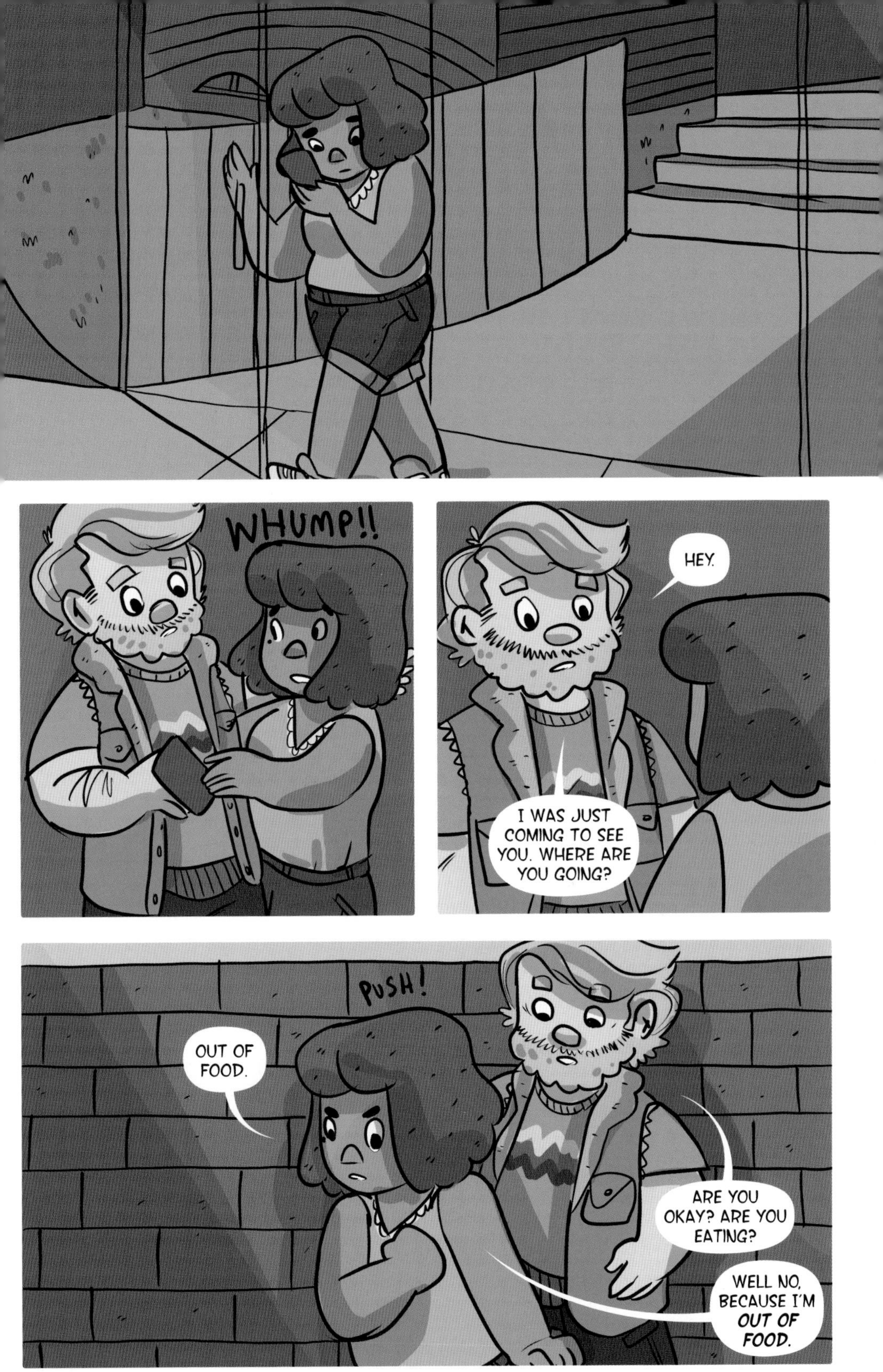
WHUMP!!
HEY.
I WAS JUST COMING TO SEE YOU. WHERE ARE YOU GOING?
PUSH!
OUT OF FOOD.
ARE YOU OKAY? ARE YOU EATING?
WELL NO, BECAUSE I'M ***OUT OF FOOD.***

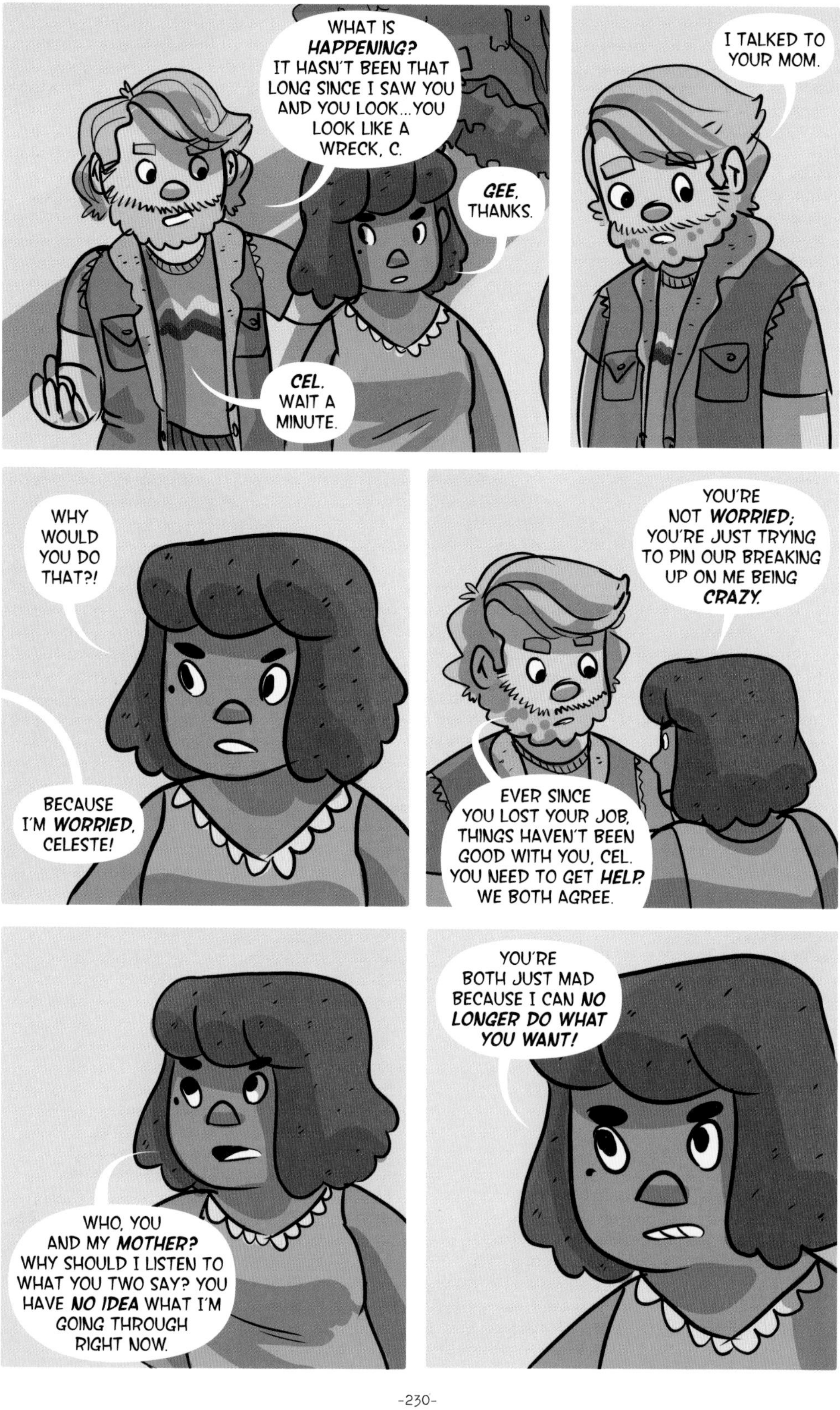
WHAT IS HAPPENING? IT HASN'T BEEN THAT LONG SINCE I SAW YOU AND YOU LOOK...YOU LOOK LIKE A WRECK, C.
GEE, THANKS.
CEL. WAIT A MINUTE.
I TALKED TO YOUR MOM.
WHY WOULD YOU DO THAT?!
BECAUSE I'M WORRIED, CELESTE!
YOU'RE NOT WORRIED; YOU'RE JUST TRYING TO PIN OUR BREAKING UP ON ME BEING CRAZY.
EVER SINCE YOU LOST YOUR JOB, THINGS HAVEN'T BEEN GOOD WITH YOU, CEL. YOU NEED TO GET HELP. WE BOTH AGREE.
WHO, YOU AND MY MOTHER? WHY SHOULD I LISTEN TO WHAT YOU TWO SAY? YOU HAVE NO IDEA WHAT I'M GOING THROUGH RIGHT NOW.
YOU'RE BOTH JUST MAD BECAUSE I CAN NO LONGER DO WHAT YOU WANT!

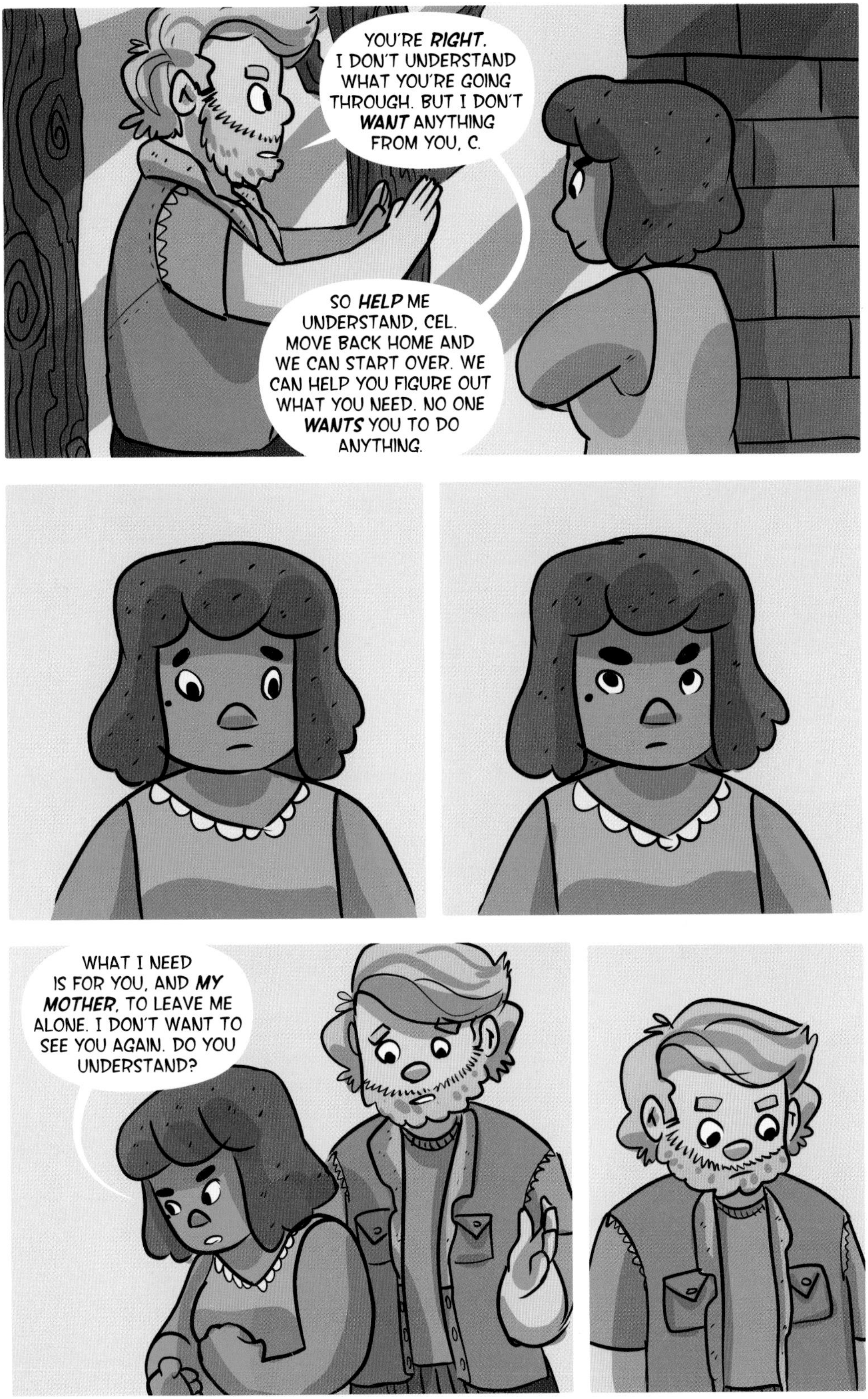
YOU'RE **RIGHT.** I DON'T UNDERSTAND WHAT YOU'RE GOING THROUGH. BUT I DON'T **WANT** ANYTHING FROM YOU, C.
SO **HELP** ME UNDERSTAND, CEL. MOVE BACK HOME AND WE CAN START OVER. WE CAN HELP YOU FIGURE OUT WHAT YOU NEED. NO ONE **WANTS** YOU TO DO ANYTHING.
WHAT I NEED IS FOR YOU, AND **MY MOTHER,** TO LEAVE ME ALONE. I DON'T WANT TO SEE YOU AGAIN. DO YOU UNDERSTAND?

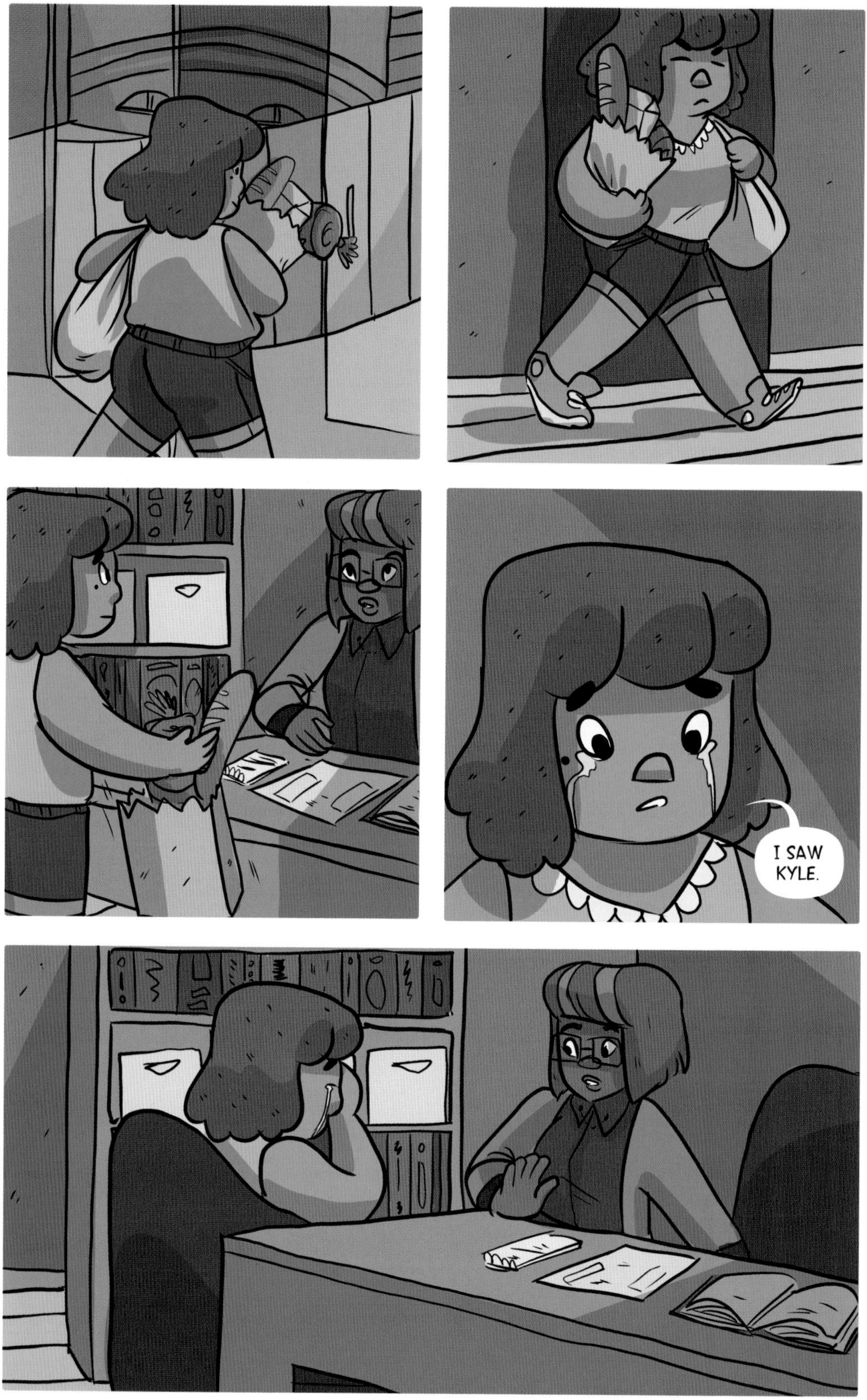
I SAW
KYLE.

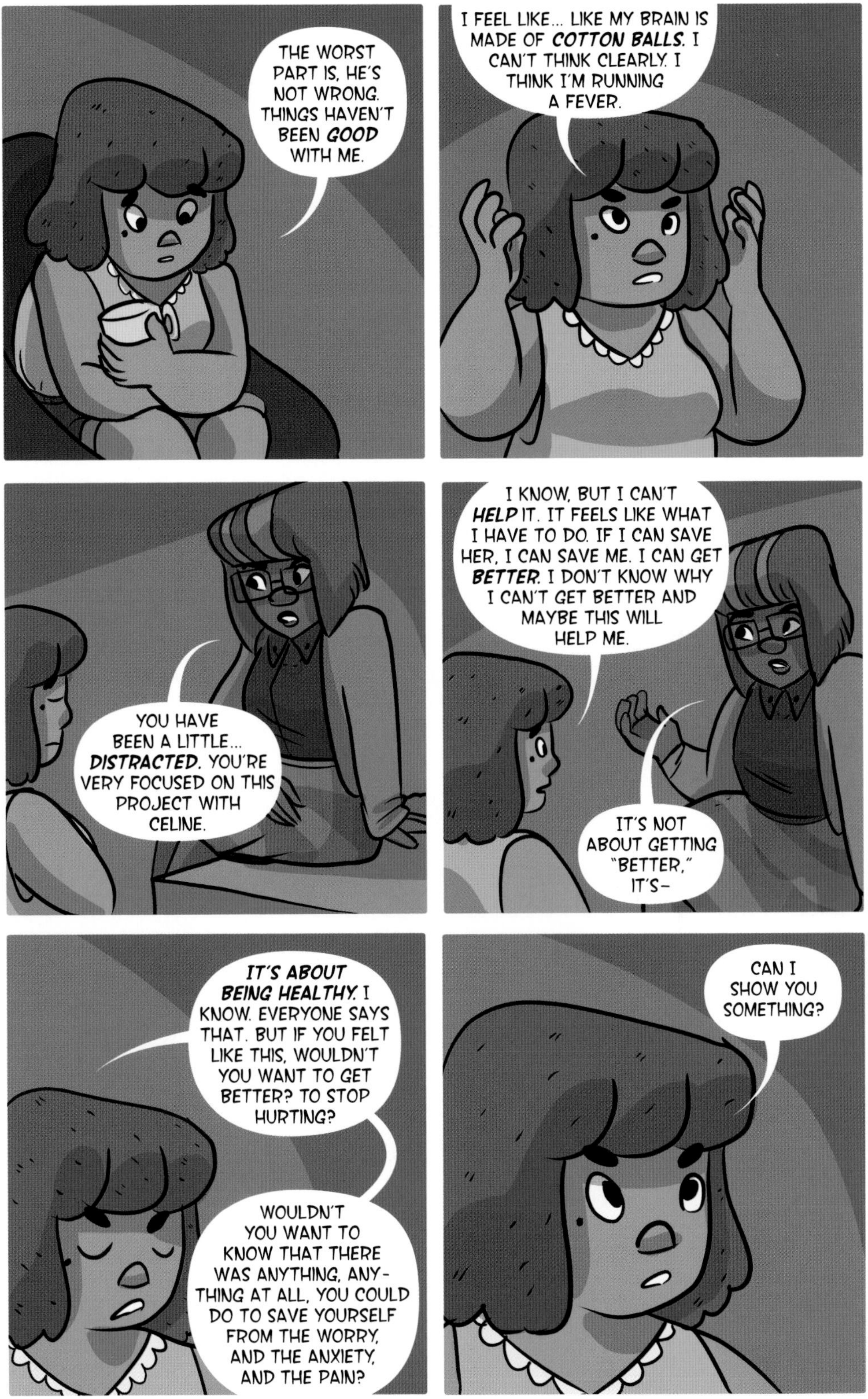
THE WORST PART IS, HE'S NOT WRONG. THINGS HAVEN'T BEEN **GOOD** WITH ME.
I FEEL LIKE... LIKE MY BRAIN IS MADE OF **COTTON BALLS.** I CAN'T THINK CLEARLY. I THINK I'M RUNNING A FEVER.
YOU HAVE BEEN A LITTLE... **DISTRACTED.** YOU'RE VERY FOCUSED ON THIS PROJECT WITH CELINE.
I KNOW, BUT I CAN'T **HELP** IT. IT FEELS LIKE WHAT I HAVE TO DO. IF I CAN SAVE HER, I CAN SAVE ME. I CAN GET **BETTER.** I DON'T KNOW WHY I CAN'T GET BETTER AND MAYBE THIS WILL HELP ME.
IT'S NOT ABOUT GETTING "BETTER," IT'S–
IT'S ABOUT BEING HEALTHY. I KNOW. EVERYONE SAYS THAT. BUT IF YOU FELT LIKE THIS, WOULDN'T YOU WANT TO GET BETTER? TO STOP HURTING?
WOULDN'T YOU WANT TO KNOW THAT THERE WAS ANYTHING, ANY-THING AT ALL, YOU COULD DO TO SAVE YOURSELF FROM THE WORRY, AND THE ANXIETY, AND THE PAIN?
CAN I SHOW YOU SOMETHING?

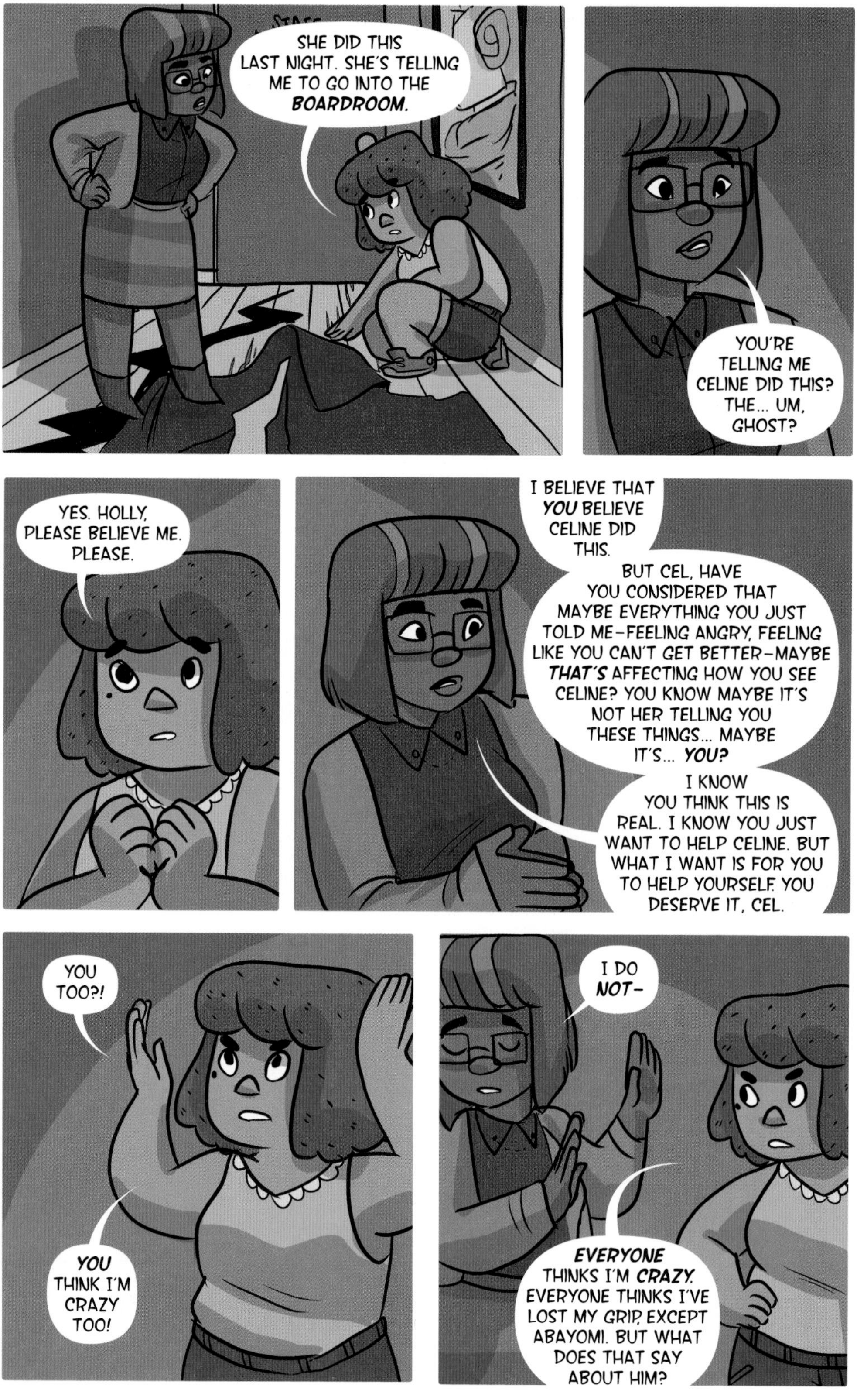
SHE DID THIS LAST NIGHT. SHE'S TELLING ME TO GO INTO THE **BOARDROOM.**
YOU'RE TELLING ME CELINE DID THIS? THE... UM, GHOST?
YES. HOLLY, PLEASE BELIEVE ME. PLEASE.
I BELIEVE THAT ***YOU*** BELIEVE CELINE DID THIS.
BUT CEL, HAVE YOU CONSIDERED THAT MAYBE EVERYTHING YOU JUST TOLD ME—FEELING ANGRY, FEELING LIKE YOU CAN'T GET BETTER—MAYBE ***THAT'S*** AFFECTING HOW YOU SEE CELINE? YOU KNOW MAYBE IT'S NOT HER TELLING YOU THESE THINGS... MAYBE IT'S... ***YOU?***
I KNOW YOU THINK THIS IS REAL. I KNOW YOU JUST WANT TO HELP CELINE. BUT WHAT I WANT IS FOR YOU TO HELP YOURSELF. YOU DESERVE IT, CEL.
YOU TOO?!
YOU THINK I'M CRAZY TOO!
I DO ***NOT—***
EVERYONE THINKS I'M ***CRAZY.*** EVERYONE THINKS I'VE LOST MY GRIP, EXCEPT ABAYOMI. BUT WHAT DOES THAT SAY ABOUT HIM?

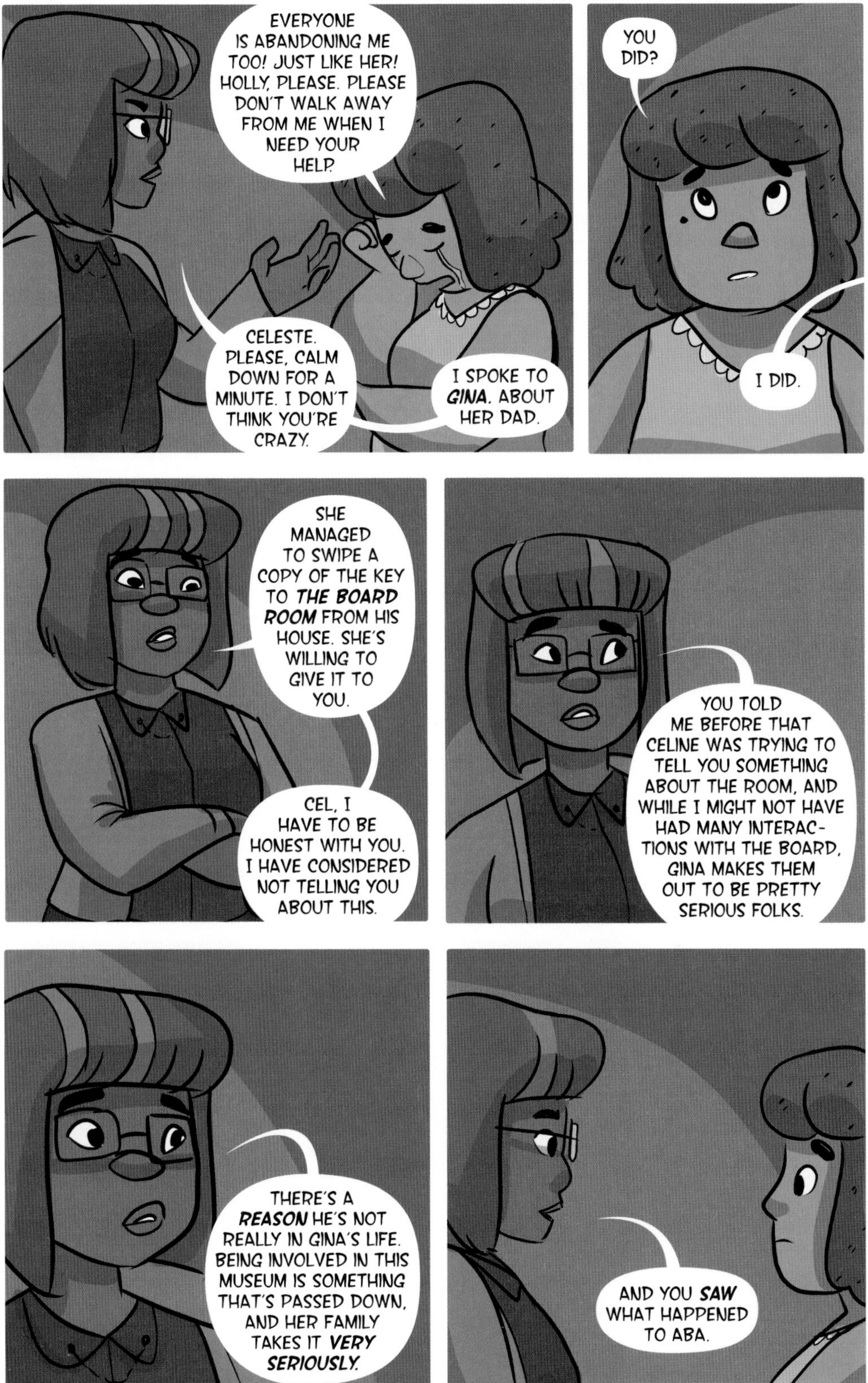

EVERYONE IS ABANDONING ME TOO! JUST LIKE HER! HOLLY, PLEASE. PLEASE DON'T WALK AWAY FROM ME WHEN I NEED YOUR HELP.
CELESTE. PLEASE, CALM DOWN FOR A MINUTE. I DON'T THINK YOU'RE CRAZY.
I SPOKE TO GINA. ABOUT HER DAD.
YOU DID?
I DID.
SHE MANAGED TO SWIPE A COPY OF THE KEY TO THE BOARD ROOM FROM HIS HOUSE. SHE'S WILLING TO GIVE IT TO YOU.
CEL, I HAVE TO BE HONEST WITH YOU. I HAVE CONSIDERED NOT TELLING YOU ABOUT THIS.
YOU TOLD ME BEFORE THAT CELINE WAS TRYING TO TELL YOU SOMETHING ABOUT THE ROOM, AND WHILE I MIGHT NOT HAVE HAD MANY INTERAC-TIONS WITH THE BOARD, GINA MAKES THEM OUT TO BE PRETTY SERIOUS FOLKS.
THERE'S A REASON HE'S NOT REALLY IN GINA'S LIFE. BEING INVOLVED IN THIS MUSEUM IS SOMETHING THAT'S PASSED DOWN, AND HER FAMILY TAKES IT VERY SERIOUSLY.
AND YOU SAW WHAT HAPPENED TO ABA.

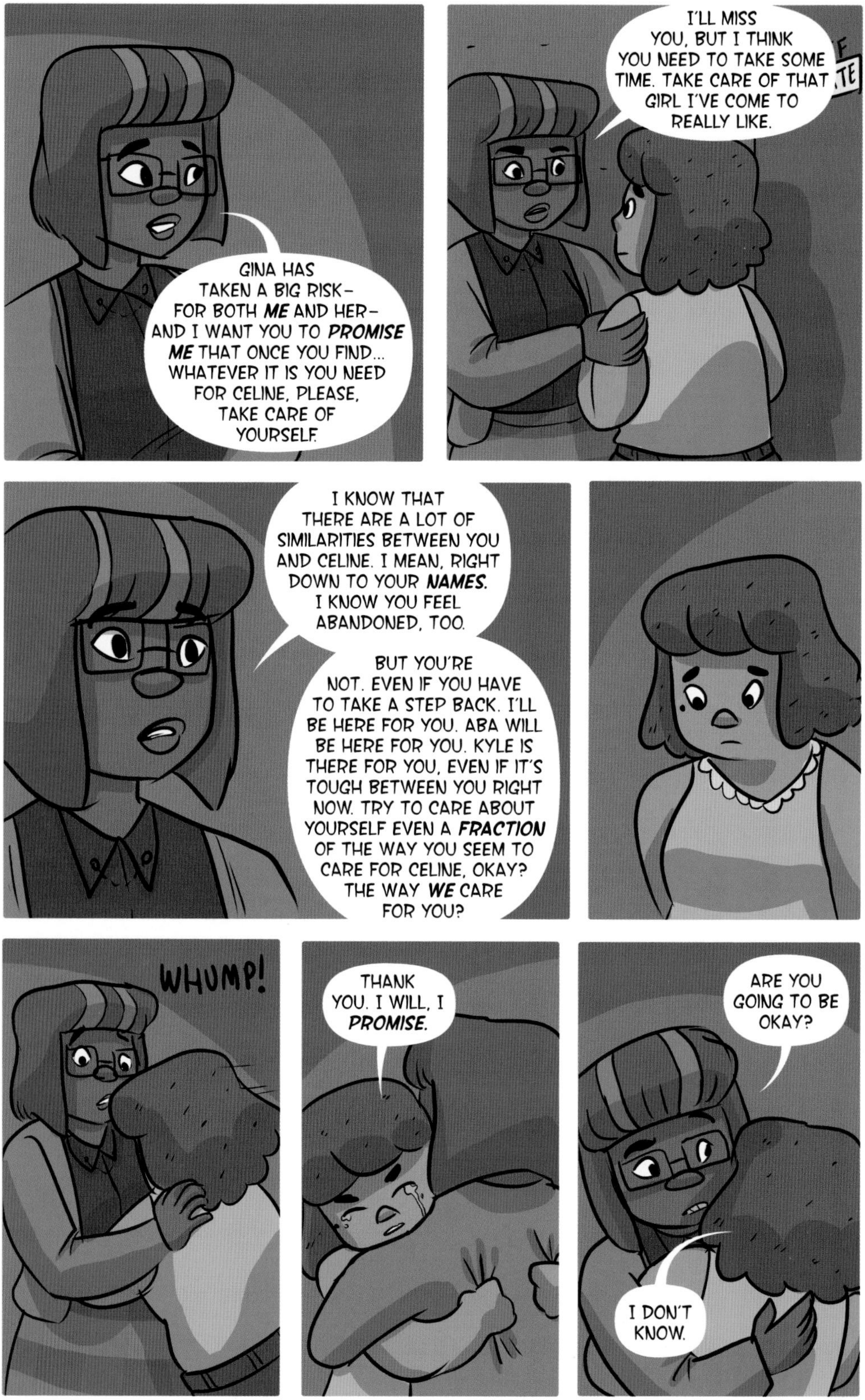
GINA HAS TAKEN A BIG RISK- FOR BOTH ME AND HER- AND I WANT YOU TO PROMISE ME THAT ONCE YOU FIND... WHATEVER IT IS YOU NEED FOR CELINE, PLEASE, TAKE CARE OF YOURSELF.
I'LL MISS YOU, BUT I THINK YOU NEED TO TAKE SOME TIME. TAKE CARE OF THAT GIRL I'VE COME TO REALLY LIKE.
I KNOW THAT THERE ARE A LOT OF SIMILARITIES BETWEEN YOU AND CELINE. I MEAN, RIGHT DOWN TO YOUR NAMES. I KNOW YOU FEEL ABANDONED, TOO.
BUT YOU'RE NOT. EVEN IF YOU HAVE TO TAKE A STEP BACK. I'LL BE HERE FOR YOU. ABA WILL BE HERE FOR YOU. KYLE IS THERE FOR YOU, EVEN IF IT'S TOUGH BETWEEN YOU RIGHT NOW. TRY TO CARE ABOUT YOURSELF EVEN A FRACTION OF THE WAY YOU SEEM TO CARE FOR CELINE, OKAY? THE WAY WE CARE FOR YOU?
WHUMP!
THANK YOU. I WILL, I PROMISE.
ARE YOU GOING TO BE OKAY?
I DON'T KNOW.

THREE DAYS LATER

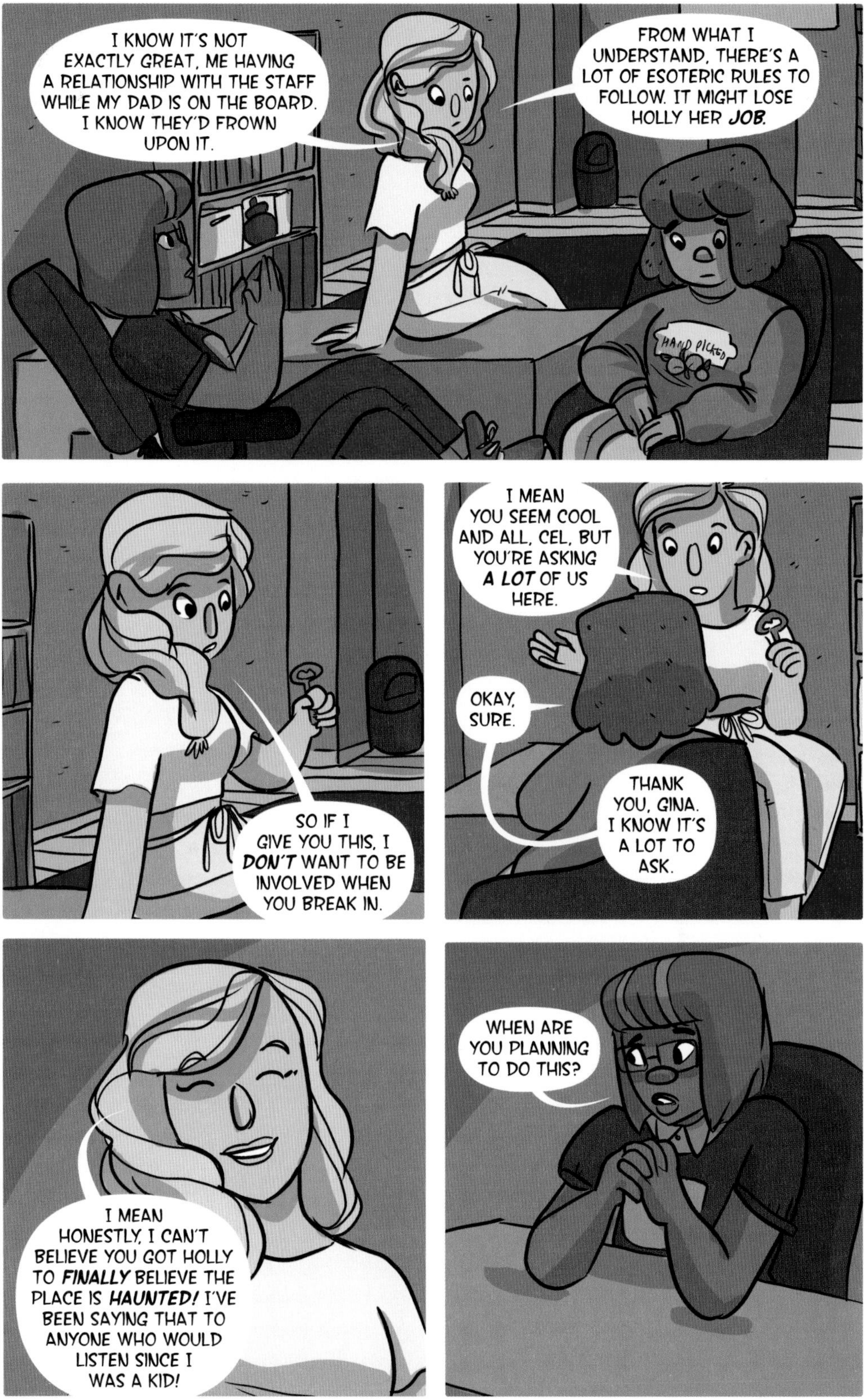
I KNOW IT'S NOT EXACTLY GREAT, ME HAVING A RELATIONSHIP WITH THE STAFF WHILE MY DAD IS ON THE BOARD. I KNOW THEY'D FROWN UPON IT.
FROM WHAT I UNDERSTAND, THERE'S A LOT OF ESOTERIC RULES TO FOLLOW. IT MIGHT LOSE HOLLY HER **JOB**.
HAND PICKED
SO IF I GIVE YOU THIS, I **DON'T** WANT TO BE INVOLVED WHEN YOU BREAK IN.
I MEAN YOU SEEM COOL AND ALL, CEL, BUT YOU'RE ASKING **A LOT** OF US HERE.
OKAY, SURE.
THANK YOU, GINA. I KNOW IT'S A LOT TO ASK.
I MEAN HONESTLY, I CAN'T BELIEVE YOU GOT HOLLY TO **FINALLY** BELIEVE THE PLACE IS **HAUNTED!** I'VE BEEN SAYING THAT TO ANYONE WHO WOULD LISTEN SINCE I WAS A KID!
WHEN ARE YOU PLANNING TO DO THIS?

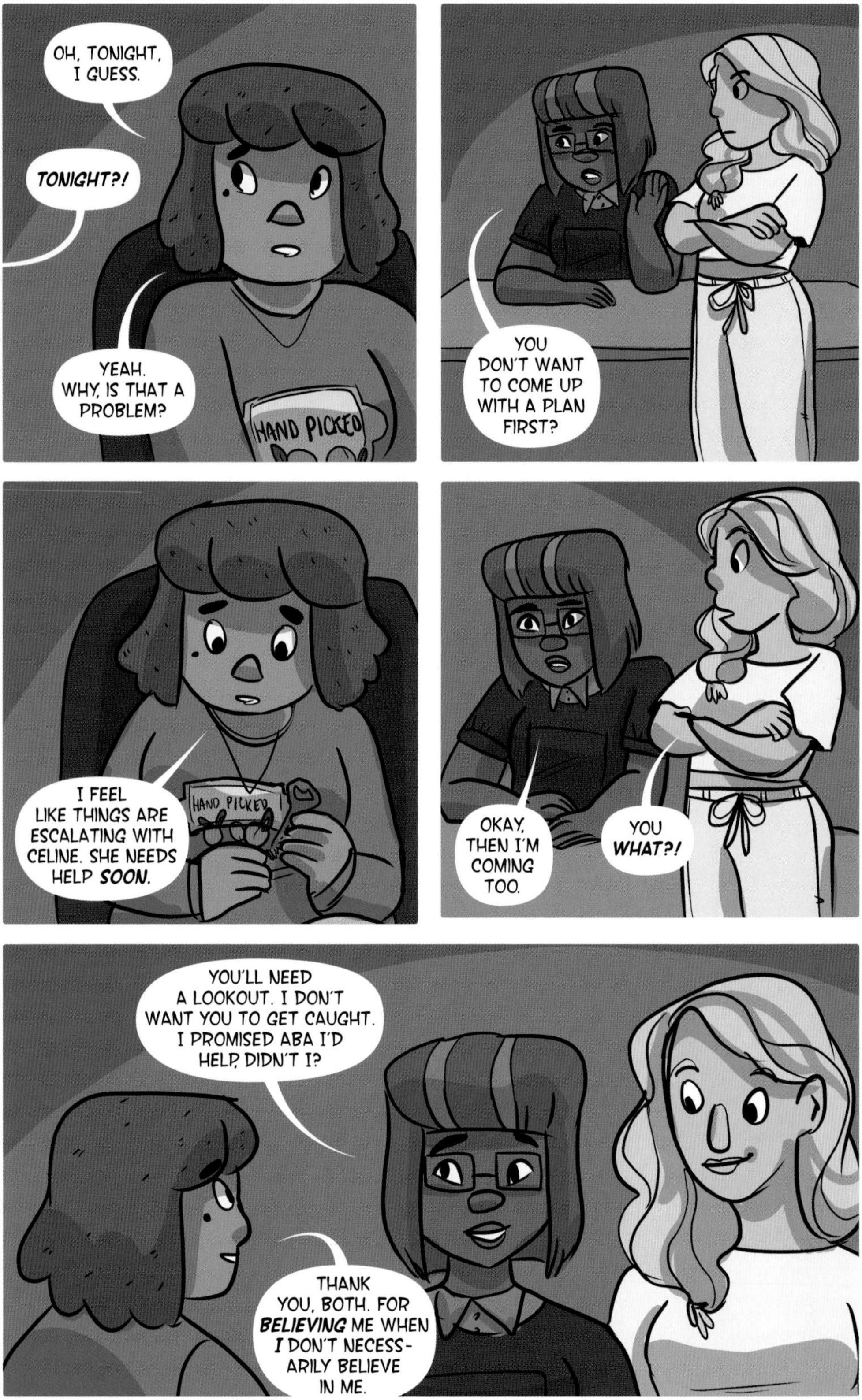
OH, TONIGHT, I GUESS.
TONIGHT?!
YEAH. WHY, IS THAT A PROBLEM?
HAND PICKED
YOU DON'T WANT TO COME UP WITH A PLAN FIRST?
I FEEL LIKE THINGS ARE ESCALATING WITH CELINE. SHE NEEDS HELP SOON.
HAND PICKED
OKAY, THEN I'M COMING TOO.
YOU WHAT?!
YOU'LL NEED A LOOKOUT. I DON'T WANT YOU TO GET CAUGHT. I PROMISED ABA I'D HELP, DIDN'T I?
THANK YOU, BOTH. FOR BELIEVING ME WHEN I DON'T NECESS-ARILY BELIEVE IN ME.

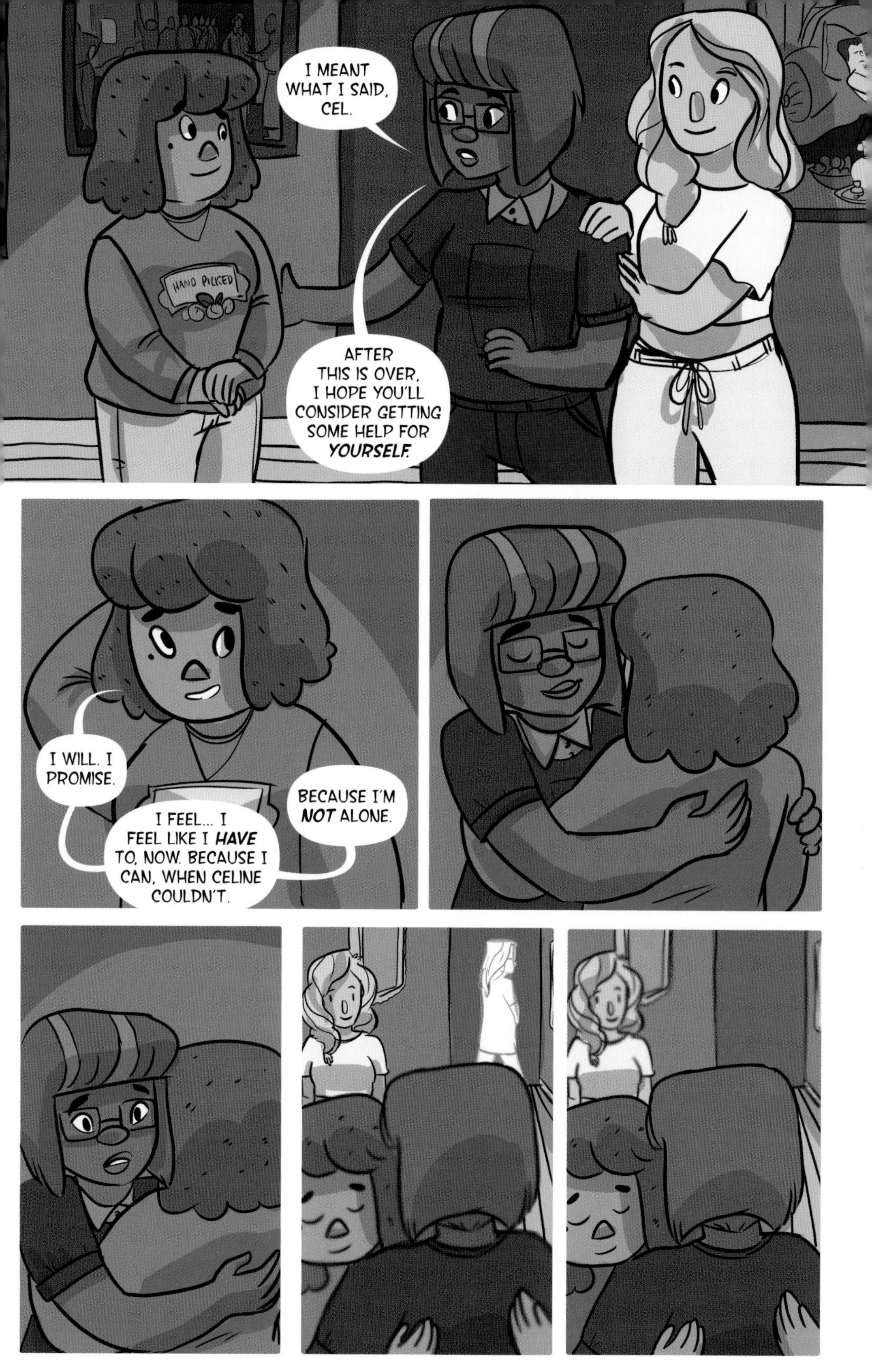
HAND PICKED
I MEANT WHAT I SAID, CEL.
AFTER THIS IS OVER, I HOPE YOU'LL CONSIDER GETTING SOME HELP FOR *YOURSELF.*
I WILL. I PROMISE.
I FEEL... I FEEL LIKE I **HAVE** TO, NOW. BECAUSE I CAN, WHEN CELINE COULDN'T.
BECAUSE I'M ***NOT*** ALONE.

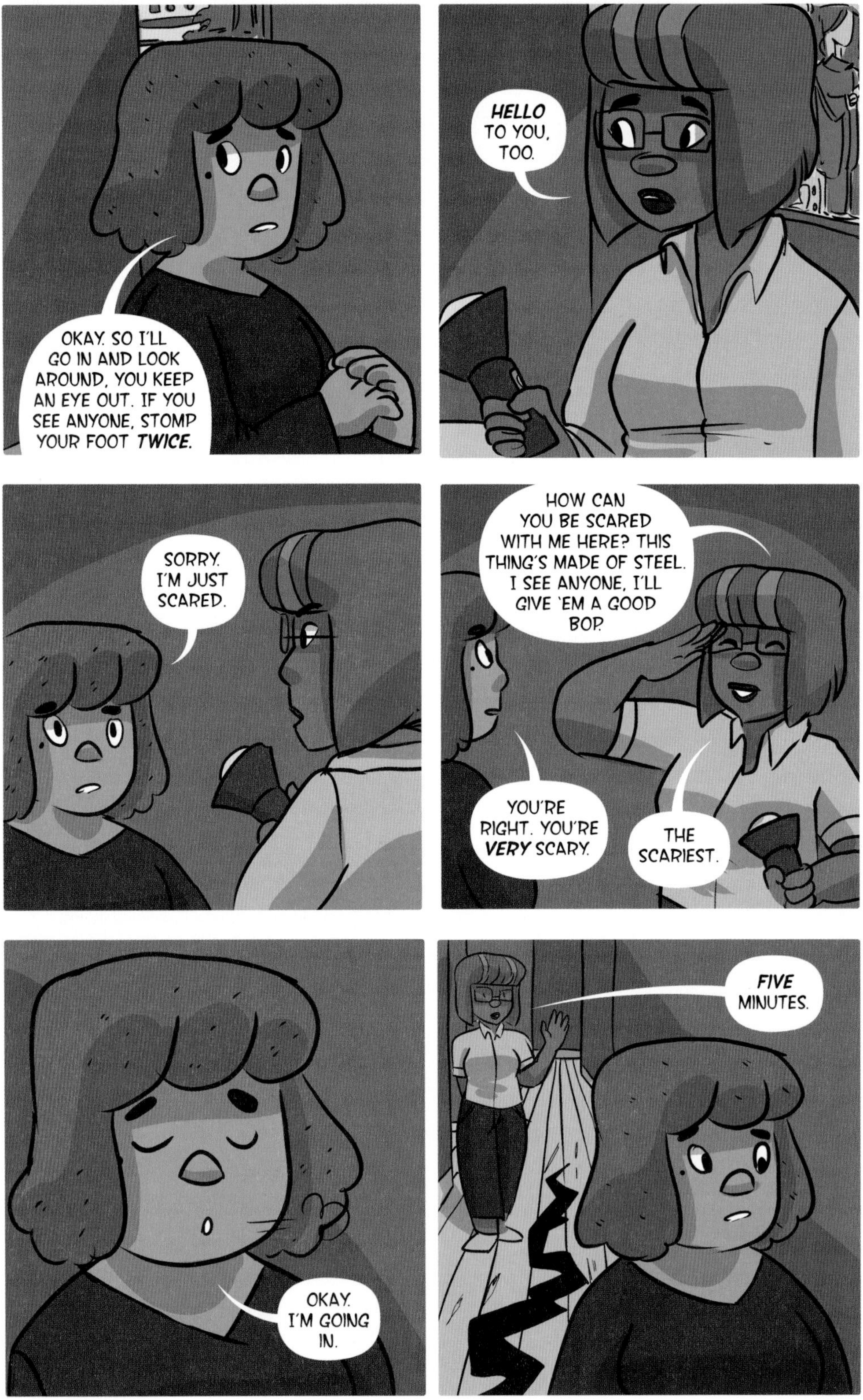
OKAY. SO I'LL GO IN AND LOOK AROUND, YOU KEEP AN EYE OUT. IF YOU SEE ANYONE, STOMP YOUR FOOT *TWICE.*
HELLO TO YOU, TOO.
SORRY. I'M JUST SCARED.
HOW CAN YOU BE SCARED WITH ME HERE? THIS THING'S MADE OF STEEL. I SEE ANYONE, I'LL GIVE 'EM A GOOD BOP.
YOU'RE RIGHT. YOU'RE *VERY* SCARY.
THE SCARIEST.
OKAY. I'M GOING IN.
FIVE MINUTES.

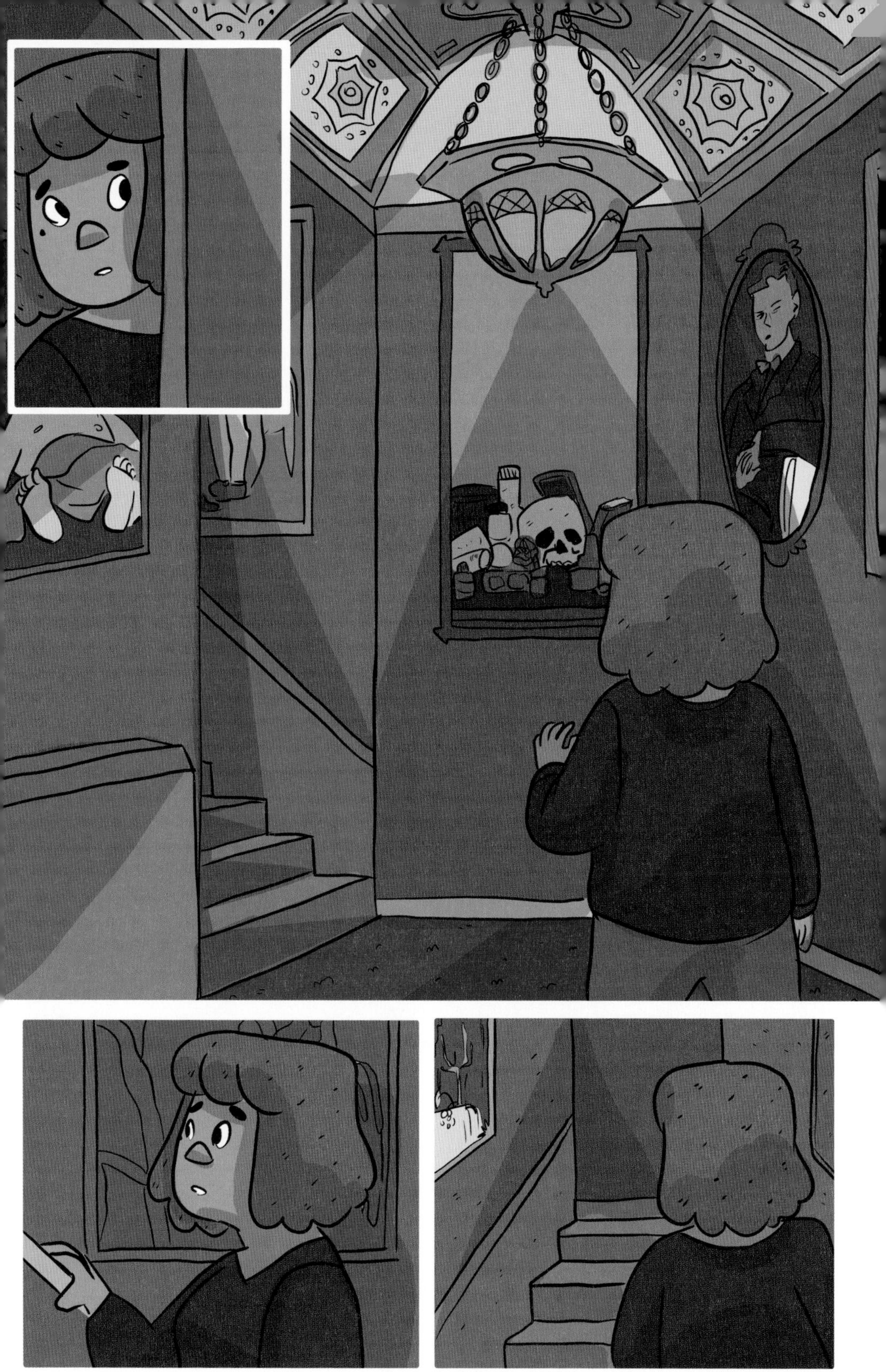

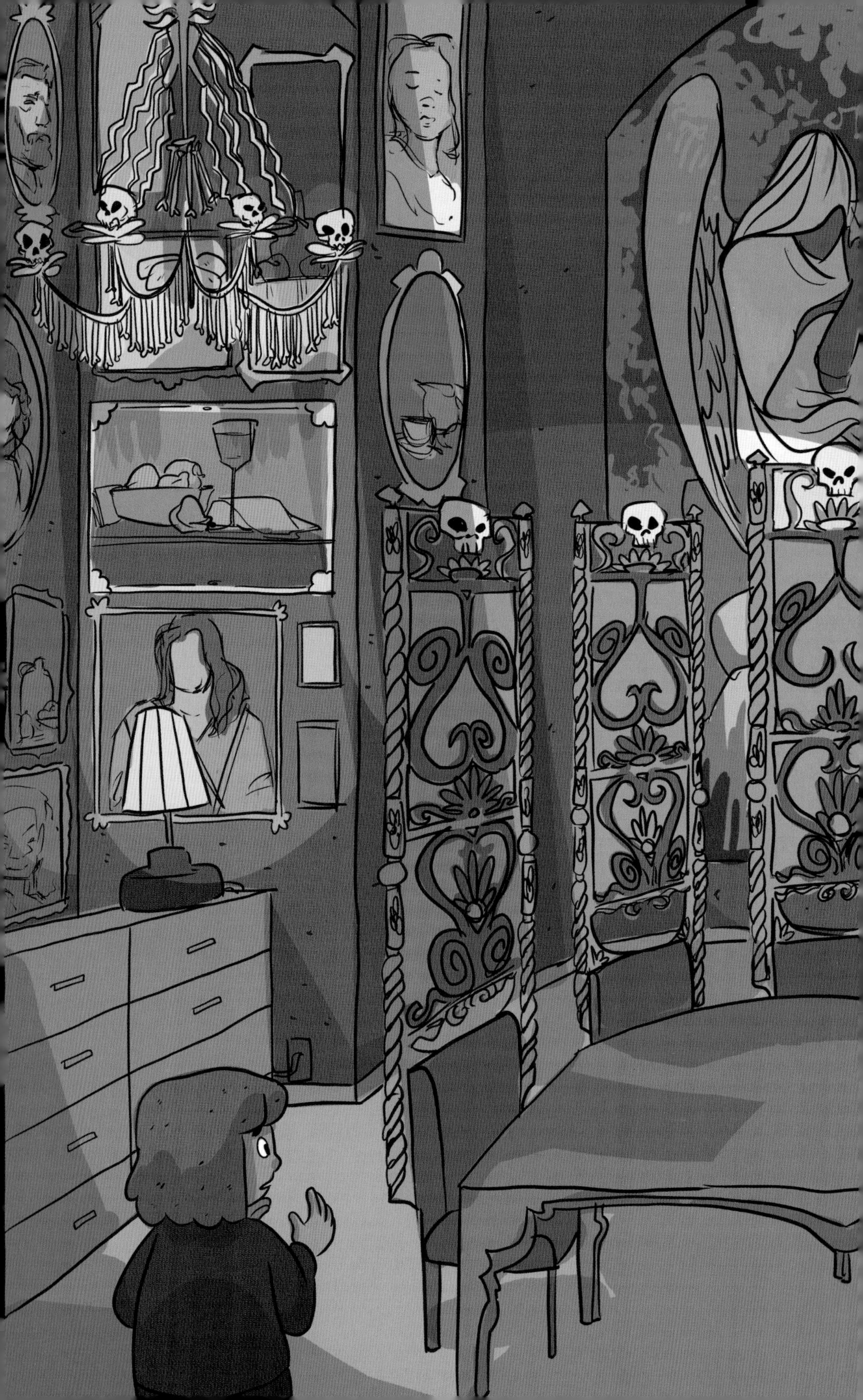

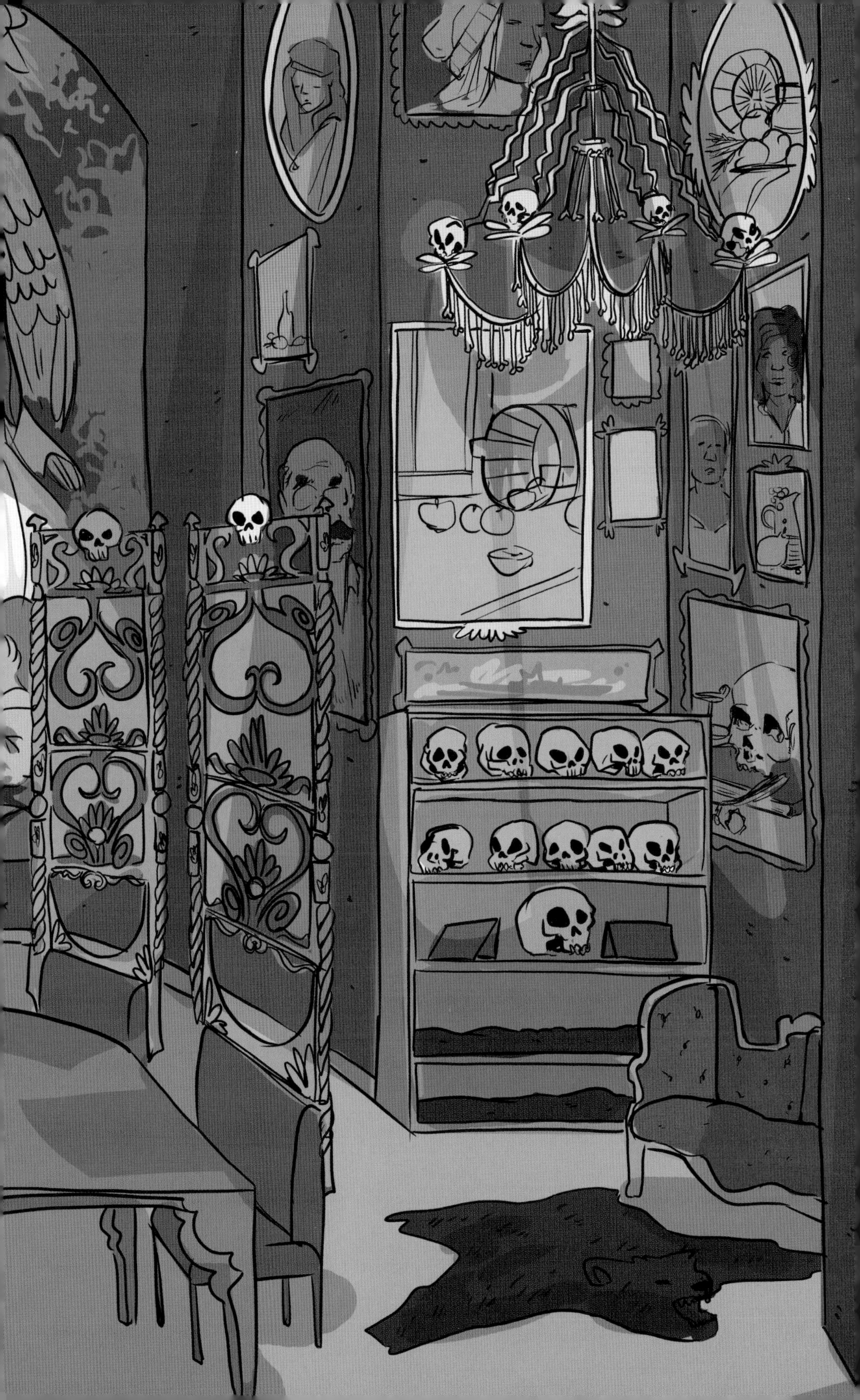

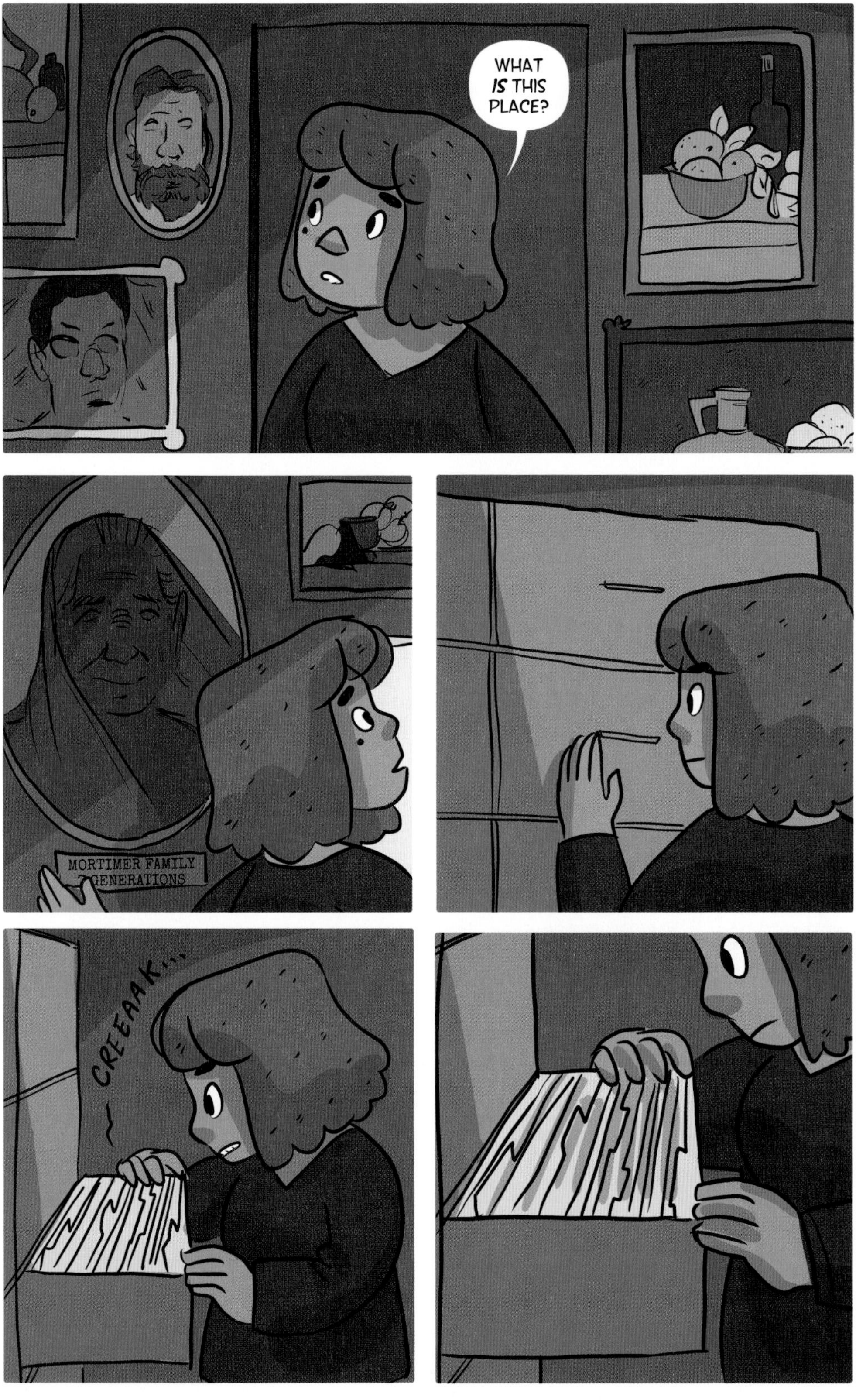

WHAT IS THIS PLACE?
MORTIMER FAMILY
GENERATIONS
CREEAAK...

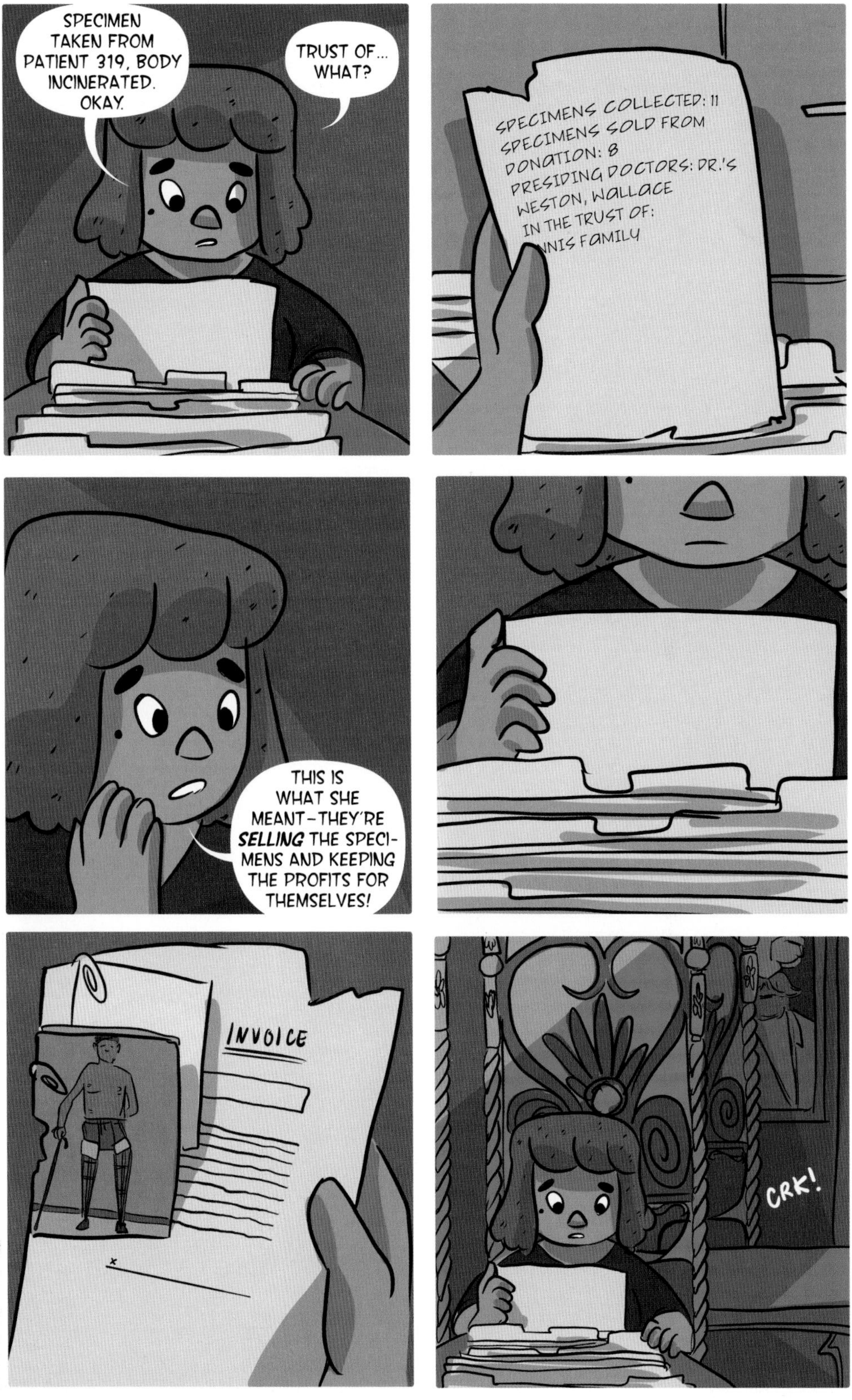
SPECIMEN TAKEN FROM PATIENT 319, BODY INCINERATED. OKAY.
TRUST OF... WHAT?
SPECIMENS COLLECTED: 11
SPECIMENS SOLD FROM DONATION: 8
PRESIDING DOCTORS: DR.'S WESTON, WALLACE
IN THE TRUST OF:
NNIS FAMILY
THIS IS WHAT SHE MEANT—THEY'RE SELLING THE SPECIMENS AND KEEPING THE PROFITS FOR THEMSELVES!
INVOICE
CRK!

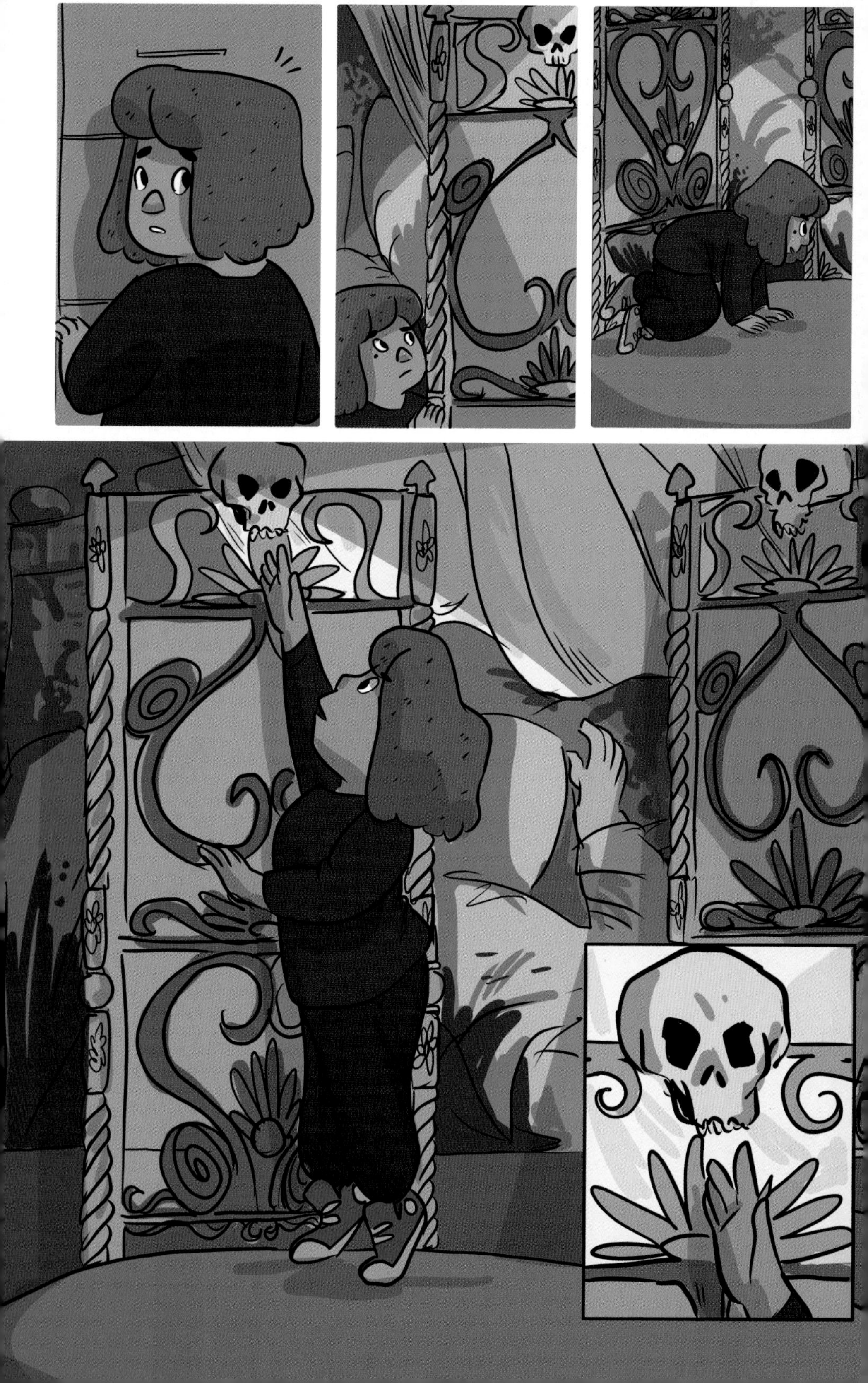

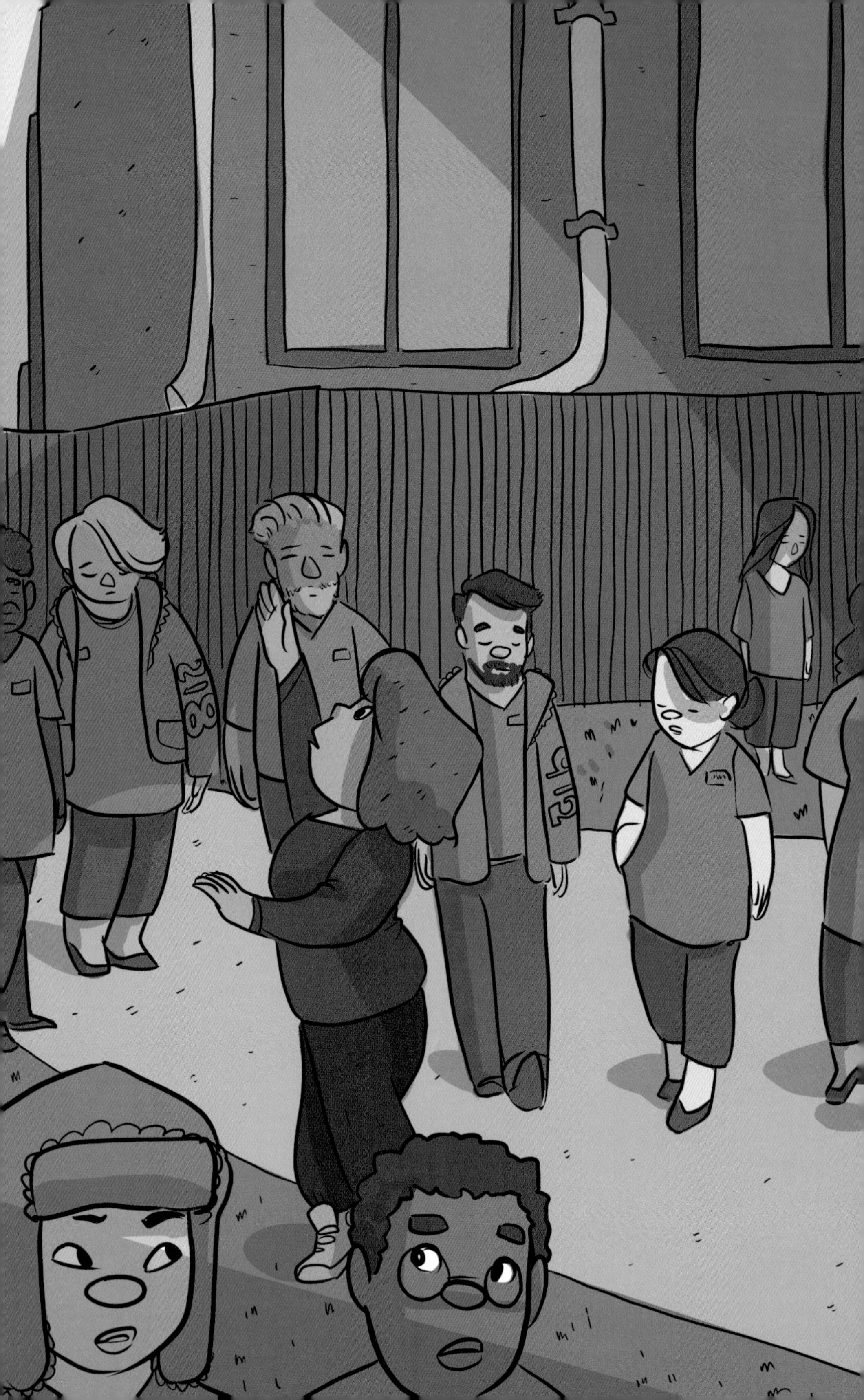

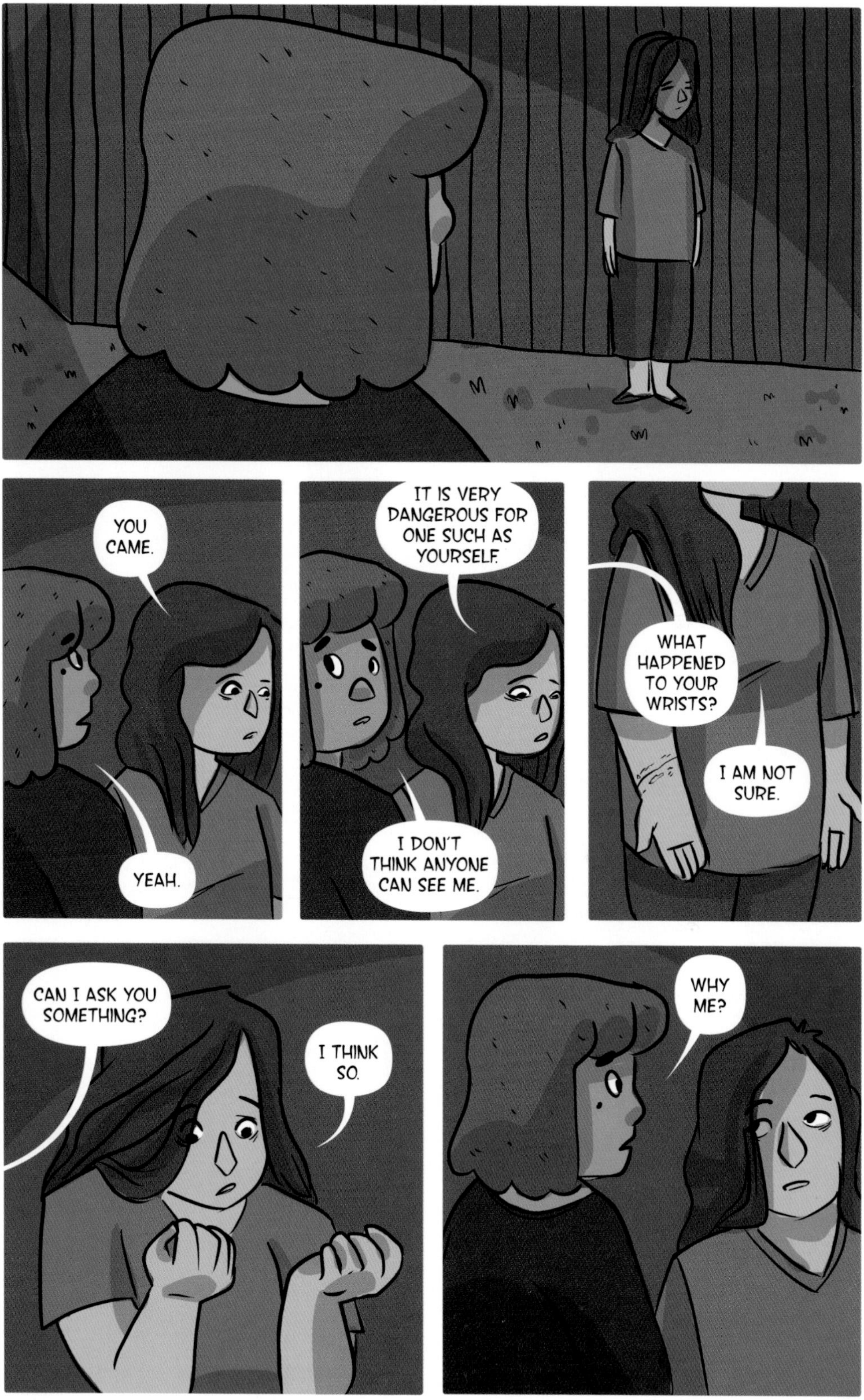
YOU CAME.
YEAH.
IT IS VERY DANGEROUS FOR ONE SUCH AS YOURSELF.
I DON'T THINK ANYONE CAN SEE ME.
WHAT HAPPENED TO YOUR WRISTS?
I AM NOT SURE.
CAN I ASK YOU SOMETHING?
I THINK SO.
WHY ME?

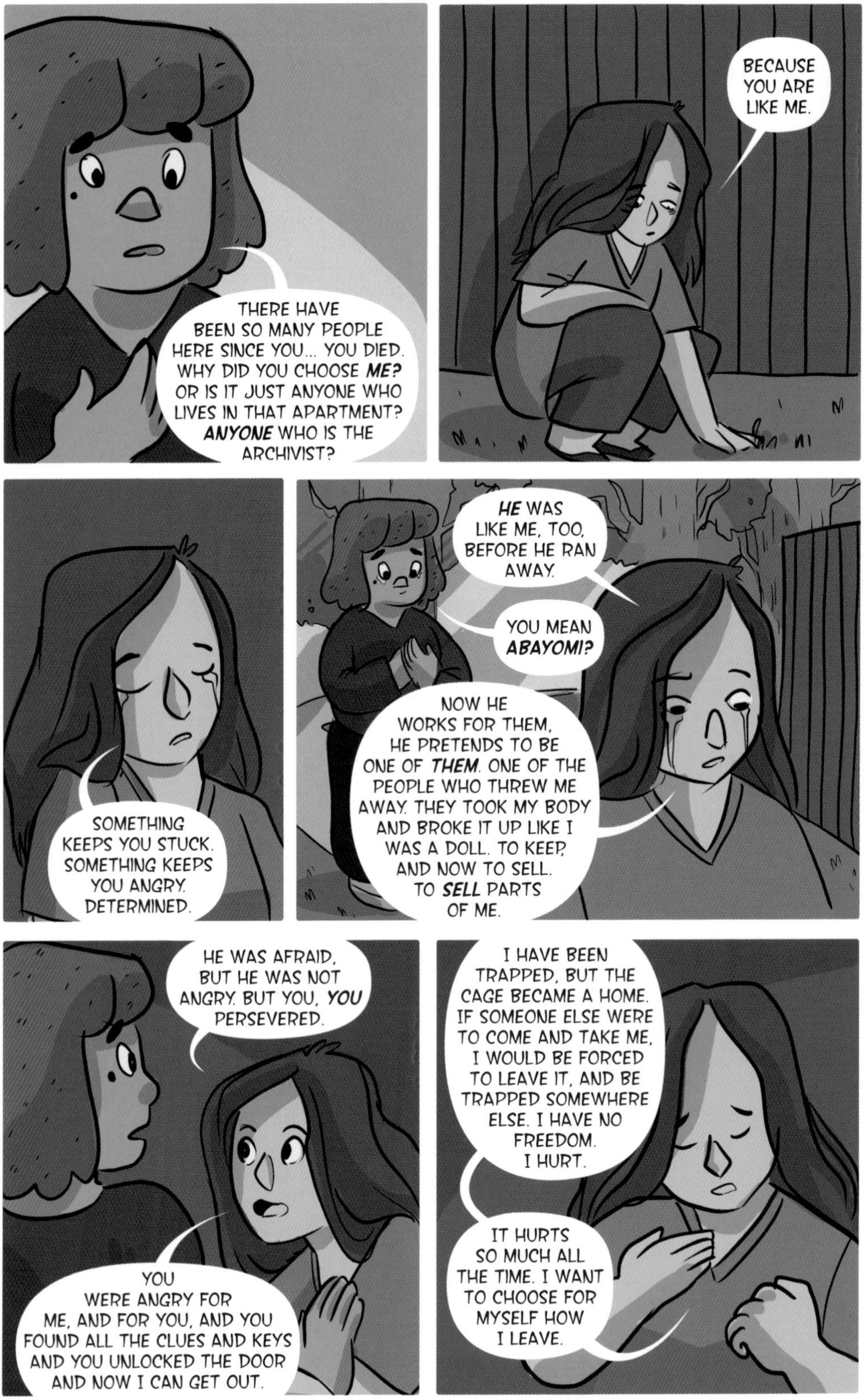
THERE HAVE BEEN SO MANY PEOPLE HERE SINCE YOU... YOU DIED. WHY DID YOU CHOOSE *ME?* OR IS IT JUST ANYONE WHO LIVES IN THAT APARTMENT? *ANYONE* WHO IS THE ARCHIVIST?
BECAUSE YOU ARE LIKE ME.
SOMETHING KEEPS YOU STUCK. SOMETHING KEEPS YOU ANGRY. DETERMINED.
HE WAS LIKE ME, TOO, BEFORE HE RAN AWAY.
YOU MEAN *ABAYOMI?*
NOW HE WORKS FOR THEM, HE PRETENDS TO BE ONE OF *THEM*. ONE OF THE PEOPLE WHO THREW ME AWAY. THEY TOOK MY BODY AND BROKE IT UP LIKE I WAS A DOLL. TO KEEP, AND NOW TO SELL. TO *SELL* PARTS OF ME.
HE WAS AFRAID, BUT HE WAS NOT ANGRY. BUT YOU, *YOU* PERSEVERED.
YOU WERE ANGRY FOR ME, AND FOR YOU, AND YOU FOUND ALL THE CLUES AND KEYS AND YOU UNLOCKED THE DOOR AND NOW I CAN GET OUT.
I HAVE BEEN TRAPPED, BUT THE CAGE BECAME A HOME. IF SOMEONE ELSE WERE TO COME AND TAKE ME, I WOULD BE FORCED TO LEAVE IT, AND BE TRAPPED SOMEWHERE ELSE. I HAVE NO FREEDOM. I HURT.
IT HURTS SO MUCH ALL THE TIME. I WANT TO CHOOSE FOR MYSELF HOW I LEAVE.

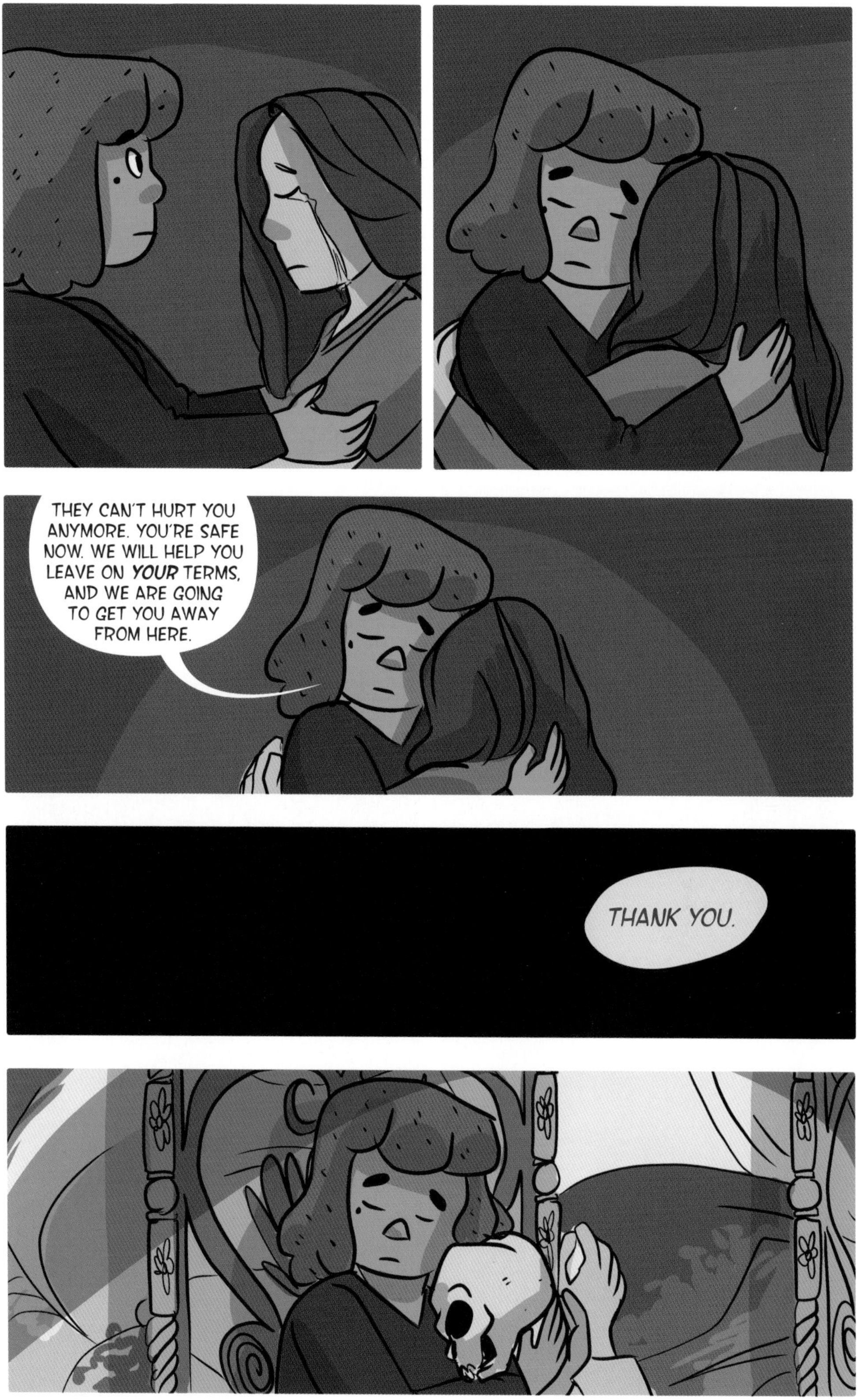
THEY CAN'T HURT YOU ANYMORE. YOU'RE SAFE NOW. WE WILL HELP YOU LEAVE ON **YOUR** TERMS, AND WE ARE GOING TO GET YOU AWAY FROM HERE.
THANK YOU.

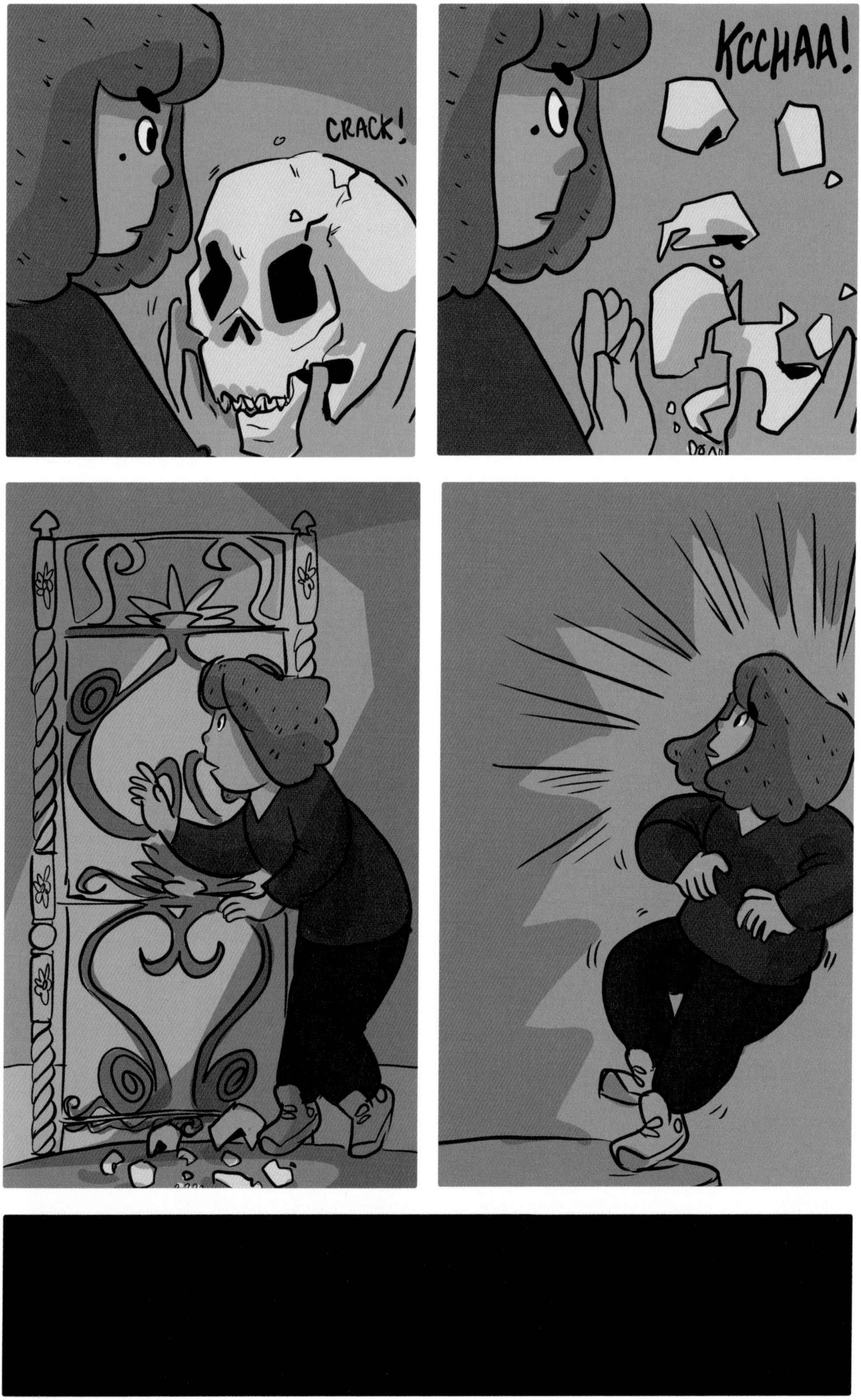
CRACK!
KCCHAA!

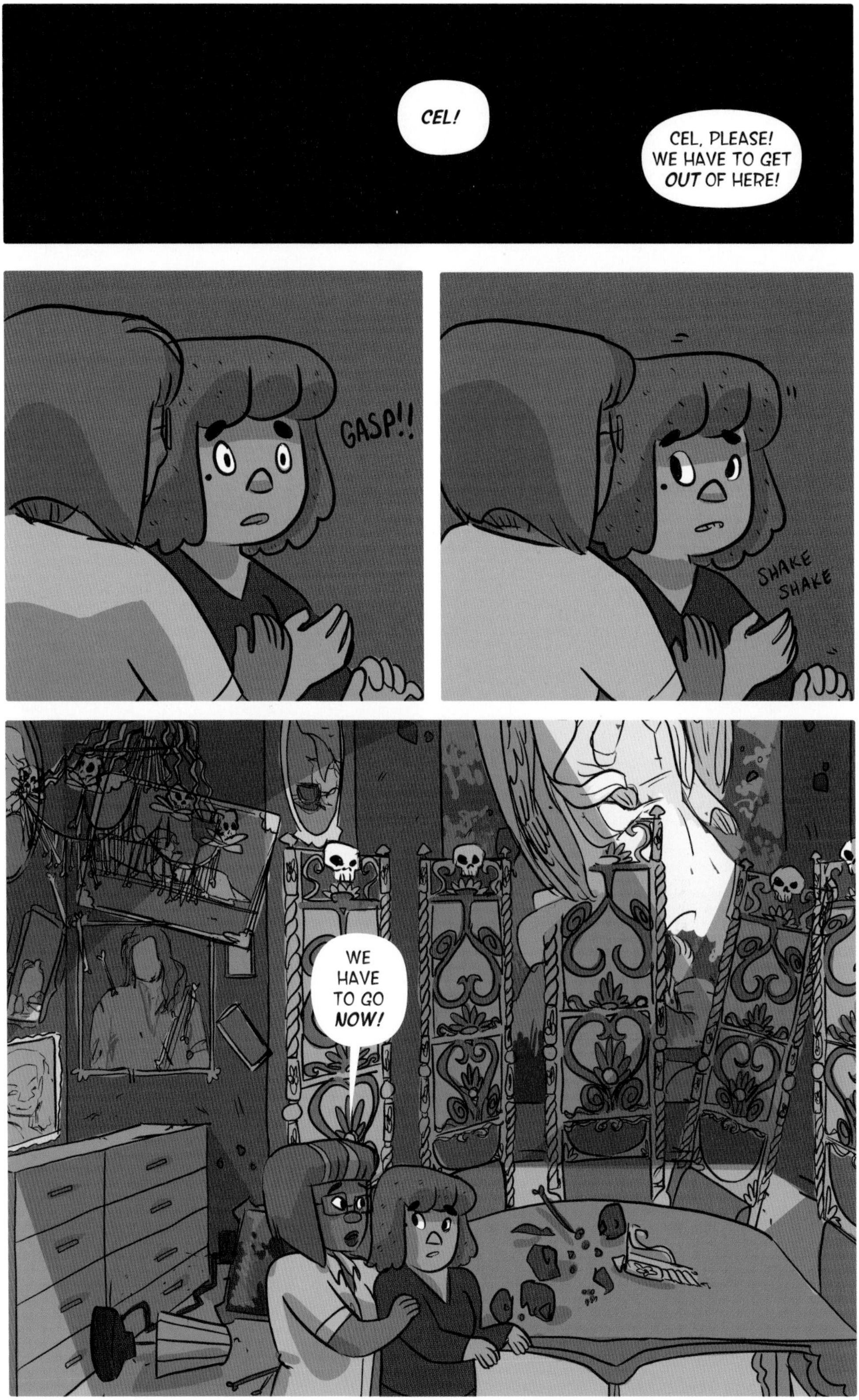
CEL!
CEL, PLEASE! WE HAVE TO GET OUT OF HERE!
GASP!!
SHAKE SHAKE
WE HAVE TO GO NOW!

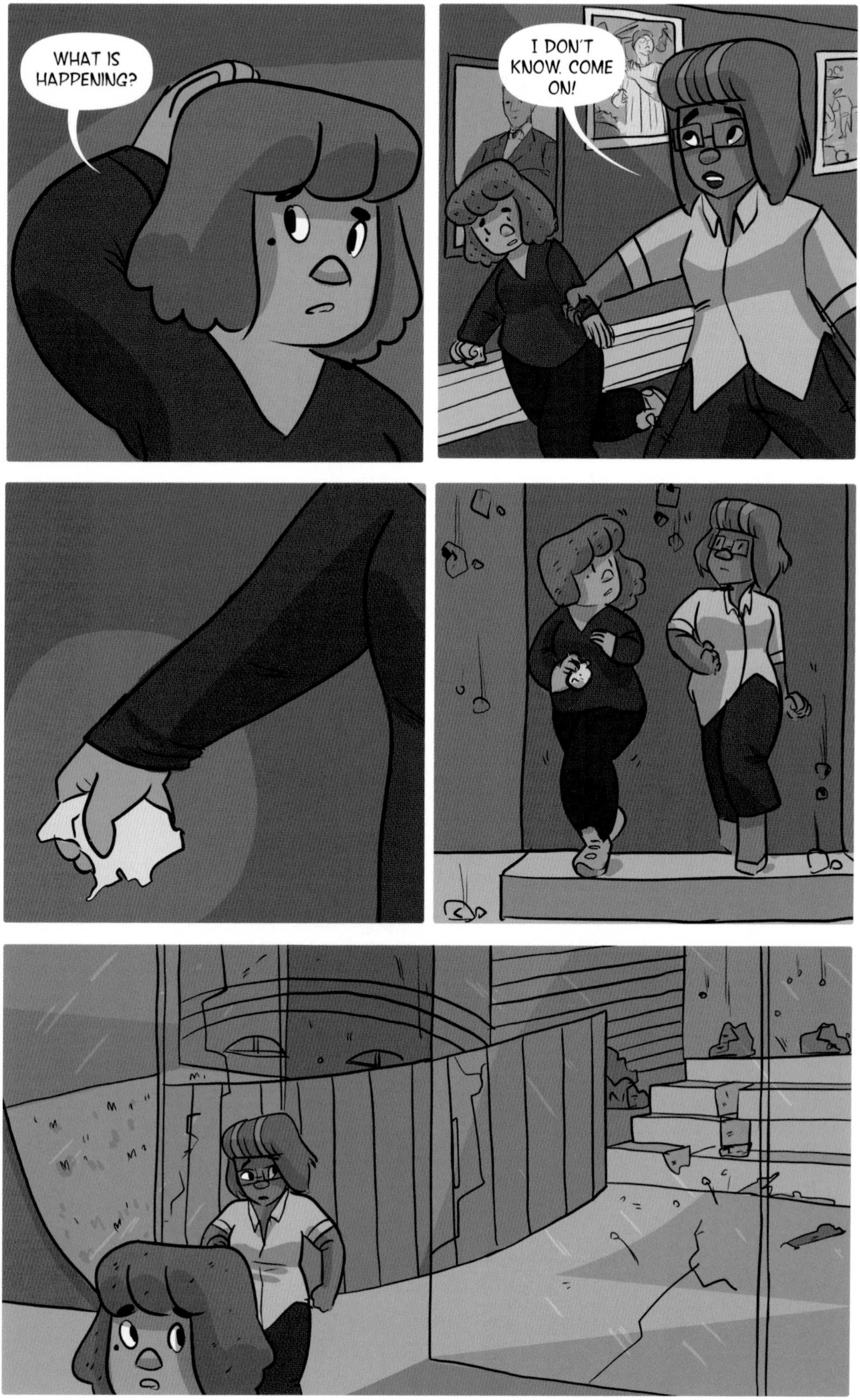
WHAT IS HAPPENING?
I DON'T KNOW. COME ON!

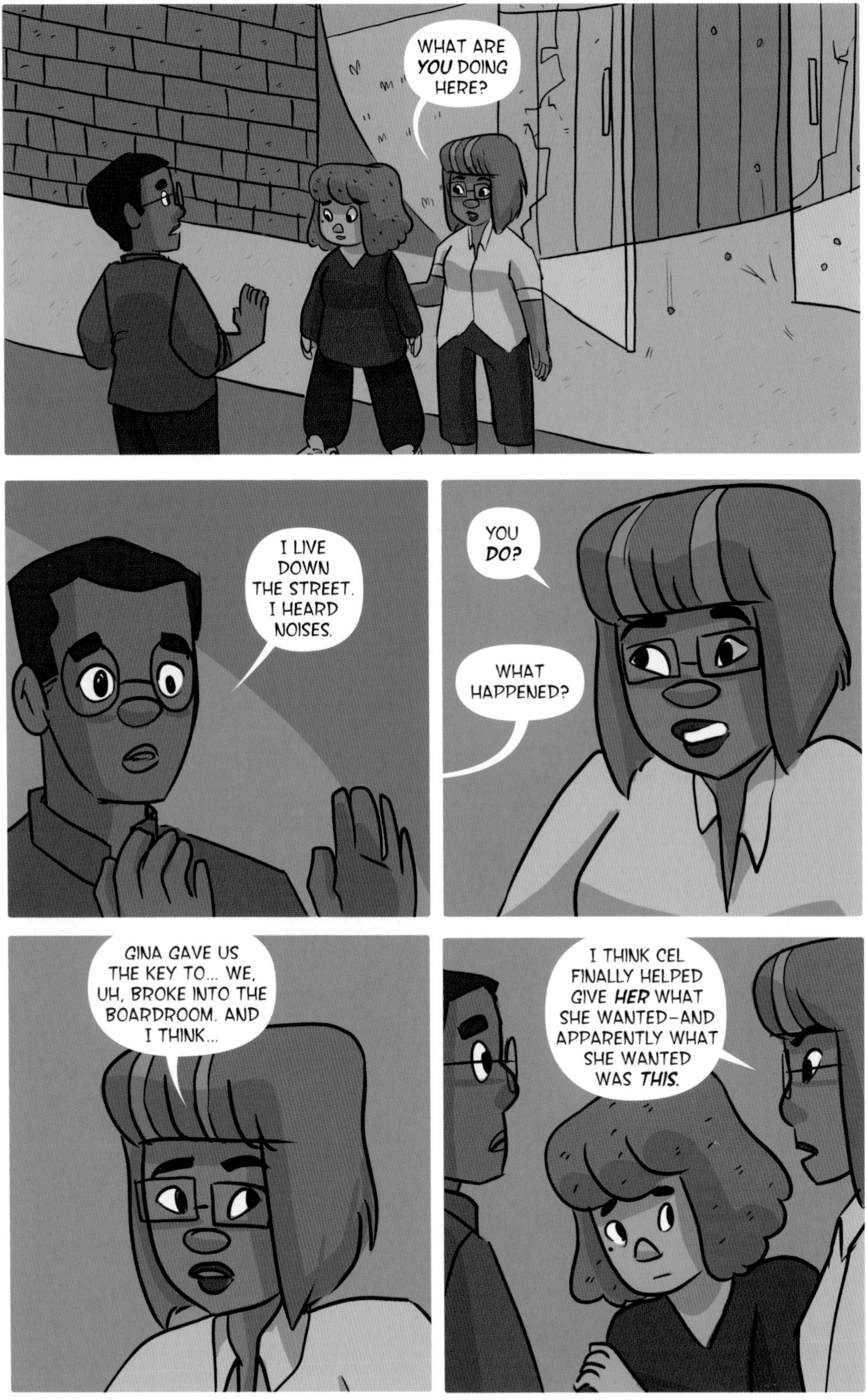
WHAT ARE *YOU* DOING HERE?
I LIVE DOWN THE STREET. I HEARD NOISES.
YOU *DO?*
WHAT HAPPENED?
GINA GAVE US THE KEY TO... WE, UH, BROKE INTO THE BOARDROOM. AND I THINK...
I THINK CEL FINALLY HELPED GIVE *HER* WHAT SHE WANTED—AND APPARENTLY WHAT SHE WANTED WAS *THIS.*

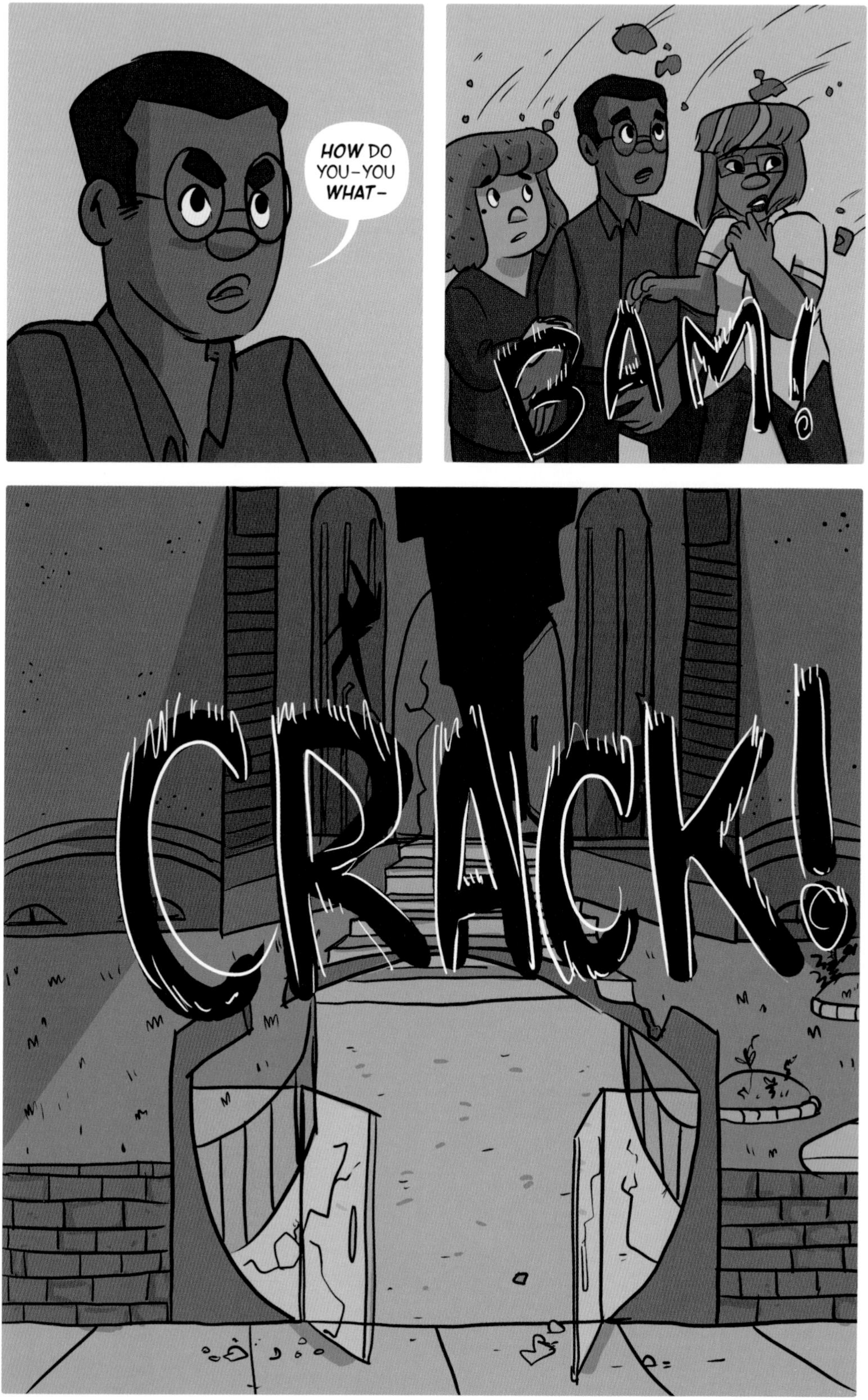
HOW DO YOU-YOU WHAT-
BAM!
CRACK!

SIX WEEKS LATER

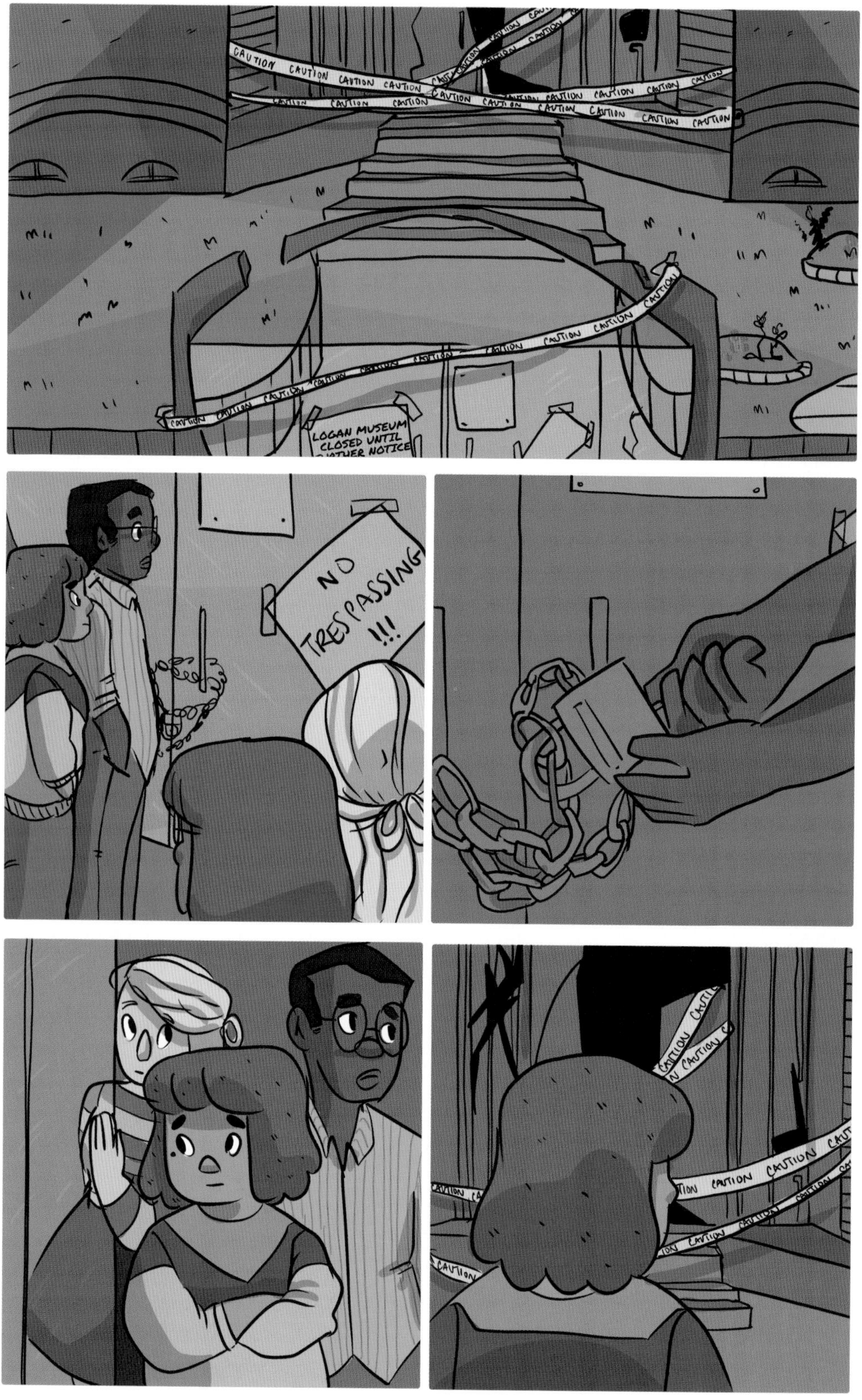
CAUTION
LOGAN MUSEUM
CLOSED UNTIL
NO TRESPASSING !!!

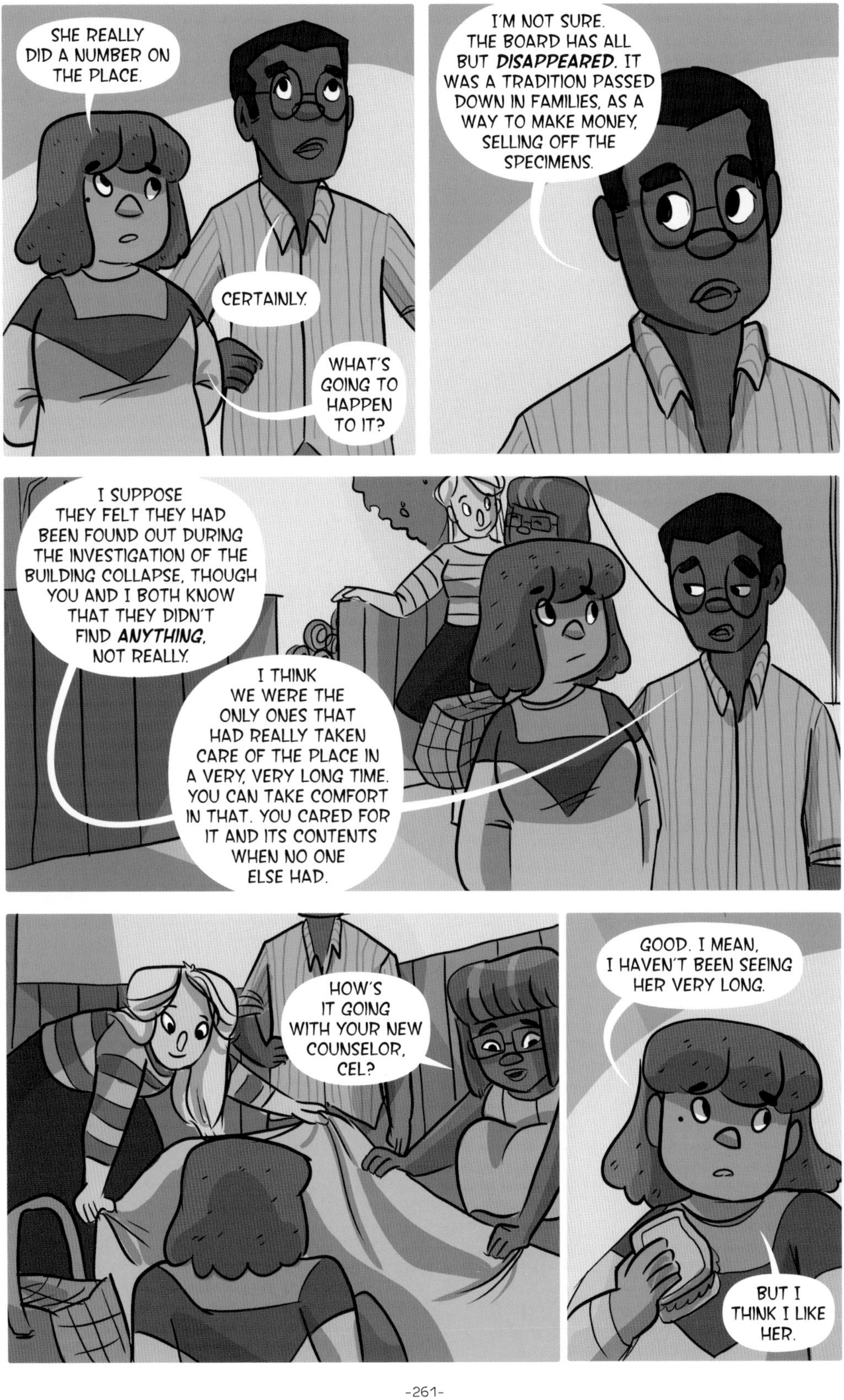
SHE REALLY DID A NUMBER ON THE PLACE.
CERTAINLY.
WHAT'S GOING TO HAPPEN TO IT?
I'M NOT SURE. THE BOARD HAS ALL BUT **DISAPPEARED.** IT WAS A TRADITION PASSED DOWN IN FAMILIES, AS A WAY TO MAKE MONEY, SELLING OFF THE SPECIMENS.
I SUPPOSE THEY FELT THEY HAD BEEN FOUND OUT DURING THE INVESTIGATION OF THE BUILDING COLLAPSE, THOUGH YOU AND I BOTH KNOW THAT THEY DIDN'T FIND **ANYTHING**, NOT REALLY.
I THINK WE WERE THE ONLY ONES THAT HAD REALLY TAKEN CARE OF THE PLACE IN A VERY, VERY LONG TIME. YOU CAN TAKE COMFORT IN THAT. YOU CARED FOR IT AND ITS CONTENTS WHEN NO ONE ELSE HAD.
HOW'S IT GOING WITH YOUR NEW COUNSELOR, CEL?
GOOD. I MEAN, I HAVEN'T BEEN SEEING HER VERY LONG.
BUT I THINK I LIKE HER.

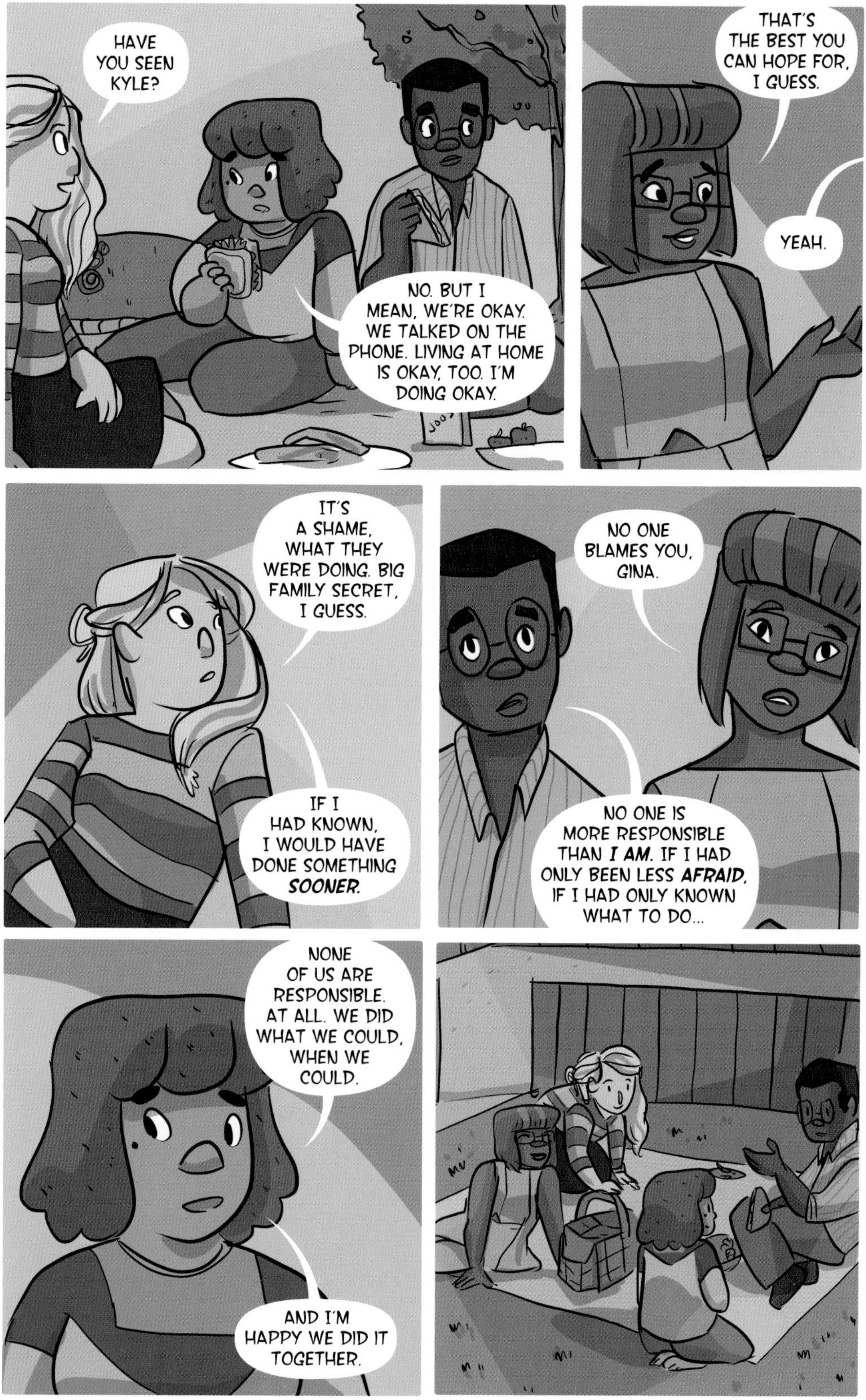
HAVE YOU SEEN KYLE?
NO. BUT I MEAN, WE'RE OKAY. WE TALKED ON THE PHONE. LIVING AT HOME IS OKAY, TOO. I'M DOING OKAY.
THAT'S THE BEST YOU CAN HOPE FOR, I GUESS.
YEAH.
IT'S A SHAME, WHAT THEY WERE DOING. BIG FAMILY SECRET, I GUESS.
IF I HAD KNOWN, I WOULD HAVE DONE SOMETHING **SOONER.**
NO ONE BLAMES YOU, GINA.
NO ONE IS MORE RESPONSIBLE THAN ***I AM.*** IF I HAD ONLY BEEN LESS ***AFRAID,*** IF I HAD ONLY KNOWN WHAT TO DO...
NONE OF US ARE RESPONSIBLE. AT ALL. WE DID WHAT WE COULD, WHEN WE COULD.
AND I'M HAPPY WE DID IT TOGETHER.

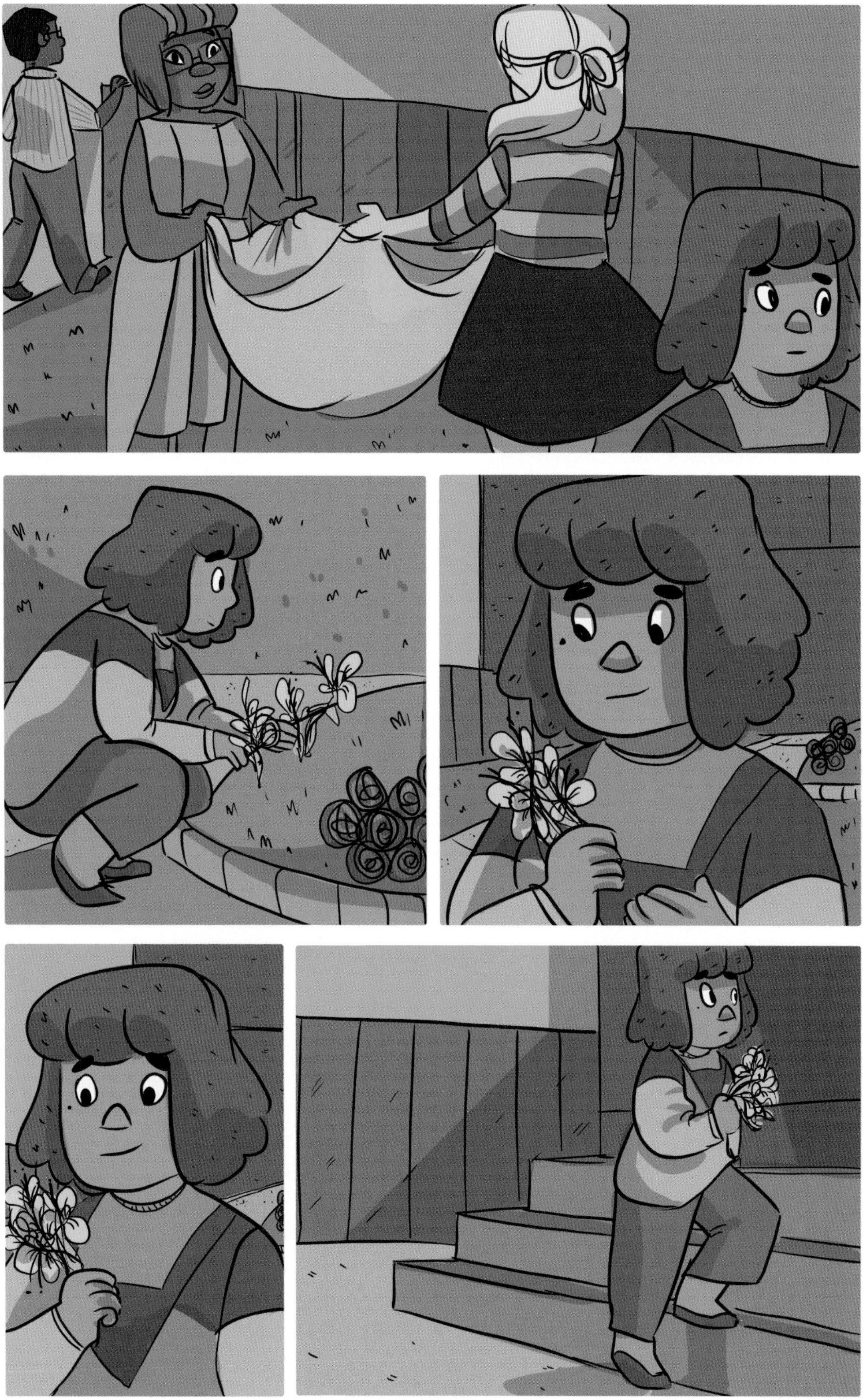

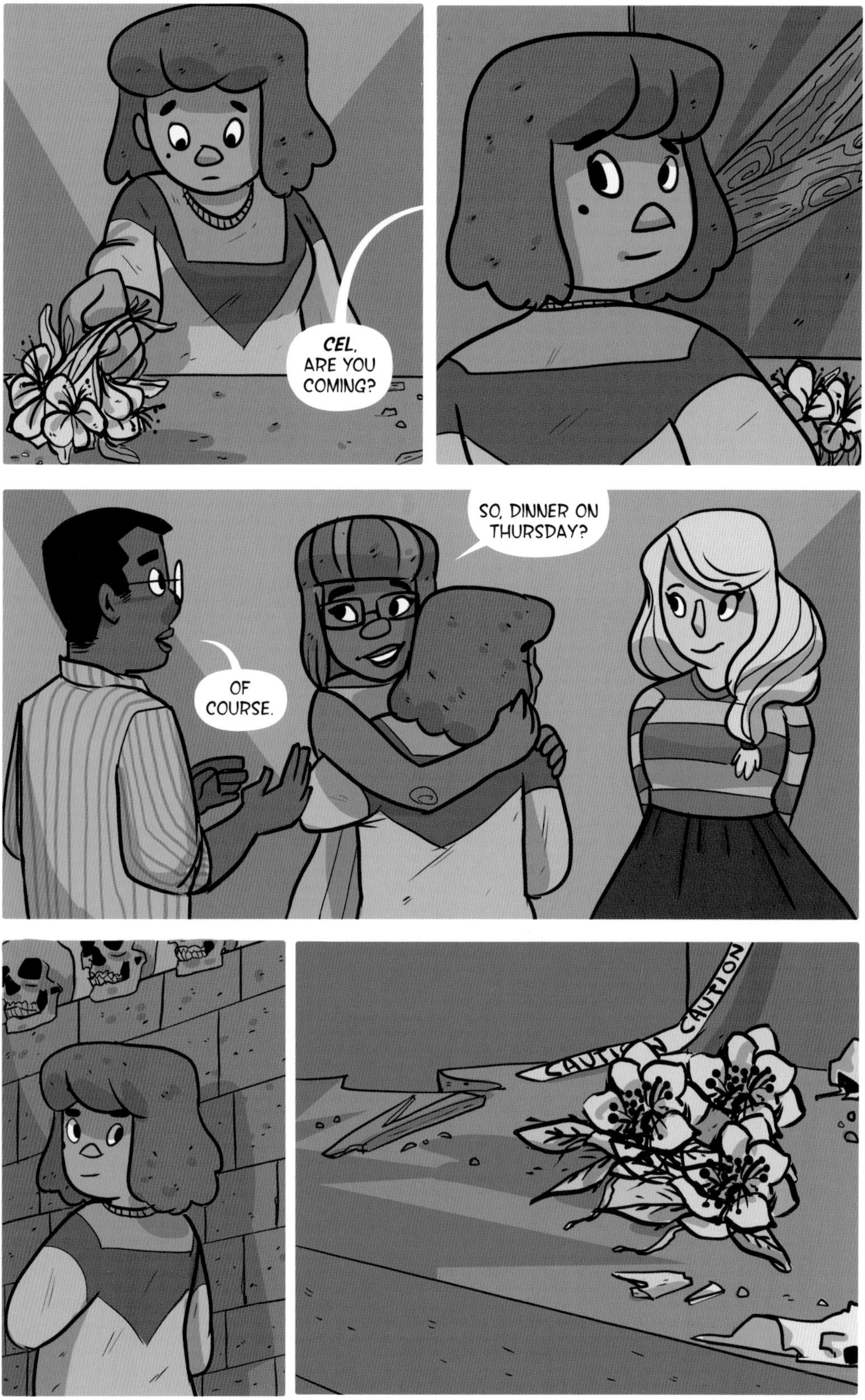
CEL, ARE YOU COMING?
SO, DINNER ON THURSDAY?
OF COURSE.
CAUTION

The End

Afterword

In 2012, I began to sketch out a story about a girl who works in a haunted museum. I was 23 years old, and I had just moved back home after leaving art school in my junior year. I spent my days feeling aimless, and found myself working part-time in a library, which I quickly took to as a replacement for the structure of school. Inside, I was depressed, anxious, and toed the line of suicidal, feeling guilty for how I was treating others and myself. It wasn't a great time.

In school, I had tailored my studio work and my writing to focus on early 19th century medical and spiritualist photography. Throughout my entire life, I'd struggled with chronic illness, depression and anxiety, and a general sense of not belonging, so I felt like something of an oddity myself, and had compassion for the subjects stiffly posed in these tintypes and albumen prints. My writing and knowledge on the subject was rewarded when I managed to land an internship in the archives of a medical history museum, where I would be helping to digitize an enormous collection of antique medical photographs, illustrations, and documents. Honored to have been allowed inside the secret rooms of the museum's library, I spent long afternoons filing away images of doctors, skeletons, and surgeries in a basement office. However, after a few months, I began to feel burnt out, desensitized to the images I was seeing, and my writing on the ethics and history of medical imagery began to suffer.

So, I decided to approach it from a different, non-academic angle, and I began to compose a little haunted house story. Celeste Walden, a cypher for myself, investigated the mysterious happenings at a medical oddities museum after dropping out of school due to her depression. Soon I had a little novella, which I submitted to the Clarion Writer's Workshop. I was soundly rejected, and so I shoved the story away, and became even more depressed.

Three years later, in a much healthier headspace, I came across the art of Steenz via The Valkyries, the female-only comic shop employees group we both belonged to. To say my love for Steenz's art was instant is no lie—I was enamored by her use of color, the way she captured facial expressions, and how it spoke to her as a person: vibrant, trend-defying, and full of a crackling wit that I wanted to have in my life. I'd never written a comic script before, but that didn't stop me from sending her a message: I have an idea for a ghost story. Will you draw it?

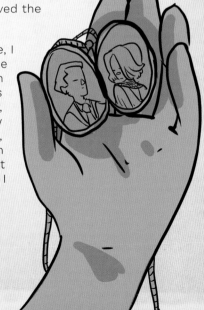

She agreed, and we set out to work. Originally intended as a webcomic, Steenz and I dove into *Archival Quality* with the idea of giving more life to Celeste, her friends, and their world. I let Steenz run free, putting flesh on the bones of my story with her art, giving Cel, Abayomi, and Holly even more depth by drawing each of them as real people with poignant emotions and, let's be real, amazing wardrobes. I learned that even if you've written prose for most of your life, writing a comic book script is a very different animal. We both grew, and improved, and changed our styles over time. The place we were at when we sent our rough ten pages to Oni for consideration is very different from where we are now.

An unexpected, but amazing, bonus to all of this was the friendship I developed with Steenz. Over the course of the past two years, we've become incredibly close, holding each other up through this process, but also connecting over our shared love of trashy television and comics. We've flown to seen each other in our hometowns, we message each other so much that if I don't hear from Steenz for more than 24 hours, I assume something is wrong. Like the relationships in *Archival Quality*, Steenz and I created an unexpected bond that has been a comfort in difficult times. I'm extremely thankful.

This book was a challenge to balance. My original novella was steeped too far in my academic background, and I wanted to make a story that could be enjoyed by those who didn't necessarily study early psychiatry (Dr. Genius, M.D., as Cel would say). As such, there are inaccuracies, fantasies, and bendings of the truth in this version of *Archival Quality* that exist to further the story and do not reflect on the actual history of medicine. I am no doctor, and while I certainly creeped out enough seatmates on the train by researching orbital lobotomies, I can't say for sure that this is scientifically sound (do not use this book as a guide for giving lobotomies). Celine's experience is only one part of history, as well: there are mountains of academic study on the way that women of color were treated in early medicine, which I felt were owed more space and nuance than I could give here. While some of the photographs you see in the book are based on real images I've encountered in my years of research, some are fabrications, while others are inspired by artists like Thomas Eakins and Matthew Barney.

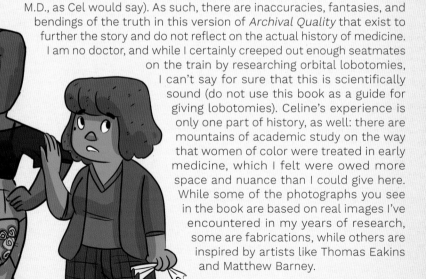

As someone who has received some form of psychiatric treatment off and on for over a decade, I wanted to open a small window into the history of mental health treatment, particularly for women, to our readers. To go through therapy is to at once give up and regain agency—you have to put the deconstruction of what you believe in the hands of a near-stranger, and then you must rebuild by yourself. You put your faith in practitioners and pills. It's scary. Cel's journey through anger, to action, to acceptance is a mirror of one that many who go through therapy experience. Overall, this is a book about freedom, peace, the death of things living and imagined. It's about freeing yourself, freeing others. Letting go of pain. I hope that if you are going through a time like Cel or Celine, you can get to a place where you can let go of some of that pain, too.

I did a lot of reading to influence this book, and I've included a few of those titles here:

Stanley Burns and Elizabeth Burns. *Stiffs, Skulls, and Skeletons: Medical Photography and Symbolism*. (Schiffer, 2014)

Asti Hustvedt. *Medical Muses: Hysteria in Nineteenth-Century Paris*. (W.W. Norton, 2011)

College of Physicians of Philadelphia. *Mütter Museum Historical Medical Photographs*. (Blast Books, 2007)

Alice Miller. *The Drama of the Gifted Child*. (3rd ed.) (Basic Books, 2008)

Richard Barnett. *The Sick Rose: Disease and the Art of Medical Illustration*. (D.A.P, 2014)

There are also many real-life museums that do an amazing job of discussing and showcasing the ethics of early medicine and psychiatry (thankfully, I know of absolutely no modern museums that operate like the creepy one in our book).

The Mütter Museum, Philadelphia, PA
The Warren Anatomical Museum, Boston, MA
New Orleans Pharmacy Museum, New Orleans, LA

And of course, the now heartbreakingly-closed Morbid Anatomy Museum in Brooklyn, NY.

-Ivy Noelle Weir
August 2017

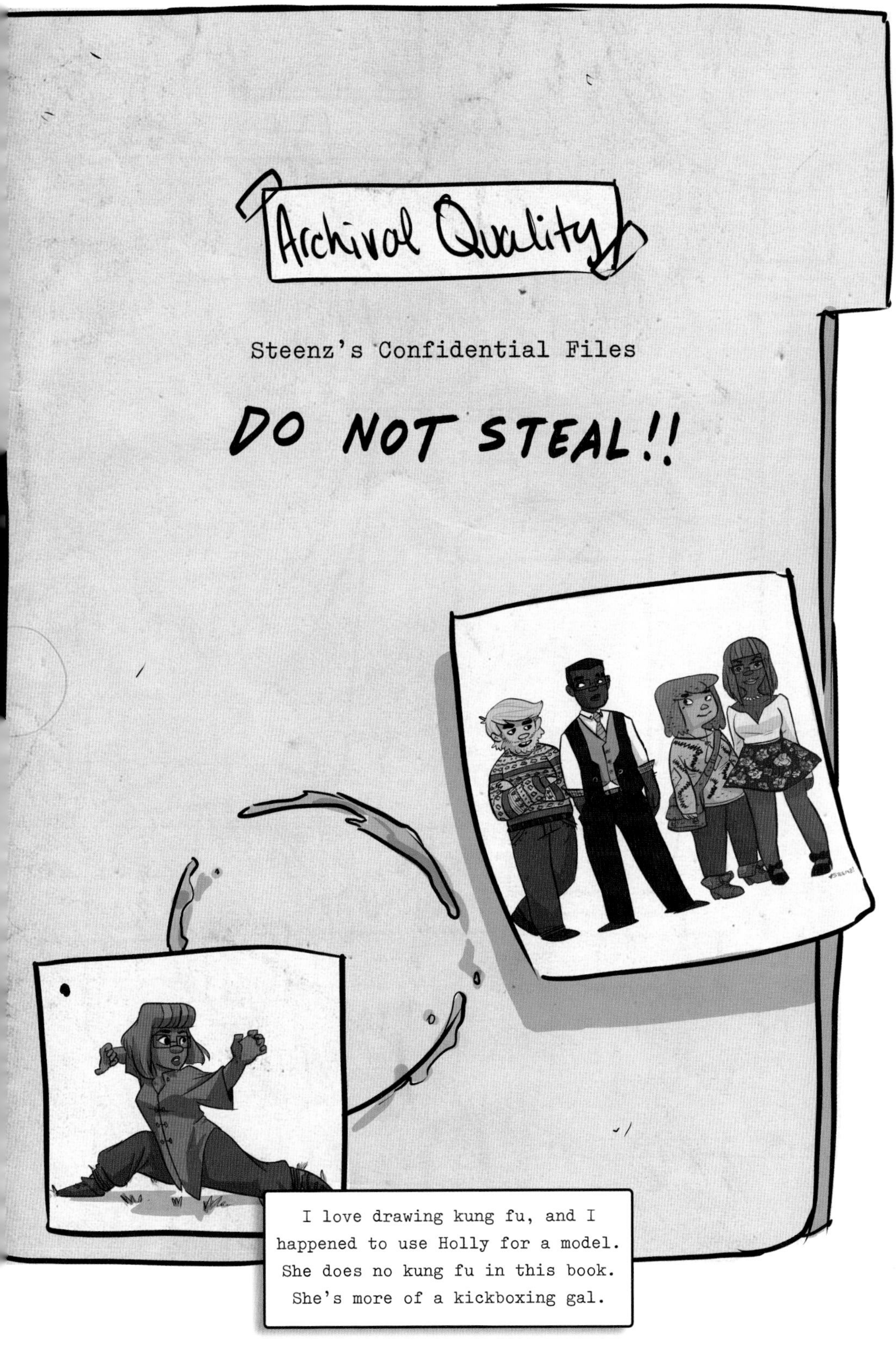
Archival Quality
Steenz's Confidential Files
DO NOT STEAL!!
I love drawing kung fu, and I happened to use Holly for a model. She does no kung fu in this book. She's more of a kickboxing gal.

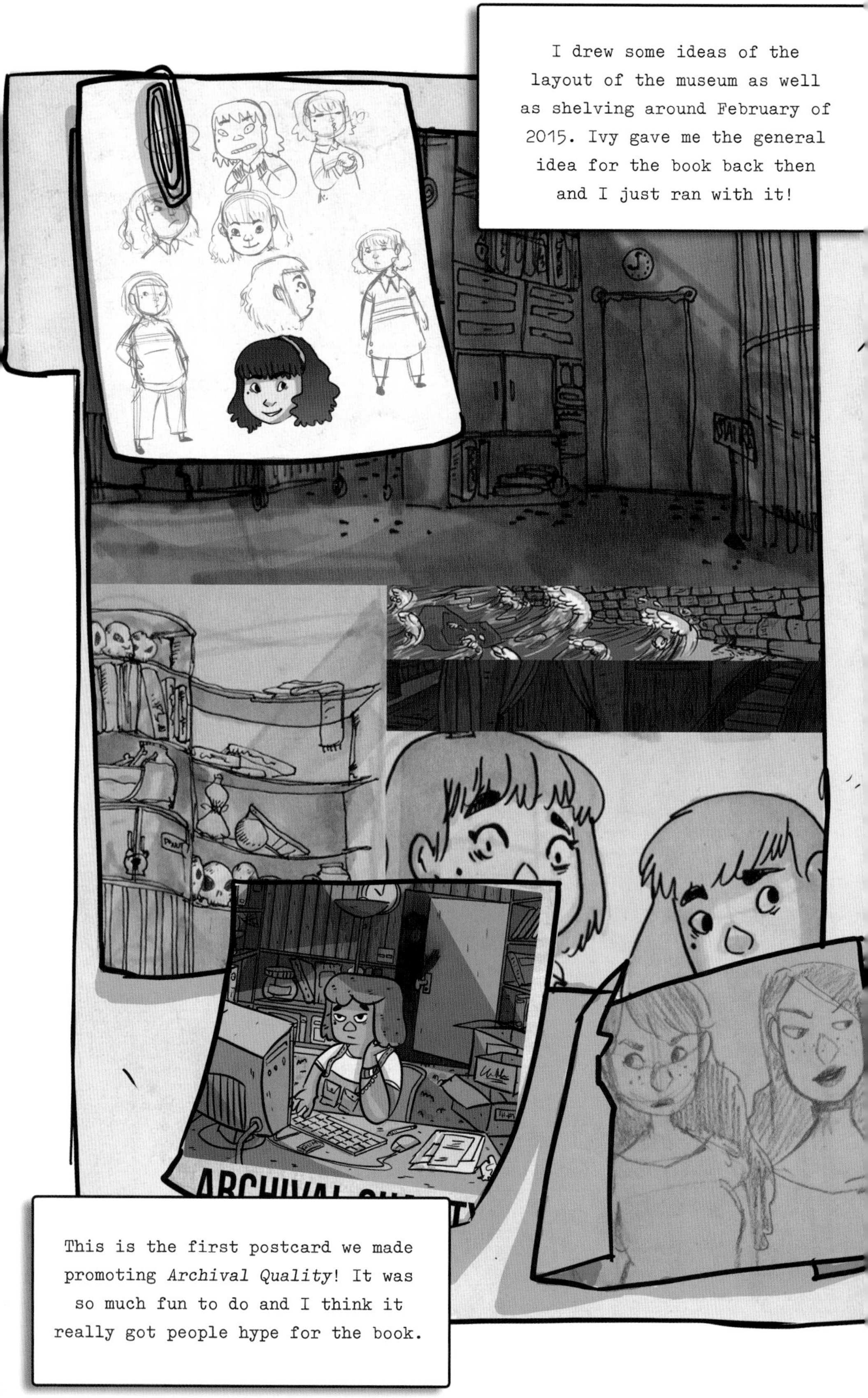
I drew some ideas of the layout of the museum as well as shelving around February of 2015. Ivy gave me the general idea for the book back then and I just ran with it!
This is the first postcard we made promoting *Archival Quality*! It was so much fun to do and I think it really got people hype for the book.

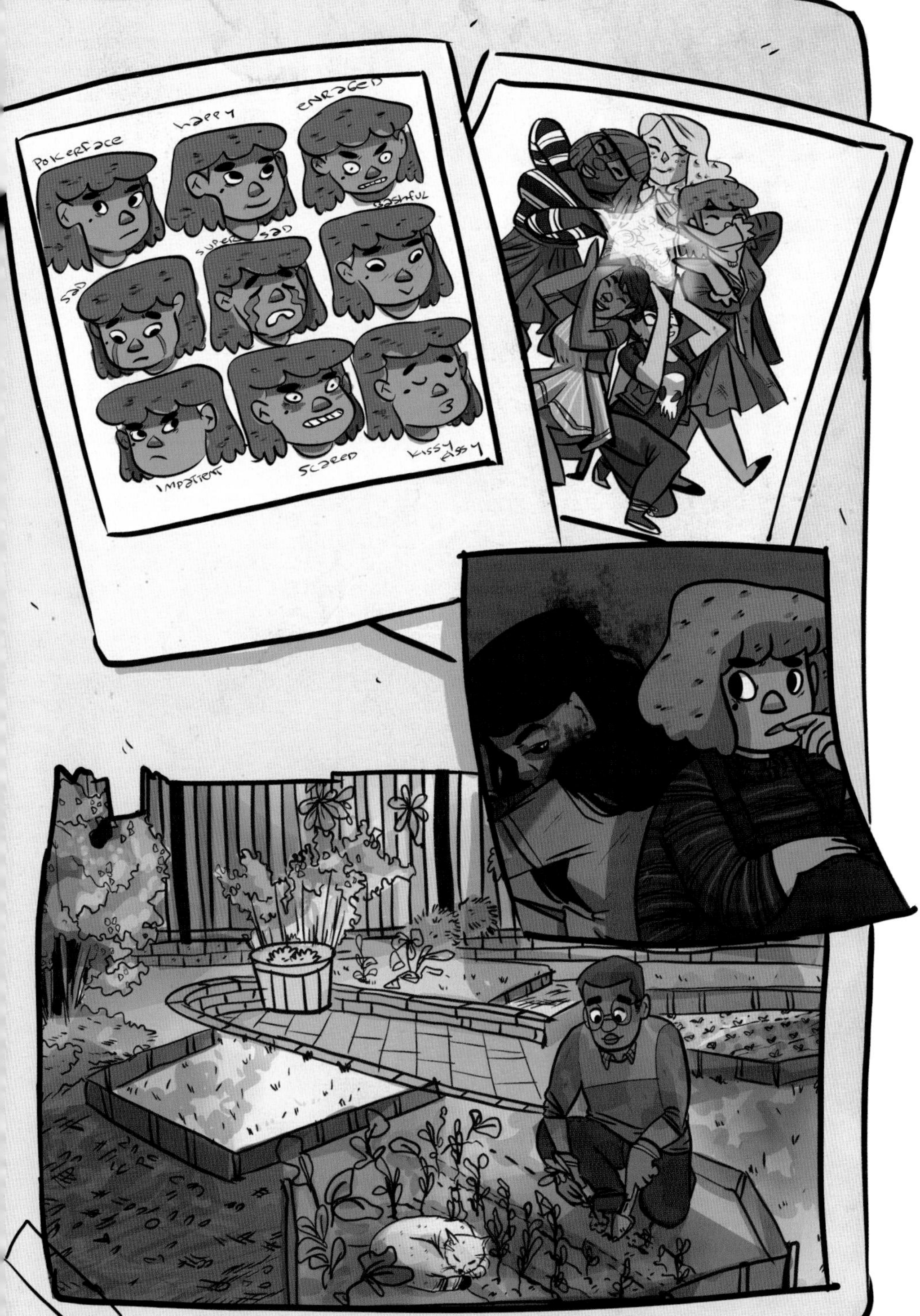

POKERFACE
HAPPY
ENRAGED
SAD
SUPER SAD
BASHFUL
IMPATIENT
SCARED
KISSY FISSY

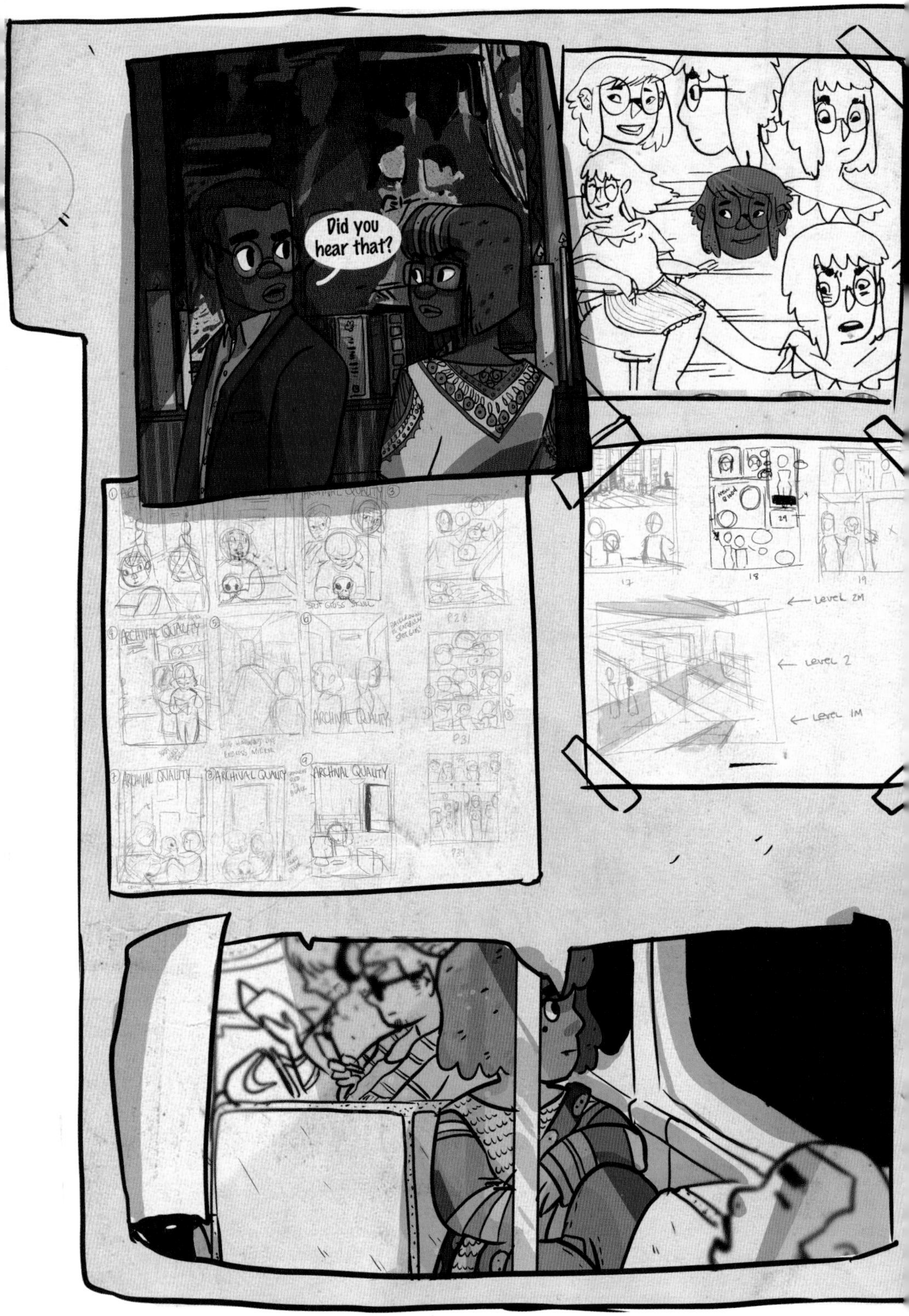
Did you hear that?
ARCHIVAL QUALITY
SPOT GLOSS SKULL
P28
ARCHIVAL QUALITY
ARCHIVAL QUALITY
P31
ARCHIVAL QUALITY
ARCHIVAL QUALITY
ARCHIVAL QUALITY
P34
17
18
19
LEVEL 2M
LEVEL 2
LEVEL 1M

When Ivy and I first worked on *Archival Quality* it was as a webcomic! But then when we decided to submit to Oni, I re-drew the first 8 pages. THEN when we started working on the book I re-drew the first 8 pages AGAIN. So I have three versions of this page spread out over 2 years of artistic growth.

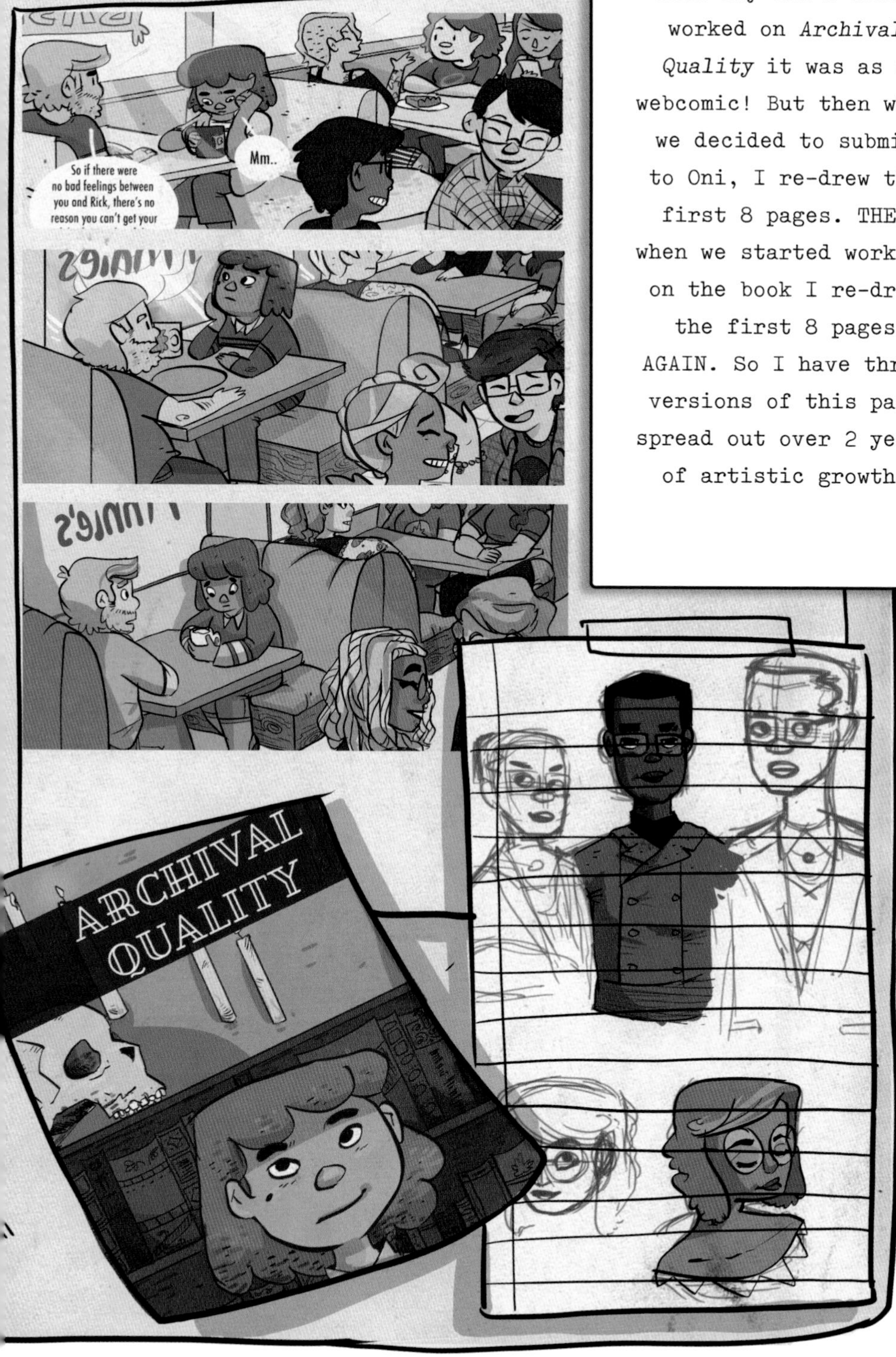
So if there were no bad feelings between you and Rick, there's no reason you can't get your
Mm..
ARCHIVAL QUALITY

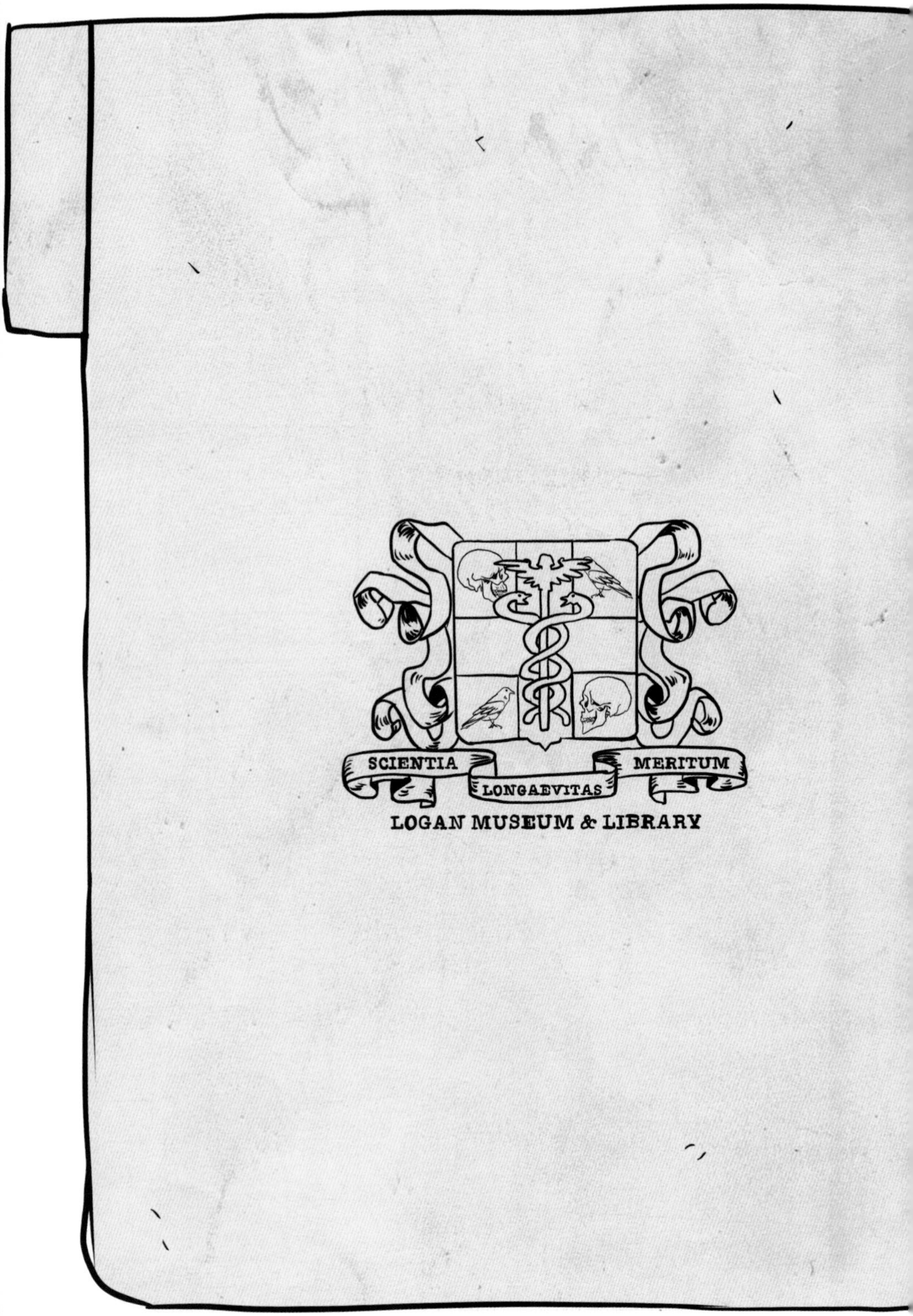
SCIENTIA
LONGAEVITAS
MERITUM
LOGAN MUSEUM & LIBRARY

IVY NOELLE WEIR

has been writing stories for her entire life, and her
essays on art, pop culture and librarianship have
appeared in a variety of outlets. In addition to her
writing, Weir is a visual artist and former librarian who
studied photography at Parsons the New School for
Design, art history at Goddard College, and holds an
MLIS from Clarion University of Pennsylvania. A native
of Philadelphia, she currently works in publishing and
lives on a crooked old street in an apartment full of
Halloween decorations with her partner and tiny dog.

(Photo by Kelsey Hoffman)

STEENZ

is an illustrator from St. Louis, MO. According to her mom, Steenz has only ever answered "an artist" when asked what she wants to be when she grows up. Here we are, years later. Steenz spends a lot of time watching reality TV, eating pizza, working at Lion Forge and drawing comics. She can officially call herself a professional artist. Steenz lives with her fiancé, Keya, and her cat, Marko. Steenz is short for Christina.

(Photo by Caitie Metz)

More titles from Oni Press!

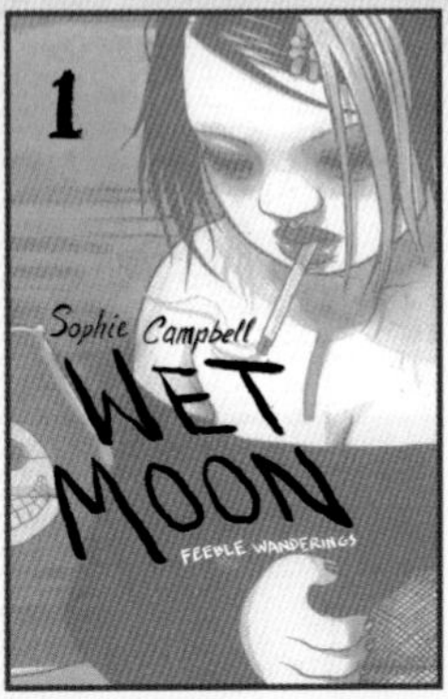
1
Sophie Campbell
WET MOON
FEEBLE WANDERINGS

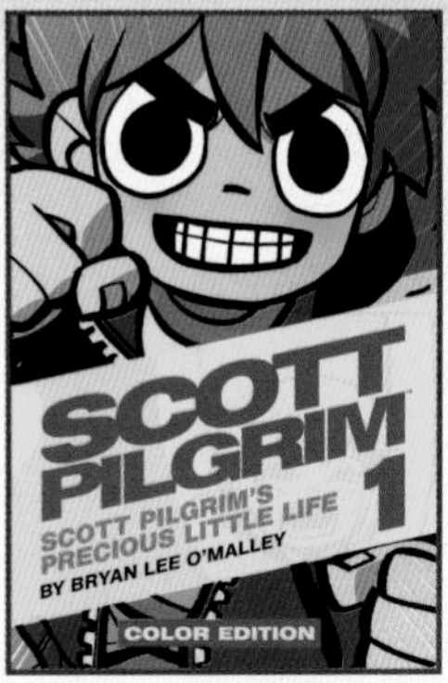
SCOTT PILGRIM 1
SCOTT PILGRIM'S PRECIOUS LITTLE LIFE
BY BRYAN LEE O'MALLEY
COLOR EDITION

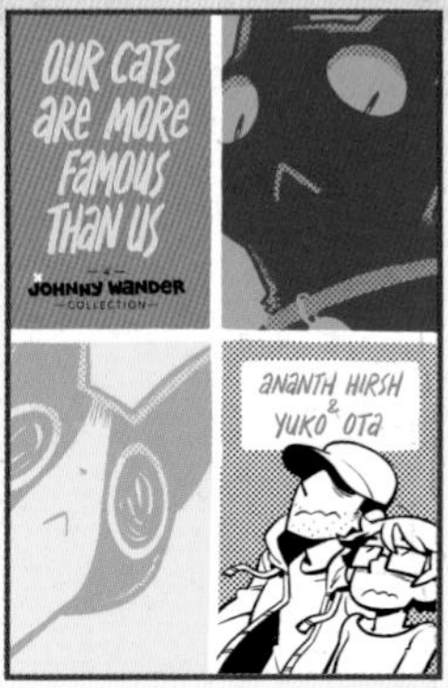
OUR CATS ARE MORE FAMOUS THAN US
JOHNNY WANDER COLLECTION
ANANTH HIRSH & YUKO OTA

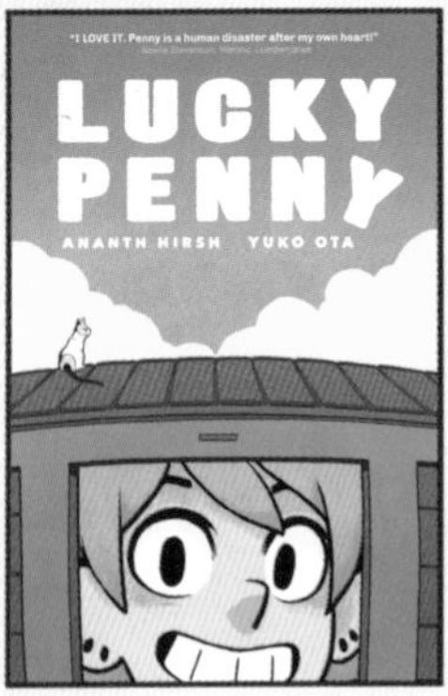
LUCKY PENNY
ANANTH HIRSH
YUKO OTA

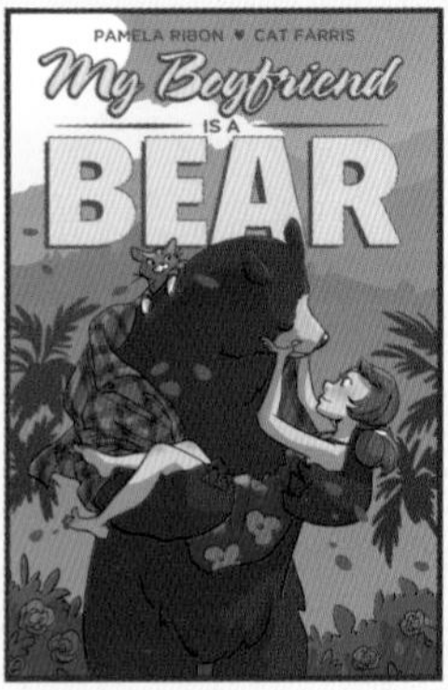
PAMELA RIBON ♥ CAT FARRIS
My Boyfriend IS A BEAR

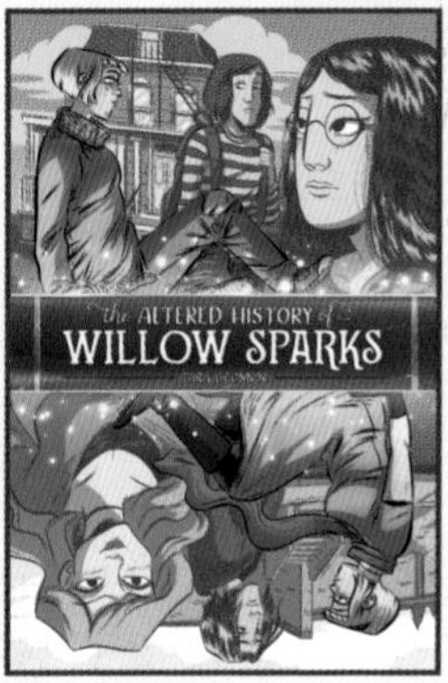
the ALTERED HISTORY of
WILLOW SPARKS

WET MOON, VOL. 1: FEEBLE WANDERINGS
By Sophie Campbell
184 pages, softcover, black and white interiors • ISBN 978-1-62010-304-3

SCOTT PILGRIM, VOLUME 1: PRECIOUS LITTLE LIFE
By Bryan Lee O'Malley & Nathan Fairbairn
192 pages, hardcover, color interiors • ISBN 978-1-62010-000-4

OUR CATS ARE MORE FAMOUS THAN US: A JOHNNY WANDER COLLECTION
By Ananth Hirsh & Yuko Ota
416 pages, hardcover, partial color interiors • ISBN 978-1-62010-383-8

LUCKY PENNY
By Ananth Hirsh & Yuko Ota
208 pages, softcover, black and white interiors • ISBN 978-1-62010-287-9

MY BOYFRIEND IS A BEAR
By Pamela Ribon & Cat Farris
176 pages, softcover, color interiors • ISBN 978-1-62010-487-3

THE ALTERED HISTORY OF WILLOW SPARKS
By Tara O'Connor
152 pages, softcover, 2-color interiors • ISBN 978-1-62010-450-7